READER'S DIGEST
SELECT EDITIONS

www.readersdigest.co.uk

The Reader's Digest Association Limited
11 Westferry Circus Canary Wharf London E14 4HE

For information as to ownership of
copyright in the material of this book,
and acknowledgments, see last page.

Printed in Germany
ISBN 978 0 276 44433 3

SELECTED AND CONDENSED
BY READER'S DIGEST

THE READER'S DIGEST ASSOCIATION LIMITED, LONDON

CONTENTS

There's nothing quite like a courtroom drama to stir the blood, and Michael Connelly's crime novels, starring defence lawyer Mickey Haller, are among the best you will ever come across. Haller is a lawyer with a conscience, which is what makes his cases so interesting. In this new story, he inherits the clients of a recently deceased Hollywood lawyer, Jerry Vincent. It's very good news, career-wise, until Haller learns that the man who killed Jerry could be coming after him.

THE BRASS VERDICT

MICHAEL CONNELLY

A man's relationship with his father is always a crucial one in his life, and its influence can be long-lasting. In this, his first book, TV presenter Richard Madeley tells the fascinating, intimate story of how three generations of males in his own family influenced one another, for good and for ill. It is a moving portrait of family life in three very different eras, as well as an inspiring story that concludes with his own immensely fulfilling experience of becoming a father.

FATHERS & SONS

RICHARD MADELEY

MOSCOW RULES

DANIEL SILVA

273

If you haven't yet discovered Gabriel Allon, Mossad agent turned art restorer, you're in for a treat. Although recently married and living in Umbria, Allon has been called back into service on a mission that will lead him across Europe to the heart of Russia, where a new generation is set on achieving supremacy over the United States—at any cost. Working in the shadows comes naturally to Allon, but the clock is ticking relentlessly and he knows that the stakes, in the spying game, have never been higher.

Under Norfolk's vast, wintry skies, miles of coastal salt-marshes are crisscrossed with treacherous muddy channels and dotted with stunted gorse. It's an area that is frequented only by sea birds and the 'twitchers' who roam the wide-open spaces. Here, a girl's remains have lain preserved for centuries, only now to be uncovered by archaeologists. Was it a ritual killing? As forensic archaeologist Ruth Galloway and Detective Harry Nelson join forces to search for two more missing girls, past and present merge in a mystery riddled with surprises.

THE CROSSING PLACES

ELLY GRIFFITHS

447

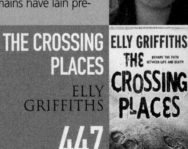

EXIT 22B

4th St →

3rd St

THE BRASS VERDICT
MICHAEL CONNELLY

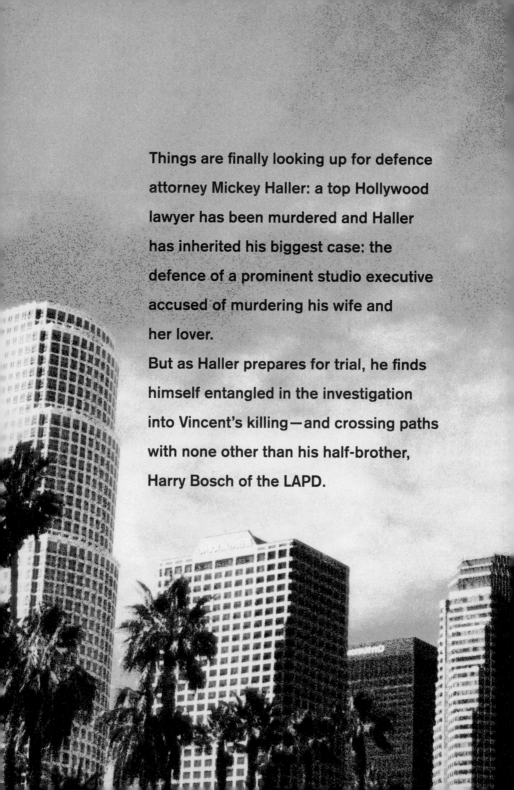

Things are finally looking up for defence attorney Mickey Haller: a top Hollywood lawyer has been murdered and Haller has inherited his biggest case: the defence of a prominent studio executive accused of murdering his wife and her lover.

But as Haller prepares for trial, he finds himself entangled in the investigation into Vincent's killing—and crossing paths with none other than his half-brother, Harry Bosch of the LAPD.

One
1992

Everybody lies.

Cops lie. Lawyers lie. Witnesses lie. The victims lie.

A trial is a contest of lies. And everybody in the courtroom knows this. The judge knows this. Even the jury knows this. They come into the building knowing they will be lied to. They take their seats in the box and agree to be lied to.

The trick if you are sitting at the defence table is to be patient. To wait. Not for any lie. But for the one you can grab on to and forge like hot iron into a sharpened blade. You then use that blade to rip the case open and spill its guts out on the floor.

That's my job, to forge the blade. To use it without mercy or conscience. To be the truth in a place where everybody lies.

I was in the fourth day of trial in Department 109 in the downtown Criminal Courts Building when I got the lie that became the blade that ripped the case open. My client, Barnett Woodson, was riding two murder charges all the way to the steel-grey room in San Quentin where they serve you Jesus juice direct through the arm.

Woodson was a twenty-seven-year-old drug dealer accused of robbing and killing two college students from Westwood. They had wanted to buy cocaine. He decided instead to take their money and kill them both with a sawed-off shotgun. Or so the prosecution said. It was a black on white crime, and that made things bad enough for Woodson—especially coming just four months after the riots that had torn the city apart. But what made his situation even worse was that the killer had weighed down the two bodies and dropped them into the Hollywood Reservoir. They stayed down for four days before popping to the surface like apples in a barrel. Rotten apples. The idea of dead bodies mouldering in a primary source of city drinking water caused a collective twist in the community's guts. When Woodson was linked by phone records to the dead men and arrested, the district attorney's office announced it would seek the death penalty.

The case against Woodson was largely constructed of circumstantial evidence—the phone records—and the testimony of witnesses who were criminals themselves. And state's witness Ronald Torrance sat front and centre in this group. He claimed that Woodson confessed the killings to him.

Torrance had been housed on the same floor of the Men's Central Jail as Woodson, in a high-power module whose sixteen single-prisoner cells opened onto a day room. Detainees had 6 a.m. to 6 p.m. access to the day room where they ate and played cards at tables under the watchful eyes of guards in an overhead glass booth. It was at one of these tables that Torrance claimed my client had confessed to killing the two Westwood boys.

On the fourth day of Woodson's trial, in direct testimony elicited by Jerry Vincent, the prosecutor, Torrance said Woodson not only confessed to the killings but furnished details that only the true killer would know.

During the testimony Vincent kept Torrance on a tight leash with long questions designed to elicit short answers. Vincent finished his direct at 11 a.m. and I began my cross. I took a big, thick file with me to the lectern.

'Mr Torrance, my name is Michael Haller. I work for the public defender's office and represent Barnett Woodson. You and Mr Woodson, you two go back a long way, correct?'

Torrance gave an *Aw shucks* smile. But I had done the due diligence on him and I knew exactly who I was dealing with. He was thirty-two years old and had spent a third of his life in jails and prisons. Under the state's three-strike law he was facing the lifetime-achievement award if convicted of charges that he robbed and pistol-whipped the female manager of a coin laundry. The crime had been committed during the rioting that ripped through the city after the not guilty verdicts were announced in the trial of four police officers accused of beating Rodney King. In short, Torrance had good reason to help the state take down Barnett Woodson.

'Well, we go back a few months is all,' Torrance said. 'To high-power module. In county.'

'You're talking about jail, correct?'

'That's right. We met for the first time in the jail.'

'Let's do the math, Mr Torrance. Barnett Woodson was transferred into the high-power module on September 5th earlier this year. Do you remember that?'

'Yeah, I remember him coming in, yeah.'

'And why were you there in high power?'

'I got a count of assault and one of robbery.'

'These alleged crimes took place during the riots, correct?'

'Yeah, I was out there like everybody else.'

'And your response to the injustice of the Rodney King verdicts was to go out and rob a sixty-two-year-old woman and knock her unconscious? Is that correct?'

Torrance looked over at the prosecution table and then past Vincent to his own lawyer sitting in the first row of the gallery. But his lawyer couldn't help Torrance now. He was on his own.

'I didn't do that,' he finally said.

'You're innocent of the crime you are charged with?'

'That's right.'

'What about looting during the riots?'

Torrance said, 'I take the Fifth on that.'

'All right, enough about you, Mr Torrance, let's get back to you and Mr Woodson. You knew the details of this double murder before you met Mr Woodson in lockup?'

'No, sir. I don't read no papers and the module's TV been broke since I got there.'

'According to the state's discovery material, you contacted the prosecution on October 2nd to report Mr Woodson's alleged confession. Does that sound right to you?'

'Yeah, that sounds right.'

'Well, not to me, Mr Torrance. You are telling this jury that a man facing the possible death penalty confessed to a man he had known for less than four weeks?'

Torrance shrugged before answering. 'That's what happened.'

'With your prior record and current charges, you are looking at fifteen years in prison if convicted, correct?'

'I don't know. I let my lawyer handle all that.'

'I see. What have you asked the prosecutor for in exchange for your testimony, Mr Torrance?'

'Nothing. I don't want nothing.'

'So you are testifying because you believe it is your duty as a citizen?' The sarcasm in my voice was unmistakable.

'That's right,' Torrance responded indignantly.

I held up the thick file. 'Do you recognise this file?'

'No. Not that I recall.'

'You don't remember seeing it in Mr Woodson's cell?'

'Never been in his cell.'

'My client had investigative documents relating to his prosecution in his cell. These contained several details you testified to this morning. You don't think that's suspicious?'

'No. All I know is that he sat there at the table and told me what he'd done. It ain't my fault people open up to me.'

'Of course not. Now can you tell the jury exactly what he said to you?'

'Well, we were sittin' there, the both of us by ourselves, and he just started talkin' about feelin' bad about what he'd done. I asked what'd you do and he told me about that night he killed two fellas.'

'Mr Torrance, you are summarising. You claim Mr Woodson confessed to the murders. So tell the jury the *exact* words Mr Woodson said to you.'

Torrance nodded as if he just realised what I was asking for. 'The first thing he said was, "Man, I feel bad." And I said, "For what, my brother?" He said he kept thinking about those two guys. I didn't know what he was talking about so I said, "What two guys?" And he said, "The two niggers I dumped in the reservoir." I asked what it was all about and he told me about blasting them with a shorty and wrappin' them up in chicken wire and such. He said, "I made one bad mistake," and I asked what it was. He said, "I shoulda taken a knife and opened up their bellies so they wouldn't float up the way they did." And that was what he told me.'

I carefully moved in with the blade. 'Did Mr Woodson use that word? He called the victims niggers?'

'Yeah, he said that.'

I hesitated as I worked on the phrasing of the next question. I knew Vincent was waiting to object if I gave him the opening. I could not ask Torrance to interpret. I couldn't use the word 'why' when it came to Woodson's meaning or motivation.

'Mr Torrance, in the black community the word nigger could mean different things, could it not?'

'Yes.'

'The defendant is African-American. As are you, correct, sir?'

Torrance started to laugh. 'Since I was born,' he said.

'When Mr Woodson used that word, did it shock you?'

Torrance thought about the question. 'Not really.'

'Why weren't you shocked, Mr Torrance?'

'I guess it's 'cause I hear it all a' time, man.'

'From other black men?'

'That's right. I heard it from white folks, too.'

'OK, Mr Torrance. Do you use that word on occasion?'

'I think I have.'

'When you have used it, who were you referring to?'

Torrance shrugged. 'Other fellas.'

'Other black men?'

'That's right.'

'Have you ever on occasion referred to white men as niggers?'

'No.'

'OK, so then what did you take the meaning to be when Barnett Woodson described the two men as niggers?'

Vincent moved in his seat, going through the body language of making an objection. But he must have known it would be useless.

'I took it that they were black and he killed 'em both.'

I looked at the judge. 'Your Honour, may I approach the witness?'

'You may,' he said.

I walked to the witness stand and put the file down in front of Torrance. It was faded orange—a colour code used by county jailers denoting private legal documents an inmate is authorised to possess. 'OK, Mr Torrance, I have placed before you a file in which Mr Woodson keeps discovery documents provided by his attorneys. I ask once again if you recognise it.'

'I seen a lotta orange files in high power. It don't mean I seen that one.'

'You are saying you never saw Mr Woodson with his file?'

'I don't rightly remember.'

'Mr Torrance, you were with Mr Woodson in the same module for thirty-two days. You testified he confided in you and confessed to you. Are you saying you never saw him with that file?'

I had backed him into a no-win corner. 'What I'm saying is I seen him with his file but I never looked at what was in it.'

Bang. I had him. 'Then I'll ask you to open and inspect it.'

The witness followed the instruction and I went back to the lectern.

'What do you see when you open the file, Mr Torrance?'

'One side's got photos of two bodies on the ground. The other side is a bunch of documents and reports and such.'

'Could you read from the first document on the right side? Just read the first line of the summary.'

'No, I can't read. I didn't get the schooling.'

'Can you read any of the words next to the boxes that are checked at the top of the summary?'

I knew that Torrance's reading had been tested during his last stint in prison and determined to be below second grade skills.

'Not really,' he said. 'I can't read.'

I walked over to the defence table and grabbed another file and a pen. I went back to the lectern and printed CAUCASIAN on the outside of the file in large block letters. I held up the file. 'Mr Torrance, this is one of the words checked on the summary. Can you read this word?'

Torrance was already shaking his head when Vincent objected to the demonstration without proper foundation and the judge sustained.

'OK, Mr Torrance,' I said. 'Let's move to the other side of the file. Could you describe the bodies in the photos?'

'Um, two men. It looks like they opened up some chicken wire and some tarps and they're laying there. A bunch a police is there investigatin' and takin' pictures.'

'What race are the men on the tarps?'

'They're black.'

'Have you ever seen those photographs before, Mr Torrance?'

Vincent stood to object but it was like holding up a hand to stop a bullet. The judge sternly told him he could take his seat. It was his way of telling the prosecutor he was just going to have to sit back and take what was coming. You put the liar on the stand, you take the fall with him.

'Mr Torrance, have you seen those photographs before?'

'No, sir, not before right now.'

'Would you agree that the pictures portray what you described earlier? That being the bodies of two slain black men?'

'That's what they look like. But I ain't seen them before.'

'Are you sure?'

'Something like these, I wouldn't forget.'

'You've told us Mr Woodson confessed to killing two black men but he is on trial for killing two white men. Wouldn't you agree that it appears he didn't confess to you at all?'

'No, he confessed. He told me he killed those two.'

I looked up at the judge. 'Your Honour, now might be a good time for the prosecutor to reacquaint his witness with the penalties for perjury.'

It was a dramatic move made for the benefit of the jury. I was expecting I would have to continue with Torrance and eviscerate him with the blade of his own lie. But Vincent stood and asked the judge to recess the trial while he conferred with opposing counsel.

This told me I had just saved Barnett Woodson's life.

'The defence has no objection,' I told the judge.

AFTER THE JURY filed out of the box I returned to the defence table as the courtroom deputy was cuffing my client to take him back to the cell.

'That guy's a lying sack of shit,' Woodson whispered to me. 'I didn't kill two black guys. They were white.'

My hope was that the deputy didn't hear that. 'Why don't you shut up?' I whispered back. 'And next time you see that lying sack of shit in lockup you shake his hand. Because of his lies the prosecutor's about to come off of the death penalty and float a deal.'

'Yeah, well, maybe I don't want no deal now. They put a damn liar on the stand, man. This whole case should go down the toilet. We can win this, Haller. Don't take no deal.'

I stared at Barnett for a moment. I had just saved his life but he wanted more. 'Don't get greedy, Barnett. I'll be back with the news.'

The deputy took him through the steel door. After the courtroom cleared Vincent and I were left looking at each other.

'So,' I said.

'First of all,' Vincent said, 'I want to make it clear that I obviously didn't know Torrance was lying.'

'Sure.'

'Why would I sabotage my own case like this?'

I waved him off. 'Jerry, don't bother. I told you in pre-trial that the guy had copped the discovery my client had in his cell. It's common sense. My guy wouldn't have said shit to your guy, a perfect stranger, and everybody knew it except you.'

'Haller, he was vetted by one of our best investigators, who told me the guy couldn't read.'

'Jerry, I'm usually pretty reasonable. I try to get along with the DA's office. But I gave you fair warning. So after the break I'm going to gut him and you're going to sit there and watch. It's called rope a dope, but when I'm done he's not the only one who's going to look like a dope. The jury's going to know that you either knew this guy was a liar or you were too dumb to realise it.'

Vincent calmly straightened his case files. He spoke in a quiet voice. 'I don't want you going forward with the cross.'

'Fine. Then cut the bull and give me a dispo I can—'

'I'll drop the death penalty. Twenty-five to life without.'

'That's not going to do it. The last thing Woodson said before they took him back was that he was willing to roll the dice. I'll go fifteen max. I think I can sell that to him.'

'No way. They'll send me back to filing buy-busts if I give you that for two cold-blooded murders. My best offer is twenty-five with parole. Not bad for what he did, killing two kids like that.'

I tried to read his face. I decided it was his best, and it wasn't a bad deal for what Barnett Woodson had done.

'I don't know,' I said. 'I think he'll say roll the dice.'

'You have to sell it to him, Haller. I can't go lower, and if you continue the cross then my career in the DA's office is finished.'

Now I hesitated. 'Wait a minute, what are you saying, Jerry? That I have to clean your mess up for you?'

'I'm saying it's a fair offer to a man who is guilty as sin. Go work your magic, Mick. Convince him. We both know you're not long for the public defender's office. You might need a favour from me someday out there in the big, bad world.'

I just stared back at him, registering the quid pro quo of the offer. I help him and somewhere down the line he helps me and Barnett Woodson does an extra couple of years in stir.

'He'll be lucky to last five years in there, let alone twenty,' Vincent said. 'What's the difference to him? But you and I? We're going places, Mickey. We can help each other here.'

I nodded slowly. Vincent was only a few years older than me but was trying to act like some kind of wise old sage.

'The thing is, Jerry, if I did what you suggest then I'd never be able to look another client in the eye again.'

I stood up and gathered my files. My plan was to go back and tell Barnett Woodson to roll the dice and let me see what I could do.

'I'll see you after the break,' I said. And then I walked away.

Two
2007

I t was a little early in the week for Lorna Taylor to be calling and checking on me. Usually she waited until at least Thursday. Never Tuesday. I picked up the phone thinking it was more than a check-in call. 'Lorna?'

'Mickey, where've you been? I've been calling all morning.'

'I went for my run. I just got out of the shower. You OK?'

'I'm fine. Are you?'

'Sure. What is—'

'You got a forthwith from Judge Holder. She wants to see you—like an hour ago.'

This gave me pause. 'About what?'

'All I know is first Michaela called, then the judge.'

Michaela Gill was the judge's clerk. And Mary Townes Holder, chief judge of the Los Angeles Superior Court, didn't call lawyers without a good reason.

'What did you tell her?'

'I said you didn't have court today and you might be on the golf course.'

'I don't play golf, Lorna.'

'Look, I couldn't think of anything.'

'It's all right, I'll call the judge. Give me the number.'

'Mickey, the judge wants to *see* you in chambers. So just go.'

'OK, I'm going. I have to get dressed.'

'Mickey? How are you really doing?'

I knew her code. I knew what she was really asking. She didn't want me appearing in front of a judge if I wasn't ready for it.

'You don't have to worry, Lorna. I'm fine. I'll be fine.'

'OK. Let me know what's going on as soon as you can.'

I felt like I was being bossed around by my wife, not my ex-wife.

'Don't worry. I will.'

AS THE CHIEF JUDGE of the Los Angeles Superior Court, Judge Mary Townes Holder did most of her work behind closed doors. Her courtroom was used on occasion but her job largely pertained to the administration of the justice system in Los Angeles County. More than 250 judgeships and forty courthouses fell under her purview. Every jury summons had her name on it and every parking space in a courthouse garage had her approval. It was Judge Holder who decided whether a judge sat in Beverly Hills or Compton, and whether they heard high-stakes financial cases in civil court or soul-draining divorce cases in family court.

I had dressed quickly in what I considered my lucky suit. It was an Italian import from Corneliani that I used to wear on verdict days. I had to take it out of a plastic bag that was hanging in the back of the closet. After that I sped downtown, thinking that I might be headed towards some sort of verdict on myself. My mind raced over the cases and clients I had left behind a year earlier. As far as I knew nothing had been left open. But maybe there had been a complaint and the judge was running her own inquiry. I entered Holder's courtroom with a lot of trepidation.

The courtroom was dark and the clerk's pod was empty. I opened the gate and was heading towards the door to the back hallway when it opened and Michaela Gill stepped through it. She ushered me in without delay.

I found the judge alone in her chambers, working at a massive desk made of dark wood. She was dressed in a maroon suit and was attractive and neat, with a slim build and brown hair kept in a short, no-nonsense style. I had never met her before but I knew she'd put twenty years in as a prosecutor before being appointed to the bench by a conservative governor.

'Mr Haller, thank you for coming,' she said. 'I'm glad your secretary finally found you.'

'She's not my secretary, Judge. But she found me. Sorry it took so long.'

'Well, you're here. I don't believe we have met, have we? I actually had a case with your father once. I was third chair, just out of USC Law. It was a murder case and they let me handle one witness. I prepared a week for my examination and your father destroyed the man on cross in ten minutes.'

I nodded. Over the years I had met older lawyers who had Mickey Haller Sr stories. I had very few of my own.

'But that's not why I called you here,' she said. 'Did you know Jerry Vincent?'

I was immediately thrown by her use of the past tense. 'Jerry? Yes, I know Jerry. What about him?'

'He's dead.'

'Dead?'

'Murdered, actually.'

'When?'

'Last night. I'm sorry. Were you close?'

It was a good question. 'We had cases against each other when he was with the DA and I was at the PD. We both left for one-man shops around the same time and over the years we worked some cases together, sort of covered for each other when it was needed.'

I had a professional relationship with Jerry Vincent. Every now and then we clicked glasses at Four Green Fields, but for me to say we were close would have been an exaggeration. I knew little about him outside of the world of law. I had heard something about a divorce a while back but had never even asked him about it.

'You seem to forget, Mr Haller, but I was with the DA back when Mr Vincent was an up-and-comer. But then he lost a big case and his star faded. I seem to recall you were the defence attorney.'

'Barnett Woodson. I got an acquittal on a double murder.'

'Then why would Jerry ever work with you?'

'Because a couple of years later he was making five times what he made with the DA. He called me up and thanked me for showing him the light.'

The judge nodded knowingly. 'He wanted the money.'

I shrugged like I was uncomfortable answering for a dead man. Then I tried to put the focus back on Jerry Vincent's murder.

'I can't believe this about Jerry. Do you know what happened?'

'He was found late last night shot to death in his car in the garage at his office. I am told the police are still at the crime scene and there have been no arrests. This comes from a *Times* reporter who called my chambers to make an enquiry about what will happen now with Mr Vincent's clients— especially Walter Elliot.'

I nodded. For the last twelve months I had been in a vacuum but it wasn't so airtight that I hadn't heard about the movie mogul murder case, one of the high-profile cases Vincent had scored over the years. Walter Elliot was the chairman/owner of Archway Pictures and a powerful man in Hollywood. He had been charged with murdering his wife and her lover after discovering them together in a Malibu beach house. The case was drawing wide media attention.

The judge broke through my reverie. 'Are you familiar with RPC two-three hundred?'

I squinted my eyes at the question. 'Uh . . . not exactly.'

'Let me refresh your memory. It is the section of the California Bar's rules of professional conduct referring to the transfer or sale of a law practice. Mr Vincent apparently named you as his second in his standard contract of representation but additionally he filed a motion ten years ago that allowed for the transfer of his practice to you should he become incapacitated or deceased.'

I just stared at her. I knew about the clause in Vincent's standard contract. I had the same in mine naming him. But the judge was telling me that I now had Jerry's cases, Walter Elliot included. Each client would be free to move on to another attorney, but I would have first shot at them.

I hadn't had a client in a year and the plan was to start back slow, not with a full case load like the one I had apparently just inherited.

'However,' the judge said, 'I've checked with some of the judges and I'm aware that you have not been practising law for almost a year. I have found no explanation for this. Before I issue the order appointing you replacement counsel, I need to be assured I'm not turning Mr Vincent's clients over to the wrong man.'

'Judge, you're right. I sort of took myself out of the game for a while. But I just started taking steps to get back in.'

Her eyes held mine. 'Why did you take yourself out?'

I spoke very carefully. 'I had a case a couple years ago. The client's name was Louis Roulet—'

'I remember the case, Mr Haller. You got shot. But I seem to remember news stories about you coming back to the job.'

'Well,' I said, 'I came back too soon. I had been gut shot, and the next thing I knew I started having pain and the doctors said I had a hernia. So I had an operation and there were complications, more pain, and, well, it knocked me down for a while. I decided the second time not to come back until I was sure I was ready.'

The judge nodded sympathetically. I guessed I'd been right to leave out my addiction to pain pills and the stint in rehab.

'Money wasn't an issue,' I said. 'I got a settlement from the insurance company. I took my time coming back, but I'm ready.'

'Then I guess inheriting an entire practice is quite convenient, isn't it?' she said in a smarmy tone.

'All I can tell you is that I'd take good care of Jerry's clients.'

The judge nodded but she didn't look at me. I knew the tell. She knew something that bothered her. Maybe she knew about the rehab.

'According to Bar records you've been disciplined several times,' she said.

'All of it ancient history, Judge. All technicalities. If you called the California Bar today, I'm sure you were told that I'm in good standing.'

She dropped her eyes to the document in front of her on the desk. 'Very well then,' she said.

She scribbled a signature on the last page. I felt the flutter of excitement begin to build in my chest.

'Here is an order transferring the practice to you,' the judge said. 'I'm going to be monitoring you. I want an updated inventory by the beginning of next week. The status of every case. After that I want biweekly updates. Am I being clear?'

'Perfectly clear, Judge. For how long do you want updates?'

Her face hardened. 'Until I tell you to stop.' She handed me the order. 'If I were you I'd get over to his office and protect my new clients from any unlawful search and seizure of their files by the police. If you have any problem you can call me.'

'Yes, Your Honour. Thank you.'

'Good luck, Mr Haller.'

I stood up and headed out of the room. Once in the hallway I read the document, confirming that what had just happened was real.

It was. It granted me immediate access to the fallen attorney's office, files, and bank accounts into which client advances had been deposited.

I pulled out my cellphone and called Lorna Taylor. I asked her to look up the address of Jerry Vincent's office. I told her to meet me there and pick up two sandwiches on her way.

'Why?' she asked.

'Because I haven't had lunch.'

'No, why are we going to Jerry Vincent's office?'

'Because we're back in business.'

I WAS IN MY LINCOLN driving towards Jerry's office when I thought of something and called Lorna back. 'I'm going to need an investigator. How would you feel if I called Cisco?'

Cisco was Dennis Wojciechowski, her significant other as of the last year. I was the one who had introduced them when I had used him on a case. Last I heard, they were now living together.

'Well, I have no problem working with Cisco. But I wish you would tell me what this is all about.'

Lorna knew Jerry Vincent as a voice on the phone. I couldn't remember if they had ever met in person. I had wanted to tell her the news in person but things were moving too quickly for that.

'Jerry Vincent is dead. He was murdered last night and I'm getting first shot at all of his cases. Including Walter Elliot.'

She was silent for a long moment before responding.

'My God . . . how? He was such a nice man.'

'I couldn't remember if you had ever met him.'

Lorna worked out of her condo in West Hollywood. All my calls and billing went through her. If there was a brick and mortar office for the law firm of Michael Haller and Associates then her place was it. But there weren't any associates and when I worked, my office was the back seat of my car. This left few occasions for Lorna to meet face to face with any of the people I associated with.

'He came to our wedding, don't you remember?'

'That's right. I forgot.'

'Did he have a family?'

'I think he was divorced. I don't know if there were kids.'

Lorna didn't say anything. We both had our own thoughts occupying us. 'Let me go so I can call Cisco,' I finally said.

'All right. What kind of sandwich do you want?'

'Stop at Dusty's and get me one of those turkey sandwiches with cranberry sauce. And get something for Cisco in case he's hungry.'

'All right.'

I hung up and called Dennis Wojciechowski's cellphone. When he answered I heard a mixture of wind and exhaust blast. He was on his bike and even though his helmet was set up with an earpiece and mike, I had to yell. 'It's Mickey Haller. Pull over.'

I waited and heard him cut the engine on his '63 pan head.

'What's up, Mick?' he asked when it finally got quiet. 'Haven't heard from you in a long time.'

Wojciechowski was a freelance defence investigator I had used on a few cases before. That was how he had met Lorna, collecting his pay. But I had known him ten years before that because of his association with the Road Saints motorcycle club, a group for which I served as a de facto house counsel. Largely because there was already a Dennis in the membership— and his last name Wojciechowski was intolerably difficult to pronounce— they christened him the Cisco Kid, riffing off his dark looks and moustache. A big, imposing man, his moustache trimmed now and going grey, Cisco was a thorough and thoughtful investigator. And he could be physically intimidating when necessary, a useful attribute.

'Where are you?' I asked. 'You on a case?'

'No, just a ride. Burbank. Why, you got something for me? You taking on a case finally?'

'A lot of cases. And I'm going to need an investigator.'

I gave him the address of Vincent's office and told him to meet me there. I knew that Vincent would have used his own investigators, and that there might be a loss of time as Cisco got up to speed on the cases, but I wanted an investigator I knew I could trust.

After closing the phone I realised I had driven right by Vincent's office on Broadway. I wasted ten minutes working my way back, catching red lights, and resolved to hire a driver again as soon as possible so I could concentrate on cases instead of addresses.

Vincent's office was in a six-storey structure simply called The Legal Center. Being so close to the main downtown courthouses meant it was a building full of trial lawyers. I saw the opening for the parking garage next door and pulled in.

As I was taking the ticket out of the machine a uniformed police officer approached my car. 'Sir, we are conducting a crime scene investigation. There's no parking on the first level. They haven't cleared the scene.'

I nodded and headed up the ramp. The first floor was empty of vehicles except for two patrol cars and a black BMW coupé being hauled onto the bed of a truck from the police garage. Jerry Vincent's car, I assumed. Two uniformed cops signalled for me to keep going up. I didn't find a space until I got to the fourth floor.

The office I was looking for was on the first floor at the front of the building. Its opaque glass door wasn't locked. I entered a reception area. Behind a counter sat a woman whose eyes were red from crying. 'Are you with the police?' she asked.

'No, I'm not,' I replied.

'Then I'm sorry, the office is closed today.'

I pulled the court order from Judge Holder out of the inside pocket of my jacket. 'Not for me,' I said.

She unfolded the document and stared at it. 'What is this?'

'That's a court order,' I said. 'My name is Michael Haller and Judge Holder has appointed me replacement counsel in regard to Jerry Vincent's clients. That means we'll be working together.'

She shook her head as if warding off some invisible threat. 'You can't do this. Mr Vincent wouldn't want this.'

I took the court papers out of her hand. 'Actually, I can. The chief judge of Los Angeles Superior Court has directed me to do this. And if you look at the contracts of representation that Mr Vincent had his clients sign you will find my name already listed as associate counsel. I know this has been a very difficult day for you. It's been difficult for me—I knew Jerry going back to his days at the DA. So you have my sympathy.'

I waited but I wasn't getting a response. I pressed on.

'I'm going to need some things to get started. First of all, Jerry's calendar. I want to put together a list of active—'

'It's gone,' she said abruptly.

'What's gone?'

'His laptop. The police told me whoever did this took his briefcase out of the car. He kept everything on his laptop.'

'You mean his calendar? He didn't keep a hard copy?'

'He kept it all on his laptop and he kept a hard copy in the old portfolio he carried. But they're both gone.'

I nodded. The missing calendar wasn't insurmountable.

'What about files? Did he have any in the briefcase?'

'I don't think so. He kept all the files here.'

'OK, good. I'll also need to see any books pertaining to the trust and operating accounts.'

'You're not going to take his money.'

'It's not—I apologise. Let's start over. What's your name?'

'Wren Williams.'

'OK, Wren, let me explain. It's not his money. It's his clients' money and until they say otherwise, his clients are now my clients. Now I need you to decide if you are with me or against me, Wren. Because if you are with me, I need you to get me the things I ask for. If you are against me, then I need you to go home now.'

'The detectives told me to stay until they were finished.'

'What detectives? Only a couple of uniforms are out there.'

'The detectives in Mr Vincent's office.'

'You let—' I didn't finish. I stepped round the counter, headed towards two doors on the back wall and picked the one on the left.

Jerry Vincent's office was large and opulent and empty. I turned in a circle until I found myself staring into the eyes of a fish mounted next to the door. The fish was a beautiful green with a white underbelly, its body arched as if it had just jumped out of the water. Its mouth was open.

THE BRASS VERDICT | 25

A brass plate said: *If I'd Kept My Mouth Shut I Wouldn't Be Here.* Words to live by, I thought.

The sound of a metal drawer being banged closed spun me back round. On the other side of the room a door was open about a foot and I could see light. I approached the lighted room quickly and pushed the door all the way open. It was the file room, a large, windowless walk-in closet with rows of filing cabinets. Two men sat at the work table against the back wall. One old, one young, they had their jackets draped over the chairs. I saw their guns and holsters and their badges clipped to their belts.

'What are you doing?' I asked gruffly.

The men looked up from their stack of files. The older detective's eyes momentarily widened in surprise when he saw me. 'LAPD,' he said. 'And I guess I should ask you the same question.'

'Those are my files and you're going to have to put them down right now.' I pulled the court order from my jacket again. 'My name is—'

'I know who you are.' The older man stood up. 'But I still don't know what you're doing here.'

I handed him the order. 'I've been appointed by the chief judge of the Superior Court as replacement counsel to Jerry Vincent's clients. You have no right to be in here, Detective. It's a clear violation of my clients' rights to protection against unlawful search and seizure. These files contain privileged attorney–client information.'

The detective flipped through the paperwork to the signature. He didn't seem impressed. 'Vincent's been murdered,' he said. 'The identity of the killer could be in one of these files. We have to—'

'No, what you have to do is get out of this file room.'

The detective didn't move a muscle. 'I consider this part of a crime scene,' he said. 'It's you who has to leave.'

'Read the order, Detective. I'm not going anywhere. Your crime scene is out in the garage and no judge in LA would let you extend it to this office. It's time for you to leave.'

'If I leave, I'm going to shut this place down and seal it.'

I hated getting into pissing matches with cops but sometimes there was no choice. 'You do that and I'll have it unsealed in an hour. And you'll be standing in front of the chief judge explaining how you trampled on the rights of every one of Vincent's clients.'

The detective smiled like he was mildly amused. He held up the court order. 'This gives you the entire practice? I guess that puts you on our list.'

'What list?'

'Our suspect list.'

'That's ridiculous. Why would I be on it?'

'You just told us why. You inherited all of the victim's clients. That's got to amount to some sort of financial windfall, doesn't it? Care to tell us where you were between eight and midnight last night?'

He grinned at me again without any warmth, giving me that practised cop's smile of judgment. His brown eyes were so dark I couldn't see the line between iris and pupil. Like shark eyes, they didn't seem to carry any light.

'I'm not even going to begin to explain how ludicrous that is,' I said. 'I didn't even know I was in line for this.'

'Don't worry, we'll be checking you out.'

'Good. Now please leave or I make the call to the judge.'

The detective picked a file up off the table and shoved it into my chest. 'Here's one of your new files, Counsellor. Don't choke on it.'

He stepped to the door and his partner followed. I had a feeling it wouldn't be the last time I saw them.

'Look, detectives, I'm sorry it's like this. I don't even know what I have here. Give me some time to—'

'We don't have time,' the older man said. 'We lose momentum and we lose the case. Do you understand what you're getting yourself into here? Whoever killed Vincent in that garage was waiting for him. They knew where he was and how to get to him. He was ambushed. If I were you, I'd watch myself with those new clients of yours. Jerry Vincent knew his killer.'

'Wait,' I said. 'You have a card? Give me a card.'

The detectives turned back. The older one pulled a card out of his pocket and gave it to me. 'That's got all my numbers.'

'Let me just get the lay of the land here and then I'll call and set something up. There's got to be a way to cooperate and not trample on anybody's rights.'

'Whatever you say, you're the lawyer.'

I looked down at the name on the card. Harry Bosch. 'Look, Detective Bosch, good luck with the case. I hope you crack it.'

Bosch nodded and there was something familiar about the physical gesture. He turned to follow his partner out.

'Detective, did we ever cross paths on a case before?'

Bosch smiled glibly and shook his head. 'No,' he said. 'If we'd been on a case, you'd remember me.'

Three

An hour later I was behind Jerry Vincent's desk with Lorna Taylor and Dennis Wojciechowski sitting across from me. We were eating our sandwiches but nobody had much of an appetite considering what had happened to the office's predecessor.

I had sent Wren Williams home. She had been unable to stop crying or objecting to my taking control of her dead boss's cases. She asked whether I was going to fire her and I told her the jury was still out but to report for work as usual the next day.

With Jerry Vincent dead and Wren Williams gone, we were left stumbling around in the dark until Lorna figured out the filing system and started pulling the active case files. From calendar notations in each file she was able to put together a master calendar—the key component in any trial lawyer's professional life. Once we had worked up a calendar I began to breathe a little easier.

The calendar was light. A few case hearings here and there but it was obvious Vincent was keeping things clear in advance of the Walter Elliot trial, which was scheduled to begin in nine days.

'So let's start,' I said. 'According to the calendar we've pieced together, I've got a sentencing in forty-five minutes. We could have a preliminary discussion, then I could leave you two here while I go to court. Then I'll come back after court and see how much farther we've gotten before Cisco and I go out and start knocking on doors.'

They both nodded, their mouths working on their sandwiches.

Lorna was as beautiful as ever. She was a stunner with blonde hair and eyes that made you think you were the centre of the universe. I had kept her on salary the whole year. I could afford it with my insurance settlement and I didn't want to run the risk that she'd be working for another lawyer when it was time for me to come back.

'Let's start with the money,' I said.

Lorna nodded. She had moved on from the active files to the bank books. 'All right, good news and bad. He's got thirty-eight thousand in the operating account and a hundred twenty-nine thousand in the trust account.'

I whistled. That was a lot of cash in the trust account. Money from clients goes into the trust account and as work proceeds is transferred to the operating account. I always want more money in the operating account, because once it's moved from the trust account, the money's mine.

'There's a reason why it's so lopsided,' Lorna said. 'He just deposited a cheque on Friday for a hundred thousand dollars from Walter Elliot.'

I tapped the makeshift calendar I'd drawn on a legal pad. 'The Elliot trial starts Thursday next week. He took the hundred up front. As soon as we're done here, see if the cheque cleared.'

'Got it.'

'If a hundred's from Elliot, who's the rest for?'

Lorna opened one of the accounting books. Each dollar in a trust fund must be accounted in regard to which client it is being held for. An attorney must be able to determine how much of a client's advance has been transferred to the operating fund and used, and how much is on reserve in trust. A hundred thousand of Vincent's trust account was earmarked for the Elliot trial. That left only twenty-nine thousand for the rest of the active cases. That wasn't a lot, considering the stack of active files we'd pulled together.

'That's the bad news,' Lorna said. 'It looks like there are only five or six other cases with trust deposits. With the rest of the active cases the money's already been moved into operating, been spent or the clients owe the firm. He's got two on pre-trial payment plans, Samuels and Henson. They're both about five thousand behind.'

I looked down at my notes. Both Samuels and Henson were on a sub-list I had drawn up while reviewing the actives. It was a listing of cases I was going to cut loose if I could. If there was something I didn't like about a case, then it went on the sub-list.

'No problem,' I said. 'We'll cut 'em loose.'

Samuels was a manslaughter DUI case and Henson was a felony grand theft. Patrick Henson momentarily held my interest because Vincent was going to build a defence around the client's addiction to prescription painkillers. He would lay out a case in which the doctor who overprescribed the drugs to Henson was the one most responsible for the consequences of the addiction he created.

I was intimately familiar with this defence because I had employed it repeatedly over the last two years to try to absolve myself of the many infractions I had committed as father, ex-husband and friend. But I put Henson into what I called the dog pile because I knew at heart the defence didn't hold up—at least not for me.

Lorna nodded and made notes. 'How many in the dog pile?'

'We came up with thirty-one active cases,' I said. 'Of those, I'm thinking only seven look like dogs.'

'You think the judge is just going to let you drop those?'

'Nope. But I'll figure something out. Anything else?'

Lorna shook her head. 'That's about it. When you're in court I'll call the bank. You want us both to be signers on the accounts?'

'Yeah, just like with my accounts.'

I hadn't considered the potential difficulty in getting my hands on the money that was in the Vincent accounts. That was what I had Lorna for. She was good on the business end in ways I wasn't.

I checked my watch. I had ten minutes before I had to get going to court. 'Cisco, whaddaya got?'

I had told him earlier to work his contacts and to monitor Vincent's murder investigation as closely as possible.

'Not a lot,' he said. 'I called a guy I know in forensics and they're still processing everything. Vincent was shot at least two times and there were no shells at the scene. A contact in communications told me the first call came in at twelve forty-three.'

'Is there a general idea of what happened?'

'It looks like Vincent worked late, which was apparently his routine every Monday. He packed his briefcase, locked up and left. He goes to the garage, gets in his car and gets popped through the driver's side window. When they found him the car was in park, the ignition on. It was in the low sixties last night. He could've put the window down because he liked the chill, or he could've lowered it for somebody coming to the car.'

'Somebody he knew.' I thought about what Detective Bosch had said. 'Nobody was working in the garage?'

'No, the attendant leaves at six. You have to put your money in the machine after that or use your monthly pass. There are licence-plate cameras where you drive in and out but there was nothing useful on the tape.'

'Who found Jerry?'

'The security guard hits the garage a couple times a night.'

I nodded, thinking the killer knew the garage.

'OK, stay on it. What about the detective?'

'Harry Bosch. Supposedly he's one of the best. Retired a few years ago and the police chief himself recruited him back. Full name is Hieronymus Bosch. Thirty-three years on the job and you know what that means.'

'No, what does it mean?'

'Well, under the LAPD's pension programme you max out at thirty years, so it makes no economic sense to stay.'

'Unless you're a man on a mission. Wait a second,' I said. 'You said Hieronymus Bosch? Like the painter?'

'I don't know about any painter. But that's his name. Rhymes with anonymous, I was told. Weird, if you ask me.'

'No weirder than Wojciechowski—if you ask me.'

'I thought you didn't know him, Mickey,' Lorna said.

'I never met him before today but the name . . . I know the name.'

'You mean from the paintings?'

I didn't want to get into a discussion of distant history. 'Never mind. I've got to get going.' I stood up. 'I'll be in Judge Champagne's court. I'm taking a bunch of the active files to read while I'm waiting.'

'I'll walk you out,' Lorna said.

I saw her throw a look at Cisco. We walked to the reception area. I knew what she was going to say but I let her say it.

'Mickey, are you sure you're ready for this?'

'Absolutely.'

'This wasn't the plan. You were going to come back slowly, take a couple cases. You're taking on an entire practice.'

'I'm not practising.'

'Look, be serious.'

'Don't you see this is better than the plan? The Elliot case is like having a billboard that says "I'm back" in big neon letters!'

'Yeah, and the Elliot case alone is so much pressure—'

'Lorna, I'm fine, I'm ready. I thought you'd be happy about this. We've got money coming in for the first time in a year.'

'I don't care about that. I want to make sure you're OK.'

'I'm more than OK. I'm excited. I feel like in one day I've got my mojo back. Don't drag me down. OK?'

She stared at me and I stared back and finally a reluctant smile peeked through her stern face. 'All right. Go get 'em.'

'Don't worry. I will.'

DESPITE THE ASSURANCES I had given Lorna, thoughts about all the work to be done played in my mind as I walked to the bridge that linked the office building with the garage. I had forgotten I'd parked on the fourth level and walked up three ramps before I found the Lincoln. I popped the trunk and put a stack of files into my bag.

The bag was a hybrid I had picked up at a store called Suitcase City while I was plotting my comeback. It was a backpack with straps I could put over my shoulders on the days I was strong. It also had a handle so I could carry it like a briefcase if I wanted. And it had two wheels and a telescoping handle so I could just roll it behind me on the days I was weak.

Lately, the stronger days far outnumbered the weak and I probably could make it with the traditional lawyer's leather briefcase. But the bag had a logo on it—a mountain ridge with SUITCASE CITY printed across it like the Hollywood sign. Skylights swept the horizon, completing the dream image of desire and hope. I think that was the real reason I liked the bag. Because I knew Suitcase City wasn't a store. It was a place. It was Los Angeles.

Los Angeles was the kind of place where everybody was from somewhere else. People drawn by the dream, people running from the nightmare. Figuratively, literally, metaphorically, everybody in LA keeps a bag packed. Just in case.

As I closed the trunk I was startled to see a man standing next to my car.

'Mr Haller, I work for the *Times* and wonder if I could talk to you about Jerry Vincent.'

I shook my head. 'I don't know anything about the case.'

'But you're taking over his clients, aren't you?'

'Who told you that?'

'Our court reporter got a copy of the order from Judge Holder. Why did Mr Vincent pick you? Were you two good friends?'

I ducked into the car but left the door open as I turned the key. 'Look, what's your name?'

'Jack McEvoy. I work the police beat.'

'Good for you, Jack. But I can't talk about this right now. You want to give me a card, I'll call you when I can talk.'

He made no move to give me a card. He just put his elbow on the car roof. 'I was hoping we could make a deal,' he said. 'I've got the police department wired and you've got the courthouse wired. You tell me what you're hearing and I'll tell you. I have a feeling this is going to be a big case.'

'You got a card?'

This time he took a card out of his pocket and handed it to me.

'OK, deal.'

I signalled him away and pulled the door closed, then started the engine.

He was still there. He called out to me just as I put the car in drive.

'Hey, Haller, love the plate.'

I waved at him as I drove down the ramp. I tried to remember which of my Lincolns I was driving. I have a fleet of three town cars left over from my days when I carried a full case load. In the last year, I'd put all three into a rotation to keep the dust out of the pipes. Part of my comeback strategy, I guess. The cars were exact duplicates, except for the licence plates.

When I got to the booth and handed in my stub, I saw a video screen next to the cash register. It showed the view from a camera located behind my car. I could see my vanity plate: IWALKEM.

I smirked. I walk 'em all right. I was heading to court to meet one of Jerry Vincent's clients for the first time. I was going to shake his hand and then walk him right into prison.

JUDGE JUDITH CHAMPAGNE was on the bench and hearing motions when I walked into her courtroom with five minutes to spare. There were eight other lawyers waiting their turn. I parked my roller bag against the rail and whispered to the courtroom deputy, explaining that I was there to handle the sentencing of Edgar Reese for Jerry Vincent. He told me the judge's motions calendar was running long but Reese would be first out for his sentencing. I asked if I could see Reese and the deputy got up and led me to the holding cell.

'Edgar Reese?' I said.

A small, powerfully built white man came over to the bars.

'My name's Michael Haller. I'm filling in for your attorney today.'

I didn't think there was much point in explaining to this guy what had happened to Vincent. It would only make Reese ask me a bunch of questions I didn't have the time or the knowledge to answer.

'Where's Jerry?' Reese asked.

'Couldn't make it. Did he go over the sentence when you pleaded out?'

'Yeah, he told me. Five years in state, out in three if I behave.'

It was more like four but I wasn't going to mess with it.

'OK, well, the judge is finishing some stuff up out there and then they'll bring you out. The prosecutor will read you a bunch of legalese, you answer yes that you understand it, and then the judge will enter the sentence. Fifteen minutes in and out.'

'I don't care how long it takes. I ain't got nowhere to go.'

I nodded and left him there. I tapped lightly on the metal door so the deputy in the courtroom would hear it. He let me out and I sat in the first row of the gallery. I opened up my case and pulled out most of the files.

The top file was Edgar Reese. I had already reviewed this one in preparation for the sentencing. It was a garden-variety drug case.

The next file belonged to Patrick Henson, the painkiller case I had told Lorna I'd be dropping. I reconsidered, and opened the file.

Henson was a twenty-four-year-old surfer from Malibu. He was a professional but on the low end of the spectrum with limited endorsements and winnings from the pro tour. In a competition on Maui he'd wiped out and crimped his shoulder. After surgery the doctor prescribed oxycodone. Eighteen months later Henson was an addict, chasing pills to chase the pain. He lost his sponsors and hit bottom when he stole a necklace from a home in Malibu to which he'd been invited by a female friend. According to the sheriff's report the necklace belonged to his friend's mother and contained eight diamonds. It was listed as worth $25,000 but Henson hocked it for $400 and went to Mexico to buy 200 tabs of oxy.

Henson was easy to connect to the caper, and film from a security camera showed him pawning the necklace. Because of its high value, he was hit with a full deck, dealing in stolen property and grand theft along with illegal drug possession.

When Vincent took Henson on, the surfer made the initial $5,000 advance payment in trade. Vincent took all twelve of his custom-made Trick Henson boards and sold them through his liquidator to collectors and on eBay. Henson was also placed on the thousand-a-month payment plan but had never made a payment because he had gone into rehab the day after being bailed out of jail by his mother. According to the file, Henson had successfully completed rehab and was working part-time at a surf camp for kids. He was barely making enough to live on.

The file was replete with motions to continue and other delay tactics while Vincent waited for Henson to come across with more cash. This was standard practice. There was a cellphone number in the file. I could call him right now. The question was, did I want to?

I looked up at the bench. There were still three lawyers waiting their turn at motions. I got up and whispered to the deputy, 'I'm going out to the hallway to make a call.'

He nodded. 'Just turn that phone off before coming back in.'

I walked out with the file, found a reasonably quiet spot and called the number. It was answered after two rings. 'This is Trick.'

'Patrick Henson?'

'Yeah, who's this?'

'I'm your new lawyer. My name is Mi—'

'Whoah, wait a minute. What happened to my old lawyer? I gave that guy Vincent—'

'He's dead, Patrick. He passed away last night.'

'Nooooo.'

'Yes, Patrick. I'm sorry. My name is Michael Haller and I'm taking over his cases. I've been reviewing your file and see you haven't made a single payment on the schedule Mr Vincent put you on.'

'Ah, man, this is the deal. I've been concentrating on staying right and I've got no money. OK? I gave Vincent all my boards. He counted it as five grand but I know those long boards were worth at least a grand apiece. He told me he got enough to get started but all he's been doing is delaying.'

'Are you staying right, Patrick? Are you clean?'

'As a whistle, man. Vincent told me it was the only way I'd have a shot at staying out of jail.'

'Jerry was right, Patrick. You got a job?'

'Man, don't you guys see? No one's going to give a guy like me a job. I'm waiting on this case and I might be in jail before it's all over. I mean, I teach water babies part-time on the beach but it don't pay me jack. I'm living out of my car, sleeping on the lifeguard stand at Sunset Beach.'

'Yeah, I know, life sucks. You still have a driver's licence?'

'That's about all I got left.'

I made a quick decision.

'OK, you know where Jerry Vincent's office is?'

'Yeah, I delivered the boards there. And my fish.'

'Your fish?'

'He took a sixty-pound tarpon I caught when I was a kid back in Florida. He said he was going to put it on the wall.'

'Yeah, well, your fish is still there. Anyway, be at the office at nine sharp tomorrow morning and I'll interview you for a job.'

'Doing what?'

'Driving me. I'll pay you fifteen bucks an hour to drive and another fifteen towards your fees. How's that?'

There was a moment of silence. 'That's good, man. I can be there for that.'

'Good. See you then. Just remember, Patrick. You gotta stay clean. If you're not, I'll know. Believe me, I'll know.'

Four

The message from Lorna Taylor was short and to the point. I got it the moment I turned my phone on after leaving the courtroom and seeing Edgar Reese get his five years. She told me she'd been in touch with Judge Holder's clerk about obtaining a court order the bank was requiring before putting Lorna's and my names on the Vincent bank accounts. The judge had agreed to draw up the order and I could walk down the hallway to her chambers to pick it up.

The courtroom was dark but Michaela Gill was in her pod next to the bench. Judge Holder still had the order with her in chambers and I asked if there was any chance I could talk to her for a few minutes. Michaela got up and went down the hallway located behind her station. At the end was the door to the judge's chambers and I watched her knock once before being summoned to enter. When she opened the door I could see a man in a chair. I recognised him as the judge's husband, an attorney named Mitch Lester.

Michaela came out carrying the court order and told me I would be allowed back as soon as the judge finished up with her visitor. I wandered the courtroom, looking around and thinking about what I was going to say to the judge. After three minutes I heard a bell tone sound at the clerk's station and Mrs Gill said I was free to go back to the judge's chambers.

When I took a seat in front of the judge she asked, 'What can I do for you, Mr Haller? You got the order?'

'Yes, Your Honour. Thank you for that. I wanted to update you a little bit and ask a question about something.'

'Please go ahead then.'

'Well, on the update. Things are going a bit slow because Vincent's laptop computer and hard copy calendar were stolen. We had to build a new calendar after pulling the active files.'

'How many active cases are we talking about?'

'It looks like there are thirty active cases. I've had a conversation with one client and it looks like I will be continuing as his lawyer.'

'Was that Walter Elliot?'

'Uh, no, I plan to talk to him later today. But, what I wanted to ask about was the police. When I got over to the office this morning I found a couple of detectives going through the files. Jerry's receptionist was there but she hadn't tried to stop it.'

'I hope you did. Those officers should have known better.'

'Yes, Your Honour, they backed off once I objected.'

She nodded. 'Then why are you here?'

'I'm wondering whether I should let them back in. The detective in charge said the evidence suggests that Vincent knew his killer and probably allowed him to get close enough to shoot him. So they were looking for potential suspects when I walked in on them.'

The judge waved her hands in a gesture of dismissal. 'And trampling on clients' rights as they were doing it.'

'They left behind a stack of files on the table. I looked them over and there were threats in those files.'

'Threats against Mr Vincent?'

'Yes. Cases in which his clients weren't happy about the outcome. There were threats and Vincent took each threat seriously enough to make a detailed record of what was said.'

The judge leaned back. 'You believe we are inhibiting the investigation by not allowing the police to do their job.'

'I was wondering if there was a way to limit the harm to clients but let the police follow the investigation.'

The judge considered this in silence, then sighed. 'I wish my husband had stayed. I value his opinion greatly.'

'Well, I had an idea. I was thinking that I could vet the files myself and draw up a list of the people who threatened Jerry. I could then pass it on to Detective Bosch and give him some of the details of the threats as well. This way he's happy, I'm happy.'

'Bosch is the lead detective?'

'Yes, Harry Bosch. He's with Robbery-Homicide.'

'You have to understand that even if you just give Bosch the names, you are still breaching client confidentiality. You could be disbarred for this.'

'Well, I believe there's a way out. One of the mechanisms of relief from the client confidentiality bond is in the case of threat to safety. I've been directly told by the lead detective on the case that it is highly likely that the identity of Jerry Vincent's killer is contained in Jerry's own files. Those files are now mine, so that information constitutes a threat to me. When I go out and start meeting these clients I could shake hands with the killer and not even know it. I feel I'm in some jeopardy here, Judge.'

'All right, Mr Haller. I believe that if you vet the files as you have suggested then you will be acting in an acceptable manner. I would like you to file a motion that explains your actions and the feeling of threat you are under. I will sign it and seal it and with luck it will never see the light of day.'

'Thank you, Your Honour.'

'Anything else?'

'Yes, Your Honour. I saw your calendar from last week out there and saw that Jerry came in on the Elliot matter. Do you mind my asking what the hearing was about?'

'It was an emergency motion. Mr Vincent came in because Judge Stanton had revoked bail and ordered Mr Elliot remanded to custody. Mr Elliot had travelled to a film festival in New York without getting permission. Mr Vincent came to me for an emergency stay of his client's incarceration. I decided to give Mr Elliot a second chance and to modify his freedom by making him wear an ankle monitor.'

'I understand, Judge. Thank you.'

I nodded and left the chambers. Harry Bosch's card was still in my pocket. I dug it out while I was going down on the elevator. I had parked in a pay lot right by Parker Center. I called Bosch's cellphone as I headed to the courthouse exit. 'It's Mickey Haller.'

There was a hesitation. 'What can I do for you?' he asked.

'How's the investigation going?'

'It's going, but nothing I can talk to you about.'

'Then I'll just get to the point. Are you in Parker Center now?'

'That's right. Why?'

'I'm heading over from the courthouse. Meet me out front. I think it will be worth your while.'

I closed the phone before he could respond. It took me five minutes to get over to Parker Center. Bosch was standing next to the memorial fountain. I saw thin white wires leading from his ears to his jacket pocket. I walked up and pulled the ear buds out.

'Shutting out the world, Detective?'

'Helps me concentrate. Is there a purpose to this meeting?'

'After you left the office today I looked at the files you'd stacked in the file room. I understand what you're trying to do. I want to help but I want you to understand my position.'

'I understand. You have to protect those files and the possible killer hiding in them because those are the rules.'

I shook my head. This guy didn't want to make it easy. 'Tell you what, Detective Bosch. Come by the office at eight o'clock tomorrow morning and I'll give you what I can.'

I think the offer surprised him. 'I'll be there.'

'OK then.' I was ready to walk away but it looked like he wasn't. 'What is it?'

'I was going to ask you if Vincent had any federal cases.'

'I don't think so. He was like me, liked to stay in state court. The feds kind of like to stack the deck. They don't like to lose.'

'OK.' He was putting something in place.

'That's it? That's all you wanted to ask?'

'That's it.'

'OK, Detective.' I clumsily put out my hand and when he shook it he appeared to feel just as awkward about it. 'Hey, there was something I was meaning to ask you, too.'

'What's that?'

'I heard your full name is Hieronymus Bosch. Is that true?'

'What about it?'

'I was just wondering, where'd you get a name like that?'

'My mother gave it to me.'

'Your mother? Well, what did your father think about it?'

'I never asked him, Counsellor. Is there anything else?'

'No, that was it. I was just curious. See you at eight.'

I left him at the memorial and headed down the block, thinking about why he had asked if Vincent had federal cases. When I turned at the corner I glanced back and saw Bosch still standing by the fountain. He was watching me. He didn't look away but I did, and I kept walking.

CISCO AND LORNA were at work in Jerry Vincent's office when I got back. I handed over the court order and told Lorna about the early appointments I had set for the next day.

'I thought you put Henson into the dog pile,' she said.

'I did. But now I moved him back.'

She put her eyebrows together the way she did whenever I confounded her—which was a lot. I asked if anything new had developed.

'A couple things. First of all, the cheque from Walter Elliot cleared.'

'Good.'

'It gets better. I found the contracts file and I took a look at Jerry's deal with Elliot. That hundred thousand deposited for trial was only a partial payment. Vincent took two-fifty up front and that's all gone. But he was getting another two-fifty for the trial, non-refundable. The rest is due on the first day of testimony.'

I nodded with satisfaction. Vincent had made a great deal. I had never had a case with that kind of money involved. But I wondered how he had blown through the first $250,000 so quickly.

'OK, all of that's good—if we get Elliot. What else do we have?'

'We had visitors. One of Jerry's investigators came by, Bruce Carlin. Jerry hired him to work the Elliot case.'

I nodded. Bruce Carlin was a former LAPD bull who had crossed to the dark side and did defence work now. A lot of attorneys used him because of his insider's knowledge of how things worked in the cop shop. I thought he was living off an undeserved reputation.

'Set up a time for him to come back in. I doubt his work is all in the files. Cisco can find out what he's got. Pay him for his time, and then cut him loose when he's no longer useful.'

'We also had a couple of clients drop by to ask for their files after they heard on the radio about Jerry's death.'

'And?'

'We stalled them. I told them only you could turn over a file and that you'd get back to them within twenty-four hours. Those are the names.'

One name was in the dog pile but the other was a public indecency case I thought I could get dismissed. 'I'll go see these two tonight. In fact, I want to hit the road with all the cases soon. Starting with Archway Pictures. I'm going to take Cisco. Gather up what you need, Lorna, and head on home. I don't want you here by yourself.'

She nodded but then said, 'Are you sure Cisco should go?' She was referring to his size and appearance—the tattoos, the boots and leather.

'Yeah, when I want to be subtle he can just wait in the car.'

Cisco nodded and seemed fine with the arrangement.

'OK,' I said. 'I guess it's time for me to be a Lincoln lawyer again. Let's hit the road.'

IN THE LAST DECADE Archway Pictures had grown from a movie industry fringe dweller to a major force. This was because of the one thing that had always ruled Hollywood. Money. As the cost of producing films grew, the major studios began to look for partners to share the cost and risk.

This is where Walter Elliot and Archway Pictures came in. On Melrose Avenue, just a few blocks from the behemoth that was Paramount Studios, Archway offered production facilities and sound stages when everything was booked at the big studios. It leased office space to would-be and has-been producers. It nurtured independent films. For a decade it limped along until luck struck twice. In a space of only three years, two of the independent films he'd backed became huge hits. Walter and his studio suddenly basked in the glow of success. Archway's cut from the two was over a hundred million dollars apiece.

With that new-found money Walter Elliot co-financed a number of productions in which the big studios were looking for partners. Over the next decade there were enough hits to double and triple his stake. He became a player, making regular appearances on the power 100 lists in industry minds and magazines. Elliot's personal wealth grew commensurately. He traded in his wife for a newer model and together they started accumulating houses. They owned seven homes and two ranches in or around LA.

Those top 100 lists came in handy when Elliot was charged with double murder. He pulled off something rarely accomplished in a murder case. He got bail. Set at $20 million, he paid in real estate.

One of the properties was a waterfront weekender on a secluded cove in Malibu. It was there that thirty-nine-year-old Mitzi Elliot was murdered with her lover in a 1,200-square-foot bedroom with a glass wall that looked out on the big blue Pacific.

The discovery file was replete with forensic reports and crime scene photographs. The death room was completely white—walls, carpet, furniture and bedding. Two naked bodies were sprawled on the bed and floor. Mitzi Elliot and Johan Rilz. The scene was red on white. Two bullet holes in the man's chest. Two in the woman's chest and one in her forehead. Though the murder weapon was missing, slugs taken from the bodies had been identified as coming from a Smith & Wesson Model 29, a .44 Magnum revolver.

Walter Elliot had been suspicious about his wife. She had announced her intentions to divorce him and he believed there was another man involved. He told the sheriff's homicide investigators that he had gone to the beach house because he thought it was a lie when she told him she was going to meet with the interior designer. He timed his approach so that he could confront her with a paramour. He loved her and wanted her back. According to the statement, he found his wife and her lover naked and already dead. It turned out that the lover was in fact the interior designer,

Johan Rilz, a German national Elliot had always thought was gay.

Elliot called 911. After he gave investigators an account of his discovery of the two bodies, he was interviewed at the Malibu substation and at the sheriff's headquarters, where in the crime lab, his hands and sleeves tested positive for high levels of gunshot residue.

I closed the file as Cisco pulled the Lincoln even with the guardhouse in front of Archway Studios. I lowered my window so I could speak to the uniformed man who stepped out.

'I'm Walter Elliot's attorney. I don't have an appointment but I need to see him right away.'

'Can I see your driver's licence?'

I passed it through the window. 'I'm handling this for Jerry Vincent.'

The guard went into the booth, slid the door closed and picked up the phone. He soon slid the door back open. 'Mrs Albrecht is Mr Elliot's executive assistant. She wants to speak to you.'

I took the extended phone. 'Hello?'

'Mr Haller, is it? What is this all about? Mr Elliot has dealt exclusively with Mr Vincent.'

'I'd rather not talk at the front gate. Can I come and see Mr Elliot?'

'Can I place you on hold while I call Mr Vincent?'

'Mrs Albrecht, Jerry Vincent's dead. That's why I'm here.'

I looked at Cisco in the rearview mirror and shrugged. The plan had been to finesse my way through the arch, then be the one to personally tell Elliot his lawyer was dead.

'Mr Haller, did you say Mr Vincent is . . . dead?'

'Yes. I'm his court-appointed replacement. Can I come in now?'

'Of course.'

We were assigned to a prime parking space in the executive lot. I went in alone, carrying Vincent's two thick files on the case. One contained discovery materials turned over by the prosecution, including the investigative documents and interview transcripts, and the other contained documents and other work product generated by Vincent during the five months he had handled the case.

I followed a sidewalk across a beautifully manicured lawn to Walter Elliot's office in Bungalow One. A Spanish-tiled entranceway led to a living room with a fireplace and a mahogany wood bar. I stepped into the middle of the room and waited.

'Mr Haller?'

I turned. Elliot's gatekeeper, Mrs Albrecht, had appeared from some unseen entrance. Elegance was the word that came to mind. She was an ageing beauty who appeared to take the process in her stride. Grey streaked through her undyed hair and tiny wrinkles seemed unchecked by injection or incision.

'Mr Elliot will see you now.'

I followed her down a short hallway to Walter Elliot's office.

Elliot was an overly tanned man with more grey hair sprouting from his open shirt collar than from the top of his head. He sat behind a large glass work table. No computer on it, though paperwork and scripts were spread across it. He had dark, piercing eyes.

'Mr Elliot, this is Mr Haller,' Mrs Albrecht said.

She signalled me to the chair across the table from Elliot. After I sat down he made a dismissive gesture and she left without another word. Over the years I had represented a couple of dozen killers. They come in all sizes and shapes, rich and poor, humble and arrogant, regretful and cold to the bone. The percentages told me that it was most likely Elliot was a killer. That he had calmly dispatched his wife and her lover and arrogantly thought he could get away with it. But there was nothing about him on first meeting that told me for sure. And that's the way it always was.

'What happened to my lawyer?' he asked.

'Somebody killed him last night in his car.'

'Where does that leave me? I'm on trial for my life in a week!'

That was a slight exaggeration. The DA's office had not announced it would seek the death penalty. But I didn't think it hurt to think in such terms. 'That's why I'm here.'

'And who are you? I've never heard of you.'

'I make it a practice not to be heard of. Celebrity lawyers bring too much attention to their clients.'

He pursed his lips. 'You're taking over Vincent's practice?'

'Let me explain, Mr Elliot. Jerry Vincent had a one-man shop. Just like I do. On occasion each of us would need another attorney to fill in here and there. If you look at the contract of representation you signed you'll find it allowed Jerry to discuss your case with me. In other words, Jerry trusted me. Earlier today the chief judge of the Superior Court issued an order placing me in custody of Jerry's cases. Of course, you ultimately choose who represents you at trial. I'm only here to tell you your options.'

Elliot shook his head. 'I really can't believe this. We were set for trial next week and I'm not pushing it back. Do you have any idea what it is like for an innocent man to have to wait and wait for justice? To read all the innuendo in the media? Look at this!' He pulled his trouser leg up to reveal the GPS monitor Judge Holder had ordered him to wear. 'I want this over!'

I nodded in a consoling manner. 'I've dealt with many clients wrongly accused,' I lied. 'The wait for justice can be almost intolerable. I spent the afternoon reviewing the files and evidence in your case. I'm confident you won't have to delay the trial, Mr Elliot. I would be more than prepared to proceed. Another attorney, maybe not. But I'd be ready.' There it was, my best pitch, most of it lies and exaggerations. 'I've studied the trial strategy Mr Vincent outlined. I wouldn't change it but I believe I can improve on it.'

Elliot nodded. 'I have to think about this. I need to talk to some people and have you checked out. Like I had Vincent checked out.'

I decided to try to force him into a quick decision. I didn't want him finding out I'd disappeared for a year. 'It's a good idea,' I said, 'but the longer you wait, the greater the chance that the judge will find it necessary to push the trial back. In the absence of Mr Vincent, he's probably already considering it. If you choose me I will tell him we're good to go.' I stood and handed him a card from my pocket. 'Those are my numbers. Call any time.'

Elliot took the card and studied it. Before I reached the office door it opened from the outside and Mrs Albrecht stood there. She smiled warmly.

'I'm sure we will be in touch,' she said.

I had a feeling that she'd heard every word that had been spoken between me and her boss.

I FOUND CISCO leaning against the Lincoln smoking a cigarette.

'That was fast,' he said.

I got inside the car in case there were cameras in the parking lot and Elliot was watching me. Cisco did the same.

'I gave it my best shot. We'll probably know something soon.'

Cisco backed out of the space and started heading towards the arch. It was hard to go from thinking about a quarter-million-dollar fee to some of Vincent's also-rans, but that was the job. I opened my bag and pulled out the other active files. The address of each client was printed neatly on each file. I quickly checked through the files looking for addresses in Hollywood. I came across the address for the woman charged with indecent exposure.

'Here we go,' I said. 'Head down Melrose to La Brea. After that stop I'll ride in the front. Don't want you to feel like a chauffeur.'

'Hey, Mick, I gotta tell you something,' Cisco said. 'Me and Lorna . . . we're gonna get married.'

I had figured they were headed in that direction. Lorna and I had been friends for fifteen years before we were married for one. It had been a rebound marriage for me and as ill-advised as anything I had ever done. We realised the mistake and somehow managed to remain close. There was no one I trusted more in the world.

'That OK with you, Mick?'

I looked in the rearview. 'I'm not part of the equation, Cisco.'

'I know but I want to know if it's *OK* with you.'

I looked out of the window, then looked back in the mirror.

'Yes, it's all right with me. But I'll tell you something, Cisco. She's one of the four most important people in my life. You have maybe seventy-five pounds on me but if you hurt her I'm going to find a way to hurt you back. That OK with you?'

He looked away to the road. 'Yeah, Mick, I'm OK with that.'

We were silent for a while after that. Cisco kept glancing at me in the mirror. 'What?' I finally asked.

'Well, I got your daughter. That makes one. And then Lorna. I was wondering who the other two were.'

Before I could answer, an electronic version of the *William Tell* Overture started to play in my hand. My cellphone said PRIVATE CALLER on the screen. I opened it up. 'Haller.'

'Please hold for Walter Elliot,' Mrs Albrecht said.

Not much time went by before I heard, 'Mr Haller?'

'I'm here. What can I do for you?' I felt the stirring of anxiety in my gut.

'Have you noticed something about my case, Mr Haller?'

'How do you mean?' The question caught me off guard.

'One lawyer. I have one lawyer, Mr Haller. I not only must win this case in court but I must also win it in the court of public opinion.'

'I see,' I said, though I didn't quite understand the point.

'In the last ten years I've picked a lot of winners. I know what people like because I know what they're thinking. And I think the public believes the more guilty you are the more lawyers you need. When I hired Mr Vincent I said, "No dream team, just you."'

'I under—'

'I've decided, Mr Haller. You impressed me when you were in here. I would like to engage your services for trial.'

THE BRASS VERDICT | 45

I calmed my voice. 'I'm glad to hear that. Call me Mickey.'

'And you can call me Walter. But I insist on one condition. We go to trial on schedule. I want to hear you say it.'

I hesitated. I wanted a delay. But I wanted the case more. 'We'll be ready to go next Thursday.'

'Then welcome aboard. What do we do next?'

'Well, I could turn around and come back.'

'I'm afraid I have meetings until seven and then a screening of our film for the awards season.'

I would have thought that his trial would trump his meetings. 'OK, give me a fax number and I'll have my assistant send over a contract. It will have the same fee structure as Jerry Vincent's.'

There was silence and I waited. If he was going to try to knock down the fee this was when he would do it. But instead he repeated a fax number I could hear Mrs Albrecht giving him.

'What's tomorrow look like, Walter?'

'Tomorrow?'

'Yes, tomorrow. We need to talk and go over things.'

I heard muffled voices as he conferred with Mrs Albrecht. 'I have a four o'clock open,' he finally said. 'Here at the bungalow.'

'OK, I'll be there. And, Walter, I want to see the crime scene. Can I get into the house in Malibu before we meet?'

Again he covered the phone and I heard muffled conversation. Then he came back on the line. 'How about eleven? I'll have someone let you in.'

'That'll work. See you tomorrow, Walter.'

I closed the phone and looked at Cisco. 'We got him.'

Five

Bosch arrived early the next morning. His peace offering was the extra cup of coffee he carried and handed me. I don't drink coffee any more—to avoid any addiction in my life—but I took it anyway, thinking maybe the smell would get me going. It was only 7.45 but I'd been in Jerry Vincent's office for more than two hours already.

I led Bosch back into the file room. He looked more tired than I felt and I was pretty sure he was in the same suit he'd been wearing the day before.

'Long night?' I asked.

'Oh, yeah.'

I told him to have a seat, and I took the other chair.

'So,' I said, picking up the yellow legal tablet on the table, 'I met with Judge Holder and worked out a plan in which we can give you what you need without actually giving you the files.'

Bosch shook his head. 'You should've told me this at Parker Center. I wouldn't have wasted my time.'

'I thought you'd appreciate this.'

'It's not going to work. How many homicides have you investigated, Haller? And how many have you cleared?'

'All right, you're the homicide guy. But as a criminal defence attorney I'm capable of discerning what constituted a threat to Jerry.'

'Look, I'm the detective. No offence, but I'm in a position here where I have to take what an amateur is giving me. I don't trust the evidence unless I find it myself.'

'Detective, you're lucky to get this much. Judge Holder wasn't interested in helping you out at all.'

'So you're saying you went to bat for me?' He said it in a disbelieving, sarcastic tone, as if it were some sort of impossibility for a defence attorney to help a police detective.

'That's right,' I said defiantly. 'I went to bat for you. Jerry Vincent was a friend. I'd like to see you take down the person who took him down. Look, do you want the list or not?'

I handed it to him. 'There are eleven names with a brief summary of each threat.'

Bosch read the first page of the legal pad. 'What else do you have?'

'What do you mean?'

'I'll run these names and see where these guys are at now. But these are dead cases. Most likely if these threats were legit they would've been carried out long ago. I'm looking for something a little more current. Something from Vincent's open cases.'

'Well, I can't help you there.'

'Sure you can. I assume you're reviewing them. You're going to come across something that doesn't fit, maybe that scares you. That's when you call me. It might save you from . . .'

He didn't finish, but the message was clear. He was trying to scare me into cooperating more than Judge Holder was allowing.

'It's one thing sharing threat information from closed cases,' I said. 'It's another thing entirely to do it with active cases. And besides that, I know you are asking for more than just threats. You think Jerry stumbled across something that got him killed.'

Bosch kept his eyes on me and slowly nodded.

'What about it being a two-way street, Detective? What do you know that you aren't telling me? What was in the laptop that was so important? What was in the portfolio?'

'I can't talk to you about an active investigation.'

'You could yesterday when you asked about the FBI.'

He squinted his dark eyes. 'I didn't ask about the FBI.'

'Come on, Detective. You asked if he had any federal cases. Why would you do that unless you have some sort of federal connection? I'm guessing it was the FBI.'

Bosch hesitated. I had a feeling I'd guessed right and my mentioning the bureau made him think I knew something. He nodded.

'OK, the killer took Jerry Vincent's cellphone. I got the call records. On the day he was killed he got three calls from the Bureau. Four days before that, there were two. He was talking to somebody over there. I can't tell who. All outgoing calls from there register on the main number. They were all short calls, none over a minute.'

'Anybody there check in on the homicide investigation?'

'Not yet. It's not their style, if you know what I mean. Now your turn. What do you have that's federal?'

'Nothing. I confirmed that Vincent had no federal cases.'

I watched Bosch do a slow burn as he realised I had played him.

'There's a rumour about a federal grand jury looking into state-court corruption. You know anything about that?'

I shook my head. 'I've been on the shelf for a year.'

'Thanks for the help.'

'Look, Detective, I don't get this. Why can't you just call over there and ask who was calling your victim?'

Bosch smiled like he was dealing with a child. 'If I call, they'll just shine me on. If this was part of a corruption probe, the chances of them talking to a local cop are between slim and none. If they're the ones who got him killed make it none.'

'How would they get him killed?'

'They kept calling. They were pressuring him. Maybe someone else knew about it and thought he was a risk.'

'What about the laptop? Is that what this is all about, something in his computer?'

'You tell me.'

'How can I tell you when I have no idea what was in it?'

Bosch nodded the point and walked out carrying the legal pad at his side. 'Have a good day, Counsellor.'

LORNA AND CISCO arrived together fifteen minutes after Bosch's departure and we convened in Vincent's office. It was another score-keeping session in which we went over what had been accomplished the night before and what still needed to be done.

With Cisco driving, I had visited eleven of Vincent's clients the night before, signing up eight of them and giving back files to the remaining three. And Walter Elliot's representation contract had already been signed and returned.

We next set the plan for the day. I told Lorna that I wanted her and Wren—if she showed up—to run down the remaining clients. I also wanted Lorna to continue building the calendar and familiarising herself with Vincent's files and financial records.

I told Cisco to focus his attention on the Elliot case with emphasis on witness maintenance. This meant that he had to take the preliminary defence witness list, which had already been compiled by Jerry Vincent, and prepare subpoenas for the law-enforcement officers and other witnesses who might be considered hostile. For the paid expert witness and others who were willingly going to testify at trial for the defence, he had to assure them that it was moving forward as scheduled, with me replacing Vincent.

'Got it,' Cisco said. 'What about the Vincent investigation? You still want me monitoring?'

'Yes, keep tabs on that and let me know what you find out.'

'I found out that they spent last night sweating somebody but kicked him loose this morning.'

'Who?'

'I don't know yet. Whoever it was is cleared for now.'

I nodded as I thought about this. No wonder Bosch looked like he had been up all night. Just then the office door swung open. Wren Williams stood tentatively in the doorway.

'Hello, Wren,' I said. 'Glad you're here. Lorna will be right out to work with you.'

'No problem,' she said. 'One of the clients was waiting when I came in. Patrick Henson.'

I looked at my watch. Five of nine, a good sign. 'Send him in.'

A young man walked in. Patrick Henson was smaller than I thought he would be. He had the requisite tan but his hair was cropped short. He wore black trousers and what probably was his best shirt. It had a collar.

'Patrick, we spoke on the phone. I'm Mickey Haller and this is my case manager Lorna. This big guy is Cisco, my investigator.'

Patrick stepped to the desk and shook our hands, his grip firm.

'I'm glad you came in. Is that your fish back there?'

Henson looked at the fish on the wall. 'Yeah, that's Betty.'

'You gave a stuffed fish a name? Was it a pet?' Lorna asked.

Henson smiled to himself. 'No, I caught it a long time ago, hung it by the front door. My room-mates and me, we'd always say, "Hellooo, Betty" when we came home. It was kind of stupid.'

'Speaking of names, do we call you Trick?' I asked.

'Nah, that was just the name my agent came up with. I don't have him any more. You can just call me Patrick.'

'OK, and you told me you had a valid driver's licence?'

'Sure do.' He reached into a front pocket, removed a thick nylon wallet and pulled out his licence. I studied it, then nodded.

'OK, Patrick, I need a driver,' I said. 'I provide the car and gas and insurance and you show up every morning at nine. I told you the pay schedule yesterday. Still interested?'

'I'm interested.'

'Are you a safe driver?' Lorna asked.

'I've never had an accident,' Patrick said.

I nodded my approval. 'When can you start?'

He shrugged. 'I don't have anything . . . whenever you want.'

'How about we start right now? Today will be a test drive.'

'Sounds good to me.'

WE TOOK THE 10 out of downtown and headed west towards Malibu. I sat in the back and opened my computer on the fold-down table. While I waited for it to boot up I told Patrick Henson how it all worked.

'My car is my office. I've got two other Lincolns just like this one. I keep them in rotation. Each one's got a printer, a fax and I've got a wireless slot card in my computer. Anything I have to do in an office I can do back here while I'm on the road to the next place. There are more than forty court-houses in LA County. Being mobile is the best way to do business.'

'I wouldn't want to be in an office either,' Patrick said.

'Damn right. Too claustrophobic.' My computer was ready and I began to customise a pre-trial motion. 'I'm working on your case right now, Patrick.'

He looked at me in the mirror. 'What do you mean?'

'Well, I reviewed your file and there's something Mr Vincent hadn't done that I think we need to do that may help.'

'What's that?'

'Get an independent appraisal of the necklace you took. They list the value as twenty-five thousand. That bumps you up to a felony. But it doesn't look like anybody ever challenged that.'

'You mean like if the diamonds are bogus there's no felony?'

'It could work out like that, but I was thinking of something else.' I pulled out his file to check a name. 'Let me ask you a question. What were you doing in the house where you took the necklace?'

He shrugged. 'I was dating the old lady's youngest daughter. I met her on the beach and was sort of teaching her to surf. There was a birthday party at the house and I was invited and the mother was given the necklace.'

'That's when you learned its value.'

'Yeah, the father said they were diamonds.'

'So then the next time you were there you stole it.'

He didn't respond.

'Patrick, I'm your lawyer now and we need to discuss the facts of the case. You stole the necklace. Tell me about it.'

'We were there alone using the pool and I said I had to go to the can, only I really wanted to check the medicine cabinet for pills. I was hurting. There weren't any downstairs so I went upstairs and looked around. I saw the necklace and just took it.'

He shook his head and I knew why. He was thoroughly embarrassed and defeated by his addiction.

'It's OK, Patrick. What did the guy say when you pawned it?'

'He said he'd only give me four bills because the chain was gold but he didn't think the diamonds were legit. I took the money. I was so messed up on the stuff I didn't care.'

'Have you talked to the girl since you were arrested?'

'No, man. We're done.' Now the eyes in the mirror looked sad and humiliated. 'The whole thing was stupid.'

I reached into my jacket pocket and pulled out a photograph. I tapped Patrick on the shoulder with it. 'Take a look at that.'

He held it on top of the steering wheel. 'What happened?'

'I tripped over a kerb. Broke a tooth, my nose, opened up my forehead. They took that in the ER as a reminder.'

'Of what?'

'I had just gotten out of my car after driving my eleven-year-old home to her mother. By then I was up to 320 milligrams of OxyContin a day.' I let him register that for a moment. 'You think what you did was stupid? I was driving my little girl around on 320 migs of hillbilly heroin.'

He was staring directly at me in the mirror.

'There's nothing you can do about the past, Patrick. Except keep it there. I'm going to help you get through the legal stuff, but it's up to you to do the hard part.'

He nodded.

'Anyway, I see something Jerry Vincent didn't see. The victim's husband gave her the necklace. His name is Roger Vogler and he's a big supporter of elected people in the county. And if the diamonds are phoney he's not going to want that coming up in court. Especially if his wife doesn't know.'

'But how's he gonna stop it?'

'Patrick, his contributions helped elect at least four members of the county board of supervisors. They control the district attorney's budget. The DA is prosecuting you. It's a food chain. If Dr Vogler wants to send a message, believe me, it will be sent. The motion I'm filing requests that we be allowed to independently appraise the evidence. You never know, the word "appraise" may stir things up.'

'That's cool! Thanks, Mr Haller.'

'You're welcome, Patrick. Can I have my picture back now?'

He handed it over and I took a look at it. The eyes were the toughest part to study. Dazed and lost, staring unsteadily at the camera. Me at my lowest point. I put it back in my pocket for safekeeping.

We drove in silence while I finished the motion, went online and sent it in. The Lincoln lawyer was back on the beat.

I looked up when we hit the tunnel that marks the end of the freeway and dumps out onto the Pacific Coast Highway. I lowered the window. I always loved the feeling I got when I'd swing out of the tunnel and see and smell the ocean.

I started seeing surfers on the swells, and saw Patrick taking glances towards the water. 'It said in the file you did rehab.'

'Yeah. It worked,' he said. 'Did you?'

'Yeah, in Laurel Canyon. You thinking about going back into surfing?'

'I don't think so. Not on a professional level. My shoulder's shot. The paddling's one thing but the key thing is getting up. I lost my move when I fucked up my shoulder. Excuse the language. Besides, I'm taking things one day at a time. They taught you that in Laurel Canyon, didn't they?'

'They did. But surfing's a one-wave-at-a-time thing, isn't it?'

He nodded and I watched his eyes trip to the mirror.

'What do you want to ask me, Patrick?'

'Um, yeah, you know how Vincent kept my fish on the wall? I was wondering if he kept any of my boards.'

I looked through his file. 'You gave him twelve boards, right?'

'Yeah, all of them.'

'Well, he gave them to the liquidator he used when he took assets from clients. The guy sold all twelve, took twenty per cent and gave Vincent forty-eight hundred dollars.'

Patrick didn't say anything. I remembered he'd said the two long boards were the most valuable. On the inventory there were two boards ten feet long. One sold for $1200 to a collector and the other for $400 on eBay. The disparity made me think the eBay sale was bogus. The liquidator had probably sold the board to himself cheap. He would then turn round and sell it at a profit he'd keep for himself. Everybody's got an angle. Including me. I knew that if he hadn't resold the board yet then I still had a shot at it.

'What if I could get you one of the long boards back?' I asked.

'That would be awesome! I just wish I had kept one, you know?'

'No promises. But I'll see what I can do.'

In another twenty minutes we pulled into the driveway of Walter Elliot's house. It was of Moorish design with white stone and dark brown shutters. A silver mid-level Mercedes was parked on the cobblestone paving.

'You want me to wait here?' Patrick asked.

'Yeah. I don't think I'll take long. Pop the trunk for me.'

I got out, went to the back to retrieve my digital camera and took a quick shot of the front of the house. Then I walked to the entrance. The door opened and Mrs Albrecht stood there.

When Walter Elliot had told me he would have someone meet me in Malibu, I hadn't expected it to be his executive assistant.

'Mrs Albrecht, how are you today?'

'Very well. Come in, please. This way.' I followed her into the great room which was larger than my entire home. It was a complete entertainment area with a glass wall on the western exposure that brought the Pacific right into the house.

'Beautiful,' I said.

'It is indeed. Do you want to see the bedroom? It's on the top floor.'

Ignoring the question, I turned the camera on and took a few shots of the living room and its view.

'Do you know who has been in here since the sheriff's department relinquished control of it?' I asked.

'Very few people. I don't believe Mr Elliot has been out here. Mr Vincent came once and his investigator came twice.'

'Let's go up to the bedroom,' I said.'

As we went up a winding white staircase with an ocean-blue banister I asked Mrs Albrecht what her first name was.

'My name is Nina. You can call me that, if you want.'

'Good. And you can call me Mickey.'

The stairs led to a door that opened into a bedroom suite the size of some courtrooms. It had twin fireplaces, a sitting area, a sleeping area and his and her bathrooms. Nina Albrecht pushed a button and the curtains split to reveal a wall of glass looking out on the sea.

The custom-made bed was double the size of a regular king. It had been stripped of the mattress. Next to the door a six-foot-square segment of carpet had been cut out and on the wall blood spatter marks had been circled and marked with letter codes.

The investigative summary in the file suggested that the naked couple had heard an intruder in the house. Rilz went to the bedroom door and opened it, only to be immediately shot down. The killer stepped over his body and Mitzi Elliot jumped up from the bed, clutching a pillow in front of her body. She was shot twice through the pillow and knocked back onto the bed. The killer pressed the barrel of the gun against her forehead for the kill shot.

I walked over to the glass doors that led out to a deck overlooking the Pacific. They were locked and I had a hard time figuring out how to open them. Nina finally came over and helped me, holding her finger down on a safety lever while turning the bolt with her other hand. The doors opened and brought in the sounds of the crashing surf. I stepped onto the deck. The surf was washing right up to the piers on which the house was built.

I walked back inside and as soon as I closed the doors I realised my phone was ringing. It said PRIVATE CALLER on the screen.

'Nina, I have to take this. Do you mind waiting downstairs?'

'No problem.'

'Thank you.' I took the call. 'Hello?'

'It's me. I'm just checking to see when you're coming by.'

'Me' was my first ex-wife, Maggie McPherson. Under a revamped agreement I got to be with my daughter on Wednesday nights and every other weekend. It was a long way from the shared custody we'd once had. But I had blown that. 'Probably around seven thirty. I have a meeting and it might run a little late.'

There was silence and I sensed I'd given the wrong answer. 'What, you've got a date?' I asked. 'What time do you want me there?'

'I'm supposed to leave at seven thirty.'

'Then I'll be there before then. Who's the lucky guy?'

'That isn't any of your business. But speaking of lucky, I heard you got Jerry Vincent's practice.' As a deputy district attorney assigned to the Van Nuys courthouse, my ex-wife was in a position to hear things about me.

'I'm his replacement. I don't know how lucky that makes me.'

'You should get a good ride on the Elliot case,' she said with a prosecutor's sneer. 'If anyone can get him off, it's certainly you.'

'I guess I won't respond to that.'

'One other thing. You're not having company tonight, are you?'

'What are you talking about?'

'Hayley said a woman was there two weeks ago. I believe her name was Lanie? She felt very awkward about it.'

'Don't worry, she won't be there. She's just a friend and she used the guest room. But for the record, I can have anybody I want over because it's *my* house. You're free to do the same.'

'And I'm also free to go to the judge and say you're exposing our daughter to people who are drug addicts.'

I took a deep breath. 'How would you know?'

'Because your daughter isn't stupid and her hearing is perfect. It was easy to figure out that your . . . friend is from rehab.'

'And so that's a crime, consorting with people from rehab?'

'It's not a crime, Michael. I just don't think it's best for Hayley.'

'I guess the one addict you're most concerned with is me.'

'Well, if the shoe fits . . .'

I almost lost it but I knew that showing anger would only hurt me. 'This is our daughter we're talking about. Don't hurt her by trying to hurt me. She needs her father and I need my daughter.'

'And that's my point. You are doing well. Hooking up with an addict is not a good idea.'

I squeezed my phone so hard I thought it might break. My words came out strangled by my own failures. 'I have to go.'

'And so do I. I'll tell Hayley you'll be there by seven thirty.'

Six

At Archway Studios we made it through the security checkpoint without any of the delay of the day before. It helped that Nina Albrecht was in the car in front of us. The studio was emptying out for the day and Patrick got a parking spot in front of Elliot's bungalow.

As I followed Nina in, she said she was taking me to the executive board-room and I could set up there while she went to get her boss. It was a big room with black leather chairs round an oval table. I took a seat and twenty-five minutes later Elliot walked in.

Nina trailed him into the room to see what she could get us for refreshment. 'Nothing,' I said before Elliot could respond. 'We need to get started.'

Elliot nodded and she left, closing the double doors behind her.

I looked across the table at my client. 'Walter, when we set a meeting let's be on time for it. There's a lot of ground to cover. For the next two weeks you have one priority. This case.'

It may have been the first time in his life he had been chided for being late, then told what to do. Finally, he nodded. 'Fair enough.'

'Good,' I said. 'Now, let's get to work.' I opened the defence file and looked at my notes on the inside flap. 'I think we're set in terms of witnesses and strategy when it comes to the state's case. What I haven't found is a strategy for putting forth your defence.'

'What do you mean? Jerry told me we were ready.'

'Maybe not,' I said. 'I know it's not something you want to see but I found this in the file.' I slid a document across to him.

He glanced at it but didn't really look at it. 'What is it?'

'A motion for a continuance. Jerry hadn't filed it, but it seems he wanted to delay the trial. The coding indicates he printed it Monday just hours before he was killed.'

Elliot shoved the document back. 'No, we talked about it and he agreed to move forward on schedule.'

'That was Monday?'

'Yes, Monday. The last time I talked to him.'

I nodded. I had noted that Vincent had billed an hour on the day of his murder. 'Was that a conference at his office or yours?'

'It was a phone call. Nina can get you the exact time.'

'He has it down at three. Why did he want a continuance?'

'He wanted more time to prepare and maybe pad his bill. I told him we were ready, like I'm telling you. We are ready!'

I sort of laughed. 'The thing is, you're not the lawyer, Walter. I am. And I'm not seeing much in terms of a defence strategy. I think that's why Jerry wanted to delay the trial. He didn't have a case.'

'No, it's the prosecution that doesn't have the case.'

'Let me explain how this works,' I said wearily. 'The prosecutor goes first and he lays out his case. We get a chance to attack it as he goes. Then we get our shot and that's when we put up our evidence and alternate theories of the crime.'

'OK.'

'And what I can tell from the files is that Jerry has counter-witnesses and cross-examination plans ready for everything the prosecution is going to put forward. But on the defence side we've got no alibi, no alternate suspects, no alternate theories, nothing. Did he ever discuss with you how he planned to roll out the defence?'

'No. We were going to have that conversation but he got killed. He said he had the magic bullet and the less I knew the better.'

I knew the term. The magic bullet was the witness or piece of evidence that you had in your back pocket that was going to either knock all the evidence down like dominoes or permanently fix reasonable doubt in the mind of every juror on the panel.

'You have no idea what this magic bullet was?'

'Just what he told me, that he found something that was going to blow the state out of the water.'

'That doesn't make sense if on Monday he was talking about delaying the trial,' I said, but my mind was on Vincent's missing laptop. Was the magic bullet there? Was it the reason for his murder?

I decided to move on. 'Well, Walter, I don't have the magic bullet. But if Jerry could find it so can I. Let's talk about an alternate theory.'

'OK. Meaning what?'

'Meaning that the state has its theory and we should have ours. The state's theory is that you were upset over your wife's infidelity and what it would cost to divorce her. So you went to Malibu and killed her and her lover. You then got rid of the murder weapon and called 911. But to back it up they have the gunshot residue and almost nothing else.'

'That test was a false positive! I never shot any weapon. And Jerry told me he was bringing in the top expert in the country to testify that the lab procedures were sloppy.'

I nodded. 'Yes, but the prosecution will counter with their own expert saying the opposite. At best, the GSR will be a wash. The prosecution will lean heavily on motive and opportunity. They'll say you knew Rilz was your wife's lover and trot out evidence indicating a divorce would cost you a hundred million dollars.'

'And it's all bull.'

'A lot of their positives can be turned into negatives. It will be a dance, Walter. We'll trade punches. We'll try to distort and destroy but ultimately they'll land more punches than we can block and that's why it's always good for the defence to float an alternative theory. We throw suspicion away from you and at somebody else. The prosecutor, Jeffrey Golantz, is a seasoned pro. He's never lost at trial. Something like twenty-seven and oh.'

Elliot nodded thoughtfully as he looked at the polished tabletop.

I checked my watch. Time had passed quickly and I needed to keep things moving if I was going to pick my daughter up on time.

'OK,' I said. 'There are other things we need to cover. I want to add a couple people to the defence team. A jury selection consultant and some-body to work with you on image and testimony.'

He shook his head. 'No jury consultant. Makes it look like you're trying to rig things.'

'Look, the person I want to hire will sit out in the gallery. No one will notice her. She just reads people's faces and looks for giveaways.'

'No, I won't pay for that mumbo jumbo.'

'Are you sure, Walter?'

I spent five minutes trying to convince him, stressing that in circumstantial cases the priority had to be in picking jurors with open minds. At the end of my plea Elliot simply clasped his hands together calmly on the table.

'Mumbo jumbo. I will trust your skills.'

BY THE TIME I dropped Patrick back at his car in downtown and headed to the Valley in heavy evening traffic I knew I was going to be late and I was heading towards another confrontation with my ex-wife. I called but she didn't pick up. When I got to her apartment in Sherman Oaks it was almost 7.40 and I found mother and daughter out at the kerb waiting. Hayley had her head down and was looking at the sidewalk.

I popped the locks as I pulled to a stop and Maggie helped Hayley in with her school backpack and overnight bag.

'Thanks for being on time,' Maggie said in a flat voice.

'No problem,' I said, just to see if it would put the flares in her eyes. 'Must be a hot date if you're waiting out here for me.'

'No, not really. Parent–teacher conference at the school.'

That got through my defences and hit me in the jaw. 'You should've told me. We could've got a baby sitter and gone together.'

'I'm not a baby,' Hayley said.

'We tried that,' Maggie said. 'Remember? You jumped on the teacher so badly about Hayley's math grade—the circumstances of which you knew nothing about—that you were asked not to come back.'

The incident sounded vaguely familiar, locked away in my oxycodone-corrupted memory banks. I didn't have a comeback.

'I have to go,' Maggie said quickly. 'Hayley, I love you. Be good for your father and I'll see you tomorrow.'

'OK, Mom.'

We drove silently down Ventura Boulevard and stopped at DuPar's, my daughter's favourite place to eat because I always let her order pancakes.

I ordered a BLT. We did her homework together which was a breeze for her and taxing for me, then I asked her what she wanted to do. I was willing to do anything—a movie, the mall, whatever she wanted—but I was hoping she'd just want to go home to my place, maybe pull out some old family scrapbooks and look at the photos.

She hesitated and I thought I knew why. 'There's nobody at my place, Hay. Lanie doesn't visit any more.'

'You mean like she's not your girlfriend any more?'

'She never was my girlfriend. Remember when I stayed in the hospital last year? We became friends and we tried to watch out for each other.'

It was the shaded truth. Lanie Ross and I had met in rehab. We continued the relationship after leaving the programme but never consummated it as a romance because we were emotionally incapable of it. Once we were in the real world I instinctively knew she wasn't going to go the distance and I couldn't make the journey to relapse with her. We went our separate ways.

'I think I just want to go home and watch TV then.'

'Good. That's what I want to do.'

We packed up her school books and I paid the bill. On the drive over the hill she said her mother had told her I had got an important new job.

'She said you had a big case and everybody would be jealous but you would do real good.'

'Your mom said that?' I was surprised but happy.

'Yeah.'

I drove for a while thinking about that. Maybe I hadn't entirely blown things with Maggie. She still respected me on some level.

'Um . . .' Hayley was looking away from me.

Children are so easy to read sometimes. If only grown-ups were the same. 'What's up, Hay?'

'Um, I was just wondering why you can't do what mom does.'

'What do you mean?'

'Like putting bad people in jail. She said your case is with a man who killed two people. It's like you always work for the bad guys.'

I was quiet for a moment. 'The man I am defending is accused of killing two people. Nobody has proved he did anything wrong. Right now he's not guilty of anything.'

She didn't respond and her scepticism was almost palpable.

'Hayley, when somebody is accused of a crime they are entitled to defend themselves. What if at school you were accused of cheating and you knew that you didn't cheat? Wouldn't you want to be able to explain?'

'I think so.'

'I think so, too. It's like that with the courts. If you get accused of a crime you can have a lawyer like me help you explain and defend yourself. It's part of the system. An important part.'

On an intellectual level I believed the argument, but on a father–daughter level it felt hollow. How could I get her to believe it when I wasn't sure I believed it any more myself?

'Have you helped any innocent people?' my daughter asked.

'A few, yes.' It was the best I could honestly say. I turned the radio on to the Disney music channel.

Maybe grown-ups were just as easy to read as their children.

Seven

After dropping my daughter off at school Thursday morning I drove directly to Jerry Vincent's office. It was still early and when I got to the garage I almost had my pick of the place. I parked on the first level and as I walked to the bridgeway I noticed a Subaru station wagon with surfboard racks on the roof.

The back windows on the wagon were tinted and I couldn't see in. I moved up to the front and looked in through the driver's side window. The back seat had been folded flat, and half the rear area was cluttered with boxes full of clothes. The other half served as a bed for Patrick Henson, lying asleep in a sleeping-bag. It was only then I remembered that he'd told me he was living out of his car and sleeping on a lifeguard stand.

I wouldn't need him until later in the morning. There was no need to roust him. I crossed into the office complex and headed down the hallway towards Jerry Vincent's office. Detective Bosch was standing in front of the door. He was listening to his music, hands in his pockets, looking pensive. He pulled out the ear buds as I approached.

'What, no coffee?' I said by way of a greeting.

'Not today. I could tell you didn't want it yesterday.' He stepped aside so I could use a key to open the door.

'Can I ask you something?' I said.

'If I said no you'd ask anyway.'

'You're probably right.' I opened the door.

'So then just ask the question.'

'All right. Well, you don't seem like an iPod sort of guy to me. Who were you listening to there?'

'Somebody I am sure you never heard of. Frank Morgan.'

'The saxophone player? Yeah, I know Frank.'

'You know him,' Bosch said in a disbelieving tone.

'Yeah, I usually drop by and say hello when he plays at the Catalina or the Jazz Bakery. My father loved jazz and back in the fifties and sixties he was Frank's lawyer. Frank got into a lot of trouble before he got straight. Ended up playing in San Quentin with Art Pepper—you've heard of him, right?'

It took Bosch a moment to recover from my surprise knowledge of Frank Morgan, the obscure heir to Charlie Parker. We crossed the reception area and went into the main office.

'So how's the case going?' I asked.

'It's going,' he said.

'I heard that before you came and saw me yesterday you spent the night in Parker Center sweating a suspect. No arrest, though?'

I sat behind Vincent's desk and Bosch stayed standing.

'Who told you that?' Bosch asked.

'I don't know,' I said. 'I must've heard it somewhere. Maybe a reporter. Who was the suspect?'

'That's none of your business.'

'What's my business with you, Detective? Why are you here?'

'I came to see if you had any more names for me.'

'What happened to the names I gave you yesterday?'

'They've checked out.'

'How could you check them all out already?'

He leaned down and put both hands on the desk. 'Because I'm not working this case alone. Every one of them is either in jail, dead or was not worried about Jerry Vincent any more. It's a dead end.'

I felt disappointed, and realised maybe I'd put too much hope into the possibility of one of those names belonging to the killer.

'Well, what can I tell you, Detective? I can't reveal anything about active cases, but here's the deal: there's nothing to reveal.'

He shook his head in disbelief.

'I mean it. There is nothing in any of them that constitutes a threat, nothing that connects to the FBI. And he had only one murder case—Walter Elliot—and there isn't anything there. Believe me, I've looked.'

I wasn't so sure I believed it as I said it but Bosch didn't seem to notice. He finally sat down on the edge of a chair. There was an almost desperate look to his face.

'Jerry was divorced,' I offered. 'Did you check out the ex-wife?'

'She's happily remarried and seven months pregnant.'

'Any other relatives? Girlfriend?'

'He was banging his secretary but there was nothing serious there. And her alibi checks out. She was also banging his investigator. And that night they were together with friends at a screening at Archway. That big-shot client of yours got them the invitation.'

I nodded and took an educated guess. 'The guy you sweated that first night was the investigator, Bruce Carlin.'

'Who told you that?'

'You just did. It's a classic love triangle. It would've been the place to start.'

'Smart lawyer. Tell me about the money.'

He'd thrown a zinger right back at me. 'What money?'

'The money in the business accounts.'

'Actually, my case manager tells me they're clean. Every penny Jerry took in is accounted for. I think Jerry probably paid himself a little too quickly but there's nothing technically wrong with that.'

I saw Bosch's eyes light up. 'He paid himself too quickly?'

'The way it works is you take on a client and you receive an advance that goes into the client trust account. It's their money but as you prepare the case, you move your fees to the operating account.'

'OK, so how did Vincent pay himself too quickly?'

'Well, it looks from the books that he liked to keep a low balance in operating. He happened to have had a franchise client who paid a large advance and that money went through the accounts pretty quickly. After costs the rest went to Vincent in salary.'

Bosch leaned towards me. 'Walter Elliot, was he the franchise?'

'I can't give out that information but it's an easy guess to make.'

Bosch nodded. I waited and he said nothing.

'Look,' I said, 'we both have rules we have to follow. I'm just doing my job. If there is nothing else I can help you with, I'll get back to it.'

He stared at me. 'Who did Vincent bribe on the Elliot case?'

The question came out of left field but I realised it was the question he'd come to ask. Everything else had been window-dressing.

'What, is that from the FBI?' I asked.

'I haven't talked to the FBI.'

'Then what are you talking about?'

'I'm talking about a payoff.'

I smiled. 'I told you, the books are clean. There's—'

'If you were going to bribe someone with a hundred thousand dollars would you put it in your books?'

'I guess you're right,' I said to Bosch. 'I wouldn't do it that way. So what aren't you telling me?'

'This is in confidence, Counsellor. But I need your help and I think you need to know this in order to help me.'

'OK.'

'Then say it.'

'Say what?' I asked.

'That you will treat this information in confidence.'

'I thought I did. Fine. I will.'

'I have Vincent's private accounts. Five months ago he accumulated a hundred grand in a personal investment account and a week later told his broker he was cashing out.'

'A hundred thousand in cash? What happened to it?'

'I don't know. But his broker asked a lot of questions to make sure there wasn't a security issue. Vincent said he needed the money to buy a boat and he'd get the best deal in cash.'

'So where's the boat?'

'There is no boat. We've checked all state transactions and asked questions all over Marina del Rey and San Pedro. We've searched his home twice and reviewed his credit card purchases. No receipts or records of boat-related expenses. No Coast Guard registration. He bought something else and Walter Elliot probably knows what it was.'

I tracked his logic and could see it coming to Walter Elliot's door. But I wasn't going to open it with Bosch looking over my shoulder. 'I think you've got it wrong, Detective.'

'I don't think so, Counsellor.'

'Well, I have no idea about all this and my client's off limits. He's not talking to you about this or anything else.'

Bosch shook his head. 'I wouldn't waste my time trying to talk to him. He used his lawyer as cover on this and I'll never be able to get past the attorney–client protection. But you should take it as a warning, Counsellor. Remember, that little trickle down your spine from the back of your neck, that's the feeling you get when you know you're in danger.'

I smiled. 'Oh, is that what that is? You've been running a game on me for two days, Detective, and it's been a waste of my time.'

I extended a hand towards the door. Bosch stood up. 'Don't kid yourself, Haller. Don't make a mistake.' He pulled a photograph from his pocket and put it on the desk. 'You recognise that man?'

It was a grainy still taken off a surveillance video. A man pushing out through the front door of a building. 'This is the Legal Center, isn't it?'

'Do you recognise him?'

The shot was taken from a distance. The man looked to be of Latin origin. He had dark skin and hair and a Pancho Villa moustache. He wore a Panama hat and an open-collared shirt beneath a leather jacket that had pulled open as he'd pushed the glass door. I could see what looked like the top of a pistol tucked into his trousers.

'Is that a gun? Is this the killer?'

'Do you recognise this man? That's all I want to know.'

'No, I don't, Detective. Happy? But that's not a great photo you've got there. Where's it from?'

'A camera on Broadway and Second. It sweeps the street and we only got this guy for a few seconds.'

I knew that the city had been quietly installing street cameras on main arteries. 'Well, it's better than nothing. You think the hair and the moustache are a disguise?'

'Let me ask the questions. Could this guy be one of your new clients?'

'I don't know. I haven't met them all. Leave me the photo and I'll show it to Wren Williams.'

Bosch reached down and took the photo back. 'It's my only copy. When will she be in?'

'In about an hour.'

'I'll come back later. Meantime, Counsellor, watch yourself.'

He pointed a finger at me like it was a gun, then turned and walked out, closing the door behind him.

I got up from the desk and started to pace the office, hands in my pockets, trying to evaluate what the information from Bosch meant.

According to Bosch, Jerry Vincent had paid a sizable bribe to a person or persons unknown. I considered the timing of Vincent's transaction. Bosch said the money transfer had gone down five months ago. Vincent's murder was just three nights ago. The distance between the two seemed to strain any possibility of a link.

But, still, I could not push the two apart and the reason for this was Walter Elliot. Through the filter of Bosch's information I now began to view my client—and myself—differently. I now saw Elliot's confidence in his acquittal coming possibly from his belief that it had already been bought and paid for. I now saw his unwillingness to delay the trial as a timing issue relating to the bribe. And his willingness to allow me to carry the torch for Vincent as a move made to get to the trial without delay. It had nothing to do with confidence in my skills and tenacity. I had simply been the one who showed up. In fact, I was perfect. Pulled out of the lost-and-found bin, dusted off and suited up and sent in, no questions asked.

Money had been paid for a specific fix and that fix was tied to the trial staying on schedule. Why must the trial remain on schedule?

I continue my pacing. The next thing I needed to consider was the photograph Bosch showed me. Early indications were that Vincent had known the person who killed him, but the man in the photograph appeared to be in disguise. The calls from the FBI were also part of the equation. What did the Bureau know and why had no agent come forward to Bosch? And the last unknown was Vincent's murder itself. He'd paid the bribe and was ready for trial. His murder certainly threatened the timetable. Why was he killed?

There were too many unknowns, but there was one conclusion that seemed clear. I was being mushroomed by my client. Elliot was keeping me in the dark about the interior machinations of the case. But that could work both ways. I decided I would do what Bosch asked; I would not question Elliot. I'd keep my head above the dark waters of the case, my eyes wide open.

I shifted focus from my thoughts to what was in front of me. I was looking directly at the gaping mouth of Patrick Henson's fish.

The door opened and Lorna entered the office to find me staring at the tarpon. 'What are you doing?' she asked.

'Thinking. Where's Cisco? Did he have breakfast?'

'Not with me, but he's here and we've got to go over what happened while you were out yesterday.'

'Then let's go to the Dining Car and have breakfast.'

Following her out, I glanced back at the big beautiful fish hanging on the wall. I thought I knew exactly how he felt.

I HAD PATRICK drive us over. Cisco and I ordered steak and eggs while Lorna had tea and honey. The Pacific Dining Car was a place where downtown power brokers liked to gather before a day of fighting it out in the nearby glass towers. The food was overpriced but good. It instilled confidence, made the downtown warrior feel like a heavy hitter.

As soon as the waiter took our order Lorna opened a spiral-bound At-A-Glance calendar on the table. 'Eat fast,' she said. 'You have a busy day.'

'Tell me.'

'All right, the easy stuff first.'

She flipped pages back and forth. 'You have a ten a.m. in chambers with Judge Holder. She wants an updated client inventory.'

'She told me I had a week,' I protested. 'Today's Thursday.'

'Yeah, well, Michaela called and said the judge wants an interim update. I think the judge is afraid you're spending all your time on Walter Elliot. Don't worry, I have a hard copy inventory—who you've met, who you signed up and calendars on all of them.'

I smiled. 'Great. What else?'

'At eleven you have an in-chambers with Judge Stanton. He wants to know if you'll be able to go next Thursday.'

'No, but Elliot won't have it any other way.'

'Well, the judge is requiring the defendant's presence.'

That was unusual. 'Did you let Elliot know? He may—'

'He knows and he'll be there. I talked to his assistant.'

'Good,' I said. 'That it?' I wanted to get to Cisco.

'Not by a long shot. Now we get to the mystery case. Yesterday afternoon Judge Friedman's clerk called Vincent's office to see if there was anyone aware of the hearing scheduled today at two. So you have a hearing for a case we not only don't have on calendar but don't have a file for either.'

'What's the client's name?'

'Eli Wyms.'

It meant nothing to me. 'Did Wren know the name?'

Lorna shook her head in a dismissive way.

'Did you check the dead cases? Maybe it was just misfiled.'

'We checked. There's no file in the office. Wyms is charged with attempted murder of a peace officer and other weapons-related charges. He was arrested May 2nd at a county park in Calabasas. He was arraigned and sent out to Camarillo. He must've been found competent because the hearing is to set a trial date.'

I nodded. From the shorthand I could read between the lines. Wyms had gotten into some sort of confrontation involving weapons with the sheriff's department, which provided law-enforcement services in Calabasas. He was sent to the state's mental evaluation centre in Camarillo. The docs determined he was competent. There would be more detail in the file but we had no file.

'No reference in the trust account deposits, I assume. Maybe Jerry took him on pro bono.'

'You know what I was thinking?' Lorna said. 'That Jerry had the file in his briefcase when he left Monday night.'

It made sense. He was preparing for the week and had a hearing on Wyms Thursday. 'Who's the prosecutor?'

'Joanne Giorgetti and I'm way ahead of you. I called her yesterday and explained our situation and asked if she wouldn't mind copying the discovery for us. She said no problem. You can pick it up after your eleven with Judge Stanton and then have a couple hours to familiarise yourself with it before the hearing at two.'

'You think of everything, Lorna. Why don't you just take over Vincent's practice and run with it? You don't need me.'

She smiled. 'I like working in the background. I'll leave centre stage for you.'

Our plates were served and I spread a liberal dose of Tabasco sauce on both my steak and the eggs. Cisco dug into his meal. I knew better than to keep him from his food so I asked Lorna how things were working out with Wren Williams.

'She's not a lot of help, Mickey. She seems to have no idea of how the office worked or where Jerry put things. If you ask me, she was working here for some other reason.'

I could have told her the reason but I didn't want to distract Lorna with gossip. I saw Cisco was mopping up his steak juice with a piece of toast. 'What do you have going, Cisco?'

'I'm working on Rilz and his side of the equation. There'll be a couple things you can use. Want to hear about it?'

'Not yet. I'll ask when I need it.' I didn't want information I might have to turn over in discovery.

'I also have the Bruce Carlin debriefing this afternoon.'

'He wants two hundred an hour,' Lorna said. 'Highway robbery, if you ask me.'

I waved off her protest. 'Just pay it. He probably has information we can use and that might save Cisco some time.'

'Don't worry, we're paying him. I'm just not happy about it. He's gouging us because he knows he can,' Lorna said.

'Technically, he's gouging Elliot and I don't think he cares.'

I turned back to my investigator.

'Cisco, you have anything new on the Vincent case?'

Cisco updated me with what he had, mostly forensic details. He said

Vincent had been shot twice in the area of the left temple. Powder burns on the skin and hair indicated the weapon was nine to twelve inches away when fired and the killer was able to cluster the impacts. Additionally, the slugs were recovered during the autopsy.

'They were twenty-fives,' Cisco said.

'They know the exact weapon yet?'

'A Beretta Bobcat. You could almost hide it in your hand.'

A completely different weapon than the one used to kill Mitzi Elliot and Johan Rilz. 'So what's all of this tell us?'

'It's a gun you take when it's going to be a head shot.'

'So this was planned. OK, what about the suspect?'

'The guy they sweated the first night?'

'No, that was Carlin they cut loose.'

Cisco looked surprised. 'How'd you find out it was Carlin?'

'Bosch told me this morning.'

'Are you saying they have another suspect?'

'He didn't have a name. He showed me a photo of a guy coming out of the building at the time of the shooting. He had a gun and was wearing an obvious disguise.'

I saw Cisco's eyes flare. It was a point of professional pride that he provided me information like that. If I'd told him about the FBI calls, he'd probably have picked the table up and thrown it through the window. 'I'll see what I can find out.'

We were finished. I put a credit card on the tab and pulled out my cellphone to call Patrick. 'Cisco, one other thing. Go to Vincent's liquidator and see if he's sitting on one of Patrick's surfboards. If he is, I want it back.'

Cisco nodded. 'I can do that. No problem.'

WAYLAID BY THE SLOW elevators in the Criminal Courts Building, I was four minutes late when I walked into Judge Holder's courtroom and hustled through the clerk's corral to her chambers.

She was behind her desk and her black robe told me she probably had a hearing scheduled soon in open court. 'Mr Haller, our meeting was set for ten o'clock. I believe you were given proper notice.'

'Your Honour. I'm sorry. The elevators in this building—'

'All lawyers take the same elevators and most seem on time for meetings. Did you bring your chequebook?'

'Yes, Your Honour. I think so, yes.'

'Well, we can do this one of two ways. I can hold you in contempt, fine you and let you explain yourself to the California Bar, or you can make a donation to the Make A Wish Foundation. It's my favourite charity. They do good things for sick children.'

I was being fined for arriving four minutes late. The arrogance of some judges was amazing. 'I like the idea of helping out sick children,' I said. 'How much do I make it out for?'

'As much as you want. And I will even send it in for you.'

I found my chequebook and wrote a cheque for $250. The judge nodded approvingly and I knew I was all right.

'Thank you, Mr Haller.' She put it on top of two others. 'They'll be sending you a receipt in the mail.'

'Like you said, they do good work.'

'Yes, they do. Now, let me ask you a question. Do you know if the police are making any headway on Mr Vincent's death?'

I wondered what I should tell the chief judge of the superior court. 'I'm not really in the loop on that. But I was shown a surveillance shot of a man I assume they're looking at as a suspect. The guy might be disguised and it looks like he has a gun. Detective Bosch came to the office with it this morning.'

The judge nodded. We were quiet for a moment and then I took from my bag the scorecard Lorna had prepared for me.

Judge Holder kept me for the next hour while I went over every case. By the time she let me go I was late for my eleven o'clock hearing. I hit the stairs and charged up two flights, wondering if it was going to cost me another donation to another favourite charity.

The courtroom was empty but Stanton's clerk was in her corral. She pointed with a pen to the open door. I quickly moved to the chambers and saw the judge behind his desk. To his left was a stenographer and across from him were three chairs. Walter Elliot was sitting in the chair to the right, the middle chair was empty and Jeffrey Golantz was in the third. I had never met the prosecutor before but he was recognisable because I had seen his face on TV and in the newspapers. In the last few years he had successfully handled a series of high-profile cases and was making a name for himself. He was the undefeated up-and-comer in the DA's office.

I loved going up against undefeated prosecutors. Their confidence often betrayed them.

'Sorry I'm late, Your Honour.' I slid into the empty seat.

'Let's go on the record now,' Stanton said, and the stenographer put her fingers on the keys of her machine.

'In the matter of California versus Walter Elliot . . . we are in chambers today for a status conference. Present is the defendant, along with Mr Golantz for the state and Mr Haller, who is here in the late Mr Vincent's stead. We're scheduled for *voir dire* next Thursday—a week from today. Mr Haller, I have received no motion from you to continue the matter while you get up to speed on the case.'

'Your Honour,' I said. 'I have spent the week getting up to speed and will be prepared to begin jury selection next Thursday.'

The judged squinted his eyes at me. 'You sure, Mr Haller?'

'Absolutely. Mr Vincent kept thorough records. I understand the strategy he built and the case has my full attention.'

The judge looked at Elliot. 'Mr Elliot, I'd like to hear that you are in full agreement and understand the risk you run in bringing in a fresh lawyer so close to trial. It's your freedom at stake here, sir.'

'Judge,' Elliot said. 'I am being persecuted and prosecuted for something I did not do. I loved my wife. I didn't kill her and it pierces my heart when I hear people on TV saying vile things about me. The sooner Mr Haller gets to prove my innocence the better.'

It was O.J. Simpson 101 but the judge nodded thoughtfully. 'Mr Golantz? What is the state's view of this?'

The telegenic deputy district attorney was handsome and dark and his eyes seemed to carry the very wrath of justice. 'Your Honour, the state is prepared for trial on schedule. But I would ask that if Mr Elliot is so sure about proceeding without delay that he formally waive any appellate redress should things not go as he predicts.'

The judge swivelled his chair. 'What about that, Mr Haller?'

'Your Honour, I don't think it's necessary for my client to waive any protections afforded to him,' I said, then argued that Elliot shouldn't have to give away his right to appellate review just because he wanted the speedy trial he was entitled to. Judge Stanton sided with Golantz, but that was OK with me. Under the Byzantine rules of law almost nothing was safe from appeal.

Next the judge gave us until Monday for submitting final discovery. The witness lists were due the day after that. This was not going to be a problem from the defence's side of the aisle. Vincent had already made two previous discovery filings and my plan was to give Golantz a witness list naming every law officer and forensic tech mentioned in the sheriff's reports. He'd have to puzzle over who I really would call to testify.

'All right,' Stanton said. 'Are we clear on everything?'

Golantz and I nodded our heads.

'OK then,' the judge said. 'We can talk about ground rules Thursday morning. I'm going to run this trial like a well-oiled machine. No surprises, no shenanigans. Are we clear?'

Golantz and I both agreed, but the judge squinted at me in suspicion. 'I'm going to hold you to that,' he said.

How come, I wondered, it's always the defence attorney who gets the judicial squint?

Eight

I got to Joanne Giorgetti's office a minute before the noon break. I knew that the DA's offices literally empty during the lunch hour. Giorgetti had a small office with most of the floor space taken up by cardboard file boxes. She handed me the Wyms file with an inch-thick stack of documents in it and told me she wouldn't oppose a continuance, considering what had happened with Jerry Vincent.

'What do you think happened to Jerry's file?' she asked.

'I think maybe it was in his briefcase, which the killer took.'

She made a cringing face. 'Weird. Why would the killer take this file?'

'Probably unintended. Jerry's laptop was in the briefcase. The killer just took the whole thing.'

'Hmmm.'

'Well, is there anything unusual about this case? Anything that would have made Jerry a target?'

'I don't think so. Just your usual, everyday crazy-with-a-gun sort of thing.'

I nodded, and thanked her again for the file.

I left the DA's office and waited ten minutes to get on an elevator with the lunch crowd. When I stepped out and came through the front doors I could see the Lincoln at the kerb waiting. I got in the back—I tell my drivers never to open the door for me—and Patrick dropped me over at Chinese Friends on Hill Street.

Wanting to get right to work I ordered a plate of the fried pork chops. They were paper-thin and delicious and I could eat them with my fingers without taking my eyes off the Wyms file. It contained copies of what the prosecutor had turned over under the rules of discovery—primarily sheriff's documents relating to the incident, arrest and follow-up investigation.

The natural starting point was the arrest report, which began with 911 calls. Multiple reports of gunfire came in from a neighbourhood next to a park in Calabasas, in an area north of Malibu.

The first deputy to respond, Todd Stallworth, had been dispatched at 10.21 p.m. to Malibu Creek State Park, where he heard the shots, called for back-up and drove in to investigate.

There were no lights in the park. As Stallworth entered on the main road the headlights of his patrol car picked up a reflection and he saw a vehicle parked in a clearing ahead. He put his spotlight on and illuminated a pick-up truck with its tailgate down. There was a pyramid of beer cans on the tailgate and what looked like a gun bag with several rifle barrels protruding from it.

Stallworth stopped his patrol car and was on the radio to the Malibu station, describing the truck, when suddenly there was a gunshot and the searchlight exploded. Stallworth killed the rest of the car's lights and crawled into some bushes, using his handheld radio to call for the special weapons and tactics team.

A three-hour stand-off ensued. Hidden in wooded terrain near the clearing, the gunman fired his weapon repeatedly but apparently his aim was at the sky. Finally, a deputy in black SWAT gear worked his way close enough to read the licence plate, which led to the name Eli Wyms, and a cellphone number. The shooter answered on the first ring and a SWAT team negotiator began a conversation.

The shooter was indeed Eli Wyms, a forty-four-year-old house painter. He was characterised in the arrest report as drunk, angry and suicidal. Earlier in the day he had been kicked out of his home by his wife, who had informed him that she was in love with another man.

Wyms told the negotiator that he had heard noises in the dark and believed he was shooting at rabid coyotes that wanted to eat him. He said he was afraid the spotlight would give his position away. He said he'd qualified as an expert marksman during the first war in Iraq. Investigators eventually collected ninety-four spent bullet casings.

Wyms did not surrender that night until he ran out of beer and told the negotiator he'd trade one rifle for a six-pack. He was turned down. He then announced that he was going to kill himself and literally go out with a bang. The negotiator tried to talk him out of it while a two-man SWAT unit moved towards his position, but soon he heard snoring on the cell line. Wyms had passed out. He was captured and taken in Stallworth's squad car to the county jail downtown.

Other documents in the file continued the saga. At his arraignment Wyms was declared indigent and assigned a public defender. The case moved slowly in the system, but then Vincent stepped in and offered his services pro bono. His first move was to ask for a competency evaluation. Wyms was carted off to the state hospital in Camarillo for a ninety-day psych evaluation. All the doctors agreed that he was competent and ready to stand trial.

In the hearing scheduled before Judge Friedman at two, a trial date would be set. To me it was a formality. One read of the case documents and I knew there would be no trial. What the day's hearing would do was set the time period I would have to negotiate a plea agreement.

It was a cut-and-dried case. Wyms would enter a plea and probably face a year or two of incarceration and mental health counselling. The only question I had was why Vincent had taken the case in the first place. It didn't fall into line with the kind of cases he usually handled, with paying or higher-profile clients.

My immediate thought was to suspect that there was a connection to the Elliot case. Vincent had found some sort of link. But on first read I couldn't nail it down. There were two general connections in that the Wyms incident had happened less than twelve hours before the beach house murders and both crimes occurred in the sheriff's department's Malibu district. But those connections didn't hold up to further scrutiny. As far as I could recall none of the names in the Wyms file were mentioned in the Elliot materials I had reviewed. The Wyms incident happened on the night shift; the Elliot murders on the day shift.

With frustration I closed the file with the question unanswered. I checked my watch and saw I had to get back to the CCB if I wanted time to meet my client in lockup before the hearing.

I called Patrick, paid for lunch and stepped out to the kerb. I was on my cell talking with Lorna when the Lincoln pulled up.

'Has Cisco met with Carlin yet?' I jumped into the back.

'No, that's at two.'

'Have Cisco ask him about the Wyms case, too. Ask him why Vincent even took it.'

'You think they're connected? Elliot and Wyms?'

'I think it but I don't see it.'

'OK, I'll tell him.'

'Anything else going on?'

'One thing. The landlord for the building wants to know if we're going to keep the office.'

I looked out of the window as we cruised across the 101 overpass back to the civic centre area. I could see the newly built Catholic cathedral and the waving steel skin of the Disney music centre. 'I don't know, Lorna. I like working from here. It's never boring. What do you think?'

'I'm not fond of putting on make-up every morning.'

Meaning she liked working out of her condo more than she liked getting ready and driving downtown to an office each day. As usual, we were on the same page.

ELI WYMS WAS STILL doped up from the three months he'd spent in Camarillo. He'd been sent back to county with a drug prescription that wasn't going to help me defend him, let alone help him answer any questions about Vincent. It took me less than two minutes in courtside lockup to decide to submit a motion requesting that all drug therapy be halted. I went back to the courtroom and found Joanne Giorgetti at the prosecution table. The hearing was scheduled to start in five minutes.

'You want a continuance, don't you?' she said.

'And a cease and desist on the drugs. The guy's a zombie.'

'I'm not sure I object to his being in that condition. He shot at an occupied sheriff's car. The state is interested in sending a message on this one.'

'I would argue that my client, panicked as he was by the coyotes, was shooting at the light on the car, not into the car. Your own documents say he was an expert marksman.'

'Well, that's an argument you could make to the jury.'

I wheeled over one of the chairs from the defence table and sat down. 'Sure, but it is probably in the state's best interest to bring this case to a close and get Mr Wyms into some sort of therapy that will help prevent this from ever happening again. So what do you say? Should we go off into a corner someplace and work this out?'

'As long as I get to pick the corner.'

'That's fine with me.' I got up to push the chair back. 'Let me ask you something. Why did Jerry Vincent take on this case?'

She shrugged and shook her head. 'I don't know.'

'Well, did it surprise you?'

'Sure. It was kind of strange, him showing up. I knew him from way back when, you know? From when he was a prosecutor.'

'Yeah, so what happened?'

'One day—a few months ago—I got notice of a competency motion on Wyms and Jerry's name was on it. I called him up and said what the hell, you know? You don't even call to say I'm taking over the case? He said he wanted to get some pro bono in and had asked the PD for a case. But I know Angel Romero, the PD who had the case originally. One day I ran into him and he asked me what was happening on Wyms. He told me that Jerry didn't just come asking for a PB referral. He went to Wyms in men's central, signed him up, and then came and told Angel to turn over the file.'

'Why do you think he took the case?'

I've learned over the years that sometimes if you ask the same question more than once you get different responses.

'I don't know. I asked him that and he didn't really answer. He changed the subject and it was all kind of awkward.'

The case was getting more mysterious. 'Joanne, what do you—'

I was interrupted by the clerk, who called court into session, and I looked up to see Judge Friedman taking the bench.

'EENIE, MEENIE, MINIE, MOE, catch a killer by the toe. If 'is lawyer's Haller let him go. Eenie, meenie, minie, moe. Hey, bro.'

Angel Romero was smiling. I'd been waiting for him in the hallway outside Judge Champagne's courtroom. I hadn't heard that jingle since he'd made it up after the not guilty verdict in the Barnett Woodson case. We bumped fists.

'What's up?' Romero asked. He'd grown up hard on the streets of East LA in a neighbourhood ruled by gangs. He had the tattoos to prove it.

'I'll tell you what's up, Angel. I want to ask you about a client you had earlier this year. Eli Wyms.'

Romero immediately recognised the case. 'Yeah, Vincent took that one off me. You got it now with him being dead?'

'I got all Vincent's cases. I just found out about Wyms.'

'Well, good luck with them, bro. What do you need to know?'

'I got a handle on the case. What I'm curious about is Vincent taking it. According to Joanne Giorgetti, he went after it. Is that right?'

Romero rubbed his chin as he checked the memory banks. I could see faint scars across his knuckles from where he'd had tattoos removed. 'Yeah, he went down to the jail and talked Wyms into it. He got a signed discharge letter. After that, the case was his. I gave him my files and was done.'

'Did he say why he wanted the case? Did he know Wyms?'

'Not that I know of. He just gave me the big wink, you know?'

'No.' I moved in closer. 'What's the big wink?'

'I asked him why he was taking on a southside homeboy who went up there in white people country and shot the place up. I thought he had some racial angle, but he just gave me the wink, like there was something else.'

'Did you ask him what?'

'Yeah, man, but he wouldn't tell me. He just said that Wyms had fired the magic bullet. I didn't know what the hell he meant.'

The magic bullet. There it was again. I could feel the blood in my veins start to move with high velocity.

I ENTERED THE OFFICE and blew right by Lorna and Cisco who were at the reception desk looking at the computer. I spoke without stopping on my way to the inner sanctum. 'If you two have any updates or anything, come in now. I'm about to go into lockdown.'

'And hello to you, too,' Lorna called after me.

But Lorna knew well what was about to happen. Lockdown was when I closed all the doors and windows, drew the curtains and killed the phones, and went to work with total absorption. There was no getting me out until I'd found what I was looking for.

I moved round Vincent's desk and dropped into the seat. I opened my bag and started pulling out the files. I viewed it as me against them. Somewhere in the files I would find the key to Jerry Vincent's last secret. I would find the magic bullet.

Lorna and Cisco came into the office soon after I was settled.

'I didn't see Wren out there,' I said, before either could speak.

'She quit,' Lorna said. 'She went out to lunch and never came back.'

'That was kind of abrupt. Did she call?'

'Yeah. She's going to be Bruce Carlin's secretary now.'

I nodded. That seemed to make a certain amount of sense.

Lorna sat down in one of the chairs. Cisco stayed standing behind her.

'One thing,' Lorna said. 'You must've touched a nerve with that motion you filed on the evidence in Patrick's case. The prosecutor's called three times today.'

I smiled. It looked like I might be able to help Patrick.

'You didn't tell me you filed motions,' Lorna said.

'From the car yesterday. I think the wife got phoney diamonds for her birthday. Now, to make sure she never knows it, they're going to float a deal to Patrick if I withdraw my request to examine the evidence.'

'Good. I think I like Patrick.'

'I hope he gets the break. What's next?'

Lorna looked at the notes on her steno book. I knew she didn't like to be rushed but I was rushing her.

'You're still getting a lot of calls from the local media. About Jerry Vincent or Walter Elliot or both. You want to go over them?'

'No. I don't have the time for any media calls.'

I looked over Lorna's shoulder at Cisco, who was still standing.

'OK, Cisco, your turn. What've you got?'

'I got with my source on Vincent and he didn't know anything about a suspect or this photo Bosch showed you.'

'Nothing? What do you think? Does Bosch know your guy's the leak and is shutting him out?'

'I don't know. But this photo was news to him.'

'Did Bosch come to show Wren the photo this morning?'

'No,' Lorna said. 'I was with her. Bosch never came in.'

I wasn't sure what any of this meant. 'Anything else?'

'Yeah. Vincent's liquidator has one of Patrick's long boards.'

'What's he want for it?'

'Nothing. Let's just say he'd like to do you the favour. I think he's hoping you'll use him for future liquidations. Somebody's supposed to bring it in to him this afternoon.'

'Thanks, Cisco. Get me an address and I'll have Patrick pick it up. Did you debrief Bruce Carlin?'

Cisco and Lorna looked at each other.

'What's wrong?' I asked.

'Carlin's messing with us,' Lorna said. 'He must've put his thinking cap on. He called at two o'clock—right after Wren called and quit—and said he wanted a flat fee or we could figure out things on our own.'

I shook my head in annoyance. 'How much does he want?'

'Ten thousand dollars.'

'You gotta be kidding me.' I looked at Cisco. 'This is extortion. Isn't there a state agency that regulates you guys?'

Cisco shook his head. 'There are all kinds of regulatory agencies but he had no deal with Vincent. We can't find any contract. So he's not required to give us anything. We simply need to hire him and he's setting his price at ten grand. It's a rip-off but it's probably legal. You're the lawyer. You tell me.'

I thought about it for a few moments, then tried to push it aside. I was still riding on the adrenaline charge I'd picked up in the courthouse. 'All right, I'll ask Elliot if he wants to pay it. Meantime, I'm going to hit the files and if I get lucky we won't need him. Thank you both for all you've been doing. Go out and have a good night.'

Lorna looked at me curiously. 'You're sending us home?'

I checked my watch. 'Why not? It's almost four thirty.'

'You're going to work here alone tonight?' Cisco asked.

'I'll lock the door and I won't let anybody in—even if I know him.'

I smiled. Lorna and Cisco didn't. I pointed to the open door to the office. It had a slide bolt at the top of the door frame and gave the idea of lockdown new meaning.

'I'll be fine. Patrick should be out there. Tell him to keep hanging. I might have something to tell him after I make that call.'

I OPENED the Patrick Henson file on my desk and looked up the prosecutor's number. I wanted to get this out of the way before I went to work on the Elliot case.

The prosecutor was Dwight Posey, a guy I had dealt with before on cases and never liked. Some prosecutors deal with defence attorneys as though they are only one step removed from their clients and, unfortunately, Posey was one of them.

'So, Haller,' he said after taking the call, 'they've got you walking in a dead man's shoes, don't they?'

'Yeah, something like that. Anyway, Dwight, I'm returning your call. Actually, your three calls. What's up?'

'I got the motion. It's sitting right here on my desk.'

'And?'

'And, uh, well, we're not going to do that, Mick. Put our evidence out there for examination.'

'Dwight, that's the beauty of the system. You don't make that decision. A judge does. That's why I put it in a motion.'

'No, actually, we do this time. We're going to drop the theft charge and just proceed with the drug charge.'

THE BRASS VERDICT | 79

I smiled and nodded. 'Only problem with that, Dwight, is that the drug charge came out of the theft investigation. So you don't have one without the other. That won't fly in any court I've ever been in.'

'Then maybe we can just talk about a disposition on the matter.'

'I'm open to it, Dwight. You should know that my client has voluntarily completed rehab, has full-time employment and has been clean for four months. He'll give his piss anytime to prove it.'

'That's really good to hear. The DA's office looks favourably on voluntary rehabilitation. Tell you what, let's make it go away. Maybe Patrick can use this opportunity to move ahead.'

'Sounds like a plan, Dwight. You're making my day.'

'OK, get me his rehab records. We'll put it in a package.'

Posey was talking about a pre-trial intervention case. If Patrick kept clean the case would go away in six months. He'd have an arrest on his record but no conviction. Unless . . .

'You willing to expunge his record?' I asked.

'Uh . . . that's asking a lot, Mickey. He did, after all, break in and steal the diamonds.'

'He didn't break in, Dwight. He was invited in. And the alleged diamonds are what this is all about, right?'

'All right, fine. We'll put it into the package.'

'You're a good man, Dwight.'

When I hung up the phone Cisco came in carrying a Post-it and a gun in a leather holster. He walked round the desk, put the Post-it down in front of me, then opened a drawer and put the weapon in it.

'What are you doing?' I said. 'You can't give me a gun.'

'It's totally legal and registered to me. I'm just storing it here.'

'I think you're overreacting.'

'Better than under-reacting. See you tomorrow.'

'Thank you. Will you send Patrick in before you go?'

'You got it.'

He left the room and Patrick soon came in.

'Patrick, Vincent's liquidator still has one of your long boards.' I handed him the Post-it Cisco had given me. 'You can go by and pick it up. Just tell him you're picking it up for me.'

'Oh man, thank you!'

'Yeah, well, I've got even better news on your case.' I went over the phone call I'd just had with Dwight and watched his eyes gain a little light.

'I have to call my mom,' he said. 'She's gonna be so happy.'

'Yeah, well, I hope you are, too.'

'I am, I am.'

'Now, the way I figure it, you owe me a couple of thousand for my work on this. That's about two and a half weeks of driving. If you want, you can stick with me until it's paid off. After that, we can see where we're at.'

'That sounds good. I like the job.' Patrick smiled broadly.

'Good, then it's a deal. One other thing. I saw you sleeping in your car in the garage this morning.'

He looked down at the floor. 'Sorry. I'll find another spot.'

'No, *I'm* sorry,' I said. 'I forgot you were sleeping in your car or a life-guard stand. I just don't know how safe it is to be sleeping in the same garage where a guy got shot the other night. If I give you an advance on your pay, would that help you get a motel room or something?'

'Um, I guess.'

I knew that living out of a motel was almost as depressing as living out of a car. 'I'll tell you what. If you want you could stay with me for a couple of weeks. Until you get a better plan going. I've got a house and you'd have your own room. Except that on Wednesday nights and every other weekend, it would be better if you stayed with a friend. That's when I have my daughter.'

He thought about it and nodded. 'Yeah, I could do that.'

I reached across the desk and signalled him to give me back the Post-it. I wrote my own address on it. 'Why don't you go pick up your board and then head over to my place. Fareholm is right off Laurel Canyon. You go up the stairs to the front porch and there's a table and chairs and an extra key under the ashtray. The guest bedroom is next to the kitchen. Just make yourself at home.'

'Thanks.' He took the Post-it and looked at the addresses.

'Look, we're only talking about a few weeks. Till you get on your feet again. Meantime maybe we can both help each other out. You know, if one of us starts to feel the pull, maybe the other one will be there to talk about it.'

'OK.'

We were quiet for a moment. I didn't tell Patrick that he might end up helping me more than I'd help him. In the last forty-eight hours the pressure was beginning to weigh on me. I could feel myself being pulled back, the desire to go to the cotton-wrapped world the pills could give me. Up front and deep down I knew I didn't want that again, and maybe Patrick could help me avoid it.

'Thanks, Mr Haller.'

'Call me Mickey. And I should be the one saying thanks.'

'Why are you doing all of this for me?'

I looked at the big fish on the wall behind him. 'I'm not sure, Patrick. But I'm hoping that if I help you then I'll be helping myself. Make sure you remember to call your mother.'

Nine

After I was finally alone I started the process the way I always do, with clean pages and sharp points. From the supply closet I retrieved two fresh legal pads and four Black Warrior pencils. I sharpened their points and got down to work.

Vincent had broken the Elliot case into two files. One file contained the state's case and the second, the defence case. The defence file was thin, as by the rules of discovery anything that went into it went to the prosecutor. I began with the thicker file, the prosecution's case. I read straight through, every page and every word. I took notes on one legal pad and drew a time and action flow chart on the other. From there, I moved on to the defence file and again read every word on every page.

When I was finished with the Elliot files I opened the Wyms case and read every document. Because Wyms was arrested following a public incident involving several uniform and SWAT deputies, this file was thick with reports —transcriptions of conversations, ballistics reports, a lengthy evidence inventory, witness statements, dispatch records and patrol deployment reports. I checked every name against the list of names from the Elliot files. I cross-referenced every address.

I found what I was looking for an hour into my second run at the files. It had been there in front of me the whole time. First in Elliot's arrest report and then on the time and action chart I had drawn myself. I called the chart the Christmas tree. It always started basic and unadorned. Just the bare bones facts of the case. Then, as I studied the case, I started hanging lights and ornaments on it. Witness statements, evidence, lab results. Soon the tree was lit up and bright. Everything about the case was there for me to see.

Walter Elliot was the trunk and all branches came from him. I had his

movements, statements and actions noted by time. On the second go-round
I started adding decorations.

> 12.40 p.m.—WE arrives at house, front door unlocked
> 12.50 p.m.—WE discovers bodies, balcony door open
> 1.05 p.m.—WE calls 911, waits outside
> 1.24 p.m.—WE calls 911 again, what's the holdup?
> 1.28 p.m.—Deputies arrive on scene, Murray (4-alpha-1) and
>   Harber (4-alpha-2)
> 1.30 p.m.—WE secured, placed in patrol car, Murray/Harber
>   search house
> 2.15 p.m.—Homicide arrives
>   First team: Kinder, Ericsson;
>   Second team: Joshua, Toles
> 2.30 p.m.—WE taken inside house, describes discovery
> 2.40 p.m.—WE transported to Malibu (Joshua/Toles)
> 4.55 p.m.—WE interview, Kinder takes lead in interview
> 5.40 p.m.—Transported to Whittier (Joshua/Toles)
> 7.00 p.m.—GSR testing
> 8.00 p.m.—Second interview, Ericsson in lead
> 8.40 p.m.—WE to men's central (Joshua/Toles)

As I had constructed the Christmas tree I kept a separate list of every
person mentioned in the sheriff's reports. This would become the witness
list I would turn over to the prosecution. From the list and the tree I could
infer what witnesses the prosecution was avoiding and possibly why. It was
while I was thinking in these terms that I felt the cold finger of revelation go
down my spine. Everything became clear and I found Jerry Vincent's magic
bullet.

Walter Elliot had been taken from the crime scene to the Malibu station
so he would be out of the way and secured while the lead detectives continued their onsite investigation. One short interview was conducted. He was
then transported to sheriff's headquarters in Whittier where his hands tested
positive for nitrates associated with gunpowder. After Kinder and Ericsson
took another shot at interviewing him he was formally placed under arrest.

Elliot was handled solely by the homicide detectives as he was moved
from crime scene to headquarters to jail. But it was how he was handled previous to their arrival that caught my eye. The uniform deputies who first
responded to the call had the designations 4-alpha-1 and 4-alpha-2 after their

names. And I had seen at least one of those designations in the Wyms file.

I quickly scanned the Wyms arrest report until my eyes came to the first 4-alpha-1 designation. Deputy Todd Stallworth had the designation written after his name. He was the deputy whose car Wyms had fired upon and who, at the end of the stand-off, had placed Wyms under arrest and taken him to jail.

I realised that 4-alpha-1 did not refer to a specific deputy, and as the Malibu district covered huge areas, I assumed that this was the fourth district for a patrol zone and alpha was the designation for a specific patrol car. It seemed the only way to explain why deputies who worked different shifts would share the same designation. Adrenaline crashed into my veins as all in a moment I realised what Vincent had been up to. I didn't need his laptop or his investigator. I knew exactly what the defence strategy was.

I pulled my cellphone and called Cisco. 'Cisco, any sheriff's deputies you know work out of the Malibu station?'

'Uh, I know one guy who used to.'

'Can you call him tonight? I need to know what the patrol designation four-alpha-one means.'

'Shouldn't be a problem. Hold on. Lorna wants you.'

I waited while she was given the phone. I could hear TV noise in the background. I had interrupted a scene of domestic bliss.

'Mickey, are you still there at the office?'

'I'm here.'

'It's eight thirty. I think you should go home.'

'I think I should too. I'll wait to hear from Cisco—he's checking something out for me—then I'll go over to Dan Tana's to have steak and spaghetti.'

She knew I went to Dan Tana's when I had something to celebrate. Usually a good verdict. 'You had steak for breakfast.'

'Then I guess this will make it a perfect day.'

'Things went well tonight?'

'I think so. Real well. I'll see you tomorrow, Lorna.'

'OK, Mickey. Have fun.'

I hung up and waited, thinking it all through again. Vincent had not taken on the Wyms case out of any obligation to the poor, he was using Wyms as camouflage. Stashing him out at Camarillo, keeping the case active. Meantime, he gathered information under the flag of the Wyms defence that he'd use in the Elliot case.

Technically, he was probably acting within bounds, but ethically it was underhand. Elliot got the magic bullet while Wyms got the zombie cocktail.

It didn't take too long before Cisco called back.

'Four-alpha is Malibu's lead car. Four for the Malibu station and alpha for . . . alpha. Priority calls go to the alpha car. Four-alpha-one would be the driver. The partner would be four-alpha-two.'

'So the alpha car covers the whole fourth district?'

'That's what he told me. Does that help, Mick?'

My theory was confirmed. A double murder and shots near a residential neighbourhood would certainly be alpha car calls.

'It does, Cisco. But it also means more work for you.'

'On the Elliot case?'

'No, not Elliot. I want you to work on the Eli Wyms case. Find out everything you can about the night he was arrested. Get me details.'

'That's what I'm here for.'

THE NIGHT'S DISCOVERY pushed the case off the paper and into my imagination. I was starting to get courtroom images in my head. Scenes of examinations and cross-examinations. I was laying out the suits I would wear. The case was coming alive inside and this was a good thing. It was a momentum thing. You time it right and you go into trial with the inescapable conviction that you will not lose.

My plan was to sit in a corner booth at Dan Tana's and sketch out some of the key witness examinations, listing the baseline questions and probable answers for each. I was excited about getting to it.

After quickly repacking the files, I killed the lights and locked the office door. I headed down the hallway and across the bridge. Just as I was entering the garage I saw a man walk up the ramp from the ground floor. He was the man in Bosch's photograph.

My blood froze. I knew the man coming towards me was the killer and that he had a gun. I swung round and started to run.

'Hey!' a voice called from behind me.

I kept running. Back across the bridge to the glass doors leading into the building. One single thought fired through every synapse in my brain. I had to get to Cisco's gun.

I shot my hand into my pocket in search of the keys, then jerked it out, currency, coins and wallet flying. As I jammed the key into the lock I could hear steps behind me. *The gun! Get the gun!*

I finally yanked the door open and bolted towards the office. I glanced behind me and saw the man catch the door just before it closed. Keys still in my hand, I reached the office door and fumbled the key in the lock. I could feel the killer closing. Finally I entered, slammed the door and threw the lock. I hit the light switch, then charged into Vincent's office.

The gun was there in the drawer. I yanked it out of its holster and went out to the reception area. Across the room I could see the killer's shape through the frosted glass. He was trying to open the door. I pointed the gun high and fired two shots into the ceiling. The sound was deafening. 'That's right!' I yelled. 'Come on in!'

The image on the other side of the glass disappeared. I heard footsteps move away, then the door to the bridge open and close. I stood stock-still, listening. There was no sound. I stepped over to the reception desk and called 911, but a recording told me I needed to hold on for the next available dispatcher. Shaking, I checked my pockets and found I hadn't lost my cellphone. Harry Bosch answered on the first ring.

'Bosch! That guy you showed me was just here!'

'Haller? What are you talking about? Who?'

'The guy in the photo you showed me today! With the gun!'

'All right, calm down. Where is he? Where are you?'

'I was leaving Vincent's office and I saw him in the garage. I ran back in and he ran after me. I fired a couple of shots—'

'You have a gun?'

'Damn right I do.'

'I suggest you put it away before somebody gets hurt.'

'He'll be the one getting hurt. Who the hell is he?'

There was a pause. 'I don't know yet. Look, I was just heading home . Sit tight and I'll be there in five minutes. Don't shoot me when I get there.'

'I won't.'

'What did he want?'

'That's a damn good question. I don't have the answer.'

'Haller, stop messing around and tell me!'

'I'm telling you! I don't know what he's after. Now get over here!' I yelled, involuntarily squeezing my hands into fists and putting a shot in the floor. I jumped as though I'd been shot.

'Haller!' Bosch yelled. 'What the hell was that?'

I pulled in a deep breath. 'Get over here and find out.'

'Did you hit him? Did you put him down?'

Without answering, I closed the phone.

BOSCH MADE IT in six minutes but it felt like an hour. A dark image appeared on the other side of the glass and he knocked sharply.

'Haller, it's me, Bosch.'

Carrying the gun at my side I unlocked the door and let him in.

'Anything since we were on the phone?' he asked.

'Haven't seen or heard him. I guess I scared his ass away.'

Bosch holstered his gun and threw me a look, as if to say my tough-guy pose was convincing no one except maybe myself.

'What was that last shot?'

'An accident.' I pointed to the hole in the floor.

'Give me that gun before you get yourself killed.'

I handed it over. 'My investigator leaves it here at night.'

Bosch looked up and his eyes found the two holes in the ceiling. He shook his head then went over to the blinds and looked out on the street. Broadway was dead out there this time of night.

'OK,' he said. 'Let's sit in your office to talk about this.'

I took a seat behind the desk. Bosch sat across from me.

'First of all, here's your stuff. I found it out there on the bridge.' From the pocket of his jacket he pulled my wallet and loose currency. He put it all on the desk.

I put my property back in my pocket. 'OK, now what?'

'Now we talk. First off, do you want to file a report on this?'

'Why bother? It's your case. Why don't you know who this guy is?'

'We're working on it.'

'That's not good enough, Bosch! Why can't you ID him?'

'Because we think he's a hitter brought in from out of town.'

'How totally fantastic! Why did he come back here?'

'Obviously, because of you. You've been in here all week. You must know something that makes you a danger to him.'

'Me? I'm telling you I don't know anything. I can't think of—'

'Come on, Haller!' Bosch barked at me. 'Your life is threatened here! Don't you get it? What've you got?'

'I told you!'

'Who did Vincent bribe?'

'I don't know and I couldn't tell you if I did.'

'What did the FBI want with him?'

'I don't know that, either!'

He started pointing at me. 'You hypocrite. You're hiding behind the law while the killer is out there. Tell me what you've got!'

'Don't point your finger at me. This isn't my job. It's your job.'

'But you had him right here. Right here! He came to either kill you or to get something from you. Something in this office that could lead to his identity.'

'All I can tell you is that all week I had my case manager, my investigator and Jerry Vincent's own receptionist in here. And none of us, Detective, *none of us*, has found the smoking gun you're so sure is here. You tell me that Vincent paid somebody a bribe. But I spent the last three hours in here looking at the Elliot file. I saw no indication he paid anybody off. In fact, I found out that he didn't *need* to bribe anybody. Vincent had a shot at winning the case fair and square.'

'What about the FBI?'

'Same answer. Nothing.'

Bosch didn't respond. I saw true disappointment cloud his face. He abruptly stood up and put Cisco's gun down on the desk. 'Keep it loaded. And if I were you I'd stop working at night.' He headed towards the door.

'That's it?' I called after him.

He spun in his tracks. 'What else do you want?'

'You want information I can't give but you give nothing back. And I'm scared as hell that's half the reason I'm in danger.'

Bosch looked like he might be about to jump over the desk at me. But then I saw him calm himself. All except for the palpitation high on his left cheek. That was his tell, and it was a tell that once again gave me a sense of familiarity.

'Damn it,' he finally said. 'What do you want to know, Counsellor? Go ahead. Ask me a question and I'll answer it.'

'I want to know about the bribe. Where did the money go?'

Bosch laughed in a false way. 'I give you a free shot and you ask me that? You think if I knew where the money went I'd be here right now? Uh-uh, Haller, I'd be booking a killer.'

'But the bribe—if there was a bribe—went down five months ago. Why was Jerry killed now? Why's the FBI calling?'

'Let me know if you come up with any answers. Anything else I can do for you? I was heading home when you called.'

'Yeah, there is. I was on my way out, too.'

He looked at me. 'What, you want me to hold your hand on the way to the garage? Fine, let's go.'

I closed the office again and we proceeded down the hall to the bridge to the garage. Bosch had stopped talking and the silence was nerve-racking. I finally broke it.

'I was going to go have a steak. You want to come? Maybe we'll solve the world's problems over some red meat.'

'Where, Musso's?'

'I was thinking Dan Tana's.'

Bosch nodded. 'If you can get us in.'

'Don't worry. I know a guy.'

BOSCH FOLLOWED ME but when I slowed on Santa Monica Boulevard to pull into the valet stop in front of the restaurant he kept going. I went in by myself and Craig, who worked the door, sat me in one of the cherished corner booths. It was a busy night but things were tapering off.

During the drive I had thought long and hard about what had just happened back at the office and now I wanted to think about how best to confront Bosch about it. It was like preparing for the cross-examination of a hostile witness.

Ten minutes later Bosch finally appeared and Craig led him to me. 'Get lost?' I asked as he squeezed into the booth.

'I couldn't find a parking space.'

'I guess they don't pay you enough for valet.'

'No, valet's a beautiful thing. But I can't give my city car to a valet. Against the rules.'

I guessed that he probably packed a shotgun in the trunk.

When the waiter came we both ordered the steak with spaghetti and red sauce on the side. Bosch ordered a beer and I asked for a bottle of water.

'So,' I said, 'where's your partner been lately?'

'He's working on other aspects of the investigation.'

'Well, I guess it's good to hear there are other aspects to it.'

Bosch studied me. 'Is that supposed to be a crack?'

'Just an observation. Doesn't seem to be much happening.'

'Maybe that's because your source dried up and blew away.'

'My source? I don't have any source,' I said.

'Not any more. I figured out who was feeding your guy.'

'I know you won't believe me, but I have no idea who or what you are talking about. I get information from my investigator. I don't ask him how he gets it.'

Bosch nodded. 'That's the best way to do it, right? Insulate yourself and then you don't get any blowback in your face. In the meantime if a police captain loses his job and pension, those are the breaks.'

I hadn't realised Cisco's source was so highly placed.

The waiter brought our drinks and a basket of bread. I drank some water as I contemplated what to say next. Bosch raised his eyebrows like he was expecting something.

'How'd you know when I was leaving the office tonight?'

He looked puzzled. 'What do you mean?'

'I figure it was the lights. You were out there on Broadway and when I killed the lights you sent your guy in.'

'I don't know what you are talking about.'

'Sure you do. The photo of the guy with the gun. It was a phoney. You set it up to smoke out your leak, then you tried to scam me with it.'

Bosch shook his head and looked out of the booth.

'You know what your mistake was? Not coming back like you said to show the photo to Vincent's secretary. If the guy in the picture was legit, you would've shown it to her because she knows the clients better than me. But you didn't and that's how I know.'

Bosch looked towards the bar in the middle of the restaurant. The overhead TV was showing sports highlights. I leaned across the table.

'So who's the guy with a stick-on moustache? Some clown from vice? Don't you have better things to do than run a game on me?'

Finally, he looked at me. 'OK, I guess that makes you one smart lawyer. Just like the old man. I wonder why you're wasting it defending scumbags.'

I smiled. 'Is that how you like to play it? You get caught so you respond by accusing the other guy?'

Bosch laughed, his face turning red as he looked away, and his mention of my father brought a vague memory of him laughing uneasily and looking away as my mother accused him of something I was too young to understand.

Bosch put both arms on the table. 'You've heard of the first forty-eight, right? The chances of clearing a homicide diminish by almost half each day if you don't solve it in forty-eight hours. I'm coming up on seventy-two hours and I've got nothing. I was hoping I might scare something out of you.'

I sat there staring at him. 'You actually thought I knew who killed Jerry and wasn't telling?'

'It was a possibility I had to consider.'

'Damn you, Bosch.'

Just then the waiter came with our steaks. As the plates were put down Bosch stared at me with what looked like a knowing smile.

'You're an arrogant son of a bitch,' I said.

Bosch cut into his steak left-handed. He put a chunk of meat into his mouth and rested his fists on either side of his plate, fork and knife in his grips, as if guarding the food from poachers. A lot of my clients who had spent time in prison ate the same way.

'Why don't you take it easy there, Counsellor,' he said. 'I'm not used to being on your side of the line, OK? Defence attorneys have tried to portray me as stupid, corrupt, bigoted, you name it, so yes, I tried to run a game on you to solve a murder. I apologise. If you want I will have them wrap up my steak and I'll take it to go.'

I shook my head. Bosch had a talent for trying to make me feel guilty for his transgressions. 'Maybe now you should be the one who takes it easy,' I said. 'I've acted openly and honestly with you. I've told you what I could tell you. You're damn lucky I didn't put a bullet in your man's chest at the office door.'

'You weren't supposed to have a gun. I checked.' Bosch kept his head down as he worked on the steak. 'So now that we have that out of the way, will you help me?'

I blew out my breath in a laugh. 'Are you kidding? Have you heard a single thing I've said?'

'Yeah. When it's all said and done I could still use your help.'

I started cutting my steak. I took my time, savouring the first bite.

'What kind of help?'

'We draw out the killer.'

'Great. How dangerous will it be?'

'Depends. It could get dangerous. I need you to shake things up, make whoever's out there think you might be a threat to them.'

'How do we shake things up?'

'I was thinking a newspaper story. I assume you've been getting calls from the reporters. We pick one and give them an exclusive, and we plant something in there that gets the killer thinking.'

'There's a guy at the *Times*,' I said. 'I kind of made a deal with him to get him off my back. I told him when I was ready to talk I would talk to him.'

'That's a perfect set-up. We'll use him. So, are you in?'

I cut into the steak again. Blood ran onto the plate.

'Yeah,' I said. 'I'm in.'

Ten

Everybody lies.

Cops lie. Lawyers lie. Clients lie. Even jurors lie.

There is a school of belief in criminal law that every trial is won or lost in the choosing of the jury. I do know that there is probably no phase in a murder trial more important than the selection of the twelve citizens who decide your client's fate. It is also the part of the trial most reliant on the whims of fate and luck and being able to ask the right question at the right time to the right person.

Jury selection in California vs Elliot began on schedule in Judge James P. Stanton's courtroom at 10 a.m., Thursday. The courtroom was packed, half filled with the *venire*—the eighty potential jurors called randomly from the jury pool on the second floor of the CCB—and half filled with media, well-wishers and just plain gawkers.

I sat at the defence table alone with my client. Spread in front of me were three coloured markers, a Post-it pad and an open empty manila file. Back at the office I had prepared the file by drawing a grid across it. There were twelve blocks, each the size of a Post-it. Each block was for one of the twelve jurors. Some lawyers use computers to track potential jurors. They even have software that can filter information through a sociopolitical pattern-recognition program and spit out recommendations. I had been using the old-school grid system since I had been a baby lawyer in the public defender's office. A computer can't hear how someone gives an answer. It can't see someone's eyes when they lie.

The way it worked was that the judge had a computer-generated list from which he called the first twelve citizens from the *venire* and they took seats in the jury box. But they only got to keep their seats if they survived *voir dire*—the questioning of their background and views and understanding of the law. The judge asked them a series of basic questions and then the lawyers followed up.

Jurors could be removed in two ways. They could be rejected for cause if they showed through their answers or demeanour or even their life's circumstances that they could not be fair or hear the case with an open mind. There was no limit to the number of challenges for cause at the disposal of the attorneys. The second method of removal was the pre-emptory challenge, and because this trial involved murder, the prosecution and defence would have up to twenty pre-emptory challenges each. A pre-emptory challenge let the attorney strike a juror for no reason other than instinctual dislike.

The rules of *voir dire* were designed to remove bias and deception from the jury. The term itself came from the French phrase 'to speak the truth'. But this of course was contradictory to each side's bottom line. I wanted a jury biased against the state and the police. I wanted them predisposed to be on my side or easily pushed there. And, of course, the man sitting four feet from me in the courtroom wanted a diametrically opposite result.

By 10.15 the efficient Judge Stanton had welcomed the randomly selected first twelve candidates to the jury box, six men and six women. We knew where they were from, and what they did, but we didn't know their names. The judge had been adamant about protecting the jurors from public scrutiny. He had ordered that the court TV camera be mounted on the wall over the jury box so that the jurors would not be seen. He had also ruled that the identities of all prospective jurors be withheld.

The process began with the judge asking each prospective juror questions about what they did for a living and where they lived. He then moved on to questions about whether they had been victims of crime, had relatives in prison or were related to any police officers or prosecutors. He asked who had prior jury experience. The judge excused three for cause, and agreed with a fourth's plea for a hardship dismissal. The four were quickly replaced with four more random selections from the *venire*. And so it went. By noon I had used two of my pre-emptories while Golantz was holding fast.

Elliot had insisted that he be allowed to sign off on each of my pre-emptory challenges. It took extra time to explain to him why I wanted to dump a juror but each time he ultimately nodded his approval. Shortly after noon the judge broke for lunch. It being technically the first day of my first trial in over a year, Lorna Taylor had come to court to show her support. The plan was to go to lunch together and then she would go back to the office and start packing it up.

As we entered the hallway outside the courtroom I asked Elliot if he wanted to join us but he said he had to make a quick run to the studio. Lorna and I hung back and let the prospective jurors crowd onto the elevators. I didn't want to ride down with them. Inevitably one of them opens their mouth and asks something improper and you then have to go through the motions of reporting it to the judge.

When one of the elevators opened I saw the reporter, Jack McEvoy, push his way out past the jurors, scan the hallway and zero in on me. He walked directly towards me.

'Great,' I said. 'Here comes trouble. What do you want?'

'To explain.'

'What, you mean explain why you're a liar?'

'No, look, when I told you it was going to run Sunday I meant it. That's what I was told.'

'And here it is Thursday and no story in the paper and when I've tried to call you about it you don't call me back. I've got other reporters interested, McEvoy. I don't need the *Times*.'

'Look, I understand. But they decided to hold it so it would run closer to the trial. They're running it out front this coming Sunday.'

'The front page on Sunday. I'll believe it when I see it.'

I took Lorna by the arm and started leading her towards the elevators. I pushed past the reporter.

'So we're OK?' he said. 'You'll hold off on giving away the exclusive.'

'Whatever.'

I left him hanging and got on an elevator. When Lorna and I got out of the building we walked a block over to City Hall and I had Patrick pick us up there. I didn't want any prospective jurors to see me getting into the back of a chauffeured Lincoln. It might not sit well with them. I told Patrick to take us over to the French Garden on 7th Street.

'Listen,' I told Lorna, 'when you go back to the office call Julie Favreau and see if she can come tomorrow.'

'I thought Elliot didn't want a jury consultant.'

'He doesn't have to know we're using her. Take it out of general operating. I already burned through two strikes. Just tell her the bailiff will have her name and will make sure she gets a seat.'

'OK, I'll call her. Are you doing all right, Mick?'

I must've been talking too fast or sweating too much. Lorna had picked up on my agitation. I was feeling shaky and I didn't know if it was because of the growing realisation that what I'd been working towards for a year would soon be upon me.

'I'm fine, just hungry. You know how I get when I'm hungry.'

'Sure,' she said. 'I understand.'

The truth was I wasn't hungry. I was feeling the weight on me. The burden of a man's future. And it wasn't my client's future. It was my own.

BY THREE O'CLOCK on the second day of jury selection Golantz and I had traded pre-emptory and cause challenges for more than ten hours of court time. It had been a battle. We had quietly identified each other's must-have jurors and struck them without care or conscience. We had gone through almost the entire *venire* and my jury seating chart was covered with as many as five layers of Post-its. I had two pre-emptory challenges left. Golantz was down to his final one.

The panel now included an attorney, a computer programmer, two postal service employees and four retirees as well as a male nurse, a tree trimmer, an engineer and an artist. From the original twelve the engineer in seat seven and one of the retirees, in seat twelve, had somehow gone the distance. Both were white males and on my chart I had written notes about both in blue ink—my code for being cold to the defence. But their leanings were so slight that I had still not used a precious challenge on either.

The latest addition to the jury box was the artist. During Judge Stanton's general enquiries I had taken notes about her in red and grew happier and happier with her on my jury. When it was the lawyers' turn Golantz went first and asked questions he hoped would draw out a bias but the woman held her own, appearing very open-minded.

Four questions into the prosecutor's effort I felt a vibration in my pocket and reached in for my cell. I held it down below the defence table. Julie Favreau had been texting me all day from the gallery.

Favreau: She's a keeper. Don't like 8. Haven't heard enough from 10.
Kick 7 if you have to.

Juror eight was the tree trimmer. I had him in blue because of answers he gave about the police. I also thought he was anxious to be on the jury, a flag in a murder case. It signalled strong feelings about law and order and lack of hesitation about sitting in judgment.

Judge Stanton was allowing us a lot of leeway. When it was my turn to question the artist, I accepted her without further questioning. I was allowed instead to make further enquiries of juror eight. I found him deceptive and decided Favreau was right. He had to go.

When the judge asked if the prosecution and defence accepted the panel as composed, Golantz used his last pre-emptory to remove the artist. I used my second to last to remove the tree trimmer.

Two more names were called from the *venire* and a real-estate agent and one more retiree took seats eight and eleven in the box. Their answers to the questions from the judge put them right down the middle of the road.

The bottom line was that I had one pre-emptory left to use on juror seven or juror ten. The engineer or the retiree.

I asked the judge for a moment to confer with my client and slid my chart in front of Elliot. 'Walter, what do you think? We need to get rid of seven and ten but can only get rid of one.'

Elliot tapped a finger on the block for juror ten, a retired technical writer for a toy manufacturer. 'Get rid of him.'

I looked at the grid. There was a lot of blue on block ten but there was an equal amount on block seven. The engineer.

I had a hunch that the technical writer, like the tree trimmer, wanted badly to be on the jury but probably as research for a book, as he had acknowledged during *voir dire* that in retirement he was trying to write fiction. Juror seven was blue for another reason. He was listed as an aerospace engineer. In general, engineers were conservative politically and religiously, two blue attributes, and they worked for companies that relied on huge government contracts. A vote for the defence was a vote against the government. Lastly, engineers exist in a world of logic and absolutes. These were things you could not apply to a crime scene or even to the criminal justice system as a whole.

'I don't know,' I said. 'I think the engineer should go.'

'No, I like him. I've liked him since the beginning. I want him to stay.'

My eyes travelled from juror seven to ten and then back again. I was hoping for some sign, some tell that would reveal the right choice.

'Mr Haller,' Judge Stanton said. 'Do you wish to use your last challenge or accept the jury as it is now composed? I remind you, it is getting late in the day.'

My phone was buzzing. 'One more moment, Your Honour.'

I leaned into Elliot and whispered, 'Are you sure, Walter?' But what I was really doing was pulling my phone.

'Look, I make my living reading people,' Elliot whispered back.

I nodded and looked down. It was a text from Favreau.

Favreau: kick 10. Juror 7 fits prosecution profile but I see good eye contact and open face. He's interested in your story. He likes your client.

Eye contact. That settled it. I slipped the phone back into my pocket and stood up. 'Your Honour, the defence would like to thank and excuse Juror Ten at this time.'

WALKING IN A DEAD MAN'S SHOES
Attorney takes over for Murdered Colleague
The Trial of the Decade
By Jack McEvoy, *Times* Staff Writer

It wasn't the thirty-one cases dropped in his lap that were the difficulty. It was the big one with the big client and high stakes. Defence Attorney Michael Haller took over for his murdered colleague Jerry Vincent two weeks ago and now finds himself at the centre of this year's 'Trial of the Decade'.

Today testimony is scheduled to begin in the trial of Walter Elliot, the fifty-four-year-old chairman of Archway Pictures charged with murdering his wife and her alleged lover six months ago in Malibu. Haller stepped into the case only ten days ago after Vincent, forty-five, was found shot to death.

Vincent had made legal provisions that allowed Haller to step into his practice. Haller, who had been at the end of a year-long sabbatical from practising law, is the forty-two-year-old son of the late Michael Haller Sr, one of Los Angeles's storied defence attorneys in the 1950s and 1960s.

The investigation of Vincent's murder is ongoing. Detectives say there are no suspects. He was shot twice in the head while sitting in his car in the garage next to his office building in the 200 block of Broadway.

Following Vincent's death the attorney's entire law practice was turned over to Haller. His job was to cooperate with investigators within the bounds of attorney–client protections, inventory the cases and inform all active clients of Vincent's death. The majority of cases remained with Haller. By far the biggest of these is the 'Murder in Malibu' case.

The case came with one big condition. Elliot would only keep Haller if Haller agreed not to try to delay the trial.

'Walter has insisted on his innocence since day one,' Haller told the *Times* in his first interview since taking on the case. 'There were early delays and he has waited six months for his day in court.'

But whoever killed Vincent also stole his briefcase from his car. It contained Vincent's laptop computer. 'It was the central storage point for case information and strategy,' Haller said. 'The hard files in the office were incomplete and at first I thought we were dead in the water.'

But then Haller found something the killer had not taken. Vincent backed his computer up on a digital flash drive attached to his key chain. And when the testimony begins today, Haller says, 'We'll be locked and loaded and ready to go.' Legal experts expect the defence to attack the handling of evidence in the investigation and the testing procedures that determined that Elliot had fired a gun.

Deputy District Attorney, Jeffrey Golantz, who is prosecuting the case, declined comment for this story.

Eleven

The jury came out in a single-file line like the Lakers taking the basketball court. The same feeling of anticipation was in the air. They split into two lines and moved down the two rows of the jury box. They took the same seats they were in on Friday when they were sworn in.

It was almost 10 a.m. Monday. Judge Stanton had had the lawyers and the defendant back in chambers for almost forty minutes while he went over last-minute ground rules, and took the time to give me the squint and express his displeasure over the story on the front page of the morning's *Los Angeles Times*.

I turned and looked back at the gallery. The courtroom once again was packed with members of the media and the public as well as those with a blood link to the case. Directly behind the prosecution's table, Golantz had positioned Mitzi Elliot's mother. Next to her sat Johan Rilz's father and two brothers who had travelled all the way from Berlin. In the first row behind me were Lorna, Cisco, Patrick and Julie Favreau—who I'd hired to ride through the trial and observe the jury for me.

An empty fifth seat had been reserved for my daughter. My hope had been that I'd convince my ex-wife to allow Hayley to go to court with me for the day. She had never seen me at work and I thought opening statements would be the perfect time. I had even employed the Mark Twain line about taking her out of school so that she could get an education. But my ex-wife refused to allow it.

Walter Elliot had no one in the gallery. He had no children and no relatives he was close to. Because Nina Albrecht was listed on both the prosecution and defence witness lists she was excluded from the gallery until her testimony was completed. My client had plenty of associates and hangers-on that wanted to be there for him, even A-list movie actors. But I told him a Hollywood entourage would broadcast the wrong image. It is all about the jury, I told him. Every move that is made is in deference to the jury.

Judge Stanton began the proceedings by asking if any jurors had seen the *Times* story. None raised their hands and Stanton repeated an earlier reminder about not reading or watching reports on the trial. He said the trial would begin with opening statements from the opposing attorneys.

'Ladies and gentlemen, remember,' he said. 'These are statements. It's up to each side to present the evidence that backs them up. And you will be the ones at the end of the trial who decide if they have done that.'

He gestured to Golantz and said the prosecution would go first.

Handsome and impressive-looking in a black suit, white shirt and maroon tie, Golantz stood, introduced himself and got down to it.

'Ladies and gentlemen, we are here today because of unchecked greed and anger. Plain and simple. The defendant, Walter Elliot, is a man of great power, money and standing. But that was not enough for him. He did not want to divide his money and power. He did not want to turn the cheek on betrayal. Instead, he lashed out in the most extreme way possible. He did not take one life, but two. In a moment of high anger and humiliation he raised a gun and killed both his wife, Mitzi Elliot, and Johan Rilz. He believed his money and power would save him from punishment for these heinous crimes. But the state will prove to you beyond any reasonable doubt that Walter Elliot pulled the trigger and is responsible for the deaths of two innocent human beings.'

I was turned in my seat, half to obscure the jury's view of my client and half to keep a view of Golantz and the gallery rows behind him. Before his first paragraph was completed the tears were flowing from Mitzi Elliot's mother. The theatrics were prejudicial and I would need to ask the judge to move her to a seat that was less of a focal point for the jury.

I saw hard grimaces on the faces of the men from Germany. I was very interested in them and how they would appear to the jury. I wanted to see how they handled emotion. The grimmer and more menacing they looked, the better the defence strategy would work when I focused on Johan Rilz. Looking at them now, I knew I was off to a good start. They looked angry and mean.

Golantz laid his case out to the jurors, telling them what he'd be present-ing in testimony and evidence and what he believed it meant. There were no surprises. At one point I received a one-line text message from Julie

Favreau: They are eating this up. You better be good. Right, I thought. Tell me something I don't know.

There was always an unfair advantage to the prosecution built into every trial. The state has the power and the might on its side. It comes with an assumption of honesty and integrity and fairness. And anybody who has ever stepped foot into a courtroom knows that presumed innocence is just one of the idealistic notions they teach in law school. There was no doubt in my mind that I started this trial with a defendant who was presumed guilty.

Golantz lasted his entire allotted hour, leaving no secrets about his case hidden. It was typical prosecutorial arrogance; put it all out and dare the defence to try to contradict it.

The judge had told us in the pre-trial session that we would be required, while addressing witnesses, to remain at our tables or to use the lectern placed between them, but during opening statements and closing arguments we were free to use the space directly in front of the jury box—a spot called the proving grounds. Golantz finally moved to the proving grounds when it was time for his big finish and held his hands wide like a preacher in front of his flock.

'In closing,' he said, 'I urge you to take great care as you listen to the evidence and the testimony. Common sense will lead you. Remember, two people had their lives stolen from them. That is why we are here today. For them. Thank you very much.'

It was a solid beginning, if too long. I was going to get in and get out, make a few points, raise a few questions. I was going to make them like me. If they liked me they would like my case.

Once the judge gave me the nod I immediately moved to the proving grounds. I wanted nothing between me and the jury.

'Ladies and gentlemen, I know the judge already introduced me but I would like to introduce myself and my client. I am Michael Haller, the attorney representing Walter Elliot, who you see here sitting at the table by himself.'

I pointed to Elliot and by prior design he nodded sombrely.

'Now, I am not going to take a lot of time because I want to get to the testimony and the evidence. Mr Golantz wove a big and complicated picture but I am here to tell you this is not complicated. What the prosecution's case amounts to is a labyrinth of smoke and mirrors. And when we blow away the smoke and get through the labyrinth you will find that there is no fire—that there is no case against Walter Elliot. That there is more than reasonable doubt here. And that there is outrage that this case was ever brought against Walter Elliot in the first place.'

Again I turned and pointed to my client. He sat with his eyes cast downwards, writing notes. Again, prior design, depicting my client as busy, actively involved in his own defence.

I turned back to the jury. 'I counted six times that Mr Golantz mentioned the word gun in his speech. Six times he said Walter took a gun and blew away the woman he loved and an innocent bystander. Six times. But what he didn't tell you is that there is no gun. He has no gun. The sheriff's department has no gun. Mr Golantz told you that he will introduce indisputable evidence that Walter fired a gun, but let me tell you to hold on to your hats. Let's see whether that so-called evidence is indisputable.'

As I spoke my eyes washed back and forth across the jurors like the spotlights sweeping the Hollywood sky at night. I felt a certain rhythm in my thoughts, and I instinctively knew I was holding the jury.

'In our society we want our law-enforcement officers to be professional and thorough. We see crime on the news and in the streets and we know that these men and women are the thin line between order and disorder. We want our cops to step in and save the day. But that's not what happened here. The state's own evidence and testimony will show that from the start the investigators focused on Walter Elliot. All other avenues of investigation were halted or never pursued. They had a suspect and they never looked back.'

I stepped forward in front of juror number one. I slowly walked along the front of the box, hand sliding along the railing.

'Ladies and gentlemen, this case is about tunnel vision. The focus on one suspect and the complete lack of focus on anything else. And I promise you, that when you come out of the prosecution's tunnel you're going to be looking at each other and squinting your eyes against the bright light, wondering where the hell their case is. Thank you very much.'

ONCE MORE MY CLIENT eschewed lunch with me so he could get back to the studio and make his business-as-usual appearance. I was beginning to think that he viewed the trial as an annoying inconvenience in his schedule. He was either more confident than I was, in the defence's case, or the trial simply wasn't a priority. That left me with my entourage from the first row. We went over to Traxx in Union Station, far enough away from the courthouse to avoid our ending up in the same place as the jurors. I had Patrick valet the Lincoln and join us so that he would feel like part of the team.

They gave us a table next to a window that looked out on the train station's huge and wonderful waiting room. Lorna made the seating arrangements and I ended up next to Julie Favreau. Ever since Lorna had hooked up with Cisco she had endeavoured to be something of a matchmaker. But my addiction had left me with an emotional distance from people and things that I was only now beginning to close. As such, I had made it my priority to reconnect with my daughter. After that I would worry about finding a woman to spend time with.

Romance aside, Julie Favreau was wonderful to work with. 'So,' I said as I spread a napkin on my lap. 'How is my jury doing?'

'I think it's a good jury,' she said. 'Overall, I see them willing to listen to your case. We all know that they are predisposed to believe the prosecution, but they haven't shut the door on anything. I like eleven and twelve. Retirees sitting next to each other. I have a feeling they're going to bond when it gets to deliberations. You win one over and you win them both.'

'What about juror seven?' I asked. 'During selection he was all eyes. Now he won't look at me.'

Julie nodded. 'Eye contact has dropped off the chart. Like something changed since Friday. I would have to say at this point he's in the prosecution's camp.'

'So much for listening to my client,' I said under my breath.

We ordered lunch. While we waited I checked with Cisco on our witnesses and he said we were good to go. I was halfway through my grilled chicken salad when I glanced through the window into the waiting room. A grand mixture of architectural designs with an Art Deco vibe, it had rows of big leather chairs and huge chandeliers. I saw people sitting with their suitcases gathered around them.

And then I saw Bosch. He was sitting alone in the third row. He had his earphones in. Our eyes held for a moment and then he looked away. I put my fork down, put five twenties on the table and told the others to finish eating while I stepped out to make a call.

I left the restaurant and called Bosch's cell. He pulled his plugs and answered it as I was approaching the seats.

'What?' he said by way of a greeting.

'Frank Morgan again?'

'Actually, Ron Carter. Why are you calling me?'

'What did you think of the story?'

I sat in the empty seat across from him, gave him a glance, but acted like I was talking to someone far away from me.

'This is kind of stupid,' Bosch said.

'Well, I didn't know whether you wanted to stay undercover—'

'Just hang up.'

We closed our phones and looked at each other.

'Well?' I asked. 'Are we in play?'

'I think the story did what we wanted it to do. Now we wait. We won't know we're in play until we're in play.'

I nodded. 'Is it just you here? Watching me by yourself?'

'Don't worry. You have people around you that you'll never see. I've got people on your office whether you are there or not.'

And cameras. They had been installed ten days earlier, when we had thought that the *Times* story was imminent.

'Yeah, good, but we won't be there for long.'

'I noticed. Where are you moving to?'

'Nowhere. I work out of my car.'

'Sounds like fun.'

I studied him a moment. He had been sarcastic in his tone as usual. He was an annoying guy but somehow he had got me to trust my safety to him. 'Well, I've got to get to court. Any particular way you want me to act or anything I should be doing?'

'Just do what you always do. But there is one thing. Keeping an eye on you in motion takes a lot of people. So at the end of the day, when you are home for the night, call me and tell me so I can release some people.'

'OK. But you'll still have somebody watching, right?'

'Don't worry. You'll be covered twenty-four-seven. Oh, and one other thing. Don't ever approach me again like this.'

'Got it.' I stood up without looking at him. 'See ya, Detective.'

AFTER LUNCH Golantz began to present his case. He started at the very beginning, proceeding in linear fashion. The first witness was an emergency operator used to introduce the tape recordings of Walter Elliot's calls for help.

I had sought in a pre-trial motion to thwart the playing of the two tapes, arguing that printed transcripts would be clearer, but the judge had ruled in the prosecution's favour. The tapes were prejudicial to my client. When in the first call Elliot had calmly reported that his wife and another person had been murdered, there was room for an interpretation of calculated coldness that I didn't want the jury to make. The second tape was worse. Elliot sounded annoyed and also indicated that he knew and disliked the man who'd been killed with his wife.

> Dispatcher: 911, what is your emergency?
> Walter Elliot: Yeah, I called before. Where is everybody?
> Dispatcher: You called 911?
> Walter Elliot: Yeah, my wife's been shot. So's the German. Where is everybody?
> Dispatcher: Is this the call on Crescent Cove Road?
> Walter Elliot: Yeah, that's me. I called at least fifteen minutes ago and nobody's here.

Elliot said the word German with almost a sneer in his voice. I passed on questioning the dispatcher because I knew there was nothing to be gained for the defence.

Next up was Sheriff's Deputy Brendan Murray, who was driving the alpha car which responded to the 911 call. Golantz led the deputy through the discovery of the bodies in minute detail. According to Murray, the defendant showed no emotions when leading them to the bedroom. He calmly stepped over the legs of the dead man, pointed to the naked body on the bed and said, 'That's my wife. I'm pretty sure she's dead.' Murray also testified that Elliot said at least three times he had not killed them.

'Was that unusual?' Golantz asked.

'Well, we're not supposed to get involved in murder investigations,' Murray said. 'So I never asked Mr Elliot if he did it.'

I had no questions for Murray either. I waited for the next witness, Christopher Harber, Murray's rookie partner. I thought that if either of the deputies were to make a mistake it would be him. Harber's short testimony was used primarily to confirm his partner's testimony. 'Just a few questions, Your Honour,' I said.

While Golantz had conducted his direct examination from the lectern I remained at the defence table. I wanted the prosecutor to think I was just going through the motions. The truth was I was about to plant a key point in the defence's case.

'Now, Deputy Harber, when you and your partner arrived at the Elliot house you said you saw my client out front, correct?'

'That is correct.'

'OK, what was he doing?'

'Just standing there.'

'OK, now what did you know about the situation when the alpha car pulled in there?'

'Dispatch told us a man named Walter Elliot called from the house and said two people had been shot dead inside.'

'Had you ever had a call like that before?'

'No.'

'Were you scared, nervous, what?'

'The adrenaline was flowing, but we were pretty calm.'

'Did you draw your weapon when you got out of your car?'

'Yes I did. I carried it at my side.'

'Did your partner draw his weapon?'

'I believe so.'

'Did he point it at Mr Elliot?'

He hesitated. 'I don't recall. I was looking at the defendant.'

I nodded. 'To be safe, correct? You didn't know this guy.'

'That's right.'

'Is it correct to say you approached Mr Elliot cautiously?'

'That's right.'

'When did you put your weapon away?'

'After we had searched and secured the premises.'

'OK. When you were doing this, was Mr Elliot with you?'

'Yes, we needed him to show us where the bodies were.'

'Now was he under arrest?'

'No, he was not. He volunteered to show us.'

'But you handcuffed him, didn't you?'

Harber's second hesitation followed. 'He had voluntarily agreed to be handcuffed. We explained that we were not arresting him but that it would be best for his safety and ours until we secured the premises.'

'Were his hands cuffed behind his back or in the front?'

'In the back, according to procedure.'

'I know you are new on the job but how often have you handcuffed someone who was not under arrest?'

'It happens on occasion. I don't recall the number of times.'

'Now, your partner testified and you have testified that Mr Elliot on three occasions told you both that he was not responsible for the killings in that house. Right?'

'Right.'

'Was that when you were outside or inside or where?'

'That was inside when we were up in the bedroom.'

'So that means that he made these supposedly uninvited protestations of his innocence while he was handcuffed with his arms behind his back and you and your partner had your weapons drawn and ready, is that correct?'

The third hesitation. 'Yes, I believe that would be so.'

'OK, so what happened after you and your partner determined that there was no one else in the house?'

'We took Mr Elliot back outside, we sealed the house and we called detective services for a homicide call-out.'

'Good. Now, Deputy Harber, did you take the handcuffs off Mr Elliot then since he was not under arrest?'

'No, sir. It is against procedure to place a subject in the back of a sheriff's car without handcuffs.'

'OK, how long was he in the back seat of that car?'

'Approximately one half-hour while we waited for homicide.'

'And what happened when the homicide team arrived?'

'They looked in the house first. Then they came out and took custody of Mr Elliot. I mean, took him out of the car.'

'He was in custody at that time?'

'No, I made a mistake there. He voluntarily agreed to wait.'

'You are saying he voluntarily agreed to be handcuffed in the back of a patrol car?'

'Yes.'

'When did the handcuffs finally come off Mr Elliot?'

'When the detectives removed him from the car.'

'OK.' I nodded like I was finished and flipped a few pages on my pad. 'Oh, one last thing. The first call to 911 went out at one-oh-five according to the dispatch log. Mr Elliot had to call again nineteen minutes later and then you and your partner finally arrived four minutes after that.' I looked up. 'Deputy, why did it take so long to respond to what must've been a priority call?'

'The Malibu district is our largest. We had to come all the way over the mountain from another call.'

'Wasn't there another patrol car that was closer?'

'My partner and I were in the alpha car. We handle the priority calls and we accepted this one when it came in.'

'OK, Deputy, I have nothing further.'

The judge adjourned for the afternoon break. As soon as the jury had cleared the courtroom I heard a whispered voice call my name. I turned round and saw Lorna, who pointed towards the back of the courtroom. There was my daughter and her mother squeezed into the back row. My daughter waved to me and I smiled back.

Twelve

I met them in the hallway outside the courtroom. Hayley hugged me and I was overwhelmed that she had come. I saw an empty wooden bench and we sat down.

'How long were you guys there?' I asked. 'I didn't see you.'

'Not that long,' Maggie said. 'Her last school period was PE so I decided to pull her out early. We saw most of your cross with the deputy.'

I looked from Maggie to our daughter, sitting between us. She had her mother's looks; dark hair and eyes, skin that held a tan long into the winter. 'What did you think, Hay?'

'Um, I thought it was really interesting. You asked him a lot of questions. He looked like he was getting mad.'

'Don't worry, he'll get over it.'

I looked over her head at my ex-wife and nodded my thanks. She had put aside any anger for me and put our daughter first.

'Do you go back in there?' Hayley asked.

'Yes, this is just a little break so people can get something to drink or use the bathroom. We have one more session.'

She nodded towards the courtroom door. People were starting to go back in. 'Um, Daddy? Did that man kill somebody?'

'Well, honey, we don't know. He is accused of that, yes, and a lot of people think he did. But nothing has been proven yet. Remember how I explained that?'

'I remember.'

'Mick, is this your family?'

I looked over my shoulder and froze. Walter Elliot was smiling warmly, expecting an introduction.

'Uh, hi, Walter. This is my daughter, Hayley, and this is her mom, Maggie McPherson.'

'Hi,' Hayley said.

Maggie nodded and looked uncomfortable. Walter made the mistake of thrusting his hand out to her. She shook it once quickly. When his hand moved towards Hayley, Maggie jumped up and pulled her from the bench. 'Hayley, let's go to the rest room before court starts again.'

She hustled Hayley off and Walter watched them go. I stood up. 'Sorry, Walter, my ex-wife's a prosecutor. She works for the DA.'

His eyebrows climbed his forehead. 'Then I guess I understand why she's an ex-wife.'

I told him to go on back into the courtroom and walked to the rest rooms. Maggie and Hayley were coming out.

'We're going to head home,' Maggie said. 'She's got a lot of homework and I think she's seen enough for today.'

I could've argued but I let it go. 'OK. Hayley, thanks for coming. It means a lot to me.'

'OK.'

I bent down and kissed her on the top of the head, then pulled her in close for a hug. I looked up at Maggie. 'Thanks for bringing her.'

Maggie nodded. 'For what it's worth, you're doing good in there.'

'It's worth a lot. Thank you.'

She shrugged and let a small smile slip out. That was nice.

I watched them walk to the elevators, knowing they weren't going home to my house and wondering how I had messed up my life so badly. 'Hayley!' I called after them.

My daughter looked back at me.

'See you Wednesday. Pancakes!'

She was smiling as an elevator opened. My former wife was smiling too. I pointed at her. 'You can come too.'

She nodded. 'We'll see,' she said.

IN ANY MURDER TRIAL the main witness for the prosecution is the lead investigator. Because there are no living victims to tell the jury what happened, it falls on the lead to speak for the dead. The lead investigator puts everything together, makes it clear and sympathetic. His job is to sell the case and like any transaction it is often as much about the salesman as it is about the goods being sold.

Golantz called the case's lead investigator to the stand after the afternoon break. It was a stroke of genius and master planning. John Kinder would hold centre stage until the jurors went home with his words to consider over dinner and into the night.

Kinder was a large, affable black man who spoke with a fatherly baritone. He slipped reading glasses on the end of his nose when referring to the binder he carried. Between questions he would look over the rims at Golantz or the jury. His eyes seemed kind and wise.

With Golantz's precise questioning and a series of blowups of crime scene photos, Kinder led the jury on a tour of the murder scene. It was purely clinical and methodical but with his authoritative voice, he came off as something akin to a professor teaching Homicide 101.

I objected here and there when I could in an effort to break the Golantz/Kinder rhythm. My client, it appeared, was barely paying attention. He was writing notes on a legal pad but I saw the heading *Foreign Distribution*. I whispered, 'This guy's killing us up there.'

Elliot whispered back, 'I think we're doing fine. You've had a good day.'

I shook my head. He was well aware that I had the magic bullet in my gun, but nothing is a sure thing when you go to trial. And a murder trial is the biggest gamble of them all.

After the crime scene investigation was covered, Golantz moved to Elliot, basically confirming Murray's testimony. Finally he asked, 'Where did Elliot lead you in the house, Detective Kinder?'

'He walked us straight upstairs to the bedroom. I asked if he'd been anywhere else in the house and he said no.'

'Did that seem unusual or inconsistent to you?'

'Well, I thought it was odd that he'd gone directly up to the bedroom without looking around the ground floor. It also didn't jibe with what he told us when we got back outside. He pointed at his wife's car, which was parked out front, and said that was how he knew she had somebody with her in the house. I asked him what he meant and he said that she parked out front so that Johan Rilz, the other victim, could use the garage. They had stored a bunch of furniture in the garage and that left only one space. He said the German had hidden his Porsche in there.'

'And what was the significance of that to you?'

'It showed deception. He'd told us he hadn't been anywhere but the bedroom but it was pretty clear to me that he'd looked in the garage.'

Golantz nodded emphatically, driving home the point. The prosecutor continued to lead Kinder through the investigation up until he cleared the crime scene and interviewed Elliot at the Malibu station. This set up the introduction of a videotape I knew was unremarkable in terms of content. What was important to the prosecution about the tape was Elliot's demeanour. He appeared as calm as a summer sunset and that made him look like an ice-cold killer.

A video screen was set up in front of the jury box and Golantz played the ten-minute tape. There were no hard questions and the interview ended with Kinder presenting the search warrant that granted the sheriff's department access to test Elliot's hands, arms and clothing for gunshot residue.

Elliot smiled slightly as he replied. 'Have at it, gentlemen. Do what you have to do.'

Golantz used a remote to freeze the image of Elliot's catch-me-if-you-can smile on the screen. That was the image he wanted the jurors to take with them. 'Your Honour,' he said. 'I think now would be a good time to break for the day. I will be moving with Deputy Kinder in a new direction after this.'

The judge agreed, adjourning court after once more admonishing the jurors to avoid all media reports on the trial.

I stood at the defence table and watched the jurors file out. 'Walter, what do you have going tonight?' I asked.

'A small dinner party, then the first cut of a film my studio is producing with Johnny Depp playing a detective.'

'Well, call and cancel it all. You're having dinner with me.'

'I don't understand.'

'Yes, you do. You've been ducking me and that was OK because I didn't want to know what I didn't need to know. Now we're in trial and I need to know everything, Walter. We're going to talk tonight, or you're going to hire another lawyer.'

I saw his face grow tight with anger. In that moment I knew he could be a killer, or at least someone who could order it done.

'You wouldn't dare,' he said.

'Make your calls,' I said. 'We'll take my car.'

WITH A THIRTY-SECOND PHONE CALL Elliot got us a private booth at the Water Grill over by the Biltmore and had a martini waiting on the table for him when we got there. As we sat down I asked for a bottle of flat water and some sliced lemon.

I sat across from Elliot and watched him study the menu.

'You called it a dinner meeting,' he said. 'Aren't you going to look?'

'I'm having what you're having, Walter.'

He put the menu to the side. 'Fillet of sole.'

He signalled a waiter and ordered for us both, adding a bottle of Chardonnay to come with the fish. He then clasped his hands on the table and looked expectantly at me.

'This better be good,' he said.

'Walter, this *is* going to be good. This is going to be where you stop hiding from me. If I know what you know I'm not going to get sandbagged. I'm going to know what moves Golantz is going to make before he makes them.'

Elliot nodded as though he agreed. 'I did not kill my wife or her Nazi friend,' he said. 'I have told you that from day one.'

'That's not good enough. I said I want to know what really happened, Walter, or I'm going to be moving on.'

'Don't be ridiculous. No judge is going to let you walk away in the middle of a trial.'

'You want to bet your freedom on that, Walter? If I want off this case I will find a way off it.'

He hesitated. 'You should be careful of what you ask for. Guilty knowledge could be a dangerous thing.'

I leaned across the table to him. 'Walter, I'm your lawyer. You can tell me what you've done and it stays with me.'

The waiter brought a bottle of water and a side plate of sliced lemon. Elliot waited until he had filled my glass and moved away.

'What is going on is that you have done an excellent job preparing my defence and all in two weeks. Astonishing!'

'Drop the bull!' I said it too loud.

Elliot looked outside the booth and stared down a woman at a nearby table who had heard me. 'You'll have to keep your voice down,' he said. 'The bond of attorney–client confidentiality ends at this table.'

I looked at him. I knew he was reminding me of what I had already assured him of, that what was said here stayed here. Was it a signal that he was willing to finally talk? I played the only ace I had. 'Tell me about the bribe Jerry Vincent paid.'

I detected shock in his eyes, then a knowing look as the wheels turned inside. Then I saw a flash of regret. I wished Julie Favreau had been sitting next to me. She could have read him better.

'That is a very dangerous piece of information to be in possession of,' he said. 'How did you get it?'

I obviously couldn't tell him I got it from a detective. 'You could say it came with the case. I have all Vincent's records. It wasn't hard to figure out that he funnelled a hundred thousand of your advance to an unknown party. Is the bribe what got him killed?'

Elliot raised his martini glass with two fingers clenching the delicate stem and drank what was left in it. 'I think it is safe to say a confluence of events led to Jerry Vincent's death.'

'Walter, I need to defend you. And to protect myself.'

He nodded. 'I think you may have found the reason for his death. It was in the file. You even mentioned it to me.'

'I don't understand. What did I mention?'

'He planned to delay the trial. You found the motion. He was killed before he could file it.'

I tried to put it together. 'That got him killed? Why?'

Elliot leaned towards me. He spoke in a tone just above a whisper. 'OK, you asked for it and I'll tell you. Yes, there was a bribe. He paid it and everything was fine. The trial was scheduled and all we had to do was be ready to go. But then he changed his mind and wanted to delay.'

'Why?'

'I think he actually thought he could win without the fix.'

It appeared that Elliot didn't know about the FBI's phone calls and apparent interest in Vincent. If he had, now would have been the time to mention it. The FBI's focus on Vincent would have been as good a reason as any to pull out of the jury scheme.

'So delaying the trial got him killed?'

'That's my guess, yes.'

'Did you kill him, Walter?'

'I don't kill people.'

'You had him killed.'

Elliot shook his head. 'I don't *have* people killed, either.'

A waiter moved up to the booth with a tray and a stand. He deboned our fish, plated them and put them on the table along with a fresh martini. He uncorked the wine and asked if Elliot wanted to taste it. Elliot shook his head.

'OK,' I said when we were left alone. 'Who was bribed?'

Elliot downed half his new martini in one gulp. 'That should be obvious, when you think about it. A trial that cannot be delayed. Why?'

My eyes stayed on him but I was no longer looking at him. I went inside to work the riddle. Ticking off the possibilities—judge, prosecutor, cops, witnesses, jury—I realised that there was only one place where a bribe and an unmovable trial intersected. 'There's a sleeper on the jury,' I said. 'You got to somebody.'

Elliot let me run with it and my mind swept along the faces in the jury box. 'Number seven. You wanted him. Who is he?'

Elliot gave me a half-smile and took his first bite of fish before answering. 'I have no idea and don't really care to know. But he's ours. And he's no sleeper. He's a persuader. When it gets to deliberations he will go in there and turn the tide. With the case Vincent built and you're delivering, it probably won't take more than a little push. They will never convict me, Mickey. Never.'

I pushed my plate aside. I couldn't eat. 'Walter, no more riddles. Tell me how this went down.'

Elliot poured himself a glass of wine. 'This is a long story, Mickey. Would you like wine to go with it?' He held up the bottle.

I shook my head. 'No, Walter, I don't drink.'

'I'm not sure I can trust someone who doesn't take a drink from time to time.' Chuckling, he drank heavily and began his story.

'When you come to Hollywood it doesn't matter who you are as long as you've got money. I came twenty-five years ago but it wasn't my money.'

'I thought the story was that you came from a family that owned a phosphate shipping operation in Florida.'

He nodded. 'All true, but it depends on your definition of family.'

It slowly came to me. 'Are you talking about the mob?'

'I'm talking about an organisation with a tremendous cash flow that needed legitimate businesses to move it through and legitimate front men to operate those businesses. I was an accountant. I was one of those men.'

It was easy to put together. Florida twenty-five years ago. The heyday of the uninhibited flow of cocaine and money.

'I was sent west,' Elliot said. 'I had a story and I had suitcases full of money. And I loved movies. I knew how to pick 'em and put 'em together. I took Archway and turned it into a billion-dollar enterprise. And then my wife . . .'

A look of sad regret crossed his face.

'What, Walter?'

'The day after our twelfth anniversary—after our prenuptial agreement was vested—she told me she was getting a divorce.'

I nodded. With the prenup vested Mitzi Elliot would be entitled to half of Elliot's holdings, only his holdings actually belonged to the organisation. And it wasn't the type of organisation that would allow half its investment to walk out of the door in a skirt.

'I tried to change her mind,' Elliot said. 'She was in love with that Nazi bastard and thought he could protect her.'

'The organisation had her killed.'

'I wasn't supposed to be there that day,' Elliot said. 'I was told to stay away, to make sure I had a rock-solid alibi.'

'Why'd you go then?'

His eyes held on mine. 'I still loved her in some way. I went out there to try to stop it, maybe be the hero, win her back. I don't know. But I was too late. They were both dead when I got there.'

'Then came Jerry Vincent,' I said. 'Tell me about the bribe.'

'I don't have a lot to tell. My corporate attorney hooked me up with Jerry and he was fine. We worked out the fee arrangement and then he came to me—this was early on—and said he had been approached by someone who could salt the jury. You know, put someone on the jury who would be for us. He would be a skilled persuader—a con man. The catch was that the trial would have to stay on schedule so that this person would end up on my jury.'

'And you and Jerry took the offer.'

'We took it. This was five months ago. At the time I didn't have much of a defence. I didn't kill my wife but it seemed the odds were stacked against me. We had no magic bullet . . . and I was scared. So we took the offer.'

'How much?'

'A hundred thousand up front. Jerry inflated his fee and I paid him and then he paid for the juror. Then it was going to be another hundred for a hung jury and two-fifty for an acquittal. These people had done it before.'

I thought of the FBI. 'Were Jerry's trials fixed before?'

'He didn't say and I didn't ask. But then the Monday before he was killed he told me he was going to delay the trial. He said he had the magic bullet and was going to win without the sleeper.'

'And that got him killed.'

'It had to be. I don't think these kind of people just let you change your mind and pull out of something like this.'

'Did you tell anyone Jerry was going to delay the case?'

'No.'

'Then who did Jerry tell?'

'I don't know. He wouldn't say who he made the deal with.'

I had to end this and get away by myself to think. I glanced at my untouched fish and wondered if I should take it to go for Patrick.

'You know,' Elliot said, 'not to put any more pressure on you, but if I get convicted I'm dead.'

I looked at him. 'The organisation?'

He nodded. 'A guy gets busted and normally they wipe him out before he even gets to court. But they wipe me out and they lose Archway, the real estate, everything, so they're hanging back and watching.' He drained his glass. 'Mick, the things I've told you could get you killed in a heartbeat. Just like Jerry. Remember that.'

He waved down a waiter and asked for the check.

I WAS THANKFUL my client liked his martinis before dinner and his Chardonnay during and after. I wasn't sure I'd have got what I got from Elliot without the alcohol loosening his tongue. But afterwards I didn't want him pulled over on a DUI in the middle of a murder trial. I drove him home while Patrick followed.

'Walter,' I said to him, 'despite everything you told me tonight, I'm going to do my best for you.'

'Then you believe I'm innocent.'

I hesitated. 'I believe you didn't shoot your wife and Rilz. I'm not sure that makes you innocent, but that's all I need.'

Elliot lived in Beverly Hills in a gated estate in the flats south of Sunset. He pushed a button on his car's ceiling and we slipped through the steel entry gate, Patrick coming in right behind in the Lincoln. We got out and I gave Elliot his keys and said good night.

The internal gears were working all the way to my house. I sat gazing out of the back window. It wasn't hard to figure out how Jerry Vincent's deal was done. The question was who did it.

Elliot had admitted several crimes over dinner. But I was his lawyer and these admissions would remain confidential under the bonds of the attorney–client relationship. The exception to this rule was if I was endangered by my knowledge or had knowledge of a crime that had not yet occurred. The bribe had already occurred, but the crime of jury tampering had not yet occurred. That wouldn't take place until deliberations, so I was duty-bound to report it, even though Elliot apparently was convinced that the threat of my meeting the same end as Jerry would keep me in check.

I thought about all this, then realised I wouldn't have to report the intended crime if I were to stop it from happening.

I looked around. We were on Sunset coming into West Hollywood and I saw a familiar sign. 'Patrick, pull over in front of Book Soup. I want to run in for a minute.'

Patrick pulled the Lincoln to the kerb in front of the bookstore and I jumped out. I went in the door and back into the stacks, found an empty alcove and called my investigator.

'Cisco, it's me. Where are you?'

'At home. What's up?'

'Lorna there?'

'No, she went to a chick flick with her sister.'

'I want you to do something you may not want to do. If you don't, I understand. Either way I don't want you to talk about it with anybody. Including Lorna.'

There was a hesitation before he answered. 'Who do I kill?'

We both laughed and it relieved some of the night's tension. 'We can talk about that later but this might be just as dicey. I want you to shadow juror number seven.'

BY THE TIME Patrick pulled the car into the garage below my house, it was almost ten o'clock. We walked up the stairs to the front deck. I was beat after a fourteen-hour day, but my adrenaline kicked in when I saw a man in one of the deck chairs. I put my arm out to stop Patrick from advancing, the way a parent would stop a child from stepping into the street.

'Hello, Counsellor.'

Bosch. I relaxed. We stepped up onto the porch and I unlocked the door to let Patrick in, then closed the door and turned to Bosch.

'Nice view,' he said. 'Defending scumbags got you this place?'

I was too tired to do the dance with him. 'What are you doing here, Detective?'

'I figured you might be heading home after the bookstore.'

'Well, I'm done for the night. You can give your team the word, if there really is a team.'

'After court you had dinner with your client at Water Grill. You both had the fillet of sole and your client drank liberally, which resulted in you driving him home in his car. On your way back you stopped by Book Soup and made a phone call you obviously didn't want your driver to hear.'

I was impressed. 'OK, then never mind that. I get it. They're out there. What do you want, Bosch? What's going on?'

Bosch stood up and approached me.

'I was going to ask you the same thing,' he said. 'What was Walter Elliot so hot and bothered about tonight at dinner? And who'd you call in the back of the bookstore?'

Thirteen

My turn at Detective Kinder did not come until late on Tuesday, after the prosecutor had spent several hours delving into the defendant's marriage, the discovery of the recently vested prenuptial agreement, and Elliot's efforts before the murders to determine how much money and control of Archway Pictures he would lose in a divorce. Kinder had also established that Elliot had no credible alibi for the estimated time of the murders. And he described the many unfounded leads that were called in and dutifully checked out.

These details worked in my favour. I thought the jury—and Julie Favreau confirmed this by text message—was bored by the minutiae. But all in all, Golantz and Kinder appeared to have done a thorough job of nailing my client to the murders and by midafternoon the young prosecutor was satisfied enough to say, 'No more questions, Your Honour.'

It was now finally my turn and I moved to the lectern.

'Detective Kinder, I know we'll hear from the medical examiner later but you testified that you were informed after the autopsy that the time of death of Mrs Elliot and Mr Rilz was estimated to be between eleven a.m. and noon.'

'That is correct.'

'Was it closer to eleven or closer to noon?'

'It's impossible to tell. That's just the time frame.'

'Once you had that frame, you proceeded to make sure the man you had already arrested had no alibi, correct?'

'I wouldn't put it that way, no. I would say that it was my obligation to continue to investigate the case. In carrying out that obligation I determined according to multiple interviews as well as gate records that Mr Elliot left Archway Studios, driving by himself, at ten forty that morning. This gave him plenty of time to—'

'Thank you, Detective. You've answered the question.'

'I haven't finished my answer.'

Golantz asked if the witness could finish his answer and Stanton allowed it. Kinder continued in his Homicide 101 tone. 'This gave Mr Elliot plenty of time to get to the house within the estimated time of death.'

'Did you say plenty of time to get there?'

'Enough time.'

'Earlier you described making the drive yourself several times. When was that?'

'The first time was one week after the murders. I left Archway at ten forty and arrived at the Malibu house at eleven forty-two.'

'Did you know you were taking the same route as Mr Elliot?'

'I didn't. I just took what I considered the most obvious and quickest route that somebody would take.'

'Los Angeles traffic can be very unpredictable, can it not?'

'Yes.'

'Is that why you drove the route several times?'

'One reason, yes.'

'Detective, you testified that you drove the route five times and got to the Malibu house each time before noon, right?'

'Correct.'

'Now, tell the jury how many times you began the route but broke off when you knew you weren't going to make it.'

'That never happened.'

There had been a slight hesitation. I was sure the jury picked up on it. 'Detective, if I were to produce records that showed you started at the Archway gate at ten forty in the morning seven times and not five would those records be false?'

'No.'

'Thank you. Detective, tell us how many of these test drives you broke off before reaching the house in Malibu.'

'There were two.'

'Which ones?'

'The second time and the last time—the seventh.'

'You stopped these because you knew you'd never make it to the house within the murder window, correct?'

'No, one time I was called back to the office to conduct an interview and the other time I heard a radio call and diverted to back up a deputy.'

'Why didn't you document these in your driving time report?'

'I didn't think they were germane because they were incomplete tests.'

'So we only have your word about what caused you to stop them before reaching the Elliot house, correct?'

'That would be correct.'

I had flogged him enough on this front. But I hoped I had raised at least a question of trust. I decided to hit Kinder with a punch he wouldn't see coming.

I asked the judge for a moment and went to the defence table. I bent down to my client's ear. 'Just nod like I am telling you something really important,' I whispered.

Elliot did as instructed and then I picked up a file, went to the lectern and opened it. 'Detective, at what point did you determine that Johan Rilz was the primary target of this double murder?'

Kinder opened his mouth to respond, then sat back and thought for a moment. 'At no point did I ever determine that.'

'He was at no point front and centre in your investigation?'

'Well, he was the victim of a homicide. That made him front and centre in my book.'

'Then him being front and centre explains why you went to Germany to investigate his background, correct?'

'I did not go to Germany.'

'What about France? His passport indicated he lived there before coming to the United States.'

'We didn't believe it was necessary. We'd asked Interpol for a background check and it came back clean.'

'What is Interpol?'

'It stands for International Criminal Police Organisation. It links the police in more than a hundred countries.'

'Did you directly check with the police in Paris, where Rilz lived five years ago?'

'No, we relied on our Interpol contacts for background.'

'The Interpol check was for a criminal arrest record, correct?'

'That was included, yes. I'm not sure what else.'

'If Mr Rilz had worked for the Paris police as an informant on a drug case, would Interpol have given you this information?'

Kinder's eyes widened for a split second. 'I don't know.'

'Law-enforcement agencies usually don't give out the names of their confidential informants willy-nilly, do they?'

'No, they don't. It might put the informants in danger.'

'So being an informant in a criminal case can be dangerous?'

'On occasion, yes.'

'Detective Kinder, have you ever investigated the murder of a confidential informant?'

Golantz stood up and asked for a sidebar conference. The judge signalled us up and we huddled.

'Mr Golantz?' the judge prompted.

'Judge, nothing in any of the defence's discovery even hints at what Mr Haller is asking the witness about.'

The judge swivelled in his chair. 'Mr Haller?'

'Judge, this was a sloppy investigation that—'

'Save it for the jury. Whaddaya got?'

I put a computer print-out from the file in front of the judge, positioning it so it was upside down to Golantz.

'A story in *Le Parisien* four and half years ago. It names Johan Rilz as a witness for the prosecution in a major drug case. He was used by the Direction de la Police Judiciaire to make buys and get inside knowledge of the drug ring. And these guys over here never even—'

'Mr Haller, this is in French. Do you have the translation?'

'Sorry, Your Honour.' I put a second sheet down.

Golantz twisted his head as he tried to read it. 'How do we know this is the same Johan Rilz? This isn't an official document.'

I put a last sheet down. 'This is a photocopy of a page from Rilz's passport from the state's own discovery. It shows Rilz left France for the United States one month after this story. Plus the article has his age right and says he was making drug buys for the cops out of his business as an interior decorator. It obviously is him, Your Honour. He put a lot of people over there in jail.'

Golantz shook his head in a desperate way. 'This is a violation of the rules of discovery and is inadmissible. You can't sit on this, then sucker-punch the state with it.'

The judge swivelled his view and gave me the squint.

'Your Honour, if anybody sat on anything it was the state. I think the witness did know about this and *he* sat on it.'

'That is a serious accusation, Mr Haller,' the judge intoned. 'Do you have evidence of that?'

'Judge, the reason I know about this at all is by accident. On Sunday I noticed my investigator had run all the names associated with this case through the LexisNexis search engine using the computer I'd inherited with Vincent's law practice. The default setting was for English language search only. Having looked at the photocopy of Rilz's passport in the discovery file, I did the search including French and German and came up with this article in about two minutes. I find it hard to believe I found something the entire sheriff's department, the prosecution and Interpol didn't know about. Judge, the defence is certainly feeling like the damaged party here.'

I couldn't believe it. The judge swivelled to Golantz and gave him the squint. The first time ever. I shifted to my right so that a good part of the jury had an angle on it.

'What about that, Mr Golantz?' the judge asked.

'It's absurd. Anything we've found has gone into the discovery file. I'd like to ask why Mr Haller didn't alert us to this yesterday.'

I stared deadpan at Golantz. 'If I'd known you were fluent in French I'd have given it to you, Jeff. I was handed that translation ten minutes before I started my cross.'

'All right,' the judge said. 'What are you going to do about verifying this information, Mr Haller?'

'I'm going to put my investigator on it to do the job the sheriff's department should have done six months ago.'

'We're obviously going to verify it as well,' Golantz added.

The judge held up a hand. 'OK,' he said. 'Mr Haller, I'll allow you to lay the foundation for this during the presentation of the defence if you can verify the report and the identity. I think we are done here, gentlemen.'

The judge rolled back into position and the lawyers returned to theirs. I noticed the courtroom clock said ten minutes until five.

I stood at the lectern. 'Judge, I look forward to exploring Mr Rilz's activities in France during the defence phase of the trial. Until then I have no further questions for Detective Kinder.'

I sat down. The judge announced that court was recessed.

I watched the jury file out, then glanced to the gallery. All three Rilz men were staring at me with hardened, dead eyes.

CISCO CALLED ME at home at ten o'clock. He said he was nearby in Hollywood and that he could come right over. He said he already had some news about juror number seven.

After hanging up I told Patrick that I was going out on the deck to meet privately with Cisco. I put on a sweater, grabbed the file I'd used in court earlier and went out to wait for my investigator.

The Sunset Strip glowed like a blast furnace over the shoulder of the hills. I'd bought the house in a flush year because of the view the deck offered of the city. It never ceased to entrance me, day or night.

'Hey, Boss.'

I jumped and turned. Cisco had climbed the stairs and come up behind me without my even hearing him. He must've come up the hill on Fairfax, killed the engine and freewheeled down to my house.

I pointed him to the small table and chairs under the roof's eave. He sat down and looked through the window into the living room. The television was on and Patrick was in there watching the extreme sports channel on cable. People were doing flips on snowmobiles.

'Is that a sport?' Cisco asked.

'To Patrick, I guess.'

'How's it working out with him?'

'It's working. He's staying a couple weeks. Tell me about number seven?'

He pulled a small journal out of his back pocket. 'His name is David McSweeney and almost everything he put on his J-sheet is false.'

The J-sheet, filled out as part of the *voir dire* process, carried the prospective juror's name, profession and area of residence by zip code as well as a checklist of basic questions. In this trial the name would've been excised.

'Give me some examples.'

'Well, according to the zip he lives down in Palos Verde. Not true. I followed him directly to an apartment off Beverly over behind CBS.' Cisco pointed south in the direction of the CBS television studio. 'I had a friend run the plate on the pick-up he drove home from court—David McSweeney, same address—then run his driving licence and shoot me over the photo. McSweeney is our guy.'

'Cisco, your prints are going to be all over this.'

'Chill, man. My guy doesn't use his terminal or user ID when he does these jobs for me. He cadged an old lieutenant's password. So we're safe, OK?'

'All right,' I said. 'What else?'

'Well, he's got an arrest record and he checked the box that said he'd never been popped before. Assault with a deadly weapon in '97 and conspiracy to commit fraud in '99. No convictions is all I know right now.'

I wanted to know how arrests for fraud and ADW could result in no convictions, but if Cisco pulled records he'd have to show ID. 'Let it go for now. You got anything else?'

'Yeah, I'm telling you, I think it's all phoney. He says he's an engineer with Lockheed and they don't have a David McSweeney in the Lockheed phone directory.' He raised his hands palm up. 'So what's going on? Don't tell me that scumbag prosecutor put a sleeper on the jury.'

'It's better if I don't tell you. Did you see this guy with anybody?'

'Not so far. I've only been with him since five.'

'OK, Cisco, you did good. You can drop it and go back to this.' I slid the file across to him.

He smiled slyly. 'What did you tell the judge at the sidebar?'

I had forgotten he had been in the courtroom. 'I told him I redid the search to include French. I even printed the story out again on Sunday so I would have a fresh date on it. Where's the translator you used on the print-out?'

'Probably in her dorm over in Westwood. She's an exchange student I came up with on the Net.'

'Well, call her and pick her up because you're going to need her tonight to translate. They're what, nine hours ahead over there in Paris? At midnight start calling all the gendarmes who worked that drug case and get one of them on a plane over here. Spend whatever needs to be spent. Just get him here as soon as possible.'

'You want me to call you tonight when I have it set up?'

'No, I need my beauty rest. Just call me in the morning.'

Fourteen

On Monday morning I had my Corneliani suit on. I was sitting next to my client ready to begin to present his defence. Jeffrey Golantz sat at his table ready to thwart my efforts. And the gallery behind us was maxed out once again. But the bench in front of us was empty. The judge was sequestered in his chambers and running almost an hour behind. Something had come up, but we had not yet been informed. We had seen sheriff's deputies escort a man I didn't recognise into chambers and then out again.

'Jeff, what do you think?' I finally asked across the aisle.

Golantz looked over at me. He was wearing his nice black suit but he had been wearing it every other day and it wasn't as impressive any more. He shrugged. 'No idea.'

The prosecution's case had strung out through the entire previous week. I had helped with a couple of protracted cross-examinations but for the most part it had been Golantz engaging in overkill. He kept the medical examiner on the stand for nearly an entire day explaining in excruciating detail how and when the victims died. He kept Walter Elliot's accountant on the stand for half a day explaining how much Walter stood to lose in a divorce. And he kept the sheriff's forensic tech on for nearly as long explaining his finding of high levels of gunshot residue on the defendant's hands and clothes.

In between he conducted shorter examinations of lesser witnesses and then finished Friday afternoon with a tearjerker. Mitzi Elliot's lifelong best friend testified about Mitzi confiding her divorce plans, the fight that followed between husband and wife, and the bruises on Mitzi's arms the next day. She never stopped crying during her hour on the stand.

The trial would move to the defence phase the following Monday. I spent the weekend strategising and preparing my two anchor witnesses: my GSR expert and a jet-lagged French police captain. Now I was ready to go but there was no judge on the bench.

'What's going on?' Elliot whispered.

I shrugged. 'Your guess is as good as mine.'

A deep furrow had settled into Elliot's brow. He knew something was up. I looked back into the gallery and noticed that behind the prosecution table there was a gap in the spectators. No Germans. I was about to ask Golantz where Rilz's family members were when a uniformed sheriff's deputy walked up to the rail behind him and beckoned him with a document.

'Excuse me, are you the prosecutor?' the deputy said. 'Who do I talk to about this?'

Golantz got up and walked over to take a look at the document.

'It's a defence subpoena. Are you Deputy Stallworth?'

'That's right.'

'Then you're in the right spot.'

'No, I'm not. I didn't have anything to do with this case.'

'You weren't at the house? What about the perimeter or traffic control?' I could see the wheels begin turning but it was going to be too late when he figured things out.

'I was home asleep. I work midnight shift.'

'Hold it a second.' Golantz went back to his desk and checked my final witness list. 'What is this, Haller?'

'What's what? He's on there. He's been on there for two weeks.' I got up and went to the rail. 'Deputy Stallworth, I'm Michael Haller, the one who summoned you. If you wait out in the hall I'll try to get you in and out as soon as court starts.'

The deputy looked over at Golantz for help but the prosecutor was whispering into a cellphone. 'Look,' I said, 'just go out into the hall and I'll—'

The clerk was signalling us to the judge's chambers. Golantz ended his call and got up. I turned from Stallworth and followed him.

The judge sat behind his desk in his black robe. 'Gentlemen,' he said. 'Have a seat and I'll tell you what's going on.'

Golantz and I sat side by side. Stanton clasped his hands on top of a folded piece of paper in front of him. 'We have an unusual situation involving juror misconduct,' he said. 'My office received a letter Thursday addressed personally to me. Unfortunately, I didn't get a chance to open it until after court on Friday. The letter said—well, here is the letter. I've already handled it but don't either of you touch it.'

He unfolded the piece of paper and allowed us to read it.

Judge Stanton, you should know that juror number seven is not who he says he is. Check Lockheed and check his prints. He's got an arrest record.

The letter looked like it had come out of a laser printer. 'Did you keep the envelope it came in?' I asked.

'The postmark is Hollywood. I didn't talk to number seven yet. I conferred with a few other judges on the matter and was prepared to bring it up with counsel this morning. The only problem is juror seven didn't show up today.'

That brought a pause to both Golantz and myself.

'He's not here?' Golantz said. 'Did you send deputies to—'

'Yes, I sent court deputies to his home and his wife told them that he was at work. They went over to Lockheed and found the man and brought him here. He was not juror number seven. We had seven in the computer as Rodney L. Banglund, but the man who has been sitting for two weeks in seat number seven is not Rodney Banglund. We don't know who he was and now he's missing.'

'What does this do?' I asked. 'Do we have a mistrial?'

'I don't think so. I think we bring the jury out, we explain that number seven's been excused and we drop in the first alternate. Meantime, the sheriff's department makes damn sure everybody else in that box is who they're supposed to be. Mr Golantz?'

'I think the state would be prepared to continue.'

'Mr Haller?'

I nodded approval. The session had gone as I'd hoped. 'I've got witnesses from Paris. My client doesn't want a mistrial.'

'OK, go on back out and we'll get this thing going in ten minutes.'

Elliot was all over me when I got to the defence table. 'What happened? What's going on?'

'Juror number seven didn't show up and the judge found out he was a phoney,' I whispered.

Elliot stiffened. 'My God, what does this mean?'

'The trial continues with an alternate juror, but there'll be an investigation of who number seven was. Hopefully, Walter, it doesn't come to your door.'

'But we can't go on now. You have to get a mistrial.'

I saw the pleading look on my client's face and realised he'd never had any faith in his defence. 'The judge said no on a mistrial. Don't worry, Walter. We're going to win fair and square.'

The clerk called the courtroom to order and the judge bounded up the steps to the bench. 'Back on the record with California versus Elliot,' he said. 'Let's bring in our jury.'

THE FIRST WITNESS for the defence was Julio Muniz, a freelance video-grapher from Topanga Canyon who got the jump on the rest of the media on the day of the murders. I quickly established through my questions how Muniz listened to police scanners in his home and car, picked up addresses for crime scenes and took film he then sold to local news broadcasts.

'What did you do when you arrived at the Elliot house?' I asked.

'Well, I noticed they had some suspect in the patrol car so I got my camera out.'

I introduced the digital video cassette Muniz used that day as the first defence exhibit and rolled the video screen and player in front of the jury. I put in the cassette and hit play. It had been previously spooled to begin at the point that Muniz began shooting outside the Elliot house. Using a remote, I froze the image. Elliot was in the rear passenger-side seat. He was leaning forward because his hands were cuffed behind his body and it made sitting awkward.

'OK, Mr Muniz, let me draw your attention to the roof of the patrol car. What do you see painted there?'

'I see the car's designation. It is four-A or four-alpha.'

'Did you recognise that designation? Had you seen it before?'

'Well, I had actually seen the four-alpha car earlier that day.'

'And what were the circumstances of that?'

'I had heard on the scanner about a possible hostage situation in Malibu Creek State Park. I shot that about two a.m.'

'So about twelve hours before you were videoing the activities at the Elliot house you shot this hostage situation?'

'That's correct.'

'And the four-alpha car was involved in this earlier incident?'

'Yes, when the suspect was finally captured around five a.m. he was transported in four-alpha. The same car. That footage comes earlier on the same tape.'

'Then let's see,' I said.

Golantz immediately stood, objected and asked for a sidebar. The judge waved us up and I brought the witness list.

'Your Honour,' Golantz said angrily. 'The defence is sandbagging. There's been no indication in discovery or otherwise of intent to explore some other crime with this witness.'

I calmly slid the list in front of the judge. 'It clearly says Muniz would testify about video he shot on May 2nd, the day of the murders. The video at the park was shot on May 2. Mr Golantz could have talked to this witness and checked out his videos.'

The judge studied the list for a moment and nodded. 'Objection overruled. You may proceed, Mr Haller.'

I went back and reversed the video and started to play it. It was a night shoot and the images were grainy. Finally, it came to footage showing a man with his hands cuffed behind his back being placed into a patrol car. A deputy closed the door. As the car drove by the camera I froze the image. The light of the camera illuminated the roof of the car as well as the man in the back seat.

'Mr Muniz, what's the designation on the roof of that car?'

'Again it's four-A or four-alpha.'

'And the man being transported, where is he sitting?'

'In the rear right passenger seat.'

'Is he handcuffed?'

'His hands were cuffed behind his back. I shot it.'

'Now is he in the same position in the patrol car that Mr Elliot was in when you videotaped him about twelve hours later?'

'Yes, he is. Exact same position and seat.'

'Thank you, Mr Muniz. No further questions.'

Golantz passed on cross-examination. There was nothing that could be attacked. Muniz stepped down and I called Deputy Todd Stallworth to the stand.

Stallworth looked beat as he came into the courtroom. I quickly established that he was driving the alpha car in the Malibu district during the first shift on the day of the murders. His style was getting old with me. This time I slapped the list down in front of the judge.

'Judge, Deputy Stallworth is clearly listed under law-enforcement personnel. The explanation, as before, says he'll testify about his activities on May 2nd. That's all I put down because I never talked to him.'

Golantz tried to maintain his composure. 'Judge, from the start of this trial the defence has relied on trickery and deception to—'

'Mr Golantz,' the judge interrupted. 'Don't say something you can't back up. This witness, just like the first one, is right there on this list in black and white. You better watch yourself.'

Golantz stood with his head bowed. 'Your Honour, the state requests a brief recess,' he said in a quiet voice.

'Your Honour,' I cut in. 'I object to any recess. He just wants to grab my witness and turn his testimony.'

'Now *that* I object to,' Golantz said.

'No recess,' the judge said. 'Objection overruled.'

We returned to our places and I played the cut showing the handcuffed man being placed in the back of the 4-alpha car at Malibu Creek State Park. I froze the image as before. 'Deputy Stallworth, is that you driving that car?'

'Yes, it is.'

'Who is the man in the back seat?'

'His name is Eli Wyms.'

'Was he handcuffed because he was under arrest?'

'Yes. He was arrested for trying to kill me for one. And for the unlawful discharge of a weapon.'

'How many counts of unlawful discharge of a weapon?'

'I can't recall the exact number.'

'How about ninety-four?'

'That sounds about right. He shot the place up.'

'So you took him to the nearby Malibu station?'

'No, I transported him to the county jail downtown.'

'How long did that take? The drive, I mean.'

'About an hour.'

'And then you drove back to Malibu?'

'No, first I had four-alpha repaired. Wyms had taken out the side lamp. While I was downtown I went to the motor pool. They only have a couple guys work midnight watch so that took up the rest of my shift.'

'So when did the car return to Malibu?'

'At shift change. I turned it over to the day-watch guys.'

I looked down at my notes. 'Deputies Murray and Harber?'

'That's right.'

'Deputy, when you turn the car over from shift to shift, do you clean it out or disinfect the car in any way?'

'You're supposed to. Realistically, unless you've got puke in the back seat, nobody does that. Cars get taken out of rotation once or twice a week and the motor guys clean them up.'

'Did Eli Wyms puke in your car?'

'No, I would've known.'

'OK, Deputy Stallworth, let me see if I've got this right. Eli Wyms was arrested for shooting at you and firing at least ninety-four other shots that morning. His hands were cuffed behind his back and he was transported by you downtown. In the video Mr Wyms can be seen in the rear passenger-side seat. Did he stay there for the hour-long ride downtown?'

'Yes, he did. I had him belted in.'

'Deputy, I noticed on the tape that you did not place Mr Wyms's hands in plastic bags. Why is that?'

'Didn't think it was necessary. The evidence was overwhelming that he had fired the weapons in his possession.' Stallworth yawned. 'We weren't worried about gunshot residue.'

'Thank you, Deputy. I hope you can go and get some sleep now.'

I sat down and left the witness for Golantz but he knew exactly where I was going with this now and there was little he could do to stop me. He passed on cross-examination and the judge adjourned for lunch.

Dr Shamiram Arslanian was a surprise witness. Not in terms of her appearance at trial, but in terms of her physical appearance. Her name and pedigree in forensics conjured an image of a woman deep, dark and scientific. A white lab coat and hair back in a knot. But she was a vivacious, blue-eyed blonde with an easy smile. She was telegenic, articulate and confident but never arrogant. The one-word description for her was likable.

I had spent most of the weekend with Shami, as she preferred to be called. We had gone over the evidence, her testimony for the defence, and her expected cross-examination late in the game to avoid discovery issues. So she was kept in the dark about the magic bullet until the last moment.

There was no doubt that she was a celebrity gun for hire. She had once hosted a show on Court TV and she charged a celebrity-level fee as well. For four days in Los Angeles to study, prepare and testify, she would receive a flat rate of $10,000 plus expenses. I knew after spending ten minutes with her that she was worth every penny. Her personality was going to win over the jury and her facts were going to seal the deal.

I heard the low hum of recognition in the courtroom as my witness made her entrance from the back, holding all eyes as she walked to the witness stand. She wore a navy-blue suit that fitted her curves snugly and accentuated her cascade of blonde curls. Even Judge Stanton seemed infatuated.

After she took the oath I went to the lectern with my legal pad. 'Good afternoon, Dr Arslanian. How are you?'

'I'm doin' just fine. Thanks for asking.'

'Before we go over your curriculum vitae I want to get something out of the way up front. You are a paid consultant to the defence, is that correct?'

'I'm paid to be here, not paid to testify to anything other than my own opinion, whether it's in line with the defence or not. That's my deal and I never change it.'

'OK, tell us where you are from, Doctor.'

'I live in Ossining, New York, right now. I was born and raised in Florida and spent a lot of years in the Boston area.'

'Shamiram Arslanian doesn't sound like a Florida name.'

She smiled brilliantly. 'My father is one hundred per cent Armenian. That makes me half-Armenian and half-Floridian. My father said I was Armageddian when I was a girl.'

Many in the courtroom chuckled politely.

'What is your background in forensic sciences?' I asked.

'Well, I got my master's at the Massachusetts Institute of Technology in chemical engineering, then a PhD in criminology awarded from John Jay College.'

'When you say awarded does that mean it's honorary?'

'Hell, no,' she said forcefully. 'I worked my butt off.'

This time laughter broke out across the courtroom and even the judge smiled before politely tapping his gavel. I checked the jury and saw all twenty-four eyes looking at my witness with rapt attention.

'What are your undergraduate degrees?'

'I got one from Harvard in engineering and one from the Berklee College of Music at the same time.'

'You have a music degree?' I said with feigned surprise.

'I like to sing.'

More laughter. The hits kept coming. One surprise after another.

Golantz finally stood. 'Your Honour, the state would ask that the witness provide testimony regarding forensics, not music or things not germane to this trial.'

Stanton grudgingly asked me to keep my examination on point. Golantz won but everybody now viewed him as a spoilsport.

I asked a few questions that revealed that Dr Arslanian currently worked as a teacher and researcher at John Jay and finally brought her testimony to her study of the gunshot residue found on Walter Elliot's body and clothing on the day of the murders in Malibu.

'Now, Dr Arslanian, the state's forensic witness testified that tabs wiped on Mr Elliot's hands, sleeves and jacket tested positive for certain elements associated with gunshot residue. Do you agree?'

'Yes. For elevated levels of barium, antimony and lead.'

'What does elevated levels mean?'

'That you'd find some of these materials on a person whether they'd fired a weapon or not. From everyday life.'

'So are elevated levels of all three materials required for a positive result in gunshot-residue testing?'

'Yes, that and concentration patterns.'

'Can you explain what you mean by concentration patterns?'

'Sure. When a gun discharges there is an explosion in the chamber that sends gases out of the barrel as well as any little crack and opening. The escaping gases propel microscopic elements backwards onto the shooter.'

'And that's what happened in this case, correct?'

'Based on the totality of my investigation I can't say that.'

I raised my eyebrows in surprise. 'But, Doctor, you said you agreed with the state's conclusion that there was gunshot residue on the defendant's hands and sleeves.'

'I do agree. But that wasn't the question you asked.'

I took a moment as if to retrace my question. 'Dr Arslanian, are you saying that there could be an alternate explanation for the gunshot residue on Mr Elliot?'

'Yes, I am.'

We were there. It was time to shoot the magic bullet.

'Did your studies of the materials provided by the defence lead you to an alternate explanation?'

'Yes, they did. It is very highly likely, in my opinion, that the residue was transferred there inadvertently by contact.'

'What does transfer by contact mean?'

'It means the material alights on a surface after it's discharged from the gun. If that surface comes into contact with another, some of the material will transfer. This is why suspects in gun crimes often have their clothes removed for preservation and study. Some agencies put evidence bags over people's hands to preserve and guard against transference.'

'Can this material be transferred more than once?'

'Yes, it can, with depreciating levels. This is a solid material. It has to be someplace at the end of the day. I have conducted numerous studies and found that transference can repeat and repeat. It's all a matter of how much you start with.'

I nodded. 'OK, Doctor, with these theories in mind can you tell us what happened in the Elliot case?'

'I can. When Mr Elliot was handcuffed and placed in the back of the four-alpha patrol car, his hands, arms and clothing were in direct contact with gunshot residue from another case. Transfer would have been inevitable.'

Golantz quickly objected, saying I had not laid the groundwork for such an answer. I told the judge I intended to do that now and asked to set up the video equipment again.

Dr Arslanian had edited the video shot by Julio Muniz into one demonstration video. Using it as a visual aid, I carefully walked my witness through the defence's theory of transference.

'A man who had fired weapons at least ninety-four times was placed in that seat,' she said. 'Ninety-four times! He would have literally been reeking of gunshot residue.'

Then it was time to bring in the big prop to drive Dr Arslanian's testimony home. 'Doctor, did you draw any other conclusions from your analysis of the GSR evidence that supported the theory of transference?'

'Yes, I did. Can I use my mannequin to demonstrate?'

The judge granted permission without objection from Golantz and I wheeled Dr Arslanian's mannequin in front of the jury. A full body model with manipulating limbs, hands and fingers, it was made of white plastic and was dressed in blue jeans and a dark blue, collared shirt beneath a University of Florida football windbreaker.

Handing a wooden gun and collapsing pointer to Dr Arslanian, I went back to the lectern. 'OK, what do we have here, Doctor?'

'This is Manny, my demo mannequin. Manny, this is the jury.'

There was a bit of laughter and the lawyer even nodded hello.

'Manny's a Florida Gator fan?'

'Uh, he is today. His clothes are exact duplicates of what Mr Elliot was wearing.'

'Why do we need Manny here, Doctor?'

'Because an analysis of the SEMS tabs collected by the sheriff's forensic expert can show us why the gunshot residue on Mr Elliot did not come from his firing of a weapon.'

'The state's expert explained these procedures last week but I'd like you to refresh us. What is a SEMS tab?'

'The GSR test is conducted with round tabs whose sticky side is patted on the test area to collect all the surface microscopic material. The tabs then go into a scanning electron microscope or SEMS and we see or don't see the barium, antimony and lead.'

'OK, then do you have a demonstration for the jury?'

'Yes, I do.' Dr Arslanian extended her pointer. 'Mr Guilfoyle, the sheriff's forensic expert, took eight different coded samples from Mr Elliot's body and clothes.' She pointed to the locations of the samples. 'Tab A was the top of the right hand, Tab B the top of the left. Tab C was the right sleeve of Mr Elliot's windbreaker and D was the left sleeve. Then we have tabs E and F being the right and left front panels of the jacket and G and H being the chest and torso portions of the shirt.'

'OK, what did you learn from your analysis of the tabs?'

'I learned that the levels of gunshot residue greatly differed.'

'How so?'

'Well, tabs A and B which came from Mr Elliot's hands were where the highest levels of GSR were found. From there we get a steep drop-off—tabs C, D, E and F with much lower levels and no GSR reading on tabs G and H.'

'What did that tell you, Doctor?'

'First, comparable readings coming from both hands indicates that the weapon was fired in a two-handed grip.' She pulled the mannequin's hands together and out to the front. She then bent them round the wooden gun. 'But a two-handed grip would also result in higher levels of GSR on the sleeves of the jacket in particular and the rest of the clothes as well. The tabs processed by the sheriff's department show the opposite.'

'So, in your expert opinion, what does it mean?'

'A compound transfer exposure. The first exposure occurred when he was placed with his hands and arms behind his back in the four-alpha car. After that the material was on his hands and arms and some of it was trans-ferred onto the front of his jacket during normal hand and arm movement.'

'In your expert opinion, Doctor, is there any way he could have got this pattern of GSR by discharging a firearm?'

'No, there is not.'

'Thank you, Doctor Arslanian. No further questions.'

I returned to my seat and Walter Elliot whispered, 'The best ten thousand dollars I've ever spent.'

I didn't think I'd done so bad myself. Golantz asked the judge for the afternoon break. I couldn't imagine he had much in his arsenal or he'd have got up and charged right after my witness.

After the jury and the judge had vacated the courtroom, I sauntered over to the prosecutor's table. Golantz was writing out questions on a legal pad. He didn't look up at me. 'What?' he said.

'The answer's no.'

'To what question?'

'The one you were going to ask about a plea agreement.'

Golantz smirked. 'You're funny, Haller. So what, you've got an impres-sive witness. The trial's a long way from over.'

'And I've got a French police captain who's going to testify tomorrow that Rilz ratted out seven of the most dangerous, vindictive men he's ever investigated. Two of them happened to get out of prison last year.'

Golantz put his pen down and finally looked up at me. 'Yeah, I talked to your Inspector Clouseau yesterday. It's pretty clear he's saying whatever you want him to say.'

'So, where are Rilz's family?' I asked.

'I told them that they had to be prepared for your building a defence by crapping all over the memory of their son and brother, using Johan's problems in France to try to get his killer off and depicting him as a German gigolo who seduced rich men and women all over Malibu. You know what the father said?'

'No, but you'll tell me.'

'He said that they'd had enough of American justice and were going home.'

I tried to retort with a clever comeback. I came up empty.

'Don't worry,' Golantz said. 'I'll tell them the verdict.'

I went out to the hallway and saw my client in the centre of a ring of reporters. Feeling cocky after the success of Dr Arslanian's testimony, he was now working the big jury—public opinion.

'All this time they've concentrated on coming after me, the real killer's been out there running around free!' he said.

I was about to grab him when Cisco intercepted me first. 'Come with me,' he said.

We walked down the hallway away from the crowd.

'What's up, Cisco? I was wondering where you've been.'

'I got the report from Florida. Do you want to hear it?'

I had told him what Elliot had told me about fronting for the so-called organisation. Elliot's story had seemed sincere enough but in the light of day I reminded myself of a simple truism—everybody lies—and told Cisco to see what he could do about confirming it.

'Give it to me,' I said.

'I used a PI in Fort Lauderdale. I wanted to go with a guy I trusted. Elliot's grandfather founded a phosphate shipping operation seventy-eight years ago, then Elliot's father worked it. Elliot didn't like getting his hands dirty and sold it a year after his father died. Newspaper articles put the sale at about thirty-two million.'

'What about organised crime?'

'My guy couldn't find a whiff of it. Looked to him like it was a good, clean operation—legally, that is. Elliot's lying.'

I nodded. 'OK, thanks, Cisco.'

He headed off to the elevators and I was left to stare at my client holding forth with the reporters. A slow burn started in me and it gained heat as I waded into the crowd to get him.

'OK, that's all, people,' I said. 'No further comment.'

I walked Elliot down the hall, shooing away reporters. Smiling gleefully, he pumped a fist into the air. 'Mick, it's in the bag. She was outstanding in there. I mean, I want to marry her!'

'Yeah, that's nice but let's see how she does on cross before you buy the ring, OK?'

Another reporter came up and I told her to take a hike, then turned back to my client. 'Listen, Walter, we need to talk.'

'OK, talk.'

'I had a private investigator check out your Florida story and I just found out it was bull. You lied to me, Walter, and I told you never to lie to me.'

He looked annoyed with me for taking the wind out of his sails.

'Why did you lie to me, Walter? Why'd you spin that story?'

He shrugged. 'The story? I read it in a script once, actually.'

'But I'm your lawyer. You can tell me anything. I asked you to tell me the truth and you lied to me. Why?'

He finally looked me in the eyes. 'I knew I had to light a fire under you. Come on, Mickey. Let's not get—'

He was turning to go into the courtroom but I grabbed him roughly by the arm. 'What fire did you light?'

'You're hurting my arm.'

I relaxed my grip but didn't let go. He put an 'aw, shucks' grin on his face. 'Look,' he said. 'I needed you to believe I didn't do it. It was the only way to know you would bring your best game. I told you I could read people, Mick. I knew you needed something to believe in. If I was a little guilty but not guilty of the big crime then it would give you your fire back.'

They say the best actors in Hollywood are on the wrong side of the camera. At that moment I knew that was true. I knew that Elliot had killed his wife and her lover and was even proud of it.

'Where'd you get the gun?'

'Oh, I'd had it. Bought it under the table at a flea market in the seventies. I was a big Dirty Harry fan and I wanted a forty-four Mag. I kept it at the beach house for protection.'

'What really happened in that house, Walter?'

'I went out there to confront her and whoever she was with every Monday. But when I got there I realised it was Rilz. She'd passed him off as gay, had him to dinners and parties with us and they probably laughed about it later. It got me mad. Enraged. You should have seen the look on their faces when they saw that big gun.'

I stared at him for a long moment. I'd had clients confess before, but usually they were crying, wringing their hands, battling the demons their crimes had created inside. But not Walter. He was cold to the bone.

'How'd you get rid of it?'

'I had somebody with me and she took the gun, the rubber gloves and my first set of clothes down the beach, walked to the highway and caught a cab.'

I had a flash vision of Nina Albrecht easily unlocking the door to the deck when I couldn't figure it out. It showed a familiarity with her boss's bedroom that struck me the moment I saw it.

'I never counted on the transference. I thought I was clean and that would be the end of it.' He shook his head at such a close call.

I looked down at the floor, scuffed by a million people who had trod a million miles for justice. 'Did you kill Jerry Vincent?'

'No. But it was a lucky break because I ended up with a better lawyer. Thank God for lawyers like you.'

Fifteen

That night I sent Patrick to the movies because I wanted the house to myself. I wanted no interruption. It was not so that I could prepare for what very likely would be the last day of the trial. I had the French police captain primed for that. And it was not because I now knew my client was guilty. I could count the truly innocent clients I'd had over the years on one hand. Guilty people were my speciality. But I was feeling bruised because I'd been used. And because I'd forgotten the basic rule: everybody lies.

I was feeling bruised, too, because I could not stop thinking about Rilz's father and brothers. About what they had told Golantz about their decision to go home. They were not waiting for the verdict if it first meant seeing their dead loved one dragged through the sewers of the American justice system. I didn't feel very good about myself or the work I would perform the next day.

It was in these moments that I felt the strongest desire to return to old ways. To find that distance again. To take the pill for the physical pain that I knew would numb me to the internal pain. It was in these moments that I realised that I had my own jury to face and that the coming verdict was guilty, that there would be no more cases after this one.

I went outside to the deck hoping the city could pull me out of the abyss into which I had fallen. The night was cool and crisp and clear. Los Angeles was spread out in front of me in a carpet of lights.

After a while a memory washed through me and somehow I smiled. It was one of my last memories of my father. An antique glass ball passed down through my mother's family had been found broken beneath the Christmas tree. My mother brought me to view the damage and to give me the chance to confess. By then my father was sick and wasn't going to get better. He had moved his work—what was left of it—home to the study next to the living room. Through the open door I heard his voice in a sing-song rhyme.

In a pickle, take the nickel . . .

I knew what it meant. Even at five years old I was my father's son in blood and the law. I refused to answer my mother's questions. I refused to incriminate myself.

Now I laughed out loud as I looked at the city of dreams. I leaned down, elbows on the railing, and bowed my head.

'I can't do this any more,' I whispered to myself.

The *William Tell* Overture suddenly burst from the open door behind me. I stepped inside and looked at the cellphone on the table. It said PRIVATE CALLER. At the last moment I took it.

'Is this Michael Haller, the lawyer?'

'Yes, who is this?'

'This is Los Angeles Police Officer Randall Morris. Do you know an individual named Elaine Ross, sir?'

I felt a fist grip my guts. 'Lanie? What's wrong?'

'Uh, sir, I have Miss Ross up here on Mulholland Drive and she shouldn't be driving. In fact, she sort of passed out after she handed me your card.'

Lanie Ross. She had fallen back. An arrest would put her back into the system and probably cost her another stay in jail and rehab.

'Which jail are you taking her to?'

'I gotta be honest. I'm code seven in twenty minutes. If I take her down to book her I'm looking at two more hours. If you send somebody for her, I'm willing to give her the break.'

'Thank you, Officer. I'll come if you give me the address.'

'You know where the overlook is above Fryman Canyon? We're right there. Make it quick.'

Fryman Canyon was only a few blocks from the converted-garage guesthouse where a friend allowed Lanie to live rent-free. I could get her home and walk back to retrieve her car. I left the house and drove along Laurel Canyon up the hill to the top and took a left on Mulholland, then followed the serpentine road west for half a mile.

My cellphone buzzed as I'd been expecting it to. 'What took you so long to call, Bosch?' I said by way of a greeting.

'I've been calling but there's no cell coverage in the canyon,' Bosch said. 'Is this some kind of test? Where the hell are you going? You called and said you were done for the night.'

'I gotta call. A . . . client of mine got busted up here at the Fryman Canyon overlook. The cop's giving her a break if I drive her home.'

'Who was the cop?'

'Randall Morris.'

'OK, pull over until I can check it out.'

'Pull over? I'm already here.'

The overlook was on the Valley side. I took a right to turn in and drove by the sign. I didn't see Lanie's car or a police cruiser. The parking area was empty. 'Damn!'

'What?' Bosch asked.

I hit the heel of my palm on the steering wheel. Morris hadn't waited. 'She's not here. He took her to jail.'

Now I'd have to figure which station Lanie had been transported to and spend the night arranging bail.

I put the car in park and got out and looked around. The lights of the Valley spread out below the precipice for miles and miles.

'Bosch, I gotta go. I have to try to find—'

I saw movement to the left. I turned and saw a crouching figure coming out of the brush. He was dressed in black and a ski mask was pulled down over his face. As he straightened he raised a gun.

'Wait a minute,' I said. 'What is—'

'Drop the phone!'

I dropped it and raised my hands. 'Are you with Bosch?'

The man moved quickly towards me and shoved me. I stumbled to the ground and felt him grab the back of my jacket collar. 'Get up! Now!' He started pulling me up.

'OK, I'm getting up.' The moment I was on my feet I was shoved forward in front of my car lights. 'Where are we going? What is—'

I was shoved again. 'You ask too many questions, lawyer.'

He pushed me towards the precipice. I knew it was almost a sheer drop-off. I tried to dig my heels in but the man shoved harder. He was going to run me off the edge into the blackness of the abyss.

'You can't—'

Suddenly there was a shot. The man yelped and fell into the brush. Then came voices and shouting.

I dived face down to the dirt and put my hands over my head. I heard more yelling, the sound of running, vehicles roaring across the gravel. When I opened my eyes I saw blue lights flashing.

'Counsellor,' a voice above me said. 'You can get up now.'

I craned my neck to look up. It was Bosch, his shadowed face silhouetted by the stars above him.

'You cut that one pretty close,' he said.

THE MAN IN THE MASK yelped in pain as they handcuffed him. 'My hand! My hand is broken!'

I climbed to my feet and saw men in black windbreakers moving about like ants on a hill. Some raid jackets said LAPD but most had FBI across the back. Soon a helicopter came overhead and lit the clearing with a spotlight.

Bosch stepped over to the FBI agents huddling round the man in the mask. 'Was he hit?' he asked.

'No, the round hit the gun,' an agent said. 'We're still looking for it.' They pulled the man up into a standing position.

'Let's see who we've got,' Bosch said.

The ski mask was unceremoniously yanked off. Bosch turned and looked back at me.

'Juror number seven,' I said. 'He didn't show up today and the sheriff's department was looking for him.'

Bosch turned back. 'Hold him right there.'

Signalling me to follow him, he walked over to my car. I got my question in first. 'What just happened?'

'What happened was we just saved your life.'

'I know that, but where did all these cops come from? You said you'd let your people go at night after I was tucked in. And what's the FBI doing here?'

'Things were different tonight. Let's talk about juror number seven. Why didn't he show up today?'

'You should probably ask him that. All I can tell you is that this morning the judge said he got an anonymous letter saying he was a phoney. And he lied about having a record.'

'Why did he want to kill you?' Bosch asked.

I raised my empty hands. 'I don't know. Maybe because of the story we planted. Wasn't that the plan, to draw him out?'

'I think you're holding out on me, Haller.'

'You're the one holding out. What's the FBI doing here?'

'They've been in it from the start.'

'Right and you just forgot to tell me.'

'I told you what you needed to know.'

'Well, I need to know it all or my cooperation with you ends now. That includes being any sort of witness.'

He smiled in frustration. 'Come on, man, cool your jets. Don't be throwing empty threats around.'

'We'll see how empty it is when I start stringing out the federal grand jury subpoena. I can argue client confidentiality all the way to the Supreme Court. Your pals in the Bureau are going to wish you'd come clean when you had the chance.'

Bosch thought a moment and pulled me by the arm. 'All right, tough guy, come over here.'

We walked to a spot in the parking area even further from the law-enforcement ant hill. Bosch started to talk.

'The Bureau contacted me after the Vincent murder and said he'd been a person of interest. That's all. A person of interest. He was one of the lawyers whose name came up in their look at the state courts. Nothing specific, just based on rumours, things he had supposedly told clients he could get done, connections he claimed to have. They invited him in as a cooperating witness and he declined. They were increasing the pressure on him when he got hit.'

'So you joined forces. Isn't that wonderful? Thanks for telling me.'

'Like I said, you didn't need to know. If it wasn't for the Bureau right now you could be lying down there at the bottom of the mountain.'

I tried to accept that reality. And the reality that I had been used as a pawn from the beginning—by my client and Bosch and the FBI. Bosch signalled over an agent who was now standing nearby.

'This is Agent Armstead. He's been running the Bureau's side of things and he's got some questions for you.'

'Why not?' I said. 'Nobody answers mine. I might as well answer yours.'

Armstead was young, with a precision military haircut. 'Mr Haller, your cooperation will be greatly appreciated. Is juror number seven the man Vincent paid the bribe to?'

I looked at Bosch with a *Who is this guy?* expression.

'Man, how would I know that? I wasn't part of this thing. You want an answer to that, go ask him.'

'Don't worry. We will. What were you doing here, Mr Haller?'

'I told you people. I told Bosch. I got a call from somebody who said he was a cop. He said he had a woman I know personally up here and she was under the influence and that I could come up and drive her home and save her from getting booked.'

'We checked that name you gave me on the phone,' Bosch said. 'Randall Morris is on gang detail in South Bureau.'

I nodded. 'Yeah, well I think it's pretty clear that it was a fake call, but he knew my friend's name and he had my cell.'

'How did he get the woman's name?' Armstead asked.

'Good question. I don't know. Go ask McSweeney.'

I immediately realised I had slipped up. I wouldn't know that name unless I had been investigating juror number seven. Bosch looked at me curiously. I was saved by someone yelling from the brush, 'I've got the gun!'

Bosch pointed a finger at my chest. 'Stay right here.'

I watched Bosch and Armstead trot over and join a few of the others as they bent down to study the found weapon under a flashlight. Then the *William Tell* Overture started to play behind me and I saw my phone on the gravel, its tiny screen glowing like a beacon. I went over and took the call.

'Cisco, I gotta call you back.'

'Make it quick. I've got some good stuff.'

I closed the phone and watched Bosch step over to McSweeney and whispered something into his ear. He didn't wait for a response. He just walked back towards me. I could tell even in the dim moonlight that he was excited. Armstead was following behind him.

'The gun's a Beretta Bobcat like we were looking for on Vincent,' he said. 'Put this together for me, Haller. If the ballistics match why'd he want to kill you, too?'

'I don't know.'

'How did he know your friend's name on the phone?'

'I don't know that either.'

'Then what good are you?' Bosch asked.

It was a good question. 'Look, Detective, I—'

'Don't bother, man. Why don't you just get in your car and get the hell out of here? We'll take it from here.'

He started walking away and Armstead followed. I hesitated and then called out. Bosch came back alone.

'No bull,' he said impatiently. 'I don't have the time.'

'OK, this is the thing,' I said. 'I think he was going to make it look like I jumped. Like a suicide.'

Bosch considered this and then shook his head.

'You've got the case of the decade, man. You're hot. You're on TV. And you've got a kid to worry about. Suicide wouldn't sell.'

I nodded. 'Yes, it would.'

He looked at me and said nothing, waiting for me to explain.

'I'm a recovering addict, Bosch. The story would go that I couldn't take the pressure of the case and the attention and I jumped. It makes me think that . . .'

'What?'

I pointed across the clearing towards juror number seven.

'That he and whoever he was doing this for know a lot about me. They did a deep background. They came up with my addiction and Lanie's name, then they came up with a solid plan for getting rid of me. I guess they think I know too much.'

'Do you?'

Before I could answer McSweeney started yelling. 'Hey! Over there! I want to make a deal.'

'My tip?' I said. 'Go strike while the iron's hot. Before he remembers he's entitled to a lawyer. But before you go you owe me one answer. You were supposed to cut the surveillance down to one car for the night. But this is the whole enchilada. What changed your mind?'

Bosch signalled to Armstead to go to McSweeney. 'You really haven't heard, have you?'

'Heard what?'

'You get to sleep late tomorrow, Counsellor. There's no trial any more. Your client's dead. Somebody took Elliot and his girlfriend out when they came home from dinner. His electric gate wouldn't open and when he got out to push it somebody put a bullet in the back of his head. He hit Nina Albrecht in the car.'

I took a half-step back in shock.

'I got tipped from a friend at the medical examiner's and figured somebody might be cleaning the slate tonight. I figured I ought to call the team back. Lucky for you I did.'

I stared right through Bosch. 'Yeah,' I said. 'Lucky for me.'

THERE WAS NO LONGER A TRIAL but I went to court on Tuesday to see the case through to its official end. I took my place next to the empty seat Walter Elliot had occupied for the past two weeks. The news photographers who had been allowed access to the courtroom seemed to like that empty chair. They took a lot of photos of it.

Jeffrey Golantz sat across the aisle. He was the luckiest prosecutor on earth. He had left court one day thinking he was facing a career-hobbling loss and came back the next with his perfect record intact. He had nothing to say to me as we waited for the judge.

But there was a lot of talk in the gallery. People were buzzing with news of the murders of Walter Elliot and Nina Albrecht. No one made mention of the attempt on my life. Bosch and Armstead had asked me to keep quiet so they could move slowly with their cooperating suspect. I was happy to cooperate myself. To a point.

Judge Stanton took the bench promptly at nine. His eyes were puffy and he looked like he'd had very little sleep. The jury was brought in and if any of them knew what had happened they weren't showing it. Several checked out the empty seat beside me as they took their own.

'Ladies and gentlemen, good morning,' Stanton said. 'At this time I am going to discharge you from service in this trial. As I'm sure you can see, Mr Elliot is not in his seat at the defence table. This is because the defendant was the victim of a homicide last night.'

Half the jurors' mouths dropped open in unison.

'I know that to all of you this is rather shocking news,' Stanton told the jurors. 'Be assured that the authorities hopefully will soon bring the individual or individuals responsible to justice. You'll learn all about it when you read the paper or watch the news. I want to thank you for your service. You are excused.'

We stood one last time for the jury. After they filed through the doorway the judge thanked Golantz and me for our professional demeanour during the trial, and quickly adjourned court. I stood motionless for the longest time after he left the courtroom. Golantz approached me with his hand out and without thinking I shook it.

'No hard feelings, Mickey. You're a damn good lawyer.'

Was, I thought. 'Yeah,' I said. 'No hard feelings.'

'Take care of yourself.' He clapped me on the shoulder and pushed through the gate. I was sure there would be a throng of media out in the hall and he'd tell them that in some strange way justice had been served. Live by the gun, die by the gun. Or words to that effect.

I gave him a good lead and then followed. The reporters were surrounding him and I was able to hug the wall and escape notice. I went down three landings into the hallway on ten, then walked to Judge Holder's courtroom and entered.

Michaela Gill was in the clerk's pod. I asked if I could see the judge for a few minutes.

'But I don't have you down for an appointment,' she said.

'I know that, Michaela, but I think the judge will want to see me. Is she back there? Can you tell her I only want ten minutes. Tell her it's about the Vincent files.'

She picked up the phone and gave my request, then told me I could go right to her chambers.

The judge was behind her desk. 'Well, Mr Haller,' she said. 'It's certainly been an eventful day. Have a seat.'

I sat in the familiar chair. 'Thank you for seeing me, Judge.'

'What can I do for you?' She started scribbling signatures on a series of documents.

'I just wanted you to know I will be resigning as counsel on the rest of the Vincent cases.'

She put her pen down and looked at me. 'What?'

'I'm resigning. I came back too soon or probably should have never come back at all. But I'm finished.'

'That's absurd. Your defence of Mr Elliot has been the talk of this courthouse. I watched parts of it on television. I don't think many observers would have bet against an acquittal.'

I waved the compliments away.

'Anyway, Judge, it doesn't matter. It's not really why I'm here. I want you to know that I know. And soon everybody else will as well.'

'What are you talking about? What do you know, Mr Haller?'

'That you are for sale and that you tried to have me killed.'

She barked out a laugh. 'Is this some kind of joke?'

'No, it's no joke.'

'Then, Mr Haller, I suggest you compose yourself. If you go around this courthouse making outlandish accusations there will be severe consequences. Maybe you're right. You're feeling the stress of coming back too soon from rehab.'

I smiled. I could tell by her face she realised her mistake.

'How'd you know I was in rehab, Judge? Better yet, how did juror number seven know how to lure me from home last night? You had me backgrounded, set me up and sent McSweeney to kill me. Last time I saw him he was playing "Let's Make a Deal" with the federal government.'

It hit her like a punch in the gut. I knew it wasn't going to endear me to Bosch or Armstead, but I didn't care. Neither of them was the guy who had been used like a pawn and had nearly taken the high dive off Mulholland. I was that guy and that entitled me to confront the person I knew was behind it.

'My investigator traced McSweeney,' I said. 'Nine years ago he was arrested for an ADW and who was his attorney? Mitch Lester, your husband. The next year he was popped again for fraud and Mitch was on the case. There's the connection. It makes a nice little triangle, doesn't it? You planted the sleeper on my jury. Jerry Vincent paid you but changed his mind after the FBI came sniffing around. You couldn't run the risk that Jerry might try to deal a judge to them so you sent McSweeney. Then, when it all turned to crap yesterday, you sent McSweeney after Elliot and Albrecht, then me. How am I doing, *Judge*? I miss anything so far?'

She stood up. 'This is absurd. Get out of my chambers.'

'The whole house is going to fall. The FBI has McSweeney. You're about to trade that black robe for an orange jumpsuit.'

'Get out or I will call security and have you arrested!'

She pointed to the door. I calmly stood up. 'Sure, I'll go. And I may never practice law again in this courthouse, but I'll come back to watch you prosecuted. You and your husband.'

The judge stared at me, the anger in her eyes slowly changing to fear. Her arm dropped. I left her standing there.

I took the stairs all the way down. Ten flights. At the bottom I pushed through the doors, pulled my phone and told Patrick to bring the car round. Then I called Bosch.

'I didn't want to wait around a year and a half while the Bureau made its case. Sometimes justice can't wait, Detective.'

'What did you do, Haller?'

'I had a conversation with Judge Holder—yes, I figured it out. If I were you, I'd hurry up your case and keep tabs on her. She doesn't seem like a runner, but you never know. Have a good day.'

I closed the phone. It felt good to turn the tables on him, make him and the FBI do the dancing at the end of the string.

Sixteen

Bosch knocked on my door early Thursday morning. I hadn't combed my hair yet but I was dressed. He, on the other hand, looked like he had pulled an all-nighter.

'I wake you?' he asked.

I shook my head. 'I have to get my kid ready for school. What's up, Detective?'

'I thought you'd be interested in knowing where things stand.'

'Sure. Let's sit out here. I don't want her hearing this.' I patted down my hair as I walked towards the table.

'I don't want to sit,' Bosch said. 'I don't have a lot of time.' He turned and leaned his elbows down on the railing.

I changed direction and did the same thing right next to him. 'I don't like to sit when I'm out here either.'

'I have the same sort of view at my place,' he said. 'Only it's on the other side.'

'I guess that makes us flip sides of the same mountain.'

He turned his eyes from the view to me for a moment. 'Something like that,' he said.

'What's happening? I thought you'd be too angry to tell me.'

'Truth is, I think the Bureau moves too slowly myself. They didn't like what you did very much but it got things rolling.' Bosch straightened up and leaned back on the railing, the city behind him. 'The grand jury came back with indictments last night. Holder, Lester, Carlin, McSweeney and a supervisor in the jury office who gave them computer access. We're taking them all down this morning, so keep it under your hat.'

It was nice he trusted me enough to tell me before the arrests. 'Is it solid?' I asked. 'Holder *is* a judge. You better have it nailed down.'

'McSweeney gave it all up. We've got phone records, money transfers. He even taped her husband's conversations.'

I nodded. 'I didn't know Carlin was hooked up in this.'

'He goes way back with the judge and she used him to approach Vincent. Vincent used him to deliver the money. Then when Vincent got cold feet Carlin got wind of it and told the judge.'

'Got wind of it how? Wren Williams?'

'Yeah, we think he got close to her to keep tabs on Vincent.'

'What about McSweeney? He just did what he was told?'

'McSweeney was a con man before he was a killer. I don't think we're getting the whole truth but he says the judge explained that either Vincent went down or they all did. Besides, she promised to increase his cut.'

I nodded. 'So what are the indictments?'

'Conspiracy to commit murder, corruption. More down the road. McSweeney's been on four juries in seven years. Two acquittals and two hangers. Three courthouses.'

I whistled. 'This is going to be huge.'

'Biggest one I've ever had.' He glanced over his shoulder. 'You've got the Sunset Strip and I've got Universal,' he said.

I heard the door open and looked back to see Hayley peeking out. 'Dad? Is everything all right?'

'Everything's fine. Hayley, this is Detective Bosch. He's a policeman.'

'Hello, Hayley,' Bosch said. I think it was the only time I had ever seen him put a real smile on his face.

'Hi,' my daughter said.

'Hay, did you eat your cereal?' I asked.

'Yes.'

'OK, then you can watch TV until it's time to go.'

She disappeared inside and closed the door.

'She's a cute kid,' Bosch said.

I nodded.

'I gotta ask you a question,' he said. 'You sent that anonymous letter to the judge, didn't you?'

'If I say yes am I going to become a witness?'

'No. I just want to know if you did the right thing.'

Ultimately I wanted him to know. 'Yeah, that was me. I didn't expect Judge Stanton to consult other judges.'

'He called up the chief judge and asked her advice.'

'It's gotta be what happened,' I said, shaking my head. My own actions had almost brought about my own demise in the form of a 300-foot dive off Mulholland. 'I guess I was stupid.'

'You're still standing. After today none of them will be.'

'There's that. What kind of deal did McSweeney cut?'

'No death penalty and consideration. If everybody goes down he'll probably get fifteen and do thirteen.'

'Pretty good deal for three murders,' I said.

'One murder,' Bosch corrected. 'He didn't kill Elliot and Albrecht. Those two didn't match up.'

'What are you talking about?'

'It was a different weapon.'

I was stunned silent. 'Does Beverly Hills have any ideas?'

'Yeah, they're pretty sure but they'll never make a case.'

The hits kept coming. One surprise after another. 'Who?'

'The family of Johan Rilz. They took care of it.'

'How do they know that?'

'Lands and grooves. The bullets were nine-millimetre Parabellums. Brass jacket and casing and manufactured in Germany. Beverly Hills PD took the bullet profile and matched them to a C96 Mauser, also manufactured in Germany. They're thinking it's almost like somebody was sending a message.'

'A message from Germany. What will happen now?'

Bosch shrugged. 'I know a couple of detectives who'll get a nice trip to Germany out of it. They'll go through the motions and the due diligence. But if the hit was done right, nothing will happen.'

'How'd they get the gun over here?'

'It could be done. Through Canada or *Der* Fed-Ex if it absolutely, positively has to be there on time.'

I didn't smile. I was thinking about Elliot and the equilibrium of justice. Somehow Bosch seemed to know what I was thinking.

'Remember what you said when you told me you had told Judge Holder you knew she was behind all of this?'

I shrugged. 'What did I say?'

'You said sometimes justice can't wait.'

'And?'

'And you were right. Sometimes it doesn't wait. In that trial Elliot looked like he was going to walk. So somebody decided to deliver his own verdict.

Back when I was riding patrol you know what we called a killing that came down to simple street justice?'

'What?'

'The brass verdict.'

I understood. We were both silent for a long moment.

'Anyway, that's all I know.' Bosch pushed his weight off the railing. 'I gotta go put people in jail. It's going to be a good day.'

'It's funny you coming here today,' I said. 'Last night I decided I was going to ask you something the next time I saw you.'

'Yeah, what's that?'

I thought a moment then nodded. It was the right thing to do. 'Flip sides of the same mountain . . . do you know you look a lot like your father?'

He said nothing. He just nodded and turned to cast his gaze at the city. 'When did you put that together?'

'Technically, last night when I was looking at old photos and scrapbooks with my daughter. But I think on some level I've known it for a long time. We were looking at photos of my father. They kept reminding me of somebody and then I realised it was you. Once I saw it, it seemed obvious.' I stared out at the city with him.

'Most of what I know about him came from books,' I said. 'A lot of different cases, a lot of different women. But there are a few memories that aren't in books and are just mine. I remember coming into the office he set up at home when he got sick. There was a painting framed on the wall—a print actually. *The Garden of Earthly Delights*. Weird, scary stuff for a seven-year-old . . . He held me on his lap and made me look at it and told me that it wasn't scary. That it was beautiful. He tried to teach me the painter's name. Hieronymus Bosch. Rhymes with anonymous, he told me.'

I wasn't seeing the city out there. I was seeing the memory. I was quiet for a while after that. It was my half-brother's turn. Eventually, he leaned his elbows down on the railing and spoke.

'I remember that house,' he said. 'I visited him once. Introduced myself. He was on the bed. He was dying.'

'What did you say to him?'

'I just told him I'd made it through. That's all. There wasn't really anything else to say.'

Like right now, I thought. What was there to say?

'You've known all these years. Why didn't you ever make contact? I have another half-brother and three half-sisters. They're yours, too.'

Bosch gave an answer I guessed he'd been telling himself for a few decades.

'I don't know. I didn't want to rock anybody's boat. Most of the time people don't like surprises. Not like this.'

For a moment I wondered what my life would be like if I had known about Bosch. Maybe I would've been a cop instead of a lawyer. 'I'm quitting, you know.'

'Quitting what?'

I wasn't sure why I had said it. 'My job. The law. You could say the brass verdict was my last verdict.'

'I quit once. It didn't take. I came back.'

'We'll see.'

Bosch glanced at me and then put his eyes back out on the city. It was a beautiful day with low-flying clouds and a cold air front had compressed the smog to a thin amber band. The sun had just crested the mountains and was throwing light out on the Pacific. We could see all the way to Catalina.

'I came to the hospital that time you got shot,' he said. 'I wasn't sure why. I saw on the news that it was a gut shot and I knew those could go either way. I thought maybe if they needed blood or something I could . . . I figured we matched, you know? Anyway there were all these reporters and cameras. I ended up leaving.'

I smiled and then I started to laugh. I couldn't help it.

'What's so funny?'

'You, a cop, volunteering to give blood to a defence attorney. I don't think they'd let you back in the clubhouse if they knew.'

Now Bosch smiled. 'I guess I didn't think about that.'

And just like that both our smiles disappeared and the awkwardness of being strangers returned. Eventually Bosch checked his watch. 'The warrant teams meet in twenty minutes. I gotta roll.'

'OK.'

'I'll see you around, Counsellor.'

'I'll see you around, Detective.'

He went down the steps and I stayed where I was.

I STAYED OUT on the deck after that and looked at the city as the light moved across it. Many different thoughts filtered through my head and flew off into the sky like the clouds up there. Remotely beautiful and untouchable. Distant. I was left feeling that I would never see Bosch again. That he would have his side of the mountain and I would have mine and that's all there would be.

After a while I heard the door open and footsteps on the deck. I felt my daughter's presence by my side and I put my hand on her shoulder.

'What are you doing, Dad? Are you all right?'

'I'm fine. Just looking.'

'What did that policeman want?'

'Just to talk. He's a friend of mine.'

We were silent a moment before she moved on. 'I wish Mom had stayed with us last night,' she said.

I squeezed the back of her neck. 'One thing at a time, Hay. We got her to have pancakes with us, didn't we?'

She thought about it and gave a nod. She agreed. Pancakes were a start.

'I'm going to be late if we don't go,' she said. 'One more time and I'll get a conduct slip.'

I nodded. 'Too bad. The sun's just about to hit the ocean.'

'Come on, Dad. That happens every day.'

'Somewhere, at least.'

I went in for the keys, locked up, and we went down the steps to the garage. By the time I backed the Lincoln out and had it pointed down the hill, I could see the sun was spinning gold on the Pacific.

MICHAEL CONNELLY

Born: Philadelphia, USA
Film adaptation: *Blood Work*, 2002
Motto: 'Everybody counts or nobody counts'

Q: What's the first book you can remember reading?

A: I can't remember the first book. I think the first *important* book I remember reading was *To Kill a Mocking Bird* by Harper Lee.

Q: Did you enjoy school? What is your most vivid memory of it?

A: I did not enjoy school but at least knew the value of it. My best and most vivid memory is being told that I would be allowed to graduate despite my poor work.

Q: Did you always want to be an author?

A: I went to university to learn building construction. Two years in, I discovered the work of Raymond Chandler and decided to be a writer.

Q: What were the first pieces of writing that you produced?

A: In high school I had a short-story assignment that was supposed to have irony in it. I wrote a mystery called 'The Perfect Murder'. I got an A grade. It was narrated by a guy who has supposedly committed the perfect murder. At the end, the reader realises he is writing this story in prison. That's high-school irony, I guess.

Q: Who do you most admire and why?

A: My daughter because she has an unbiased, unfettered view of the world. She is innocent and hopeful.

Q: What jobs did you have before you started writing?

A: Since the end of my schooling, I have been a professional writer in one capacity or another. Before that, I did many different jobs from dishwasher to salmon-server on a buffet line to bagging groceries to delivering dry-wall to construction sites.

Q: Where do you write?

A: I write in an office that is a very controllable environment. It has black-out curtains and ways for me to avoid knowing what time of day it is. I like to escape into the writing and not know whether it is 3 p.m. or 3 a.m. I like to avoid outside influences.

Q: Typewriter, word processor or pen?

A: I write on a laptop because it is fast. The key to writing is rewriting and the computer makes it easier to do.

Q: What's the greatest influence on your writing?

A: At the moment, I would say a small group of real detectives I have been spending a lot of time with. They work on old, unsolved cases and are very passionate and committed. The nobility of their mission is very influential on me as a person and a writer. I want to get some of that nobility into my life and my work.

Q: If your house was burning down, what would you save?

A: My family. The rest could go up in flames. (Except I do have a first edition of *The Big Sleep* that I might try to grab on the way out. It could probably put my daughter through college.)

Q: What do you do when you are not writing? How do you relax? What are your hobbies?

A: I like to fish.

To read the full interview go to: Michael Connelly *at* www.orionbooks.co.uk

THE HARRY BOSCH FILE

Defence lawyer Mickey Haller might be the hero of *The Brass Verdict*, but he shares the limelight with Connelly's best-loved and longest-running detective, Harry Bosch, who turns out to be his half-brother. Here are some facts about Harry:

- He is named after the 15th-century Dutch artist, Hieronymus Bosch.
- During service in Vietnam, he was a 'tunnel rat', a specialist who infiltrated underground mazes used by the Vietcong. He has a rat tattoo on his right shoulder, dating from that time.
- We meet him first in *The Black Echo* (1992), when he is a detective with the Los Angeles Police Department.
- He joined the force aged eighteen, having gone AWOL from the army.
- He was posted first to Robbery Homicide, but later joined the Hollywood detectives.
- He is left-handed.

- He wears his gun on his left hip when he is not expecting a tactical situation.
- He likes jazz.
- His personal motto is, like Connelly's: 'Everybody counts or nobody counts.'

FATHERS & SONS

RICHARD MADELEY

'The real connective strand that binds together my father, grandfather and me only became fully clear to me during the writing of this book. It can be expressed in a mantra that I am certain never left my grandfather's lips: "To understand all is to forgive all."'

Richard Madeley

Preface

I was twenty-one when my father died, suddenly and with no warning. His last morning on earth was spent at the office. By lunchtime the symptoms of coronary thrombosis must have been unmistakable, because Dad did what many men are strangely compelled to do when their hearts give notice of imminent convulsion—he headed for home. He managed to drive himself to his front door, fumbled desperately with the key, staggered inside and collapsed into my appalled mother's arms.

He had three minutes to live.

Dad said that his arms and hands were tingling and he felt very cold. Mum settled him on a sofa, called an ambulance and rushed upstairs for blankets. When she got back to him, he was now struggling to breathe but, ever the journalist, a career he'd begun thirty years before, managed to gasp: 'My expenses from last week . . . they're in the glove box.'

My mother urged him to lie still and wrapped her arms around him. This was to prompt my father's last words: 'Do you have to lean on me so bloody hard?' he gasped, before his life winked out with the sudden totality of a power cut. The light of my mother's life had been snapped off with a querulous rebuke.

Like most sudden deaths, my father's triggered multiple impacts. My mother, still a relatively young woman in her early forties, now faced the prospect of completely rebuilding her life. My sister Elizabeth and I had to face up to the prospect of a future without a father's guidance and love. But for one member of the family, the death of Christopher Madeley on the afternoon of August 8, 1977, would shroud what remained of his own life in speechless sorrow. Geoffrey Madeley, my father's father, never recovered from the loss of his youngest son—a son he never once told he loved.

Geoffrey, Christopher, Richard and Jack. Fathers and sons, four generations strung together like beads on the twisting double helix of their shared DNA. The story you are about to read spans a century, from 1907 to the present day; a hundred years of unprecedented change and transformation during which the roles of men and women within the family were fundamentally altered.

Men now face major challenges to their traditional position in the home. The lines between motherhood and fatherhood have become blurred, and that burgeoning new science of our era—psychology—has ushered in a new age of self-awareness and analysis. Today's fathers must surely have more insight into their roles as parents than previous generations, and yet they are probably just as confused as their forefathers were.

So begins our expedition: a survey of the lives of Madeley men that may chart a map of sorts for other fathers and sons. Some of the details have been blurred not only by time but by subtly differing family accounts. I have tried to reconcile these.

But be in no doubt: these are true stories.

Chapter 1

My grandfather awoke on a feather bed in a bare room that smelt of apples. His ten-year-old mind struggled to remember where he was. Then consciousness returned; he was in the orchard room of his uncles' and aunt's farmhouse. He, his parents and his six brothers and sisters were halfway to Liverpool. They'd said goodbye to their old home in Worcester the day before and packed their belongings onto a horse-drawn cart. This was a place called Shawbury. Mother and Father had told them they had one more day's journey before they would see the great ship that was to carry them all across the sea.

Geoffrey turned to discuss this thrilling prospect with the brother he had shared the bed with, but the other was up and gone. As Granddad hurriedly dressed, he wondered why the house was so still and quiet. Everyone should be up and preparing to leave by now. They'd meant to set off at dawn, but the sunlight slanting through the window onto the brass bedstead told him that morning had broken hours ago. Why hadn't anyone thought to wake him? Surely they couldn't have forgotten him!

Not quite. As the small boy trotted and then ran from room to room, each as silent and empty as the last, the children and parents whose names he called out in increasing desperation and panic were already long gone on the road to Liverpool. My grandfather had not been forgotten.

A deal had been done. He had been left behind.

THE WHOLE THING was Bulford's fault. Mr Bulford, from Birmingham, was the money-man in a partnership with my great-grandfather, Henry George Madeley. Henry was a farmer's son from Shropshire but had no intention of working on the land. As soon as he could he left the farm in the care of his two bachelor brothers and spinster sister and with Bulford's backing opened a grocery store in Worcester's Mealcheapen Street. Business was brisk enough for Henry to marry and live comfortably with his wife Hannah at the family home half a mile away, in Stanley Road. By 1907 their seven children ranged from baby Cyril to fifteen-year-old Douglas, with ten-year-old Geoffrey coming in at number three.

Bulford called Henry to a meeting. He was sorry to inform him that he had decided to retire from business and would therefore be removing all his capital from their joint venture forthwith. He was sure Henry would do very well by himself.

Henry was stunned. He tried his best to find a new backer but there were no takers. He had to come up with something, fast, or his family would be out on the street. There was always the farm . . .

Henry's brothers, William and Thomas, were still up in Shropshire with their sister, Sarah. She looked after the two men while they worked the tenancy on Kiln Farm. With its tiny herd of a few dairy cattle it wasn't exactly a goldmine, but maybe something could be worked out.

Kiln Farm stood close to the village of Shawbury, about seven miles outside Shrewsbury. A century ago, it was a remote place to live. A few miles to the south rose the dark, barrow-shaped hump of a prehistoric volcano, the Wrekin. Standing like teeth along the western horizon lay the Stretton Hills, and behind them, Wales. Kiln Farm nestled in the shallow, almost saucer-like depression of the Shropshire Plain.

Henry had absolutely no intention of returning to live there, and still less of going back to work on the land. But he began to think his brothers might be willing to help him in other ways. There was nothing to keep him and his family in Worcester. Come to think of it, there was nothing to keep them in England at all. Henry knew people who had emigrated to Canada and by all accounts were getting along very well there, thank you. Why shouldn't the Madeleys do the same?

For one, currently, insurmountable reason. He had no money to buy transatlantic tickets, and no money to get his family established once they had arrived. But surely a loan of some sort could be arranged? William was his brother, after all.

Henry went back to Kiln Farm. Alone. He had no collateral to offer, he explained to William, other than his word. William told him collateral would, unfortunately, be required, but not to worry. He had a proposal of his own to make . . .

The farm had been full of happy noise the night before. Of course, the little ones didn't really know what was going on. Cyril was still a baby and not even talking yet. Katherine, who was three, Doris, eight, and William, five, seemed to think they were off on holiday somewhere and Geoffrey could understand why—it *did* feel as if they were off on holiday, only, well, somehow much *bigger* than that. He and his two older brothers, Douglas and thirteen-year-old John, knew exactly what was happening. They were all about to emigrate. Leave for Canada, and never come back, not like you had to from a holiday.

Geoffrey went to sleep dreaming of silver dollars and snow.

A few hours later, running in increasing panic through the empty bedrooms, he realised everyone's bags had gone. Everyone's but his. He rushed downstairs to find his aunt and uncles sitting by the kitchen fire. Uncle William said they had something to tell him.

So what was Henry's 'arrangement'? It was certainly William, the eldest brother, who would have set the terms. He would advance the money for one-way passages to Canada for everyone except Geoffrey. At ten years old, the boy would soon be strong enough to help out on the farm, and young enough to give the maximum years of service before reaching his majority.

William threw in a couple of sweeteners. When Geoffrey was twenty-one, he would be 'allowed' to visit his family in Canada. Of course, it was up to him whether he came back to England or not, but if he did, and assuming he was up to the job, he would be promoted to farm manager. If by then William had succeeded in his ambition to buy the farm, he would leave it to Geoffrey in his will. That was the offer. Henry could take it or leave it.

Henry took it. At what stage he broke the terrible news to his wife we do not know. But we do know that Hannah was distraught. Years later her youngest child, Cyril, would visit my grandfather in England and describe to him their mother's 'awful grief' at having to leave her beloved boy behind.

SOME YEARS BEFORE he died I asked my grandfather who had given the news to him. He maintained a wonderful silence for so long that I thought I had offended him. Then finally he said, so quietly that I could barely hear: 'It was a very long time ago. They all thought they were doing their best.' But he confided in my parents that it was his Uncle William who delivered the *coup de grâce*.

At the time, Granddad later revealed, the shock of being abandoned was total. He said the panic and fear were so intense as he grasped the depths of his betrayal and sacrifice, he could scarcely breathe. Not that he meekly accepted his fate without a fight. That night, after a day spent speechless with shock, he was put to bed by candlelight. Geoffrey waited for the household to fall asleep. As soon as he was certain, he slipped out of bed and dressed. He had formed a plan: he would leave the house and follow the pitch-black lane to the village. Once there he would knock at the first house with lights still burning and ask for directions to Liverpool. He'd start walking and, with luck, hitch a ride on a cart or wagon after daybreak. He could remember the name of the ship and he'd find it somehow and . . . well, his parents would have to take him, wouldn't they?

It was a hopeless plan. It is almost fifty-five miles from Shawbury to Liverpool and he would quickly have become lost, but he was too little and too desperate to understand that. Or to unpick the lock on the stout wooden door at the foot of the stairs which had been thoughtfully turned with a key. A key that was, of course, no longer there.

IT IS DIFFICULT for us today to fully appreciate just how rudimentary and isolated ordinary rural life was as recently as the early decades of the twentieth century.

My grandfather's new home was a brick-built Victorian farmhouse set in fields sloping down to the River Roden, which rolled slowly towards the Severn a few miles downstream. Across the river lay the village, reached by an ancient stone bridge. There was a pub, the Fox and Hounds, which served local ale brewed in the sleepy town of Wem nearby, a village store, the church and some cottages.

There was no electricity or gas supply, and no mains water. One of the first tasks assigned to my grandfather was to 'pump up' first thing each morning, vigorously working the long wooden handle of the well pump behind the farmhouse to fill the waiting jugs and basins.

There was no car, no telephone and no radio. Newspapers were more or less unavailable, unless someone walked or took a cart into Shrewsbury or Wem, and why would anyone want to do that? Work filled each day and bedtime was decreed by the setting of the sun.

Few visitors came to the farm. Geoffrey's new guardians were unmarried and childless, so there were no playmates on hand for him there. How Granddad must have yearned for the sound of his brothers' and sisters' laughter, and the touch of his mother's hand. The double blow to his self-esteem of first being abandoned and then having to accept that he had, in effect, been bargained away, must have been devastating. In one of his rare descriptions of the situation he confided just two succinct words to me. He had been, he said in his usual quiet tones, 'utterly miserable'.

He was not treated like a slave, or a servant. He was, after all, family, and his guardians would be answerable for his upbringing. But he had undoubtedly become something dangerously close to a chattel: a human being who had, effectively, been bought and paid for. His spinster aunt seems to have done her best to welcome, calm and befriend the child who had so suddenly and unexpectedly entered her life. Approaching middle age, Sarah Madeley had long ago given up hope of marriage and bearing children of her own, and now fate had delivered her a son, of sorts. Meanwhile the boy, instantaneously deprived of a mother's love and attention, reached out with both hands for a substitute.

Sarah, I am sure, had no choice but to accept the situation concerning Geoffrey, and tried to help him adjust to his new life. She had no experience of bringing up children, but my grandfather probably gave her a few guidelines based on the things his mother used to do. Back in the never-to-be-regained world of Stanley Road, Hannah had a tradition of making rice pudding every Sunday. It was not long before Sarah was replicating the recipe, and remembering, too, to serve Geoffrey's portion complete with its 'Mary Jane'—the obscurely named skin of browned milk and sugar that always formed on the surface and which was his favourite part.

But neither of her brothers could replace Henry in Geoffrey's affections.

Meanwhile, as 1907 turned into 1908, Granddad had no option but to make the best he could of the hand his father and uncle had dealt him. He went to the church school in Shawbury, where his superior city education elevated him to the top of the class. The headmaster was a Mr Caswell, whose wife also taught there, and their darkly pretty daughter Maudie was in Granddad's class. They quickly became childhood sweethearts, and that, together with friendships with other boys, must have gone some way to easing the burden of his loneliness.

But the greatest soothing influence, then and for the rest of his life, was music. Geoffrey had begun piano lessons in Worcester when he was six and was allowed to continue them in Shawbury. By the age of twelve he was accomplished enough to be invited to play church organ in the neighbouring hamlet of Morton Mill.

Music became my grandfather's lifeline, his salvation. When he was playing, or attending the classical recitals that were one of the mainstays of rural entertainment, he was transported from Kiln Farm and the dull heartache that never seemed to leave him. Long before the age of counselling and therapy, my grandfather took reassurance and comfort from Handel, Beethoven, Chopin and Strauss.

SLOWLY THE SEASONS TURNED, and what remained of my grandfather's childhood gradually unwound with them. Occasionally a letter would arrive from Ontario, where Henry and Hannah had settled with their six remaining children. Geoffrey must have replied to these missives but nothing survives of the correspondence. Meanwhile, he was growing up. He left Shawbury school and was sent to a private school in the nearby village of Astley. William paid the fees—four pounds and ten shillings a term—but not for long. A year later Granddad was deemed to be adequately educated and, more importantly, finally strong enough to begin working full-time on the farm. He was now fourteen years old.

Did William pay him? Up to a point. He was 'all found' with his bed and board, and he told my mother that William allowed him one shilling a week. As Sunday was a day of rest—as far as it could be on a working farm—my grandfather was effectively earning tuppence a day: less than three pounds a year. With an iron will, he denied himself whatever small pleasures such a tiny wage might afford him, and hoarded virtually every penny. He had a picture, which burned bright and sharp in his mind, of a day seven years in his future: the heart-stopping moment when he would walk into a Liverpool shipping office and, with his own money, buy himself a ticket to Canada.

By the time Granddad left school, Kiln Farm had seen its herd of dairy cows swell to a modest seven heads. Butter and milk were sold at the door. Mixed crops were grown and, gradually, the teenager settled into the time-less rhythm of the seasons. He discovered, slightly to his surprise, that he was rather good at farming. In fact, he began to suspect that he might have something of a flair for it. He had his own private ideas on how to increase yield and productivity. He was also good with figures. Arithmetic and maths had been his strong subjects at school and now he was developing a head for business. Perhaps when he eventually got to Canada he would have a set of skills that would be valued there. How proud his mother and father would be of him.

Each spring, the adolescent boy would tick off another birthday on his private, inner calendar. By the time he reached sixteen, on April 8, 1913, his goal at last seemed to be within sight. Five more years before he would be twenty-one and free to rejoin his family abroad. It would be the happiest year, he was certain, of his whole life, the point where everything would come gloriously right at last.

It would be 1918. The final, apocalyptic year of the Great War.

Chapter 2

Like most young men in 1914, my grandfather thought the outbreak of war with Germany was rather exciting. This scrap with the Kaiser had been a long time coming and it was time to get it over with. The Royal Navy and British Army were second to none. Our battleships, and an array of crack regiments, would swiftly carry the day. Everyone said so. The whole thing would be over by Christmas.

Rarely in British history has the national mood been so catastrophically at odds with impending reality. The delusion that the coming conflict would be swift, decisive and glorious pervaded every level of society. Young men—and not-so-young men—were falling over themselves to enlist, if necessary lying about their age and medical condition in order to fight for King and Country.

Life at Shawbury was largely unaffected at first. Geoffrey was seventeen now, and reckoned the whole shooting match would be over long before he got a sniff of the action. But disquieting rumours of unexpected setbacks on what had become known as the Western Front began to filter back. Newspapers—more people in Shawbury seemed to be reading them these days—persisted with their jingoistic, upbeat tone, but word of mouth was spreading as the first wounded began to straggle home.

One morning, long after the harvest and as the winter wheat was being sown, a neighbour called at Kiln Farm, clutching a copy of *The Times*. The man was shaking his head in disbelief as he pointed to a seemingly endless list of British dead and missing. 'It was so long my uncles said it was obviously a mistake,' Granddad recalled. 'It must be a list of the wounded, not those killed in action, and the paper should be ashamed of all the unnecessary grief and suffering it had caused.'

There was no mistake. As 1914 dissolved darkly into 1915, Geoffrey Madeley began to realise, for the second time in his life, that events beyond his control were again shaping his destiny. But this time he would meet fate on his own terms. One fine morning he put on his best suit, walked into Shrewsbury, and enlisted.

HIS FIRST MILITARY SHOCK was an entirely pleasant one. The King's shilling was payable on a daily basis, unlike William's weekly offering, and overnight Geoffrey saw his income increase sevenfold. Eighteen-year-old Private Madeley spent his first night in the army at Shrewsbury barracks, and two days later got his marching orders. Far from being packed off to the slaughterhouse across the Channel, he was posted in the opposite direction, to northeast England. Cavalry was still considered to be a battlefield option and that gave my grandfather, with his experience of horses on the farm, an intermission between the harshness of his life so far and the horrors that would shortly follow.

Sixty-odd years later, when I was working as a television reporter, I filmed a story at beautiful Druridge Bay in County Durham. I mentioned it to Granddad. 'Isn't that near where you were stationed for a while during the first war?'

I can still see the look of delight that spread like sunlight across his face. He told me of golden hours galloping along the seven-mile beach. Service life seemed like a paid holiday. And for the first time he had the companionship and friendship of comrades. Those boys who reminded him of Douglas and John were not blood brothers, but a band of brothers nonetheless. Suddenly, life wasn't so bad.

It couldn't last. Cavalry training was abandoned when the British and

Germans realised horses weren't much use against machine guns. Granddad found himself back on a troop train, this time taking him to the trenches. His train pulled into Crewe Station for its last stop before the embarkation points. As coal and water were taken on, men wrote final letters home; others smoked cigarettes and made attempts at gallows humour. My grandfather stared out of the window at another train.

It was crammed with troops also bound for France. But there was something different about these soldiers, or at least their uniforms. Granddad suddenly realised they were Canadians, sent to help the mother country in her hour of need. He knew from a recent letter from his mother that his two older brothers had joined up back in Toronto. Could they be on board?

Granddad shouldered his way through the packed carriage to the officers' compartment.

'Permission to speak, sir.'

'Carry on.'

'That train across there, sir . . . it's full of Canadians.'

'What of it?'

'My brothers, sir . . . they're serving in a Canadian division. I'd like to cut across and see if they're on board.'

The officers must surely have thought this boy was on a wild-goose chase but permission was granted anyway. My grandfather doubled over to the other platform and climbed onto the Canadian train. He began pushing down the carriages, calling their names.

'Is there a Douglas or a John Madeley on board? Does anyone know a Douglas Madeley or a John Madeley . . .'

He found Douglas and John sitting together in the same carriage.

I don't know how he recognised them. Perhaps he had been sent a recent photograph; perhaps their faces were still discernibly those of the boys who had slipped away from him in the night so many years before. Perhaps another soldier pointed them out.

But it was an electrifying encounter. Geoffrey was looking into the eyes of his dear brothers, faces he had not seen for ten long and lonely years. They stared back, dumbfounded, at their lost brother, who they remembered as a little boy and who was now a strapping young man of twenty in uniform. An incredible coincidence had reunited them as they were all poised to plunge into the whitest heat of war.

It must have seemed like a miracle.

The Madeley brothers knew the chances all three would emerge unscathed from France were slim. But they would have made no mention of that. Their hurried, snatched conversation (how strange Douglas's and John's Canadian accents must have sounded to Geoffrey!) ended with promises to write and, God willing, perhaps meet in France. Then my grandfather had to go. His train was leaving, and he walked back to it in a daze.

He never saw Douglas again. The eldest Madeley boy went into action a few weeks later in the Canadian Corp's assault on Vimy Ridge. He was killed on the first day. John also took part in the battle, but survived.

Douglas Madeley lies somewhere near Vimy Ridge. His name is carved on the Canadian war memorial there. It is all that is left of him.

MY GRANDFATHER was a typical veteran of the Great War in that he rarely spoke about what it was like to be at the centre of the bloodiest conflict in history. But much later, in old age, one or two stories slipped out.

One recalled a ferocious German assault barely held off by his trench, the attackers surging so close to his position that he could see every detail of their faces as they fell to his platoon's frantic rifle fire. Afterwards, my grandfather stared in disbelief at the shreds of skin smoking and peeling from his right hand; the bolt of his Lee Enfield .303 had become almost red-hot during the intense firing.

Then there was the sight of a comrade, one arm cleanly shot off by a burst of machine-gun fire, running in tight circles, screaming, before collapsing in death.

One especially vivid glimpse into hell took place on a warm summer's afternoon when Granddad was sent with a message to the field hospital. When he got there he heard peculiar growling noises coming from behind a tent. Curious, he went to see what it was.

Four or five men were suspended, upside down, from meat hooks clipped to a metal A-frame. They were in the last stages of lockjaw—tetanus—and as their spines arched in the agonising death throes, medics thought some small relief could be found by inverting them.

When I was about fifteen I asked my grandfather if, as a young man barely twenty, he had been afraid of dying. Actually, I didn't. By then I had learned that direct questions about his experiences in the trenches never got a reply; one had to pose them as more thoughtful musings. I said something like, 'I expect a lot of you—especially the younger ones—would have been very shocked and afraid. One minute you were safe in England, the next you were in the lines, fighting for your lives.'

After the long pause that always followed such not-so-subtle attempts to get him to describe his experiences, he answered, 'Well, you see . . . we didn't really talk about all that. No point. I think there was a silly song at the time, "We're here because we're here because we're here." Everyone was in the same boat and you just had to get on with things and do your best . . .'

And beyond this handful of stories and comments, my grandfather's war withdraws itself into a privacy. Except after he had told me about the men dying of tetanus, I asked another question. I can clearly remember the scene: we were standing in a glade in an autumnal Epping Forest, foraging for sweet chestnuts. Finally he spoke: 'Believe me, Richard . . . that was nothing like the worst of it.'

God knows what appalling secrets my grandfather—and millions like him—kept locked inside their heads. Some literally went mad, others withdrew into an interior world for the rest of their lives. Granddad probably saw himself as a survivor. He had lost part of one foot, from a machine-gun burst, and would be permanently deaf in one ear after a shell landed close to his trench. Both wounds were more or less hidden disabilities and with home-made incisions in his shoe leather, he managed to walk without a limp.

But he was twenty-one and at last the master of his own destiny. He now had more than enough money to pay his own way to Canada and rejoin his family. No one and nothing could stop him.

The British Army had other ideas, and sent him to fight the IRA.

IRELAND WAS IN TURMOIL. After the failure of the uprising in 1916, elections two years later saw the establishment of the Dáil Eireann—the first underground Irish Parliament. By the time Geoffrey's troop ship was crossing the Irish Sea, the war of independence was in full flow. It would be another two years before the Anglo-Irish Treaty recognised partition.

The reluctant soldier wanted to be in Ontario, not the Emerald Isle. Granddad chafed at the dreary routine of guard duty and patrol, and constantly badgered his superiors to find out when he would get his discharge papers: later that same year, 1919, he was told.

My grandfather's final assignment for King and Country would be the weekly Church Parade. He wound on his puttees for the last time and marched with the others down the main street of the little town they garrisoned. After morning service they went as usual into the wooden hut next to the church to take tea and cakes, served by the staunchly pro-British local ladies. On this last Sunday, as Granddad said his goodbyes to the smiling women, he suddenly felt deeply uneasy. He couldn't work out what it was, but something was definitely not right.

He went outside, lit a cigarette, and tried to think. Then it came to him. All morning, he realised, ever since leaving barracks, he'd had a sense of being secretly watched. He couldn't explain it and later, as he packed his kit, handed in his rifle and ran to catch the boat train to England, he forgot all about it. He was done with the army and the army was done with him.

Later, my grandfather thought some kind of sixth sense had whispered to him that day. He believed that an IRA reconnaissance unit had probably been keeping them under surveillance and he had been subconsciously aware of it.

A few weeks later, Church Parade was far from routine. The IRA had set up a machine gun in the hedge opposite the church and delivered their savage rebuke to the hated occupiers. If my grandfather had spent many more days in the army, they would probably have been his last on earth.

GEOFFREY SETTLED his affairs in Shawbury and in September 1919, nearly eighteen months behind schedule thanks to a combination of the Kaiser and the IRA, he finally boarded a ship bound for Canada. He was, he realised, sailing across a wide ocean towards a deeply uncertain future. There had been very little communication with his parents in the years after they left, although they had written to let him know that his eldest brother had been killed in France.

Henry and his family had put down roots in the little town of St Thomas, close to the shores of Lake Erie and at the heart of the Great Lakes Peninsula. This was tobacco-growing country, surprisingly hot and humid in summer, but true to the stereotypical image of Canada in winter when thick snow blanketed the ground for months.

Granddad must have written to let them know he was coming, or perhaps sent a telegram. A series of trains and buses brought him to St Thomas and the address his family had been living at for the last few years. He stood stock-still outside the simple frame-built house on a quiet street and stared at the front door. Finally he stepped forward and knocked.

A pause. Then steps approaching from the other side; a woman's tread. The handle rattling and turning; the door swinging open.

Geoffrey looked into the eyes of a middle-aged woman.

His mother's eyes.

She stared at him and slowly shook her head. 'Oh . . . I'm so sorry, I never buy anything at the door.' She closed it in his face.

The last exchange of photographs across the Atlantic had obviously failed to imprint my grandfather's mature features on his mother's memory. In her mind's eye she still saw him as the little boy she had last seen twelve years earlier.

Geoffrey had sometimes wondered if he would recognise his parents when he saw them again. It never crossed his mind that they might not recognise him. None of his fantasies about this moment had included this scenario. Eventually, he knocked again.

Now the woman looked annoyed. He spoke quickly, before she could send him away a second time.

'It's me, Mother. I'm your son. I'm Geoffrey.'

Slowly, Hannah saw the man standing on her doorstep as the boy she once knew. Her eyes widened and she put her hands to her mouth.

'Mother . . . are you all r—'

'Geoffrey . . . oh, *Geoffrey*!'

Her child had crossed the years, a war and an ocean to come home to her. He had come home to her.

MY GRANDFATHER moved in with his family that same afternoon. The coming days were utterly, blissfully happy. He was 'home'. But, unlike the return of the prodigal son, this was the homecoming of a young man to the prodigal parents. Forgiveness could only flow one way—from him to them.

What mature, unbounded forgiveness it was! Henry and Hannah must have been profoundly grateful (and secretly not a little relieved) to find the boy they left behind so apparently free of anger. Geoffrey had every right to ask about what had been done to him and why, but he had not made his journey to deliver judgment or apportion blame. Long ago he had decided to try to understand his father's great dilemma of 1907. It would be pointless now to condemn Henry's solution to it; Geoffrey's betrayal could never be undone. But it could be healed.

And it was. Despite the passing of the years, the Madeleys were still a relatively young family. The death of Douglas at twenty-five on Vimy Ridge left Henry and Hannah with six children; five siblings for Geoffrey to get to know again. Baby Cyril was now twelve; Katherine was fifteen, William seventeen, Doris twenty, and John, the surviving eldest, twenty-five. They welcomed my grandfather back with open arms and open hearts.

Granddad spent his first months in Canada earning dollars to go travelling. He picked up some casual labour on the tobacco farms and in local factories, and stayed with his parents and siblings. There was a lot of catching up to do. By the late summer of 1920 the long-severed connection with his family was almost fully restored. He felt confident and relaxed enough to tell them that he was heading off for a while.

The harvest season had arrived. Geoffrey began by fruit-picking on Ontario's farms, then crossed into Manitoba to help bring in the wheat. He did the same in the great dust bowl of Saskatchewan—Canada's Kansas— and by winter he had reached Calgary and the foothills of the Rockies.

At some point along the way, he met The Girl. Of all the figures in my grandfather's past, it is she who remains the most elusive, and yet she would have a profound bearing on the rest of his life.

Who was she? My father knew only that she was the first woman his father fell in love with, that Geoffrey asked her to marry him, and that she had said 'yes'. But he would lose The Girl as surely as he had lost his family years before—only this time, for good. Why?

Because Geoffrey went back to Kiln Farm.

Chapter 3

Before Geoffrey sailed for Quebec, his uncle had extracted an agreement from him. William was on the point of buying the farm from the Charleton Estate, which was being broken up. He persuaded his nephew to promise to return after a year or so, and become farm manager. It seems an odd, even unnecessary commitment for Geoffrey to have made. But I suppose he would have been feeling insecure about his reception in St Thomas, and had no idea if the new life in Canada would suit him.

Now, happier than at any time in his life and deeply in love, he must have been kicking himself. Because his girlfriend had agreed to marry him on one condition—they must live in Canada. The Girl came from a large and close family. She knew that transplanting to England would almost certainly mean she would never see her parents or brothers and sisters again.

What was he to do?

We can be reasonably certain that Geoffrey wrote to William and explained how the land lay. He knew he had made a promise and if necessary he would keep his word, but . . . surely William could understand.

William's response was swift and calculated. Now, unlike the verbal agreement he had made with Henry back in 1907, the ageing farmer made a commitment to my grandfather in writing: *Come back now*, Geoffrey read, *and you'll inherit the lot when I die. Every brick, field and head of cattle. It's all here, waiting for you. Just come back. And, yes—you did give me your word that you would do so.*

Quite why William was so determined to bring Granddad back to Kiln Farm, I have never really understood. There must have been other candidates to run the business. I think it was a deep-rooted sense of posssessiveness. For years he had virtually owned the boy, a near-chattel that he had paid good money for. So, he thought he could fly the coop, did he? Well, William would see about that.

Oddly enough, William's offer to leave Kiln Farm lock, stock and barrel to Geoffrey didn't weigh particularly heavy in my grandfather's decision to return to Shropshire. He would have come back anyway. He was, he explained to my mother years later, a man of his word. If William wouldn't release him from it, he had no choice in the matter.

Many would now laugh at such old-fashioned morality. But back then, the imperative was sufficiently strong for Geoffrey to do something that, in our sentimental, romantic age, we would consider unthinkable. He gave up the love of his life. Not that he didn't try to persuade The Girl to come with him; not that she didn't try to convince him to stay. But it was no use. Steel hawsers of convention, duty and circumstance dragged them apart.

A few weeks after receiving his uncle's letter, Geoffrey found himself on a ship headed back to England. His brokenhearted fiancée had released him from his promise; his anguished parents had said their bewildered goodbyes and, as he watched the icebergs drift past the liner as it steamed east from the mouth of the St Lawrence, he knew that, once again, William had succeeded in parting him from the ones he loved.

GRANDDAD ARRIVED BACK at Shawbury as a young man in his mid-twenties. He had seen more pain, loss and heartbreak than many experience in a lifetime. Perhaps it was for the best that he had come back to the farm. Land was land. Land couldn't betray you or leave you. And he would inherit these acres one day. They would be undisputedly his, for ever. No one could take that away from him.

So Geoffrey, in self-protection, began to shut down emotionally. It was a spontaneous, subconscious reaction to one heartbreak too many. His soul had been bruised too often. Back at Kiln Farm, he slipped quickly into a familiar routine. Sarah was overjoyed to see him; she had greatly missed her nephew. William was William, and got on with the business of handing over the day-to-day running of the farm.

Geoffrey felt increasingly that his adventures in Canada were taking on a dreamlike quality. Had he really been engaged to be married? The Girl wasn't answering his letters. Sometimes he found himself wondering if she had ever existed. Shawbury, with its familiar reality, was quietly reclaiming him from the New World and delivering him back to the Old.

To his surprise, he found he wasn't willing to fight the process. Perhaps the numbing of his emotions would turn out to be a positive, an unlooked-for anaesthetic for a bruised heart. And meanwhile there was the soothing balm of his music. He began playing piano again at local recitals, and one evening was asked to accompany a young woman with a light, pleasant voice. She was a couple of years younger than him, and pretty, with soft, dreamy eyes and a creamy complexion. Her name was Kate Edwards, although, she confided in Geoffrey, everyone called her Kitty. She lived on her parents' farm a few miles from Shawbury—close enough for the two of them to meet again.

After a brief courtship Geoffrey found himself engaged for a second time. Kate's parents had three daughters, part of a cursed generation of women. The slaughter of 1914–18 had decimated the young male population, so when Kate Edwards became Kate Madeley, the gathered wedding guests could practically hear the collective sigh of relief from the bride's side of the little country church. Not only was she safely off the shelf, she was marrying one of the catches of the county, a young man who was well travelled, musically accomplished, only lightly scarred by war—externally, at any rate—and with excellent prospects.

He was also undeniably attractive. Geoffrey was lean and stood over six foot tall. Intelligent eyes looked out of a well-proportioned face. Perhaps there was something a little distant about those eyes, but they could also twinkle with humour. For most of the year he was lightly tanned from working outdoors, and he had large, sensitive hands. Kitty used to love to watch them as they moved smoothly and confidently over a piano keyboard.

Yet the marriage soon ran into trouble. It is difficult to be precise about the reasons, but there was tension in the farmhouse from the start. Sarah was accustomed to running the place for the men; my grandmother Kitty's arrival transformed this simple arrangement into a knotty equation. As Geoffrey's new wife, she would have expected to assume control over domestic matters, but where did that leave Sarah? The atmosphere became charged and volatile. Kitty—spirited, feisty, with a strong sense of her own worth—decided she'd had enough.

One morning, after a spectacular row with her husband over some household matter, a heavily pregnant Kitty walked out. My grandfather's marriage seemed over when it had barely begun.

Kitty's journey home passed into family legend. I have an image of her: she is striding across pastures and meadows, tearful but determined. I can see her as she clambers over stiles and fences, clutching her swollen belly, startling the cows grazing on the lush Shropshire grass. They lift their heads to stare at the young woman as she passes through them like a weeping apparition.

At last, an exhausted Kitty reaches her parents' farm and sweeps into her mother's kitchen, telling her tale through heaving sobs.

'I've left him, Mother! I've left him! I cannot bear it any longer . . . I have left Geoffrey and I am never going back.'

But if Kitty had expected a sympathetic welcome, she was in for a shock. Her mother heard her out, and then delivered an iron verdict to her sniffling daughter. This merciless lecture on the facts of life was, my grandmother wryly recalled, like having a bucket of cold water poured over her head. She told me the whole story one summer's evening as she and I moved a huge pile of logs from the farmyard into a barn.

Firstly, Kitty was crisply informed, there was the minor matter of her wedding vows—promises made before God. Eighty years ago, Christian doctrine was the powerful glue that bonded society together. My great-grandmother would have been appalled by her daughter's defiance before God, and perhaps even a little frightened by it. And Kitty was pregnant. This was the worst possible time to cast aside the protection of a husband. Even if she did insist on divorce—which was out of the question, by the way—what man would want a woman with another man's child?

No, Kitty was told, you must go back and make your peace with Geoffrey. It's your duty—to him and to God.

So she went.

Marriages displaying early cracks can be split apart by the birth of a baby. But in my grandparents' case the arrival of their first son, James, in

1924, seems to have brought them close again, for the time being at least. Theirs would always be a somewhat volatile marriage. My father once said it mirrored the seasons, sometimes sunny, sometimes icy.

Certainly Kitty now had a clearly defined role, as the first new mother Kiln Farm had seen in many years.

The focus of daily life must have shifted seismically. The farmhouse had long felt a sterile place—strange, considering it was the hub of a cycle of life that revolved with its fields and cowsheds and stables. But now it had a nursery, and a purpose and a point beyond mere business.

Geoffrey, staring at himself in his shaving mirror the day after his firstborn had been safely delivered, must have considered the question all men do on such momentous mornings.

What sort of a father would he make?

It was a difficult one. His own father had been on another continent for much of Geoffrey's childhood and William had hardly been an ideal replacement role model. Although my grandfather was fully reconciled with Henry, theirs was a relationship between adults. He really had no examples to follow.

Oh, well. He would just have to do his best.

Granddad was twenty-seven when James was born. He was just shy of thirty when a second son, John, arrived. Perhaps the vivid reality of fatherhood, with two lively little boys running around the farm, was reassuring; Geoffrey saw that life could offer more than forced goodbyes and sudden partings.

John was a bright, inquisitive boy. Before he was three, he became fascinated by the weekly ritual of paying the farm hands their wages. The night before payday the little boy insisted on polishing the copper pennies and silver sixpences, shillings and florins. Only then was his father allowed to count them out in gleaming towers on the kitchen table. To the child, they looked like piles of treasure.

One gusty, chilly morning in early spring, John and James were sent to play in the orchard that stood behind the house. A dry, cold wind flowed down from the Welsh hills on the horizon, but John had removed his coat as he ran around in the deceptive sunshine. Later, he began to shiver and complained of a headache. He was put to bed and remained there the following day, suffering from a 'chill'. By evening he was running a high temperature and starting to breathe strangely. The doctor was called; the Madeleys' second son was diagnosed with pneumonia, and William and Kitty were advised to prop the child up on pillows during the night to help drain fluid from John's chest.

The next day, he died. He was four years old.

CHILD MORTALITY was common right up to the Second World War, when the increasingly widespread availability of antibiotics and mass immunisation changed things. But John's illness was so abrupt, so casual in its easy, invisible arrival and swift, pitiless departure that my grandparents could scarcely comprehend what had happened. The shock stayed with them for the rest of their lives. Decades later, when my sister and I were driven on visits to Shawbury with our parents, the last mile of the journey was always accompanied by the same solemn instructions.

'Don't talk with your mouths full. Comb your hair before coming down to breakfast. And don't mention John.'

There were no photographs of him to be seen anywhere in the house; it was almost as if he had never been. Only once did I catch a glimpse of him. My grandmother kept an ancient wooden-bound chest in the farm's living room, full of the bric-a-brac of half a century.

I was fascinated by this trunk and one afternoon, when rain fell from the sky in pounding torrents, my grandmother gave me permission to rummage through it. I was about nine years old.

Once I had excavated the disappointing top layer of old women's magazines, knitting patterns and yellowing bills for obscure farm machinery, things got interesting. The barrel and lock of a rusting .410 shotgun—no stock—and a mouldering gun-cleaning kit that smelt of crushed walnuts. Clanking mole traps, all springs and chains and sharp snapping jaws. A medium-sized cannonball with the faded label: 'Moreton Corbett—Civil War'. And finally, right at the bottom, hidden by a faded embroidered cushion, a little glass jar with a brass top. It might have once contained perfume or face cream, but as I held it up to the rain-streamed window I could see it was filled with tiny balls of silver and gold paper: the kind of foil that used to line cigarette packets. There were dozens of them, and I poured a few out. What could they mean?

Suddenly a hand fell on my shoulder and I yelped with shock, scattering the little balls over the floor. My grandmother bent down and picked them up wordlessly, dropping them carefully back into the jar and gently screwing the lid back on. When she'd finished, she looked at me.

'They were John's,' she said simply. 'His money. He was too little when he . . . well, he was too little to have real money, you see, so he made his own.' She gestured. 'The gold ones were pennies and the silver ones were shillings. When his father paid the men their wages, John used to pretend to do the same with these.'

The next day, helping my grandfather move sacks of grain, I asked him with the directness of childhood, 'What happened to John, Granddad?'

He stood quite still for a few moments and then slowly sat down on one of the dusty bags. He lit a cigarette, considered it, and then he began to tell me about that March day in the orchard, two brothers running between the trees, and Death beckoning one of them. When he'd finished, he said he'd stack the rest of the bags by himself. I never asked about John again.

John's death was, I believe, the psychological tipping point for my grandfather. Since the age of ten he had done his best to deal with the worst fate and circumstances could do to him. He had been determined, tenacious and, on occasion, magnificently, heroically, non-judgmental. A tough self-reliance had seen him through tests and challenges that would have brought other men to their knees.

But this . . . this was too much. This wasn't fair. Yet again, someone he loved had been snatched from him. Would this be the way of it to the end of his days? Loving and losing, loving and losing, over and over again?

Geoffrey had wondered what sort of a father he would make. After John's death, my grandfather quietly withdrew into an emotional fortress. The drawbridge was raised. Life would go on, but Geoffrey would not have his heart broken again. For the time being, he had placed it beyond reach.

Chapter 4

John died when my father was still a baby. Just over a year earlier, on May 2, 1928, the village midwife had delivered the Madeleys' third son in the front room of a crooked half-timbered cottage next to Shawbury's church. The village and countryside around it had barely changed from the day Geoffrey had arrived there, twenty-one years before.

It was still a quiet rural backwater. A few more families owned cars but many did not. By no means all farms and cottages had electricity, and oil lamps and candles could still be seen glowing through windows after dark. Something of the nineteenth century lingered about the place.

But appearances were deceptive. Christopher Holt Madeley arrived in a world trembling on the brink of enormous change. In 1928, America issued its first television licences, and radio stations began transmitting pictures along with sound. Meanwhile ordinary US citizens had discovered the stock market and were making paper fortunes.

The month after my father was born, Amelia Earhart became the first woman to fly across the Atlantic. By September ,Alexander Fleming had stumbled upon penicillin. Mass entertainment was revolutionised with the arrival of the talkies and at a place called Berchtesgaden in the Bavarian mountains, Adolf Hitler was busy dictating the second volume of *Mein Kampf* to Rudolf Hess.

A few months later, Wall Street crashed.

BY THE TIME CHRISTOPHER was four, the Great Depression had the world by the throat and Kiln Farm teetered on the brink of foreclosure. Money was so tight that all luxuries and fripperies—not that these had ever featured particularly prominently—were eliminated. But one small weekly treat for my father survived. Denied sweets or pocket money, he nevertheless received, every Sunday, a small chocolate-covered biscuit wrapped in silver paper. His mother bought it on Saturdays at the village shop and it stood in solitary splendour on the kitchen dresser until after lunch the next day, when it was solemnly handed to the little boy.

My father loved these biscuits, but after a while felt that supply was simply not keeping up with demand. He decided that with a little sacrifice, foresight and patience, he could improve matters considerably. He had watched his mother picking fruits from her orchard, and sowing seeds in her vegetable garden. Why not plant a chocolate-biscuit tree?

That Sunday he denied himself his treat and took it to a quiet corner of the orchard. He scraped a small hole and crumbled the biscuit into it. Earth was brushed back over the top, and my father retired to await developments.

Every morning he ran to see if the first shoots were pushing up; each day brought disappointment. By the following Sunday he was torn; should he eat his next biscuit or plant it again? After lunch, he decided to ask his mother for advice.

Dad later told me that the reaction his innocent enquiry provoked was the first great shock of his life. Not his mother's response—Kitty listened carefully to her son's dilemma and then dissolved into helpless laughter. But Geoffrey, sitting in an armchair behind his Sunday paper, began to tremble with rage.

He rose and took a cane from a cupboard. Face dark with anger, he accused his son of 'wicked waste' and drew him into the parlour for a measured beating. The punishment lasted for at least a minute and my father would say it was at this precise point in his life that any nascent desire to sow crops was comprehensively extinguished.

It was the first time Geoffrey had thrashed his youngest son, and it would not be the last. The beatings continued until that delicate moment of balance was reached|: the point where a boy realises he has grown powerful enough to consider the merits of striking back.

THE DARK GODS OF corporal punishment are complex and mysterious. It is tempting to assume that Geoffrey's extraordinarily violent response to a tiny infraction had its roots in his own childhood. There must have been a great deal of buried anger in him. He had worked so hard to rationalise everyone's behaviour and forgive it; and there had to have been a price to pay for that. Certainly my father thought so. Although like many men of his generation Dad shied away from over-analysing anyone's behaviour— including his own—he knew cause and effect when he saw it.

As he grew older and learned more about his father's fractured journey to manhood, my father was able, to some extent, to forgive Geoffrey's dramatic swings from emotional *froideur* to hot-blooded rage. If he concluded that his father was unconsciously lashing out against his own childhood experiences, he kept that to himself.

But these almost ritualised punishments—the sacred stick broadcasting its mute warning from corner or cupboard; the appointed place of execution (always the parlour where the best furniture was)—were not peculiar to Kiln Farm. Most parents still imposed discipline on their children according to the Victorian mantra of 'spare the rod and spoil the child'. Fathers— and mothers too—cheerfully wielded straps, canes, belts, rulers and shoes on their erring sons and daughters and would have been astounded to be told they were child-abusers.

GEOFFREY'S EXPLOSIVE REACTION to a wasted biscuit should, in fairness, be placed in the context of the Depression. He was under ferocious financial pressure; neighbouring farms were going to the wall and Kiln Farm could be next. He had built his herd up to fifty head of cows with an impressive daily milk yield but local dairies were going under too and frequently there was no one to collect the brimming churns. Granddad would wait as long as he could and then, in defeat, pour hundreds of gallons of perfectly good milk straight down the drains. My father and his older brother stood with the farm hands, watching in silence as the creamy white torrent frothed and gurgled away. It was heartbreaking.

The Depression forced Geoffrey to postpone plans to buy Kiln Farm's first tractor, so huge horses still hauled the ploughs, harrows and seed machines. This was a job my father loved to help with, and he struck up a great friendship with the biggest beast of the lot, a magnificent black-maned giant called Captain.

Captain was devoted to my father. At the end of the working day he would whinny loudly for him from his stable and only settle down after the boy had come to say good night. Once he escaped from a carelessly locked stable door and trotted up to the drawing-room window. Christopher was practising his scales on his father's highly prized baby grand (bought sec-ondhand before the Depression and one of Kiln Farm's few luxuries). There was a crunch and tinkling of glass, and he looked up to see Captain's great head pushing into the room like the figurehead on the prow of a ship, nostrils flared, teeth bared, lips curled back in a sloppy, happy grin of greeting.

Other animals were less friendly. When Christopher was about four years old, he went to pet Rex, the farm dog. It was a hot day and the big black Labrador was sleeping in his kennel (there was no question of dogs being allowed in the house). Rex was startled when the little boy's hand suddenly materialised through the doorway. He flew out and clamped his jaws on my father's face.

There was pandemonium as farm hands rushed to pull the dog off. When they managed to free my father, the damage looked bad. He was bleeding from both eyes and screaming that he couldn't see.

The village doctor quickly established that it was simply blood that had temporarily blinded the child, and dressed and disinfected the deep bites around my father's eyes. But the attack left lasting damage to his sight. Almost as soon as the wounds had healed, he complained of headaches and not being able to 'see proper'. An optician in Shrewsbury diagnosed astig-matism. It seems likely that the bites had disturbed the shape of the surface of both eyes, and my father had to wear glasses for the rest of his days.

As my father grew up he often struggled to be happy. He had the companionship of James, of course, but his brother was four years older and had his own interests and circle of friends. He also seemed to have, my father thought, an easier and more open relationship with their father. James, a talented farmer, was destined to run Kiln Farm in years to come.

Christopher loved his parents and assumed they loved him, but as he got older it was hard to be sure. There was a near-total absence of demonstrative affection. Kitty was more outgoing than her husband in this regard, but not by much. My father told me he always felt his relationship with his mother was characterised by formality.

But Kitty was an earth mother compared with what, by now, was Geoffrey's almost complete emotional withdrawal. As a small boy, my father gradually became aware that his friends' fathers were different from his own. He would see them ruffling their sons' hair, swinging them in the air, playing games with them, tickling them, even kissing them—but nothing remotely like that had ever happened to him. It confused him. Once he was playing at a friend's house when the boy's father returned from a short business trip. His son rushed out into the lane—'Daddy-Daddy-Daddy!'— to be swept up in a bear hug.

My father walked home thoughtfully, and made a plan.

A short time later, Geoffrey had to spend a night or two on business in Shrewsbury. On the evening of his return his youngest son waited patiently by the wooden garden gate that opened into the lane. It was almost dark when the tall figure finally emerged from the gathering dusk, smartly suited and wearing his best trilby.

My father took a deep breath and ran down the road towards him, waving and shouting. But when father and son reached each other, a terrible awkwardness descended. After a few moments, the little boy resolutely stepped forward and hugged his father's knees. There was absolutely no response. Finally he let go and stared down, utterly defeated, at Geoffrey's shiny town shoes. There was a long moment. Perhaps my grandfather felt chastened by the sight of the forlorn child before him, because he suddenly knelt down and put one arm stiffly around his son's shoulder for a brief moment. Then he stood up and walked on.

That was it. The first and last occasion in my father's childhood when his father made the slightest gesture of physical affection towards him. Dad never forgot it. Until the day he died he could remember every detail of the moment: the 'pinking' of the blackbirds roosting in the dim hedgerow, the evening star beginning to shimmer in the darkening sky, the smell of his father's tobacco pouch.

When my father first told me this story I felt almost guilty. I was about nine or ten and I felt guilty because it was clear to me—and to him—that my own relationship with my grandfather was much better than my father's had been.

GRANDDAD AND I were pals, mates. He did what endears any adult to a child: he took an interest in me. He also treated me as an equal. He taught me how to play draughts and sometimes I would beat him. He didn't mind.

I loved him and always looked forward to our visits to Shawbury. My grandmother was perhaps a little distant with me in my earlier years; she doted on my sister, probably because Kitty had never had a daughter. But when I stopped being an irritating little boy (she didn't call me Richard: I was always 'Wretched') Kitty and I grew close, too.

I think my father took vicarious pleasure from all this. I also believe I was a kind of surrogate son for Geoffrey, in the narrow sense that he could demonstrate the affection to me that had been locked away inside him for all those years. When he ruffled my hair or kissed me in greeting or farewell, he was also doing it, belatedly, to my father.

Even so, they never managed any more than a handshake.

There can be no doubt that we children, and our cousins, James's son and daughter, helped to defrost the atmosphere at Kiln Farm. I remember happy family parties there, my father and grandfather laughing delightedly together, or falling into a deep discussion about their shared love of classical music.

But if Geoffrey was unable to demonstrate love, he was nevertheless a good provider for his family. By the mid-1930s he had steered the farm through the worst of the Depression. The atmosphere at Kiln Farm became more optimistic and, perhaps best of all, he and Kitty had the place to themselves and their children. At some stage Sarah and her brothers had moved to a cottage of their own nearby, to give the growing family more room. My grandmother was mistress of her own house at last.

Up to a point.

Sarah still kept a protective, almost maternal eye on Geoffrey and made regular visits to Kiln Farm to check that Kitty wasn't frittering away her husband's money.

William was now an old man, and in failing health. He still took a close interest in the business, but appeared satisfied with his nephew's running of the farm. So he should have been. By 1936 Geoffrey had continued to build up his herd of prime dairy cattle. Profits were good. The Madeley acres had never been so productive; Geoffrey thought that William must be proud of what he was achieving.

He couldn't have been more wrong. Just a week after his last meeting with William, the old uncle died.

The will was read.

William hadn't left Geoffrey a thing.

MY GRANDFATHER was dizzy with shock. What had he done to deserve this second great betrayal in his life? There had been no argument with his uncle, no rift. Geoffrey racked his brains, trying to remember if there had been some hint of the catastrophe that was about to explode in his face. He could think of none.

He faced ruin. All those years of grinding labour—for nothing. A brave new life and a great love in Canada rejected—for nothing. His word of honour put above the yearning of his heart—for nothing. Not since he was ten years old had Geoffrey felt so confused and cast aside.

William had not left Kiln Farm to his sister. That would have almost certainly undermined his extraordinary decision to disinherit Geoffrey; at the very least, in due course Sarah would have left the farm to her nephew in her own will. Cleverly, thoughtfully, and with a kind of wicked capriciousness, the will divided Kiln Farm into equal parts. And bequeathed them to each of Geoffrey's siblings in Canada.

Every brick, field and head of cattle. Just come back . . . you did give me your word . . .

William's treachery was grotesque. In his confusion, Geoffrey could only think, wildly, that his success in running the farm had made his uncle jealous. I think my grandfather was wrong. I am convinced that William's perfidy sprang out of a terrible obsession with control. As I have said, I don't think he ever really ceased to regard my grandfather as his personal possession, a pawn on the chessboard he could move at his pleasure or sacrifice at his whim. Leaving Kiln Farm to my grandfather would have been a poor endgame for William; it would be a final, irrevocable transfer of control from him to his chattel. And William just couldn't do it. He just couldn't bear to release the boy from his power.

So he did the next best thing. He transferred it to others.

THE FIRST THING Sarah did when she heard the news was to hire a lawyer. The will had to be challenged, she said. It was monstrous. Right was right, and her brother had done a dreadful thing. Granddad wasn't hopeful, and the lawyer swiftly confirmed that the will was legally watertight. Now the focus switched to Canada. Geoffrey looked west, and waited.

Opinion about what to do was divided amongst the Madeleys in Canada. Some siblings wanted to sell their share of Kiln Farm at once; others were conscious of the moral dilemma with which they had been presented.

This latter group pointed out that the prosperous farm they had been jointly bequeathed was only a going concern because of their brother's sacrifice and hard work. The opposing forces countered that Uncle William's last will and testament should be respected. Legally the place was now theirs, and they had their own growing families to consider.

According to my parents, it was Geoffrey's youngest sister, Katherine, who banged heads together at a crisis meeting. There was to be no more talk of anyone selling off their parcel of Kiln Farm on the open market. She would never speak again to anyone who did such a thing. They were entitled to their inheritances, but only up to a point, and certainly not at the price of their brother's happiness and security. They owed him everything.

Katherine prevailed. Back in England, Sarah paid for a lawyer to draw up contracts allowing Geoffrey to buy back Kiln Farm from his brothers and sisters. Under its terms, he took ownership of Kiln Farm in 1937 although the deeds were, for some reason, retained by Sarah. They were finally passed to him on her death fourteen years later, in 1951.

I have often wondered how he managed to regard the 'buy back' agreement with such apparent equanimity. He had forgiven his parents for abandoning him; now he forgave his siblings for presenting him with a bill for what was rightfully his.

Why? Because I think my grandfather had grasped one of the most fundamental truths of human experience: the extraordinary healing power of forgiveness. Geoffrey had been sundered from his family once; he had no intention of allowing it to happen a second time. So he made the necessary sacrifices and accommodations.

GEOFFREY, KITTY, James and Christopher huddled round their wireless set one Sunday morning in September 1939 and listened to Chamberlain's weary voice telling them they were at war.

Kitty wasn't greatly disturbed by the Prime Minister's announcement, although she thought the poor man sounded very tired. But she knew her eldest son couldn't be called up for at least a couple of years, and Christopher four years after that. Her husband was already too old at forty-two. The Madeley men should be safe this time and, anyway, the thing was bound to be over soon. France had a huge army and we had a navy. There was an RAF aerodrome at Shawbury now and Kitty had been summoned outside by her sons to see the new fighter planes being put through their paces high in the skies above the Shropshire Plain.

To begin with, it seemed Kitty's optimism was justified. For months, nothing much happened. Perhaps Hitler's bluff had been called. Some people said an honourable truce should be announced and everyone could just go home.

May arrived. Dad woke one morning to hear his father coming back into the house from the dawn milking. There were the usual start-of-the-day noises—the fireplace being raked out from the night before; pots and pans banging on the kitchen range. Suddenly everything went quiet. Then, his father's voice bellowing from the foot of the stairs: 'Come down, everyone, now! It's on the wireless! It's started!'

German soldiers had swept into the Low Countries at dawn. The fight was on.

The phoney war hadn't just ended; it was being blasted into oblivion by events that followed each other with dizzying speed. Within a few weeks Belgium had capitulated, France had fallen and the British were fighting a desperate rearguard action in the Pas de Calais so its army could escape across the Channel. Dunkirk was a catastrophe and a deliverance. But with most of its battered army's equipment left behind, many wondered if Britain would fare any better than France if Germany invaded.

My grandfather and his neighbours working other farms in Shropshire and in the Welsh Marches met in secret soon after the fall of France. This was before the formation of the LDV—the Local Defence Volunteers, which would later become the Home Guard—and most of these men had served on the Western Front a quarter of a century before. They had a fair idea of what living in enemy-occupied territory would be like.

THE GERMANS DIDN'T INVADE but they visited Shawbury nevertheless. By the time Christopher entered his teens, the Blitz had begun. Manchester and Liverpool lay roughly sixty miles north, and the village was almost directly under the Luftwaffe bombers' flight path. The air raids went on night after night, and people would go outside to listen to the great flying armadas rumbling their way to their targets.

The sound of bombs pulverising the big industrial cities to the north rarely carried as far as Shawbury but the vibrations did. My father always knew when the attacks had started because the heavy balls on his brass bedstead would start to judder and jangle in sympathy with the colossal explosions more than fifty miles away.

One winter night in 1942, Liverpool was that night's target and the bombing had begun earlier than usual. The familiar vibrations had been making the house tremble for about an hour when they were overlaid by something else—the drone of an approaching plane. The steady rise and fall of its engines marked it as a German bomber.

The Madeleys were having their evening meal. Conversation came to an abrupt halt and everyone lifted their eyes to the ceiling.

'What the devil does he want here?'

Kitty stared at her husband. 'Perhaps the aerodrome, Geoffrey?'

'Maybe. He'll have a job finding it—it's cloudy and there isn't a moon.'

By now the plane had throttled back its engines and dropped down closer to the village. It began circling patiently, flying round and round as it sought its target. My grandfather, still staring at the ceiling, said, 'His navigator must be trying to work out where the airfield is by dead reckoning. He can't possibly see it in the blackout.'

At last the pilot seemed to give up. His engine revs increased and the plane began to fly away to the south, its mournful droning gradually fading.

'Thank God,' my grandmother said, 'he's leaving.'

'Or lining up for his bombing run,' came her husband's reply.

He was right. The engine noise suddenly increased again. This time there was no tentative circling—the plane was coming in fast and low.

'Everyone to the arches!'

These were a row of thick, red-brick arches set low in a kind of demi-cellar at the back of the house. I have no idea what they were originally for but that night they were tiny, one-man air-raid shelters.

Within seconds the first bomb began to fall with a tearing, rushing sound. There was an enormous crash somewhere near and then the sound of another bomb, which seemed to be falling through the air even closer than the first. It landed barely a hundred yards to the southwest in the field next to the farm. The explosion shook the entire building to its foundations and the crouching family felt the percussive wave punch through them. Another bomb exploded further away, the plane roared back up into the sky, and the attack was over.

The Luftwaffe pilot missed the RAF base, but his stick of bombs had neatly bracketed Kiln Farm. There was no damage to anyone or anything and, once this had been established, Shawbury was rather proud of itself. My father said it was one of the most exciting nights of his life and my grandfather was always happy to tell the tale, complete with sound effects.

The crater caused by the closest bomb is still there but not as apparent as when I was a child. I used to make my grandfather take me to it and insist he go over every thrilling detail of that night. Once I told him I wished I'd been there when it happened. He gave me a long look.

'How odd to want to be blown up . . .'

The bombing of Kiln Farm marked the end of the first major chapter of my father's life. A new phase was about to begin.

His father was going to drop a bombshell of his own.

Chapter 5

By the time he was fifteen, Chris, as he now preferred to be called, had given up any hope of forging closeness with his father. If his relationship with Kitty had been characterised by cool formality—something that was slowly thawing as he got older—that with Geoffrey remained deep in permafrost. There was simply no reaching the man and Chris had stopped trying.

There were points of contact, however. My grandfather had an extensive collection of 78s—scratchy recordings of some of the world's best orchestras and opera singers. He retired into the parlour most evenings to listen to them and Chris would often creep in and join him. There was no need for conversation; the dialogue was provided by the great composers.

Chris and his father enjoyed discussing politics and the course of the war, which had been going atrociously. After the fall of France, the British suffered setback after setback. Few would admit it aloud, but by 1942 it appeared extremely likely that the German/Japanese axis was going to win the war. America's entry after Pearl Harbor changed everything. By 1943 the tide had turned; shipping losses were down, North Africa was retaken, and the Russians launched sweeping counterattacks against the Wehrmacht. Now the talk was of a different invasion—that of Nazi-occupied Europe by the Allies.

Throughout these changing fortunes of war, Chris had been educated at Wem Grammar School, an establishment in a quintessential small country town. By 1943 he was in the fifth form and was enjoying himself there. He'd started going out with girls, to the cinema in Shrewsbury mostly, and had a relaxed approach to the looming School Certificate exams and his studies in general. He began staying out for longer and coming home later. One of Geoffrey's farmer friends saw the lad smoking a Woodbine in the Fox and Hounds, his arm round a girl.

His parents decided he was going off the rails. Something had to be done. Geoffrey and Kitty went to see a local clergyman to discuss their 'wayward' youngest. The man had connections with a minor public school known for its old-fashioned approach to discipline. It was miles distant, tucked away in a remote corner of rural Staffordshire. Would the Reverend find their boy a place there?

At first the clergyman was uneasy. He told them that, at fifteen, their son would find it extremely difficult to adapt to the rigours of life in an English public school. Most boys at such establishments had been sent away from home when they were quite small, to prep schools. They had become accustomed to long separations from their families and knew how to navigate the closed, claustrophobic, arcane world of a boarding school. By contrast, Christopher would be completely out of his depth and, worse, a Johnny-come-lately. An outsider. Boys could be very . . . inconsiderate to outsiders. Perhaps it would be best to leave him where he was.

But my grandparents were determined. So letters were sent, fees negotiated, and before the end of the holidays, the business was settled. There merely remained the minor matter of informing the boy concerned.

Geoffrey called my father into the parlour.

'We're sending you to Denstone.'

'What's Denstone? I'm sorry, Father, I don't understand.'

'It's a boarding school in Staffordshire. About fifty miles from here.'

'But . . . but I go to Wem. What's wrong with that?'

'Nothing. It's you there's something wrong with. You're becoming a slacker. Denstone will put a stop to that.'

'But . . . I don't want to go away, Father. And I'm not a slacker. I want to stay here, with, with . . . everyone. I shall be terribly unhappy, I know I shall.

I swear I'll work harder at Wem. Please don't send me away, please . . . surely Mother doesn't agree with this?'

'She thinks it's a very good idea.'

'I won't go. You can't make me.'

Geoffrey smiled faintly and left the room. His son burst into hot tears of anger, frustration and sheer disbelief.

My father often described to me the day he left Shawbury for Denstone. It was the following Sunday. He and his mother took the bus into Shrewsbury, Christopher with a brown suitcase resting on his lap. All his other things would follow on in a trunk. As they neared the station he implored Kitty to change her mind.

'I still don't understand what I'm supposed to have done wrong, Mother. Please, please, please, don't do this to me. I'll do anything you and Father want . . . I'll study all day on Saturdays . . . I won't go to the cinema during term . . .'

Why did his parents do it? Why send him into exile, sever him from Kiln Farm, Shawbury, and all his friends and familiars? It was an extraordinary decision and he never understood it. He never forgave them for it, either, although he managed to pretend to, much later.

Geoffrey is the key to understanding such an apparently inexplicable event. Fathers can be jealous of their sons and I wonder if Geoffrey was finding it increasingly difficult to reconcile his own childhood privations with my father's growing freedoms and pleasures.

I am sure Geoffrey persuaded himself that he was banishing Christopher to a better place for his own good, but I don't believe that was his underlying, subconscious motive. Indeed, it's possible that at a deeper level he was re-enacting his own childhood abandonment, but in mirror image. Instead of the boy being left behind, he was sent away: the long-ago sin against the father visited on the son.

After the bus had arrived at Shrewsbury Station, Kitty waited on the eastbound platform with her boy for the Stoke train. By now my bewildered father had abandoned his pleading and stood, utterly dejected and in complete silence, beside her. He simply could not understand what was happening. It made no sense to him at all.

At last his train arrived and he climbed very slowly into the carriage and turned round to look at his mother through the open door.

Kitty banged it shut with a crisp, 'Goodbye, dear. See you at the end of term.' And with that she walked back through the barriers and out of sight.

WHEN HE ARRIVED at Denstone, a Gothic construction consisting of a forbidding central block with twin wings, on either side, my father was greeted formally by the matron and informed he was one of the first to arrive. Hadn't his parents told him classes didn't start for several more days? He would have to manage with bread and margarine for his supper and see himself to bed. Sheets and pillows were still down in the laundry so he'd have to make do with blankets.

And with that the fifteen-year-old boy was left with half a candle, a sliver of soap and a basin of cold water for the morning.

Almost everything the clergyman back in Shawbury had cautioned his parents about turned out to be depressingly accurate. My father spoke with a distinct 'country' accent. This was quickly picked up on by the other boys as they began returning from holiday and they immediately dubbed him 'our country cousin'.

Most of them had been together as a unit for years; some had been at the same prep schools. Dad was a classic outsider. Unfortunately, Kitty had bought him school trousers in the wrong shade of grey; it was too late to do anything about it now and in Denstone's isolated and enclosed world such trivialities assumed tribal significance.

There were the usual induction ceremonies, more normally associated with the arrival of younger boys. Dad presented an opportunity for one last hurrah before such japes became beneath everyone's dignity. Most nights he would find his bed drenched in water; his clothes were stolen while he slept and stuffed in the nearest cistern.

But Dad was a grammar school boy and he knew the ropes. He'd been expecting this and adopted a stoical attitude. They weren't bad boys at heart and after a while the ragging began to flag. But it came to an abrupt end after someone went too far.

A special school assembly had been called to celebrate an Allied victory and the boys were instructed to make sure their trousers were meticulously pressed for the occasion. They used an old army trick. Trousers were folded with great care at bedtime and placed under the hard mattress. Done properly, the creases should be ruler-straight by morning.

That night someone gently eased Chris's trousers from their makeshift press, rolled them into a ball, and put them back.

He arrived at the ceremony looking as if he'd slept in a hedge and was instantly removed for his first thrashing at Denstone. The maximum six strokes, too. There was disobedience, and then there was unpatriotic disobedience. Men were dying for their country and the new boy had shown gross disrespect.

There was an uncomfortable silence in the dormitory that night when my father walked in. He removed his glasses, placed them carefully on his bed and turned round.

'Who did it?'

After a pause one of the older boys stood up.

'I did, country cousin. So, what of it?'

'So I fight you.'

My father was an unknown quantity to the others where fighting was concerned. They sat up in their beds with interest. Someone went to the door to keep watch.

'Come on then . . .'

Chris wasn't especially known for fighting at Wem, but he'd never lost an encounter. Since he was small, he had watched his father's farm hands settle their differences with their fists and one of them, a Dubliner called Jacob, had given him a little tuition and advice.

'Don't go worryin' about style, sorr. Just go on in loik a haymaker in a hurricane an' ye'll be foin. Watch now . . . loik this . . .'

Now, farmyard met Queensbury. Thirty seconds later, Queensbury was on the floor looking as crumpled as my father's trousers had that morning.

There were astonished murmurs around the room as my father attempted to disguise his trembling limbs by climbing into bed and pretending to read a book.

'Bloody *hell*!'

'I say, country cous—I mean, Madeley . . . well done!'

'Yes, hats off. No more nonsense, then.'

But this small victory, and the space it won him, was cold comfort to my father. He had no interest whatsoever in public school life and traditions. He did form a couple of semi-friendships but realised the only thing he and these boys had in common was a hatred of Denstone.

And as his first term there crept into winter with agonising slowness, he had plenty of time to reflect on the fact that he had three more years of this to come. Three years, stuck in this place! Everything about it was awful. It was freezing cold and the food was terrible—terrible. Rationing was biting hard and Denstone had no access to the occasional illicit comforts of the black market.

My father wrote home requesting food parcels. Butter, eggs, cream, cake and preserved meats arriving from Shawbury on a regular basis made Chris Madeley everyone's new best friend. But he wasn't much of a one for bought popularity and shared things out without favour.

He began to suffer from chronic loneliness.

When my father died, I was just old enough to handle probate and most of the other sad business connected with his passing. Naturally, I had to go through his personal papers. One letter, still in its envelope, caught my eye. It was addressed in my father's handwriting to: *Mrs G Madeley, Kiln Farm, Shawbury, Salop* and marked *Private*.

> *December 1943*
> *Dearest Mother,*
>   *I cannot tell you how much I look forward to coming home for Christmas. It seems so long since I was at Shawbury and I cannot wait to see you all again.*
>   *Mother, I have tried so very hard not to write this letter but after three months spent here at Denstone I simply feel I must.*
>   *Mother, I truly loathe it here. The other boys are nothing at all like me or my friends at Shawbury or Wem and I miss them so much. I am so lonely here and the teachers are awful. Remember old Mr—who the School Board insisted retire because he was so doddery? Well, Mother, they are all just like that here.*
>   *I do not feel I am getting the education you and father are paying for, and Wem Grammar is so much less costly for you. Please let me stay home after Christmas and go back there.*
>   *There are other matters here which I do not like but cannot explain to you. Will you talk to Father for me? I am so miserable here.*
>   *Looking forward to seeing you all in a week or two,*
>   *Your loving son, Christopher*

The 'other matters' my father obliquely referred to in his letter concerned a small clique of older boys—mostly sixth-formers but a few from his own year too—who preyed on smaller boys for sexual gratification. Christopher had seen nothing like this during his school career so far and it shocked him profoundly. His classmates, who had grown up with this sort of thing, advised him to ignore it but he couldn't.

One day he was in the washrooms and heard sounds of distress coming from a cubicle. Two seniors were in there with a much younger boy. They hadn't bothered to lock the door.

My father dragged the two sixth-formers out but before he could do anything else they ran off. The junior scurried away too.

That evening, the clique's ringleaders dragged my father into a classroom and beat him to the floor. He was given a thorough kicking and by the time they fled he was barely conscious. He was left with temporary tinnitus and something else that until then he thought would have been impossible: an even deeper loathing for Denstone.

Christopher tried to discuss his letter with his mother when he came home, but she repeatedly changed the subject. A conversation with Geoffrey about it was obviously out of the question. It made for a tense, strained Christmas at Shawbury and, with a corrosive mix of frustration, resentment and anger boiling inside him, Christopher was put on the train back to Denstone in January 1944. He felt powerless, unloved and completely rejected.

Dad never directly discussed with me the damage done to him by his parents' strange, ruthless decision to send him away. He kept such conversations for my mother, and after he died she told me how massively destabilised he had been by what he saw as his parents' betrayal. It shook his confidence in himself, left his self-worth at rock bottom, and took him years to recover from.

My father, as an adult, always went to great lengths to avoid discussing Denstone with his parents. My sister and I were explicitly ordered never to bring the subject up during visits to our grandparents. But this keep-the-peace tactic eventually backfired; in the absence of any reproof on the matter my grandparents gradually persuaded themselves that they had done a wonderful thing for their youngest boy.

'Of course, Chris loved Denstone,' my grandmother would announce comfortably over Sunday lunch at the farm. 'It was the making of him, I always like to think. You were so grateful we got you in there, weren't you, darling? You really should think of sending Richard there, you know.'

My father, beet-red, would make anguished noises in his throat and my mother would smoothly change the subject. Although I don't think that, deep down, he ever truly pardoned his parents for causing him such pointless unhappiness, he tried his best to pretend to. Perhaps that was enough.

The Denstone years crawled by and Christopher's childhood was almost at an end. There can be no question that it had been a boyhood doubly blighted, first by his father's implacable emotional withdrawal and then by this inexplicable exile to purgatory, a sentence with no appeal.

Chris was now in the upper sixth at Denstone and impatiently nearing the end of his three years there. He had increasingly taken refuge in literature and music and begun dabbling at writing. A few local newspapers had accepted letters and articles from him, mostly reviews of local concerts or reports on college sporting fixtures. Meanwhile his status as prefect brought with it slightly more privileges and freedoms.

The war was coming to its exhausted end. Kitty had been right about one thing: the conflict would be over before my father was old enough to be called up. Dad carried his suitcase out of Denstone's gates for the last time in the summer of 1945. By a long-held agreement with himself, he made a point of not looking back.

Chapter 6

Christopher's final school report arrived in the same post as his National Service call-up papers. He didn't give a damn about Denstone's last verdict on him but he did care passionately about what was inside the brown government envelope.

My father had set his heart on joining the RAF. The damage done to his eyes by the farm dog all those years before meant he couldn't hope to be a pilot, but he dearly wanted to be part of the so-called junior service, unencumbered as it was by the centuries of tradition which dominated and stifled the Army and Navy.

In a rare moment of empathy, Geoffrey offered to open the letter from the War Office.

'Thanks, Dad. Go on, then . . .'

His father read it carefully, then peered over his glasses at his son.

'It's the Royal Flying Corps for you, Christopher.'

My father burst out laughing and pumped his father's hand. They grinned at each other for a moment, then looked away, embarrassed.

MANY YOUNG MEN dreaded doing National Service. Not my father. He thought he'd gone on holiday. Twenty-four months' compulsory service in the RAF was a doddle after his three years at Denstone. The rigidity of service life, which frustrated and oppressed so many others, seemed like a relaxed and benevolent regime compared to the dark tunnel from which he had just emerged.

Luckily he was in Signals, which meant he was on the inside loop of camp life. He and his fellow telegraphists received and transmitted all official messages and requests from the aerodrome radio shack. Dad enjoyed being in the know before most other people. It was the nascent journalist in him. He liked being the one to pass it on, too, and his thoughts on what he might do after his discharge began to crystallise.

By happy coincidence he was posted to Shawbury and enthusiastically picked up the threads of his old life there, including spending as much time at Kiln Farm as duties permitted. Like his father before him, he saw no point in berating his parents for their failures. By tacit agreement, the subject of Denstone was avoided. What was done was done. Nothing could change the past. My father looked ahead now. He had a plan.

He was going to be a reporter.

IN 1948, MY FATHER came out of the RAF, bought a stuttering, evil-smoking Norton motorbike for five pounds and joined the *Whitchurch Herald* as a cub reporter. A year later, bored of writing up weddings, obituaries and agricultural shows, he transferred to the *Shrewsbury Chronicle*. A lot more was going on in the county town, but to his frustration most of his stories were cut to ribbons. Not because he was over-writing; everyone's copy was slashed. There was an acute shortage of newsprint in postwar Britain. Painstakingly written articles and features were savagely subbed down or bit the dust entirely.

Dad grew sick of it. Everyone did. Then one day a colleague confided over a pint that he'd cracked the problem. He was taking a job in Canada.

'They've got newsprint coming out of their ears over there, Chris. You can't move for bloody trees in Canada. I've got a pal working on the *Toronto Star*—forty pages every edition! I'm off. You should give it some serious thought, too.'

Canada. There was no rationing, while shortages in Britain were getting worse by the week. There was even talk of bread being put on the points system. Bread! You wouldn't think we'd won the war . . .

As Chris rode back to Kiln Farm that evening, he could think of nothing but Canada. Since the end of the war his parents had made the first of many visits to Canada to see Geoffrey's family, while James took care of the farm. Chris was sure the Madeleys over there could put him up for a while.

By the time he was kicking out the stand on the Norton by the back door of the farmhouse, his mind was made up. He had some savings—more than enough for his fare. He was going.

He saw Geoffrey coming out of the dairy shed after the evening's milking. Chris hesitated a moment, then hurried across the farmyard to break the news to his father.

MY FATHER WAS FULLY AWARE that a strange family pattern was repeating itself as his ship was shepherded out of the River Mersey by Liverpool's pilot boats. He thought about Henry's family making exactly the same departure more than forty years before, and of Geoffrey's hopeful voyage to find them thirteen years later.

But these fathers and sons had crossed the Atlantic with different imperatives. Henry was escaping bankruptcy and ruin. Geoffrey was chasing the dream of being reunited with his long-lost family. Now Chris was turning his back on his own parents.

They had supported his decision to emigrate but he sensed something approaching regret as well. His father appeared more reluctant than Kitty to see his youngest son go, although it was hard to be sure. Geoffrey's emotions were as inscrutable as ever, but Chris thought he could detect sadness in his father's voice when they talked over his plans.

Dad and I spoke about this years later, just a few months before he died. I was in no doubt. 'I think Granddad realised that deep down he loved you,' I told him. 'You can't compare going to Denstone with emigrating to Canada, Dad. No wonder he seemed upset. Given the way he knew he'd treated you he probably thought he'd never see you again.'

My father became quite thoughtful after this conversation. Later that evening, he did something almost unheard of. He telephoned Shawbury 'just for a chat' with his father.

It's never too late to salvage something from the wreckage.

Before setting sail for Quebec, Chris had been in touch with the Thomson newspaper group's Toronto office. They ran a string of titles over there and, after some hard lobbying, he was offered a reporter's job in the city. They'd found him digs near the offices; he was, his editor-to-be said in a telegram, 'all set'.

Bad weather in the mid-Atlantic slowed the ship down, as did an unusually heavy crop of icebergs off Newfoundland. When Chris's bus arrived in Toronto he was several days late.

He reported direct to his newspaper and was shown to the deputy editor's office. It was empty.

Eventually a harassed-looking man in shirtsleeves and glasses hurried in. He shook hands with my father and offered him a cigarette.

'Good trip over?'

'Well, apart from the storms and some icebergs. That's why I'm a bit late. I—'

The other man waved expansively. 'Sure, sure, these things happen. I had to sail to London last year for the paper and the same thing happened to me. Missed my story. Almost lost my job, ha ha!'

There was an uncomfortable pause, and then the deputy took a deep breath and delivered the *coup de grâce*. 'See here, Madeley, it's like this. A deadline is a deadline. You missed yours—not your fault—and . . . well, I'm afraid the job's gone to another guy. Sorry. Nothing personal.'

The interview was over and Chris found himself in an elevator going back down to the lobby. Half an hour before he thought he had a job and somewhere to live. Now he was literally out on the street.

To his credit, he didn't panic, though he felt horribly winded and humiliated. What would he tell his colleagues back home on the paper? Or his parents, come to that? Sacked before he'd even walked through the door.

He went to a drugstore, bought every newspaper in the place, traded some of his dwindling dollars for dimes and settled in for a long haul at the payphone. He had to get a job.

Perhaps a note of desperation had slipped into his voice, perhaps it was because he was calling from a public phone and had to keep inserting coins as the pips sounded, but Chris received increasingly short shrift from the newspapers he dialled. After a while he hung up and went for a coffee.

He toyed briefly with the idea of calling one of several relatives who lived in Ontario to beg a bed for a few nights, but he felt too ashamed and embarrassed. He had to fix this on his own.

He ended his first day in Toronto with the promise of a job selling men's underwear in a downtown department store, and the payment of a month's rent on a filthy bedsit across the city.

Not exactly what he had come three and a half thousand miles for.

MOST OF US CAN remember a run of particularly bad luck in our lives or careers, or both. Now, fortune resolutely refused to shine on my father. It was partly bad timing on his part. Thousands of Canadian servicemen were being demobbed every month and they got first pick of the jobs. Several times he was convinced he had landed a position in some newsroom only to be told at the last minute that a local man had belatedly entered the frame and taken priority.

It was the same in men's underwear. After a few weeks Chris was quietly let go in favour of a local man just out of the army.

Sometimes, at harvest time, he took a bus into the tobacco country outside the city and earned a few dollars picking leaves. He enjoyed this; it reminded him a little of home. It also reminded him that he couldn't afford to buy cigarettes any more. He was economising on food, too; photographs of him at this time show my father to be disturbingly gaunt.

But he was stranded. He had come to Canada optimistically on a one-way ticket, and going back home wasn't an option. Years later he would ruefully say to me: 'Never travel anywhere without your fare home in your back pocket. Not anywhere.'

By the autumn of 1950, he was in an extremely tight spot. The tobacco harvest was over and he was flat broke, reduced to patrolling the sands of Lake Ontario with his Leica camera—a twenty-first birthday present from his parents—taking photos of children on donkey rides and hustling their parents to buy them at a dollar a shot. Most politely declined. Then, out of the blue, his beach-bum existence threw him a break.

It was a warm October afternoon and a large, prosperous family had gathered on the sands. The father was dressed in an immaculate tan suit, his pretty wife in a spreading dress cinched in tightly at the waist. Their children were in cool crisp cotton and a uniformed nanny and a chauffeur fussed in attendance. The glamorous party appeared to be waiting for someone to show up.

My father drifted over.

'Goddamned reporters,' growled the paterfamilias, glaring around him. 'Where the hell are they? I told 'em, three o'clock at the pier.'

Chris's scalp tingled as he felt the electric crackle of opportunity.

'Excuse me . . . I'm a newspaperman. Freelance. I write and I take photos. Can I be of help?'

The other man looked the scarecrow up and down and then grinned. 'You sure can, Limey. My company's just taken over a coupla big employers in Sault Ste Marie and Tillsonburg. Saved a lot of jobs. Big story. Local papers want pictures of the saviour of Ontario and his family, but it looks like their reporters can't follow directions worth a damn.'

He fished in his pocket and pulled out a list of newspaper titles.

'Here they are—all syndicated. Just send your shots and words to them. Think you can do it? We gotta be outta here in five minutes.'

Dad grabbed his pictures, dashed down some quotes, and headed for the darkroom that a sympathetic friend—a more successful freelance photographer who shared his tenement block—allowed him to borrow.

He was back in business. There was a central pool for syndicated copy but he bypassed that, calling each paper in turn and insisting on speaking to the editor. He offered to write subtly different stories for each title so it looked like they'd had a staff man on the job, and sent a series of alternative photos to the picture desks too, so they could claim exclusives.

He was by-lined in some editions and by the end of the day had landed a contract as a reporter/photographer for the *Woodstock Sentinel Review*, Tillsonburg bureau. Tillsonburg was a medium-sized tobacco town ninety miles southwest of Toronto and about twelve miles from Lake Erie.

My father's break would lead to an encounter with a red-headed, eighteen-year-old actress.

My mother.

HIS NEW EMPLOYERS were an even smaller outfit than the *Whitchurch Herald*. But at least Chris was a big fish in a small pond. Well, a middling fish in a minuscule pond. He was a one-man band, reporting on all the news and sport fit to cover. The pay wasn't great, but enough for him to run a car, rent a decent apartment and start buying his packets of cigarettes again.

Compared to life in grey, pinched, exhausted, rationed, postwar England, Canada was flowing with milk and honey. This part of Ontario rubbed up close and cosy against its border with America; US prosperity spilled into its neighbour's garden like water from an overflowing lake.

Sometimes Chris's news beat took him to bigger towns nearby—London, Hamilton and Detroit's Canadian twin, Windsor. He couldn't get used to the sights that surrounded him. Everything was off the scale. Huge, shiny, gas-guzzling American cars (not that their thirstiness mattered—petrol was plentiful at just a few cents a gallon). Soda parlours offering every imaginable flavour of ice cream. Drive-in movie theatres with little private speakers you hooked over your car's windows. Ice-hockey rinks, brilliantly lit for violent night-time clashes between armour-clad warriors who smashed into each other; extravagantly floodlit baseball games with pitchers and batters worshipped like gods by their roaring fans.

And television. Everyone had a television, the programmes impossibly superior to the modest transmissions Chris had occasionally glimpsed on the flickering sets still rare in England. Proper shows that everyone watched, and talked and laughed about the next day. Many were piped in direct from the States. *The Ed Sullivan Show*, live from New York—urbane, witty, modern. *The Sid Caesar Show*—side-splittingly funny. Then there were the news shows; rollicking, rolling extravaganzas of news and unabashed comment, stuffed with on-the-spot footage and hosted by charismatic men who were stars and household names in their own right.

It was dazzling, amazing. And there was the weather. Summer was insufferably hot and humid: as humid as Florida, some said, with more mosquitoes. It was because of the moisture from the Great Lakes virtually surrounding the huge inland peninsular; the same watery expanses that in winter produced unimaginable quantities of snow. Lake snow, they called it. One could draw the bedroom curtains on a dry, clear, frosty night and open them next morning to look out on a different planet. Familiar neighbourhood landmarks had vanished completely beneath a vast, shape-shifting shroud; road signs, hedges, walls and parked cars were buried beneath the earth's shining new crust.

Tillsonburg and its surrounding tobacco farms may have been a small news beat but it wasn't quiet. Whatever went on there it was my father's job to cover. He soon became fluent in the mysteries of ice hockey, baseball, basketball and Little League or Pee-Wee. Locals liked the tall Englishman with his funny accent and he started making friends. Photographs from this time show him still at his underfed skinniest, but relaxed and smiling. His trademark spectacles gave him something of a Clark Kent appearance.

One of Dad's new friends was a fellow newspaperman called Bill. He was the editor of the *Tillsonburg News*, a guy on the up-and-up. Bill drove a big red Pontiac and reportedly had a stunning girlfriend. One day he phoned Chris to beg a favour.

'Chris, I'm on a story in Toronto tonight. I promised I'd walk my girl home from the theatre—she's starring in that new play at the Town Hall. Would you be her knight in shining armour for me?'

'Of course. What's she called?'

'Mary Claire. Mary Claire McEwan. I'll tell her to look out for the beanpole in the foyer. Be there around ten. Thanks, pal.'

Dad was delayed by a story that evening and arrived at the theatre a few minutes after ten. Most of the audience and cast had already left, but as he ran up the steps to the foyer the doors opened and a petite, red-headed girl hurried out. Chris thought she looked a knockout and rather French in her smart belted raincoat.

'Mary Claire?'

'Yes. If you're Chris, you're late.'

'I know, I'm sorry . . . I got stuck on a story.'

'Hmm. You sound like Bill.'

My father worked hard to make up lost ground as they walked to her parents' house. After a few minutes he managed to make her laugh, and flattered her by asking about the play. But suddenly she interrupted him with: 'We're here.'

They were standing in front of a frame house that faced the town cinema. Two flights of wooden steps led to a verandah and front door. Through a window he could see a woman moving about.

He couldn't hide his disappointment that they had arrived. 'So soon? But I was hoping . . .'

'What, that I have to walk halfway across town every night? Sorry, Englishman, this is the end of the line.'

He played for time. 'Look, I'd like to come and see the play. I could write a review for the paper and use a picture of you. How would that be?'

'That would be . . . very nice. Thank you. Bill's been promising to do the same thing since we opened.'

'Then I'll see you tomorrow. Good night.'

''Night.'

My father retraced his steps, thinking about how he would describe this girl in his article. If he'd known how she was describing him to her mother at that very moment, he probably would have passed out with shock.

'Play go well, dear? Want some coffee? There's some still on, I think.'

'Yes, it went fine. Thanks, I'll take a cup.'

'Bill walk you home again?'

'No, he's out of town. One of his friends did. An Englishman.'

'Oh? What's he like?'

Mary Claire sipped her coffee.

'I think we're going to be married.'

She brought him home for dinner a week after they met. This first meal with her family was one of the great turning points of my father's life. It would have an immeasurable impact on him and his attitude to fatherhood, and a profound effect on my own childhood.

Chapter 7

Chris had been so busy making his way in the world that for nearly four years he had managed to push Denstone, and his complete failure to form a demonstrative, loving relationship with his father, to the bottom of his thoughts.

But nothing is forever buried. He was still emotionally scarred. Deep down he secretly thought there must be something fundamentally wrong with him. If not, why had his parents sent him away? He must be intrinsically unlovable, he decided. Although this whirlwind romance with Mary Claire had shaken his heart—he was completely in love with her—how could she possibly love him in return?

Gradually my mother began to sense a deep well of self-doubt concealed behind her fiancé's outwardly confident manner. Englishmen were famous for their emotional reticence, she knew, so at first it wasn't surprising to her that when she asked him about his childhood and parents he was not exactly evasive, but reserved and vague.

But one evening, after the two of them had said their good-nights, she reflected on the conversation they'd had over dinner, and suddenly grasped what was missing from it.

He never spoke about his feelings. Not regarding his boyhood, anyway. Not about the past at all, in fact. With a slight shock she realised she had no idea if he had been a happy child or not, or what he thought of his parents. He simply didn't say. More to the point, he avoided saying. What could it mean? She confided in her mother, Barbara.

'It's not that I believe he's hiding something horrible. But I can tell he's unhappy about something, and I'm certain it's somehow to do with his family. I want to help him but I don't know what to say or do.'

Barbara regarded her eldest daughter calmly. 'You must get him completely on his own, choose your moment, and ask him outright. You'll get your answer, dear—either by what he says, or what he doesn't say.'

The following weekend, Chris, on Mary Claire's suggestion, hired a small motor launch and the two of them went out for the day on Lake Erie. It was now humid, sultry summer but they were cooled by the breeze puffing across the water. They ate their lunch as the little boat rocked in the slight swell of the great inland sea, and after a long companionable silence, Mary Claire decided the moment had come.

'Darling . . . what is it you won't tell me about your childhood, your life back at Shawbury?'

Years later my father would describe the question as like a door swinging open: a doorway he could shun or pass through. The choice was his.

He turned to look towards the distant shoreline, and then back at the eyes of the young woman looking solemnly into his own. The moment held itself in perfect balance a while longer and then gently dipped under his decision.

'Well . . . this will probably sound . . . I don't know. I've never spoken to a soul about it, but . . .'

For the first time in his life, hesitatingly, Chris began to describe the doubts and fears and disappointments that had haunted him for as long as he could remember. As his fiancée listened in silence, the lake murmured its accompaniment.

A dark tide that had begun to run nearly half a century earlier, flooding through two lives, father's and son's, was at last about to turn.

MARY CLAIRE'S KID BROTHER Bailey was barely a fortnight old when Chris walked into my mother's family home at 174 Broadway for the first time. Her younger sister Barbara Ann was fifteen. Mary Claire was eighteen, and the oldest child, Malcolm, twenty-two. Their mother, Barbara, was in her early forties and father Hector had just turned fifty. It was a vibrant family that cheerfully spanned five decades; a typical and triumphant product of the modern North American way—confident, affluent (Hector owned a garage and Barbara ran a hair salon), forward-looking and relaxed.

Chris had never been in a house like it. The McEwan home seemed to glow with emotional warmth. Perhaps that was because women were a strong presence—a mother and two daughters outnumbered and outgunned the men and Chris marvelled at the loving, playful atmosphere that surged around him whenever he visited his fiancée. He didn't realise it then, but his emotional DNA was being subtly re-engineered by the McEwans' family chemistry. Their immediate unfeigned fondness for him astounded him.

My father told me he experienced more demonstrative affection in one week in Tillsonburg than he had known in his entire life in Shawbury. At first he was startled and confused by the experience; quickly he came to love it, and them.

Dad was most fascinated by Hector's behaviour. On weekend visits to the McEwan home, my father would sit pretending to read a newspaper while covertly observing his future father-in-law's playful exchanges with his children as they came and went. Malcolm, though now in his early twenties, was still hugged, kissed or playfully wrestled with. The girls were kissed and teased too, and Bailey was everyone's darling, swept through the house in the interchangeable arms of his siblings or parents.

It is impossible to overemphasise the critical importance of this period for my father. Demonstrably, showing and receiving love and affection was normal. The more he observed it, the easier it looked. And not only that, the little clan on Broadway continued to make their growing affection for him abundantly plain. Mary Claire had confided in her mother and Barbara went out of her way to make the young Englishman feel loved and welcomed into the family. His confidence soared.

CHRIS AND MARY CLAIRE were married in Tillsonburg on October 13, 1951. The bridegroom was twenty-three, the bride nineteen. Ten months later my mother gave birth to a daughter—Elizabeth Barbara Madeley. Telegrams were sent: mother and baby doing fine.

But the father wasn't. Chris was still desperately thin and working extra shifts for his newspaper to earn enough to keep his little family. He was exhausted after eighteen-hour days and seemed to have no resistance to infections. Heavy smoking didn't help and after a vicious bout of bronchitis his new wife took charge.

'We can't carry on like this, Chris. You're going to wear yourself out. You *are* worn out. And Elizabeth and I hardly ever see you. We have to think of something else.'

My father nodded. 'All right. But what? It took me months to get the job I have now.'

The couple both had aunts living in Windsor, the big industrial city which stared across the border into America and 'Motown'—Detroit. My mother considered this for a while and then seized the moment.

'Let's go to Windsor—today, right now. There's plenty of work there and we can stay with our aunts while we get fixed up.'

And so my slightly bewildered father found himself catching the last train from Tillsonburg that evening with his wife and baby. Next morning the couple walked into the city's employment centre and walked out with job interviews at the Ford of Canada plant. An hour later they were on the payroll—Mary Claire was assigned to production planning, Chris, with his journalistic experience, to the communications department—in effect, the press office. He would work for Ford until the day he died.

Once again Mary Claire was my father's saviour. With kinder hours and better pay he began finally to put on some weight, and he was energised and uplifted by the turn their lives had taken.

He also had more time to spend getting to know his growing daughter. My mother says he was an infinitely gentle, tender father. Like all new fathers he had to feel his way, but he had very little experience from his own childhood to call on. He had to rely on what he'd learned in the McEwan family home. That, as it turned out, served well enough.

But my mother says he seemed to have an instinct for it anyway. Becoming a father was enormously important to him. I think he felt fatherhood, and marriage, defined him properly for the first time in his life.

But, as well as learning to define himself, Chris was also attempting to define his wife. She had harboured thoughts of returning to the stage, but he wouldn't hear of it. Today, we might call his attitude 'controlling'.

My father met my mother when she was playing the female lead in a romantic comedy, and it had involved some stage kisses. This was all very well then; now she was his wife, he could not bear the thought of her in the arms of another man. So she renounced any remaining ambitions to pursue a theatrical career, telling friends she was happy to be a wife and mother. Although this was not without a large degree of truth, there was definitely an element of pretence. Years later, when she wanted to drive, my father refused to allow it. My mother told everyone that it was a matter of cost, but again this was only partly true. The main issue was her husband's superstitious fear that a driving wife might just one day drive away from him for good.

She was quite unable to reassure him that this was nonsense, any more than she had been able to convince him she had no intention of running off with her next leading man. Her eventual response was to accede gracefully to his demand. Recently I asked her why.

'It was partly the times, Richard,' she told me. 'Things were . . . different for women. But, also, I didn't want to make him unhappy.

'Yes, I wanted to act and I wanted to drive—quite badly sometimes—but not *that* badly, you see. We were so happy together and, anyway, I'd known he was insecure when I married him, hadn't I? I loved that I had managed to take some of that insecurity away and make him stronger. Why would I want to endanger that?'

I hope he knew how lucky he was. I think so.

IF CHRIS LOOKED OUT of his new office window he could see straight into the smokestacks of mighty Detroit across the narrows that marked the Canada–US border. He began to think about transferring to America. The pay was better, opportunities were greater . . . why not?

Because of my mother's teeth.

Mary Claire cleared away her husband's supper plate in the kitchen of their little flat in Windsor, checked the baby—now more of a toddler—was still asleep, and cleared her throat. She had been dreading this conversation since getting the news that afternoon, but it had to be had.

'Darling . . . you know I went to the dentist today.'

'Sure, honey.' After several years in Canada, Chris now spoke in an unaffected North American accent.

'Well . . . it's not good news.'

'What? You're not ill with something, are you?'

Mary Claire shook her head. 'No, it's not anything serious . . . just expensive. He told me I have to have all my teeth out—*all* of them, Chris— and have false ones made and it's going to cost a thousand dollars!' She burst into tears.

Chris was aghast. 'But of course that's serious! We haven't got a thousand dollars. We haven't got a hundred dollars. It'd be cheaper to take a boat to England and get you fixed on the National Health!'

Mary Claire looked up. 'You're not serious?'

'Well, no . . . I mean, yes, it's true, we could get you seen to for free in England, but I didn't mean . . . I wasn't actually suggesting . . .'

They stared at each other. Mary Claire broke the silence.

'There's many a true word spoken in jest. I think you might be onto something. Let's sleep on it, shall we?'

The decision to sail for England was not based solely on Mary Claire's dental dilemma. Britain was finally moving out of years of austerity; rationing was almost at an end and after four years away Chris realised he was homesick. Mary Claire, though nervous about emigrating and convinced she would miss her mother terribly (indeed she did—they wrote to each other every single day and the entire McEwan clan came over from Tillsonburg to visit) had long been something of an Anglophile and was intensely curious to see the country of her husband's birth.

The decision was sealed by the news that Ford had an opening in their British press office. The job was Chris's if he wanted it.

And so it was that at the beginning of August 1954 my parents and their two-year-old daughter boarded the *Empress of France* at Montreal, bound for Liverpool.

My father was taking his young family home.

Back to Kiln Farm.

Chapter 8

The Shropshire Madeleys arrived at Liverpool to greet their wandering son and his new bride and child. Geoffrey and Kitty were there, as was Chris's elder brother Jim, with his new wife Hilda. She came from Market Drayton and she and Jim had married after Chris had emigrated. Both brothers would shortly be meeting the other's new bride for the first time.

Meanwhile, in the unloading sheds opposite, Chris and Mary Claire's luggage—everything they had in the world—had vanished without trace and their little girl was flushed and unwell.

After the drive down to Shawbury, Elizabeth, who had been increasingly restless, suddenly went into a sharp decline. The doctor was called out. His diagnosis seemed strangely and ominously fateful. On this, her very first night at Kiln Farm, Elizabeth had been struck down by precisely the same illness that had stolen John from his parents nearly thirty years before—bronchial pneumonia. The little girl was even lying in the same bedroom where the small boy had been propped up on his pillows the night before he died. A *frisson* of superstitious dread rippled through everyone.

But this was the 1950s, not the 1920s. My sister was transferred, semiconscious, to Shrewsbury Hospital where she was placed in an oxygen tent and fed antibiotics. Modern medicine duly carried the day and the family managed to shrug off the sense that dark and malign forces were at work.

But no one actually mentioned John by name.

Geoffrey and Kitty had missed their youngest boy more keenly than their letters to him ever showed. Now, they insisted that he and his wife must stay at Kiln Farm for at least a month before he started his new job at Ford's headquarters in Dagenham, Essex. So my mother had an opportunity to become familiar with this emotionally charged parcel of land, and to get to know her husband's parents.

Years later, Geoffrey would confess to her that the arrival of his son's Canadian wife had confused and unsettled him. It brought back memories of The Girl. He had been unable to persuade his first fiancée to sail to England with him, but Chris had successfully brought his own girl home. My grandfather admired this, and also my mother's determination to make the journey, leaving her own family behind.

My mother certainly made an impact on Shawbury. Her red hair and glamorous looks marked her out. She dressed in the tailored, fashionable clothes she had brought with her to a country still emerging from the so-called Age of Austerity. Because of the height difference with her husband— she was five foot four to his six foot two—she always wore high heels. The whole combined to produce a distinctly chic, Parisian look. This, and her Canadian accent, caused heads to turn in the village shop.

She made an impact on Geoffrey too. He quickly became fond of my mother, and it was the beginning of a friendship which, in later years, saw him increasingly confide in her on the long walks they took through the countryside; conversations she remembers to this day and which were of enormous value in the writing of this book.

After a week or two spent settling in, Chris drove Mary Claire into Shrewsbury for her long-dreaded appointment with the Madeley family dentist. She was ushered into the surgery. My mother shivered at the sight of the ancient pre-war dental equipment, and wished heartily that she had stayed on the other side of the Atlantic and had all her teeth pulled under gas in a modern North American dentist's.

Outside, her husband sat in the waiting room flicking through a tattered prewar copy of *Punch*. He was expecting a lengthy vigil—most of the afternoon—but suddenly the surgery door opened and my mother walked through, smiling, holding a slightly bloodied rag to a corner of her mouth.

'What's happened, Claire? You can't possibly have had all of them removed already.'

''On't need 'oo,' she answered indistinctly through the cloth before taking it away for a moment. 'He says there's nothing wrong with my teeth, except one or two at the back that were crowding the others. One more treatment and I'm fixed. That guy in Windsor was a chiseller, Chris, out for a fast buck.'

On the drive back to Kiln Farm, Chris glanced across at his wife. 'Well, it looks like we needn't have come to England after all, doesn't it?'

'Looks like it.'

There was a pause before my father spoke again. 'D'you mind?'

My mother shook her head. 'No, I don't think I do. You know I always wanted to visit England. Let's look on it as an adventure; see how things work out.'

For a moment my father couldn't speak. Then he managed a piece of understatement that was typical of him. 'OK . . . well, good. Thank you.'

By the autumn of that year my father was living in digs nearly 200 miles south of wife and child, working for the Yankee dollar. He was a public relations officer for Ford at their sprawling Dagenham plant and this enforced separation was something he and Mary Claire swiftly agreed could not be tolerated. Geoffrey loaned them the deposit on a semi standing on a busy main road in Romford, Essex, and by Christmas the young family was in residence. Later the following year, Mary Claire fell pregnant again.

Essex boy was on his way.

THE SIGHT OF FLOWERING laburnum always reminds me that my birthday is approaching. When I was small my mother would point to the bursting yellow buds on the fine tree that stood outside our back door and whisper, 'See the petals? It means your birthday's coming.'

I was a Sunday's child, arriving on May 13, 1956, in the front room of our house in Dagenham Road, Rush Green. Rush Green had once been a small village outside the market town of Romford, but by now it was almost entirely absorbed by a rapidly expanding postwar London. Traces of the countryside remained, though. Even today patches of ancient farmland survive around Romford, ploughed fields sitting bravely alongside 1930s-built housing estates and rows of shops and pubs.

Later, when I was old enough to appreciate Kiln Farm's rural appeal, these fragments of countryside that stubbornly refused to be completely swamped by bricks and concrete held a deep attraction for me. I would ride my bike around their cement-besieged perimeters, closing my ears to the roar of traffic and resolutely turning my gaze towards the narrow vistas still free of cityscape. It was then that I first realised the hold Kiln Farm had begun to exert over me, even as a young boy. As time went by, I increasingly yearned for its meadows and trees and river, the red-bricked barns and outbuildings. I still do.

My father's reaction to the birth of his first son was extravagant. Chris would race home from Dagenham as fast as his wheezing prewar Ford 8 would carry him, and, without so much as a 'Hi honey, I'm home', charge up the stairs to the nursery to stare and stare and stare at me if I were asleep, or pick me up and cradle me in his arms if I were even drowsily awake.

My mother admits to becoming quite jealous. 'You want your husband to love his new son, but you don't want to be usurped by the baby,' she told me candidly. It was sometimes over half an hour before her husband would sheepishly make his entrance downstairs and bid his wife and four-year-old daughter good evening.

More than half a century on from these exorbitant homecomings, I believe my father was plainly overcompensating. He was making it transparently clear to everyone—most of all, to himself—that the relationship with his son would not be anything like the one his father had had with him. He was going to have a demonstrative, loving relationship with his son come hell or high water.

I love him very much for that. He'd thought about it. He reversed the flow. Henry, William, Geoffrey . . . they had all, in their own ways, done so much damage. Christopher had suffered enough and learned enough to be able to work out how to repair it.

MY FIRST MEMORY is a very early one. I am lying in my pram, gazing up at a blue sky through the branches of a tree laden with white blossom. I can be scarcely more than one, and I must be under the old pear tree at the bottom of the garden where on sunny days I was parked for a nap.

The next break in the blank void of recall also involves blossom. My mother and I are looking through a window at the brilliant yellow petals on our laburnum tree. She points to it, then turns and smiles at me. 'Four tomorrow!'

Now my father drifts into view. He is always in a suit and tie. Always. And never in a shirt of any shade other than brilliant white, except when he was wearing his pyjamas. The first thing he put on in the morning was his spectacles; the lenses in heavy, black plastic frames, almost as dark as his thick hair, which he slicked back with Brylcreem after shaving. I climbed into my parents' bed most mornings and watched the daily ritual of them dressing for the day.

On Saturdays my mother had the afternoon 'off' after spending all week looking after house, husband and children, while my father entertained my sister and me.

We might walk past the gasworks to Cottons Park where there were two slides, one of them breathtakingly high and steep with a wooden hut at the top to stop children falling off, the other disappointingly low and tame. Elizabeth, four years older than me, was allowed to swoop down the 'daddy' slide while I was confined to the baby version. I argued, begged and pleaded to be allowed to scale the metal Everest with my sister. The answer was always the same.

'Not until you're six.'

Or we would go out for a drive. Sometimes we would motor as far as Epping Forest and explore. Over time we became expert at finding our way through the thousands of acres of trees. Most visitors scarcely penetrated the timber beyond sight of their cars and we would leave these timid souls far behind. We had our own 'private' glade deep in the heart of the forest where no one else ever seemed to go and where we shared undisturbed picnic lunches.

MY FATHER WAS extremely playful. I am sure the games we enjoyed were as much for his benefit as for ours; he was compensating for all that he had missed out on during his own childhood. Our little family of four would play rounders, French cricket, badminton (without a net, which made it slightly pointless) and, occasionally, on my mother's insistence, baseball.

That was just on outings. At home, my father instigated a nightly tradition that started when I was about three and continued until I was ten.

We called it 'The Play'. After supper, my father and I would retire to my parents' room, climb onto the big double bed and try to shove each other off. Simple as that. You could use arms, legs, push, pull—whatever it took. Of course my father let me win these contests and my mother, sitting downstairs, would sigh each time another thundering crash shook the house as my father toppled to the floor of the room above.

He built me a train set, and spent far more time playing with it than I did. The little electric locomotives had funnels you could put drops in, and fake smoke would stream behind the train as it chuffed around the track. My father laid in stocks of the special chemical so that rolling stock would always look realistic when we—or he—played with it. Sometimes he would drive us half a mile up the road to Crow Lane to see some real trains. The main Liverpool Street railway line ran parallel with it and we would park on top of an embankment and wait to see what my father called a 'proper' train—one pulled by a steam engine—rush past us like a snorting dragon. This was thrilling, and one day it resulted in the first great regret of my life.

One bitingly cold, snowy Saturday afternoon we saw the telltale puffs of smoke rising into the air far down the track and knew we were in luck. Soon the great black engine appeared round a distant bend and thundered towards us. I could see the fireman shovelling the coal and the driver standing on the footplate. Suddenly he noticed the tall man with two little children standing on the slope above the track and, as the distance closed, gave a huge theatrical wave.

'Come on, Richard—he's waving at us. Wave back, quickly!'

But I couldn't. It was as if a god had taken personal notice of my existence, and I froze. A moment later the chance was gone as the engine rocked past us and into a tunnel.

'What a shame . . . you won't get a chance like that again.'

I knew my father was right. I had let a wonderful opportunity to exchange waves with a train driver pass; tears of disappointment and self-recrimination sprang from my eyes. I may have been too young to understand the words *carpe diem* but I resolved to seize my chances in future. Today when I dither I tell myself: 'Remember the train driver.'

Before long the steam engines had been comprehensively replaced with electric and diesel trains and a great decade of change was under way. My mother had taught me to read and count, and one evening my father arrived home with a gleaming, freshly minted coin. 'Can you tell me what year is stamped on this, Richard?'

I studied the glittering sixpence for a few moments. 'Um . . . it's 1961.'

'Yes. Well done. You can keep it. In fact, it's time you started getting pocket money like your sister. I'll give you sixpence every week from now on, all right?'

So far, then, so good. Chris was turning out to be the very model of a modern father. Putting aside what today we describe as 'quality time' for his children. Taking them out by himself once a week. Excelling in the demonstrative affection department—he was extravagant with his kisses and cuddles. I don't think a day went by when I wasn't swept into the air in a bear hug, had a huge raspberry trumpeted on my neck (unfailingly hilarious, this), or was showered with kisses at bedtime. The only occasions these offerings were muted were when we stayed at Shawbury, or if my grandparents visited us. Then a touch of formality entered the atmosphere; there was a faint air of reserve about my father and he would be less boisterous with his children. I didn't mind; it was simply part of having to 'be polite' when Grandma and Granddad were around.

On the long drives from Romford to Shawbury, my parents would inevitably discuss my grandparents and my father's upbringing. My sister and I would shamelessly eavesdrop, even to the point of demanding, 'Speak up!' or 'What was that again? I didn't catch it.' My parents were usually tolerant and would merely flash the occasional warning glance over their shoulders. 'Not a word about this at Shawbury, you two . . .'

My father's openness and affection meant that, by the time I was about seven, I thought I'd worked out how he'd react in most situations involving me and I loved him in an uncomplicated, trusting way. But things weren't that simple. There was still a lot of unresolved damage caused by the past. Dad had done extraordinarily well in laying many of his ghosts—and I wish he were alive today so I could tell him that—but he was still haunted by pernicious phantoms and they were about to make an appearance.

THE FAMILY HAD SETTLED down in front of our black and white television set (we always called it a television set, not the telly or TV) to watch comedian Harry Worth's weekly show. A big treat for me—Harry came on after my bedtime but I was allowed to stay up to watch him.

The BBC continuity announcer was introducing the programme when suddenly the screen cut away to a caption that read 'Newsflash'. I was sitting on my father's lap and rocked slightly as he sat up straighter. A newsreader appeared, holding a piece of paper.

'We are getting reports that President Kennedy has been shot in Dallas, Texas. The President is believed to have been wounded and has been taken to hospital. We will bring you more on this when we can.' There was a pause and then the screen faded slowly to black.

Before either of my parents could say a word, the screen brightened again and the newsreader was back, being handed a fresh piece of paper. For a few moments he looked dumbly at it, and then cleared his throat.

'I am very sorry to have to tell you . . . that President Kennedy is dead.' I felt my father's entire body stiffen and my mother gave a little wail. Newscaster and nation stared blankly at each other for a few moments longer until the screen darkened again.

The trauma that swept around the world was fully represented in our small living room. My parents clung to each other in instant, overwhelming grief. My mother kept whispering, 'Oh-oh-oh-oh-oh-oh,' and my father pressed one hand to his eyes, tears dripping through his fingers. My sister and I stared at them in awe, but particularly at my father. These were the first sobs we had ever seen wrung from him.

Next morning my mother succumbed to a vicious migraine and had to stay in bed. My sister and I dressed in our smartest clothes and my father put on his darkest suit. We took a train into London and joined the long queue outside the American embassy to sign the hastily arranged book of condolence. When it was full it would be sent to Jackie Kennedy. We seemed to shuffle slowly forward for hours in the cold November wind, but at last we were in a little anteroom and my father was handed a gold fountain pen by a man in a black coat.

Dad produced the scrap of paper on which he had drafted his message to the newly widowed woman across the Atlantic, and copied it carefully onto the page. Then we went home.

It was my first experience of the death of an icon. Seventeen years on I was old enough to understand the wave of shock and emotion that swept the world when John Lennon was shot; curiously, another seventeen years later, Princess Diana was killed. As had been the case with Kennedy and Lennon, millions would remember exactly where they were and what they were doing when they heard the news that the princess was dead. The dreadful news was followed by a mass outpouring of public grief.

But at seven, I struggled to comprehend my parents' distress. They tried to explain but it made no sense. President Kennedy had never been to our house and my mother and father had not met him. Why then did they keep crying in the days after he died?

As I GREW OLDER, I came gradually to understand, and even vicariously to share, something of their emotion. Kennedy was the great postwar visionary of my parents' generation. To them, he was a hero and the antithesis of the clapped-out politics that had led to two world wars. Now I can see that my father identified with Kennedy. He wore the same style of single-breasted suit, the same narrow sober ties of silver and speckled grey, and white shirts with gleaming cuffs that always protruded a discreet inch or so beyond his jacket's sleeves.

Women like my mother adored the First Lady too, and eagerly copied her fashion style. My mother was a dab hand at her Singer sewing machine and skilled at running up her own outfits. Women's magazines often gave away patterns based on Jackie's latest look and my mother would go out and buy the material. A couple of evenings later, she would sashay into our living room with a 'Well, what do you all think?' and there was Jackie Kennedy's latest party frock on display in Dagenham Road.

What with my father's Kennedy-esque power suits and my mother's copied outfits, sometimes, when they when out together, they looked as if they were off to a party on Capitol Hill.

As I grew up I was increasingly puzzled that my personal memories of the day Kennedy died should be so vivid. I was only seven. Lots of people my age have no recall of it at all.

Now I believe it is because another trauma occurred almost immediately afterwards; a personal one so shocking to me that it fixed this period in my childhood in my mind for ever.

The first time my father thrashed me.

I SUPPOSE I MUST have been smacked a few times by both my parents up to this point, but I can't really remember it. I do have an image of my grand-mother rapping me over the knuckles with a walking stick for saying I was 'sick of this damn weather'—swearing of any kind was not tolerated at Kiln Farm—but it didn't really hurt, and neither was it meant to.

I wish I could remember exactly what I did wrong that prompted the first thrashing, but that particular mental home video stubbornly refuses to roll. The tape only starts after my infraction, with my father pointing a finger at me. His hand is trembling with rage and his face is dark.

'Wait here.'

So I stand calmly in the living room, obediently waiting while he goes out into the garden. I am not particularly frightened. I am familiar with my father's occasional outbursts of temper and hearing his baritone crack as he bellows at full volume, but the worst that has ever happened is to be sent to my room for a couple of hours, or early to bed.

Today, I hear the shed door grating open. There is a stiff point where the wood tries to jam against the garden path and it always makes the same groaning rasp as it is forced open. The unmistakable sound will soon come to have a Pavlovian effect on me, producing a weakness in the knees, a spasm in the belly and a suddenly dry mouth. This first day, it's just our shed door being opened.

My father is back, holding one of the garden canes I help him plant in his vegetable patch every spring. I can't imagine why he has brought one into the house.

'Turn around.'

I obey, wondering what's going on. There is a painting on the wall in front of me, of an autumnal Canadian lake with blue-grey rocks rising from the still, clear water. Perhaps I am going to have to count them, or—

The backs of my legs have caught fire. I hear the dry cracking of burning wood. There it is again, and now my buttocks are burning too. Another sharp crack and my back is alight. Too shocked and consumed by agony to move at first, I find I cannot breathe either. My lungs have stopped working.

I manage to stumble into a half-turn in time to see my father bringing his stick whistling through the air in a sideways arc meant to connect with my shoulder blades, but instead it meets with the muscle of my upper arm. I collapse to my knees in agony, eyes wide, mouth open as I desperately try to suck in air.

My father steps back, breathing heavily. 'Next time, do as you're told.'

As he walks out of the room again, I at last manage to drag in a juddering, shuddering gasp, but when I try to breathe out, a most surprising and disconcerting thing happens. I make a noise just like the whistle on our kitchen kettle when it boils.

And so I continue to kneel there for a while, screaming.

A NEW REGIME had begun. I quickly discerned that the beatings I was now intermittently subjected to were rarely a result of especially bad behaviour. I could tell that they stemmed from a loss of control on my father's part. He had always been prone to losing his temper and shouting at my sister and me when we were naughty, but, as far as I was concerned, that no longer seemed enough for him. He did not hit Elizabeth.

I must have known that the thrashings were excessive because, tellingly, I didn't mention them to anyone. I never confided anything about it to anyone at Rush Green Junior School, which I walked to each morning. I realised after several playground conversations about parental discipline that although many of my friends were also physically chastised, my own beatings were of a different order.

I cannot remember how frequent the thrashings were. They must have been staggered because I can distinctly recall periods where I decided they must have stopped for good. Then I would do something to enrage my father and my heart would falter as once again I stood alone in a room, listening to the distant shed door grind open.

My mother was torn. She had sworn to love, honour and obey her husband and he had a dominant 'I know best' attitude to disciplining his son. I don't think she was fully aware how hard I was being hit; I have a dim memory of my father downplaying it in a row with her about it.

When I discussed it with her recently, she told me that the issue became an increasingly serious one in her marriage. She was very unhappy about the situation, but the canings usually took place when she was not in the house—often on a Saturday—and, for some reason I still don't fully understand, I didn't tell her what had happened when she arrived home. I think I just wanted to forget the experiences as quickly as possible and pushed them to the back of my mind.

Because my father continued being a loving, indulgent parent in the sunny periods between the beatings, I was confused. As soon as an hour after a caning he would be speaking gently to me and offering apologies.

Today, I am certain that these rages were the last reflex stirrings of the abiding resentment my father felt about his own childhood. I was quite literally his whipping boy, for a time. His anger went very deep and occasionally it would consume him completely. That doesn't justify what he did to me over a two- or three-year period, but I have to reconcile his basic decency and gentleness as a father with these grotesque outpourings of violent anger.

Significantly, he never struck my sister, and certainly not my mother.

It was a strictly father–son thing.

I WAS NEARLY TEN and had bumped into my mother at the shops as I walked home from school. I persuaded her to buy a packet of Rolos for us all to share after supper that evening.

Back home watching *Blue Peter*, I called to her in the kitchen.

'Mum, can I have one of those Rolos?'

'No. After supper.'

'Go on. Just one . . .'

'Oh, all right. They're in my raincoat pocket. Just one, though.'

'Promise.'

Fifteen minutes later, as Valerie Singleton told us the programme's cat was getting over the flu, I was looking in horror at the ripped paper on the carpet in front of me. There was just one Rolo left.

I stuffed it back into my mother's pocket with the wrappings and hoped for the best. Maybe I could blame it on Elizabeth.

Later, after we'd all eaten, my mother went to get the sweets. She came back with the solitary survivor, looking more amused than cross.

'OK, who ate all of these?'

My sister had only arrived home a couple of minutes before the meal so I couldn't pin it on her. I was about to confess when I glanced at my father.

His face had gone the sinister shade of dark red I knew so well. I panicked.

'Not me. Honestly, Mum . . . Dad. Not me.'

'Come on, Richard, it couldn't have been anyone el—'

But my father interrupted her.

'I will not have you lying. I will not have it. You get one more chance. Did you eat all of them?'

I thought of the one remaining chocolate.

'Well . . . not exactly. I left—'

'Go to your room and wait.'

My mother grimaced. 'Chris, no. It's only a few sweets. We can . . .'

But her husband had already left the room. I walked silently up the stairs and waited in my bedroom, listening to the grinding of the shed door and trying to breathe normally.

My father came in with the cane.

'Wait, Dad, I was only—'

'Take off your shirt.'

This was new. I reluctantly pulled it over my head and at once the beating began. But after the first agonising strokes, delivered randomly across my chest and waist, something deep inside me revolted. I rushed at my father, kicking and punching him and trying to grab the bamboo. He thrust me off easily and a bizarre chase ensued, with me hopping round the room and over my bed, the cane whistling through the air behind me and occasionally making stinging contact.

Finally my father—not the fittest of men—gave up, completely out of breath. He hurled his stick at me and stormed out. I threw it back at him and collapsed on my bed, shocked and in tremendous pain.

The noise of the encounter must have filled the house. As did the colossal row which now took place between my parents. Elizabeth crept into my room. 'Mum says she's going to call the police.'

The row stopped suddenly and a few moments later my mother appeared in front of me.

'Put the light on, darling. I want to look at you.'

I realised I had been sitting in the growing dark and switched on my bed-side lamp, its shade askew after the exciting events of a few minutes before. My mother stared at my upper body.

'It's all right. It's all going to be all right. I'll just go and fetch some Green Ointment from the bathroom. Stay there.'

Green Ointment was the Savlon of its day and our family swore by it. My mother came back and dabbed it along the multiple weals on my arms and body, and on the fingers that had been bruised trying to snatch away my father's stick.

'Wait here, my love. I'll be back with some hot chocolate in a minute.'

She went back downstairs again and this time the only voice I could hear was hers, a low, endless monotone which for some reason my father did not interrupt. I fell asleep before the hot chocolate arrived.

The next day was a Friday: PE day for my class. There was no question of my being allowed to go to school. Although none of my injuries were serious, the marks left by the bamboo were livid and there could be no explaining them away.

My father was silent at breakfast. My mother did the talking.

'Your father is extremely ashamed of himself. He will be apologising to you later, but I am going to tell you something first. He has promised me faithfully never to hit you again. He knows what will happen if he breaks this promise. I don't believe he will, otherwise we wouldn't all be sitting here now.'

My father cleared his throat and looked at me for the first time. 'I have to go to Shrewsbury this morning, to pick up an American car. It's one of the new Ford Mustangs. The company are lending it to Prince Philip. I thought I'd stop off at Shawbury on the way. Would you like to come?'

An hour later we were belting up the M1 in a green-striped Lotus Cortina. Without moving his eyes from the road ahead he began to make the humblest apology I have ever been offered. I instinctively knew he was truly sincere, not just in his anguished regrets, but also in his passionate promises never to hit me again.

As we swept towards Kiln Farm, my father tried to explain how he thought his rages were something to do with his boyhood. He wasn't making excuses, he said; there were none to make. And after the apologies and promises, his conversation increasingly became more with himself than with me. I was not yet ten, but I detected, for the first time, the childhood source of his sporadic rages. It was an explanation that made sense even then, long before I traced the thread of betrayal and rejection running between the generations that preceded me.

Thanks to my mother's stand and his own nascent if belated insight, my father finally fixed the last part of him broken by his childhood. I long ago forgave him my involuntary part in the process.

And I got to ride back to London in a Mustang.

AS WE SPED SOUTH in the red and cream car, attracting startled looks from other drivers all the way back down the motorway, I instinctively trusted my father's promise that he would never beat me again. I put my faith in him, as sons do when their fathers make solemn vows to them. And as time went by and the cane remained absent from its cobwebbed corner in our garden shed, I realised that an unpleasant chapter had definitely closed. The bond of trust between my father and me was restored, never to be breached again.

I sometimes wonder if I have over-sentimentalised this episode, been too quick to write off the debt my father incurred. These were, after all, a series of savage assaults on a child for which he was never brought to book or punished. But the reason I forgave him then—and now—is, I think, because the contrition he displayed was without artifice. Children know when they are being emotionally manipulated, even if they are powerless to do anything about it. My father was truly humbled by the realisation of what he had done. I could see that. And perhaps my automatic act of forgiveness transferred a degree of power and control from father to son.

I don't think this unpleasant interlude in my childhood had any particularly lasting effect on me. I don't wince when I pass a bamboo trellis, I don't have bad dreams in which I am being beaten. I harbour no dark fantasy of swishing a cane myself. Children are adaptable creatures and live in the present. I dealt with the thrashings as best I could while they were happening and, when they stopped, mostly forgot about them.

And now there was a considerable distraction from the receding unpleasantness. It was 1966 and England was hosting the World Cup. Excitement at Dagenham Road was intense. My bedroom began to fill with World Cup paraphernalia: posters of the star players; collections of swap-cards featuring the entire home team; and sundry incarnations of the tournament's mascot, a cheerful, stubby cartoon lion called World Cup Willie.

My father and I hosted daily conferences at the breakfast table to discuss England's prospects, during which my mother and sister were generously allowed to listen, and even to make the occasional contribution. As we had predicted all along, England made it to the final against West Germany. Unashamed xenophobia reigned.

'If we managed to beat Hitler, we can beat that shower,' my father told me, shaving on the morning of the big game.

And we did. The final whistle blew and we all yelled ourselves hoarse. My father and I shook hands in mutual congratulation. Naturally, we forbore to claim credit for our victory. But we knew what we had achieved.

MEANWHILE I was growing up. Rush Green Junior gave way to grammar school—Coopers Company, on Tredegar Square, just off the Mile End Road in Bow. It was a ghastly place, living on its past reputation as a guild school established by the Worshipful Company of Coopers in the mid-1500s. By the time I got there in the second half of the twentieth century, Coopers was a bizarre battleground: a freakish blend of public school-style tradition and modern yobbery. Staff were baffled and intimidated by the gangs of skinheads who dominated the classrooms. Discipline was in tatters. Most of the boys were from the East End—I was one of a small contingent who commuted in from the suburbs. Our 'posh' accents—Ha! Essex boys, we!—marked us as outsiders. One by one we were picked off. I kept a low profile longer than most, partly because I was in the school rugby team.

Coopers had a knife culture long before the current street vogue for carrying blades. One day, when I was fourteen, one of my few remaining friends whispered that I was going to be 'rumbled'—cut—on my way to Mile End tube station after school. I knew he was unlikely to be joking; one boy had been beaten unconscious with a metal chair leg and another had been shot point-blank in the mouth with a .22 air pistol.

Staff were in denial about the steady rise in violence at Coopers. When I went to the headmaster's office to put myself under his protection, he dismissed me out of hand. The choice lay between having a verbal confrontation with him, or a metallic one with his pupils and an exciting trip by ambulance to Whitechapel Hospital. I chose the argument. I insisted on phoning my father at Ford's head office in Brentwood.

Like most schoolboys, I had kept the fact I was being bullied to myself. I didn't see what my parents could do about it. In any case, like most adolescents intimidated by their peer group, I felt as ashamed as I did frightened.

My father must have been surprised to get a call from his son informing him that a casual stabbing was in the offing. But he was urbane.

'Well, we can't have you coming home with puncture wounds,' he said reasonably. 'Put me on to the head, will you?'

Their conversation was brief and mostly conducted at the other end. The headmaster replaced the receiver with a curt: 'Your father will collect you in an hour. You are to remain in my office until then.'

Dad arrived soon after school finished for the day and as we drove past Tredegar Square's scruffy park, we spotted my persecutors lurking in the bushes. My father grunted. 'That's your last day at Coopers. You won't be seeing that lot again.'

'Isn't that . . . a bit cowardly?'

He glanced at me. 'Don't be idiotic. Even at Denstone I never thought I was going to be stabbed.'

You could say I left Coopers at knifepoint, but I would probably have changed schools anyway. We had recently moved out of Greater London to rural Essex, and I transferred to Shenfield Tech, soon to become one of the first of the new comprehensives. Shenfield was a 'mixed' school—what we now call co-ed—so, for the first time in three years, I was in the same class as girls. Teenage girls. I was completely tongue-tied and for months barely spoke a word to the lithe beauties who eyed me coolly across the classroom.

Brentwood was once part of a great forest that covered much of Essex. An expanse of timber to the northwest at Epping is the largest surviving chunk, but Hartswood, on the southern edge of Brentwood, is pretty big too. My parents had had an eye on the spot ever since Ford moved their HQ to the area from its massive factory in nearby Dagenham. So when a semi went on the market they snapped it up.

Our new home looked out on a dense wall of trees standing immediately opposite on the other side of the street. Only a few more houses continued along our side of the road before it was swallowed up by thick woodland on either side. A mile or so distant lay fields and ancient parkland. My hunger for the countryside, an appetite sharpened by so many holidays to Shawbury, was at last satisfied.

When I was thirteen my father, nagged incessantly by my grandfather, gave me an air rifle for Christmas. My mother hated my airgun and there was a matriarchal no-shooting decree at home. But I couldn't resist temptation and secretly crept across the road on many dawns to practise my shooting skills. Two brothers who lived next door had air guns too and we usually went together. We were never caught; our parents slept on, oblivious, and the wood was empty at such an early hour.

But, increasingly, we left our rifles behind. We were falling under the spell of a great English deciduous forest. In winter, Hartswood was pungent with the scent of decaying leaves, moss and wilting bracken. We might pick up the unmistakable rank scent of a fox and track him to his earth.

Badger setts were harder to find but when snow fell it was easier to follow their spoor home, a dugout usually hidden under an old tree root in a clay bank. We marked where the animals slept and when spring and summer came spent hours watching their young playing. Sunset was the best time to see the fox cubs; you needed at least a half-moon to see badgers. I loved these expeditions. Most of all, I looked forward to describing them to my grandfather on my next visit to Shawbury.

He always listened with grave attention, followed by precise questions and, finally, his advice on woodcraft. 'If you hear jays starting to scream in the distance, they've like as not seen a fox moving under the trees. Stay still and you'll probably see him too, as long as you're downwind of him.'

For my fourteenth birthday, Granddad gave me *The Book of British Birds*, inscribed, 'To my fellow bird-watcher'. His present didn't embarrass me in the slightest, something which surprises me a little now. After all, it was 1970 and I was increasingly immersed in the rock and pop culture. I was growing my hair long—to my father's utter consternation—and learning to play guitar under the instruction of a teacher who had once accompanied Paul Simon on stage. I was even part of a rudimentary folk-rock band, called, appallingly, 'Alchemy'.

Yet I was secretly delighted to be described by my grandfather as a 'bird-watcher'. I emphasise the word 'secretly'—this was not a soubriquet I could possibly share with friends. But I cherished the bond that was forming between us and I basked in the old man's approval. I took *The Book of British Birds* to bed with me most nights and studied it carefully, particularly the section on species that lived on farmland.

Today, I understand the dynamic that was shaping my emerging friendship with Geoffrey. We had discovered common ground. We may have been discussing jays or pigeons or green woodpeckers; what we were really doing was developing shared language. We could just as well have been discussing football; it was the form of our conversations, not the content, that really mattered. We had become friends and delighted in each other's company on our long walks through Kiln Farm's fields and spinneys.

Geoffrey had plenty of time to spare for such moments. A few years earlier, soon after he turned sixty, he had been poleaxed by a near-fatal heart attack. He recovered, but after this my Uncle Jim ran Kiln Farm.

It left my grandfather with a lot of time on his hands. He went on long walks around Shawbury—doctor's orders—and my mother often joined him. It was on these long rambles that he began increasingly to confide in her. He told her how he had felt when he realised his family had gone to Canada without him; about the girl he fell in love with there years later; about William's betrayal. He even spoke a little of John, and the pain of losing his little boy. But not much about this: the subject of John remained deeply painful territory.

Classical music became an even greater comfort to him than before. My father bought him a modern hi-fi unit, and the two of them listened to classical music together, eyes closed, lost in the discourse of the great composers. Of course, stereo sound was no use to my grandfather. He had been deaf in one ear since the trenches and could only hear in mono.

Once, I watched them sitting side by side in armchairs pushed together in the middle of the room, with speakers on either side, and heard my grandfather ask, 'Where's the soloist, Chris?'

His son pointed to a corner. 'Over there.'

My grandfather nodded. 'Extraordinary.'

It was the way they were able to communicate emotionally. Timeless music had become an alternative language they appreciated together. After one long session, they slowly opened their eyes and shyly nodded and smiled at one another. They understood what the other had felt. It was a touching moment to witness.

BY NOW I WAS SIXTEEN and clear on what I wanted to do. Go to university to study English, and then get a graduate trainee placement on some newspaper. I was going to be a reporter, like my dad.

In June 1972 I sat my final O level—the GCSE of the day—and dashed off a letter to my local paper. I suggested to the editor of the *Brentwood Argus* that he let me spend a few weeks in his newsroom, making tea, fetching and carrying generally, and getting a flavour of life on a weekly title.

The reply was curt. His reporters were far too busy news-gathering to keep an eye on some sixteen-year-old lad and anyway they made their own tea, thanks. I could come in for a quick chat if I liked, though.

My father coached me on questions to ask and a few days later I sat in the editor's office, surrounded by inky proofs, newsroom rotas and expense claims that lay in a tray marked 'Abandon all hope ye who enter here'. Every single person I glimpsed in the newsroom next door was smoking furiously and hammering away on ancient Underwood typewriters.

I can't recall much about the interview but I do remember how it ended. The editor eyed me up speculatively before saying, 'I've got a cub reporter's job going. Was going to advertise. Yours if you want it. Three-year apprenticeship. Start tomorrow. Pay's rubbish, but you can fiddle your expenses a bit. What do you say?'

I said I needed to discuss it with my parents and tottered out onto the street. The editor's sash window on the first floor above slid up with a crash

affection for them all. When I try to help one of them with their problems, I don't add or subtract a little extra tender loving care depending on which one carries my DNA and which one doesn't.

When their mother and I made our wills, I didn't think of putting a little extra aside for the two children whose cells come from the Madeley gene pool. If either of us had suggested it, the other would have thought they had gone mad.

They are all our children. Equal shares for all, in love and treasure.

I GRITTED MY TEETH and held on tight to my squirming, kicking, yelling son as I edged my way between tables towards the restaurant exit. Jack was five now, and if I'd had hopes he would grow up as biddable and easy-going as his brothers, those hopes had faded long ago. He could be a little sod.

'Help! Somebody help me!'

'He's just doing it for effect,' I said tersely to a group of concerned diners as I sidled past, trying to keep Jack's flying feet from kicking anyone in the head. 'Everything's under control, I assure you. Excuse me, can I just . . . thank you.'

When it came to iron wills, Jack could have given Stalin a few useful pointers. He had the unyielding determination of a world-class tyrant. Once he had decided to do something—or more usually, to not do something—nothing and no one was allowed to stand in his way.

Jack's battlefield of choice was the dining table. He regarded being asked to sit down at one as a personal and grievous affront to his *amour propre* and his inviolable right to self-determination.

Today's outbreak of hostilities had begun that morning with a typical opening skirmish.

'What are we doing today, Daddy?'

'We're going out for Sunday lunch.'

'*No. No*. We're not, not, *not*!'

At least you couldn't accuse Jack of ambiguity in such matters.

'Yes we are. At a lovely little pub in the country, a place called the Trough of Bowland, where—'

'*Hate* the toffobolly.'

'The Trough of Bowland. You've never been there, Jack, so you can't possibly hate it, can you?'

'Yes, yes, I *can*.'

Two hours later we were trying and failing to enjoy Sunday lunch. As were most of the other diners, thanks to Jack. He was using his usual tried and trusted tactics—rhythmically kicking the table, noisily refusing to eat, and demanding, over and over: 'Want to go *home*!'

'This is awful, Richard,' Judy whispered as people at other tables looked across with increasing hostility. 'He's ruining it for everyone . . . perhaps we'd just better go.'

'No. We mustn't give in to him. Appeasement never works.'

'Oh, don't be ridiculous. This is Lancashire in 1990, not Munich 1938.'

I glared at my son, now blowing noisy bubbles through a straw and throwing ice from his Coke at his sister opposite.

'Jack!'

He glared back. 'Want to *go*!'

'Right, that's it, mister. You're going all right. I'm taking you out to the car. You can sit in there while we have our lunch in peace.'

Shoulders at nearby tables sagged with relief.

Exile was our ultimate sanction and Jack hated it. Deprived of his audience he would usually subside after a few minutes and be brought back to the table, docile enough. He'd know he'd lost a battle but not the war, and there would be other campaigns to fight.

But he never went without a struggle. Today, as I picked him up and put him over my shoulder, he called dramatically, 'No! Not the car!'

Faces turned. What was that man about to do to his little boy?

Jack's radar was good. He picked up the signals and exploited them straight away, stretching out his hands beseechingly to the room behind me.

'Not the car,' he sobbed piteously. 'Not the car, Daddy!'

There were stirrings among the tables. 'Is everything . . . all right?' a woman asked as we passed.

'It's all right, everyone,' I said with forced cheeriness. 'Situation completely under control. He's just playing to the gallery.' I sounded like Basil Fawlty, Judy told me later.

Was that a smile of secret triumph lurking on my son's face as I strapped him into his car seat, and left him for a few minutes while I had a cigarette? It certainly looked like one. But when I returned he appeared contrite.

'Sorry, Daddy.'

'All right. Promise to be good now?'

'Promise.'

Hmm. That's what Napoleon said after his first great defeat and exile. He was already planning his comeback at Waterloo.

WE DIDN'T NEED a child psychologist to work out what was driving Jack's determination to call the shots at the dinner table. There were two fundamental reasons, aside from that iron will of his.

His brothers. The twins were ten years older than Jack and the poor kid was stuck in a never-ending game of catch-up with them. He yearned to have their freedoms, to be given a golden pass that would allow him access to all areas of their comparatively privileged lives. It must have been deeply frustrating for him to have to bob along so far behind in their wake.

His sister. Chloe had arrived when Jack was only thirteen months old. He was simply too young to understand what was going on, other than to instinctively grasp the primary point: that his position had been usurped. There was a new baby demanding his parents' attention, and why should he do anything but resent it? The day after Chloe was born I took Jack into St Mary's to see his mother and meet his new sister. I'd tried to tell him what was happening but when they're barely one year old you might as well try to explain how Parliament works.

We arrived in Judy's room, where she was feeding the baby. Jack looked astonished. When I lowered him onto the bed, he kicked out at them with his foot and started to cry. A textbook case of sibling rivalry.

Jack, then, was a completely different kettle of fish from his brothers: stroppier, angrier, endlessly assertive. Where Tom and Dan were content to negotiate with the world, Jack was more likely to chuck down the gauntlet and challenge it to a fight.

I had rather more to do with bringing up Jack than his mother did in the first couple of years after Chloe was born. Judy was necessarily occupied with the baby, and then succumbed to a vicious bout of postnatal depression, which caused her to quietly withdraw into herself for many months before we realised what was happening to her and sought help.

Trying to work out what made my little fireball of a boy work was a challenge. The key, I slowly discovered, was to roll with the punches as much as possible. He wasn't particularly badly behaved; he was simply trying to carve out his own niche in our complicated little family. Although his endless declarations of independence could be draining, it was usually wise to let his little storms blow themselves out. And I also learned that, with Jack, forewarned was defused. He hated surprises or suddenly announced plans. So if on Saturday I casually announced we were all going out for lunch the following day, the scale of his opposition was mute; it didn't interfere with his immediate plans and, anyway, tomorrow was another day. He'd still be grumpy at table, granted, but his full-scale guerrilla campaigns of disruption became things of the past.

Anyway, if they returned there was always The Car.

IN THE SUMMER OF 1996 we moved to London, with the transfer of our morning show from Liverpool to the capital. The money two successful TV careers had provided bought us a large house up on one of London's ancient hills, in heavily wooded Hampstead. Not a 'mansion' as some newspapers claimed, but a comfortable family home nevertheless.

It stood facing a scrap of preserved medieval fields, the remnant of what used to be Wyldes Farm. Constable, Turner and Gainsborough once lodged at the farmhouse—which still stands—to paint in the clear country air high above toxic London, escaping its stench and smoke and disease. Now the surviving meadows, hedgerows and trees were part of a turn-of-the-century addition to the more famous heath, the Heath Extension.

It felt safe there; as safe as Old Broadway had. Families walking dogs and throwing Frisbees roamed the fields opposite. We thought it a perfect place to bring up our children, and after a long interval I again had my little make-believe corner of countryside to look at. I woke up the morning after we'd moved in and felt like a pigeon back in its loft.

The twins had stayed behind in Manchester to begin their degree courses, but came down for our first Christmas in London.

On Christmas Day afternoon I left Judy and nine-year-old Chloe in the kitchen and wandered into the television room, where Tom and Dan were watching Rory Bremner's alternative Queen's speech. Jack poked his head round the door, holding his main present, a remote-control car.

'Can I take this onto the heath? I want to see how far it goes before the signal packs in.'

I glanced through our front window. There were plenty of Christmas Day walkers out on the frosty meadow opposite.

'Sure. But stay in sight of the house and don't be too long—we'll be eating soon.'

'OK, Dad.' And he was gone.

Tom and Dan were sitting on a sofa next to the window that looked out onto the heath. 'Just keep an eye on Jack, would you?' I asked them.

'Sure.' They turned round every now and then to check on their ten-year-old brother.

After a few minutes, Tom stood up and peered out for a little longer.

'Has Jack come back in?' he asked me over his shoulder. 'Only I can't see him any more.'

I came over to the window. The field was much emptier now; only a few figures moved against a background of skeletal trees and an already darkening midwinter sky. Jack must have come back. I went through to the kitchen where Judy and Chloe were.

'Has Jack come in?'

They looked vaguely at me and shook their heads. 'Don't think so.'

I went to the front door and opened it. I cupped my hands to my mouth. 'Jack!'

My voice echoed back to me, but that was the only reply. I went to the bottom of the stairs and called up to his bedroom.

'Jack! Are you up there?'

Nothing. A faint sensation of unease moved deep inside and I went back to the kitchen.

'I can't find Jack. Seriously, Judy, he's vanished. He's not in the house, or the garden, or on the heath.'

'He must be. You can't have looked properly, that's all.' I went back to the open front door and stared out again. It was darker now, and there was nothing moving out there.

'*Jack!*'

I crossed the road onto the grass. I heard voices and suddenly a couple walking their dog materialised out of some bushes. I jogged over to them.

'Have you seen a boy in a blue jumper? He'll have been playing with a remote-control car . . . a red one.'

They shook their heads. 'No, sorry.'

'Is he there?' Judy called from our front steps. For the first time she sounded worried.

'No.'

By now Tom and Dan were making a room-by-room search of the house. I rejoined Judy on our front steps as the twins clattered breathlessly down the stairs.

'Not there.'

'Not there.'

Judy turned to me, white and wide-eyed.

She said it first. What we'd both started thinking, at the edges of our minds.

'We've lost him. Some bastard must have seen him playing with his truck and gone over and said to him, "Hey—I've got one of those in my car. Come and have a look." Oh God, Richard, he's been taken, he's been taken.'

I looked wildly around me. We'd warned our children time without number not to go off with strangers, but it happens. A couple of years before, Jack had been on his bike in Old Broadway and had ridden straight into a car cruising slowly down the street. He wasn't hurt and we were in the house, oblivious. A few minutes later he ran in to tell us what had happened and finished with the words, 'But I did cry a bit and the lady sitting next to the man driving put me on her knee and cuddled me. She was very kind, Mummy.'

I'd had visions of a latter-day Hindley and Brady on the prowl and exploded. 'You never, *ever* get into a strange car. Not *ever*!'

Now it looked like he had, and this time the Big Bad Wolf really was behind the wheel. I had a sudden, vivid image of my son panicking in some paedophile's car, now miles away somewhere on the North Circular. I pushed it away.

'Hang on. Let's think. Is there anywhere he could have gone? What about Ronnie and Jan?'

They used to live in our house. They had only moved a few hundred yards up the road, and had sons around Jack's age.

They'd become friends. Jack always asked us if he wanted to call on them but perhaps, in all the excitement of Christmas Day, he'd forgotten. I grabbed my mobile phone and punched in their number. Jan answered.

'Oh hi, Richard—Merry Christmas!'

I could hear party noises and the squeal of children's voices.

'Jan, is Jack there?'

My voice had cracked slightly, and she sounded startled as she said quickly, 'Why? What's wrong?'

'Is he there?'

'I don't think so. But the house is full of kids. Hold on, I'll check.'

She left the receiver swaying on the end of its flex and I heard it bumping lazily against the wall. Time seemed to slow and settle along with the swinging phone. Then it snapped back into gear as the receiver rattled. Jan was back on the line.

'No, he's definitely not here—he hasn't been round for a couple of days. Is everything OK?'

That was that, then. The last door behind which our son might have been standing had slammed shut. Game over. Try again.

I stared at my wife. 'I'm calling the police.'

She nodded hopelessly and sagged against the doorframe.

As I was about to complete the triple sequence, I suddenly remembered one last door we hadn't tried. Our neighbours, an American couple, had a dog, a big grey Weimaraner called Sophie. Sometimes Jack went round to play with her. He always checked with us first, but . . .

I walked up their front path, praying fiercely. 'God, let him be here. If you don't, we've lost him. Make him be here.'

I pressed the doorbell but couldn't hear anything. It didn't seem to be working, so I hammered on the door with my fist. I turned away in despair, reaching for my phone again, but suddenly heard the faint sound of voices as a distant door opened. Footsteps approached and a lock and chain rattled.

The front door swung open and a blast of warmth and smell of cooking hit me. Our neighbour, Sandy, cracker hat askew and glass of wine in hand, swayed slightly before me. 'Hey, Richard! Merry Christmas!'

'Is Jack here?'

She blinked in surprise.

'Sure, didn't you know? He's out back with Sophie getting her to chase his new truck. We were just going to . . .' She stared at me. 'Richard . . . are you OK?'

My legs had given way and I was breathing oddly.

'We've been . . . we couldn't find him, Sandy. He was on the heath and then . . . he wasn't. We looked everywhere. We thought he'd been . . .'

Her eyes widened.

'Oh my God, I'm so sorry, we thought you knew he was here . . . I'm so sorry.'

Sophie came rushing out barking furiously, Jack on her heels.

'Hi, Dad. Is our dinner ready? They've nearly finished theirs here . . .'

When I'd been Jack's age there was a big fire at the gasworks at the end of Crow Lane. My mates and I watched, thrilled, as the fierce jet of flame thundered from a ruptured pipe directly onto one of the gasometers, blistering the paint and turning the metal beneath it a dull red. We'd managed to sneak through the police cordon and were up nice and close to the action. Then we were spotted, bundled into a squad car and driven home.

My mother's language, when the officers on the doorstep explained what her son had been up to, was unprecedented.

Thirty years later, on another doorstep, history repeated itself.

Word for word.

I WILL NEVER FORGET the animal intensity of my emotions over that thirty minutes on a Christmas Day; the relentless acceleration of dread and fear, culminating in the absolute certainty that my son had been abducted. Even now my heart trembles at the memory of it, and yet all was well, nothing was wrong; happy endings all round. But what a glimpse into darkness those minutes provided; a very facsimile of hell.

I said happy endings all round—not quite. The flash of completely unreasonable anger I felt towards my son when I found him at last was almost as fierce as the panic that preceded it, and it took a while to fade. Perhaps, too, there was a faint echo of my father's propensity to explode with rage. I don't know. I assumed at the time this was a one-way passage of emotion; a strictly father-to-son, adult-to-child reaction. But a few years later I discovered this was wrong.

We were celebrating my niece's eighteenth birthday at a restaurant called the Blue Strawberry. Our sprawling family party had commandeered a huge table and, as is usual when we all gather together, the conversational volume control was set to eleven. I was having a fierce argument with my sister's husband about the current television remake of *The Forsyte Saga*. He'd just made rather a good point and I intended to counter it. So I swallowed the entire chunk of rare beef I'd just forked into my mouth, wanting to return to the fray without delay.

I opened my mouth, but no words came. The slick piece of meat had wrapped itself snugly across the top of my windpipe, and I couldn't make a sound. Neither could I breathe.

Choking—proper choking, I mean, not the coughing and spluttering we all make when something goes down the wrong way (if you can cough and splutter, you're OK)—is the most extraordinarily sinister physical experience I have ever had. I must have exhaled just before swallowing so I had very little air in my lungs; no reservoir of oxygen to compress upwards to punch out the obstruction. I sat in complete silence, trying to work out what to do. My brother-in-law thought I'd been silenced by his rapier thrust and turned to talk to someone else.

In the middle of this raucous family gathering, I was trapped in my own little world.

I wrapped my arms round myself and tried to squeeze my ribcage in a sort of self-delivered bear hug. No dice. Then I thrust hard backwards into my chair and strained every muscle to try and deliver a cough. Not even the tiniest hack. My chest was locked in paralysis.

By now I'd started to drool slightly and black spots were beginning to appear in front of my eyes. Uh-oh.

Still no one noticed anything was wrong, even though I hadn't spoken for at least thirty seconds (unheard of). I pushed my chair back with a crash and stood up, bending low over the table and hammering it as hard as I could with my fists, not to attract attention but in an instinctive attempt to dislodge the blockage. It didn't work but people now looked across at me curiously.

'What on earth's he doing?'

My face was beginning to turn as blue as the proverbial strawberry and Peter suddenly shouted, 'Christ—he's choking!'

Uproar. Fists crashing on my back (Judy's). Bigger fists (Pete's). Still the thing in my throat wouldn't budge, and now the dark spots were multiplying into a grey blizzard.

Strangely, the initial panic that had swept through me now faded, and I was able to think perfectly clearly. I remember telling myself: 'This is a stupid way to die' and a very high whine began droning in my head, exactly like a mosquito hovering over one's ear on a hot summer night.

Still the pounding behind me went on, and still my respiratory system was stuck in stubborn lockdown.

Then I heard a new noise, not from inside my head but from the rapidly shrinking world in front of me as my peripheral vision shorted out. It was the sound of glasses and bottles being scattered as my sister, on the far side of the room, leapt onto the table and strode across it yelling, 'Get out of the way!' with all the authority of the teacher that she is.

Elizabeth jumped down behind me and wrapped her arms round my lower chest, making a hard fist just below the sternum. Ah, I thought almost lazily, the old Heimlich manoeuvre. Good for sis.

Doctors say if you find yourself having to administer the Heimlich manoeuvre, you shouldn't be afraid to break a few ribs in the process, and my big sister certainly wasn't. The violent squeeze she delivered made all those thumps on my back feel like kindly pats.

But it didn't work. Not in the slightest degree. She tried again and again, but my trachea stubbornly refused to release its grip on the intruder it had decided was trying to infiltrate the lungs beneath.

It's called the drowning reflex. A sphincter muscle at the top of the wind-pipe instantly seals the tube shut when water tries to get in. If you're drown-ing it's the body's way of buying a little extra time for you to get to the surface or be rescued, because the moment you inhale water, you're pretty much finished. But the trachea can't tell the difference between drowning and choking, and the conscious brain can't override the primitive reflex that's been triggered deep in the cerebral cortex. This evolutionary conundrum was now in the process of efficiently killing me, albeit in a companionable silence.

Liz had started to panic. From what seemed like a great distance I heard her screaming, 'Help! Somebody help me!' I remembered Jack's performance in another restaurant a long time ago, and smiled inwardly. I was quite calm now, and resigned. Another final coping reflex, apparently. A little home-brewed morphine to ease the crossing.

I managed to lift my head slightly as the light finally began to fade away altogether, and saw my daughter weeping hysterically on the far side of the table, her face pressed into her hands. I couldn't see Judy—she was behind me—but Jack was turned to the wall, beating it with both palms. I felt terribly sorry for all of them, having to see this awful finale, but was perfectly relaxed nevertheless. It was just time to go, that was all.

Perhaps it was my legs finally giving way that did it. As I buckled towards the floor, my sister gave another despairing squeeze, the strongest yet. Muscle power combined with gravity, and the rock in my throat moved for the first time since I'd swallowed it nearly three minutes before. I managed to gulp in a tiny gasp of air before my stupid, suicidal windpipe jealously grabbed the lump back again.

Liz felt it. 'I think it's coming!' She gave another vicious heave.

Now I had a little air to work with I managed a tiny cough at the same time and up shot the vile—and by now almost liquid—piece of meat, into my mouth. I spat it out and sucked in the biggest lungful of air in my entire life. Sound and vision flickered for a moment and then snapped back to normal. All systems go.

Laughter. Tears. Cheers. I hugged my sister, I hugged my wife, I hugged my sister again. Chloe was suddenly in my arms too.

'Oh, Daddy, I thought you were dying . . .'

'I can assure you I was,' I croaked, 'but it's all right now. I'm fine.'

Then Jack appeared in front of me, cheeks wet with tears, hair wild, face contorted with fury. He pointed a trembling finger right into my own face.

'*Never. Eat. Again.*'

There was a moment's pause and then everyone except Jack cracked up. He looked round in angry confusion.

'I mean, never eat *meat* again . . . I'm serious, Dad. Don't ever do that again . . . please.' And he burst into tears.

He was easily the most affected person in the room. Jack was sixteen when his pa nearly expired before his very eyes, but even now, in his twenties, he looks up in alarm if I so much as clear my throat while I'm eating. His anger with me that day was an interesting reflection of my own with him the Christmas he went missing. Perhaps men instinctively resent having their deepest emotions disturbed unnecessarily; an atavistic sense that their feelings have been toyed with needlessly.

Judy certainly wasn't angry with Jack when I discovered him next door that Christmas Day. She was just suffused with relief. Meanwhile, within minutes of my sister saving my life, both Elizabeth and Judy were making dry jokes at my expense about what had just happened. Even Chloe started teasing me before we'd even left the restaurant.

Jack, though, sat in brooding silence. Even today, I don't think he has quite forgiven me. Whenever the subject comes up, his face sets and he becomes monosyllabic before, usually, leaving the room. I frightened him that day, badly, and he's still not quite over it. Come to think of it, neither am I. I tend to steer clear of roast beef now.

Now, AS MY SON moves into his adulthood, I feel as if I stand on one of the great fault lines of my life, an elevated ridge between tectonic plates. Ahead lies the future, mostly a smooth, featureless land. But when I turn around I look across a continent sculpted and scarred by the unalterable past.

From here I can see the road that winds through a century of my paternal family history. Jack and I stand in the foreground.

Behind us, in the middle distance, is Christopher, and further away, looking sadly at his son, Geoffrey. Distant but discernible, Henry stands, frozen in his moment of decision more than one hundred years ago. A choice he could neither revise nor revisit.

Henry's abandonment of his son at Kiln Farm conferred an icy childhood on the boy. In turn, a glacier ground its way into my father's life.

Perhaps Geoffrey could have tried harder to block or divert the freezing flow, but fate—and Uncle William—conspired against him.

When my father arrived in Canada he found a way to escape the cold past. That was thanks to my mother and the warmth of her family life there. Emotionally defrosted, Christopher did everything he could to reinvent himself and become a loving father to his children.

He wasn't entirely successful. The suppressed rage that found an outlet in my beatings took a long time to subside. And my father never regained the self-belief that had been extinguished by his father's lack of affection.

But he did enough. He did enough. His children grew up secure in their father's love, and that was a huge achievement, a true reversal of fortune.

I have often wondered how the consequences that flowed from the fateful decision made by 'Mr Bulford from Birmingham', when he withdrew his capital from the business he shared with my grandfather so long ago, may have rippled into my life and influenced my behaviour as a father.

For example, my father lacked self-confidence; as a consequence, I have too much of it. That can be dangerous (and overconfidence is not an attractive quality, either). I am certain it was at the root of my catastrophic oversight at a supermarket checkout when I was in my early thirties. I forgot to pay for a stack of items in the front section of my trolley, because my mind was in overdrive planning the rest of a busy busy day. I thought I could handle everything and anything and forgot that the devil lurks in the detail. I ended up having to argue my innocence before a judge and jury.

As I have become older, I have had to fashion tools to hack away at the hubris to which I am prone. My marriage has helped me do this; Judy is inclined to pessimism and this has acted as a gentle but constant counterweight to my sometimes overweening optimism.

I loathe corporal punishment, for what I think are obvious reasons. I believe I would have always hated the idea of visiting such cruelty on my son. Just as Christopher swore to himself that he would show his children love in a way that his father could not, I promised myself, even when I was a boy, that I would never inflict the pain and humiliation of a thrashing on my own son.

But the real connective strand that binds together my father, grandfather and me only became fully clear to me during the writing of this book. It can be expressed in a mantra that I am certain never left my grandfather's lips, although he followed its dictum faithfully from the moment he was left behind in 1907. It is a creed that allowed him to be reconciled with his family in Canada two decades later.

To understand all is to forgive all.

On the very morning of Geoffrey's abandonment, William and Thomas and Sarah explained to the frantic boy standing before them the exact nature of the agreement with Henry. From that moment he had not the slightest doubt that he had been pawned by his father, and that the ticket with his name on it could only be redeemed when he was twenty-one. From the very first, he understood the fate that had befallen him and who was responsible for it. And yet he forgave them all.

My father, in his turn, understood the reasons his father had slowly evolved into a man who found it so difficult to demonstrate affection. He knew Geoffrey's story well enough; he told it to me enough times, and sympathetically too. But like his father before him, he had no interest in playing the blame game.

The one thing he never really understood was why he'd been packed off to Denstone, but he chose to write that riddle off and refused to take his father to task about it. Instead, he tried all his life to build bridges with Geoffrey. And he succeeded. They both succeeded in the end. They found a language through which they could, at last, communicate emotionally. Music was the salve and blessing that healed and united Geoffrey and Christopher. I saw it with my own eyes.

And me?

To understand all is to forgive all.

My father's extraordinary confessional to his young son on the road from London to Shawbury the morning after he had beaten me so recklessly and severely, was a defining moment in both our lives. I instinctively accepted the explanation for his behaviour, and trusted his sincerity when he promised me it would never be repeated.

I understood and I forgave. He never gave me cause to regret that.

And Jack?

I think it's time my son spoke for himself.

Epilogue

I never met my grandfather Christopher and so, for reasons that I'm sure are more to do with my short attention span than with my dad withholding information, I never knew the story of his life, or his father's.

The occasional conversation I had with Dad about Chris and Geoffrey left me with a vague awareness of my great-grandfather's abandonment, but in my mind our family history was always coloured with an atmosphere of mystery and adventure. They were merely bedtime stories, or casual but interesting and insightful anecdotes Dad would relate to me whenever we found ourselves on a day out together, or sharing a long car journey.

If I'm brutally honest, up until a few years ago, I couldn't even remember my grandfather's first name. I would constantly confuse it with my mother's dad's. This other grandfather also died before I was born, and his name, too, had little meaning for me. In fact, if anyone were to have shown me a photo of the two men, I would have had a tough time deciding who was who.

Then, one afternoon in 2001, Dad came back from his mother's house with a collection of photographs documenting his childhood, adolescence and early professional life. I remember sifting through them, smiling and cringing at the woeful 1970s progressive folk-rock haircut he sported throughout his late teens and early twenties. It was weird seeing him at the same stage of life that I was now passing through—the same awkward, lanky teenager I saw each time I looked in the mirror.

These glimpses of my own father's youth—hanging out with his mates, smoking cigarettes, generally messing around—had a distinct and profound impact on me. They provided me with a strange comfort. I was a difficult teenager, and I think between the ages of fifteen and seventeen my dad and I found our relationship under strain for the first time. As Christopher had lamented to his wife years before, there was simply 'too much testosterone in the house'.

Looking at those photos allowed me to see my dad in an entirely different light. However much I deny it, however much I try to ignore it, Dad and I are pretty much identical in terms of our character traits. For example, our tempers are bloody awful. Although Dad has had nearly three decades more than me to work on his inner Zen, we both get needlessly wound up by small and insignificant provocations.

In short, I was able to see my dad as a person, a human being as opposed to simply my father. I think this understanding was a seminal point in our relationship, and one that brought us undeniably closer.

As I glanced through those old, dusty photos, I gained my first proper understanding that my dad had . . . well, actually had his own dad. This may sound ridiculously naive, and of course I knew that my father had not been raised single-handedly by my grandma. But every third or fourth photo that I came across depicted my father with a tall, smartly dressed man with strong features, a wide grin and broad shoulders.

To see my elusive grandfather staring back at me, happy, smiling and alive, triggered a strange feeling of emotional connection. I could suddenly see my dad, not as a father, but as a son. And in the strangest way, I at last saw my grandfather, Christopher, for the first time.

A sense of guilt began to build within me. I felt selfish and self-absorbed. I had never given Christopher any thought. The idea that I was part of a legacy, of sorts—that my life and upbringing was inexorably linked with such recent generations—had never even occurred to me before. As to what kind of father he had been to my own, I hadn't a clue.

Now I know. The pages preceding these have provoked a similar, but much stronger, reaction to the one I had years ago when I flicked through those old family photographs. The life of my great-grandfather Geoffrey—permeated with a constant feeling of loss, disappointment and abandonment—is an unimaginable world away from the comfortable, affectionate upbringing afforded to me. The bleak and harsh reality he was confronted with at such a vulnerable age encompassed not only loss but, obviously, a deep sense of betrayal. Henry's decision was by no means an easy one, but it is hard to imagine any father now resorting to such cold, sad practicality. But this is the problem, for me. I find it hard to imagine because the relationship I have with my father is a loving one, built on a mutual feeling of trust and care. Essentially, I know that Dad will always be there for me. As I will for him. This may sound cheesy or clichéd, but it is sincere—absolute certainties that I hold very close to my heart.

I was fascinated by the sentence my father used to describe Christopher's reconciliation with his own father: 'It's never too late to salvage something from the wreckage.' Henry's 'deal' with his brother spawned deep-rooted psychological issues that I think are, even now, being confronted by my dad. *Fathers & Sons* is an exploration of the power of forgiveness. Geoffrey forgave Henry, Christopher forgave Geoffrey, and Dad forgave Christopher. The only difference with me is, I have nothing to forgive.

Jack Madeley, June 2008

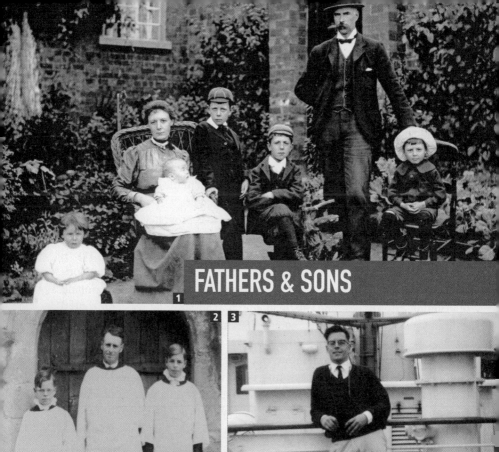

FATHERS & SONS

Left page: 1 The Madeleys, *c.* 1902. From left: Doris, Hannah (holding William), John and Douglas. Henry stands, hand on Geoffrey's chair. **2** Shawbury Church, *c.* 1935. From left: Christopher, Geoffrey, James. **3** Christopher on the boat to Canada (1950) and **4** working as a journalist. **Right page: 5** Christopher and Mary Claire Madeley, October 1951. **6** Richard with his father. **7** Richard and Judy, November 21, 1986, with, from left: Dan, Tom and Jack.

MOSCOW RULES

DANIEL SILVA

Gabriel Allon is semiretired from the Israeli secret service and enjoying a honeymoon in Umbria when his old friend and mentor, Ari Shamron, asks him to investigate the death of a journalist in the French Alps.

The mission takes Allon to the Côte d'Azur, to rural England and, ultimately, to Russia's capital, awash with new oil wealth and bulletproof Bentleys. It's a dangerous place, where Allon must play by Moscow Rules if he hopes to stay alive.

Chapter 1

Courchevel, France

The invasion began, as it always did, in the last days of December. They came by armoured caravan up the winding road from the floor of the Rhône Valley or descended onto the treacherous mountaintop airstrip by helicopter and private plane. Billionaires and bankers, oil tycoons and metal magnates, supermodels and spoilt children: the moneyed elite of a Russia resurgent. They streamed into the suites of the Cheval Blanc and commandeered the big chalets along the Rue de Bellecôte. They booked Les Caves nightclub for private parties and looted the glittering shops of the Croissette. By New Year's Eve, the conquest was complete. Courchevel, the exclusive ski resort in the French Alps, was once more under Russian occupation.

Only the Hôtel Grand Courchevel managed to survive the onslaught from the East. Hardly surprising, for, at the Grand, Russians were quietly encouraged to find accommodation elsewhere. Her rooms were thirty in number, modest in size and discreet in appointment. One did not come to the Grand for gold fixtures and suites the size of football pitches. One came for a taste of Europe as it once was. Gentlemen wore jackets to dinner and waited until after breakfast before changing into their ski attire. The Internet had not yet arrived at the Grand, but her guests did not seem to mind.

The entrance was heated by a well-tended wood fire, and the reception was a cramped alcove with brass hooks for the room keys and pigeonholes for mail and messages. Adjacent to reception, near the Grand's single wheezing lift, stood the concierge desk. Early in the afternoon of January 2, it was occupied by Philippe, a former French paratrooper. Philippe cast his seasoned concierge's eye over the list of pending arrivals. It contained a single entry: *Lubin, Alex. Arriving by car from Geneva. Booked into Room 237. Ski rental required.*

Philippe cleared his throat discreetly. An impeccably groomed head poked from reception. It belonged to Ricardo, the afternoon manager.

'I think we have a problem,' Philippe said calmly.

Ricardo frowned. He was a Spaniard from the Basque region. He didn't like problems. 'What is it?'

Philippe held up the arrivals sheet. 'Lubin, Alex. Twelve nights. Ski rental required. Who took this reservation?'

'I believe it was Nadine.'

Nadine was the new girl. She worked the graveyard shift. And for the crime of granting a room to someone called Alex Lubin without first consulting Ricardo, she would do so for all eternity.

'Perhaps we can dump him on our competitors,' said the manager. Though senior in rank, Ricardo was twenty years Philippe's junior and had come to rely heavily upon the older man's experience and judgment.

'Not possible. There isn't a room to be had between here and Albertville.'

'Then I suppose we're stuck with him—unless, of course, he can be convinced to leave on his own.'

'What are you suggesting?' asked Philippe.

'Plan B, of course.'

'It's rather extreme, don't you think?'

'Yes, but it's the only way.'

Philippe accepted his orders with a crisp nod and began planning the operation. It commenced at 4.12 p.m., when a grey Mercedes sedan pulled up at the front steps and sounded its horn. Philippe remained at his pulpit for a full two minutes before heading outside. By now the unwanted Monsieur Alex Lubin was standing angrily next to the open boot. He had a face full of sharp angles and pale blond hair.

The concierge frowned at the two large nylon suitcases in the boot as if he had never seen such objects before, then greeted the guest with a glacial warmth. 'May I help you, monsieur?'

The question had been posed in English. The response came in the same language, with a distinct Slavic accent. 'I'm checking into the hotel.'

'Really? I wasn't told about any arrivals this afternoon. I'm sure it was just a slip-up. Why don't you have a word with my colleague at reception? I'm confident he'll be able to rectify the situation.'

Lubin murmured something under his breath and tramped up the steep steps, where he recited his confirmation number to the perplexed-looking duty manager. Try as he might, Ricardo was unable to locate the reservation in question. The problem was finally resolved only to be followed by another. Due to an oversight by the housekeeping staff, the room was not yet ready. 'It will just be a few moments,' Ricardo said in his most silken voice. 'My colleague will place your bags in the storage room. Allow me to show you to our lounge bar.'

Sadly, Ricardo's optimism that the delay would be brief turned out to be misplaced. Indeed, ninety additional minutes would elapse before Lubin was shown, *sans bagages*, to his room. In accordance with Plan B, there was no bathrobe for trips to the wellness centre, no vodka in the minibar and no remote for the television. The heater was roaring. Philippe slipped out through the door, with a promise that the bags would be delivered shortly. Ricardo was waiting for him as he came out of the lift.

'What do you think?' asked Ricardo. 'Mobster, spy or hit man?'

It didn't matter, thought Philippe gloomily. The walls of the Grand had been breached by a Russian. *Resistance* was now the order of the day.

HAD THEY WITNESSED the first few moments of Lubin's stay, they would have felt certain in their belief that a miscreant was in their midst. How else to explain that he removed all the drawers from the chest and the bedside tables and unscrewed all the bulbs from the lamps and the light fixtures? Or that he stripped bare the deluxe queen-size bed and prised the lid from the telephone? Or that, having completed his rampage, he then returned the room to the near-pristine state in which he had found it?

It was because of his profession that he took these rather drastic measures, but Aleksandr Viktorovich Lubin was neither a mobster nor a spy, nor a hit man, only a practitioner of the most dangerous trade one could choose in the brave New Russia: the trade of journalism. His magazine, *Moskovsky Gazeta*, was one of the country's last investigative weeklies. Its reporters and photographers were watched and harassed constantly, not only by the Kremlin's secret police but by the private security services of the powerful oligarchs they attempted to cover. Courchevel was now crawling with such men, men who operated by the creed of Stalin: *Death solves all problems. No man, no problem.*

Confident the room had not been tampered with, Lubin settled himself at the writing desk and removed a file folder from his dog-eared leather briefcase. It had been given to him the previous evening by Boris

Ostrovsky, the *Gazeta*'s editor-in-chief. Their meeting had taken place on a bench in the Arbatskaya Metro station.

I'm going to give you only part of the picture, Ostrovsky had said, handing Lubin the documents with practised indifference. *It's for your own protection. Do you understand, Aleksandr?* Lubin had understood perfectly. Ostrovsky was handing him an assignment that could get him killed.

Lubin opened the file now and examined the photograph that lay on top of the dossier. It showed a well-dressed man with cropped dark hair and a prizefighter's rugged face standing beside the Russian president. Attached to the photo was a thumbnail biography—wholly unnecessary, because Lubin could recite the particulars of Ivan Borisovich Kharkov's career from memory. *Son of a senior KGB officer . . . graduate of Moscow State University . . . boy wonder of the KGB's Fifth Main Directorate . . .* As the empire was crumbling, Kharkov had left the KGB and earned a fortune in banking during the anarchic early years of Russian capitalism. He had invested in energy, raw materials and property, and by the dawn of the millennium had joined Moscow's growing cadre of newly minted multimillionaires.

Lubin flipped to the next page of the dossier, a glossy photograph of 'Château Kharkov', Ivan's winter palace in Courchevel.

He spends the winter holiday there along with every other rich and famous Russian, Ostrovsky had said. *Watch your step. Ivan's goons are all former Spetsnaz and I don't want you to end up like Irina Chernova.*

Irina Chernova was the journalist from the *Gazeta*'s main rival who had exposed one of Kharkov's shadier investments. Two nights after the article appeared, she was shot dead in her apartment building.

Ivan usually operates behind tightly closed doors. Courchevel is one of the few places where he actually moves around in public. We want you to follow him, Aleksandr. We want to know who he's meeting with. Who he's skiing with. Who he's taking to lunch. Get pictures when you can, but never approach him. Ivan's security boys can smell a reporter a mile away.

Ostrovsky had then handed Lubin an envelope containing airline tickets, a rental-car reservation and hotel accommodations. *Check in with the office every couple of days*, Ostrovsky had said. *And try to have some fun. Your colleagues are all very jealous. You get to go to Courchevel and party with the rich and famous while we freeze to death in Moscow.*

On that note, Ostrovsky had risen to his feet and walked away. Lubin had slipped the dossier into his briefcase and broken into a drenching sweat. He was sweating again now. *The damn heat!* The furnace was still blazing away. He was starting to reach for the telephone to lodge another complaint when finally he heard a knock. He flung open the door without bothering to ask who was on the other side. *A mistake*, he thought immediately, for standing in the semidarkness of the corridor was a man of medium height, dressed in a dark ski jacket, a woollen cap and mirrored goggles.

Lubin was wondering why anyone would wear goggles inside a hotel at night when the first blow came, a vicious sideways chop that seemed to crush his windpipe. The second strike, a well-aimed kick to the groin, caused his body to bend in half at the waist. He was able to emit no protest as the man slipped into the room and closed the door soundlessly behind him. Nor was he able to resist when the man forced him onto the bed and sat astride his hips. The knife that emerged from the inside of the man's ski jacket entered Lubin's abdomen just below the ribs and plunged upwards towards his heart. As his chest cavity filled with blood, Lubin watched his own death reflected in the mirrored lenses of his killer's goggles. The assassin rose from the bed and calmly collected the dossier. Aleksandr Lubin felt his heart beat a final time as his killer slipped silently from the room. *The heat*, he was thinking. *The damn heat . . .*

IT WAS SHORTLY after seven when Philippe finally loaded Monsieur Lubin's bags onto the lift. Arriving at Room 237, he found the DO NOT DISTURB sign hanging from the latch. In accordance with the conventions of Plan B, he gave the door three thunderous knocks. Receiving no reply, he drew his passkey from his pocket and entered, just far enough to see two size-twelve Russian loafers hanging a few inches off the end of the bed. He left the bags in the entrance hall and returned to the lobby.

'Passed out drunk,' he reported back to Ricardo.

The Spaniard glanced at his watch. 'It's early, even for a Russian.'

'We'll let him sleep it off. In the morning, when he's good and hung-over, we'll initiate Phase Two.'

The Spaniard smiled. No guest had ever survived Phase Two.

Villa dei Fiori, Umbria

The Villa dei Fiori, a thousand-acre estate in the rolling hills between the Tiber and Nera rivers, had been a possession of the Gasparri family since the days when Umbria was still ruled by the popes. There was a large and lucrative cattle operation and an equestrian centre, and the hillsides were ablaze with sunflowers, olive groves and a small vineyard that contributed several hundred pounds of grapes each year to the local cooperative. Everywhere, there were dogs: a quartet of hounds that roamed the pastures, devouring fox and rabbit, and a pair of neurotic terriers that patrolled the perimeter of the stables with the fervour of holy warriors.

The villa itself stood at the southern edge of the property and was reached by a long gravel drive lined with towering umbrella pines. In the eleventh century, it had been a monastery. There was still a small chapel, and a walled interior courtyard, whose heavy wood and iron doors looked as though they had been built to withstand pagan assault. At the base of the house was a large swimming pool enclosed by walls of Etruscan stone.

Count Gasparri, a faded Italian nobleman with close ties to the Vatican, did not rent out the villa, nor did he make a habit of lending it to friends and relatives, which was why the staff were surprised by the news that they would be playing host to a long-term guest.

'His name is Alessio Vianelli,' the count informed Margherita, the house-keeper, by telephone from his office in Rome. 'He's working on a special project for the Holy Father. You're not to disturb him. You're not to talk to him. But, most important, you are not to tell a soul he's there. As far as you're concerned, this man is a nonperson. He does not exist.'

'And where shall I put this nonperson?' asked Margherita.

'In the master suite, overlooking the swimming pool.'

'What time should we expect him?'

'He refuses to say. He's rather vague, our Signor Vianelli.'

He arrived in the dead of night—sometime after three, according to Margherita, who was in her room above the chapel and woke at the sound of his car. She glimpsed him briefly as he stole across the courtyard in the moonlight, a dark-haired man, thin as a rail, with a duffle bag in one hand and a Maglite torch in the other. He read the note she had left at the entrance to the villa, then slipped inside. A moment later, a light came on in the master bedroom, and he appeared at the window. For several tense seconds, they gazed at each other across the courtyard. Then he gave her a single soldierly nod and drew the shutters closed with an emphatic thump.

They greeted each other properly the next morning at breakfast. After an exchange of polite but cool pleasantries, he said he had come to the Villa dei Fiori for the purposes of work, though he neglected to say precisely what sort of work he would be doing. He asked Margherita not to enter his rooms under any circumstances and informed Anna, the cook, that he would be seeing to his own meals. When recounting the details of the meeting for the rest of the staff, Margherita described his demeanour as 'standoffish'. Anna was far less charitable in her depiction. 'Unbearably rude,' she said. 'The sooner he's gone, the better.'

His life quickly acquired a strict routine. After a spartan breakfast of espresso and dry toast, he would set out on a long march round the estate. At first, he snapped at the estate dogs when they followed him, but eventually he seemed resigned to their company. He walked through the olive groves and the sunflowers and even ventured into the untamed woods.

After his walk, he would prepare a light lunch—usually a bit of bread and local cheese. Then, after a vigorous swim in the pool, he would settle in the garden with a bottle of Orvieto and a stack of books about Italian painters. Not once did he set foot outside the estate.

As the days ground gloriously past, Alessio Vianelli, and his mysterious work on behalf of the Holy Father, became something of an obsession for the staff of the villa. Margherita thought him a missionary recently returned from some hostile region of the world; Anna suspected a fallen priest who had been cast into Umbrian exile; but Isabella, the ethereal half-Swede who oversaw the horse operation, believed him to be a reclusive theologian at work on an important Church document. Carlos, the Argentine cowboy who tended the cattle, reckoned he was an agent of Vatican intelligence. 'Take a look into his eyes, if you dare,' Carlos said. 'He has the eyes of a man who knows death.'

During the second week, there was a series of events that clouded the mystery further. The first was the arrival of a tall young woman with riotous auburn hair and eyes the colour of caramel. She called herself Francesca, spoke Italian with a pronounced Venetian accent, and proved to be a much-needed breath of fresh air. She rode the horses—'Quite well, actually,' Isabella informed the others—and secretly encouraged Anna to cook. Whether they were husband and wife was unclear. Margherita, however, was sure of two things: Signor Vianelli and Francesca were sharing the same bed, and his mood had improved dramatically since her arrival.

And then there were the delivery trucks. The first dispensed a white table of the sort found in professional laboratories; the second, a large microscope with a retractable arm. Other parcels arrived in rapid succession: two large easels of varnished oak from Venice, woodworking tools, dowels, brushes, professional-grade glue, a case of chemicals, lamps and several dozen vessels of pigment.

Finally, three weeks after Signor Vianelli's arrival in Umbria, a dark green panel van eased its way slowly up the tree-lined drive, followed by an official-looking Lancia sedan, whose licence plates spoke of links to the Holy See. From the back of the van emerged a vast, ghastly painting depicting a man being disembowelled. It was soon propped on the two large easels in Count Gasparri's drawing room.

Isabella, who had studied art history before devoting her life to horses, recognised the canvas immediately as Poussin's *Martyrdom of St Erasmus*. Commissioned by the Vatican in 1628, it now resided in the Vatican Museum. That evening, at the staff dinner, she announced that the mystery was solved: Signor Alessio Vianelli was a famous art restorer retained by the Vatican to save a painting.

His days took on a distinctly monastic rhythm. He toiled on the canvas from dawn till midday, slept through the heat of the afternoon, then worked again from dusk until dinner. For the first week the painting remained on the table, where he examined the surface with a microscope and made a series of detailed photographs. Then he transferred the canvas to the easels and began removing the surface grime and yellowed varnish, using a swab fashioned from cotton wool and a wooden dowel. It was a tedious task.

When he had finished removing the old varnish, he covered the canvas in a coat of isolating varnish and began the final phase of the restoration, retouching those portions of the painting that had been lost to time and stress. So perfect was his mimicry of Poussin that it was impossible to tell where the French painter's work ended and his began. He even added faux craquelure, the fine webbing of surface cracks, so that the new faded flawlessly into the old.

Isabella knew enough of the Italian art community to realise Signor Vianelli was no ordinary restorer. No wonder the men of the Vatican had entrusted him with their masterpiece. But why was he working here instead of the state-of-the-art conservation labs at the Vatican?

She was pondering this question, one brilliant afternoon in early June, when she saw the restorer's car speeding down the drive, disappearing behind a cloud of dust. Isabella spent the remainder of the afternoon wrestling with a new question. Why, after remaining a prisoner of the villa for five weeks, was he suddenly leaving? Though she would never know it, the restorer had been summoned by other masters. As for the Poussin, he would never touch it again.

Assisi

Few Italian cities handle the crush of summer tourists more gracefully than Assisi. The packaged pilgrims arrive in midmorning and shuffle politely through the sacred streets until dusk, when they are herded once more onto coaches and whisked back to their hotels in Rome.

The restorer watched a group of overfed German stragglers tramp wearily through the stone archway of the Porto Nuova; then he walked along the Corso Mazzini to the Piazza del Comune. At the edge of a fountain sat a girl in faded blue jeans and a gauzy cotton top. She pushed her sunglasses onto her forehead and looked away as the restorer set off down the narrow street.

The restaurant to which he had been instructed to come was about a hundred yards from the Basilica di San Francesco. He told the hostess he was meeting a man called Monsieur Laffont and was immediately shown onto a narrow terrace with sweeping views of the Tiber Valley. At the end of the terrace was a small patio with a single private table. Potted geraniums stood along the edge of the balustrade and overhead stretched a canopy of flowering vines. Seated before an open bottle of white wine was a man with cropped strawberry-blond hair and the heavy shoulders of a wrestler. His real name was Uzi Navot, and he held a senior post in the secret intelligence service of the State of Israel. He was also one of the few people in the world aware that the Italian art restorer known as Alessio Vianelli was actually an Israeli named Gabriel Allon.

'Nice table,' said Gabriel, as he took his seat.

'It's one of the fringe benefits of this life. We know all the best tables in all the best restaurants in Europe.'

Gabriel poured himself a glass of wine and nodded slowly. They did know all the best restaurants, but they also knew all the dreary airport lounges, all the stinking rail platforms and all the moth-eaten transit hotels.

Gabriel looked down towards the other tables. The girl from the piazza was now seated alone near the entrance. Her menu was open but her eyes were slowly scanning the other patrons. An oversized handbag lay at her feet with the zipper open. Inside the bag, Gabriel knew, was a loaded gun.

'Who's the *bat leveyha*?'

'Tamara,' said Navot. 'She's new.'

'She's also very pretty.'

'Yes,' said Navot, as though he'd never noticed that before. 'She was the only girl available at short notice.'

'Just make sure you behave yourself, Monsieur Laffont.'

'The days of torrid affairs with my female escort officers are officially over.' Navot removed his spectacles and laid them on the table.

They were highly fashionable and far too small for his large face. 'Bella has decided it's time we finally get married.'

'So that explains the new glasses. You're the chief of Special Ops at King Saul Boulevard now, Uzi. You should be able to choose your own glasses.'

King Saul Boulevard, usually referred to simply as 'the Office', was the long-time address of Israel's foreign intelligence service, and the men from Special Ops were the ones who did the jobs no one else wanted, or dared, to do. They were executioners, kidnappers and blackmailers; men of intellect and ingenuity with a criminal streak wider than the criminals themselves.

'I thought Bella had grown weary of you,' Gabriel said.

'Your wedding to Chiara managed to rekindle her belief in love. At the moment, we are in tense negotiations over the time and place.' Navot frowned. 'I'm confident it will be easier to reach agreement with the Palestinians over the final status of Jerusalem than it will be for Bella and me to settle on our wedding plans.'

Gabriel raised his wineglass and murmured, '*Mazel tov*, Uzi.'

'That's easy for you to say,' Navot said gloomily. 'You see, Gabriel, you've set the bar rather high for the rest of us. Imagine, a surprise wedding, perfectly executed—the dress, the food, even the place settings, exactly what Chiara wanted. And now you're spending your honeymoon at an isolated villa in Umbria restoring a painting for the pope. How's a mere mortal like me ever supposed to live up to that?'

'I had help.' Gabriel smiled. 'Special Ops really *did* do a lovely job with the arrangements, didn't they?'

'If our enemies ever find out Special Ops planned a wedding, our reputation will be ruined. The Old Man sends his love, by the way.'

'I'm sure he does,' Gabriel said absently. 'How is he?'

'He's beginning to grumble. He thinks your security arrangements at the villa are less than satisfactory.'

'Precisely five people know I'm in the country: the Italian prime minister, the chiefs of his intelligence and security services, the pope and the pope's private secretary.'

'He still thinks the security is inadequate, given recent developments.'

'What recent developments?'

Navot placed his big arms on the table and leaned forward a few inches.

'We're picking up some rumblings from our sources in Egypt. It seems Sheikh Tayyib is rather upset with you for foiling his plan to bring down the Mubarak government. He's instructed all Sword of Allah operatives in Europe and the Middle East to begin looking for you at once.

'As you might imagine, since hearing these reports the Old Man has become fixated on one single thought: why is Gabriel Allon, Israel's avenging angel and most capable secret servant, now to be found on an estate in the hills of Umbria restoring a painting for the pope?'

Gabriel looked out at the view. The sun was sinking towards the distant hills in the west, and the first lights were coming up on the valley floor.

'The angel is on his honeymoon,' he said, his gaze still focused on the valley. 'And the angel is in no condition to work again.'

'We don't get honeymoons, Gabriel—not proper ones anyway. As for your physical condition, God knows you went through hell at the hands of the Sword of Allah in London. No one would blame you if you left the Office for good this time.'

'No one but Shamron, of course.'

Navot picked at the tablecloth but made no reply. It had been nearly a decade since the celebrated Israeli spy master Ari Shamron had done his last tour as chief, yet he still meddled with the affairs of the Office as though it were his personal fiefdom.

'Shamron wants me locked up in a cage in Jerusalem,' Gabriel said. 'He thinks that if he can make my life miserable enough, I'll have no other choice but to take over control of the Office.'

'There are worse fates in life. Many would give their right arm to be in your position.' Navot lapsed into silence, then added, 'Including me.'

'Play your cards carefully, Uzi, and someday the job will be yours.'

'That's the way I got the job as chief of Special Ops—because you refused to take it. It's not easy living in your shadow, Gabriel.'

'If they didn't think you were worthy of the job, Uzi, they would have found someone else.'

Navot changed the subject. 'Let's have something to eat,' he suggested.

'Is that it, Uzi? Surely you didn't come all the way to Umbria just to tell me that people wanted me dead?'

'Actually, we were wondering whether you might do us a favour.'

'What sort of favour?'

Navot opened his menu and frowned. 'My God, look at all this pasta.'

'You don't like pasta, Uzi?'

'I love pasta, but Bella says it makes me fat.' He massaged the bridge of his nose and put on his new eyeglasses.

'How much weight do you have to lose before the wedding, Uzi?'

'Thirty pounds,' Navot said sullenly. 'Thirty pounds.'

THEY LEFT THE RESTAURANT in darkness and joined a procession of brown-robed Capuchin friars filing slowly along the narrow street towards the Basilica di San Francesco. A cool wind was chasing about the vast fore-court. Uzi Navot lowered himself onto a stone bench and spoke of death.

'His name was Aleksandr Lubin. He worked for a magazine called *Moskovsky Gazeta*. He was killed in a hotel room in Courchevel a few days after Christmas.'

Gabriel sat down next to Navot and watched two boys playing football near the basilica.

'The *Gazeta* claimed that Lubin went to Courchevel on holiday, but the French police concluded that he was there on an assignment. Unfortunately, there was nothing in his room to indicate what it might be.'

'How did he die?'

'A single stab wound to the chest. No one heard a thing. It's a small hotel with poor security.'

'Russian journalists are dropping like flies these days, Uzi. What does this have to do with us?'

'Three days ago, our embassy in Rome received a phone call from a man claiming to be Boris Ostrovsky, the *Gazeta*'s editor-in-chief. He said he had an important message regarding a grave threat to the security of the West and to the State of Israel. He said he will explain the nature of this threat only to a specific agent of Israeli intelligence.'

The flash of a camera illuminated the forecourt like lightning. Navot and Gabriel stood in unison and started towards the basilica. Five minutes later, after descending a long flight of steps, they were seated in the gloom of the Lower Church before the Tomb of St Francis.

'We tried to explain to Ostrovsky that you weren't free to take a meeting at the moment, but I'm afraid he's not the sort to take no for an answer,' Navot continued. 'King Saul Boulevard has determined that he is a credible figure, and they're eager to hear what he has to say.'

'I'm on my honeymoon, remember? Let someone else do it, Uzi.'

A nun in full habit materialised out of the gloom and pointed towards a sign that forbade talking in the area surrounding the tomb. Gabriel apologised and led Navot into the nave, where a group of Americans were listening intently to a lecture by a cassocked priest. No one appeared to notice the two Israeli spies conversing softly before a stand of votive candles.

'Where is he staying?' Gabriel asked.

'He's barricaded in a room at the Excelsior. He'll be in Rome until the day after tomorrow; then he's heading back to Russia. He's made it clear he wants no contact from us in Moscow.'

Navot drew a photograph from the breast pocket of his blazer and handed it to Gabriel. It showed a balding, overweight man in his early fifties.

'We've given him a set of instructions for a surveillance detection run tomorrow afternoon. He's supposed to leave the hotel at one thirty sharp and visit four destinations: the Spanish Steps, the Trevi Fountain, the Pantheon and the Piazza Navona. When he gets to Navona, he'll walk around the piazza once, then take a table at Tre Scalini. If he's under watch, we walk away. But if he's clean, we'll tell him where to go next.'

'And where's that? A safe flat?'

Navot shook his head. 'I'd rather do it someplace public—someplace where it will look like you're just two strangers chatting.' He hesitated, then added, 'Somewhere a man with a gun can't follow.'

'Ever heard of the Moscow Rules, Uzi?'

'I live by them.'

'Perhaps you recall rule three: assume everyone is potentially under opposition control. It's quite possible we're going to a great deal of trouble to meet with a man who's going to spoonfeed us a pile of Russian shit.' Gabriel looked at the photograph. 'Are we sure this man is really Ostrovsky?'

'Moscow Station says it's him.'

Gabriel placed the photograph in his shirt pocket. 'In order to get back into Italy, I had to make a solemn promise to the Vatican and the Italian services. No operational work of any kind on Italian soil.'

'Who says you're going to operate? It's just a conversation.'

'With a Russian editor who just lost one of his reporters to a professional assassin in Courchevel.' Gabriel shook his head slowly. 'I don't know about you, Uzi, but I don't think it's exactly good karma to lie to a pope.'

'Shamron is our pope and Shamron wants it done.'

Gabriel led Navot from the basilica, and they walked together through the darkened streets, with the *bat leveyha* trailing quietly after them. Gabriel had to admit he was curious about the nature of the message the Russian wanted to deliver. The assignment had one other potential windfall.

It could be used as leverage to get Shamron off his back once and for all. As they crossed the Piazza del Comune, he listed his demands.

'I listen to what he has to say, file a report and then I go back to the villa in Umbria and finish my painting. OK? No more complaints from Shamron. No more warnings about my security.'

Navot hesitated, then nodded his head. 'You can go back to Umbria and restore paintings to your heart's content. No more complaints from Shamron. No more warnings from me or anyone else about the legion of terrorists who wish you dead.'

'Is Ostrovsky under surveillance by assets from Rome Station?'

'We put him under watch within an hour of the first contact.'

'Tell them to back off, or you'll run the risk of telegraphing our interest to anyone else who might be watching him.'

'Done.'

'I need a watcher I can trust. Someone like Eli. Where is he?'

'On a dig somewhere near the Dead Sea.'

'Get him on the sunrise express out of Ben-Gurion. Tell him to meet me for lunch at Piperno. Oh, and tell him to have a bottle of Frascati and a plate of *filetti di baccalà* waiting.'

Villa dei Fiori, Umbria

To restore an Old Master painting, Gabriel always said, was to surrender oneself body and soul to the canvas and the artist who had produced it. The painting was always the first thing in his thoughts when he woke and the last thing he saw before dropping off to sleep. And he could never walk past a restoration in progress without stopping to examine his work.

He switched off the halogen lamps now and climbed the stone steps to the first floor. Chiara was propped up on one elbow in bed, leafing distractedly through a thick fashion magazine. Her skin was dark from the Umbrian sun and her auburn hair was moving faintly in the breeze of the open window. She turned the page of her magazine. 'Did you boys have a nice time?'

'Where's your gun?'

She lifted the corner of the bedcover and the walnut grip of a Beretta 9mm shone in the light of her reading lamp. Gabriel would have preferred the weapon to be more accessible, but he resisted the impulse to chide her. Chiara routinely outscored him in accuracy on the firing range—a rather remarkable achievement, considering the fact she was the daughter of the chief rabbi of Venice and had spent her youth in the tranquil streets of the city's ancient Jewish Ghetto. Officially, she was still an Italian citizen. Her association with the Office was a secret, as was her marriage to Gabriel. She covered the Beretta and flipped another page.

'How's Uzi?'

'He and Bella are going to get married.'

She closed her magazine. 'So is that why Uzi came all the way to Italy to see you? To tell you he was getting married?'

'The Sword of Allah has hung a contract round my neck. Shamron is concerned about our security.'

'That sounds like something that could have been handled with a phone call, darling. Surely Uzi had more to say than that.'

'He wants me to run an errand for him in Rome.'

'Really? What sort of errand?'

'It's need-to-know, Chiara.'

'Good, Gabriel, because I need to know why you would interrupt our honeymoon to run off on an assignment.'

'It's not an assignment. I'll be back tomorrow night.'

'What's the job, Gabriel? And don't hide behind silly Office rules. We've always told each other everything.' She paused. 'Haven't we?'

Gabriel sat down on the edge of the bed and told her about Boris Ostrovsky and his request for an audience.

'And you agreed to this?' She gathered her hair into a bun and patted the bed distractedly for a clasp. 'Am I the only one who's considered the possibility that you're walking straight into a trap?'

'It may have crossed my mind.'

'Why didn't you just tell them to send a stand-in? Surely Uzi can find someone who looks enough like you to fool a Russian journalist who's never seen you in person before.' Greeted by Gabriel's silence, Chiara supplied her own answer. 'Because you're curious as to what he has to say, aren't you?'

'Not enough to interrupt my honeymoon.'

Chiara gave up trying to find the clasp and allowed her hair to tumble about her shoulders once more.

Gabriel walked over to the wardrobe and took down a small overnight bag. Chiara watched silently. 'Will you really be back tomorrow night?' she asked.

'If everything goes according to plan.'

'When was the last time an assignment went according to plan?' She took hold of the Beretta and held it out to him. 'Do you need this?'

'I have one in the car.'

'Who's going to be watching your back?'

'Eli's flying to Rome in the morning.'

'Let me come with you.'

'I've already lost one wife to my enemies. I don't want to lose another.'

'So what am I supposed to do while you're gone?'

'Make sure no one steals the Poussin. His Holiness will be rather miffed if it vanishes while in my possession.'

Chapter 2

Rome

To call it a safe flat was no longer accurate. Indeed, Gabriel had spent so much time in the pleasant apartment near the top of the Spanish Steps that the lords of Housekeeping, the division of the Office that handled secure accommodation, referred to it as his Rome address. There were two bedrooms, a large, light-filled sitting room and a spacious terrace that looked west towards St Peter's Basilica.

Two years earlier, Gabriel had been standing at the side of His Holiness Pope Paul VII when the Vatican was attacked by Islamic terrorists. More than seven hundred people were killed that October afternoon, and the dome of the basilica had nearly been toppled. At the behest of the CIA and the American president, Gabriel had killed the two Saudis who masterminded the operation. The pope's powerful private secretary, Monsignor Luigi Donati, knew of Gabriel's involvement in the killings and tacitly approved.

It had rained during the night, and the pavements of the Via Gregoriana were still damp as Gabriel stepped from the foyer. He turned right and descended the Spanish Steps to the piazza, where he drank his first cappuccino of the day. After deciding that his return to Rome had gone unnoticed by the Italian security services, he hiked back up the Spanish Steps, climbed aboard a Piaggio motorbike, and sped off down the Via Veneto.

The Excelsior Hotel stood near the end of the street, near the Villa Borghese. Gabriel parked on the Corso d'Italia and locked his helmet in the rear storage compartment, before putting on a pair of dark wraparound sunglasses and heading back to the Via Veneto on foot. He walked nearly the length of the boulevard to the Piazza Barberini, then crossed over to the opposite side and headed back towards the Villa Borghese. Along the way, he spotted four men he assumed to be plain-clothes American security—the US Embassy stood at Via Veneto 121—but no one who appeared to be an agent of Russian intelligence.

Gabriel walked into the Excelsior and lifted the receiver of a house phone. When the operator came on the line, he asked to speak to a guest named Boris Ostrovsky and was connected to his room right away. The phone was answered by a man speaking English with a pronounced Russian accent. When Gabriel asked to speak to someone named 'Mr Donaldson', the Russian-speaking man said there was no one there by that name and hung up.

Gabriel left the connection open for a few seconds and listened for the sound of a transmitter on the line. Hearing nothing suspicious, he hung up and walked to the Galleria Borghese. He spent an hour looking at paintings and checking his tail for signs of surveillance. Then, at 11.45, he climbed aboard the Piaggio again and set off towards Piperno. The *filetti* and Frascati were waiting when he arrived. And so was Eli Lavon.

'I THOUGHT you were supposed to be on your honeymoon.'

'Shamron had other ideas.'

Eli Lavon smiled and pushed a few strands of wispy hair from his forehead. Despite the warmth of the Roman afternoon, he was wearing a tweed jacket and an ascot at his throat. Even Gabriel, who had known Lavon for more than thirty years, sometimes found it difficult to believe that the brilliant, bookish little archaeologist was actually the finest street surveillance artist the Office had ever produced. He still lectured at the Academy, but these days his primary work address was Jerusalem's Hebrew University, where he taught biblical archaeology.

'Uzi tells me you're working in the Judaean Desert. I hope it wasn't something too important,' Gabriel said as he took a large bite of the fried fish.

'Only one of the most significant archaeological expeditions in Israel in the past twenty years. But instead of being there with my colleagues, sifting through the relics of our ancient past, I'm in Rome with you.' Lavon's brown eyes flickered around the piazza. 'Do you have a picture?'

Gabriel removed the photograph from his shirt pocket and placed it on the table. Lavon shoved on a pair of half-moon reading glasses and scrutinised the image carefully. 'These Russians all look the same to me,' he said, and slipped the photo into the breast pocket of his jacket.

Gabriel briefed Lavon on the assignment as they ate the last of the fish.

'And if he's clean when he gets to Tre Scalini?' Lavon asked. 'What happens then?'

'I want you to have a go at him in that fluent Russian of yours. Back him into a corner and see if he breaks.'

'And if he insists on talking to you?'

'Then you tell him to visit one more Roman tourist attraction.'

'Which one?'

'I doubt that your friend His Holiness will be pleased if he ever finds out you used his church for a clandestine meeting,' Lavon said, after hearing Gabriel's answer.

'It's a basilica, Eli. And His Holiness will never know a thing.'

'Unless something goes wrong.'

'It's my honeymoon. What could go wrong?'

THEY FINISHED their lunch and departed aboard the Piaggio scooter. Gabriel dropped Lavon near the Excelsior and rode to the Piazza di Spagna, where he took a window table at Caffè Greco. He appeared to be engrossed in his copy of *La Repubblica* as Boris Ostrovsky came strolling along the Via Condotti. Lavon was trailing fifty yards behind. He was still wearing his ascot, which meant he had seen no sign of surveillance.

Gabriel finished his coffee while checking Lavon's tail, then paid the bill and rode to the Trevi Fountain. He was standing near Neptune's rearing seahorse when Ostrovsky shouldered his way through the crowds and stood alongside the balustrade. The Russian dipped his handkerchief into the water and used it to dab the perspiration from his forehead. Then he dug a coin from his pocket and flung it into the fountain before turning and walking away. Gabriel glimpsed Lavon as he started after him. He was still wearing his ascot.

The third stop on the itinerary was a slightly shorter walk, but the portly Russian appeared weary by the time he finally laboured up the front steps of the Pantheon. Gabriel watched Ostrovsky stroll once round the interior of the rotunda, then stepped outside onto the portico, where Lavon was leaning against a column.

'What do you think?' Gabriel asked. 'Is there anyone following him?'

Lavon shook his head. 'Clean as a whistle.'

IT HAD BEEN a Roman racetrack once. Indeed, the baroque structures along its elliptical perimeter were built upon the ruins of ancient grandstands. There were no chariot races now in the Piazza Navona, only a never-ending carnival-like atmosphere that made it one of the most popular squares in all of Rome. Eli Lavon was pretending to watch a cellist performing Bach's Suite No. 1 in G Major, but, in reality, his gaze was focused on Boris Ostrovsky, who was settling at a table, fifty yards away, at Tre Scalini. The Russian ordered only a small bottle of mineral water, which the white-jacketed waiter took an eternity to deliver. Lavon took one final look around the square, then walked over and sat across from the Russian.

'You really should order something more than water, Boris. It's bad manners,' Lavon said in rapid Russian.

Ostrovsky responded in the same language. 'I'm a Russian journalist. I don't take beverages in public unless they come with a cap on them.'

He regarded Lavon and frowned, as though he had decided the small man in the crumpled jacket could not possibly be the legendary Israeli agent. 'Who are you?'

'None of your business.'

Another frown. 'I did everything I was told to do. Now, where is Allon?'

'What makes you think we would ever let you anywhere near him? No one summons Gabriel Allon. It's always the other way around.'

A waiter sauntered over to the table; Lavon, in respectable Italian, ordered two coffees and a plate of *tartufi*. Ostrovsky was perspiring freely now and glancing nervously around the piazza.

'Who are you afraid of, Boris?'

'The *siloviki*,' he said.

'The *siloviki*? I'm afraid my Russian isn't that good, Boris.'

'I'm surprised you haven't heard the word before. It's how we refer to the former KGB men who are now running my country. If you cross them, they will kill you.'

'Relax, Boris. You're clean. No one followed you here.'

'How do you know?'

'We're good at what we do.'

'They're better, my friend. They've had a lot of practice.'

'All the more reason why you're not going anywhere near Allon. Give me the message, Boris, and I'll give it to Allon. It's safer that way.'

'The message I have to deliver is of the utmost gravity. I meet with Allon or I go back to Moscow in the morning and meet with no one at all. The choice is yours.' Greeted by silence, the Russian pushed his chair away from the table and stood. 'I risked my life coming here. Many of my fellow journalists have been murdered for far less.'

'Sit down,' Lavon said calmly. 'You're making a scene.'

Ostrovsky sat down.

'Is this your first time in Rome?' Lavon asked.

Ostrovsky nodded his head.

'Then allow me to give you some advice on your next destination.'

AT THE HEART of St Peter's Square stands the Egyptian Obelisk, brought to Rome from Egypt by Emperor Caligula in the year AD 37. To protect the Obelisk from terrorists and other modern threats, it is now surrounded by a circle of stubby brown barriers of reinforced concrete. Gabriel sat atop one as Boris Ostrovsky appeared at the outer edge of the piazza. He watched the Russian's approach, then turned and headed towards the row of magnetometers located near the front of the basilica. After enduring a brief wait, he passed through them without so much as a ping and started up the sunlit steps towards the portico.

Of the basilica's five doors, only the Filarete Door was open. Gabriel allowed himself to be swallowed up by a large band of cheerful Polish pilgrims and was propelled into the vast nave. He was standing before the Papal Altar as Boris Ostrovsky came in from the portico.

The Russian walked over to the Chapel of the Pietà. After spending just thirty seconds pretending to marvel at Michelangelo's masterpiece, he continued up the right side of the nave and paused again, this time before the Monument to Pope Pius XII. Because of the statue's position, the Russian was temporarily shielded from Gabriel's view. Gabriel looked towards the opposite side of the nave and saw Lavon standing near the entrance of the Vatican Grottoes. Their eyes met briefly; Lavon nodded and Gabriel set off for where the Russian was waiting.

When Gabriel entered the enclave where the statue is located he saw that Boris Ostrovsky was on his knees before the pedestal, with his face lifted sharply towards the ceiling and his hands raised to his neck.

Gabriel moved quickly to Ostrovsky's side. His eyes were bulging and frozen in terror, and his hands appeared to be locked round his own throat, as though he were attempting to strangle himself. He wasn't, of course; he was only trying to breathe. Ostrovsky's affliction wasn't natural. In fact, Gabriel was quite certain the Russian had been poisoned. Somehow an assassin had managed to get to him, despite all their precautions.

Gabriel eased Ostrovsky to the floor and spoke quietly into his ear while attempting to prise his hands loose. Three African nuns gathered round and began to pray, along with a crowd of curious bystanders. Within thirty seconds, the first officers of the Vatican's police force had arrived to investigate. By then, Gabriel was no longer there. He was walking calmly down the steps of the basilica, with Eli Lavon at his side.

'He was clean,' Lavon was saying. 'I'm telling you, Gabriel, he was clean.'

Vatican City

It took just one hour for the death in St Peter's to reach the airwaves of Italy and another hour for the first report to appear in a roundup of European news on the BBC. By eight o'clock the corpse had a name; by nine an occupation. At 9.30 p.m. Rome time, global interest in Ostrovsky's death increased dramatically when a spokesman for the Vatican Press Office issued a terse statement suggesting the dead man was a Russian journalist who appeared to have died as a result of foul play. The announcement ignited a frenzy of activity in newsrooms around the world, and by midnight there were satellite broadcast trucks lining the Via della Conciliazione from the Tiber to St Peter's Square.

A young priest was standing just inside St Anne's Gate, chatting with a Swiss Guard, when Gabriel approached. The priest greeted him with a nod, then turned and escorted him up the Via Belvedere. They entered the Apostolic Palace and stepped into a waiting lift that bore them up to the third floor. Monsignor Luigi Donati, private secretary to His Holiness Pope Paul VII, was waiting in the frescoed loggia. He was six inches taller than Gabriel and blessed with the dark good looks of an Italian film star.

'Please tell me you didn't actually kill a man in my basilica,' Donati murmured after he had banished the young priest with a curt wave.

'I didn't kill anyone, Luigi.'

The monsignor frowned, then handed Gabriel a manila file folder stamped with the insignia of the Vigilanza, the Vatican's police force. Gabriel lifted the cover and saw himself, cradling the dying figure of Boris Ostrovsky. There were other photos beneath: Gabriel walking away as the onlookers gathered round; Gabriel slipping out through the Filarete Door; Gabriel at the side of Eli Lavon as they hurried together across St Peter's Square. He closed the file and held it out towards Donati like an offertory.

'I would be eternally grateful if you would be so kind as to drop those prints and any other copies in the nearest pontifical shredder.'

'I will,' Donati said icily. '*After* you tell me everything you know about what transpired here this afternoon.'

Donati removed a cigarette from his elegant gold case, tapped it impatiently against the cover, then ignited it with an executive gold lighter. There was very little that was clerical in his demeanour and, not for the first time, Gabriel had to remind himself that the tall figure standing before him was actually a priest. Brilliant, uncompromising and notoriously short of temper, Donati was one of the most powerful private secretaries in the history of the Roman Catholic Church. He ran the Vatican like the CEO of a Fortune 500 company, a management style that had won him few friends behind the walls of the Vatican.

'It's been a long time since I've been to confession, Luigi.'

'Try it,' Donati said. 'It's good for the soul.'

Gabriel may have harboured serious doubts about the benefits of confession, but he had none when it came to the trustworthiness of Luigi Donati. The former Jesuit knew how to keep a secret and so, as they walked the silent halls of the Apostolic Palace together, Gabriel told him everything.

'Do I have to remind you that we had an agreement? We asked the Italian authorities to allow you to reside in the country under a false identity. We gave you work and accommodation and in exchange for this, we asked only that you refrain from any and all work for your former employer.'

Gabriel offered an uninspired version of the 'Navot defence'—that it was not really an operation, only a conversation.

Donati dismissed it with a wave of his hand. 'You gave us your word, Gabriel, and you broke it. Not only that, you've laid a potential scandal on our doorstep and that's the last thing we need right now.'

'The difficult questions will be directed towards Moscow, not the Vatican.'

'Let's hope you're correct. I'm obviously no expert, but it appears Ostrovsky was poisoned by someone.' Donati paused. 'Someone who apparently didn't want him talking to *you*.'

Gabriel nodded. 'Ostrovsky told us he was afraid of the *siloviki*. It's the word Russians use to describe the gang of former KGB men who've set up shop inside the Kremlin. He also told us that the information he had concerned a grave threat to the West and to Israel.'

'What sort of threat?'

'He didn't get a chance to tell us that.'

Donati clasped his hands behind his back thoughtfully and looked down at the marble floor. 'For the moment, Ostrovsky's death is a matter for the police and security services of the Vatican, but I anticipate pressure will build rather quickly for us to grant the Italian authorities primacy in the investigation. If we refuse, we'll be accused of engaging in a cover-up. The press will spin wild theories about dark forces at play behind the walls of the Vatican. Which brings us back to the photographs of you inside the basilica at the time of Ostrovsky's death.'

'What about them?'

'Shredding the prints is only a temporary solution. The images are stored permanently in the memory of our computers. And don't even think about asking me to delete them. I won't countenance the destruction of evidence.'

'No one is going to recognise me from those images, Luigi. There's only one way the Italians will find out I was there.'

'Don't worry, Gabriel. Your secret is safe with us. Three people know of your involvement: the Holy Father, myself and the Vigilanza detective leading our investigation, who is sworn to secrecy.'

'If it's all right with you, I'd like to have a word with the inspector.'

'About what?'

'It's possible the security cameras picked up someone other than me.'

'Who?'

'The man who killed Boris Ostrovsky, of course.'

ISPETTORE MATEO CASSANI, a trim figure in a well-cut dark suit, was waiting in the reception foyer of the Vatican Central Security Office. He regarded Gabriel with a pair of weary, bloodshot eyes, then extended his hand. 'Welcome back, signore. Come with me, please.'

They headed down a narrow corridor and paused briefly in an open doorway. Inside, two uniformed Vigilanza officers were seated before a wall of video monitors.

'This is our main observation room,' Cassani said. 'Everything is recorded and stored digitally. For all eternity,' he added with a tired smile. 'Just like the Holy Mother Church.'

'I was afraid of that.'

'Don't worry, signore. I know who you are and I know what you did the day those terrorists attacked this place. The Church lost four cardinals and eight bishops that day. And if it wasn't for you, we might have lost a pope.'

They left the observation room and entered a cramped office. Cassani sat down before a computer and invited Gabriel to look over his shoulder.

'Monsignor Donati told me you wanted to see every image we had of the dead Russian,' Cassani said.

Gabriel nodded. The detective clicked the mouse and the first image appeared, a shot of St Peter's Square, taken from a camera mounted atop the left flank of Bernini's Tuscan Colonnade. The shot advanced at the rate of one frame per second until the time code at the bottom left of the screen reached 15:47:23.

Cassani pointed to the top right-hand corner. 'There's Signor Ostrovsky. He enters the square and makes his way directly to the security checkpoint.' Cassani glanced at Gabriel. 'It's almost as if he were intending to meet someone inside.'

They watched as Boris Ostrovsky moved across the square, with Eli Lavon following carefully in his wake. Ninety seconds later, as Ostrovsky was passing the Obelisk, he slipped out of the range of that camera and into the range of another mounted near the Loggia of the Blessings. A few seconds later, he was surrounded by a group of tourists. A solitary figure approached from the left side of the image; rather than wait for the group to pass, he shouldered his way through it. The man appeared to bump several members of the group, including Ostrovsky, then headed off towards the entrance to the square.

Gabriel watched the final three minutes of Boris Ostrovsky's life. Precisely sixty-seven seconds after his arrival, he fell to his knees before the statue and began clutching his throat. Gabriel appeared twenty-two seconds after that, advancing spirit-like across the screen, one frame per second. The detective appeared moved by the sight of Gabriel lowering the dying Russian carefully to the floor.

'Did he say anything to you?' the detective asked.

'No, nothing. He couldn't speak,' Gabriel said. 'Take it back to the shot at fifteen fifty.' The Vatican detective did as Gabriel requested and for the second time they watched as Ostrovsky advanced towards the basilica. And as the solitary figure approached him from the left . . .

'Stop it right there,' Gabriel said suddenly. Cassani immediately clicked pause. 'Can you enlarge the image?'

'I can,' Cassani said, 'but the resolution will be poor.'

'Do it anyway.'

The Vatican detective clicked on the enlarge icon. The resolution, as promised, was nebulous at best. Even so, Gabriel could clearly see the right hand of the solitary figure wrapped round Ostrovsky's right arm.

'Has anyone examined Ostrovsky's body yet?'

'I gave it a brief examination to see if there were any signs of physical trauma or wounds. There was nothing.'

'If you check again, I suspect you'll find a very small perforation to the skin of his upper arm. It's where the assassin injected him with a Russian poison that paralyses the respiratory system within minutes. It was developed by the KGB during the Cold War. But there's something I need from you first.' Gabriel tapped the screen. 'I need to know what time this man entered the square and which direction he went when he left. And I need the five best pictures of him you can find.'

HE WAS A PROFESSIONAL, and, like all professionals, he had been aware of the cameras. He had lowered his guard just once, at 15:47:33, ten seconds after Ostrovsky had first been picked up by Vatican surveillance on the edge of the square. The image showed a sturdy-jawed man with wide cheekbones, heavy sunglasses and thick blond hair.

Eli Lavon examined the photograph by the glow of a streetlight at the top of the Spanish Steps. Fifty yards away, an Office security team was searching the safe flat for traces of toxins or radioactive material.

'I stand by what I said. Ostrovsky was clean. I didn't see anyone following him. There's no way I could have missed someone who looks like this.'

'Maybe Ostrovsky was clean, but we weren't.'

'You're suggesting they were watching the watchers? But how did they know we were going to be there, Gabriel?'

'Ostrovsky's probably been under watch in Moscow for months. When he came to Rome, he made contact with our embassy on an insecure line. Someone from the other side picked up the call. The assassin is a pro. He knew we wouldn't go near Ostrovsky without sending him on a surveillance detection run. And so he ignored the target and watched us instead. He must have been following me. I missed him, Eli. It's my fault Ostrovsky died a miserable death on the floor of the basilica.'

Ben-Gurion Airport, Israel

There is a VIP reception room at Ben-Gurion Airport that few people know about. Reached by an unmarked door near passport control, it has walls of Jerusalem limestone, furnishings of black leather and a permanent odour of burnt coffee. When Gabriel entered the room the following evening, he found it occupied by a single man, seated at the edge of his chair, his large hands resting atop an olive-wood cane. He was dressed, as always, in a pair of pressed khaki trousers and a white Oxford cloth shirt with the sleeves rolled up. His head was bullet-shaped and bald, and his ugly wire-framed spectacles magnified a pair of blue eyes that were no longer clear.

Gabriel kissed Ari Shamron on the top of the head. 'Why didn't you just let someone from Transport pick me up?'

'I was in the neighbourhood.'

'You live in Tiberias! You're retired now. You should be spending time with Gilah to make up for all those years you weren't around.'

'I'm *never* going to retire!' Shamron thumped the arm of his chair for emphasis. 'As for Gilah, it was she who suggested I come here to wait for you, to get me out of the house for a few hours. She said I was underfoot.'

Shamron closed his hooded eyes for a moment and gave a ghost of a smile. His loved ones, like his power and influence, had slowly slipped through his fingers. His son was a brigadier general in the Israel Defence Force's Northern Command and used almost any excuse to avoid spending time with his father, as did his daughter. Only Gilah, his long-suffering wife, remained faithfully by his side, but even she found his constant presence a burden. His real family were men like Gabriel, Navot and Lavon— men whom he had recruited and trained, men who operated by a creed, even spoke a language, written by him. They were the secret guardians of the State, and Ari Shamron was their overbearing, tyrannical father.

'I devoted my life to building and protecting this country and I assumed that my family would forgive my sins of absence. I was wrong, of course.'

'And now you want to inflict the same outcome on my life.'

'You're referring to the fact I've interrupted your honeymoon?'

'I am.'

'Your wife is still on the Office payroll. She understands the demands of your work. Besides, you've been gone for over a month.' Shamron squeezed his deeply lined face into a heavy frown. 'Do you know what I did for my honeymoon?'

'Of course I do. The whole country knows.'

Shamron smiled. It was an exaggeration, of course, but only a slight one.

'Gilah and I were married in April of 1947, at the height of the War of Independence. I put my foot on a glass, our friends and family shouted, "*Mazel tov*," then I kissed my new wife and went back to my unit.'

'They were different times, Ari.'

'Not so different. We were fighting for survival then and we fight for survival now.' Shamron scrutinised Gabriel for a long moment through his spectacles. 'But you already know that, don't you, Gabriel? That's why you didn't simply ignore my message recalling you.'

'I should have ignored your original summons. Then I wouldn't be back here in this dreary room.'

'I wasn't the one who summoned you. Boris Ostrovsky did. Then he had the terrible misfortune of dying in your arms. The least you can do is to find out who killed him and why.'

Gabriel glanced at his wristwatch. 'Did Eli make it in all right?'

They had travelled back on separate planes and by different routes.

'Eli's already inside King Saul Boulevard being debriefed. When they're finished with him, they'd like a crack at you. As you might expect, they're unhappy about the way things turned out in Rome. But that can wait until tomorrow. Come,' he said, 'I'll take you home.'

An armoured Peugeot limousine was waiting outside. They climbed into the back and headed towards the Judaean Hills.

'There were developments in Rome after you boarded your flight. The Italian Ministry of Justice sent a letter to the Vatican, formally requesting permission to take over the investigation, and they agreed immediately.'

'Donati has promised to keep my name out of it. Ostrovsky was killed by a professional Russian assassin in St Peter's Square.' Gabriel removed a manila folder from the side flap of his bag and handed it to Shamron. 'And these pictures prove it.'

Shamron examined the photos. 'It's a brazen act, even by Russian standards. Ostrovsky must have known something very important for them to resort to this.'

'I take it you have a theory?'

'Unfortunately, we do.' Shamron slipped the photos back into the file folder. 'Our friends in the Kremlin have been selling sophisticated weapons systems to the rogue regimes of the Middle East at an unprecedented rate. We've been picking up reports that the Syrians and the Kremlin are about to close a major deal involving an advanced Russian missile known as the Iskander. It's a road-mobile weapon with a range of one hundred and seventy miles, which means Tel Aviv would be well within Syria's range. I don't need to explain the ramifications of that to you.'

'It would alter the strategic balance in the Middle East overnight.'

Shamron nodded his head slowly. 'And unfortunately, given the track record of the Kremlin, it's only one of many unsettling possibilities. The entire region is bristling with rumours of some kind of new deal *some-where*. But so far we've been unable to come up with anything we can take to the prime minister. I'm afraid he's beginning to get annoyed.'

'It's part of his job description.'

'And mine.' Shamron smiled humourlessly. 'All of this goes to explain why we were so interested in having you meet Ostrovsky in the first place. And why we would now like you to travel to Russia to find out what Ostrovsky intended to say to you.'

'*Me?* I've never set foot in Russia. I don't even speak the language.'

'You have something more important than local knowledge.'

'What's that?'

'A name and a face that the staff of *Moskovsky Gazeta* will recognise.'

'Chances are, the Russian security services will recognise it, too.'

'We have a plan for that,' Shamron said. The Old Man smiled. He had a plan for everything.

THERE WERE SECURITY AGENTS at either end of Narkiss Street, a quiet, leafy lane in the heart of Jerusalem, and another standing watch outside the entrance of the little apartment house at number 16. Gabriel, as he crossed the foyer with Shamron at his heels, didn't bother checking the postbox. He never received mail, and the name on the box was false. As far as the bureaucracy of the State of Israel was concerned, Gabriel Allon did not exist.

Uzi Navot was seated on the living-room couch in Gabriel's apartment, with his feet propped on the coffee table and an Israeli diplomatic passport in his right hand. He handed it over for inspection. Gabriel opened the cover and looked at the photograph. It showed a silver-haired man with a neat grey beard and glasses. The silver hair was the handiwork of a stylist who worked for Identity. The grey beard was his own.

'Who's Natan Golani?' Gabriel asked.

'A mid-level functionary in the Ministry of Culture. He specialises in building artistic bridges between Israel and the rest of the world: peace through art, dance, music and other pointless endeavours.'

'Has he ever been to Russia?'

'No, but he's about to.' Navot removed his feet from the table and sat up. 'Six days from now, the Deputy Minister of Culture is scheduled to travel from Jerusalem to Russia for an official visit. We've prevailed upon him to become ill at the last moment, and Natan Golani will go in his place.'

'What's the purpose of his trip?'

'It may have escaped your notice, but UNESCO has declared this "the decade for the promotion of a culture of peace and nonviolence for the children of the world".'

'You're right, Uzi. Somehow I missed that.'

'In furtherance of that noble goal, it holds a conference each year to assess progress. This year's conference will be held in St Petersburg.'

'How many days of this nonsense do I have to sit through?'

'Three,' said Navot. 'Your speech is scheduled for day two of the conference. Your remarks will focus on a groundbreaking new programme we've instituted to improve cultural ties between the Israelis and our Arab neighbours. Many of those in attendance will not hear your remarks, however, because, as is customary, they will walk out of the hall en masse as you mount the rostrum, denouncing you as an oppressor and an occupier.'

'I've never enjoyed speaking to large crowds anyway. What then?'

'At the conclusion of the conference, our ambassador to Russia, who happens to be an old friend of yours, will invite you to visit Moscow to sample the cultural delights of the capital. The true purpose of your visit, however, will be to establish contact with one Olga Sukhova. She's one of Russia's best-known and most controversial investigative journalists. She's also the acting editor-in-chief of *Moskovsky Gazeta*. If there's anyone at the *Gazeta* who knows why Boris Ostrovsky went to Rome, it's Olga.'

'Which means she's probably under full-time FSB surveillance. And as a visiting Israeli diplomat, I will be, too.'

The Russian Federal Security Service, or FSB, had assumed most of the functions of the KGB, including counterintelligence. Though the FSB liked to present itself to the outside world as a modern European security service, it was staffed largely by KGB veterans and even operated from the KGB's notorious old headquarters in Lubyanka Square.

'Obviously,' said Navot, 'we'll have to be a bit creative.'

'How creative?' Gabriel asked warily.

'Nothing more dangerous than a dinner party. Our ambassador has agreed to host a small affair at the official residence while you're in town. It will be an interesting mix of Russian journalists, artists and opposition figures, including Olga Sukhova.'

'What makes you think she'll come? Dinner at the home of the Israeli ambassador is hardly a coveted invitation, even in Moscow.'

'Unless it comes attached with a promise of an exclusive scoop of some sort. But you must let us worry about what that is.'

'And if she comes?'

'Then you will pull her aside for a private conversation within the secure environment of the residence. And you will reveal yourself to her in whatever manner you deem appropriate and prevail upon her to share anything she knows about why Boris Ostrovsky went to Rome to see you.'

Navot reached back into his attaché case and withdrew a file. Gabriel opened it and removed Olga Sukhova's photograph. She was an attractive woman in her mid-forties, with sleek Slavic features, ice-blue eyes and satiny blonde hair swept over one shoulder. He closed the file and looked at Shamron, who had been standing before a pair of open French doors, twirling his old Zippo lighter between his fingertips as he listened.

'There *are* worse ways to spend an evening, Gabriel. At the very least, you'll pick up whatever information you can about why the journalists at the *Gazeta* are being targeted. Then you can go back to your villa in Umbria—back to your wife and your painting.'

'And what happens if the FSB doesn't fall for your little ruse?'

'Your diplomatic passport will protect you.'

'The Russian Mafia and FSB assassins don't bother much with diplomatic niceties. They shoot first and worry about the political fallout later.'

'Moscow Station will be watching your back from the moment you land in St Petersburg,' Navot said. 'But if things start to look dicey, we can always arrange for an official security detail for you.'

'What makes you think Moscow Station would ever see it coming, Uzi? A man brushed against Boris Ostrovsky in Rome yesterday afternoon and before anyone knew what had happened he was dead.'

'Your protection isn't your diplomatic passport,' Shamron said. 'It's the reputation of the Office. The Russians know that if anyone lays a finger on you, no Russian agent anywhere in the world will ever be safe again.'

'A war against the Russian services is the last thing we need now.'

'They're selling advanced weaponry to countries and terror groups that wish to exterminate us. We're already at war with them. You have a lot to do in the next six days. The Deputy Minister of Culture is expecting you in his office tomorrow morning at ten, when he'll brief you thoroughly on your *other* mission in Russia. Behave yourself at that conference, Gabriel. It's important you do nothing to make our position at the UN any worse than it already is.'

St Petersburg

Pulkovo 2, St Petersburg's ageing international airport, had thus far been spared the wrecking ball of progress. The cracked tarmac was dotted with forlorn-looking Soviet-era planes, and the structure itself looked more like a factory complex or prison than a hub of modern air travel. Gabriel entered the terminal and was pointed towards passport control by an information hostess who seemed annoyed by his presence. After being formally admitted into Russia, he made his way to baggage reclaim, where he waited the statutory hour for his luggage.

In the arrivals hall, Gabriel was accosted by a large Russian woman wearing a red shirt with UNESCO written across her ample breast. She adhered a name tag to his lapel and directed him to a bus waiting outside in the traffic circle. The interior was already crowded with delegates. Gabriel found a seat near the rear of the coach, next to a sullen-looking Norwegian.

The woman in the red UNESCO shirt stood at the front of the bus, microphone amplifying her voice, and pointed out the landmarks: the statue of Lenin, with his hand extended, as though he were forever attempting to hail a cab; the stirring monuments to the Great Patriotic War; the towering temples of Soviet central planning and control.

Though capitalism had taken Russia by storm, the concept of customer service had not. Gabriel stood in a queue for twenty minutes at the reception desk of the Astoria Hotel before finally being processed by a flaxen-haired woman who made no attempt to conceal her loathing of him. He carried his own bags to his room. He didn't bother searching it; he was playing by the Moscow Rules now. Assume every room is bugged and every telephone call monitored. And don't look back. You are never completely alone.

And so Natan Golani attached his laptop to the complimentary high-speed data port and read his email, knowing full well that the spies of the FSB were reading it, too. And he called his ersatz wife in Tel Aviv and listened dutifully while she complained about her ersatz mother, knowing full well the FSB was enduring the same tedious monologue. Then he changed into casual clothing and plunged into the soft Leningrad evening. He dined surprisingly well at an Italian restaurant next door and was later tailed by two FSB watchers, whom he nicknamed Igor and Natasha, as he strolled the Neva embankment through the endless dusk of the white nights. In Palace Square, he paused to gaze at a wedding party drinking champagne at the foot of the Alexander Column, before turning back to the Astoria, with Igor and Natasha trailing silently after him beneath the midnight sun.

THE FOLLOWING MORNING Natan Golani threw himself into the business of the conference. He was seated at his assigned place in the grand hall of the Marble Palace when the conference commenced and he remained there, translation headphones on, long after many of the other delegates were gathering in the bars of the Western hotels. He did the working lunches and made the rounds of the afternoon cocktail receptions. He did the endless dinners and never once bowed out of the evening entertainment.

He mounted the dais in the grand hall at the end of the second day's session and, as Uzi Navot had forecast, many of the delegates immediately walked out. Those who remained found the speech quite unlike anything they had ever heard from an Israeli representative before. The French delegate referred to Monsieur Golani as 'a true man of culture and the arts', and everyone agreed that a new wind seemed to be blowing from the Judaean Hills.

There was no such wind blowing, however, from the headquarters of the FSB. Their break-in artists searched his hotel room each time he left, and their watchers followed him wherever he went. During the final gala at the Mariinsky Theatre, an attractive female agent flirted shamelessly with him and invited him back to her apartment. He politely declined and left the Mariinsky with no company other than Igor and Natasha, who were by now too bored even to bother concealing their presence. When he returned to his hotel room, he found the message light winking on his telephone.

It was the Israeli ambassador, insisting that he come to Moscow.

'You have to see the place to believe it, Natan! Billionaires, dirty bankers and gangsters, all swimming in a sea of oil, caviar and vodka! We're having a dinner party on Thursday night—just a few brave souls who've had the chutzpah to challenge the regime. And don't *think* about trying to say no, because I've already arranged it with your minister.'

He erased the message, then dialled Tel Aviv and informed his ersatz wife that he would be staying in Russia longer than expected. She berated him for several minutes, and, as she slammed down the phone in disgust, Gabriel imagined the FSB listeners having a good laugh at his expense.

Moscow

In the bar of the Savoy Hotel, the sharp boys and their bodyguards were drinking cold beer instead of vodka. Their black Bentleys and Range Rovers waited just outside the entrance, engines running for a quick getaway. Conservation of fuel was hardly a priority in Russia these days. Petrol, like nearly everything else, was in plentiful supply.

At 7.30 p.m., Gabriel came down to the lobby dressed in a dark suit and diplomatic silver tie. Stepping from the entrance, he scanned the faces behind the wheels of the parked cars before heading down the hill to the Teatralnyy Prospekt. After consulting a hotel street map—needlessly, because his route was well planned in advance—he made his way to a large open-air esplanade at the foot of the Kremlin walls. Passing a row of kiosks selling everything from Soviet hockey jerseys to busts of Lenin and Stalin, he turned to the left and entered Red Square, where the last of the day's pilgrims stood outside the entrance to Lenin's Tomb.

He crossed the square towards the candy-cane domes of St Basil's Cathedral, then followed the eastern wall of the Kremlin down to the Moscow River. He gave his map another pointless glance as he set out across the Moskvoretsky Bridge. At the far end, the Russian president smiled disagreeably at Gabriel from a billboard three storeys in height. He was scheduled to face the Russian 'electorate', such that it was, at the end of the summer. There was little suspense about the outcome; the smiling man on the billboard had long ago purged Russia of dangerous democratic tendencies, and was the new tsar in everything but name.

On the other side of the river lay Zamoskvoreche, a pleasant district that had retained some of the atmosphere of nineteenth-century Moscow. Gabriel walked past flaking imperial houses and onion-domed churches until he came to the walled compound at Bolshaya Ordynka 56. He held his credentials up to the fish-eye lens of the camera and heard the electronic locks immediately snap open. As he stepped into the embassy compound, he glanced over his shoulder and saw a man in a car across the street raise a camera and blatantly snap a photograph. Apparently, the FSB intended to intimidate the guests as they arrived.

Inside the drab compound, a youthful security guard greeted Gabriel cordially by his cover name and escorted him into the foyer of the small apartment building that housed most of the embassy's personnel. The ambassador was waiting on the top-floor landing as Gabriel stepped out of the lift. A polished career diplomat whom Gabriel had seen only in photographs, he threw his arms round Gabriel and shouted, 'My God, Natan! Is it really you? You look as though you've been travelling an age. St Petersburg surely wasn't as bad as all that.' He thrust a glass of champagne into Gabriel's hand. 'As usual, you're the last to arrive. Mingle with the masses. We'll chat later after you've had a chance to say hello to everyone.'

Gabriel hoisted his most affable diplomatic smile and, glass in hand, waded into the noisy smoke-filled sitting room.

He met a famous violinist who was now the leader of a ragtag opposition party called the Coalition for a Free Russia. He met a playwright who had revived the time-tested art of Russian allegory to criticise the new regime.

He met a film-maker who had recently won a major human rights award in the West for a documentary about the gulag. He met a brave essayist who had been nearly beaten to death by a band of Unity Party Youth.

And finally, ten minutes after his arrival, he introduced himself to a reporter from *Moskovsky Gazeta*, who, owing to the murders of two colleagues, had recently been promoted to the post of acting editor-in-chief. She wore a black sleeveless dress and her bangles clattered like wind chimes as she extended her hand towards Gabriel and gave him a melancholy smile. 'How do you do, Mr Golani,' she said primly. 'My name is Olga Sukhova.'

The photograph Uzi Navot had shown him a week earlier had not done justice to Olga's beauty. With translucent eyes and long, narrow features, she looked to Gabriel like a Russian icon come to life. He was seated at her right during dinner but managed only a few brief exchanges of conversation, largely because the documentary film-maker monopolised her attention. Gabriel found himself in the clutches of an ancient dissident, who treated him to a lecture on the history of Russian political opposition.

As the waiters cleared the plates, Olga gave him a smile. 'I'm afraid I feel a cigarette coming on,' she said. 'Would you care to join me?'

They rose from the table together under the crestfallen gaze of the film-maker and stepped onto the small terrace. It was empty and in semidarkness; in the distance loomed one of the 'Seven Sisters', the monstrous Stalinist towers that still dominated the Moscow skyline. 'Europe's tallest apartment building,' she said without enthusiasm. 'Everything in Russia has to be the biggest, the tallest, the fastest or the most valuable. We cannot live as normal people.' Her lighter flared. 'Is this your first time in Russia, Mr Golani?'

'Yes,' he answered truthfully.

'And what brings you to our country?'

You, he answered truthfully again, but only to himself. Aloud, he said that he had been drafted on short notice to attend the UNESCO conference. And for the next few minutes he spoke glowingly of his achievements. He glanced over his shoulder, into the ambassador's dining room, and saw no movement to indicate that their privacy was about to be interrupted.

'We have a common acquaintance,' he said. 'Actually, we *had* a common acquaintance. I'm afraid he's no longer alive.'

She lifted the cigarette to her lips and held it there as though it were a shield protecting her from harm. 'And who might that be?' she asked.

'Boris Ostrovsky,' Gabriel said calmly.

Her gaze was blank. The ember of her cigarette was trembling slightly in the half-light. 'And how were you acquainted with Boris?' she asked.

'I was in St Peter's when he was murdered.' He gazed directly at her, assessing whether her fear was authentic. Deciding it was indeed genuine, he pressed on. 'I was the reason he went to Rome. I held him while he died.'

'I'm sorry, Mr Golani, but you are making me extremely uncomfortable.'

'Boris wanted to tell me something, Miss Sukhova. He was killed before he could do that. I think you may know what it was.'

'I'm afraid not. No one on the staff knew why Boris was in Rome.'

'We know he had information, information that was too dangerous to publish here. Information about a threat to the West and Israel.'

She glanced through the open doorway into the dining room. 'I suppose this whole evening was staged for my benefit so you could meet me somewhere you thought the FSB wouldn't be listening.' She placed her hand suggestively on his forearm and leaned close. She spoke again in little more than a whisper. 'You should know that the FSB is *always* listening, Mr Golani. In fact, two of the guests your embassy invited tonight are on the FSB payroll.'

She released his arm and moved away. Then her face brightened suddenly. Gabriel turned and saw the film-maker advancing towards them, with two other guests. Cigarettes were ignited, drinks were fetched, and within a few moments they were all four conversing in rapid Russian.

Gabriel was convinced he had overplayed his hand, but as he turned to leave he felt her hand once more upon his arm. 'The answer is yes,' she said.

'I'm sorry?'

'You asked whether I would be willing to give you a tour of Moscow tomorrow. And the answer is yes. Where are you staying?'

'At the Savoy.'

'I'll call you in the morning.'

Chapter 3

Novodevichy Cemetery, Moscow

She wanted to take him to Novodevichy Cemetery. *To understand Russia today*, she said, *you must first know her past. And to know her past, you had to walk among her bones.* She telephoned the Savoy and suggested they meet at three. Gabriel, playing the role of Natan Golani, spent much of the day touring the Kremlin and the Tretyakov Gallery. Then, at 2.45, he stepped onto the escalator of the Lubyanka Metro and took a train to Sportivnaya Station. His FSB watcher emerged into the hazy sunlight first and went to the left. Gabriel turned to the right and entered a chaotic outdoor market selling cheap goods from the former republics of central Asia. A man in his early thirties was trailing a few steps behind Gabriel as he arrived.

Olga Sukhova was waiting at the entrance of the cemetery, a bouquet of carnations in her arms. 'Your timing is impeccable, Mr Golani.' She kissed Gabriel formally on both cheeks and smiled warmly. 'Come with me. I think you're going to find this fascinating.'

She led him up a shaded footpath lined with tall elm and spruce. The graves were on either side: small plots surrounded by iron fences; tall sculpted monuments; redbrick niche walls covered in pale moss. For a moment, Gabriel was almost able to forget they were being followed.

'The cemetery used to be inside the Novodevichy Convent, but at the turn of the last century the Church decided that there were too many burials taking place inside the monastery's walls so they created this place.' She spoke to him in English, loudly enough that those around them could hear. 'Playwrights and poets, monsters and murderers, they all lie together here in Novodevichy. One can only imagine what they talk about at night when the gates are closed and the visitors all leave.' She stopped before a tall grey monument with a pile of wilted red roses at its base. 'Do you like Chekhov, Mr Golani?'

'Who doesn't?'

'He was one of the first to be buried here.' She took him by the elbow. 'Come, I'll show you some more.'

They drifted slowly together along the tranquil footpath. A few feet away a woman with a beige anorak tied round her waist pointed a digital camera directly at Gabriel and Olga.

'You were followed here.' Olga gave him a sideways glance. 'But, then, I suppose you already know that, don't you, Mr Golani? Or should I call you Mr Allon?'

'My name is Natan Golani. I work for the Israeli Ministry of Culture.'

'Forgive me, Mr Golani.'

She managed a smile. She was dressed casually in a snug-fitting black pullover and a pair of blue jeans. Her suede boots made her appear taller than she had the previous evening. Their heels tapped rhythmically along the pavement as they walked slowly past the graves.

The musicians Rostropovich and Rubinstein; the writers Gogol and

Bulgakov; the Party giants Khrushchev and Kosygin; Molotov, signatory to the secret pact that condemned Europe to war and the Jews of Poland to annihilation . . .

'There's no place quite like this to see the striking contradictions of our history. These men gave us everything, and when they were gone we were left with nothing: factories that produced goods no one wanted, an ideology that was tired and bankrupt. All set to beautiful words and music.'

Gabriel looked at the bouquet of flowers. 'Who are those for?'

She stopped before a small plot with a low, unadorned stone monument. 'Dmitri Sukhova, my grandfather. He was a playwright and a film-maker. Had he lived in another time, under a different regime, he might have been great. Instead, he was drafted to make cheap Party propaganda for the masses. His reward was to be buried here, among true Russian genius.'

She crouched next to the grave and brushed pine needles from the plaque. 'You have his name,' Gabriel said. 'You're not married?'

She shook her head and placed the flowers gently on the grave. 'I'm afraid I've yet to find a countryman suitable for marriage and procreation. The New Russian man buys himself a mistress and winters in Zermatt and Courchevel and summers in the South of France. I prefer to spend my summers at my grandfather's dacha. I grow radishes and carrots there. I still believe in my country. I don't need to holiday in the exclusive playgrounds of Western Europe to be a contented, self-fulfilled New Russian woman.'

She had been speaking to the grave. Now she turned her head and looked over her shoulder at Gabriel. 'You must think I'm terribly foolish.'

'Why foolish?'

'Because I pretend to be a journalist in a country where there is no longer true journalism. Because I want democracy in a country that has never known it—and, in all likelihood, never will.'

She stood upright and brushed the dust from her palms. 'To understand Russia today, you must understand the trauma of the nineties. Everything we had, everything we had been told, was swept away. Russians are a paternalistic people. They believe in the Orthodox Church, the State, the Tsar. They associate democracy with chaos. Our president understands this. He uses words like "managed democracy" and "State capitalism", but they're just euphemisms for something more sinister: fascism. Look around you, Mr Golani. The history of Russia is nothing but a series of convulsions. We cannot live as normal people. We never will.'

She looked past him, into a darkened corner of the cemetery. 'They're watching us very closely. Hold my arm, please, Mr Golani. It is better if the FSB believes you are attracted to me.'

He did as she asked. 'Perhaps fascism is too strong a word,' he said.

'What term would you apply to our system?'

'A corporate state,' Gabriel replied without conviction.

'I'm afraid that is a euphemism worthy of the Kremlin. Yes, our people are now free to make and spend money, but the State still picks the winners and the losers. Our leaders use our oil and gas to bully our neighbours. They have all but eliminated the opposition and an independent press, and those who dare to protest are beaten openly in the streets. Our children are being coerced into joining Party youth organisations. They are taught that America and the Jews want to control the world—that America and the Jews want to steal Russia's wealth and resources.'

She turned to face him. 'I believe in my Russia, Mr Golani, and I want no more acts of evil committed in my name. Neither did Boris Ostrovsky. That is why he wanted to talk to you. And that is why he was murdered.'

'Why did he go to Rome, Olga? What did he want to tell me?'

She reached up and touched his cheek with her fingertip. 'Perhaps you should kiss me now, Mr Golani. It is better if the FSB is under the impression we intend to become lovers.'

THEY DROVE TO THE OLD ARBAT in her car, an ancient pea-soup-green Lada with a dangling front bumper. She knew a place where they could talk, a Georgian restaurant with stone grottoes and waiters in native dress. It was loud, she assured him.

She left the car in a flagrantly illegal space near Arbat Square and they walked to the restaurant. It was so noisy that Gabriel had to lean across the table a few degrees to hear her speak. She was talking about an anonymous tip the *Gazeta* had received before the New Year. A tip from a source whose name she could never divulge . . . 'This source told us that an arms dealer with close ties to the Kremlin was about to conclude a major deal that would put some very dangerous weapons into the hands of some very dangerous people.'

'What kind of people?'

'The kind you have been fighting your entire life, Mr Golani. The kind who have vowed to destroy your country, who fly aircraft into buildings.'

'Al-Qaeda?'

'Or one of its affiliates.'

'What type of weapons?'

'We don't know.'

'Are they conventional?'

'We don't know. But we can't rule *anything* out, Mr Golani.' She was silent for a moment, then managed a cautious smile. 'Perhaps it would be better if I simply told you what I *do* know.'

She was now gazing at him intently. Gabriel heard a commotion to his left and glanced over. Two ageing mobsters and their high-priced professional dates were being shown to the neighbouring table. Olga took note and continued speaking. 'The source who provided us with the initial tip about the sale is impeccable. But we couldn't print a story based on a single source. You see, unlike many of our competitors, the *Gazeta* has a reputation for accuracy. We've been sued many times by people who didn't like what we wrote about them but we've never lost, not even in the kangaroo courts of Russia.'

'So you started asking questions?'

'We sent one of our reporters to Courchevel to follow the arms dealer in question. The dealer owns a chalet there.'

'The reporter was Aleksandr Lubin?'

She nodded her head slowly. 'Aleksandr was murdered within a few hours of his arrival. Obviously, it was a warning to the rest of the *Gazeta* staff to back off. I'm afraid it had the opposite effect. We kept digging and though we were able to uncover much about the arms dealer's operations in general, we were never able to pin down the specifics of a deal. Finally, the matter was taken out of our hands entirely. Quite unexpectedly, the owner of the *Gazeta* decided to sell the magazine, pressured into the sale by the Kremlin. Our new owner recently announced that he was not interested in hard news or investigative journalism. The *Gazeta* was now going to focus on celebrity news, the arts and life in the New Russia.'

'I assume the time of the sale wasn't a coincidence.'

'No, it wasn't. Our new owner is an associate of the arms dealer. In all likelihood, it was the arms dealer who put up the money. Only in Russia.'

She reached into her handbag and withdrew a pack of cigarettes and a lighter. 'Do you mind?'

Gabriel shook his head, and glanced around the restaurant. There were no signs of any watchers. Olga lit her cigarette.

'The sale of the magazine presented us with a dilemma. We believed the story about the missile sale to be true, but we now had no place to publish it. We decided to make our findings known to the West through a trusted figure inside Israeli intelligence.'

'Why me? Why not tell the CIA?'

'It is no longer wise for members of the press to meet with American officials, especially those who also happen to work for the CIA.'

'And so he decided to leave the country and contact us in Rome?'

'In keeping with the new mission of the *Gazeta*, he said he wanted to do a piece about Russians at play in the Eternal City. After he arrived in Rome, he made contact with your embassy and requested a meeting. Obviously, the arms dealer and his security service were watching.'

'Who is he? Who is the arms dealer?'

She said a name, then picked up the wine list and opened the cover. 'Let's have something to drink, shall we? Do you prefer red or white?'

THE WAITER brought the wine. It was Georgian, blood red and very rough. Gabriel's thoughts were now elsewhere. The name Olga had just spoken was familiar to him, of course. Everyone knew the name Ivan Kharkov.

'What do you know about him, Mr Golani?'

'The basics. Former KGB turned Russian oligarch. Passes himself off as a legitimate businessman. Lives mainly in London and France.'

'Those *are* the basics. May I give you a more thorough version of the story?' Gabriel nodded his head. Olga held her wineglass near her face with both hands. Between them, a candle flickered in a red bowl. It added blush to her pale cheeks. 'Ivan's father was high-ranking KGB. *Very* high-ranking. In fact, when he retired, he was the chief of the First Main Directorate, the foreign espionage division. Ivan spent a good part of his privileged childhood abroad. He had blue jeans and Rolling Stones records, while ordinary Soviet teenagers had Communist propaganda and Komsomol weekends in the country. Like all the children of Party elite, he was automatically granted a place at a top university. In Ivan's case, it was Moscow State. After graduation, he was admitted directly into the ranks of the KGB, assigned to the Fifth Main Directorate. Do you know about the Fifth Main Directorate, Mr Golani?'

'It was responsible for internal security functions: border control, dissidents, artists and writers.'

She nodded. 'Don't forget it was responsible for persecuting Jews too, Mr Golani. Rumour has it Ivan was very diligent in that regard.

'Ivan benefitted from the magic hand of his famous father and was promoted rapidly through the ranks of the directorate. Then came Gorbachev and glasnost and perestroika, and overnight everything in our country changed. Young entrepreneurs were allowed to start cooperatives and private banks. Against all odds, many of these young entrepreneurs actually started to make money. This didn't sit well with our secret overlords at Lubyanka, who decided they had no option but to go into business for themselves. They needed an energetic young man of their own, a young man who knew the ways of Western capitalism.'

'Ivan Kharkov.'

She raised her glass in salutation to his correct answer. 'With the blessing of his masters at Lubyanka, Ivan was allowed to leave the KGB and start a bank. Within months his new bank was raking in millions of dollars in profit, almost all of it due to State business. Then the Soviet Union crumbled, and when the State-owned enterprises were auctioned off, Ivan gobbled up the most lucrative assets and factories. When property in Moscow could be purchased for a song, Ivan snatched up some of the gems. Ivan never had any illusions about the reason for his astonishing success. He had been helped by the magic hand of the KGB, and he was very good at keeping the magic hand filled with money.'

A waiter appeared and began laying small dishes of Georgian appetisers on the table. When he'd gone, she resumed her lecture.

'One of the State assets Ivan scooped up in the early nineties was a fleet of cargo planes and container vessels. They didn't cost him much, since at the time most of the planes were sinking into the ground at airfields around the country and the ships were turning to rust in dry dock. Ivan bought the facilities and the personnel necessary to get the fleet up and running again, and within a few months Ivan's ships and planes were filled with lucrative cargo moving to and from troubled foreign lands, no questions asked.'

'Russian weapons,' said Gabriel.

Olga nodded. 'And not just AK-47s and RPG-7s, though they are a substantial part of his operation. Ivan deals in the big-ticket items, too: tanks, antiaircraft batteries, attack helicopters, even the occasional frigate or out-of-date MiG. He hides now behind a respectable veneer as one of Moscow's most prominent property developers, but beneath it all, he's nothing but a gunrunner and a thug.'

'If we're going to find out whether Ivan has really made a deal with al-Qaeda, we have to get inside his network,' Gabriel said. 'And to get inside Ivan's network, we need the name of your original source.'

'You can't have it, Mr Golani. Two people are already dead. I'm afraid the matter is closed.' She looked down at her menu. 'We should eat something, Mr Golani. It's better if the FSB thinks we're actually hungry.'

For the remainder of dinner, Olga spoke of books recently read, films recently viewed and the coming election. When the bill came, they engaged in a playful tussle, male chivalry versus Russian hospitality, and chivalry prevailed. It was still light out; they walked directly to Olga's car, arm in arm for the benefit of any spectators.

'Would you be so kind as to see me to my door, Mr Golani?' she said as they climbed into the old Lada. 'I'm afraid my building isn't as safe as it once was.'

'It would be my pleasure.'

'It's not far from here. There's a Metro stop nearby. You can—'

Gabriel placed a finger to her lips and told her to drive.

OLGA'S APARTMENT BUILDING was known as K-9, but the local English-speaking wits called it the House of Dogs. Built in the footprint of an H, it had thirty-two floors, six entrances and a large transmission tower on the roof with blinking red warning lights. It was not a home, thought Gabriel, but a storage facility for people. 'Which doorway is yours?'

'Entrance C.'

'Pick another.'

'But I always go through C.'

'That's why I want you to pick another.'

They entered through a doorway marked B and struck out down a long corridor with a cracked linoleum floor. Every other light was out, and from behind the closed doors came the sounds and odours of too many people living too closely together. Arriving at the lifts, Olga stabbed at the call button and gazed at the ceiling. A minute elapsed. Then another.

'It's not working.'

'What floor do you live on?'

'The eleventh.'

'Where are the stairs?'

With a glance, she indicated round the corner. Gabriel led her into a dimly lit stairwell that smelled of stale beer, urine and disinfectant. 'Believe it or not, it used to be much worse,' she said.

Gabriel mounted the first step and started upwards, with Olga at his heels. For the first four floors, they were alone, but on the fifth they encountered two girls sharing a cigarette and on the seventh two boys sharing a syringe. On the tenth they walked through shards of broken glass.

By the time they reached the eleventh-floor landing, Olga was breathing heavily. Gabriel reached out for the latch, but before he could touch it, the door flew away from him as though hurled open by a blast wave. He pushed Olga into the corner and managed to step clear of the threshold as the first rounds tore the dank air. Olga began to scream but Gabriel scarcely noticed. He was now pressed against the wall of the stairwell. He felt no fear, only disappointment. Someone was about to die. And it wasn't going to be him.

The gun was a P-9 Gurza with a suppressor screwed into the barrel. It was a professional's weapon, though the same could not be said for the dolt who was wielding it. Perhaps it was overconfidence on the part of the assassin, or perhaps the men who had hired him had neglected to point out that one of the targets was a professional himself. Whatever the case, the gunman blundered through the doorway with the weapon exposed in his outstretched hands. Gabriel seized hold of it and pointed it safely towards the ceiling as he drove the man against the wall. The gun discharged harmlessly twice before Gabriel was able to deliver a vicious knee to the gunman's groin, followed by a crushing elbow to the temple. Leaving nothing to chance, after prising the Gurza from the gunman's now-limp hand, Gabriel fired two shots into his skull, the ultimate professional insult.

Amateurs, he knew, tended to kill in pairs, so when he heard the sound of crackling glass rising up the stairwell he pulled Olga out of the line of fire and was standing at the top of the stairs as the second man came round the corner. Gabriel put him down as if he were a target on a training range: three shots to the body, one to the head for style points.

He stood motionless for a few seconds, until he was certain there were no more assassins, then turned round. Olga was cowering on the floor, next to the first man Gabriel had killed. His head was covered by a black balaclava. Gabriel tore it off, revealing a lifeless face with a dark beard.

'He's Chechen,' Olga said.

'You're sure?'

Before Olga could answer, she leaned over the edge of the stairs and was violently sick. In the distance, he could hear the first sirens of the police.

'They'll be here any minute, Olga. We're never going to see each other again. You must give me the name. Tell me your source before it's too late.'

THE FIRST OFFICERS to arrive were members of a Moscow City Militia public-security unit, the proletariat of the city's vast police apparatus. A stubble-chinned sergeant took a brief statement from Olga, whom he appeared to know by reputation, then turned his attention to the dead men.

'Chechen gangsters,' he declared with disgust. He gathered a few more facts, including the name and nationality of Miss Sukhova's foreign friend, and radioed the information to headquarters. At the end of the call, he ordered his colleagues not to disturb the scene and confiscated Gabriel's diplomatic passport, hardly an encouraging sign.

The next officers to appear were members of the GUOP, the special unit that handles cases related to organised crime and contract killings. The team leader called himself Markov. No rank. No first name. Just Markov. Unlike the sergeant, Markov spoke a bit of English. His first questions were directed not at the famous reporter from the *Gazeta* but at Gabriel. He seemed most interested in hearing how a middle-aged Israeli diplomat had managed to disarm a professional assassin, shoot him twice in the head, then kill his partner. Listening to Gabriel's account, his expression was one of open scepticism. He slipped Gabriel's passport into his coat pocket and said they would have to continue this conversation at headquarters.

'I must protest,' Gabriel said.

'I understand,' said Markov sadly.

For reasons never made clear, Gabriel was handcuffed and taken by unmarked car to a busy Militia headquarters. There, he was led into the central processing area and placed on a wooden bench. Shortly after 1 a.m., Markov reappeared. He ordered Gabriel to stand, removed the handcuffs, and led him into an interrogation room. Gabriel's possessions—his wallet, diplomatic passport, wristwatch and mobile—were laid out neatly on a table. Markov picked up the phone and called up the directory of recent calls.

'You dialled your embassy before the first Militia officers arrived.'

'That's correct. It's standard procedure in a situation like this.'

'Are you often in situations like this?'

Gabriel ignored the question. 'I am a diplomat of the State of Israel, entitled to every and all diplomatic protection and immunity. I assume an officer of your rank and position would realise that my first responsibility is to contact my embassy and report what has transpired.'

'Did you *report* that you killed two men?'

'No.'

'Did it slip your mind?'

'We are instructed to keep telephone communications brief in all situations. I'm sure you understand.'

'Who's *we*, Mr Golani?'

'The ministry.'

'I see.'

Gabriel thought he could see a trace of a smile.

'I want to see a representative of my embassy immediately.'

'Unfortunately, due to the special circumstances of your case, we're going to have to detain you a little longer.'

Gabriel focused on a single word: *detain.*

'What special circumstances?'

Markov led Gabriel silently out of the room. This time, he was locked in a fetid holding cell with a pair of bloodied drunks. Gabriel found a relatively clean spot along one wall and lowered himself cautiously to the concrete floor. He sat with his arms wrapped round his shins, trying to shut out the sounds around him—the slamming of doors, the shouting of orders, the cries of a man being beaten. He wondered whether Olga was somewhere in this building or whether she had been taken elsewhere due to the 'special circumstances' of this case. Was she even alive, or had she suffered the same fate as her colleagues? As for the name Olga had spoken to him in the stairwell of the House of Dogs, he pushed it to a far corner of his memory and concealed it beneath a layer of gesso and base paint.

It was Elena . . . Elena was the one who told me about the sale.

Elena who? Gabriel thought now. *Elena where? Elena nobody . . .*

Finally, one sound managed to penetrate his defences: the sound of Markov's approaching footsteps. 'Responsibility for your case has been transferred to another department,' he said grimly.

'Which department is that?'

'Face the wall and place your hands behind your back.'

'You're not going to shoot me in front of all these witnesses, are you?'

'Don't tempt me.'

Gabriel did as instructed. A pair of uniformed officers entered the cell, reattached the handcuffs, and led him outside to a waiting car. It sped through a maze of side streets before finally turning onto a broad, empty avenue. Gabriel's destination now lay directly ahead, a floodlit fortress of yellow stone looming atop the low hill: Lubyanka, headquarters of the FSB.

GABRIEL HAD EXPECTED a period of isolation in a cell where Lubyanka's blood-soaked history could chip away at his resistance. Instead, he was pushed roughly into the building, causing him to tumble helplessly down a flight of stairs. That, plus a well-aimed kick to the kidney, left him clutching himself in agony. He was then taken directly to an interrogation room and forced into a chair before a rectangular table of pale wood. Seated on the other side was a man in a grey suit with a pallor to match. He wore a neat little goatee and round, wire-framed spectacles. Whether or not he was trying to look like Lenin, the resemblance was unmistakable. He was several years younger than Gabriel—mid-forties, perhaps—and looked educated, intelligent. A man of words rather than violence. Gabriel considered himself lucky. Given his location, he could have done far worse.

'I am a diplomat of the State of Israel,' Gabriel said.

'So I'm told. You might find this difficult to believe, but I am here to help you. You may call me Sergei. It is a pseudonym, of course. Just like the pseudonym that appears in your passport.'

'You have no legal right to hold me.'

'I'm afraid I do. You killed two citizens of Russia this evening.'

'Because they tried to kill *me*. I demand to speak to a representative of my embassy.'

'In due time, Mr . . .' He made a vast show of consulting Gabriel's passport. 'Ah, here it is. Mr Golani.' He tossed the passport onto the table. 'Come now, Mr Golani, we are both professionals. Surely we can handle this rather embarrassing situation in a professional manner.'

'I've given a complete statement to the Militia.'

'I'm afraid your statement raises many more questions than it answers.'

'What else do you need to know?'

Sergei produced a thick file; then, from the file, a photograph. It showed Gabriel, five days earlier, walking through the airport in St Petersburg.

'What I need to *know*, Mr Golani, is exactly what you are doing in Russia. And don't try to mislead me. If you do, I will become very angry. And that is the last thing you want.'

THEY WENT THROUGH IT ONCE; then they went through it again. The sudden illness of the deputy minister. Natan Golani's hasty recruitment as a stand-in. The meetings and the speeches. The receptions and the dinners. Each contact, formal or casual, was duly noted, including the woman who had tried to seduce him during the final gala at the Mariinsky Theatre.

'You were originally scheduled to return to Tel Aviv the morning after the UNESCO conference concluded.'

'That's correct.'

'And why did you suddenly decide to extend your stay in Russia?'

'Our ambassador here is an old friend. He suggested I come to Moscow for a day or two.'

'For what purpose?'

'To see him, of course—and to see Moscow.'

'What did he say to you exactly, your friend the ambassador?'

'He said I had to see Moscow to believe it. He said it was filled with billionaires, dirty bankers and Russian gangsters. He said it was a boom town. He said something about a sea of oil, caviar and vodka.'

'Did he mention a dinner party?' He tapped the file with his index finger.

'I'm sure he mentioned it. He said there would be some people from the opposition there.'

'Is that how he described the guests? As members of the *opposition*?'

'Actually, I think he referred to them as "brave souls" who've had the chutzpah to challenge the regime.'

'And why did he feel it necessary to throw such a party? Was it his intention to meddle in the internal affairs of the Russian Federation?'

'I can assure you no meddling took place. It was just dinner and pleasant conversation.'

'Who was in attendance?'

'Why don't you ask the agents who were watching the embassy that night? They photographed everyone who entered the compound.'

The interrogator smiled. 'Who was in attendance, Mr Golani?'

Gabriel listed the names to the best of his recollection. The last name he recited was Olga Sukhova.

'Was that the first time you and Miss Sukhova had met?'

'Yes.'

'You seem to have hit it off quite well.'

'We were seated next to each other at dinner. We had a very pleasant conversation.'

'Did you discuss the recent murders of her colleagues?'

'The topic might have come up. I can't remember.'

'What *do* you remember, Mr Golani?'

'We talked about Palestine and the Middle East. We talked about the war in Iraq. We talked about Russia and the coming election.'

'What did Miss Sukhova say about the election?'

'She said Russian politics are nothing more than professional wrestling. She said the winners and losers are chosen in advance. She said the president and the Russian Unity Party will win in a landslide. The only question is, how many votes will they steal in order to achieve their goals.'

'The Russian Federation is a democracy. Miss Sukhova's political commentary, while entertaining, is slanderous and completely false.' He paused. 'Did you and Miss Sukhova spend any time alone at the party?'

'Olga said she needed a cigarette. She invited me to join her.'

'There were no cigarettes among your possessions tonight.'

'That's hardly surprising, given the fact that I don't smoke.'

'But you joined her in any case?'

'Yes.'

'Because you wanted to have a word alone with her?'

'Because I was attracted to her—and, yes, because I wanted to have a word alone with her, in a place no one else could hear.'

'Where did you go?'

'The terrace.'

'How long were you alone?'

'A minute or two, no more.'

'What did you discuss?'

'I asked if I could see her again. If she would give me a tour of Moscow.'

'Did you also tell her you were a married man?'

'We'd already discussed that.'

'Whose idea was it to visit Novodevichy?'

'Hers.'

'Did you travel to the cemetery together?'

'No, I met her there.'

'Which grave did you visit first?'

'It was Chekhov's.'

'Describe it for me.'

Gabriel closed his eyes, as if trying to summon an image of the gravestone, but instead he heard the voice of Olga whispering softly into his ear. *You mustn't give them her name*, she was saying. *If Ivan discovers it was Elena who betrayed him, he'll kill her.*

THEY FORGED ON TOGETHER—for how long, Gabriel could only guess. At times, they wandered through unexplored territory. At others, they retraced their steps over familiar ground. Trivial inconsistencies were pounced upon as proof of treachery, minor lapses in memory as proof of deceit. There is a strange paradox to an interrogation: it can often impart more information to the subject than to the officer posing the questions. Gabriel had concluded that his opponent was but a small cog in a much larger machine. His real enemies resided elsewhere. Since he was supposed to be dead by now, his very presence in Lubyanka was something of an inconvenience for them. One factor would determine whether he survived the night: did they have the power to reach into the basement of Lubyanka and kill him?

The interrogator's final questions were posed with the bored air of a traffic policeman recording the details of a minor accident.

'I take it you've killed before, Mr Golani?'

'Like all Israeli men, I had to serve in the IDF. I fought in Sinai in 1973 and in Lebanon in 1982.'

'So you've killed many innocent Arabs?'

'Yes, many.'

'You are not who you say you are, Mr Golani. Your diplomatic passport is false. The sooner you confess your crimes, the better.'

The interrogator placed the cap on his pen and screwed it slowly into place. It must have been a signal, for the door flew open and the four handlers burst into the room. They took him down a flight of stairs and placed him in a cell no larger than a broom closet. It stank of damp and faeces. If there were other prisoners nearby, he could not tell, for when the windowless door was closed, the silence, like the darkness, was absolute.

He placed his cheek against the cold floor and closed his eyes. Olga Sukhova appeared in the form of an icon, head tilted to one side, hands folded in prayer. *If you make it out of Russia alive, don't even think about trying to make contact with her. She's surrounded by bodyguards every minute of the day. Ivan sees everything, hears everything. He is a monster.*

HE WAS SWEATING one minute and shivering violently the next. His kidney throbbed with pain, and he could not draw a proper breath because of the bruising to his ribs from when he had been thrown down the stairs. When he groped the interior of the cell to see if they had left him a blanket, he found only four slick walls instead. He closed his eyes and slept. In his dreams, he walked through the streets of his past and encountered many of the men he had killed. They were pale and bloodless, with bullet holes in their hearts and faces.

He woke finally to the sight of torches blazing in his face. The men holding them lifted him to his feet and frog-marched him up several flights of steps. Gabriel tried to count, but soon gave up. Five? Ten? Twenty? He couldn't be sure. He feared they were about to hurl him from the roof—Lubyanka had a long history of such unfortunate *accidents*—but then he was in the cold night air, being shunted into the back of a black van. His hands were freed briefly, only to be restrained again a few seconds later when they were attached to a steel loop in the roof. Then the doors closed with a deafening thud and the van lurched forward.

Where now? he thought. *Exile or death?*

HE HEARD NO SIRENS to indicate they were under escort, and the driver appeared to be obeying traffic rules, such as they were. At one long stop, he heard the sound of laughter, and he thought of Solzhenitsyn. *The vans . . .* That was how the KGB had moved the inhabitants of the Gulag Archipelago—at night, in ordinary-looking vans, invisible to the souls around them, trapped in a parallel world of the damned.

It was impossible to guess in which direction they were travelling. Twice the van stopped and twice Gabriel could hear Russian voices raised in anger. He supposed even an unmarked FSB van had trouble moving through the countryside without being shaken down by *banditi* and traffic police looking for bribes.

The third time the van stopped, the doors swung open and a handler entered the compartment. He unlocked the handcuffs and motioned for Gabriel to get out. A car had pulled up behind them; the interrogator whom he knew as Sergei was standing in the glow of the parking lamps, stroking his little beard as though deciding on a suitable place to carry out an execution. Then Gabriel noticed his suitcase lying in a puddle of mud. The interrogator nudged the bag towards Gabriel with the toe of his shoe and pointed towards a smudge of yellow light on the horizon.

'The Ukrainian border. They're expecting you.'

'Where's Olga?'

'I suggest you get moving before we change our minds, Mr *Allon*. And don't come back to Russia again. If you do, we will kill you. And we won't rely on a pair of Chechen idiots to do the job for us.'

Gabriel picked up his suitcase and started towards the border. He waited for the crack of a pistol and the bullet in his spine, though he heard nothing but the sound of the car and van turning round. With their headlights gone, the heavy darkness swallowed him. He kept his eyes focused on the yellow light and walked on. And, for a moment, Olga was walking beside him. *Her life is now in your hands*, she reminded him. *If Ivan ever finds out his own wife was my source, he won't hesitate to kill her.*

Chapter 4

'Wake up, Mr Golani. You're almost home.'

Gabriel opened his eyes slowly and gazed out of the window of the first-class cabin. Below, the lights of the Coastal Plain lay in a glittering arc along the edge of the Mediterranean.

He turned his head a few degrees and looked at the man who had awakened him. He was twenty years younger than Gabriel, with eyes the colour of granite and a fine-boned, bloodless face. The diplomatic passport in his blazer pocket identified him as Baruch Goldstein of the Israeli Ministry of Foreign Affairs. His real name was Mikhail Abramov. A former member of the Sayeret Metkal special forces, he had one other attribute that had made him the perfect candidate to escort Gabriel back to Israel. He had been born in Moscow to a pair of dissident scientists and spoke fluent Russian.

They had been travelling together for the best part of a day. After crossing the border, Gabriel had surrendered himself to a waiting team of Ukrainian security officers, the SBU. These men had taken him to Kiev and handed him over to Mikhail and two other Office security men. From Kiev, they had driven to Warsaw and boarded the El Al flight to Ben-Gurion.

Gabriel tried to sit up, but his kidney began to throb again. He closed his eyes and waited for the pain to subside.

'You should have watched your step on those KGB stairs.'

'It's called the FSB now, Mikhail. The KGB doesn't exist any more.'

'Where did you ever get that idea? They were KGB when I was growing up in Moscow and they're KGB now.' He glanced at his watch. 'We'll be on the ground in a few minutes.'

Gabriel leaned back against the headrest and closed his eyes until the cabin shuddered with the impact of a hard landing.

When the plane had taxied to a halt, Gabriel rose to his feet and collected his bag from the overhead locker, then followed Mikhail and the others down the stairs. While the rest of the passengers filed into the airport, Gabriel headed towards a waiting Peugeot limousine, and climbed into the back seat.

Shamron examined the dark bruise along Gabriel's cheek. 'I suppose you don't look bad for someone who survived Lubyanka. How was it?'

'The rooms were on the small side, but the furnishings were lovely.'

'Perhaps it would have been better if you'd found some other way of deal-ing with those Chechens besides killing them.'

'I considered shooting the guns out of their hands, Ari, but that sort of thing really only works in the movies.'

'I'm glad to see you emerged from your ordeal with your fatalistic sense of humour intact. A team of debriefers is waiting for you at King Saul Boulevard. I'm afraid you have a long night ahead of you.'

'I'd rather go back to Lubyanka than face the debriefers tonight.'

Shamron gave Gabriel a paternalistic pat on the shoulder.

'I'll take you home, Gabriel. We'll talk on the way.'

Jerusalem

They still had much ground to cover when they arrived at Gabriel's apart-ment in Narkiss Street. Despite the fact it was after midnight, Shamron invited himself upstairs for coffee. Gabriel hesitated before inserting his key into the lock.

'Go ahead,' Shamron said calmly. 'We've already swept it.'

'I think I like fighting Arab terrorists better than Russians.'

'Unfortunately, we can't always choose our enemies.'

Gabriel entered the apartment first and switched on the lights. Everything was exactly as he had left it a week earlier, including the half-drunk cup of coffee he had left in the kitchen sink. As he poured the now-mouldy remnants down the drain, he said, 'How *did* you get me out?'

'When it became clear to our ambassador and the Moscow Station chief that the FSB had no intention of respecting your diplomatic passport, we decided to go on the offence. Shin Bet regularly monitors the movements of Russian Embassy employees. As it turned out, four of them were drinking heavily in the bar of the Sheraton Hotel. A mile from the hotel, they were pulled over for what appeared to be a routine traffic stop. It wasn't, of course.'

'So you kidnapped four Russian diplomats and held them hostage in order to coerce them into releasing me.'

'We Israelites invented tit for tat. Besides, they weren't just diplomats. Two of them were known intelligence officers. When we received confir-mation from the Ukrainians that you'd made it safely across the border, we released them from custody.'

Gabriel went into the kitchen and saw to the coffee. 'Where is Olga now?'

'Back in her apartment, surrounded by security guards. She's as safe as one can be in Russia, which is to say not terribly safe at all. Eventually, she might want to consider a new life in the West.' His eyes settled on Gabriel. 'Is she as good as she appears, or is it possible she's something else entirely?'

'She's golden, Ari. She's a gift from the intelligence gods. She agreed to help us at great risk to herself, remember. And I was allowed to leave. Olga is still in Moscow. If the Kremlin wants her dead, they'll kill her. And there's nothing those security guards can do to protect her.

'How much do we have on Ivan Kharkov?' Gabriel asked as they sat down at the kitchen table.

'Plenty,' said Shamron. 'Ivan's been active in Lebanon for years. He makes regular deliveries to Hezbollah, but he also sells weapons to Palestinian and Islamist factions operating inside the refugee camps.'

'What kind of weapons?'

'The usual. Grenades, mortars, RPGs, AK-47s—and bullets, of course. *Lots* of bullets.'

'Which means Ivan Kharkov has an established track record of selling weapons directly to terrorist organisations.'

'Without question. He has the connections to lay his hands on the most dangerous weapons in the world. Chemical. Biological. Even nuclear weapons aren't out of the question. We know that agents of al-Qaeda have been scouring the remnants of the old Soviet Union for years looking for nuclear material or even a fully functioning nuclear device. Maybe they've finally found someone willing to sell it to them.'

Shamron spooned sugar into his coffee and stirred it slowly. 'The Americans might have better insight into the situation. It's my recommendation we dump this in their lap as soon as possible and wash our hands of the affair. I want you to go to Washington and see your friend Adrian Carter. Tell him everything you learned in Moscow. Give them Elena Kharkov. Then get on the next plane to Umbria and finish your honeymoon.'

'What do you think the Americans will do with this information?'

'I suspect they'll go cap in hand to the Kremlin and plead with the Russian president to block the sale.'

'And he'll tell the Americans that Ivan is a legitimate businessman with no ties to the illegal international arms trade. He'll dismiss the intelligence as an anti-Russian slur spread by Jews conspiring to keep Russia backward and weak.' Gabriel shook his head slowly. 'We should regard the Russian president and his intelligence services as adversaries and act accordingly.'

'So what exactly are you suggesting?'

'That we have a quiet word with Elena Kharkov and see if she knows more than she told Olga Sukhova. She spends the majority of her time in London, Ari. We can get to her.'

'And so can Ivan. She's surrounded by his security goons night and day. All her communications are probably monitored. What do you intend to do? Invite her to tea? Drop her an email?'

'I'm working on that part.'

'Just know Ivan is three steps ahead of you. There's been a leak from somewhere in his network and he knows it. Any approach to his wife is going to set off alarm bells. One misstep and you could get her killed.'

'So we'll just have to do it quietly.'

'*We?* I seem to remember a conversation we had a few days ago during which you berated me for interrupting your honeymoon. Now you want to run an open-ended operation against Ivan Kharkov?'

'Let's just say I have a personal stake in the outcome of the case.'

Shamron sipped his coffee. 'Something tells me your new wife isn't going to be pleased with you.'

'She's Office. She'll understand.'

'Just don't let her anywhere near Ivan,' Shamron said. 'Ivan likes to break pretty things.'

Georgetown

The CIA sent a plane for him, a Gulfstream G500, with leather club chairs, in-flight action movies and a well-stocked galley. It touched down at Andrews Air Force Base in the equatorial heat of midday and was met in a secure hangar by a pair of Agency security agents who took him to a graceful redbrick town house in Georgetown. Waiting in the entrance hall was a man of retirement age, dressed in a navy-blue blazer and crumpled gabardine trousers. He had the tousled thinning hair of a university professor and a moustache that had gone out of fashion with disco music.

'Gabriel,' said Adrian Carter, extending his hand. 'So good of you to come.'

'You're looking well, Adrian.'

'And you're still a terrible liar.' He looked at Gabriel's face and frowned. 'I assume that lovely bruise is a souvenir of your night in Lubyanka?'

'I wanted to bring you something, but the gift shop was closed.'

Carter gave a faint smile and took Gabriel by the elbow. 'I thought you might be hungry after your travels. I've arranged for some lunch.'

They entered the living room. It was a formal Georgetown salon, rectangular and high-ceilinged, with French doors overlooking a small terrace.

Carter wandered over to the buffet and selected a ham sandwich and a ginger ale. Gabriel drew a cup of black coffee from a silver pump-action thermos and sat in a wing chair next to the French doors.

'Shamron tells me Ivan has been a bad boy again,' Carter said as he sat down and balanced his plate on his knees. 'Give me everything you've got. I love stories about Ivan. They serve as helpful reminders that there are some people in this world who will do absolutely anything for money.'

It wasn't long after Gabriel began his briefing that Carter seemed to lose his appetite. He placed his partially eaten sandwich on the table next to his chair and sat motionless. Little about his demeanour suggested that he was one of the most powerful members of Washington's intelligence establishment—or that before he became director of the CIA's national clandestine service, he had been a field man of the highest reputation.

'I wish I could say your story sounded like the ravings of an angry wife,' Carter said. 'But I'm afraid it dovetails with some alarming intelligence we've been picking up over the past few months.'

'What sort of intelligence?'

'Chatter,' said Carter. 'More to the point, a specific phrase that has popped up several times over the past few weeks—so many times, in fact, that our analysts are no longer willing to dismiss it as mere coincidence.'

'What's the phrase?'

'The Arrows of Allah. We've seen it about a half-dozen times now, most recently on the computer of a jihadi who was arrested in Copenhagen. The suspect had tried to delete an email that said something about "the arrows of Allah piercing the hearts of the infidels", or sentiments to that effect. Ivan's main stomping ground is Africa. But he's made lucrative forays into the Middle East and Latin America as well. Ivan is willing to provide the dictators, the warlords and the guerrilla fighters with whatever they want, and, in turn, they're willing to pay him whatever he asks. He's responsible for more death and destruction than all the Islamic terrorists of the world combined. And now he trots around the playgrounds of Europe, safe in the knowledge that we can't lay a finger on him.'

'Why didn't you ever go after him?'

'We tried during the nineties. We noticed that much of the Third World was burning, and we started asking ourselves a single question: who was pouring the gasoline on the flames? The Agency started tracking the movement of suspicious cargo planes around Africa and the Middle East. Before long, we had a good idea where all the weapons were coming from.'

'Ivan Kharkov.'

Carter nodded. 'We established a working group at the National Security Council to come up with a strategy for dealing with the Kharkov network. Since he had violated no American laws, our options were extremely limited. By the time the Clinton administration left town, the Kharkov network was still in business. And when the new crowd settled into the White House, they barely had time to figure out where the bathrooms were before they were hit with 9/11. Suddenly, Kharkov didn't seem so important any more.'

'Because you needed Russia's help in the fight against al-Qaeda?'

'Exactly,' said Carter. 'Ivan is former KGB. He has powerful benefactors. To be fair, even if we *had* pressed the Kremlin on the Kharkov issue, it probably wouldn't have done any good. On paper, there are no ties between Ivan Kharkov the legitimate oligarch and Ivan Kharkov the international arms trafficker. Ivan is a master of the corporate front.'

Carter fished a pipe and a pouch of tobacco from the flap pocket of his jacket and loaded the bowl of his pipe. 'In a perfect world,' he continued, 'I suppose we would go to the Russian president and ask him for help. But the current president of Russia is anything but a trustworthy ally. He's a dangerous man. He wants Russia to be a superpower again. He wants to challenge American supremacy around the globe. He's sitting atop a sea of oil and natural gas, and he's willing to use it as a weapon. I lived through the end of the first Cold War. We're not there yet, but we're definitely heading in that direction. If we're going to track down those weapons, we'll have to do it *without* Russia's help.'

'I prefer it that way. We Jews have a long history of dealing with Russians.'

'So how do you suggest we proceed?'

'I want to arrange a meeting with Elena Kharkov.'

Carter raised an eyebrow. 'I suggest you proceed carefully, Gabriel. Otherwise, you might get her killed.'

'Thank you, Adrian. That really hadn't occurred to me.'

'Forgive me,' said Carter. 'How can I help?'

'I need every scrap of intelligence you have on Ivan's network. And I mean *all* of it, Adrian—especially National Security Agency intercepts of Ivan's telephone communications. And don't just give me the transcripts. I need to get inside his head. And to get inside his head, I need to hear his voice.'

'You're talking about a great deal of *highly* classified material. It can't be turned over to an officer of a foreign intelligence service on a whim, even you. I have to run it through channels. But I'll do my best to get it to you within twenty-four hours. What else do you need?'

'A Russian speaker.'

'Believe it or not, we've still got a few of those.'

'Actually, I have one in mind. I need you to get him into the country right away.' Gabriel told him the name.

'Done,' said Carter. 'Where will you set up shop? At your embassy?'

'I've never been fond of embassies.' Gabriel looked around the room. 'This will do nicely. But do me a favour, Adrian. Ask your techs to remove all the cameras. I don't want them watching me while I shower.'

It took Adrian Carter the better part of the next morning to secure the authorisation necessary to release the Kharkov files into Gabriel's custody. Then several additional hours elapsed while they were gathered, sorted and purged of anything remotely embarrassing to the CIA or the US government. Finally, at seven that evening, the material was delivered to the Georgetown house. Carter stopped by with a draconian release form that threatened criminal prosecution and many other forms of punishment if Gabriel shared the documents or their contents with anyone else.

'That's ridiculous. How can I operate without *sharing* the intelligence?'

'Just sign it,' Carter said. 'It doesn't mean what it says. It's just the lawyers being lawyers.'

Gabriel scribbled his name in Hebrew across the bottom of the form and handed it to Eli Lavon, who had just arrived from Tel Aviv. Lavon signed it without protest and gave it back to Adrian Carter.

'No one is allowed in or out of the house while this material is on the premises. And that includes you two. Don't think about trying to sneak out, because I've got a team of watchers on N Street and another in the alley.'

For the remainder of the evening, and late into the night, Gabriel and Eli were treated to the sound of Ivan Kharkov's voice. They listened while he negotiated with the mayor of Moscow over a prime piece of riverfront property where he wished to develop a shopping mall. They listened while he coerced a fellow Russian businessman into surrendering his share of a lucrative Bentley dealership. They listened while he threatened to castrate the owner of a London removals company over damage to his mansion in Belgravia incurred during the delivery of a Bösendorfer piano.

When not tending to his far-flung business empire, Ivan juggled his many women. There was Yekatarina, the supermodel whom he kept for personal viewing in an apartment in Paris. There was Tatyana, the Aeroflot flight attendant who saw to his needs each time their paths happened to intersect, and there was poor Ludmila, who had come to London looking for a way out of her dreary Siberian village and had found Ivan instead. She had believed Ivan's lies and, when cast aside, had threatened to tell Elena everything. Ivan threatened to have her killed.

Occasionally, they would be granted a reprieve from Ivan by the voice of Elena, who became ensnared in NSA's net each time she used one of Ivan's phones. She was silk to Ivan's steel, decency to Ivan's decadence. She raised their two children without Ivan's help and, for the most part, passed her days free of Ivan's boorish company. Ivan bought her large houses and gave her endless piles of money to fill them with expensive things. In return, she was permitted to ask nothing of his business or personal affairs.

An hour before dawn, Gabriel was reading an excruciatingly dull cable by the CIA station chief in Angola when Lavon poked his head round the door.

'I think I may have just found a way for us to talk to Ivan's wife.'

'SHE'S OBSESSED with Mary Cassatt,' Gabriel said.

They were walking along the towpath at the edge of the Chesapeake and Ohio Canal. Gabriel wore faded jeans and a plain white pullover; Carter, a nylon tracksuit and a pair of pristine running shoes.

'Is that one of Ivan's girlfriends?' Carter asked.

'She's a painter, Adrian. An Impressionist painter.'

'Forgive me, Gabriel. I've been somewhat busy since 9/11. I can give you chapter and verse on the one hundred most dangerous terrorists in the world, but I can't tell you the title of the last movie I saw.'

'You need to get out more, Adrian.'

'Tell that to al-Qaeda,' he said. 'I take it Mary Cassatt was French?'

'American, actually. She moved to Paris in 1865 and fell under the spell of the Impressionists. Her speciality was tender portraits of women and children—intriguing, since she was childless herself. Her work is a bit sentimental for my taste, but it's popular with collectors.'

'Like Elena Kharkov?'

Gabriel nodded. 'Based on what we heard in the intercepts, she owns at least six Cassatts already and is in the market for more. She's on first-name terms with every significant dealer in Paris, London and New York, including the director of the Impressionist and Modern Art department at Christie's in London, who coincidentally I knew in another life.'

'I take it you're planning to renew your professional relationship?'

'One step at a time, Adrian. But after listening to those intercepts, I'm convinced that if a painting by Mary Cassatt were to come quietly onto the market, Elena Kharkov would jump at the opportunity to have a look.'

'And you would be standing next to it when she did?'

'Or one of my associates. Someone with a pleasing demeanour and a deep passion for the paintings of Mary Cassatt. Someone who won't make Elena's bodyguards nervous.'

'Should I assume this encounter would take place on British soil?'

'You should.'

'That means you're going to have to bring the British into the picture. Ivan and his entourage are under full-time MI5 surveillance whenever they're in London. But I suspect our British cousins will be more than willing to cooperate. They've been pressing us to do something about Ivan for years,' Carter said. 'This agent with a deep passion for Mary Cassatt, do you have someone in mind for the job?'

'I'm inclined to use a woman, someone who could pass as an American or a Brit. We have several suitable candidates but none with expertise in art.'

'As you may recall, we have someone who might fit the bill,' Carter said. 'She has a PhD in art history from Harvard and she's done a job like this before. She's even operated with your service on a couple of occasions.'

'It might be complicated, Adrian.'

'Because she's secretly in love with you?' Carter glanced at Gabriel to see his reaction but received only a blank stare in return. 'She's a big girl, Gabriel. And she's a true professional.'

'Where is she?'

'Still at the Counterterrorism Center at Langley, which means she's technically under my control. If you want her, she's yours.'

'Poor choice of words, Adrian.'

'I was speaking in a professional sense, of course.'

Gabriel walked in silence for a moment. 'Obviously, she's perfect for the job. But are you sure she's ready to go back into the field?'

'I'm given regular updates on her progress. The Agency psychiatrist we assigned her says she's coming along nicely. She's had no problems adapting to her new cover identity, and her superiors have given her extremely high marks. Do you want to use her?'

'I'll know after I talk to her—somewhere the Agency isn't listening.'

'That narrows our options considerably.' Carter made a show of careful consideration. 'How about Dumbarton Oaks? The gardens, at noon.'

THE SUN HAD BURNED through the morning haze by the time Gabriel presented himself at the entrance of Dumbarton Oaks and it had grown appallingly hot. He purchased an admission ticket from a man in a booth, and a few minutes after noon, he made his way to a distant corner of the gardens, where he found an attractive woman in her early thirties seated on a wooden bench, a paperback open in her lap. She wore a simple cotton sundress and sandals. Her blonde hair had grown out since he had seen her last; her alabaster skin was beginning to turn red from the intense sun. She looked up sharply as Gabriel approached, but her face remained expressionless.

'Did you spot Adrian's watchers?' asked Sarah Bancroft.

He kissed her cheek and led her towards the shade of a nearby trellis. 'Let's hear it.'

'Woman with the sunhat, man with the plaid Bermuda shorts, the couple wearing matching "I Love New York" shirts.'

'Very good. But you missed the two boys in the dark sedan on R Street.'

'They might as well have just waved hello to me as I came inside.'

They sat down together, but even in the shade there was little relief from the heat. Sarah pushed her sunglasses into her hair and brushed a trickle of perspiration from her cheek. Gabriel gazed at her in profile while her eyes flickered restlessly around the gardens. The daughter of a wealthy Citibank executive, Sarah Bancroft had spent much of her childhood in Europe, where she had acquired a European education along with a handful of European languages and impeccable manners. She had returned to America to attend Dartmouth and, later, after spending a year studying at the Courtauld Institute of Art in London, went on to earn a PhD in art history at Harvard. While finishing her dissertation, she began dating a young lawyer named Ben Callahan, who had the misfortune of boarding United Airlines Flight 175 on the morning of September 11, 2001. He managed to make one telephone call before the plane plunged into the South Tower of the World Trade Center. That call was to Sarah. Gabriel had recruited her and given her the chance to fight back against the murderers. With Carter's blessing, and with the help of a lost Van Gogh, he had inserted her into the entourage of a Saudi billionaire named Zizi al-Bakari and ordered her to find the terrorist mastermind lurking within it. She had been lucky to survive. Her life had never been the same since.

'I was afraid you wouldn't come,' he said.

'Why? Because in the midst of a very tense operation I committed the unprofessional act of confessing my true feelings for you?'

'That was one reason.'

'You don't have to worry, Gabriel. I'm over you now.' She looked at him and smiled. 'The question is, do you really want me tagging along on another operation?'

'Why wouldn't I?'

'Because your lovely new Italian bride might not approve.' She adjusted the thin straps of her sundress. It clung to her breasts in a way that could cause even the most faithful eye to wander. 'You know, for a man of your many gifts, your knowledge of women is shockingly deficient.'

'I make up for it in other ways.'

She gazed at him for a moment as though he were a dull student. 'The last person Chiara wants to see in the field again is *me*.'

'You were a guest at our wedding.'

'One of the worst days of my life. And I've had some pretty terrible days.'

'But you're over me now?'

'Not even a flicker of interest.'

Gabriel gazed across the gardens and asked what Carter had told her.

'Only that you're going after Ivan Kharkov.'

'Know much about him?'

'He's not formally under the purview of the Counterterrorism Center at Langley, but he probably should be. We went to war in Iraq, in part, because we feared that Saddam might be willing to supply the terrorists with sophisticated weaponry or even weapons of mass destruction. But these days terrorists can go to a nonstate actor like Ivan and for the right money he'll sell them whatever they want and route it to them through one of his customers in Africa or Latin America.' She continued, 'What do you need me to do this time?'

'Memorise the CIA's files on Ivan and his network, and read everything you can about Mary Cassatt. Adrian will tell you the rest.'

'Kharkov and Cassatt? Only a Gabriel Allon operation could feature a combination like that.' She lowered her sunglasses. 'Should I assume you'll need me to go undercover again?'

'Yes, you should.'

A silence fell between them, heavy as the midday heat. 'If you don't want to do it, Sarah, just tell me. You've done more than enough already.'

She looked at him and smiled. It was a brave smile, thought Gabriel.

'And miss all the fun?' She fanned herself dramatically with her book. 'Besides, I'd do just about anything to get out of here for a few days. I can't stand Washington in the summer.'

Chapter 5

London

Number 7 Mornington Terrace was a postwar apartment block overlooking the railway tracks of Euston Station. When Gabriel rang the bell of Flat 5C, the door opened a few inches and a pair of grey eyes regarded him coolly over the chain. They didn't look pleased to see him.

Free of the chain, the door swung open a more hospitable distance. Gabriel stepped inside and took stock of his surroundings: a dreary little bedsit, with a cracked linoleum floor and flea-market furnishings. The man waiting inside looked as though he had wandered into the flat by mistake. He wore a pinstriped suit and a Burberry raincoat. His hair had been blond once; now it had the cast of pewter. It gave him the appearance of a model in a magazine advertisement for fine cognac, the older millionaire type who puts himself about with younger women.

Graham Seymour didn't have time to pursue women, though. As deputy director of MI5, the British Security Service, he had more than enough work on his desk to keep him occupied. His country was now home to several thousand Islamic extremists with known terrorist connections. And just to keep things interesting, Russian espionage activities in London were now at levels not seen since the end of the Cold War.

Seymour must have arrived just before Gabriel because the shoulders of his coat were still beaded with raindrops. He tossed it wearily over the back of a chair and held out his hand. The palm was facing up. 'Hand it over.'

Gabriel exhaled heavily and surrendered his passport. Seymour opened it and frowned. 'Martin Stonehill. Place of birth: Hamburg, Germany.' Seymour handed the passport back.

Gabriel slipped it back into his coat pocket and looked around the room. 'Do you use this for all your high-level liaison meetings, Graham, or is this palace reserved for Israeli visitors?'

'Don't get your nose bent out of joint. It was all we could find at short notice. Besides, it was you who refused to come to Thames House.'

Thames House was MI5's riverfront headquarters near Lambeth Bridge. 'I really like what you've done with the place, Graham.'

'It's been in the family for years. We use it mainly as a crash pad and for debriefing sources and penetration agents.'

'What sort of penetration agents?'

'The sort that we slip into potential terrorist cells.'

'Any of your sources picking up any whispers about Russian arms headed this way?'

'The Americans aren't the only ones who've been hearing chatter about the Arrows of Allah. We've intercepted references to them as well.'

In the galley kitchen, an electric kettle began to spew steam. Gabriel walked over to the window and peered out at a passing West Coast Main Line train while Seymour saw to the tea. He returned with two cups, black for Gabriel, milk and sugar for himself.

Seymour lowered himself hesitantly onto the couch and placed his cup on a scratched coffee table. 'Adrian gave me the basics of what you picked up in Moscow. Why don't you fill me in on the rest?'

Gabriel told Seymour everything, from the murder of Boris Ostrovsky in Rome to his interrogation and deportation from Russia.

'My, my, but you *do* get around. And to think you managed all that with only three dead bodies. That's something of an accomplishment for you.' Seymour blew thoughtfully into his tea. 'So what are you proposing? You want to pull Elena Kharkov aside for a private chat about her husband's operations? Easier said than done, I'm afraid. She doesn't put a toe outside her Knightsbridge mansion without a full complement of bodyguards.'

'Actually, that's not exactly true. There's someone in London she talks to on a regular basis—someone who might be willing to help.'

'He's a British citizen, I take it?'

'Quite.'

'Is he honestly employed?'

'I suppose that depends on your point of view. He's an art dealer.'

'Where does he work?'

Gabriel told him.

'Oh dear. This could be a bit ticklish.'

'That's why I'm here, Graham. I wouldn't dream of operating in London without consulting you first.'

'Spare me.'

'I think we should have a little look under his fingernails before we make any approach. The art world is filled with a lot of shady characters.'

'*We?* No, Gabriel, *we* won't go anywhere near him. The Security Service will handle this matter with the utmost discretion.'

'How soon can you start?'

'I'll have a man on him by lunch,' Seymour said. 'I propose we meet once a day to review the watch reports.'

'Agreed.'

'We can do it here if you like.'

'Surely you jest.'

'Your choice, then.'

'St James's Park. Six o'clock. The benches on Duck Island.'

Graham Seymour frowned. 'I'll bring the breadcrumbs.'

GABRIEL'S PRIMARY TARGET during those first days of the operation was Alistair Leach, director of Impressionist and Modern Art at the august Christie's auction house. He was a good and decent man who became ensnared in the affair through no fault of his own, other than his serendipitous proximity to evil.

Few lives are lived without a trace of sin, and fewer still can stand up to the scrutiny of an MI5 telephone tap and a full-time complement of MI5 watchers. Any intelligence officer with a modicum of conscience knows it can be a disquieting experience to rifle through the drawers of a man's life, and Seymour made certain it was done with the gentlest hand possible. His listeners eavesdropped on Leach's telephone conversations with a forgiving ear, his watchers stalked their quarry from a respectable distance, and his burrowers dug through Leach's phone records, bank statements and credit-card bills with the utmost sensitivity. It did not take long for the bugs to reveal why Leach spent so little time at his Kentish Town residence. The listeners began referring to his wife, Abigail, only as 'the Beast'.

During this phase of the affair, Gabriel took up residence in an Office safe flat in Bayswater Road, where he caught up on his rest and let his bruised body heal. He slept late, then spent the remainder of his mornings dawdling over coffee and the newspapers. After lunch, he would take long walks around Central London, ending up each day at Duck Island in St James's Park.

Graham Seymour appeared promptly at six o'clock the first two evenings, but on the third he arrived forty-five minutes later, muttering about his director-general being in a snit. He immediately opened his stainless-steel attaché case and handed Gabriel a photograph. It showed Alistair Leach strolling the pavements of Piccadilly with a woman at his side.

'Who is she?'

'Rosemary Gibbons. She's an administrator in the Old Master Paintings department at Sotheby's. For obvious reasons, both personal and professional, they keep their relationship highly secret. As far as we can tell, it's strictly platonic. To tell you the truth, my watchers are actually rooting for poor Alistair to take it to the next level. Abigail is an absolute fiend.'

'Where are they now?'

'A little wine bar in Jermyn Street. Quiet table in the far corner.'

'You'll get me a picture, won't you, Graham? A little something to keep in my back pocket in case he digs in his heels?'

Seymour ran a hand through his grey locks, then nodded.

'I'd like to move on him tomorrow,' Gabriel said. 'What's his schedule?'

'Appointments all morning at Christie's, then he's attending a meeting of something called the Raphael Club. We have a researcher checking it out.'

'You can tell your researcher to stand down, Graham. I can assure you the members of the Raphael Club do nothing more seditious than drink far too much wine and bemoan the shifting fortunes of their trade.'

'Shall we do it before the meeting or after?'

'*After*, Graham. Definitely after.'

THE MEMBERS of the Raphael Club began trickling into Green's Restaurant and Oyster Bar shortly before one the following afternoon. Oliver Dimbleby, a lecherous independent dealer from Bury Street, arrived early, but then Oliver always had a gin or two at the bar alone, just to get the mood right. The unscrupulous Roddy Hutchinson came next, followed by Jeremy Crabbe, director of Old Master Paintings from Bonhams. A few minutes later came a pair of curators, one from the Tate and another from the National. Then, at one sharp, Julian Isherwood, the Raphael Club's founder, came teetering up the front steps, looking hung-over.

By 1.20, the guest of honour—at least in the estimation of Gabriel and Graham Seymour, who were sitting across the street from Green's in the back of an MI5 surveillance van—had not yet arrived. Seymour telephoned the MI5 listeners and asked whether there was any recent activity on Leach's work line or his mobile.

'It's the Beast,' explained the listener. 'She's giving him a list of errands he's to run on the way home from work.' At 1.34, a surveillance team in King Street reported that he had just left Christie's, and shortly afterwards a team inside Green's reported that Leach had joined the proceedings and that the white Burgundy was now flowing.

The luncheon was three hours and fifteen minutes in length, and the final wine count was four bottles of Sancerre, four bottles of a Provençal rosé and three bottles of an excellent Montrachet. The bill, estimated at 'somewhere north of fifteen hundred pounds' by the team inside the restaurant, was collected by means of a passed plate, with Oliver Dimbleby cracking the whip. Alistair Leach tossed a couple of hundred quid onto the plate as it passed beneath his nose and he finished his last glass of wine.

They clustered briefly outside in Duke Street before going their separate ways. Alistair Leach started back towards Christie's but he would get no farther than the corner of Duke Street, for it was there that Graham Seymour had chosen to make the scoop. The task was handled by an operative named Nigel Whitcombe, who had a face like a parson and the grip of a blacksmith.

Leach offered only token resistance as he was led towards a waiting MI5 Rover. 'Mind telling me what this is all about?' he asked meekly as the car pulled away from the kerb.

Whitcombe's smile was like balm. 'Relax, Alistair. You're not in any trouble. We just need to borrow some of your connections and expertise.'

'Any idea how long we'll be?'

'I suppose that depends on you.'

'I'll need to call Abigail if we're going to be late. She worries, you know.'

Yes, thought Whitcombe. *We know all about Abigail.*

TWENTY MINUTES after he was plucked from King Street, Alistair Leach was shown into the drawing room of a hastily leased mews house not far from Sloane Square. It was a pleasant room with good books on the shelves and good whisky on the trolley. The blinds were partially open and the agreeable light of late afternoon was filtering through the slits and making striped patterns along the wood flooring. Graham Seymour was slowly pacing up and down. Gabriel was seated in front of a television monitor in an upstairs bedroom, with two MI5 technicians for company, one called Marlowe and the other called Mapes. Inside the Service, they were better known as M&M Audio and Video.

Whitcombe instructed Leach to sit on the couch, then sat next to him. On the coffee table was a single sheet of paper. Graham Seymour drew a pen from his pocket and held it towards Leach like a loaded gun.

'Be a love, Alistair, and sign that for me. It's a copy of the Official Secrets Act. You needn't bother reading it, since the wording isn't terribly important. Rest assured, it gives us the right to lock you away in the Tower if you ever breathe a word of what is about to transpire here. You're not to talk about it with anyone. Not with your colleagues. Not with Abigail. Not with any other friend with whom you share the occasional intimacy.'

Leach looked up sharply, and for an instant Gabriel feared that Seymour had played his ace when a jack would have done the trick. Then Leach looked at Whitcombe, who nodded gravely.

'What have I done?' Leach asked, pen to the document. 'Shortchanged Inland Revenue? Misbehaved on the Tube? Said something nasty about the current occupant of Number Ten?'

'You're fortunate enough to have been born in a free country,' said Seymour. 'You can say anything you like—within certain limits, of course. You're here not because of your own actions but because of your association with a man who is a rather serious threat to British national security.'

'Where's *here*?' Leach looked around the room. 'And who are *we*?'

'The *here* is not important. This is all temporary. As for the *we*, that's a bit more permanent. We're from the Security Service, sometimes referred to as MI5. I'm Charles.' He nodded towards Whitcombe. 'This is Gerald.'

'And this *association* of mine that's a threat to national security? Who might that be? My newsagent? The bloke who brings us coffee at the office?'

'It's one of your clients, actually.'

'I'm afraid one encounters all sorts in a business like mine and not all of them are candidates for sainthood.'

'The client I'm talking about need never apply for admission to God's heavenly kingdom, Alistair. He's not your average robber baron or hedge-fund thief. He's an arms dealer who is about to conclude a transaction that could make the London bombings seem like child's play.'

'Does he have a name?'

'You don't get to know his name yet—not until you've agreed to help us.'

'But what can *I* do? I sell paintings.'

'We're asking you to make a telephone call, Alistair. Nothing more. For that telephone call, you will be handsomely compensated. More important, we are giving you the opportunity to help defend your country and the world from an enemy that thinks nothing of slaughtering innocents.'

Seymour stopped walking. His eyes were concealed by shadow. 'Shall I go on, or should we run you home to Abigail and pretend this encounter never took place?' Leach shifted uneasily in his seat.

'Go on,' he said, to no one in particular.

Seymour resumed his pacing. 'Because the threat is international, our effort to counter it is international as well. You are about to meet an officer from the intelligence service of another country, a country allied with our own in the struggle against terrorism. What's more, it is quite possible you will recognise this gentleman from your professional life. The document you signed covers your contact with this man as well as us.'

'Please tell me he isn't a bloody American.'

'Worse, I'm afraid.'

'The only thing worse than an American is an Israeli.'

Whitcombe gave Leach an admonitory tap on the side of the knee.

'Have I put my foot in it?' Leach asked.

'I'm afraid so,' said Seymour.

'You won't say anything to him, will you? They *do* tend to get their back up at even the slightest insult.'

Seymour gave a ghost of a smile. 'It will be our little secret.'

GABRIEL ENTERED the drawing room and, without a word, lowered himself into the armchair opposite Leach.

'Dear heavens, you're—'

'I'm no one,' said Gabriel, finishing the sentence for him. 'You don't know me. You've never seen me before in your life. Are we clear, Alistair?'

Leach looked at Seymour and appealed for assistance.

Seymour said, 'Answer his question, Alistair.'

'But I *do* know his name. He's Mario Delvecchio. He cleans pictures for juicy Julian Isherwood. He's the best. Paints like an angel and can authenticate a work simply by running his fingers over the brushstrokes.'

Gabriel silently handed Leach a single sheet of paper. 'Read this.'

'What is it?'

'A transcript of a phone conversation.'

Leach did as instructed, then looked up. 'Where did you get this?'

'It's not important.'

'Tell me where you got this or this conversation is over.'

Gabriel capitulated. In recruitments it was sometimes necessary to accept small defeats in order to secure ultimate victory. 'It was given to us by the Americans.'

'The Americans? Why in God's name are they tapping my phone?'

'Don't be grandiose,' Seymour interjected. 'They're not tapping *your* telephone. They're tapping *hers*.'

'Are you trying to tell me Elena Kharkov is an arms dealer?'

'Ivan Kharkov is the arms dealer,' Gabriel said. 'Elena just gets caught when she happens to place a call from one of the phones they're monitoring. If it makes you feel any better, no one bothered to read the transcript—until I came along. But let's put all that aside and focus on what's important. You were talking to her about a painting that day—a painting by Mary Cassatt.'

'Elena has a thing for Cassatt. An obsession really. Buys anything that comes on the market. I thought I'd managed to prise loose a painting for her from a minor collector—a picture called *Two Children on a Beach*. The collector kept us hanging for several weeks before finally telling me that he wasn't ready to sell. I placed a call to Elena and got her machine. She called me back and I gave her the bad news.'

'Did you ever tell Elena the name of the owner?'

'You know better than to ask that, Signor Delvecchio.'

Gabriel looked at Graham Seymour, who had wandered over to the shelves and was pulling down books for inspection. 'Who is he, Alistair? And don't try to hide behind some claim of dealer-client privilege.'

'Can't do it,' said Leach obstinately. 'He wishes to remain anonymous.'

Nigel Whitcombe made a church steeple with his fingertips and pressed it thoughtfully against his lips. 'And if the owner was aware of the stakes involved? I suspect he might actually relish the chance to help us. I suspect the owner is a patriot, Alistair.' A pause. 'Just like you.'

'Boothby,' Leach said, after a lengthy silence. It was as if the name had popped suddenly into his memory. 'Sir John Boothby. Lives in a big Edwardian pile on a hundred acres in the Cotswolds. The father worked for your lot. Rumour has it he had a wonderful war.'

Seymour twisted his head round. 'You're not talking about Basil Boothby, are you?'

'That's him. Ruthless bastard, from what I hear.'

'Basil Boothby was one of the legends of the Service. He was involved in our deception programme during the Second World War. Ran captured German spies back to their masters in Berlin.'

'I'm wondering whether there's a chance that Sir John might have had a change of heart,' Gabriel said. 'It might be time to have another go at him.'

'He's not going to sell that painting—at least not to Elena Kharkov.'

'Why not?'

'Because in a moment of professional indiscretion, I may have mentioned that the prospective buyer was the wife of a Russian oligarch. Boothby's father spent the final years of his career battling KGB spies.

The old man didn't hold with Russians. Neither does Sir John.'

'Perhaps we can convince him to see the error of his ways.'

'Good luck. But remember, if that Cassatt changes hands, I get my cut.'

'How much are you getting these days, Alistair?' asked Gabriel.

Leach smiled. 'You have your secrets, signor, and I have mine.'

Chapter 6

Chipping Campden, Gloucestershire

Havermore, the ancestral home of the Boothby family, lay five miles to the northwest of the picturesque market town of Chipping Campden. At its zenith, the estate had sprawled over eight hundred acres of Cotswold pastures and wooded hills and had employed several dozen men and women. Its fortunes had dwindled in recent years, along with those of the family that owned it. All but a hundred acres had been sold off, and the manor house had fallen into a state of rather alarming disrepair. As for the staff, it now consisted of a single farmhand called Old George Merrywood and a plump housekeeper named Mrs Lillian Devlin.

She greeted Gabriel and Graham Seymour early the next afternoon and informed them that Sir John was eagerly awaiting their arrival. They found him standing before an easel in the East Meadow, flailing away at a dreadful landscape. Boothby and Seymour shook hands cordially and regarded each other for a moment in silence. They were of similar size and shape, though John Boothby was several years older. His thick grey hair and tangled eyebrows gave him the appearance of a bottlebrush come to life.

'This is an associate of mine,' Seymour said, his hand resting on Gabriel's shoulder. 'He works for an intelligence service in the Middle East whose interests occasionally intersect with our own.'

'So you're an Israeli, then,' said Boothby, shaking Gabriel's hand.

'I'm afraid so,' replied Gabriel contritely.

'No apologies necessary around here, my dear fellow. I have no quarrel with Israelis—*or* Jews, for that matter. We Europeans dropped you into the swamp, didn't we? And now we condemn you for daring to stand your ground.' He released Gabriel's hand. 'But do I get to know your name?'

'His name is Gabriel Allon, Sir John.'

Boothby gave a wry smile. 'I thought it was you. An honour, Mr Allon.'

He returned to his easel. He looked morosely at the painting. 'Bloody awful, isn't it? I can never seem to get the trees right.'

'May I?' asked Gabriel.

Surprised, Boothby handed him the brush. Gabriel worked on the painting for thirty seconds, then stepped aside.

'Good Lord! But that's bloody *marvellous*. You're obviously a man of considerable talent.' He took Gabriel by the arm. 'Let's go up to the house, shall we? Mrs Devlin has made a roast.'

THEY ATE OUTSIDE on the terrace beneath an umbrella that gave their faces the sepia colouring of an old photograph. Gabriel remained largely silent during the meal while Graham Seymour talked at length about Boothby's father and his work during the Second War. Gabriel was left with the impression that Boothby the Younger did not necessarily enjoy hearing about his father—that he had spent his life living in the shadow of Basil Boothby's wartime exploits. It wasn't until Mrs Devlin served the coffee that he finally asked why Seymour and his friend from Israel had come all the way to Havermore to see him. But when Seymour commenced a somewhat meandering explanation, Boothby's patience finally wore thin.

'Come, come, Graham, we're all men of the world here. If you want me to sign a copy of the Official Secrets Act, I'll find the pen myself. But please spare me the bullshit.' He looked at Gabriel. 'You Israelis are known for your bluntness. Be blunt, for God's sake.'

'We've picked up intelligence that a Russian arms dealer named Ivan Kharkov may be about to sell some very dangerous weapons to the terrorists of al-Qaeda. Is that blunt enough for you, Sir John?'

'Quite.' He scratched his grey head and made a show of thought. '*Kharkov?* Why do I know that name?'

'Because his wife wants to buy your *Two Children on a Beach*.'

'Ah, yes. I remember now. The wife's name is Elena, isn't it?' He sat back in his chair. 'Listen, gentlemen, perhaps I'm not as foxy or devious as my old father was, but what *exactly* are you asking me to do?'

'I need to arrange a meeting with Elena Kharkov.' Gabriel paused to look around at the landscape. 'And I'd like to do it at Havermore.'

'Why do you need to meet with Elena Kharkov?'

'We have strong reason to believe Mrs Kharkov is aware of her husband's plans and does not approve,' Gabriel said. 'And we also believe she may be receptive to a quiet approach.'

'A recruitment? Is that what you're suggesting? You want to ask Elena Kharkov to betray her husband—*here*, in my home?'

'It's perfect, actually.'

'I must say, I'm rather intrigued by the idea. Who's going to make the actual pass at her?'

'Your American niece.'

'But I don't *have* an American niece.'

'You do now.'

'And what about *me*?'

'I suppose we could get a stand-in,' Seymour said. 'One of our older officers, or perhaps even someone who's retired.' He lapsed into silence. 'I suppose there is *one* other alternative, Sir John. *You* could play the role yourself. Your father was one of the greatest deceivers in history. Deception is in your genes.'

'And what happens if Ivan Kharkov ever finds out? I'll end up like that poor bloke Litvinenko, dying an agonising death in University College Hospital with my hair falling out.'

'We'll make certain Ivan never gets anywhere near you. And the fact that you were never married and have no children makes our job much easier.'

'Well, if you truly believe I'm up to the job, it would be my honour to do it.'

'Excellent,' said Seymour. 'That leaves only the small matter of the painting itself. If Elena Kharkov wants to buy it, we have to sell it to her.'

Boothby brought his hand down on the table hard enough to rattle the china and the crystal. 'Under no circumstances am I selling that painting to the wife of a Russian arms dealer.'

Gabriel patted his lips with his napkin. 'There is another possible solution—something your father would have enjoyed.'

'What's that?'

'A deception, of course.'

THEY HIKED UP the grand central staircase beneath yellowed portraits of Boothbys dead and gone. The nursery was in semidarkness when they entered; Boothby pushed open the heavy curtains, allowing the golden Cotswold light to stream through the tall, mullioned windows. It fell upon two matching children's beds, two matching children's dressers, two matching hand-painted toy chests and *Two Children on a Beach* by Mary Cassatt.

'My father bought it in Paris between the wars. My mother and sisters adored it, but, to be honest, I never much cared for it.'

Gabriel walked over to the painting and stood before it in silence, right hand to his chin, head tilted slightly to one side. Then he licked three fingers of his right hand and scrubbed away the surface grime from the chubby knee of one of the children. Boothby frowned.

'I say, Gabriel. I hope you know what you're doing.'

Gabriel took two steps back from the painting. 'I'm going to need a place to work for a few days. Somewhere quiet where I'm not going to be disturbed.'

'There's an old gamekeeper's cottage at the north end of the property. I did a bit of renovation a few years back, converted the entire second floor into a studio. I think you'll find it to your liking.'

'Please tell Mrs Devlin that I'll see to my own cleaning.' Gabriel resumed his appraisal of the Cassatt, one hand pressed to his chin. 'I don't like people watching me while I work.'

THE FOLLOWING MORNING, Gabriel gave MI5 an operational shopping list the likes of which it had never seen. Whitcombe volunteered to fill it. His first stop was L. Cornelissen & Son in Great Russell Street, where he collected a large order of brushes, pigment, medium, ground and varnish. Next, it was up to Camden Town for a pair of easels, then over to Earl's Court for three commercial-grade halogen lamps. His final two stops were just a few doors apart in Bury Street: Arnold Wiggins & Sons, where he ordered a lovely carved frame in the French style, and Dimbleby Fine Arts, where he purchased a work by a largely unknown French landscapist. Painted outside Paris in 1884, its dimensions were twenty-nine inches by thirty-eight inches, the same as the Cassatt canvas.

By afternoon, the painting and the supplies were at Havermore, and Gabriel was soon at work in the old gamekeeper's cottage. After subjecting the Cassatt to a surface examination, he covered the painting with a translucent paper and carefully traced the image beneath. When the sketch was complete, he removed it and made several thousand tiny perforations along the lines he had just drawn. He then transferred the tracing to the second canvas—which had been stripped bare and covered in a fresh ground—and carefully sprinkled charcoal powder over the surface. A moment later, when he removed the paper, a ghost image of *Two Children on a Beach* appeared on the surface.

Gabriel then placed the easels side by side, with Cassatt's original on the left, and immediately prepared his first palette. He worked slowly for the first few days, but as he grew more accustomed to Cassatt's style, he was able to apply the paint to the canvas with increasing confidence and swiftness.

Though the painting consumed most of Gabriel's attention, Ivan and Elena Kharkov were never far from his thoughts. NSA redoubled its efforts to intercept all of Ivan's electronic communications, and Adrian Carter arranged for a man from London Station to make regular trips to Havermore to share the take.

Ivan spent his days largely sequestered in his walled mansion in Zhukovka, west of Moscow. Only once did he venture outside the country: a day-trip to Paris to spend a few hours with Yekatarina, his mistress. He phoned Elena three times from Yekatarina's bed to say that his business meetings were going splendidly. One of the calls came while she was dining with two companions at the exclusive Café Pushkin, and the moment was captured by an Office watcher with a miniature camera. Gabriel couldn't help but be struck by the melancholy expression on her face.

One salient operational fact still eluded Gabriel: the precise date Ivan and Elena were planning to visit Knightsbridge next. But finally, an MI5 team monitoring the Kharkov mansion in Rutland Gate witnessed the delivery of a large consignment of vodka, champagne and wine—strong evidence, they argued, of Ivan's impending return. The next day, NSA intercepted a telephone call from Ivan to Arkady Medvedev, the chief of his personal security service. Buried within a lengthy discussion about the activities of a Russian rival was the nugget of intelligence for which Gabriel had been so anxiously waiting: Ivan was coming to London in a week on business. After leaving London, he would travel to the South of France to take up residence at his sumptuous summer palace near Saint-Tropez.

That evening, Gabriel ate dinner while standing before the canvas. Shortly after nine, he heard the sound of car tyres crunching over the gravel drive. He walked over to the window and peered down as a tall woman with pale blonde hair emerged with a single bag slung over her shoulder. She came upstairs to the studio and stood at his shoulder while he worked.

'Watch your brushwork on the hands, Gabriel. It's a bit too impasto.'

'My brushwork, as usual, is flawless.'

'How foolish of me to suggest otherwise.' She smothered an elaborate yawn. 'I'm running on fumes.'

'You can sleep here tonight, Sarah, but tomorrow, you're moving up to the main house. Uncle John is expecting you.'

'What's he like?'

'I wouldn't want to spoil the surprise.'

'If you need any more advice, don't hesitate to wake me.'

'I think I can manage on my own.'

Sarah kissed his cheek and slipped silently through the doorway.

Gabriel pressed the play button on a small portable stereo and stood motionless while the first notes of *La Bohème* filled the room. Then he tapped his brush against the palette and painted alone until midnight.

SIR JOHN BOOTHBY was introduced to his American niece over breakfast the following morning. Gabriel swiftly sketched the missing chapters of their long and cordial relationship. Though Sarah's mother, now deceased, had been foolish enough to marry a Wall Street banker, she had made certain her daughter maintained strong connections to England, which is why Sarah had spent summers at Havermore, and why she still made an annual pilgrimage to the estate now that she was in her thirties.

As a young girl, she had stayed in the nursery and formed a deep bond with *Two Children on a Beach*. Therefore, it would be natural for Sarah to show Elena Kharkov the painting rather than her uncle, who had never really cared for it. Uncle John's task would be to assist in the separation of Elena from her bodyguards while she went upstairs to view the painting. Gabriel estimated they would have ten minutes. Any more than that, he reckoned, and the bodyguards would start getting jumpy.

With Sarah's arrival, the pace of the preparations increased dramatically. Cameras and microphones were installed around the house and the grounds, and a makeshift command post was created in the hayloft of the barn, where the feeds were monitored and recorded. Sarah spent her mornings 'reacquainting' herself with the estate. She spent many pleasant hours with her uncle, familiarising herself with the vast old manor house, and led herself on long walks around the estate with Punch and Judy, Boothby's poorly behaved Pembroke Welsh corgis, trotting at her heels.

Mrs Devlin pronounced her 'the most delightful American I've ever met'. She knew nothing of Sarah's alleged blood relationship to her employer— indeed, she had been told by Sir John that Sarah was the daughter of an American friend and had recently gone through a nasty divorce. *Poor lamb*, she commented one afternoon to Old George Merrywood as they watched Sarah emerge from the dappled light of the North Wood with the dogs at her heels. *What idiot would ever let a girl like that slip through his fingers?*

In the evenings, Sarah would wander out to the gamekeeper's cottage to discuss the recruitment of Elena Kharkov with Gabriel.

'Remember, Sarah,' he said, 'two people are already dead because of her. You can't force the issue. Just open the door and let her walk through it. If she does, get as much information as you can about Ivan's deal and try to arrange a second meeting. Whatever you do, don't let the first encounter last longer than ten minutes. You can be sure the bodyguards will be watching the clock. And they report *every*thing to Ivan.'

The following morning, Graham Seymour called from Thames House to say that Ivan Kharkov's plane was due to arrive at Stansted Airport at 4.30 p.m. After hanging up the phone, Gabriel applied the final touches of paint to his version of *Two Children on a Beach*. Three hours later, he removed the canvas from its stretcher and carried it downstairs to the kitchen, where he placed it in a 350-degree oven. Sarah found him there twenty minutes later, leaning nonchalantly against the counter, coffee mug in hand. 'What's that smell?' Gabriel glanced down at the oven. Sarah peered through the window, then looked up in alarm.

'Why are you baking the Cassatt?'

Just then the kitchen timer chimed softly. Gabriel removed the canvas from the oven and allowed it to cool slightly, then laid it face-up on the table. With Sarah watching, he took hold of the canvas at the top and bottom and pulled it firmly over the edge of the table, down towards the floor. He examined the surface for a moment, then, satisfied, held it up for Sarah to see. The combination of heat and pressure had left the surface covered by a fine webbing of fissures and cracks.

'Amazing,' she whispered.

'It's not amazing,' he said. 'It's craquelure.'

Whistling tunelessly to himself, he carried the canvas upstairs to his studio, placed it back on the original stretcher, and covered the painting with a thin coat of yellow-tinted varnish. When the varnish had dried, he summoned Sarah and John Boothby to the studio and asked them to choose which canvas was the original, and which was the forgery.

After several minutes of careful comparison, both agreed that the painting on the right was the original, and the one on the left was the forgery.

Smiling, Gabriel removed the painting on the right from its easel and mounted it in the new frame. Sarah and John Boothby, humiliated over being duped, carried the forgery up to the main house and hung it in the nursery. Gabriel climbed into the back of an MI5 car and, with Nigel Whitcombe at his side, headed back to London. The operation was in Alistair Leach's hands now.

London

Gabriel knew that discretion came naturally to those who work in the high-lands of the art trade, but even he was surprised by the extent to which Alistair Leach had remained faithful to his vow of silence. Indeed, after more than a week of relentless digging and observation, MI5 had found no trace of evidence to suggest he had broken discipline in any way.

Gabriel gave Whitcombe a cheque for one hundred thousand pounds and a brief script. 'Tell him not to blow his lines, Nigel. Tell him expectations couldn't be higher.'

Graham Seymour had insisted on using Thames House as a command post, and Gabriel reluctantly agreed. The ops room was a hushed chamber of blinking monitors and twinkling lights, staffed by earnest-looking young men and women.

At 2.17 p.m., he was informed by Graham Seymour that the stage was now set and the performance ready to commence. Gabriel made one final check of the video monitors and nodded his head. Seymour leaned forward into a microphone and ordered the curtain to be raised.

THE HANDSOME young man's card identified him as Jonathan Owens, asso-ciate editor of something called the *Cambridge Online Journal of Contemporary Art*. He claimed to have an appointment, though the recep-tionist in the lobby of Christie's could find no record of it in her logbook. 'Would it be too much trouble to actually ring him?' the young man asked through a benedictory smile. 'I'm sure he's just forgotten to notify you.'

'I'm sure you're right,' said the receptionist. 'Give me a moment, please.' She picked up the receiver and punched in a four-digit extension. 'Owens,' she said, repeating the name. 'Jonathan Owens, *Cambridge Online Journal of Contemporary Art* . . . Yes, that's him, Mr Leach . . . Lovely manners.' She hung up and handed the visitor a temporary guest identification badge, which he affixed to his lapel. 'Third floor, dear. Turn left out of the lift.'

He stepped away from the receptionist's desk and boarded a waiting lift. Alistair Leach was waiting in the doorway of his office with a somewhat baleful expression on his face.

'What can I do for you, Mr *Owens*?'

Nigel Whitcombe closed the door and handed Leach the script. 'Think you can do it cold, Alistair, or do you want to run through it a time or two?'

'I do this for a living. I think I can manage it on my own.'

Leach lifted the receiver of his telephone and dialled the number from memory. Ten seconds later, Gabriel's operation truly took flight.

'Elena, darling, it's Alistair Leach from Christie's. Am I catching you at a perfectly dreadful time?'

He hadn't, of course. In fact, at the moment her mobile rang, Elena Kharkov was having tea with her seven-year-old twins, Anna and Nikolai, at the café atop Harrods department store. Her Russian bodyguards were seated at an adjacent table.

She appeared to recognise the number in the caller-ID screen and was already smiling when she lifted the phone to her ear.

The conversation that followed was forty-nine seconds in length and was intercepted at multiple transmission points and by multiple services, including the US National Security Agency, Britain's GCHQ and even by the Russian eavesdropping service, which made nothing of it.

Gabriel and Graham Seymour listened to it live by means of a direct tap on Leach's line at Christie's. When the connection went dead, Graham Seymour looked at Gabriel and smiled.

'Congratulations, Gabriel. Looks like you've managed to get your hooks into her.'

Chipping Campden, Gloucestershire

It was 5.30 that same evening when Mrs Devlin entered the library at Havermore, bearing a silver tray with a glass of whisky in the centre of it. Sir John was reading the *Telegraph*. He always read the *Telegraph* at this time of day; like most idle men, he kept to a strict regime.

'If you've nothing else for me, Sir John, I'll be going home now. Your dinner's in the oven,' said the housekeeper.

He took a sip of the whisky and said, 'What are we having tonight?'

'Rack of lamb.'

'Divine,' he murmured. Mrs Devlin bade him a good evening and started towards the door. Boothby lowered his newspaper. 'Oh, Lillian?'

'Yes, Sir John?'

'We'll be having a visitor tomorrow afternoon.'

'*More* visitors, Sir John?'

'I'm afraid so. She won't be staying long. She's just going to have a look at the painting in the nursery.'

The painting in the nursery . . . The painting that had spent a week in the gamekeeper's cottage, in the possession of the man whose presence she had been told to say nothing about.

'I see,' she said. 'Shall I make a batch of scones?'

'She's not exactly a *scone* person, if you catch my meaning.'

'I'm not sure I do, Sir John.'

'She's a *Russian*, Lillian. A very well-to-do Russian. I doubt she'll be staying for tea.' Mrs Devlin remained rooted in the doorway. 'Something bothering you, Lillian?'

'May I speak bluntly, Sir John?'

'You usually do.'

'Is there something going on at Havermore that you're not telling me?'

'Many things, I suppose. You'll have to be a bit more specific.'

'The odd man in the gamekeeper's cottage. The girl who claims to be the daughter of your American friend. The men doing the electrical work all through the house. Old George is convinced they're up to no good!'

'Old George sees conspiracies everywhere, Lillian.'

'And now you're thinking about selling that beautiful painting to a *Russian*? Your poor father would be spinning in his grave.'

'I need the money, Lillian. *We* need the money.'

Mrs Devlin tugged sceptically on her apron. 'I'm not sure I believe you, Sir John. I think something important is going on in this house. Something to do with secrets, just like when your father was alive.'

Boothby gave her a conspiratorial look over his whisky. 'If you would rather not be here when the Russians arrive—'

'I'll be here, Sir John,' she said quickly.

'What about Old George?'

'Perhaps we should give him the afternoon off, sir.'

THE TWO ARMOURED MERCEDES limousines flashed down the terraced High Street of Chipping Campden, past the quaint shops and the old limestone church, and roared out of town again on Dyers Lane.

At the once-grand estate known as Havermore, there was no visible evidence to suggest that anyone was aware of the cars' rapid approach. As Mrs Devlin, in contravention of Sir John's direct orders, was putting the final touches to a tray of fresh scones, strawberry jam and clotted cream, Sir John was sequestered in the library. As for the young woman known to them as Sarah Crawford, she was coming up the footpath from the East Meadow, with Punch and Judy watching her back like tiny tan bodyguards.

Only in the hayloft of the tumbledown barn were there hints that something truly out of the ordinary was about to take place. Four men were there, seated before a bank of video and audio monitors, watching the video image of the young woman entering the kitchen. She playfully dipped a finger into Mrs Devlin's fresh cream, then passed through a pair of double doors and made her way into the entrance hall. She wore only a hint of blusher on her alabaster cheeks and cat-eyed spectacles instead of contact lenses. *Your beauty must pose no challenge to Elena's*, she had been told. *Elena's not used to finishing second at anything.*

At precisely 4.04, the armoured limousines turned through the gates of Havermore and started up the long drive. The men in the hayloft saw them first, followed by Sir John, whose library window gave him a superb outpost from which to monitor their approach. Sarah, from her position in the entrance hall, could not see the cars but heard them a few seconds later as they came prowling into the gravel forecourt.

Two powerful engines went silent, several doors opened, and six young bodyguards with faces of chiselled marble emerged. The men in the hayloft knew their names. Three were Oleg, Yuri and Gennady: Elena Kharkov's permanent detail. The other three were Vadim, Vasily and Viktor: 'the three Vs', as they were known to Kharkov watchers the world over. Their presence at Havermore was curious, since they served almost exclusively as Ivan's praetorian guard.

Having established a loose perimeter round the lead Mercedes, two of the guards opened the rear doors. Elena Kharkov emerged from the driver's side, a radiant flash of lustrous dark hair and green silk. Then, from the passenger side, came a sturdy male figure, well dressed, with hair the colour of steel: the man who was supposed to be otherwise engaged on a conference call with Zurich.

The men in the hayloft attempted to warn Sarah—they had hidden a tiny audio speaker in the entrance hall for just such a contingency— but she had already opened Havermore's impressive door and was stepping into the forecourt. Punch and Judy scampered past her ankles and shot across the gravel like a pair of honey-coloured torpedoes towards the most authoritative-looking member of the entourage. The three Vs formed a wall in front of their target: Ivan Kharkov.

He was standing calmly behind them, an expression of mild bemusement on his heavy features. Sarah used a moment of mock anger at the dogs to help conceal her shock at seeing the monster face to face for the first time. She seized the dogs by the collars and gave them each a firm shove on the hindquarters towards the house, then turned and extended her hand to Ivan.

'I'm afraid herding instincts take over when they see a large group of people,' she heard herself say. 'I'm Sarah Crawford.'

Ivan's right hand rose from the seam of his trousers. It looked, thought Sarah, like a manicured mallet. It gave her hand a testing squeeze and quickly released it. 'You're an American,' he pointed out.

And you forgot to tell me your name, she thought.

'Actually, I'm only half American.'

'Which half?'

'The self-centred half, according to my uncle. This is his home. I'm just visiting.'

'Where do you live in America?'

'Washington, DC. And you?'

'I like to think of myself as a citizen of the world, Miss Crawford.'

A citizen of the world, perhaps, but exposure to the West had yet to buff away the last traces of KGB English. It was surprisingly fluent but still flecked with the intonation of a Radio Moscow propagandist.

He was proud of his English, thought Sarah, just like he was proud of his armoured limousines, his bodyguards, his handmade suit and the rich after-shave that hung around him like a vaporous cloud. Yet no amount of Western clothing and cologne could conceal the fact that he was a KGB hood who had stumbled onto a mountain of money.

Almost as an afterthought, he lifted his left hand and, with his eyes still fixed on Sarah, said, 'My wife.' She was standing several feet away, sur-rounded by her own palace guard. She was taller than Ivan by an inch or two and held herself with the erect carriage of a dancer. Her skin was pale, her eyes liquid green, her black hair allowed to fall loosely about her shoul-ders. As for the prospect of Sarah's beauty posing a challenge to Elena's, there was little chance of that, for at forty-six years she was still a strikingly attractive woman.

She extended her hand. 'It's a pleasure to meet you, Sarah. I'm Elena Kharkov.' Her accent, unlike Ivan's, was authentic and rich, and completely beguiling. 'I believe Alistair told you I would be coming alone. My hus-band decided to join me at the last minute.'

'Actually, Alistair told me a *woman* would be coming alone. He didn't give me a name. He was very discreet, Mrs Kharkov.'

'And we trust that you will be discreet as well,' Ivan said. 'It is important that we conduct our business transactions in privacy.'

'You may rest assured my uncle feels the same way, Mr Kharkov.'

As if on cue, Boothby emerged, with Punch and Judy now swirling noisily at his feet. 'Did my ears deceive me,' he trumpeted, 'or is it true that the
great Ivan Kharkov has come to Havermore? That dolt from Christie's told
me to expect a VIP, but no one of your stature.' He took Ivan's hand in his
own and pumped it vigorously. 'It is indeed an *honour* to have you here, Mr
Kharkov. I *do* admire your accomplishments. I knew you were a man of
many interests, but I never knew art was one of them.'

Ivan's face broke briefly into something approaching a genuine smile.
Ivan, they knew, was vulnerable to flattery, even from tattered English
landed gentry. 'Actually, my wife is the expert when it comes to art,' he
said. 'I just felt like getting out of London for a few hours.'

'Oh, yes, of course. Can't stand London any longer, what with the traffic
and the terrorism.' He turned and gestured towards the façade of
Havermore. 'This has been in my family for five generations. I'd love to
give you a tour while our two art experts have a look at the painting.'

A glance passed between Ivan and Elena: coded, secure, inscrutable to an
outsider. She murmured a few words in Russian; Ivan responded by looking
at Boothby and nodding. 'I'd love a tour,' he said. 'But we'll have to make it
brief. I'm afraid my wife tends to make decisions quickly.'

'Brilliant!' said Boothby. 'Allow me to show you the grounds.'

He lifted his hand and started towards the East Meadow. Ivan, after a
brief hesitation, followed after him, with the three Vs flying close behind in
tight formation. Boothby looked at the bodyguards and politely objected.

'I say, but is that really necessary? I can assure you that you have no enemies here. The most dangerous things at Havermore are my martinis.'

Ivan murmured a few words in Russian to the bodyguards. When he
started towards the meadow a second time, they remained motionless.
Elena watched her husband's departure in silence, then looked at Sarah.

'I'm sorry about the security, Miss Crawford. Ivan insists they stay by my
side wherever I go. I imagine that it must seem very exciting to be surrounded by men in dark suits. I can assure you it is not.'

Sarah was momentarily taken aback by the intimacy of her words.
They constituted a betrayal. *A small one*, thought Sarah, *but a betrayal
nonetheless*. 'A woman in your position can't be too careful,' she said. 'But
I can assure you that you are among friends here.'

Boothby and Ivan disappeared round the corner of the house. Sarah
placed her hand gently on Elena's arm, then spoke: 'Would you like
to see my uncle's Cassatt, Mrs Kharkov? It is still in the nursery. My

uncle thought you would enjoy seeing it in its original setting.'

'I would *love* to see your uncle's Cassatt, Miss Crawford.'

When they started towards the portico, the bodyguards remained motionless.

IN THE HAYLOFT of the barn, the four men standing before the video monitors moved for the first time in three minutes.

'Looks like Uncle John just saved our arses,' said Graham Seymour.

'His father would be very proud.'

'Ivan's not the world's most patient man. I suspect we'll have five minutes with Elena at most.'

'I'd kill for five minutes.'

'Let's hope there's no killing today, Gabriel. Ivan has all the guns.'

ELENA ENTERED the room first. Sarah closed the door, then walked over to the window and pushed open the curtains. The golden light fell upon *Two Children on a Beach* by Gabriel Allon. Elena gasped.

'It's glorious,' she said. 'I must have it.'

Sarah allowed a silence to fall between them. She lowered herself onto the bed nearest the window and, with her eyes cast downwards, absently ran her hand over the Winnie the Pooh spread. Seeing her reaction, Elena said, 'My God, I'm so sorry. You must think I'm terribly spoilt.'

'Not at all, Mrs Kharkov.' Sarah made a show of looking around the nursery. 'I spent every summer in this room when I was a little girl. That painting was the first thing I saw in the morning and the last thing I saw at night. The house just won't feel the same without it.'

'I can't take it from you, then.'

'You must,' Sarah said. 'My uncle has to sell it, and I want it to go to someone who loves it as much as I do. Someone like *you*,' she added.

Elena turned back to the painting. 'I'd like to have a closer look at it before I make a final decision. Would you help me take it down, please?'

'Of course.'

Sarah rose to her feet and, passing before the window, glanced downwards towards the meadow. Boothby and Ivan were still there, Boothby with his arm extended towards some landmark in the distance, Ivan with his patience clearly at an ebb. She walked over to the painting and, with Elena's help, lifted it from its hooks and laid it flat upon the second bed. Elena then drew a magnifying glass and a small Maglite torch from her handbag and examined first the signature in the bottom left corner of the painting, then the surface. Her examination lasted three minutes. When it had ended, she switched off the Maglite and slipped it back into her handbag.

'This painting is an obvious forgery,' she said.

She regarded Sarah's face carefully for a moment as if she realised Sarah was a forgery, too.

'Please tell me who you are, Miss Crawford.'

Sarah opened her mouth to respond, but before she could speak, the door swung open and Ivan appeared in the threshold, with Boothby at his shoulder. Ivan stared at Elena for a moment; then his gaze settled on Sarah.

'Is something wrong?' he asked.

It was Elena who answered. 'Nothing's wrong, Ivan. Miss Crawford was just telling me how much the painting means to her and she became understandably emotional.'

'Perhaps they've had a change of heart.'

'No, Mr Kharkov,' Sarah said. 'I'm afraid we have no choice but to part with it. The painting belongs to your wife now—if she wants it, of course.'

'Well, Elena?' Ivan asked impatiently. 'Do you want it or not?'

Elena ran her fingers over the faces of the children, then looked at Sarah. 'It's one of the most extraordinary Cassatts I've ever seen.' She turned to Ivan. 'I must have it, my love. Please pay them whatever they ask.'

London

Precisely how Ivan Kharkov had managed to slip past the vaunted watchers of MI5 was never determined to anyone's satisfaction. Gabriel paid little attention to the recriminations and post-mortems because by paying $2.5 million for a painting she knew to be a forgery, Elena had shown herself to be receptive to a second approach. Which was why Adrian Carter boarded his Gulfstream jet and came to London.

'Sounds as if you had an interesting afternoon in the Cotswolds, Gabriel. How do you think Elena was able to tell the painting wasn't real?' They were seated together on Gabriel's bench in St James's Park.

'She owns several other Cassatts, which means she spends a great deal of time around them. She knows how they look, how they *feel*. Her instincts must have told her that the painting was a forgery.'

Gabriel stood up, followed by Carter, and together they set out along the Horse Guards Road.

'Where's the painting now?'

'Still at Havermore. Elena's shippers are coming to collect it. She told Alistair Leach she intends to hang it in the children's room at Villa Soleil, their villa in Saint-Tropez.'

'I take it Saint-Tropez is now in your travel plans as well?'

'It's not what it once was, but it's still the only place to be in August.'

'You can't set up shop there without first getting your ticket punched by the French services. And, knowing the French, they're going to want in on the fun. They're understandably angry with Ivan. His weapons have spread a great deal of death and destruction in parts of Africa where the Tricolore used to fly and where the French still wield considerable influence.'

'They can't come in, Adrian. The circle of knowledge is already too wide on this operation for my comfort. And if it widens again, the chances of Ivan and the FSB getting wind of it increase substantially.'

'We're back on speaking terms with the French, and the president would like to keep it that way. Which means that you're not to take any action on French soil that might bring yet another euro shit-storm down upon our heads. We have to go on the record with the French, Gabriel.'

'OK, but they aren't likely to be pleased with my terms.'

'Let's hear them.'

'They will be granted no formal role. In fact, my wish is that they do nothing more than stay out of the way. That means shutting down any surveillance operations they might be running on Ivan. If his security gorillas see a bunch of French agents in Saint-Tropez, alarm bells will go off.'

'What do you need from us?'

'Continued coverage of all of Ivan's communications. Make sure someone is sitting on the account twenty-four hours a day—someone who can speak Russian. I'm thinking about giving Sarah a Russian-American boyfriend. I can do Russian-Israeli on short notice, but not Russian-American.' Gabriel handed Carter an envelope. 'He'll need a full set of identification, of course, but he'll also need a cover story that can stand up to the scrutiny of Ivan and his security service.'

They turned into Great George Street. Carter paused in front of a newsstand and frowned at the morning papers. Osama bin Laden had released a new videotape, warning of a coming wave of attacks. It might have been dismissed by the intelligence professionals as an empty threat had the statement not contained four critical words: *the Arrows of Allah.*

'He's promising the autumn is going to be bloody,' Carter said. 'The fact that he was specific about the timing is noteworthy in itself. It's almost as if he's telling us there's nothing we can do to stop it. 'We're telling the media that we see nothing new or unusual in the tape. Privately, Gabriel, we're shitting bricks. We know they want to hit us again before the president leaves office. Expert opinion is convinced this plot may be the one. Which means you have a limited amount of time.'

'How limited?'

'End of August, I'd say. Then we raise the terror warning to red and go on war footing.'

'The moment you do, we lose any chance of getting to Elena.'

'Better to lose Elena than live through another 9/11. Or *worse*.'

They were walking towards the river now. Carter looked to his right and saw the North Tower of Westminster Abbey aglow in the bright sunshine, but his thoughts were clearly focused on the unpleasant meeting he was about to conduct on the other side of the English Channel.

'You know, Gabriel, you get the easy job. All you have to do is convince Elena to betray her husband. I have to go cap in hand to the Frogs and beg them to give you and your team the run of the Riviera.'

'Be charming, Adrian. I hear the French like that.'

'You have to give them *something*, Gabriel. They won't agree otherwise.'

'Tell them they can cook for us. That's the one thing they do well.'

'Be reasonable.'

Gabriel stopped walking. 'Tell them that if we manage to block Ivan's sale, we'll make sure all the credit goes to the French intelligence services.'

'You know something?' Carter said. 'That might actually work.'

Chapter 7

Saint-Tropez

The village of Saint-Tropez was nothing but a sleepy fishing port on the Côte d'Azur when, in 1956, it was the setting for a film called *And God Created Woman*, starring Brigitte Bardot. Nearly overnight, Saint-Tropez became one of the most popular resorts in the world, an exclusive playground for the fashionable, the elite and other assorted euro millionaires. Though it had fallen from grace in the eighties and nineties, it had seen a revival of late, particularly among the newly rich invaders from the East: the Russians.

In the hills above the Old Port are a number of *villages perchés*, where it is almost possible to imagine Saint-Tropez does not exist. One such village is Gassin. Small and quaint, it is known mainly for its ancient windmills— the Moulins de Paillas—and for its stunning views. A mile or so beyond the windmills is an old stone farmhouse. The rental agency described it as a steal at thirty thousand euros a week; a man with a German passport and money to burn took it for the remainder of the summer. He then informed the agent he wanted no cooks, no maid service, no gardeners and no inter- ruptions of any kind. He was a film-maker at work on an important project. When the agent asked what type of film it would be, the man mumbled something about a period piece and showed the agent to the door.

The other members of the film-maker's 'crew' trickled into the villa like scouts returning to base after a long time behind enemy lines. All had sailed under Gabriel's star before and leaped at the chance to do so again.

First came Gabriel's two Russian speakers, Eli Lavon and Mikhail Abramov. Next it was a man with short black hair and pockmarked cheeks named Yaakov Rossman, a battle-hardened case officer from the Arab Affairs Department of Shin Bet. Then Yossi Gavish, a tall, balding intellec- tual from the Office's research division who had read classics at Oxford and still spoke Hebrew with a pronounced British accent.

Finally, this rather motley, all-male troupe was graced by the presence of two women. The first, Rimona Stern, was an army major with sandstone- coloured hair who served in Israel's crack military intelligence service. The second was dark-haired and carried herself with the quiet air of early widowhood: Dina Sarid, a veritable encyclopedia of terrorism from the Office's history division, who could recite the time, place and casualty count of every act of violence ever committed against the State of Israel. Dina herself had been seriously wounded when a Hamas terrorist deto- nated his suicide belt aboard a number 5 bus in Tel Aviv some years ago, and she still walked with a slight limp.

For the next few days, the lives of Gabriel and his team stood in stark contrast to those of the man and woman they were pursuing. While Ivan and Elena Kharkov entertained wildly at their palace on the Baie de Cavalaire, Gabriel and his team took delivery of a large consignment of weaponry, listening devices, cameras and communications gear. While Elena and Ivan Kharkov cruised the waters of the Golfe de Saint-Tropez aboard their 263-foot motor yacht, Gabriel and his team hid miniature cam- eras with secure transmitters near the gates of Villa Soleil. And while Ivan and Elena dined lavishly at Villa Romana, Gabriel and his team plotted a meeting they hoped to conduct at the earliest date.

The first step towards creating the circumstances of that meeting occurred when Mikhail climbed into a red Audi convertible and drove to the Côte d'Azur International Airport in Nice. There, he met an attractive young American woman arriving on a flight from London Heathrow: Sarah Crawford of Washington, DC, lately of the Havermore estate, Gloucestershire. Two hours later, they checked into their suite at the Château de la Messardière, a five-star hotel located a few minutes from the *centre ville*. The bellhop who showed the young couple to their room reported to his colleagues that they could barely keep their hands off one another. The next morning, while the guests were partaking of a buffet breakfast, the chambermaids found their king-size bed in a shambles.

THEY DRIFTED through the same world but along distinctly parallel planes. When Elena and the children chose to remain cloistered at the Villa Soleil, Sarah and her lover would spend the day poolside at the Messardière—or 'the Mess', as they referred to it privately. And when Elena and the children chose to spend the day frolicking in the gentle surf of Tahiti Beach, Sarah and her lover would be stretched out on the sands of the Plage de Pampelonne instead. And at night, when Elena and Ivan dined at Villa Romana or one of the other Russian haunts, Sarah and her lover would dine quietly at the Mess—in close proximity to their room, lest the urge to ravage each other grow too strong to resist.

It proceeded in this seemingly directionless fashion until the fourth day, when Elena decided to have lunch at Grand Joseph. She reserved early—a requirement in August, even for the wife of an oligarch—and although she did not know it, her call was intercepted by an NSA spy satellite.

Elena took a seat with her back turned discreetly to the room, while her bodyguards settled at either end of the table. They took only scant notice of the postcard that arrived with her bottle of rosé, though it sent a jolt of fear the length of Elena's body. She concealed it with a look of mild displeasure, then picked up the card and read the note scribbled on the back:

Elena,
I hope you're enjoying the Cassatt. May we join you?
Sarah

Wineglass in hand, Mikhail at her side, Sarah gazed calmly across the crowded dining room towards Elena's long back. The postcard was still in Elena's grasp. She was gazing down at it with an air of mild curiosity, as was Oleg, her chief bodyguard. She laid the postcard down and turned slowly to survey the room. Twice, her gaze passed over Sarah with no visible sign of recognition. Elena Kharkov was a child of the Party, Sarah thought. She knew how to scan a room for watchers before making a meeting. She knew how to play the game by the Moscow Rules.

On its third sweep over the room, her gaze finally settled on Sarah's face. She lifted the postcard dramatically and opened her mouth wide in a show of surprise. The smile was forced, but her bodyguards could not see it. Then, before they could react, she was on her feet and manoeuvring between the tightly packed tables. Sarah stood to greet her; Elena kissed her on each cheek and pressed her mouth to Sarah's ear. The right ear, Sarah noted. The one her bodyguards couldn't see. 'What a wonderful surprise!' Then, in a quiet voice that caused a cavernous ache in Sarah's abdomen, 'You'll be careful, won't you? My husband is a very dangerous man.'

Elena released her grip on Sarah and looked at Mikhail, who had risen to his feet and was standing at his chair. She appraised him carefully, extended a bejewelled hand while Sarah saw to the introduction.

'This is my very good friend Michael Danilov. Michael and I work in the same office in Washington. If any of our colleagues found out we were here together, there would be a terrible scandal.'

Elena smiled. 'It's a pleasure to meet you, Michael.'

'The pleasure is mine, Mrs Kharkov. I've been an admirer of your husband's success for some time.'

Hearing Mikhail's accent, Elena's face took on an expression of surprise. It was contrived, Sarah thought, just as her smile had been a moment earlier. 'You're a Russian,' she said, not as a question but as a statement of fact.

'Actually, I'm an American citizen now, but, yes, I was born in Moscow. My family moved to the States not long after the fall of communism.'

'How fascinating.' Elena looked at Sarah. 'You never told me you had a Russian boyfriend.'

'It's not exactly the sort of thing one reveals during a business transaction. Besides, Michael is my secret. He doesn't really exist.'

'I love conspiracies,' Elena said. 'Please, you must join me for lunch.'

'Are you sure it's not an imposition?'

'Are *you* sure you want to have lunch with my children?'

'We would love to have lunch with your children.'

'Then it's settled.'

Elena summoned Jean-Luc, the maitre d', with an imperious wave of her hand and, in French, asked him to add another table to the banquette so her friends could join her. There followed much frowning and pouting of lips. The only solution, he ventured cautiously, was for Mrs Kharkov's *two* friends to trade places with *two* of Mrs Kharkov's entourage.

The exchange of places was swiftly carried out after which Elena's two bodyguards sat sulking at the far end of the table, one with a mobile phone pressed to his ear. Sarah tried not to think about whom he was calling. Instead, she kept her gaze focused on the children. They were miniature versions of their parents: Nikolai, fair and compact; Anna, lanky and dark. 'You should see photographs of Ivan and me when we were their age,' Elena said, as if reading Sarah's thoughts. 'It's even more shocking.'

'It's as if you produced exact duplicates.'

'We did, right down to the shape of their toes, though Anna is much more independent than I was as a child, and my precious Nikolai is much sweeter than his father. Ivan accuses me of babying him. Ivan's father was distant and authoritarian, and I'm afraid Ivan is as well. Russian men don't always make the best fathers.' She looked at Mikhail and, in Russian, asked, 'Wouldn't you agree, Michael?'

'My father was a mathematician,' he replied, also in Russian. 'His head was too filled with numbers to think much about his son. But he was gentle as a lamb, and he never touched alcohol.'

'Then you should consider yourself extremely lucky. A weakness for alcohol is another trait our men tend to pass on to their sons.' She raised her wineglass and spoke in English again. 'Although I must confess I have a certain weakness for cold rosé on a warm summer day.'

'A weakness I share myself,' Sarah said, raising her glass.

'Are you staying here in Saint-Tropez?'

'Just outside,' said Sarah. 'At the Château de la Messardière.'

'I hear it's very popular with Russians.'

'Let's just say that no one expressed any surprise at my accent there,' Mikhail replied.

Elena turned her gaze from Mikhail to Sarah. 'By the way, the answer to your question is yes.'

Sarah was momentarily confused. Elena tapped the postcard with her fingertip. 'The Cassatt,' she said. 'I *am* enjoying it. In fact, I'm enjoying it a great deal. I'm not sure whether you know this, Sarah, but I own six other Cassatt paintings and I think this might actually be my favourite.'

'I'm glad you feel that way. It takes away some of the sting of losing it.'

'You must come and see it. It's here, you know.'

'We wouldn't want to impose.'

'Not at all. In fact, I insist that you come tomorrow. You'll have lunch and a swim.' Then, almost as an afterthought, she added, 'And you can see the painting, of course.'

As the waiter placed a plate of *steak haché avec pommes frites* in front of each child, Elena instructed Sarah and Mikhail to have a look at the menu and was opening her own when her mobile phone began to chime. She drew it from her handbag and looked at the display screen before lifting the cover. The conversation that followed was brief and conducted in Russian.

When it was over, she closed the phone and, with a smile filled with false light, said, 'Ivan was planning to take his yacht out to sea this afternoon but he's decided to join us for lunch instead. He's just over in the harbour. He'll be here in a minute or two.'

'How lovely,' said Sarah.

Elena closed her menu and shot a glance at the bodyguards. 'Yes,' she said. 'Ivan can be very thoughtful when he wants to be.'

THOUGH IVAN had been standing just three hundred yards away at the moment he placed the call, he came by armoured Mercedes rather than on foot, lest one of his enemies was lurking amid the sea of humanity shuffling listlessly along the quays of the Old Port. The car parked a few feet from Grand Joseph's entrance, and Ivan waited in the back seat another fifteen seconds, long enough to ignite a murmur of intense speculation inside the restaurant as to his identity, nationality and profession. Then he emerged in an aggressive blur, like a prizefighter charging from his corner to finish off a hapless opponent, and entered the restaurant. He wore loose-fitting trousers of black linen and a shirt of luminous white cotton. His iron hair shone with a fresh coat of oil, and round his thick left wrist was a gold watch the size of a sundial.

The faces of Nikolai and Anna brightened with the unexpected appearance of their father, and Ivan's face softened momentarily in response. He said something to them in Russian that made the children both burst into laughter and caused Mikhail to smile. Ivan appeared to make a mental note of this. Then his gaze flashed over the table like a searchlight and came to rest on Sarah. The last time Ivan had seen her, she had been cloaked in Gabriel's dowdy clothing. Now she wore a thin peach-coloured sundress that clung to her body. Ivan admired her unabashedly.

'Saint-Tropez obviously agrees with you, Sarah,' he said. 'Is this your first time here?'

'Actually, I've been coming to Saint-Tropez since I was a little girl.'

'You have an uncle here, too?'

'*Ivan!*' snapped Elena.

Sarah smiled. 'No, just a long-time love affair with the South of France.'

Ivan frowned. He didn't like to be reminded of the fact that anyone, especially a young Western woman, had ever done anything before him.

'Aren't you going to introduce me to your friend?' he asked.

Mikhail rose and held out his hand. 'My name is Michael Danilov. Sarah and I work together in Washington.'

Ivan took the proffered hand and gave it a bone-crushing squeeze. 'Michael? What kind of name is that for a Russian?'

'The kind that makes me sound less like a boy from Moscow and more like an American.'

'To hell with the Americans,' Ivan declared. 'I assume your real name is Mikhail?'

'Yes, of course.'

'Then Mikhail you shall be, at least for the remainder of the afternoon.' He seized the arm of a passing waiter. 'More wine for the women, please. And a bottle of vodka for me and my new friend, *Mikhail.*'

HE ENTHRONED HIMSELF on the luminous white banquette, with Sarah to his right and Mikhail directly opposite. With his left hand, he was pouring icy vodka into Mikhail's glass as though it were truth serum.

'So you and Sarah are friends?' he asked.

'Yes, we are,' Mikhail answered.

'What kind of friends?'

Once again Elena objected to Ivan's forwardness. Ivan ignored her. Mikhail stoically drained his glass of vodka and, with a sly Russian nod of the head, implied that he and Sarah were very good friends indeed.

'You're staying in Saint-Tropez together?' Ivan asked, refilling the glass.

'We are,' Mikhail answered. 'At the Château de la Messardière.'

'You should come stay with us at Villa Soleil. We have a guesthouse. Actually, we have three guesthouses, but who's counting?'

You're counting, Sarah thought, but she said politely, 'That's very kind of you to make such a generous offer, Mr Kharkov, but we really couldn't impose. Besides, we paid for our room in advance.'

'It's only money,' Ivan said dismissively. He tried to pour more vodka into Mikhail's glass, but Mikhail covered it with his hand.

'I've had quite enough, thanks. Two's my limit.'

Ivan acted as though he had not heard him and doled out a third. The interrogation resumed. 'I assume you live in Washington, too?'

'A few blocks from the Capitol.'

'Do you and Sarah live together?'

'*Ivan!*'

'No, Mr Kharkov. We only work together.'

'And where is that?'

'At the Dillard Center for Democracy. It's a nonprofit group that attempts to promote democracy around the world.'

'I believe I've heard of this organisation. You poked your nose into the affairs of Russia a few years ago.'

'We have a very active programme in Eastern Europe,' Sarah said. 'But our Russia initiative was closed down by your president.'

'He was right to close you down. Why is it you Americans feel the need to push democracy down the throats of the rest of the world?'

'You don't believe in democracy, Mr Kharkov?'

'Democracy is fine for those who wish to be democratic. But there are some countries that simply don't want democracy. Iraq is a fine example. You went into Iraq in the name of establishing a democracy in the heart of the Muslim world, a noble goal, but the people were not ready for it.'

'And Russia?' she asked.

'We *are* a democracy, Sarah. Our parliament is elected.'

'Your system allows for no viable opposition, and, without a viable opposition, there can be no democracy.'

'Perhaps not your kind of democracy. But it is a democracy that works for Russia. And Russia must be allowed to manage its own affairs without the rest of the world criticising our every move.'

Elena cautiously suggested a change of subject. 'Ivan has many friends in the Russian government,' she explained. 'He takes it rather personally when they're criticised.'

'I meant no disrespect, Mr Kharkov. And you raise interesting points.'

'But not valid ones? I repeat, Sarah, the day of Russian democracy has already arrived. But my wife is correct, as usual. We should change the subject.' He looked at Mikhail. 'Why did your family leave Russia?'

'My father felt we would have more opportunities in America.'

'And did he find his opportunities?'

'He taught high-school mathematics in New York.'

'A schoolteacher? He went all the way to America to become a schoolteacher? What kind of man forsakes his own country to teach school in another? You should undo your father's folly by coming back to Russia. We need talented people like you to help build our country's future. Perhaps I could find a position for you in my own organisation.'

'I'm quite happy where I am, but thank you for the offer.'

'But you haven't heard it yet,' he said and smiled. It was as pleasant as a sudden crack in a frozen lake.

Once again, Elena offered an apology. 'You must forgive my husband's reaction. He isn't used to people saying no to him.' Then to Ivan, 'Try again tomorrow, darling. They're coming over for the afternoon.'

'Wonderful,' he said. 'I'll send a car to collect you from your hotel.'

'We have a car,' Mikhail countered. 'I'm sure we can find our way.'

'Don't be silly. I'll send a proper car to collect you.'

Gassin, France

At the old stone villa outside Gassin, dinner that evening had been a hasty affair: baguettes and cheese, a green salad, roasted chickens from the local charcuterie. At one end of the table lay a tourist brochure advertising deep-sea fishing trips. It might have looked like ordinary refuse were it not for the brief message, hastily scribbled over a photograph of a young boy holding a tuna twice his size. It had been written by Mikhail and passed to Yaakov, in a classic manoeuvre, in the town square. Eli Lavon was gazing across the table at Gabriel, his chin resting in his palm, like a grandmaster pleading with a lesser opponent either to move or capitulate.

'Maybe it's the travel arrangements that bother me most,' Lavon said finally in an attempt to prod Gabriel into action. 'Maybe I'm not comfortable with the fact that Ivan won't let them come in their own car.'

'Maybe he doesn't want strange cars on his property. Strange cars can contain strange electronic equipment. They can even contain bombs.'

'Or maybe he wants to take them on a surveillance detection run before he lets them onto the property. Or maybe he'll just skip the professional niceties and kill them immediately instead.'

'He's not going to kill them, Eli.'

'Of course not,' said Lavon sarcastically. 'After all, it's not as if he didn't kill a meddlesome reporter in broad daylight in St Peter's.' He held up a print-out of an NSA intercept. 'Five minutes after Ivan left that restaurant, he was on the phone to Arkady Medvedev, his security chief, telling him to run a check on Mikhail's father and the Dillard Center.'

'And when he does, he'll find that Mikhail's father was indeed a teacher who immigrated to America in the nineties, and that the Dillard Center occupies a suite of offices on Massachusetts Avenue in Washington.'

'Ivan knows about cover stories, and he certainly knows about front organisations. The KGB had a network of fronts all round the globe.'

Gabriel, with his silence, conceded the point.

'Cancel lunch,' said Lavon. 'Arrange another bump.'

'There's no way Ivan would believe that another chance encounter is only a coincidence. We've flirted long enough. Elena's clearly interested. It's time to start talking about consummating the relationship. And the only way we can talk is by going to lunch at Ivan's house.'

Villa Soleil, Saint-Tropez

Next day, the heat arrived. It came from the south on a scalding wind, fierce, dry and filled with grit. From the Baie de Pampelonne down to Cap Cartaya, beachgoers huddled motionless beneath their parasols or sat simmering in the shallows. At noon, the local radio reported that it was officially the hottest day ever recorded in Saint-Tropez. All agreed the Americans were to blame.

Villa Soleil, Ivan Kharkov's estate on a rocky outcrop overlooking the Baie de Cavalaire, seemed to have been spared the full force of the heat's fury. Immediately behind its twelve-foot walls lay a vast circular drive where nymphs frolicked in splashing fountains and flowers erupted in gardens groomed to hotel-brochure perfection. The villa itself was more palace than home, an endless series of loggias, marble corridors and cavernous sitting rooms where white curtains billowed in the constant breeze. Each wing of the house seemed to have its own unique view of the sea. And each view, thought Sarah, was more breathtaking than the last.

They finally came upon Elena at the end of a long, cool colonnade with a chequerboard marble floor. She wore a strapless top and a floor-length wrap that shimmered with each breath of wind. Ivan stood next to her, a glass of wine sweating in his grasp. Once again, he was wearing black and white, but this time the colours were reversed: black shirt, white trousers. They greeted each other with the casualness of an old friendship renewed. Before treating Sarah to a damp kiss and a blast of his rich aftershave, he placed his wine-glass on the plinth of a statue. It was female, nude and Greek. For the moment, Sarah thought spitefully, it was the world's most expensive coaster.

It was immediately clear that Elena's invitation to a quiet lunch and swim had been transformed by Ivan into a more extravagant affair. On the terrace below, a table had been set for twenty-four. Several pretty young girls were already cavorting in a pool the size of a small bay, watched over by a dozen middle-aged Russians lounging about on chaises and divans. Ivan intro-duced his guests as if they were simply more of his possessions. One of the girls was Yekatarina, Ivan's supermodel mistress, a gaunt, pouty child of nineteen, all arms, legs and breasts, coloured to caramel perfection. She gazed hard at Sarah, as though she were a potential rival, then leaped into the pool like a dolphin and disappeared beneath the surface.

Sarah and Mikhail settled themselves between the wife of a nickel mag-nate, who looked deeply bored, and a timber trader, who was genial but dull. Ivan and Elena returned to the colonnade, where more guests were arriving in boisterous packs. Several frosted bottles of vodka appeared; dance music pulsated from invisible speakers. On the terrace, a second table was set for lunch, then a third. Elena moved effortlessly from group to group, kissing cheeks and refreshing drinks, but Ivan remained aloof, gazing upon the merriment as though it were a performance arranged for his own private amusement.

It was nearly three o'clock by the time he summoned them all to lunch. By Sarah's count, the guests now numbered seventy in all. She sat next to Mikhail at Ivan's end of the table, where they were well within his sphere of influence and the scent of his cologne. It was a gluttonous affair; Ivan ate heavily but without pleasure, stabbing punitively at his food, his thoughts remote. At the end of the meal, the guests rose from the table and filed down to the pool for a final swim. Ivan seized Mikhail's wrist as he stood.

'Don't go so quickly,' he said. 'You promised to give me a chance to con-vince you to come home to Russia and work for me.'

'I'm not sure I remember that promise.'

'But I remember it quite clearly and that's all that matters.' He stood and smiled charmingly at Sarah. 'I can be rather persuasive. If I were you, I would begin planning a move to Moscow.'

He guided Mikhail to a distant corner of the terrace and sat with him in the shade of a cupola. Sarah looked at Elena. Anna and Nikolai had emerged from the villa and were now seated on her lap.

'You look like a painting by Mary Cassatt.'

'I'll take that as a compliment.'

Elena kissed Anna's cheek and whispered something to her daughter that caused her to smile and nod. Then she whispered something to Nikolai, with the same result.

'Are you saying naughty things about me?' Sarah asked playfully.

'The children think you're very pretty.'

'Please tell the children I think they're very pretty as well.'

'They were also wondering whether you would like to see their room. It contains a new painting, and they're very anxious for you to see it.'

'Please tell the children that I would like nothing more.'

'Come, then,' said Elena. 'The children will show us the way.'

They flitted in and out of the colonnade like starlings and hopscotched along the chequerboard marble floor. At the top of the sweeping main staircase, Anna took hold of Sarah's hand and pulled her down a glorious corridor filled with buttery light. It ended at the children's room, where *Two Children on a Beach* hung next to a similarly sized portrait of a young dancer by Degas. Elena Kharkov, former employee of the Hermitage Museum in Leningrad, slipped effortlessly into tour-guide mode.

'They knew each other quite well, Cassatt and Degas. I thought it was appropriate they be together.' She looked at Sarah and gave a faint smile. 'Until two weeks ago, I was certain the Degas was actually painted by Degas. Now I'm not so sure.'

Elena sent the children off to play, and a heavy silence fell over the two women. Overhead, a camera peered down at them like a gargoyle.

'Who are you?' Elena asked. 'And why are you in my home?'

Sarah glanced up at the camera.

'Don't be frightened,' said Elena. 'Ivan is watching but not listening. Microphones, remember, would pick up *everyone's* voices, including Ivan's. And their signals could also be intercepted by intelligence services.' She paused. 'Who are you? And who do you work for?'

Sarah stared straight ahead at Gabriel's immaculate brushstrokes. *Under no circumstances are you to tell her your real name or occupation when you're on hostile territory*, he had said. *Your cover is everything. Wear it like body armour, especially when you're on Ivan's turf.*

'My name is Sarah Crawford. I work for the Dillard Center for

Democracy in Washington. We met for the first time in the Cotswolds, when you purchased this painting by Mary Cassatt from my uncle.'

'Quickly, Sarah. We haven't much time.'

'I'm a friend, Elena. A good friend. You have something you want to tell us about your husband. I'm here to listen.'

Elena was silent for a moment. 'He's quite fond of you, Sarah. Was it always your intention to seduce my husband?'

'I assure you, Elena, your husband has absolutely no interest in me.'

'How can you be so certain?'

'Because he's brought his mistress into your house.'

Elena's head turned sharply towards Sarah. 'Who is she?'

'Yekatarina.'

'How do you know he's seeing her? It's not possible. She's a child.'

'That *child* is staying in a suite at the Carlton Hotel. Ivan is paying her bills. And we know because we follow him. And we listen to him. Did you see those pearls she was wearing today?' Elena gave an almost imperceptible nod. 'He gave those pearls to her in June when he went to Paris. You remember his trip to Paris, don't you, Elena? He said he needed to go for business. It was a lie, of course. He went there to see Yekatarina. He called you while he was in her apartment. You took the call while you were having lunch with friends at Café Pushkin. We have a photograph if you'd like to see it.' Elena was forced to absorb this news of her husband's treachery with a tranquil smile—Ivan's cameras were watching. Sarah was tempted to spare her the rest. She didn't, out of loathing for Ivan.

'Yekatarina thinks she's the only one, but she's not. There's a flight attendant called Tatyana. And there was a girl in London named Ludmila. I'm afraid Ivan treated her very badly. Eventually, he treats them all badly.'

Elena's eyes filled with tears.

'You mustn't cry, Elena. Ivan might be watching us. You have to smile while I tell you these awful things.'

Elena went to Sarah's side and their shoulders touched. Sarah could feel her trembling. Whether it was from grief or fear, she could not tell.

'How long have you been watching me?'

'It's not important. It's only important that you finish what you started.'

Elena laughed softly to herself, and her gaze swept over the surface of the painting while her fingertips explored the texture of the faux craquelure.

'You had no right to pry into my private life.'

'We had no choice.'

Elena lapsed into silence.

Place the sales contract carefully before her and lay the pen next to it. But don't pressure her into signing. She has to reach the decision on her own. Otherwise, she's no use to us.

'He wasn't always like this,' Elena said. 'Even when he worked for the KGB. You might find this hard to believe, Sarah, but Ivan was really quite charming when I first met him.'

'I don't find it hard to believe at all. He's still quite charming.'

'When he wants to be.' She was still touching the craquelure. 'When I first met Ivan, he told me he worked in some dreary Soviet agricultural office. A few weeks later, after we'd fallen in love, he told me the truth.'

'What happened?'

'The money happened. The money changed everything. It's changed Russia, too. Money controls our lives. And the pursuit of money prevents us from questioning the actions of our so-called democratic government.'

Elena reached towards the face of one of the children in the painting, the little boy. 'Whoever did this is quite good,' she said. 'I assume you know him?'

'Very well, actually.' A silence. Then, 'Would you like to meet him?'

'Who is he?'

'It's not important. It's only important that you agree to see him. He's trying to save innocent lives. He needs your help.'

Elena's finger moved to the face of the other child. 'How will we do it? Ivan sees everything.'

'I'm afraid we're going to need to tell a small lie.'

'What kind of small lie?'

'I want you to spend the rest of the afternoon flirting with Mikhail,' Sarah said. 'Mikhail will tell you everything you need to know.'

Chapter 8

Villa Soleil, Saint-Tropez

The storms had come down from the Maritime Alps after midnight and had laid seige to Ivan's fortress on the Baie de Cavalaire. Elena had not been woken by the violent weather. Having endured two sleepless nights already, she had taken twice her normal dose of sedative. Now, she woke grudgingly and in stages, like a diver rising to the surface from a great depth.

For some time she lay motionless, eyes closed, head throbbing, unable to recall her dreams. A gust of cool wind moved in the curtains and made shadows dance and play for her on the walls of the bedroom. Like all the rooms of the house, it was far too large for familial or marital intimacy, and now, alone in the cavernous space, Elena felt a prisoner to its vastness.

As a child of a senior Communist Party official, she had lived a life of Soviet privilege—a life of special stores, plentiful food and clothing, and trips abroad to other Warsaw Pact countries. Yet nothing in her charmed upbringing could have prepared her for the extravagance of life with Ivan. Her husband liked to pretend this grand palace by the sea was a reward for his capitalist ingenuity and hard work. In truth, she knew it had been acquired through corruption and connections to the old order. And it was awash in blood. Some nights, in her dreams, she saw the blood. It flowed in rivers along the endless marble corridors and spilled like waterfalls down the grand staircases. The blood shed by men wielding Ivan's weapons. The blood of children forced to fight in Ivan's wars.

She glanced at the clock on her bedside table. It was nearly noon.

Gradually her headache receded. With its departure, she was granted a sudden clarity of vision. She thought of the woman she knew as Sarah Crawford. And of Mikhail. She did not know precisely who they were; she knew only that she had no choice but to join them. For the innocent who might die, she told herself now. For Russia. For herself. *For the children . . .*

Another gust of wind stirred the long curtains, bringing with it the sound of Ivan's voice. Elena wrapped herself in a silk robe and walked onto the terrace overlooking the swimming pool and the sea. Ivan was supervising the cleanup of the storm damage, barking orders at the groundskeepers like the foreman of a chain gang.

Elena slipped back inside before he could see her and quickly entered the large sunlit chamber he used as his office. Though the rules of their marriage were largely unspoken, this room, like all of Ivan's offices, was a forbidden zone for both Elena and the children. He had been there already that morning; it was evident in the stench of cologne that hung on the air. Two identical mobile phones lay on the leather blotter, power lights winking. She picked up one of the phones and clicked to the directory of the ten most recently dialled numbers. One number appeared three times: *3064006.* With another click of a button, she dialled it again now.

Ten seconds later, a female voice answered in French, 'Good morning. Carlton Hotel. How may I direct your call?'

'Yekatarina Mazurov.'

'One moment, please.'

Then, two rings later, another female voice: younger, Russian.

'Ivan, darling, I thought you would never call. Can I come with you on the trip, or is Elena going to be with you? Ivan . . . what's wrong?'

Elena calmly terminated the call. Then, from behind her, came another voice: Russian, male, taut with quiet rage.

'What are you doing in here?'

She spun round, telephone still in her hand. Ivan stood in the doorway.

'I told my mother I would call her this morning.'

He walked over and removed the phone from her grasp, then reached into the pocket of his trousers and handed her another. 'Use this one,' he ordered.

'What difference does it make which phone I use?'

Ignoring her question, he inspected the surface of the desk to see if any-thing else had been disturbed. 'You slept late,' he said. 'I don't know how you managed to sleep through all that thunder and lightning.'

'I wasn't feeling well.'

'You look well this morning.'

'I'm a bit better, thank you.'

'Aren't you going to call her?'

'Who?'

'Your mother.'

Ivan was a veteran of such games and far too quick for her. Elena slipped past him and carried the phone back to bed.

'What are you doing?'

She held up the phone. 'Calling my mother.'

'But you should be getting dressed. Everyone's meeting us in the Old Port at twelve thirty. We're spending the afternoon on the boat, remember?'

'I'm sorry, Ivan. It must have slipped my mind. Who have you invited?'

He rattled off a few names, all Russian, all male.

'I'm not sure I'm up to it, Ivan. If it's all right with you, I'll stay with the children. Besides, you'll have more fun if I'm not there.'

He didn't bother to protest. Instead, he consulted his gold wristwatch, as if checking to see if there was still time to reach Yekatarina.

'What are you going to do with yourself all day?' he enquired casually.

'I'm going to lie in bed and read the newspapers. Then, if I'm feeling well enough, I'll take the children into town. It's market day. You know how much the children love the market.'

The market: Ivan's vision of hell on earth. He made one final indifferent attempt to change her mind before retiring to his private bathroom suite to shave and shower. Ten minutes later, freshly clothed and scented, he headed downstairs. Elena, still in bed, switched on the television and scrolled through the channels to the closed-circuit shot from the security cameras at the front gate. Ivan was climbing into the back of his car, talking on his mobile phone and wearing the smile he reserved for Yekatarina.

She switched off the television and swung her feet to the floor. *Don't stop now*, she told herself. *If you stop, you'll never find the courage to start again. And whatever you do, don't look back. You're never alone.* Those final words were not her own. They had been spoken by the man she knew as Mikhail. The man who would soon become her lover.

Elena heard his instructions now, soft but assured, as she took the final banal steps towards betrayal. She bathed in her swimming-pool-sized Jacuzzi tub, singing softly to herself. She took great care applying her make-up and appeared to struggle finding a hairstyle she deemed suitable. Her wardrobe seemed to be the source of similar vacillation, for she tried on and discarded a half-dozen outfits before settling on a simple cream-coloured Dior dress. The rejects she flung onto the bed, just as Michael had instructed. Evidence of romantic indecision, he had called it.

Finally, at one o'clock, Elena informed Sonia, the nanny, and the children that she would be going to town for a few hours. Then she ordered Oleg to prepare a car and security detail. On the way she occupied her time by telephoning her mother in Moscow. Oleg made no attempt to conceal the fact he was eavesdropping. When the call was over, she switched off the phone and dropped it into her handbag. As she climbed out of the car on the Avenue du Marechal, she hung the bag over her left shoulder, just as she had been told to do. Left shoulder meant she was ready to join them.

She entered the Place Carnot at the southeast corner and, with Oleg and Gennady trailing a few paces behind, started into the crowded outdoor market. In the clothing section, she bought matching cashmere sweaters for Ivan and Nikolai and gave the parcel to Oleg to carry. Then she headed towards the food stalls in the centre of the square, where she paused to watch a man with a grizzled face preparing ratatouille. A young woman with dark hair materialised briefly at her side; she murmured a few words in English, then melted once more into the crowds.

Elena purchased a half-kilo of the ratatouille and handed the container to Gennady, then continued across the square, towards the Boulevard Louis

Blanc. An Audi convertible, bright red, was parked on the corner. Michael was behind the wheel, face tilted towards the sun. Elena tossed her handbag onto the passenger seat and quickly climbed inside. As the car shot forward, she kept her eyes straight ahead. Had she looked over her shoulder, she would have seen Oleg, red-faced, screaming into his mobile phone. And Gennady chasing after them on foot, the ratatouille still in his hand.

The Massif des Maures, France

'Where are you taking me?'

'Somewhere we can be alone.'

'We don't have much time. You can be sure Ivan is already looking for us,' she said.

'Try not to think about Ivan. For now, there's no one but us.'

Mikhail drove very fast but without anxiety or visible exertion, working the gear stick with liquid smoothness. He was no computer technician, Elena thought. She had spent enough time in the company of elite soldiers to realise when she was in the presence of a fellow traveller.

The terrain grew more rugged as they headed inland, into the highlands of the Massif des Maures. To their right lay a dense forest of pine and eucalyptus; to their left, a bottomless green gorge. She thought how terrible it was that she had never been here until now. And she vowed that one day, when this was over, she would bring the children here without their bodyguards for a picnic. *The children* . . . It had been a mistake to think of them now. She wanted to phone Sonia and make certain they were safe. Instead, she focused on the wind in her hair and the warm sunlight on her skin. A married woman who is about to give herself to another man does not destroy the ache of sexual anticipation by telephoning her children. She thinks only of the moment, and to hell with the consequences.

They entered a village with a name she didn't recognise. A Rubensesque girl sat astride a motor scooter outside a *tabac*. She flicked her headlamp twice as they approached and entered the road ahead of them. They followed her for another mile, then turned together onto a dirt track lined with twisted olive trees, their silver-green leaves shimmering like coins in the gentle breeze. At the end of the track was a tiny stucco villa. Mikhail switched off the engine.

'Remember how it looks, Elena. It's important you're able to recall small details. Ivan will expect that when he questions you.'

'Where are we?'

'Somewhere in the mountains. You're not exactly sure. We were attracted to one another from the moment we met at Grand Joseph. Ivan didn't notice because he was thinking about Yekatarina. You were vulnerable; I could see that. I just had to think of some way to get you alone. I knew a hotel wouldn't do, so I took the liberty of renting this place from a local estate agent for the week.'

He removed the keys from the ignition. 'You did everything the way we asked? You dialled Yekatarina's room at the Carlton? You left clothes all over your room for Ivan and the housekeepers to see?'

'I did everything.'

'Then you have nothing to worry about. You'll tell Ivan that you've had suspicions about Yekatarina for a long time and that these suspicions were confirmed by the numbers you found on his mobile phone. You'll tell him I made a pass at you the afternoon we came to the villa. That you were so angry and hurt that you were unable to resist. You'll tell him you wanted to punish him and that the only way was to give your body to another man. He's going to be furious, of course, but he'll have no reason to doubt your story since he knows he is guilty of the sins you accuse him of. In due time, he'll forgive you.'

'He might forgive me but not you.'

'I'm none of your concern. I can look after myself.'

He opened the door. 'Time to go inside, Elena. There's someone inside who's very anxious to meet you.'

It was the antithesis of Villa Soleil, a small, tidy space of whitewashed walls, terracotta floors and rustic Provençal furniture. Seated at a rough-hewn wood table was a man of indeterminate age and nationality, with a long nose and the greenest eyes Elena had ever seen. He rose slowly to his feet and extended his hand as she approached.

'Meet the man who painted your Cassatt, Elena,' Mikhail said. 'I am about to commit the grave professional sin of telling you his real name, which is Gabriel Allon. He wants you to know it because he admires you deeply and does not wish to lie to you. You are in the presence of royalty, Elena—at least as far as our world is concerned. I'll leave you to it.'

Mikhail withdrew. Gabriel looked at Elena in silence for a moment, then, with a glance, invited her to sit. He retook his seat on the opposite side of the table and folded his hands before him.

'I would like to begin by thanking you,' he said.

'For what?'

'For having the courage to come forward. We're here because of you, Elena. Because you summoned us.'

'But I didn't summon you. I didn't *summon* anyone.'

'Of course you did. You summoned us with Olga Sukhova. And with Aleksandr Lubin. And with Boris Ostrovsky. Whether you realised it or not, Elena, you sent them to us. But you gave them only a part of the story. Now you have to tell us the rest.'

There was something in his accent she could not quite place. He was clearly a man who had lived in many places. A man with many names.

'Who do you work for?'

'I am employed by a small agency answerable only to the prime minister of Israel. But your husband's actions have caused an international crisis. And the response to this crisis has been international as well.'

'Is Sarah an Israeli, too?'

'Sarah is an American. She works for the Central Intelligence Agency.'

'And Mikhail?'

'Mikhail was born in Moscow. He left when he was a young boy and moved to Israel. His family left Russia because of men like your husband. And now your husband is planning to sell very dangerous weapons to people who are sworn to destroy us.'

'How much do you know?'

'Very little, unfortunately. Otherwise, we wouldn't have upended your life by bringing you here today. We know only that your husband has entered into a deal with the Devil. He's killed at least two people to keep that deal a secret. And others will surely die as well, unless you help us.' He reached out and took her by the hand. 'Will you help us, Elena?'

'What do you want from me?'

'I want you to finish what you started when you arranged to meet with your old friend Olga Sukhova. I want you to tell me the rest of the story.'

SHE BEGAN by setting the scene, as much for her own benefit as for his. It was autumn, she said. She and Ivan were staying at their country dacha north of Moscow. 'Ivan received a phone call late in the evening. After hanging up, he told me some business associates would be coming to the house in a few hours for an important meeting. He didn't identify these business associates and I knew far better than to ask. For the rest of the evening, he was on edge. Anxious. Pacing. I knew the signs. Ivan always gets very excited before a big dance.'

'Dance?'

'Forgive me, Mr Allon. Dance is one of the code words he and his men use when discussing arms transactions. "We have to make final arrangements for the *dance*." "We have to book a hall for the *dance*." "How many chairs will we need for the *dance*?" I'm not sure who they think they're deceiving with this nonsense but it certainly isn't me.'

'And did Ivan's visitors actually come that evening?'

'Technically, it was the next morning. Two thirty, to be exact.'

'Describe the scene for me. Carefully, Elena. The smallest details can be important.'

'There were eight of them in all, plus a team of Ivan's bodyguards. Arkady Medvedev was there as well. Arkady is the chief of my husband's personal security service.'

'Where was the delegation from?'

'They were from Africa. Sub-Saharan Africa.'

'Which country?'

'I couldn't say.'

'Did you meet them?'

'I'm *never* allowed to meet them. I was upstairs in our bedroom.'

'Were you ever able to hear their voices?'

'Sometimes. Their leader was a giant of a man. He was a baritone. His voice made the walls vibrate. He had a laugh like thunder.'

'You're a linguist, Elena. If they spoke another European language, what would it be?'

'French. Most definitely French. It had that lilt, you know?'

They drank first, she said. By the time the hard bargaining began, the guests were always well lubricated, and Ivan made no effort to control the volume of their voices, especially the voice of their baritone leader.

Elena began to hear words and terms she recognised: *AKs. RPGs. Mortars. Specific types of ammunition. Helicopter gunships. Tanks.*

'Before long they were arguing about money. The prices of specific weapons. Commissions. Bribes. Shipping and handling. I knew enough about my husband's business dealings to realise they were discussing a *major* arms deal—most likely with an African nation that was under international embargo. You see, Mr Allon, Ivan fills a very specific need. His customers cannot purchase arms legally on the open market. And that's why the poorest nations on earth pay vastly inflated prices for the weaponry they use to slaughter each other.'

'How long did these men stay in your home?'

'Until early the next morning. When they finally left, Ivan came upstairs to our room. He was soaring. It was bloodlust. He crawled into bed and practically raped me. He needed a body to pillage. He settled for mine.'

'When did you realise this deal was different?'

'Two nights later. I answered a phone I shouldn't have answered. And I listened long after I should have hung up. Simple as that.'

'Who was on the line?'

'Arkady Medvedev. He said there was a problem with final arrangements for the big dance.'

'What sort of trouble?'

'Big trouble. Merchandise-gone-astray trouble. Ivan had a tradition after big transactions. The blowout, he called it. A night on the town for the clients, all expenses paid. Drinks in the hottest bars. Dinner in the trendiest restaurants. A nightcap with the most beautiful young girls Moscow had to offer. The blowout with the African delegation was a rampage. It began at six in the evening and went straight through till nine the next night, when they finally crawled back to their beds at the Ukraina Hotel and passed out.

'The blowouts served another purpose beyond building customer loyalty. They allowed Ivan and his security service to gather intelligence on clients when their defences were compromised. Within five minutes of dumping the Africans at the Ukraina, he was on the phone to Ivan.

'Arkady is normally a very cool customer. But not that night. He was agitated. It was obvious he'd picked up something he wasn't happy about. I should have hung up, but I couldn't bring myself to take the telephone from my ear. So I covered the mouthpiece and held my breath.'

'Why didn't Ivan know you were on the line?'

'I suppose we picked up separate extensions at the same moment. It was luck. Stupid, dumb luck. If it hadn't happened, I wouldn't be here now.'

'What did Arkady tell Ivan?'

'He told him that the Africans were planning to resell some of the supplies from the big dance at a substantial markup to a third party. And this *third party* wasn't the usual sort of African rebel rabble.' She lowered her voice and furrowed her brow. '"They are the worst of the worst, Ivan,"' she said, imitating Arkady's voice. '"They are the sort who fly aircraft into buildings and blow up backpacks on subways, Ivan. The ones who kill women and children, Ivan. The head choppers. The throat slitters."'

'Al-Qaeda?'

'He never used that name but I knew who he was talking about. He said it was essential that they cancel the deal because the merchandise in question was too dangerous to be placed in the hands of just anyone. There could be blowback for Russia, he said. Blowback for Ivan.'

'How did Ivan react?'

'My husband shared none of Arkady's alarm. Quite the opposite. Ivan insisted that, in light of the new information, they had to renegotiate the package. If the Africans were planning to resell at a substantial markup, then Ivan wanted his cut. In addition, there was the potential for more money to be earned on shipping and handling.'

'Did Ivan ever suspect you'd eavesdropped on the call?'

'He never did or said anything to make me think so.'

'Was there another meeting with the Africans?'

'They came to our house in Zhukovka the next evening, when they'd sobered up. It wasn't as cordial as the first gathering. Ivan told the Africans he knew all about their plans and that unless they agreed to give him his fair share of the deal, the merchandise was off the table. The baritone giant screamed back at him for a while but eventually buckled to Ivan's demands for more money. The next night, before they flew home, there was another blowout to celebrate the *new* deal. All sins had been forgiven.'

'The merchandise in question—how did they refer to it?'

'They called them needles. In Russian, the word needle is *igla*. I believe the Western designation for this weapon system is SA-18. It's a shoulder-launch antiaircraft weapon.'

'The SA-18 is one of the most dangerous antiaircraft weapons in the world. But are you sure, Elena? Are you *sure* they used the word *igla*?'

'Absolutely. I'm also certain that my husband didn't care whether hundreds, or perhaps even thousands, of innocent people might die because of these weapons. What was I supposed to do with knowledge such as this?'

'What *did* you do?'

'What could I do? Go to the police? Go to the FSB? My husband *is* the FSB. His network operates under the protection and the blessing of the FSB. If I had gone to the FSB, Ivan would have heard about it five minutes later. And my children would have grown up without a mother.'

Her words hung there for a moment, an unnecessary reminder of the consequences of the game they were playing.

'I had to find some other way of telling the world what my husband was planning to do. I needed someone I could trust not to reveal the fact that I was the source of the information. I knew such a person; I'd studied languages with her at Leningrad and now she is a famous reporter in Moscow. I believe you're familiar with her work.'

GABRIEL HAD BEEN less than forthright with Elena about one aspect of the debriefing: he was not the only one listening. Thanks to a pair of small, concealed microphones and a secure satellite link, their conversation was being beamed live to four points around the globe: King Saul Boulevard in Tel Aviv, the headquarters of both MI5 and MI6 in London, and the CIA's Global Ops Center in Langley, Virginia.

Adrian Carter had at first appeared somewhat bored by the transmission, as though he were listening to a dull programme on the radio. That changed, however, when Elena uttered the word *igla*. As a Russian speaker, Carter did not need to wait for Elena's translation to understand the significance of the word. Without listening to the rest of her explanation he picked up the extension of a hotline that rang only on the desk of the director of the CIA.

'The Arrows of Allah are real,' Carter said. 'Someone needs to tell the White House. *Now*.'

ELENA AND GABRIEL adjourned to the terrace, shaded by a pair of umbrella pines. An olive grove spilled into a small gorge, and on the opposite hillside stood two tiny villas that could have been rendered by the hand of Cézanne. Somewhere in the distance, a child was crying for its mother. Elena tried to ignore it while she told Gabriel the rest of the story: her quiet lunch with Olga Sukhova; Aleksandr Lubin's murder in Courchevel; the near breakdown she had suffered after Boris Ostrovsky's death in St Peter's.

'I shut myself off from the outside world. I stopped watching television. I stopped reading the newspaper. I was afraid—afraid that I would learn an aeroplane had been shot down, or another journalist had been murdered because of me. Eventually, as time went by, I was able to convince myself it had never actually happened. There *was* no delegation of warlords who had come to my home to buy weapons. There was no secret plan to divert a portion of the consignment to the terrorists of al-Qaeda. In fact, it had all been a bad dream. A misunderstanding. Then I got a telephone call from Alistair Leach about a painting by Mary Cassatt. And here I am.'

On the other side of the ravine, the child still wailed. 'Won't *someone* help that poor thing?' she said, adding, 'Do you have children, Mr Allon?'

He hesitated, then answered quietly, 'I had a son. A terrorist put a bomb in my car because I killed his brother. My wife and son were inside.'

'And your wife?'

'She survived.' He gazed silently across the gorge for a moment. 'It might have been better if she hadn't. She was burned very badly in the fire.'

'My God, I'm so sorry. I shouldn't—'

'It's all right, Elena. It was a long time ago.'

On the other side of the ravine, the child fell silent. Gabriel seemed not to notice, for all his concentration was now focused on the task of opening a bottle of rosé. He filled a single glass and handed it to Elena.

'Drink some. It's important you have wine on your breath when you go home. Ivan will expect that.' She raised the glass to her lips and watched the pine trees moving in the faint breeze.

She obeyed, then asked, 'So, what is to be done? What are we going to do about the missiles my husband has placed in the hands of murderers?'

'You've given us a tremendous amount of information. If we're lucky— *very* lucky—we might be able to find them before the terrorists carry out an attack. It will be difficult, but we'll try.'

'Try? What do you mean? You have to stop them.'

'It's not that easy, Elena. There's so much we don't know. Which country in Africa was your husband dealing with? Have the missiles been shipped? Have they already reached the hands of the terrorists? Is it already too late?'

'I'm sorry,' she said. 'I feel like such a fool. I thought that by simply telling you about the deal, you would have enough information to find the weapons before they could be used. But what have I accomplished? Two people are dead. My friend Olga is a prisoner in her Moscow apartment. And my husband's missiles are still out there somewhere.'

'I didn't say it was impossible. Only that it was going to be difficult.'

'What else do you need?'

'A paper trail would help. Invoices. Shipping records. Transit documents. Wire transfers. Anything we can lay our hands on to track the sale of the merchandise.'

She was silent for a moment. Her voice, when finally she spoke, was barely audible. 'I think I know where that information might be,' she said.

Gabriel looked at her. 'Where, Elena?'

'In Moscow. After the fall of the Soviet Union, Ivan bought a large apartment in the House on the Embankment to use as a pied-à-terre. He keeps a private office there. I also assume he uses it as a place to take his lovers, when I'm at the estate in Zhukovka. I've been there only a few times. It's filled with ghosts, that building. The residents say that if you listen carefully at night, you can still hear the screaming.'

'I know the building you're talking about. The big one on Serafimovicha Street with the Mercedes-Benz star on top. It was built for the most senior members of the *nomenklatura* in the early thirties. During the Great Terror, Stalin turned it into a house of horror.'

'You've obviously done your homework.' She peered into the wineglass. 'Stalin murdered nearly eight hundred residents of that building, including the man who lived in my husband's apartment.'

'Where's the flat?'

'On the ninth floor, overlooking the Kremlin. He and Arkady keep a guard on duty there twenty-four hours a day. The doors to Ivan's office have a wood veneer over bombproof steel. There's a keypad entrance with a biometric fingerprint scanner. Only three people have the code and fingerprint clearance: Ivan, Arkady and me. Inside the office is a vault, same keypad and biometric scanner, same password and procedure. All my husband's secrets are in that vault, stored on disks with KGB encryption software.'

'Are you allowed to enter his office?'

'Under normal circumstances only with Ivan. But, in an emergency, I can enter alone.'

'What kind of an emergency?'

'The kind that could happen if Ivan ever fell out of favour with the men in the Kremlin. Under such a scenario, he assumes that he and Arkady would be arrested together. It would then be up to me, he said, to make certain his files never fall into the wrong hands.'

'Are you supposed to remove them?'

She shook her head. 'The interior of the vault is lined with explosives. Ivan showed me where the detonator button was hidden and taught me how to arm and fire it. The explosives had been carefully calibrated to destroy the contents of the safe without causing any other damage.'

'What's the password?'

'He uses the numeric version of Stalin's birthday: December the 21st, 1879. But the password alone is useless. You need my thumb as well. I'm the only one who can get inside the vault.'

Gabriel stood and walked to the low stone parapet at the edge of the terrace. 'There's no way for you to take those disks without Ivan finding out. And if he does, he'll kill you.'

'He won't be able to kill me if he can't find me. And he won't be able to find me if you do a good job of hiding me away.' She paused for a moment to allow her words to have their full impact. 'And the children, of course. You would have to get my children away from Ivan.'

Gabriel turned slowly round. 'Do you understand what you're saying? Your life as you know it will be over, Elena. No more winters in Courchevel. No more summers in Saint-Tropez. No more endless shopping excursions in Knightsbridge. You'll never be able to set foot in Russia again. And you'll spend the rest of your life hiding from Ivan. Are you really willing to give up everything in order to help us?'

'What am I giving up, exactly? I'm married to a man who has sold a cache of missiles to al-Qaeda and has killed two journalists in order to keep it a secret. A man who holds me in such contempt that he thinks nothing of bringing his mistress into my home. My life is a lie. All I have are my children. I'll get you those disks and defect to the West. All you have to do is get my children away from Ivan. Just promise me that nothing will happen to them.'

She reached out and took hold of his wrist, her eyes blazing. 'Surely a man who can forge a painting by Mary Cassatt, or arrange a meeting like this, can think of some way of getting my children away from their father.'

'You were able to see through my forgery.'

'That's because I'm good.'

'You'll have to be more than good to fool Ivan. You'll have to be perfect. And if you're not, you could end up dead.'

'I grew up in a Party family. I know how to beat them at their own game. I know the rules. You just have to think of some way to get me back to Moscow that won't make Ivan suspicious.'

'And then we have to get you out again. *And* get the children.'

'That, too.'

He added more wine to her glass and sat down next to her.

'I hear your mother hasn't been well.'

'How did you hear that?'

'Because we've been listening to your telephone conversations.'

'She has dizzy spells. She's been begging me to come to see her.'

'Perhaps you should. After all, it seems to me a woman in your position might actually want to spend some time with your mother, given everything your husband has put you through.'

'Yes, I think I might.'

'Can your mother be trusted?'

'She absolutely loathes Ivan. Nothing would make her happier than for me to leave him.'

'She's in Moscow now?'

Elena nodded. 'We brought her there after my father died. Ivan bought her a lovely apartment in a new building on the Kutuzovsky Prospekt.'

'I'm going to need a letter,' Gabriel said. 'It will have to be in your own hand. It will also have to contain enough personal information about you and your family to let your mother know for certain that you wrote it.'

'And then?'

'Mikhail is going to take you home to your husband. And you're going to do your best to forget this conversation ever happened.'

AT THAT SAME MOMENT, in a darkened operations room at King Saul Boulevard in Tel Aviv, Ari Shamron cast a lethal glance at Uzi Navot. 'Tell me something, Uzi. When did I authorise a defection?'

'I'm not sure you ever did, boss.'

'Send the lad a message. Tell him to be in Paris by tomorrow night. Tell him I'd like a word.'

Grand Joseph, Saint-Tropez

It was the part of the day that Jean-Luc liked best: the truce between lunch and dinner, when he treated himself to a pastis and calmly prepared the battle plan for the evening. Running his eye down the reservation sheet, he could see it was going to be an arduous night: an American rapper with an entourage of ten, a disgraced French politician and his new child bride, an oil sheikh from Abu Dhabi. For the moment, though, the dining room of Grand Joseph was a tranquil sea of linen, crystal and silver, undisturbed, except for the red Audi convertible parked directly outside the entrance, in violation of a long-standing city ordinance.

Jean-Luc drank from his glass of pastis and took a closer look at the two occupants of the car. The man behind the wheel was in his early thirties and was wearing sunglasses. He was attractive in a vaguely Slavic way and appeared quite pleased with himself. Next to him was a woman, several years older but no less attractive. Her dark hair was done up in a haphazard bun. Her dress looked slept in. Lovers, concluded Jean-Luc. No doubt about it. What's more, he was certain he'd seen them in the restaurant quite recently.

The couple talked for a moment longer before finally giving each other a kiss that put to rest any lingering doubt over how they had spent their after-noon. A moment later, the woman was standing alone on the sunlit cobbles of the square watching the Audi speed off. Then she turned and headed towards Joseph's entrance. It was then Jean-Luc realised that she was none other than Elena Kharkov. But where were her bodyguards? And why was she kissing another man in the middle of the Place de l'Hôtel de Ville?

She entered a moment later, her hips swinging a little more jauntily than usual. '*Bonsoir*, Jean-Luc,' she sang, as though there was nothing out of the ordinary, and Jean-Luc sang '*Bonsoir*' in return, as though he hadn't seen her giving mouth-to-mouth to blondie boy not thirty seconds earlier. She set her handbag on the bar and withdrew her mobile. After dialling a number and murmuring a few words in Russian, she closed the phone with an angry snap.

'Can I get you anything, Elena?' Jean-Luc asked.

'A glass of Sancerre would be nice. And a cigarette if you have one.'

'I can do the Sancerre but not the cigarette. It's the new law.'

'What's the world coming to, Jean-Luc?'

'Hard to say.' He poured a generous measure of Sancerre into a glass and placed it in front of her. She was raising it to her lips when two Mercedes sedans screeched to a stop in the square. She dropped a twenty on the bar.

'Thanks anyway, Jean-Luc.'

'It's on the house.'

She rose to her feet, swung her bag over her shoulder, and headed defi-antly towards the door, like a freedom fighter mounting a guillotine. As she stepped outside into the sunlight, the rear door of the first car was flung open and a thick arm pulled her roughly inside. The cars then lurched for-ward and vanished in a black blur. Jean-Luc watched them go, then looked down at the bar and saw that Elena had neglected to take the money. He slipped it into his pocket and raised his glass in a silent toast to her bravery. *To the women*, he thought. *Russia's last hope.*

WHEN MICHAEL DANILOV drove into the forecourt of the Château de la Messardière that evening, it was clear by his expression he had no clue of the distress he had caused his lover. He handed his keys to the valet and strode into the marble lobby, where Sarah Crawford waited anxiously. Those who witnessed the blow would later attest to the purity of its sound. It was delivered by her right hand and connected squarely with his left cheek. Because it was rendered without warning or verbal preamble, it caught the recipient and witnesses by complete surprise—all but the two

Russian security men, employees of one Ivan Kharkov, who were drinking vodka in the far corner of the bar.

The blond man made no effort at apology or reconciliation. Instead, he climbed back into the red Audi and headed at great speed to his favourite bar in the Old Port, where he contemplated the tangled state of his affairs over several chilled bottles of Kronenbourg. He never saw the Russians coming; even if he had, he was by then in no condition to do much about it. Their assault, like Sarah's, commenced without warning or preamble, though the damage it inflicted was far more severe. When it was over, a waiter helped him to his feet and made an ice pack for his wounds. A gendarme strolled over to see what the fuss was about; he took a statement and asked if the victim wanted to press charges.

'What can you do to them?' the blond man responded. 'They're Russians.'

He spent another hour drinking at the bar, then returned to the hotel. Entering his room, he found his clothing flung across the floor and a lipstick epithet scrawled across the bathroom mirror. He remained at the hotel one more day, licking his wounds, then sped off in his car to a destination unknown. Management was pleased to see him leave.

Chapter 9

Paris

The 7.28 p.m. TGV train from Marseilles eased into the Gare de Lyon ten minutes ahead of schedule. Gabriel crossed the deserted arrivals hall with his overnight bag in hand, and hailed a taxi on the Boulevard Diderot. The address he gave the driver was several blocks away from his true destination, which was an apartment house on a quiet street near the Bois de Boulogne.

It had been two years since he had set foot in the safe flat on the fourth floor, yet nothing had changed: the same drab furniture, the same stained carpeting, the same blackout curtains. Adrian Carter and Uzi Navot were gazing at him curiously from their seats at the cheap dinette set, as though they had just shared a private joke they did not want him to overhear.

A few seconds later, Ari Shamron came marching through the kitchen door, a cup and saucer balanced in his hand, his ugly spectacles propped on his bald head like goggles. He was wearing his usual uniform, khaki trousers and a white Oxford cloth shirt with the sleeves rolled up to the elbow. Something about being back in the field always did wonders for Shamron's appearance and he looked fitter than he had in some time.

He paused for a moment to glare at Gabriel, then continued into the sitting room, where a cigarette was smouldering in an ashtray on the coffee table. Gabriel stabbed it out.

'What do you think you're doing?' Shamron asked.

'You're not supposed to be smoking.'

'How can I quit smoking when my most accomplished operative is planning to go to war with Russia?' He put his cup and saucer down and angrily prowled the room. 'You were authorised to arrange a meeting with Elena Kharkov and debrief her on what she knew about her husband's illicit arms dealing. You performed that task admirably, but you vastly overstepped your authority, my son. You had no right to discuss a break-in operation in the heart of Moscow. Nor were you authorised to enter into an agreement to secure the defection of Elena Kharkov.'

'What was I supposed to do, Ari? Tell her we weren't interested in getting our hands on her husband's most precious secrets after all?'

'No, Gabriel, but you could have at least *consulted* your superiors first.'

'There wasn't time to consult my superiors. Ivan was tearing Saint-Tropez to pieces looking for her.'

'And what do you think he's going to do if you take Elena and the children away from him?' Shamron answered his own question with a slow shake of his bald head. 'Ivan Kharkov is a powerful man with powerful friends. Even if you did somehow manage to get Elena and those computer disks, Ivan will retaliate hard. Diplomats will be expelled en masse. Relations between Russia and the West will go into the deep freeze.'

'Diplomatic *sanctions*? When did the great Ari Shamron ever let the threat of diplomatic sanctions deter him from doing what was right?'

'More times than you'll ever know. But I'm not concerned only with the diplomatic fallout. Ivan Kharkov has proven himself to be a man of violence and he'll lash out at us if you steal his wife and children. He has access to the most dangerous weapons in the world. It doesn't take a devious mind to concoct a scenario in which Ivan's former KGB hoods sprinkle a few vials of polonium around Tel Aviv and a few thousand innocent people die as a result. What would you say then?'

'I would say that it's our job to make sure that never happens. And I would remind you of your own words: that our decisions should never be based on fear but what is in the long-term security interests of the State of

Israel. Surely you're not suggesting that it isn't in our interests to take down Ivan Kharkov? He operates his little shop of horrors with the full blessing, cooperation and protection of the Kremlin. I say we let the Russians impose their diplomatic sanctions. And then we hit back hard.'

'Is it your intention to personally reignite the Cold War?' Shamron asked. 'Because that is exactly what you're asking for.'

'The Russians have already done that. And if Ivan Kharkov wants to get in line with the rest of the psychotics who wish to do us harm, then let him.'

For Adrian Carter's benefit, they had been speaking English. Now Shamron switched to Hebrew. 'Is that really what you want at this stage of your life, my son? Another determined enemy who wishes you dead?'

'I can look after myself.'

'And what about your new wife? Can you look after her, too? Every second of every day? Remember what happened to Leah? She survived the first bombing, but the Palestinians were able to get to her a second time, at the psychiatric hospital in England, where you thought she'd be safe.'

'What about Eichmann?' Gabriel asked quietly. He had spoken in Hebrew, though at the mention of the murderer's name Adrian Carter's head perked up a bit, like a student roused from a slumber during a dull lecture.

'What *about* Eichmann?' Shamron asked stubbornly.

'Did you consider the diplomatic consequences before plucking him from that bus-stop in Argentina?'

'Of course we did. We were afraid the world would condemn us as criminals and kidnappers. We were afraid there would be severe fallout that our young and vulnerable state wasn't prepared to withstand.'

'But, in the end, you took that bastard down. You did it because it was the right thing to do, Ari. Because it was the *just* thing to do.'

'We *did* it because we had no other choice, Gabriel. If we'd requested extradition, the Argentines would have refused and tipped off Eichmann. And then we would have lost him for ever.'

'Because the police and security services were protecting him? Just like the FSB and the Kremlin are protecting Ivan.'

'Ivan Kharkov isn't Adolf Eichmann. I lost most of my family to Eichmann and the Nazis. So did you.'

'Tell that to the thousands who've died in the wars stoked by Ivan's guns.'

'I'll let you in on a little secret, Gabriel. If Ivan were to stop selling the warlords guns today, someone else would do it for him tomorrow.' Shamron lifted his head towards Carter. 'Who knows? Perhaps it will be your good friend Adrian. He and his government poured weapons into the Third World whenever it suited their needs. And we've been known to sell to some pretty atrocious customers ourselves.'

'Congratulations, Ari.'

'For what?'

'Achieving a new personal low,' Gabriel said. 'You have just compared our country to the worst man in the world in order to win an argument.'

Gabriel could see that Shamron's resistance was beginning to weaken. He decided to press his advantage. 'I'm doing this, Ari, but I can't do it without your support.' He paused, then added, 'Or your help.'

'Who's stooping to personal lows now? Have you given any thought to where you're going to put her?'

'I was thinking about moving her into my apartment in Narkiss Street, but I really don't have room for her *and* the children.'

Shamron remained silent, but by his dour expression let it be known he didn't find the remark even faintly amusing.

'I never really contemplated keeping her in Israel, Ari. She would have to go to America.'

'Drop her in Adrian's lap? Is that your solution? Elena Kharkov has grown accustomed to a lifestyle few of us can even contemplate. She'll become a problem. Most defectors do.'

Shamron looked to Adrian Carter for affirmation, but Carter knew better than to inject himself into the middle of a family quarrel.

'At the moment, the long-term well-being of Elena and her children is the least of your problems. First you have to devise a way of getting her back into Russia without Ivan becoming suspicious.'

Gabriel dropped an envelope on the coffee table.

'What's that?' Shamron asked.

'Elena's ticket home to Moscow.'

Shamron slipped on his spectacles and removed the letter from the envelope. He had no trouble reading it; Russian was one of his many languages. When he had finished, he inserted the letter back into the envelope.

'It's not a bad start, Gabriel, but how are you going to get her into that apartment without Ivan's private security service sounding the alarm? How are you going to get her out of the country with those disks? And how are you going to keep Ivan occupied while you kidnap his children?'

Gabriel smiled. 'We're going to steal his aeroplane.'

Shamron dropped Elena's letter on the table. 'Keep talking, my son.'

IT DID NOT TAKE LONG for Shamron to fall under Gabriel's spell. He sat motionless in his chair, his hooded eyes half closed. Adrian Carter sat next to him, his face still an inscrutable mask. At the conclusion of the briefing, it was Carter who spoke first.

'I've never regarded myself as having any particular insights into the French, but, based on our last meeting, I'm confident they'll play ball with you. The French security services have never been averse to bending the law a little when it suits their purposes.'

Shamron's eyes moved to Gabriel. 'I don't suppose I have to ask who's going to serve as Elena's chaperone.'

'She won't do it unless I go with her.'

'Why did I know that was going to be your answer?'

'He can go in on his American passport. The Russians wouldn't dare to touch him,' interjected Carter.

'I doubt very much that the thugs who work for Ivan would be intimidated by a passport, even an American one, Adrian.'

Shamron's gaze moved from Carter to Gabriel.

'Do I need to remind you, Gabriel, that your friend Sergei made it clear when he released you from Lubyanka that the FSB knew exactly who you were and what would happen if you ever set foot in Russia again?'

'I'm just there for the ride. It's Elena's show. All she has to do is walk into the House on the Embankment, grab the files, and walk out again.'

'What could possibly go wrong with a plan like that?' Shamron asked sardonically of no one in particular. 'How many of your brave associates do you intend to take along with you on this venture?'

Gabriel recited a list of names. 'We can send them in as El Al crew and cabin staff. Then we'll all fly out of Moscow together when it's over.'

Adrian Carter was nodding his head slowly. Shamron had settled into his Buddha-like pose and was staring at Navot, who was staring back at him in return.

'We'll need the approval of the prime minister,' Shamron said.

'He'll do whatever you tell him to do,' said Gabriel. 'He always does.'

'And God help us all if we create another scandal for him.' Shamron's gaze flickered from Navot to Gabriel and back again. 'Would you boys like to handle this yourselves, or would you like some adult supervision?'

'We'd love your help,' Navot said. 'But are you sure Gilah won't mind?'

Shamron shrugged. 'I think she could use a few days to herself. This might be hard to believe, but I'm not the easiest person to live with.'

Gabriel and Navot immediately began to laugh, while Adrian Carter tried to stifle the impulse to join them.

'Enjoy yourselves at my expense,' Shamron murmured. 'But one day you'll be old, too.'

THE SERIOUS PLANNING began the following morning when Adrian Carter returned to the gated government guesthouse off the Avenue Victor Hugo. The negotiations went smoothly, and by that evening the DST, the French internal security service, had taken formal control of the Kharkov watch. Gabriel's troops were stood down—all but Dina Sarid, who remained at the villa in Gassin to serve as Gabriel's eyes and ears in the south.

It soon became clear to the DST that a pall had descended over Villa Soleil. There were no more parties, no more drunken day-trips aboard *October*, and the name 'Kharkov' did not grace the reservation sheets of Saint-Tropez's exclusive restaurants. Indeed, for the first three days of the French watch, Ivan and Elena were not seen at all.

Because the DST was operating on home soil, they were highly attuned to the gossip swirling through the bars and cafés. According to one rumour, Ivan was planning to put the villa up for sale, then put to sea to heal his wounded pride. According to another, he was planning to divorce Elena and leave her begging for kopeks in the Moscow Metro. There was a rumour he had beaten her black and blue. There was even a rumour he had killed her with his bare hands and dumped her body high in the Maritime Alps. All such speculation was put to rest, however, when Elena was spotted strolling along the Rue Gambetta at sunset, absent of any signs of physical or emotional trauma, but with a large contingent of bodyguards.

At the little apartment in the sixteenth arrondissement of Paris, these events were taken as confirmation that 'the small lie to cover the big lie' had been believed. The flat had become a beehive of hushed activity with surveillance photos and watch reports taped to the walls, a large-scale map of Moscow with flags and stickpins and routes marked in red. Early in the operation, Shamron seemed content to play the role of *éminence grise*. But he gradually began to assert himself in ways that might have bred resentment in men other than Gabriel and Uzi Navot. They took advice others might have discarded for no reason other than pride. But more than anything, the two men cherished the opportunity to be in the field one more time with the legend.

In their final hours before the operation began in earnest, Shamron paced the room in silence, moody and distracted.

'You must prepare yourself for the prospect she won't come out of that building,' he said. 'And if she doesn't come out, it means she's been caught. Then you can be sure Arkady Medvedev will start looking for accomplices. If, heaven forbid, she falls into their hands, there's nothing we can do for her. Don't even think about going into that building after her, Gabriel. Your first responsibility is to yourself and your team. Do you understand me?'

'I understand.'

Shamron stopped his pacing and seized Gabriel's face in both hands with unexpected force. 'I destroyed your life once, Gabriel, and I won't allow it to happen again. If something goes wrong, get to the airport and get on that plane.'

Gabriel glanced at his wristwatch in the fading late-afternoon light. It was nearly five o'clock. The operation was about to commence. And not even Shamron could stop it now.

Moscow

It was a few minutes after seven when the house telephone in Elena's mother's apartment on the Kutuzovsky Prospekt rattled softly. Svetlana Federov was seated in her living room at the time, watching yet another televised election speech by the Russian president. The voice on the other end of the line was familiar: Pavel, the concierge. It seemed she had a visitor. 'A *gentleman* caller,' added Pavel. 'Calls himself Feliks.'

'What does he want?'

'Says he has a message. Says he's a friend of your daughter.'

'What's he look like?'

'A pile of old clothes. But he has flowers and chocolates. Godiva chocolates, Svetlana. Your favourite.'

'Send him up, then.'

'He's on his way.'

She went into the kitchen and looked for something suitable to serve. There were no pastries or cakes in the pantry, only a tin of English tea biscuits, a souvenir from her last dreadful trip to London to see Elena. She was arranging biscuits neatly on a plate when she heard the ping of the bell. Opening the door, she was greeted by the sight of an odd-looking little man in his early sixties, with a head of wispy hair and the small, quick eyes of a terrier. His clothing was indeed rumpled, but appeared to have been chosen with care. There was something old-fashioned about him; he looked as though he could have stepped from an old black-and-white movie, she thought. His manners were as dated as his appearance.

'I do hope I'm not catching you at an inconvenient time,' he said.

'I was just watching the president making a speech on television.'

'Oh, really? What was he talking about?'

'I'm not sure. They're all the same.'

The visitor handed her the flowers and the chocolates. 'I took the liberty. Elena told me how you adore truffles.'

'How do you know my daughter?'

'I'm a friend, Mrs Federov. A trusted friend.'

'She sent you here?'

'That's correct. I need to discuss something important with you.' He lowered his voice. 'Something concerning Elena's well-being.'

'Is she in some sort of danger?'

'It would really be better if we spoke in private, Mrs Federov.'

She regarded him suspiciously for a long moment before finally stepping to one side. He moved past her without a sound.

Geneva

The night manager of the Hôtel Métropole handed over an electronic key and informed Gabriel that his wife had already checked in and was upstairs awaiting his arrival. He found her seated in a wingback chair in the window, her gaze focused on the Jet d'Eau, the towering water fountain in the centre of Lake Geneva. Her El Al uniform, crisp and starched, hung from the rod in the wardrobe. Candlelight reflected softly in the silver-domed warmers of a room-service table set for two. Gabriel lifted a bottle of chilled Chasselas from the ice bucket and poured himself a glass.

'I expected you an hour ago,' she said.

'The traffic leaving Paris was miserable. What's for dinner?'

'Chicken Kiev,' she said without a trace of irony in her voice. 'The butter's probably congealed by now.'

Gabriel placed his hand on top of one of the warmers. 'It's fine. Can I pour you some wine?'

'I shouldn't. I have a four o'clock call. I'm working the morning flight from Geneva to Ben-Gurion, then the afternoon flight from Ben-Gurion to Moscow.' She looked at him for the first time. 'You know, I think it's possible El Al flight attendants might actually get less sleep than Office agents.'

'I'll tell Uzi to bear that in mind next time he's handing out field assignments.' He poured her a glass of wine. 'Have a little. It's good for the heart.'

She accepted the glass and raised it in Gabriel's direction. 'Happy anniversary, darling. We were married five months ago today.' She took a drink of the wine. 'So much for our honeymoon in Italy.'

'Five months isn't really an anniversary, Chiara.'

'Of course it is, you dolt.' She looked out at the fountain again.

'Are you angry with me because I'm late for dinner, Chiara, or is something else bothering you?'

'I'm angry because I don't feel like going to Moscow tomorrow.'

'Then don't go.'

She shot an annoyed look at him, then returned her gaze to the lake. 'Ari gave you numerous opportunities to extricate yourself from this affair, but you chose to press on. Why, Gabriel? After everything you've been through, why would you prefer to do a job like this rather than hide out in a secluded villa in Umbria with me?'

'It's not fair to put it in those terms, Chiara.'

'Of course it is. You told me it was going to be a simple job. You were going to meet with a Russian journalist in Rome, listen to what he had to say, and that was going to be the end of it.'

'It would have been the end of it, if he hadn't been murdered.'

'So you're doing this for Boris Ostrovsky?'

'I'm doing this because we need to find those missiles.'

'You're *doing* this, Gabriel, because you want to destroy Ivan.'

'Of course I want to destroy Ivan.'

'Well, at least you're being honest. Just make sure you don't destroy yourself in the process. If you take his wife and children, he's going to pursue them to the ends of the earth. And us, too.'

'We should eat, Chiara. After all, it's our anniversary.'

She looked at her wristwatch. 'It's too late to eat. That butter will go straight to my hips.'

'I was planning a similar manoeuvre myself.'

'Promises, promises.' She drank some more of the wine. 'Did you enjoy working with Sarah again?'

'You're not going to start that again, are you?'

'Let the record show, Your Honour, that the witness refused to answer the question.'

'Yes, Chiara, I did enjoy working with Sarah again. She performed her job admirably and with great professionalism.'

'And does she still adore you?'

'Sarah knows I'm unavailable. And the only person she adores more than me is you.' He sighed. 'For God's sake, Chiara. Yes, Sarah had feelings for me once, feelings that surfaced in the middle of a dangerous operation. I don't happen to share those feelings because I'm quite madly in love with you. I proved that to you, I *hope*, by marrying you.' He took her face in his hands and kissed her. 'This will all be over in forty-eight hours. Then we can go back to Italy, and no one, not even Ivan, will be able to find us there.'

'No one but Shamron.' She kissed him again. 'I thought you were planning a manoeuvre that had something to do with my hips.'

'You have a very long day tomorrow.'

'Put the table outside in the hall, Gabriel. I can't make love in a room that smells like Chicken Kiev.'

Villa Soleil, Saint-Tropez

They had arrived at an uneasy truce. It had taken seventy-two hours of interrogation, screaming and malicious threats. Like all those who have been betrayed, he demanded to be told the details, demanded to know how many times they had made love. 'Twice,' she confessed. 'He wanted to do it a third time but I told him I had to be going.'

Mikhail's predictions had proven accurate; Ivan's rage had subsided once he realised he had brought the mess upon himself. He sent a team of bodyguards to eject Yekatarina from her suite at the Carlton Hotel, then began to deluge Elena with apologies, promises, diamonds and gold. Elena appeared to accept the acts of contrition. The matter was now closed, they declared jointly over dinner at Villa Romana.

Many of Ivan's gestures were surely hollow. Many others were not.

He spent less time talking on his mobile phone and more time with the children. He brought her coffee each morning and read the papers in bed instead of rushing into his office to work. And when her mother called that morning at seven o'clock, he did not grimace the way he usually did but handed Elena the phone with genuine concern on his face. The conversation that followed was brief. Elena hung up and looked at Ivan in distress.

'What's wrong?' he asked.

'She's very sick again, darling. She needs me to come right away.'

IN MOSCOW, Svetlana Federov gently returned the receiver to its cradle and looked at the man she knew as Feliks.

'She says she'll be here later this evening.'

'And Ivan?'

'He wanted to come with her, but Elena convinced him to stay in France with the children. He was kind enough to let her borrow his plane.'

He smiled. 'Knowing your son-in-law, he'll have you and your building under surveillance within the hour. Do you remember what you're supposed to say if anyone asks about me?'

'I'm to tell them that you were a con artist—a thief who had come to swindle an old woman out of her money.'

'There really are a lot of unscrupulous characters in the world.'

'Yes,' she said. 'One can never be too careful.'

IN THE AFTERMATH of the most recent terrorist attacks in London, many improvements in security and operational capabilities had been made to the American Embassy in Grosvenor Square, one being a sparkling new operations centre located in a bunker-like annexe beneath the square itself. At precisely 6.04 a.m. London time, a message from Eli Lavon was handed to Adrian Carter. Carter, after reading it, handed it to Shamron, who in turn handed it to Graham Seymour. 'Looks like we're on,' said Seymour.

Carter activated a secure line to Paris. '*Bonjour*, gentlemen. The ball is now heading towards your side of the court.'

Villa, Soleil, Saint-Tropez

This time there was no indecision in her grooming. Elena bathed hastily, expended little effort on her hair and make-up, and dressed in a rather simple but comfortable trouser-suit. She put on more jewellery than she might otherwise have worn on such an occasion and took several thousand dollars' worth of euros and rubles from the wall safe. She knew that Ivan would not find this suspicious; Ivan always encouraged her to carry a substantial amount of cash when travelling alone.

She took a final look around the room, picked up her overnight bag and started downstairs. Sonia and the children had gathered to see her off; she held the children for longer than she should have and ordered them with mock sternness to behave for their father, who was standing outside in the drive, scowling impatiently at his wristwatch. Elena kissed each child one final time, then climbed into the back of the Mercedes with Ivan. She glanced once over her shoulder as the car shot forward and saw the children weeping hysterically. Then the car passed through the security gate and they disappeared from sight.

IVAN WAS PREOCCUPIED during the drive, and for that Elena was grateful. He passed the journey alternately talking on his mobile or staring silently out of his window. As they sped through the northern fringes of Cannes, Elena found herself thinking about Ivan and Yekatarina making love in their suite at the Carlton. Ivan must have been thinking the same thing, because he took hold of her hand and said he was sorry for everything that had happened. Elena heard herself say she was sorry, too. Then she looked out of the window and began counting the minutes until she would be free of him.

Twenty minutes later, they were walking into the air-conditioned office of Riviera Flight Services at the Côte d'Azur International Airport. Standing behind the counter was a man in his mid-thirties with receding blond hair.

Ivan went to check in. 'Kharkov,' he said. 'Leaving for Moscow at eleven.'

The young man hoisted a bureaucrat's troubled smile. 'That's not going to be possible, Monsieur Kharkov. I'm afraid there's a rather serious problem with your aircraft.'

'What sort of problem?' asked Ivan.

'A paperwork problem,' answered the young man. 'Your crew has been unable to produce two very important documents: an RVSM authorisation letter and a Stage Three certificate. The DGAC will not allow your plane to depart without them.'

The DGAC was the Direction Générale de l'Aviation Civile, the French equivalent of the Federal Aviation Administration.

'That's outrageous!' snapped Ivan. 'I've taken off from here dozens of times and *never* been required to produce those documents before.'

'I understand your frustration, Monsieur Kharkov, but I'm afraid rules are rules. Unless your crew can produce an RVSM authorisation and Stage Three certificate, your aircraft isn't going anywhere.'

'Get someone from the DGAC on the phone.'

'The DGAC has made its position clear on this matter. They will have nothing further to say until they see those documents.'

'We have an emergency in Moscow. My wife's mother is very ill. She has to get there right away.'

'Then I would suggest that your crew do their utmost to find those documents. In the meantime, your wife might consider flying commercial.'

'*Commercial?*' Ivan brought his palm down on the counter. 'My wife can't fly commercial. We have security issues to consider.'

'Then I doubt that she'll be going to Moscow today, monsieur.'

Elena moved cautiously to the counter. 'My mother is expecting me, Ivan. I can't disappoint her. I'll just fly commercial.'

The clerk gestured towards his computer. 'I can check departure times and seat availability, if you would like.'

Ivan frowned, then nodded his head. The clerk sat down at the computer and punched a few keys. A moment later, he shook his head slowly.

'I'm afraid there are no seats available on any direct flights to Moscow today.' He tapped a few more keys. 'But there is one other option. There's a Swiss International Air Lines flight departing in an hour for Geneva. Madame Kharkov can then catch the two p.m. Swissair flight from Geneva to Moscow arriving at eight this evening.'

Ivan looked at Elena. 'It's a very long travel day. Why don't you wait until I get the paperwork straightened out?'

'I've already told my mother I am coming tonight. I don't want to disappoint her, darling. You heard her voice.'

Ivan looked at the clerk. 'I need three first-class seats: one for my wife and two for her bodyguards.'

A few more taps at the keyboard. Another shake of the head. 'There's only one first-class seat available on each flight and nothing in economy. But I can assure you Madame Kharkov will be perfectly safe.'

'Which terminal does Swissair depart from?'

'Terminal One.' The clerk picked up the telephone. 'I'll let them know you're on the way.'

The young DST case officer watched Ivan and Elena depart before speaking into the handset, because it was not to the offices of Swissair that he had placed the call, but to his superior, who was sitting in the back of an ersatz service van just outside. Upon receiving the call, the officer in the van flashed word to the operations room in London. The news arrived on Gabriel's PDA while he was pretending to look at Rolex watches in an airport duty-free shop. He left the shop and wandered slowly towards his gate.

IN A SUDDEN RUSH of gallantry, Ivan stood with her in the queue at the ticket counter and argued with the poor agent over the details of her itinerary. As she was preparing to pass through security, he apologised once again for the damage he had done to their marriage. She kissed him one final time and, upon reaching the other side, turned to wave goodbye. Ivan was already walking away, bodyguards at his side, telephone pressed to his ear.

For the next half-hour, Elena revelled in the mundane. She located her gate. She drank a café crème at a crowded bar. She bought a stack of magazines. But mainly she just walked. For the first time in many years, Elena was *alone*. Not truly alone, she thought, for surely someone was watching her, but free of the cloying presence of Ivan's bodyguards, at least for a few hours. Soon she would be free of them for ever. She just had to run one small errand in Moscow first.

Her seatmate on the flight was a sunburnt Swiss gnome, who passed the time frowning at numbers. Lunch was a wilted sandwich and a bottle of warm mineral water; Elena ate everything on her tray and thanked the bewildered air hostess profusely for her kind service.

It was nearly 1.30 by the time the plane touched down in Geneva. When she arrived, she heard an announcement saying that Swissair Flight 1338 to Moscow was in final boarding. She arrived at her next gate with five minutes to spare and accepted a glass of champagne from the chief bursar as she settled into her first-class seat. This time her seatmate was a man in his mid-fifties with thick grey hair and the tinted eyeglasses of someone who suffered from light sensitivity. He was writing in a leather portfolio as she sat down and seemed to take no notice of her. As the plane was climbing rapidly over the Alps, he tore a single sheet of paper from the portfolio and gave it to her. It was a tiny pen-and-ink copy of *Two Children on a Beach*. Elena turned and looked at him in disbelief.

'Good afternoon, Elena,' said Gabriel. 'It's so good to see you again.'

Moscow

Arkady Medvedev's was a uniquely Russian story. A former breaker of dissident heads from the Fifth Main Directorate of the KGB, he had been going to seed in the shattered remnants of his former service when, in 1994, he received a telephone call from an old underling named Ivan Kharkov. Ivan had a proposition: he wanted Medvedev to construct and oversee a private security service to protect his family and his burgeoning global financial empire. Medvedev accepted the offer without a second thought.

For fifteen years, Arkady Medvedev had served Ivan well, and Ivan had been more than generous in return. His base earnings now stood at more than one million dollars a year—not bad for a former secret policeman who hadn't had two rubles to rub together after the fall of communism.

If there was one drawback to working for Ivan, it was his knack for telephoning at the absolutely worst moments. True to form, the call came just as Medvedev and Oxana, his twenty-three-year-old girlfriend, were about to jointly scale a summit of pleasure. Medvedev reached for the phone, and brought the receiver reluctantly to his ear. The conversation that followed, though brief, thoroughly spoiled the mood.

'What's the problem, Arkady?' Oxana asked, when the call was over.

The *problem*, he thought, was Elena Kharkov. She was arriving in Moscow that evening for an emergency visit. Ivan was suspicious about her motives and wanted her watched. He wanted no more stunts like the one in Saint-Tropez. And neither did Arkady Medvedev. He looked at Oxana and told her to get dressed. Five minutes later, as she was slipping out of his apartment, he started moving his teams into place.

ELENA ORDERED WHITE WINE; Gabriel, black coffee. They both decided to try the ravioli with wild mushroom reduction. Elena took a single bite and nibbled on her bread instead.

'You don't like the food?' Gabriel asked.

'It's not very good.'

'It's actually much better than the usual fare. When was the last time you flew commercial?'

'It's been a while.' She gazed out of the window. 'I suppose I'm a little like Russia itself. I went from having almost nothing to having almost everything. We Russians never seem to get it just right.'

She brushed a strand of hair from her face and asked casually where she was to be hidden after the defection. Gabriel answered in the same manner.

'On Sunday, instead of flying back to Nice, you're going to board a plane to Tel Aviv. You'll stay in Israel a day or two at most.'

'And then?'

'The Americans have assumed responsibility for your resettlement. It's a bigger country with far more places to hide than Israel. The man who is in charge of the case is a friend of mine. He'll take very good care of you and the children. But I'm afraid it won't be anything like the lifestyle to which you've become accustomed.'

'Thank God for that.'

'You might think that now, but it's going to be a rude awakening. Ivan will file for divorce in a Russian court. He'll be able to divorce you in absentia and leave you and the children penniless.' He paused. 'Unless we can lay our hands on a bit of his money in the next two days.'

'I don't want any of Ivan's money. It's blood money.'

'Then do it for your children, Elena.'

She looked at the sketch he had given her—the two children on a beach. 'There's a safe-deposit box in Zurich where he usually keeps a couple of million in cash. You could empty it out for me before Ivan freezes it.'

'Do you know the number and password?' She nodded her head. 'Give them to me, Elena—for your children.' She recited them slowly, then looked at him curiously. 'Don't you want to write them down?'

'It's not necessary.'

'You have a spy's memory, just like Ivan.' She picked at her food without appetite. 'I must say, today's performance went extraordinarily well. You should have seen Ivan's face when he was informed his plane couldn't take off. I assume you have the next act well choreographed, too?'

'We do.' A pause. 'But I want to give you a last chance to bow out, Elena. And no hard feelings if you do.'

'I'm going to finish what I started,' she said. 'For Aleksandr Lubin. For Boris Ostrovsky. And for Olga.'

Gabriel signalled to the flight attendant and asked her to remove their food. Then he placed his briefcase on the tray table and opened the combination locks. He removed four items: a small plastic spray bottle, a device that looked like an MP3 player and a second rectangular device, along with a short USB connector cord.

'We've put together a schedule for your final hours in Moscow. Pay close attention to everything I have to tell you. We have a lot of ground to cover.'

THE FLIGHT touched down at Sheremetyevo punctually at 8.05 p.m. Elena left the plane first and walked a few paces ahead through the terminal, with her handbag over her left shoulder and her overnight bag rolling behind her. Arriving at passport control, Gabriel joined a queue for unwanted foreigners, and by the time he was finally admitted into the country Elena was gone.

As soon as word of Gabriel and Elena's arrival in Moscow reached the operations centre in Grosvenor Square, at 6.19 p.m. local time, Graham Seymour stood up from his chair and rubbed the kinks out of his lower back. 'Nothing more to be done tonight. What say we adjourn to the Grill Room of the Dorchester for a celebratory supper? My service is buying.'

'I don't believe in mid-operation celebrations,' Shamron said. 'Especially when I have three of my best operatives on the ground in Moscow and three more on the way.'

Carter placed a hand on Shamron's shoulder. 'Come on, Ari. There's nothing you can do now except sit there all night and worry yourself to death.'

'Which is exactly what I intend to do.'

Carter frowned and looked at Graham Seymour. 'We can't leave him here alone. He's barely housebroken.'

'How would you feel about an Indian takeaway?'

'Tell them to go easy on the spices. My stomach isn't what it used to be.'

Chapter 10

Moscow

With just one week remaining until election day, there was no escaping the face of the Russian president. It hung from every signpost and government building in the city centre. It stared out from the front pages of every Kremlin-friendly newspaper and flashed across the newscasts of the Kremlin-controlled television networks. The president himself campaigned as though he were waging a real election rather than a carefully scripted folly.

The Kremlin had allowed two other candidates the privilege of contesting the election, but most Russians could not recall their names. The Coalition for a Free Russia, the only real organised opposition force, had no candidate but plenty of courage. As the president was addressing an afternoon rally in Dinamo Stadium, they gathered in Arbat Square for a counter rally, at the end of which one hundred members of Free Russia were in police custody and another hundred were in the hospital. Evidence of the bloody melee was still strewn about late that afternoon as Gabriel headed towards the river.

The Cathedral of Christ the Saviour rose before him, its five golden onion domes dull against the heavy grey sky. The original cathedral had been dynamited in 1931, supposedly because it blocked Stalin's view from the windows of his Kremlin apartment. Rebuilt after the fall of communism, the cathedral was now one of Moscow's most popular tourist attractions. Gabriel decided to skip it and made his way to the river instead. Three men were standing separately along the embankment, gazing across the water towards a vast apartment building with a Mercedes-Benz star atop the roof. As Gabriel walked past, one by one the men turned and followed him.

ON THE OPPOSITE SIDE of Serafimovicha Street was a melancholy patch of brown grass and wilted trees known as Bolotnaya Square. Gabriel was seated on a nearby bench next to a fountain when Uzi Navot came and sat next to him. Yaakov Rossman and Eli Lavon stood at the edge of the fountain. Lavon was chattering away on a mobile like a movie extra in a cocktail-party scene. Yaakov was looking at the ground and smoking a cigarette.

'When did Yaakov take up smoking again?' asked Gabriel.

'Last night. He's nervous. You would be, too, if you had any sense.'

'How's our local station chief?'

'Let's just say he'll be quite happy when we get on that plane tomorrow.'

'How many cars was he able to come up with?'

'Four, like you wanted—three old Ladas and a Volga. They all run just fine.'

'Where did he get them?'

'The station picked up a small fleet of old Soviet cars for a song after the fall of communism and put them on ice. All the papers are in order.'

'And the drivers?'

'Four field hands from Moscow Station. They all speak Russian.'

'What time do we start leaving the hotel?'

'I go first at two fifty. Eli goes five minutes after that. Then Yaakov five minutes later. You're the last to leave.'

'It's not much time, Uzi.'

'It's plenty of time. If we get here too early, we might attract unwanted attention. And that's the last thing we want.' Gabriel didn't argue. Instead, he asked Navot about the situation at the apartment house on the Kutuzovsky Prospekt where Elena was now staying with her mother.

'Arkady Medvedev has placed the building under round-the-clock surveillance. Just a man in a car outside in the street. Every four hours the watcher changes.'

'Does he change the car or just the man?'

'Just the man. The car stays in place.' Navot was rubbing a sore patch above his elbow. He always seemed to develop some small physical malady whenever he was anxious about an operation. 'We should assume that the watcher will follow Elena when she leaves for the airport tomorrow night. If the watcher sees her making a detour to the House on the Embankment, he'll tell Arkady. Do you see my point, Gabriel?'

'Yes, Uzi,' Gabriel said. 'I believe I do. We have to make sure the watcher doesn't follow her. A minor traffic accident should suffice.'

ELENA KHARKOV had left her mother's apartment just once that day: a quick drive to a new gourmet market, where, accompanied by two of her body-guards, she had purchased the ingredients for a summer borscht. She had spent the remainder of the afternoon in the kitchen with her mother, playfully bickering over recipes, the way they always did.

That evening, mother and daughter sat together at the dining-room table, a candle and a loaf of black bread between them. Until now, Elena's mother had assiduously avoided any discussion of the reason behind the unorthodox visit. She broached the topic for the first time, not with words but by gently laying Elena's letter upon the table. Elena looked at it a moment, then resumed eating. 'Who was the man you sent to deliver this letter?'

'He's a friend, Mama. Someone who's helping me.'

'You're leaving your husband?'

'Yes, Mama, I'm leaving my husband.'

'Is there another woman?'

Elena nodded, eyes on her food. 'She's just a child of nineteen. I'm sure Ivan will hurt her the way he's hurt me one day, too.'

'You should have never married him. I begged you not to marry him. He's a monster. His father was a monster and he's a monster.'

'I know.' Elena tried to eat some of the soup but had lost her appetite. 'I'm sorry the children and I haven't spent more time with you the past few years. Ivan wouldn't let us. It's no excuse. I should have stood up to him.'

'You don't have to apologise, Elena. I know more than you think I know. But what I don't understand is why you came to Moscow like this.'

A tear spilled onto Elena's cheek. She brushed it away before her mother could see it.

'I have to take care of some business before I leave Ivan. I have to protect myself and the children.'

'You're not thinking about taking his money?'

'This has nothing to do with money.'

Her mother didn't press the issue. She was a Party wife. She knew about secrets and walls.

'When are you planning to tell him?'

'Tomorrow night. When I return to France.'

'Your husband isn't the sort of man who takes bad news well. Will you stay in Europe, or will you come home to Russia?'

'It might not be safe for me in Russia any more. I might have to take the children someplace where Ivan can't find them. Do you understand what I'm saying to you?'

The Party wife understood perfectly. 'Am I ever going to see them again, Elena? Am I ever going to see my grandchildren again?'

'It might take some time. But, yes, you'll be able to see them again.'

'Time? How much time? Time is not something I have in abundance.'

'I've left some money in the bottom drawer of your dresser. It's all the money I have in the world right now.'

'Then I can't take it.'

'Trust me, Mama. You have to take that money.'

Her mother looked down and tried to eat, but now she, too, had lost her appetite. And so they sat there for a long time, clutching each other's hands across the table, faces wet with tears. *We cannot live as normal people*, Elena thought. *And we never will.*

THE UNDOING of Ivan Borisovich Kharkov, property developer, venture capitalist and international arms trafficker, began with a phone call. It was placed to his Saint-Tropez residence by one François Boisson, regional director of the Direction Générale de l'Aviation Civile, the French aviation authority. It appeared, said Monsieur Boisson, that there was a rather serious problem regarding recent flights by Monsieur Kharkov's aircraft, as a result of which he summoned Monsieur Kharkov to appear at Nice Airport at one that afternoon to answer a few simple questions. If he chose not to appear, his plane would be confiscated. After a long, anti-French tirade, Ivan promised to come at the appointed hour and rang off.

Elena Kharkov learned of her husband's predicament when she telephoned Villa Soleil to wish Ivan and the children a pleasant morning. Confronted with Ivan's rage, she made a few soothing comments and assured him it had to be a misunderstanding of some sort. She then had a brief conversation with Sonia, during which she instructed the nanny to take the children to the beach.

GABRIEL WAS A MAN of unnatural patience, but now, during the final tedious hours before their assault on Ivan's vault of secrets, his patience abandoned him. It was fear, he thought. The fear that he might find himself in Lubyanka once again and that this time he might not come out alive. The fear that others might join him there and suffer the same fate. He attempted to suppress his fear with activity. He walked streets he loathed, ordered an elaborate lunch he barely touched, and, in the glittering GUM shopping mall near Red Square, purchased souvenirs he would leave behind.

Finally, at 2.30 p.m., he returned to his room at the Ritz-Carlton, booked in the name of Martin Stonehill, and dressed for combat. His only weapons were a miniature radio and a PDA. At precisely 3.03 p.m., he exited the hotel's revolving door into Tverskaya Street. After walking half a block, he stopped and thrust his hand towards the street, as if hailing a taxi. A silver Volga sedan pulled in to the kerb. Gabriel climbed inside and closed the door.

'*Shalom*,' said the man behind the wheel.

'Let's hope so.'

Gabriel looked at his watch as the car shot forward: *3.06* . . .

Time for one last goodbye, Elena. Time to get in the car.

ELENA KHARKOV slipped quietly into the guest bedroom and began to pack. At 3.20, she dialled the number of Sonia's mobile phone. Sonia answered after three rings. In the most placid voice Elena could summon, she informed Sonia the children had had enough sun and that it was time to leave the beach. Sonia offered mild protest—the children, she said, were the happiest they had been in days—but Elena insisted. When the call was over, she switched on the device that looked like an ordinary MP3 player and placed it in the outer compartment of her overnight bag. Then she dialled Sonia's number again. This time, the call wouldn't go through.

She finished packing and slipped into her mother's bedroom. The money was where she had left it, in the bottom of the dresser, concealed beneath a sweater. She closed the drawer and went into the sitting room. Her mother looked at Elena and attempted to smile. They had nothing more to say, no more tears to cry. 'You'll have some tea before you leave?'

'No, Mama. There isn't time.'

'Go, then,' she said. 'And may the angel of the Lord be looking over your shoulder.'

A bodyguard was waiting for Elena in the corridor. He carried her suitcase downstairs and placed it in the boot of a waiting limousine. As the car pulled away, Elena announced that she needed to make a brief stop at the House on the Embankment to collect some papers from her husband's office.

'I'll just be a moment or two,' Elena said. 'We'll still have plenty of time to get to Sheremetyevo in time for my flight.'

AS ELENA'S LIMOUSINE sped along the Kutuzovsky Prospekt, a second car was following it. Behind the wheel was a man named Anton Ulyanov. He worked for Arkady Medvedev. *Follow her all the way to the airport*, Medvedev had told him. *And don't lose sight of her. If you do, you'll wish you'd never been born.*

Ulyanov settled fifty yards behind the limousine and switched on some music. Nothing to do now but make himself comfortable and take a nice, boring drive to Sheremetyevo. The offending car came from Ulyanov's right, though later he would be forced to admit he never saw it. He was able to recall the moment of impact, though, a violent collision of buckling steel and shattering glass that sent the airbag exploding into his face.

Nice

Upon his arrival at Côte d'Azur International Airport, Ivan Kharkov was escorted into a windowless conference room with a rectangular table and photographs of French-built aircraft on the wall. The man who had summoned him, François Boisson, was nowhere to be seen; indeed, a full thirty minutes would elapse before Boisson finally appeared. Offering neither explanation nor apology for his tardiness, the balding French bureaucrat placed a thick file at the head of the conference table and sat for an uncomfortably long period before finally bringing the proceedings to order.

'After your aircraft was refused permission to take off from this airport, we began a review of your flight records and passenger manifests. Unfortunately, in the process we have discovered some serious discrepancies.'

'What sort of discrepancies?'

'It is our conclusion, Monsieur Kharkov, that you have been operating your aircraft as an illegal charter service. Unless you can prove to us that is not the case I'm afraid your aircraft will be confiscated immediately.'

'Your accusation is complete nonsense,' Ivan countered.

Boisson sighed and slowly opened the file. The first item he produced was a photograph of a Boeing Business Jet. 'Is this your aircraft, Monsieur Kharkov?' He pointed to the registration number. 'N7287IK?'

'Of course it's my plane.'

Boisson touched the N on the tail number. 'Your aircraft carries American registry,' he pointed out. 'When was the last time it was in the United States?'

'I couldn't say for certain. Three years at least. But as you know, Monsieur Boisson, aircraft owners carry American registry because it ensures a high resale value.'

'But according to your own records, you are *not* the owner of N7287IK.'

'What are you talking about?'

'Your own aircraft registration lists the owner of N7287IK as a Delaware-based firm called, oddly enough, N7287 LLC. Obviously, N7287 LLC is a corporate shell maintained to give your plane the illusion of American ownership. Technically, the president of N7287 LLC is an attorney in Delaware named Charles Hamilton. He is also the owner by proxy of the aircraft you claim is yours. Isn't that correct, Monsieur Kharkov?'

'*Technically*,' snapped Ivan, 'that *is* correct, and I lease it from him, but these sorts of arrangements are common in private aviation.'

'Common, perhaps, but not entirely honest. Before we continue with this inquiry, I must insist you prove that you are the actual owner of the Boeing Business Jet with the tail number N7287IK. Perhaps you could telephone your attorney and put him on the phone to me?'

'But it's Sunday morning in America.'

'Then I suspect he'll be at home.'

Ivan swore in Russian and picked up his mobile phone. The call failed to go through. Two further attempts proved futile.

'I sometimes have trouble in this building myself,' Boisson said apologetically. He pointed towards the telephone at the far end of the conference table. 'Feel free to use ours. I'm sure it's working just fine.'

ARKADY MEDVEDEV received the call from an obviously dazed Anton Ulyanov while he was relaxing in his apartment in the Sparrow Hills. After hanging up, Medvedev immediately dialled the number for Elena's driver and received no answer. After a second unsuccessful attempt, he tried to reach Luka Osipov, the head of Elena's small security detail, but with the same result. He slammed down the receiver in frustration and stared glumly out of the window towards central Moscow. *A summons to appear at Nice Airport . . . a crash on the Kutuzovsky Prospekt . . . and now Elena's bodyguards weren't answering their phones . . .* It wasn't a coincidence. Something was going on. But for the moment, there wasn't a damn thing he could do about it.

THE DEPARTURE of the Kharkov children from Pampelonne Beach did not go according to schedule, which surely would come as no surprise to any parent of small children. First there were the demands for a final swim. Then there was the struggle to get two sand-covered seven-year-olds into dry clothing suitable for the journey home. And finally there were the obligatory histrionics during the long walk to the cars.

As a result of the delays, it was 1.45 p.m. before Sonia Cherkasov, the Kharkovs' long-suffering nanny, managed to get the children and bodyguards into their cars. They followed their usual course: inland on the Route des Tamaris, then south along the D93 towards the Baie de Cavalaire. As they emerged from the traffic island east of Ramatuelle, a gendarme stepped suddenly into the road ahead of them and raised a white-gloved hand.

The gendarme knew it was pointless to address the Russian driver in the lead car in French. In heavily accented English, he informed the driver that he had been travelling well in excess of the speed limit. The driver's response—that everyone speeds in the South of France in summer—did not sit well with the gendarme, who demanded to see the driver's operating permit, along with the passports of every occupant of the two vehicles.

'We didn't bring the passports, because we were at the beach.'

'As visitors to France, you are required to carry your passports with you at all times.' The gendarme peered into the back seat.

'Are these your children, monsieur?'

'No, they are the children of Ivan Kharkov.'

The gendarme made a face to indicate the name was not familiar to him. 'And who are you?'

'I work for Mr Kharkov. So do my colleagues in the second car.'

'In what capacity?'

'Security.'

'Am I to assume that you are carrying weapons?'

The Russian driver nodded his head.

'May I see your permits, please?'

'We don't have the permits with us. They're with the passports at Mr Kharkov's villa.'

The gendarme, upon hearing the answer, walked back to his car and lifted his radio to his lips. A second vehicle, a Renault minivan, had already arrived on the scene and shortly thereafter was joined by what appeared to be most of the Saint-Tropez force. The Russian driver, watching this scene in his rearview mirror, drew a mobile phone from his pocket and tried to call the chief of Ivan's detail, but the call failed to go through.

After three more attempts, he gave up in frustration and looked out of the window. The gendarme was now standing there, with the flap of his holster undone and his hand wrapped round the grip of his sidearm.

'Would you please remove your weapon and place it carefully on the dash of the car.' He looked at the bodyguard in the passenger seat. 'You, too, monsieur. Gun on the dash. Then I'd like you both to step out of the car very slowly and place your hands on the roof.'

'What is this all about?'

'I'm afraid we have no choice but to detain you until we can sort out the matter of your passports and weapons permits. The children and their nanny can travel together in one car. You and your three colleagues will be driven separately. We can do this in a civilised manner or, if you prefer, we can do it in handcuffs. The choice is yours, messieurs.'

Moscow

On the western side of the House on the Embankment was a small park with a pretty red church in the centre. A few yards from the church was a coppice of trees, and amid the trees was a wooden bench. Gabriel sat at one end; Shmuel Peled, embassy driver and clandestine officer of Israeli intelligence, sat at the other. Shmuel was chattering away in fluent Russian. Gabriel was not listening. He was focused instead on the voices emanating from his miniature earpiece. The voice of Yaakov Rossman, who reported that Elena Kharkov's car was now free of opposition surveillance and approaching the House on the Embankment at high speed. The voice of Uzi Navot, who reported that Elena Kharkov was now leaving her car and proceeding into the building with Luka Osipov at her shoulder. Gabriel marked the time on his wristwatch: 3.54 . . . They were already nine minutes behind schedule. *Better hurry, Elena. We all have a plane to catch.*

Word of Elena Kharkov's arrival reached London ten seconds later, not by voice but by a terse message that flashed across the billboard-sized video screen at the front of the room. Adrian Carter picked up the handset of a dedicated line to Langley and said calmly, 'She's heading into the building. Take down the phones. Everything from the Moscow River south to the Garden Ring.'

SHE CROSSED THE LOBBY with Luka Osipov at her heels and entered a small foyer with a single lift. He attempted to follow her into the waiting car but she froze him with a wave of her hand. 'Wait here,' she ordered, inserting a security key card into the slot. She pressed the button for the ninth floor while Luka Osipov stood motionless for several seconds, watching the lift's ascent play out on the red lights of the control panel.

When the doors opened on the ninth floor, another bodyguard was waiting in the vestibule. His name was Pyotr Luzhkov and, like Luka Osipov, he was a former member of the elite Alpha Group. The expression on his pasty, dull face was one of surprise. Because of the cellphone jammer concealed in Elena's luggage, her security detail had been unable to alert him that she would be stopping by. Elena greeted him absently, then pushed past him into the entrance hall. When the security man reflexively placed his hand on her arm, Elena whirled round, eyes wide with anger.

'What are you doing? How dare you touch me!'

Luzhkov removed his hand. 'I'm sorry, Mrs Kharkov. I shouldn't have placed my hand on you.'

'No, Pyotr, you should not. Wait until Ivan finds out about this!'

She set out down the hallway towards the office. The bodyguard followed.

'I'm sorry, Mrs Kharkov, but I'm afraid I can't allow you to enter the office unless your husband is with you.'

'Except in the event of an emergency. And this *is* an emergency. Go back to your post, you fool. I can't punch in the code with you looking over my shoulder.'

'If there is an emergency, why wasn't I notified of it by Arkady Medvedev?'

'You might find this difficult to believe, Pyotr, but my husband does not tell Arkady everything. He asked me to collect some important papers from his office and take them to France. Now, ask yourself something, Pyotr: how do you think Ivan is going to react if I miss my plane because of this?'

The bodyguard held his ground. 'I'm just doing my job, Mrs Kharkov. My instructions are that no one is allowed to enter that office without clearance from Mr Kharkov or Mr Medvedev. And that includes you.'

Elena sighed in exasperation. 'Then I suppose you'll just have to call Arkady and tell him that I'm here.'

She pointed to the telephone resting on a small decorative table. 'Call him, Pyotr. But do it quickly. Because if I miss my flight to France, I'm going to tell Ivan to cut out your tongue.'

The guard turned his back to Elena and snatched up the receiver. A few seconds later, he reached down, brow furrowed, and rattled the switch. 'The phone doesn't seem to be working.'

'That's odd. Try my cellphone.'

The guard placed the receiver back in the cradle and turned round, only to find Elena with her arm extended and a spray bottle in her hand. *The spray bottle that Gabriel had given her on the plane.* She squeezed the button once, sending a cloud of atomised liquid directly into his face. The guard struggled for several seconds to maintain his balance, then fell to the floor with a heavy thud.

NINE FLOORS BENEATH HER, a fat man in a grey fedora entered the foyer, cursing his mobile phone. He looked at Luka Osipov with an expression of mild frustration and shrugged his lumpy shoulders.

'The damn thing was working a minute ago, but when I got near the building it stopped. Perhaps it's the ghost of Stalin. My neighbour claims to have seen him wandering the halls at night.'

The lift doors opened; the tubby Russian disappeared inside. Luka Osipov walked over to the lobby windows and gazed into the street. At least two other people—a woman walking along the pavement and a taxi driver standing next to his car—were having obvious difficulty with their cell-phones. *The damn thing was working a minute ago, but when I got near the building it stopped. . .* Though Comrade Stalin was a man of great power, Luka Osipov doubted whether his ghost had anything to do with the sudden interruption in cellular communications. He suspected it was something far more tangible. Something like a signal jammer.

He tried his mobile once more without success, then walked over to the porter and asked to use his land-line telephone. It, too, was dead.

Luka left the porter's desk and stepped outside. The driver of the limousine had his window down. Luka poked his head through the opening and told the man in the passenger seat to go and stand guard in the foyer. Then he turned towards the Kremlin and started walking. By the time he reached the middle of the Bolshoy Kamenny Bridge, his phone was working again. The first call he made was to the Sparrow Hills.

THE FLOOR WAS HARDWOOD and recently polished. Even so, it took every bit of Elena's strength to drag the 200-pound unconscious body of Pyotr Luzhkov into the bathroom of the master bedroom. She locked the door from the inside, then made her way back to the entrance of Ivan's office.

After punching the eight-digit access code into the keypad, she placed her thumb on the scanner. An alarm chirped three times and the armoured door eased slowly open. Elena stepped inside.

The CPU, she knew, was concealed beneath the desk. Elena crouched down and pressed the power button, then plugged in the USB device that Gabriel had given her on the plane. After a few seconds, the drive engaged and the computer began to whirr.

She glanced at her wristwatch, then walked over to the bookcase on the opposite side of the room. The button was hidden behind Ivan's first edition of *Anna Karenina*. When pressed, the button caused the bookcases to part, revealing the door to Ivan's vault. She punched the same eight-digit code into the keypad and placed her thumb on the scanner pad. Three chirps sounded, followed by the dull thud of the locks.

The interior light came on automatically as she pulled open the heavy door. Ivan's secret disks, the grey matter of his network of death, stood in a neat row on a shelf. One shelf below were some of the proceeds of that network: rubles, dollars, euros, Swiss francs. She took only the disks. The disks that would help Gabriel find the missiles. The discs that would destroy her husband.

LUKA OSIPOV had gained fifteen pounds since leaving the Alpha Group and had lost much of his old physical fitness. As a result, he was breathing heavily by the time he arrived back at the porter's desk.

'I believe a woman under my protection is in grave danger in Apartment 9A at this very moment. I need you to get me inside.'

'I'm sorry, but it's against policy without a security card for the lift.'

'Do you know who I work for, you fool?'

'You work for Mrs Kharkov.'

'No, I work for *Ivan* Kharkov. And do you know what *Ivan* Kharkov is going to do if anything happens to his wife?'

The porter swallowed hard. 'I can get you up to the ninth floor but I can't get you into that apartment. Mr Kharkov doesn't let us keep a key on file.'

'Leave that part to me.'

'Good luck,' the porter said as he came out from behind his desk. 'You'll need a Red Army tank to get into that place.'

ELENA CLOSED THE BOOKCASES, removed the USB device from the computer, and switched off the power. Stepping into the hallway, she glanced at her watch: *4.02 . . .* The entire thing had taken just eight minutes. She shoved the device into the bag and punched the eight-digit code into the keypad. While the heavy door swung slowly shut, she took a last look around to make certain everything was in order and started for the door.

It was then she heard the pounding. A large male fist, interspersed with a large male palm. She thought of not answering it. But she did, in a fit of feigned outrage, with her right hand wrapped round the plastic spray bottle in her coat pocket. Standing in the vestibule, his face pale with anger, was Luka Osipov. A gun was in his hand and it was pointed directly at Elena's heart. She feared the gun might go off if she attempted to deploy the spray bottle, so she drew her empty hand slowly from her pocket and placed it on her hip, frowning at her bodyguard in bewilderment.

'Luka Ustinovich,' she said, using his patronymic. 'What's got into you?'

'Where's Pyotr?'

'Who's Pyotr?'

'The guard who's supposed to be on duty at this flat.'

'There was no one here when I arrived, you idiot. Now, let's go.' She tried to step into the vestibule. The bodyguard blocked her path. 'What game do you think you're playing, Luka? Trust me, the last thing you want is for me to miss my plane.'

The bodyguard said nothing. Instead, he reached into the lift, with the gun still aimed at her abdomen, and sent the carriage back down to the lobby. Then he pushed her into the apartment and slammed the door.

Grosvenor Square, London

Shamron's lighter flared in the gloom of the ops centre, briefly illuminating his face. His eyes were focused on the large central display screen at the front of room, where Uzi Navot's last transmission from Moscow flashed with all the allure of a dead body lying in a gutter.

BG ENTERING HOTE . . . TROUBLE . . .

BG stood for bodyguard. HOTE for House on the Embankment. TROUBLE required no translation. Trouble was trouble. A new message appeared.

AM ENTERING HOTE . . . ADVISE . . .

The initials AM stood for Arkady Medvedev. The word ADVISE meant that Gabriel's meticulously planned operation was in serious danger of crashing and burning, with significant loss of life a distinct possibility.

'They're your boys,' Carter said. 'It's your call.'

Shamron flicked ash into his cup. 'We sit tight. We give her a chance.'

Carter looked at the digital clock. 'It is now four fifteen, Ari. If your team is to have any chance of getting on that plane, they need to be in their cars and heading to the airport in the next ten minutes.'

'Aircraft are complicated machines, Adrian. A lot of little things can go wrong with them.' Shamron picked up a secure telephone connected to King Saul Boulevard, uttered a few terse words in Hebrew.

'It appears a cabin pressure warning light is now flashing in the cockpit of El Al Flight 1612, Adrian. Until that problem is resolved to the satisfaction of the captain that aircraft isn't going anywhere.'

'Well played,' said Carter.

'How long can our French friends keep Ivan tied up in Nice?'

'Monsieur Boisson is just getting started. The children, however, are another matter. What do we do about the children, Ari?'

'I wouldn't want my children sitting around a gendarmerie station, would you, Adrian?'

'Can't say I would.'

'Then let's take them. Who knows? We may need them.'

'For what?'

'I'm not going to give her up without a fight, Adrian, and you can be sure Gabriel won't either. Call the French. Get me Ivan's children.'

Carter picked up the secure line connected to the French ops centre in Paris. Shamron looked back at the message screen, where Uzi Navot's last message flashed incessantly.

THEY HAD PLACED Sonia and the children in a pleasant holding room and plied them with ice cream. A pretty young female gendarme remained with them while they watched cartoons and played a noisy game of cards. The chief duty officer made them honorary gendarmes for the day and even allowed Nikolai to inspect his firearm.

After receiving a telephone call from headquarters in Paris, the duty officer returned to the holding room and announced that it was time for everyone to go home. Anna and Nikolai greeted this news not with joy but tears; for them, the arrest and detention had been a great adventure. They were finally coaxed into leaving with a promise that they could come back to play any time they wished.

They left through a rear door that gave onto an enclosed courtyard. Several official Renaults were parked there, along with an older-model Peugeot wagon. Seated behind the wheel, wearing a white Lacoste polo, was a man with grey hair. Seeing the children, he climbed out of the car and opened the rear door. Sonia froze and turned to the duty officer.

'What's going on? Who is this man?'

'This is Monsieur Henri. He's a good man. He's going to take you and the children somewhere safe.'

'I don't understand.'

'I'm afraid Mr Kharkov is in a bit of trouble. Mrs Kharkov has arranged to place the children in Monsieur Henri's care until she returns. She has asked that you remain with them. She promises you will be extremely well compensated. Do you understand what I'm saying, mademoiselle?'

'I think so.'

'Very good. Now, get into the car, please. And try not to look so frightened. It will only upset the children.'

AT MOSCOW'S Sheremetyevo 2 Airport, Chiara was standing at her post at the check-in counter when the status window on the departure board switched from ON TIME to DELAYED. Ten feet away, in the crowded passenger lounge, 187 weary voices groaned in unison. One brave soul, a bearded Orthodox Jew in a dark suit, approached the counter and demanded an explanation.

'It's a minor mechanical problem,' Chiara explained calmly. 'The delay shouldn't be more than a few minutes.' The man returned to his seat, sceptical as to whether he had been told the truth.

Chiara turned and looked up at the board: DELAYED . . .

Walk away, Gabriel, she thought. *Turn round and walk away.*

Chapter 11

MOSCOW

The clouds opened up at the same instant Gabriel's earpiece crackled with the sound of Uzi Navot's voice.

'We're history.'

'What are you talking about?'

'The Old Man just issued the order to abort.'

'Tell him I want ten more minutes.'

'I'm not telling him anything. I'm following his order.'

'You go. I'll meet you at Sheremetyevo.'

'We're out of here. *Now.*'

'I'm not leaving.'

'Get off the radio and into your car.'

Gabriel and Shmuel Peled rose in unison and walked calmly from the park in the driving rain. Peled headed to the Volga; Gabriel, to Bolotnaya Square. Navot and Lavon joined him. Navot was wearing a waxed cap, but Lavon was hatless. His wispy hair was soon plastered to his scalp.

'Why are we here?' Navot demanded. 'Why are we standing in the rain in this godforsaken park when we should be heading to the airport?'

'Because I'm not leaving yet, Uzi.'

'Of course you are, Gabriel.' Navot tapped the PDA. 'It says right here you are: "Abort at five p.m. Moscow time and board flight at SVO." That's a direct order from the Memuneh himself.'

Memuneh was a Hebrew word that meant 'the one in charge', and in the Office it had always been reserved for one man: Ari Shamron.

'You can stand here in the park and shout at me until you're hoarse, Uzi, but I'm not leaving her behind.'

Navot seized Gabriel's upper arm and squeezed it hard. 'It's not your call, Gabriel. You made a promise to Shamron. If she doesn't come out of that building within the allotted period of time, you *leave*.'

Gabriel wiped the rain from his tinted glasses. 'What do you intend to do? Drag me to the car? It might cause a bit of a spectacle, don't you think?'

'At least it will be brief. And unlike your desire to stay here in Moscow, chances are it won't be fatal.'

'Let go of my arm, Uzi.'

'Don't tell me what to do, Gabriel. I'm chief of Special Ops, not you. And I am telling you to get into that car and come with us to the airport.'

Eli Lavon carefully removed Navot's hand from Gabriel's arm. 'That's enough, Uzi. He's not getting on the plane.'

Navot shot Lavon a dark look. 'Thanks for the support, Eli.'

'I don't want him to stay behind any more than you do. I just know better than to waste my breath trying to talk him out of it. He has a hard head.'

'He'll need it.'

Gabriel held up his wristwatch so Navot could see it. 'Five o'clock, Uzi. Better be running along. And take Eli with you. He's a fine watcher, but he's never been one for the rough stuff.'

Navot gave Gabriel a Shamronian stare. He was done arguing.

'If I were you, I'd stay away from your hotel.' He reached into his coat pocket and handed Gabriel a single key. 'I've been carrying this around in case we needed a crash pad.' He recited the street address, the building number and the number of the apartment near Dinamo Stadium. 'Once you're inside, signal the station and bar the door. We'll put in an extraction team. With luck, you'll still be there when they arrive.'

Then he turned away without another word and pounded across the rain-swept square towards his car. Lavon watched him for a moment, then looked at Gabriel. 'Sure you don't want some company?'

'Get to the airport, Eli. Get on that plane.'

'What would you like me to tell your wife?'

Gabriel hesitated a moment, then said, 'Tell her I'm sorry, Eli. Tell her I'll make it up to her somehow.'

NAVOT'S TRANSMISSION appeared on the screen of the London ops centre at 5.04 Moscow time: LEAVING FOR SVO . . . MINUS ONE . . . Adrian Carter swore softly and looked at Shamron.

'It seems you were right,' Carter said.

Shamron said nothing.

'The French say Ivan is about to blow, Ari. They say the situation at Nice is getting tenuous. They would like a resolution, one way or the other.'

'Perhaps it's time to let Ivan see the scope of the dilemma he's now facing. Tell your cyber warriors to turn the phones back on in Moscow. And tell the French to confiscate Ivan's plane. And his passport, while they're at it.'

BY THE TIME Ivan Kharkov emerged from the conference room at Côte d'Azur Airport, his anger had reached dangerous levels. It exploded into mild physical violence when he found his two bodyguards dozing on the couch. They stormed down a flight of stairs and climbed into the waiting Mercedes limousine. When the car was two hundred feet from the building, Ivan's phone rang. It was Arkady Medvedev calling from Moscow.

'Where have you been, Ivan Borisovich? Do you have any idea what's been going on?'

'The French are trying to steal my plane. *And* my passport. That's what's going on, Arkady.'

'They're trying to steal more than that. They've got your children, too. It's part of some elaborate operation against you. And it's not just going on there in France. Something's happening here in Moscow, too.'

Ivan made no response. Arkady Medvedev knew that when Ivan went dead silent it was a dangerous sign. Finally the Russian instructed his chief of security to tell him everything he knew.

'Who put her up to this?' he asked when Medvedev had finished.

'She claims she did it on her own.'

'She's lying. I need to know what I'm up against. And quickly.'

THERE WAS A TIME in Moscow, not that long ago, when a man sitting alone in a parked car would have come under immediate suspicion. But that was no longer the case. These days, sitting in parked cars, or in cars stuck in traffic, was what Muscovites did.

Gabriel was on the northern edge of Bolotnaya Square, engine running and the radio on, watching the entrance of the House on the Embankment.

Twenty minutes into his vigil, a pair of underfed Militia officers rounded the corner. Gabriel nodded cordially. For a moment, he feared they might be contemplating a shakedown. Instead, they frowned at his old Volga, as if to say he wasn't worth their time on a rainy night, and moved on. Gabriel focused his gaze on the building.

The lights in the Kharkov apartment went dark at 7.48 p.m. The woman who emerged from the building soon after had no handbag hanging over her left shoulder. Indeed, she had no handbag at all. Luka Osipov held one arm while a colleague held another. Arkady Medvedev walked behind, head lowered against the rain, eyes up and on the move.

A Mercedes waited at the kerb. Elena sat in the back seat, wedged between bodyguards; Arkady Medvedev was in the front passenger seat, a mobile phone now pressed to his ear. The car crept to the end of Serafimovicha Street, then disappeared in a black blur. Gabriel counted to five and slipped the Volga into gear.

They roared southwards out of the city on a road that bore Lenin's name and was lined with monuments to Lenin's folly. Apartment blocks—endless apartments blocks. It was as if the masters of the Communist Party, in their infinite wisdom, had decided to uproot the country's entire population and resettle it here, along a few wretched miles of the Leninsky Prospekt.

Shmuel Peled had been right about the Volga—it did run decently for a twenty-year-old piece of Soviet-made junk—but it was no match for the finest automobile Bavaria had to offer. The Volga topped out at about eighty-five, and its little wipers were altogether useless against the heavy rain and road spray.

Gabriel kept his foot pressed to the floor and his eyes fastened to the tail-lights of the Mercedes. His thoughts, however, were focused on the scene he had just witnessed. *How had he managed it?* How had Arkady convinced her to walk into the car without a fight? Was it with a threat or a promise, or some combination of both? And why were they now hurtling down the Leninsky Prospekt, into the Russian countryside?

Gabriel was pondering that final question when he felt the first impact on his rear bumper: a car, much bigger and faster than his own, headlights doused. He responded by pressing the accelerator to the floor, but the Volga had nothing more to give. The car behind gave him one more tap, almost as a warning, then moved in swiftly for the kill.

What followed was the classic manoeuvre that every good traffic policeman knows. The aggressor initiates contact with the victim, right front bumper to left rear bumper. The aggressor then accelerates hard and the victim is sent spinning out of control. How many times Gabriel's car actually rotated, he would never know. He knew only that, when it was over, the car was resting on its side in a field of mud at the edge of a pine forest and he was bleeding heavily from the nose.

Two of Arkady Medvedev's finest waded into the mud to retrieve him, though their motives were hardly altruistic. One was a skinheaded giant with a right hand like a sledgehammer. The hammer struck Gabriel only once, for once was all that was necessary. He toppled backwards, into the mud, and for an instant saw upside-down pine trees. Then the trees streaked skywards towards the clouds like missiles. And Gabriel blacked out.

AT THAT SAME MOMENT, El Al Flight 1612 was rapidly gaining altitude over the suburbs of Moscow and banking hard towards the south. Uzi Navot was seated next to the window in the final row of first class, hand wrapped round a glass of whisky, gloomily scanning the vast carpet of winking yellow lights beneath him. Lavon sat beside him, watching Chiara serving drinks from the trolley.

'Don't worry, Uzi. You did the right thing.'

'Just don't ever tell Chiara. She'll never forgive me.' Navot shook his head slowly. 'It's never a good idea to bring spouses into the field. You'd think Gabriel would have learned that by now.'

At that moment the plane knifed into the clouds and the lights of Moscow vanished. Navot pulled down his window shade and lifted the whisky to his lips.

GABRIEL OPENED his eyes slowly. *Not eyes*, he thought. *Eye*. The left eye only. The right eye, the one that had been punched by the bald giant, was swollen shut and crusted over with clotted blood.

Before attempting movement, he took stock of his situation. He was sprawled on the concrete floor of what appeared to be a warehouse, with his hands cuffed at his back. His right shoulder was pressing painfully against the floor, as was the right side of his face. Somewhere, a light was burning, but his own corner of the building was in semidarkness. A few feet away stood a stack of large wooden crates with Cyrillic markings on the sides.

He rolled onto his back and levered himself into a sitting position. The exertion of the movement, combined with the fact that he was now upright, caused his right eye to begin throbbing with catastrophic pain. He reckoned the blow had fractured the orbit around the eye. For all he knew, he no longer had an eye, just an empty crater in the front of his head.

He leaned against the wooden crates and looked around him. There were towering stacks of crates, receding into the distance like the apartment buildings of the Leninsky Prospekt. Gabriel doubted they were filled with caviar.

He heard the sound of footsteps approaching from a distance. Two sets. Both male. One man significantly larger than the other. The big man was the bald giant who had hit him. The smaller, older man had a skull that looked as if it been specially designed to withstand much blunt trauma.

'Where are the children?' asked Arkady Medvedev.

'What children?' replied Gabriel.

Medvedev nodded to the giant, then stepped away as if he didn't want his clothing to be spattered with the blood. The sledgehammer crashed into Gabriel's skull a second time. Same eye, same result. Pine trees and missiles. Then nothing at all.

Lubyanka Square, Moscow

Like almost everyone else in Moscow, Colonel Grigori Bulganov was divorced. His marriage, like Russia itself, had been characterised by wild lurches from one extreme to the other: glasnost one day, Great Terror the next. Thankfully, it had been short and had produced no offspring. Irina had won the apartment and the VW; Grigori, his freedom. Not that he had managed to do much with it.

For the most part, Grigori Bulganov worked. He worked early in the morning. He worked late into the evening. He worked Saturdays. And sometimes, like now, he could be found in his FSB office late on a Sunday night. His brief was counterespionage. More to the point, it was Bulganov's job to neutralise attempts by foreign intelligence services to spy on the Russian government and State-owned Russian enterprises. His assignment had been made more difficult by the activities of the FSB's sister service, the SVR. Espionage by the SVR had reached levels not seen since the height of the Cold War, which had prompted Russia's adversaries to respond in kind. Grigori Bulganov could hardly blame them.

Like many FSB officers, Bulganov supplemented his government salary by selling his expertise, along with knowledge gained through his work itself, to private industry. In Bulganov's case, he served as a paid informant for a man named Arkady Medvedev, the chief of security for Ivan Kharkov. Medvedev rewarded him by keeping a secret bank account in Bulganov's name filled with cash. As a consequence of the arrangement, Grigori Bulganov had been able to penetrate Kharkov's operations, legal and illicit, in a way no other outsider ever had. In Russia, such knowledge could be dangerous, which explained why Bulganov was careful to stay on Arkady Medvedev's good side. And why, when Medvedev called his cellphone at 11.15 p.m. on a Sunday, he didn't dare consider not answering it.

Grigori Bulganov did not speak for the next three minutes, as he listened to the account of what had taken place that afternoon.

'How did he get back into the country?' Bulganov asked.

'With an American passport and a crude disguise.'

'Where is he now?'

Medvedev told him the location.

'What about Ivan's wife?'

'She's here, too.'

'What are your plans, Arkady?'

'I'm going to give him one more chance to answer a few questions. Then I'm going to drop him in a hole somewhere.' A pause. 'Unless you'd like to do that for me, Grigori?'

'Actually, I might enjoy that. After all, he did disobey a direct order.'

'How quickly can you get down here?'

'Give me an hour. How many men do you have there?'

'Five.'

'That's a lot of witnesses.'

'Don't worry, Grigori. They're not the talkative sort.'

Kaluzhskaya Oblast, Moscow

When Gabriel woke next, it was to the sensation of a dressing being applied to his wounded eye. He opened the one that still functioned and saw the task was being performed by none other than Arkady Medvedev. The Russian was working with a single hand. The other held a pistol. *A Stechkin*, thought Gabriel.

'Feeling sorry for me, Arkady?'

'It wouldn't stop bleeding. We were afraid you were going to die on us.'

'Aren't you going to kill me anyway?'

'Of course we are, Allon. We just need some information from you first.'

'And who said former KGB hoods don't have any manners?'

Medvedev finished applying the bandage and regarded Gabriel in silence. 'Aren't you going to ask me how I know your name?' he asked finally.

'I assume you could have got it from your friends at the FSB. Or it's possible you saved yourself a phone call by simply beating it out of Elena Kharkov. You strike me as the type who enjoys hitting women.'

'Keep that up and I'll bring Dmitri back for another go at you.'

'He has a lot of wasted motion in his punch, Arkady. Why don't you let me give him a couple of pointers?'

'Are you serious, or is that just your Jewish sense of humour talking?'

'Our sense of humour came from living with Russians as neighbours. It helps to have a sense of humour during a pogrom. It takes the sting out of having your village burned down.'

'You have a choice, Allon. You can lie there and tell jokes all night or you can start talking.' The Russian removed a cigarette from a silver case and held the case towards Gabriel. 'Would you like one?'

'They're bad for your health.'

Medvedev closed the case. 'Are you up for a little walk, Allon? I think you might find this place quite interesting.'

'Any chance of taking off these handcuffs?'

'None whatsoever.'

'I thought you would say that. Help me up, will you? Just try not to pull my shoulders out of their sockets.'

Medvedev hoisted him effortlessly to his feet. Gabriel felt the room spin and for an instant thought he might topple over. Medvedev must have been thinking the same thing because he placed a steadying hand on his elbow.

'You sure you're up for this, Allon?'

'I'm sure.'

Medvedev dropped his cigarette and crushed it carefully with the toe of an expensive-looking Italian loafer. Then they set out together between the crates. They seemed to go on for ever, like the warehouse itself. *Hardly surprising*, Gabriel thought. *This was Russia, after all. World's largest country. World's largest hotel. World's largest warehouse.*

'What's in the boxes?'

Medvedev pointed towards a skyscraper of wooden crates. 'Those are bullets. Fifty million rounds, to be precise. Enough to kill a good portion of the Third World. There's not much chance of that, though. Your average freedom fighter isn't terribly disciplined. We don't complain. It's good for business.'

'And the rest?'

'Over there are mortars. Next to the mortars is our bread and butter: the AK-47. It helped us beat the Germans; then it helped us change the world. The Kalashnikov gave power to the powerless. Voice to the voiceless.'

They walked on for a while in silence. Gabriel knew this wasn't a tour but a death march. Arkady Medvedev wanted something from Gabriel before they reached their destination. He wanted Ivan's children.

'You should know, Allon, that everything I am showing you here is completely *legal*. We've done well. We're much bigger than our competition.'

'Congratulations. And how did you make out on the missile deal?'

Medvedev was silent for a moment. 'What missiles are you referring to?'

'The SA-18s, Arkady. The *Iglas*.'

Medvedev's tone took on a briefing-room quality. 'It is far too dangerous a system ever to be let loose into the free market. We don't deal in *Iglas*. Only a madman would.'

'That's not what I'm told, Arkady. I hear you sold several hundred to an African country. A country that was planning to forward them at a substantial markup to some friends at al-Qaeda.'

Gabriel lapsed into silence. When he spoke again, his tone was confiding. 'We know all about the *Iglas*, Arkady. We also know that you were against the sale. It's not too late to help us. Tell me where they are.'

Medvedev made no response, other than to give Gabriel a firm shove in the back. Apparently, there was one more thing they had to see.

SHE WAS SECURED to a straight-backed metal chair at the far end of the vast warehouse. Luka Osipov was standing to one side, the bald giant on the other. Her blouse was torn, her cheeks aflame from repeated slaps. She glanced at Gabriel's bandaged eye, then lowered her gaze to the floor.

'Before we begin, you should know that Mrs Kharkov has been very cooperative this evening. She has given us a full and forthright account of her involvement in this sorry affair.' Elena's face remained a stoic mask.

'Unfortunately,' Medvedev continued, 'Mrs Kharkov was unable to supply us with one critical piece of information: the location of her children. We were hoping you might tell us that now, so that Mrs Kharkov might be spared additional unpleasantness.'

'I told you, Arkady, I don't know where the children are. That information was kept from me.'

'In case you found yourself in a situation like this?' Medvedev tossed a mobile phone at Gabriel's chest. It clattered to the floor. 'Call the French. Tell them to deliver the children to Ivan's villa *tonight*, along with Ivan's passport. Then tell them to release Ivan's plane. He'd like to return to Russia immediately.'

'Let her go,' Gabriel said. 'Do what you want to me. But let Elena go.'

'So she can testify against her husband in a Western courtroom? So she can publicly bemoan how Russia is becoming an authoritarian state that once again poses a grave threat to global peace? Mr Kharkov's friends in the Kremlin might find it annoying, should such a situation occur. And Mr Kharkov tries very hard never to annoy his friends in the Kremlin.'

'I promise we won't let her talk. She'll raise her children and keep her mouth shut. She's innocent.'

'Ivan doesn't see it that way. Ivan sees her as a traitor. And you know what we do to traitors.' Medvedev placed the barrel of his gun against the back of Elena's neck. '"Seven grams of lead", as Stalin liked to say. That's what Elena is going to get if you don't order the French to let Ivan get on his plane tonight—*with* his children.'

Elena lifted her gaze from the floor and stared directly at Gabriel. 'Don't tell him a thing, Gabriel. They're going to kill me regardless of what you do. I would rather those children be raised by anyone other than a monster like my husband.' She raised her eyes towards Medvedev. 'You'd better pull the trigger, Arkady, because Ivan is *never* getting those children.'

Medvedev walked over to Gabriel and slammed the butt of the pistol into his right eye. Gabriel toppled sideways to the floor, blinded by excruciating pain. It was compounded when Medvedev buried an Italian loafer into Gabriel's solar plexus. He was lining up a second kick when a distant voice intervened in Russian. The voice was familiar to Gabriel, but in his agony he could not recall where he had heard it before. It came to him a moment later, when he was finally able to breathe again. He had heard the voice during his first trip to Moscow, in Lubyanka.

The two men had a brief but amicable debate in Russian, as if they were quarrelling over whose turn it was to pay for lunch. When the conversation concluded, two pairs of hands lifted him to his feet. It was only then that he saw the face of the man he knew as 'Sergei'. He looked much as he had that night in Lubyanka. The same grey suit. The same grey pallor. The same lawyerly eyes behind round spectacles. His little Lenin beard had recently been groomed.

'I thought I told you not to come back to Russia, Allon,' he said.

'If you had been doing your job, I wouldn't have had to.'

'And which job is that?'

'Preventing scum like Ivan from flooding the world with weapons and missiles.'

Sergei sighed heavily, as if to say this was the last way he had hoped to spend his evening. Then he took hold of Gabriel's handcuffs and gave them a sharp jerk. If Gabriel had had any feeling left in his wrists, he was certain it would have hurt like hell.

They crossed the warehouse together, Sergei trailing a step behind, and exited through a door wide enough to accommodate Ivan's freight trucks. It was raining again; three of Medvedev's men were sheltering beneath the eaves, talking quietly in Russian. A few feet away was an official FSB sedan. Sergei inserted Gabriel into the back seat and slammed the door.

He drove through a thick birch forest with a Makarov in his hand. Tucked amid the trees were dachas—not palaces like Ivan's dacha but *real* Russian dachas, surrounded by little plots of cultivated land. Gabriel thought of Olga Sukhova, tending to her radishes. *I believe in my Russia, and I want no more acts of evil committed in my name . . .*

He looked into the rearview mirror and saw the eyes of Lenin. They were searching the road behind them.

'Are we being followed, Sergei?'

'It's not Sergei. My name is Colonel Grigori Bulganov.'

'How do you do, Colonel Bulganov?'

'I do just fine, Allon. Now shut your mouth.'

Bulganov eased into a lay-by and killed the engine. After warning Gabriel not to move, he climbed out and opened the boot. He rummaged around the interior before coming over to Gabriel's side of the car. When he opened the door, he was holding a pair of rusted bolt cutters.

'What are you going to do? Cut me into little pieces?'

'Shut up and get out.' Gabriel did as he was told. Bulganov spun him round, so that he was facing the car, and took hold of the handcuffs. Gabriel heard a single snap and his hands were free.

'Would you like to tell me what's going on, Sergei?'

'I told you, Allon—it's Grigori. Colonel Grigori Bulganov.' He held out the Makarov towards Gabriel. 'I assume you know how to use this?'

Gabriel took the gun. 'Any chance of getting these cuffs off my wrists?'

'Not without the key. Besides, you'll need to be wearing them when we walk back into that warehouse. It's the only way we'll be able to get Elena out alive.' Bulganov treated Gabriel to one of his clever smiles. 'You didn't think I was actually going to let those monsters kill her, did you, Allon?'

'Of course not, *Sergei*. Why would I think a thing like that?'

'I'm sure you have a few questions.'

'A couple of thousand, actually.'

'We'll have time for that later. For now, get back in the car and pretend your hands are still cuffed.'

In the car, Gabriel peered out of the window at the dachas in the trees, wondering if Bulganov was playing some sort of game. *Possible*, he thought, *but not likely*. The colonel had just freed his hands and given him a loaded gun.

'What were you and Arkady talking about in Russian?'

'He told me he wanted information from you. He told me to take you into the woods and put a gun to your head. I was supposed to give you one more chance to talk before killing you.'

'And you agreed to this?'

'It's a long story. The point is, we can use it to our advantage. We'll go back and I'll tell Arkady you've had a change of heart. That you're willing to talk. Then, when we're close enough, I'll shoot him.'

'Arkady?'

'Yes, I'll take care of Arkady. That leaves the two other gorillas.'

Bulganov glanced into the rearview mirror. 'I hear you're not bad with a gun. Do you think you can hide that Makarov somewhere you can get to it quickly enough to keep those goons from killing us?'

Gabriel inserted the Makarov into the waistband of his trousers and concealed it with his coat. 'Keep your gun pointed at me until you're ready. When I see it move towards Arkady, I'll take that as my cue.'

'That leaves the three boys in the loading bay outside.'

'They won't stay outside for long—not when they hear the sound of gunfire. Whatever you do, don't offer them a chance to lay down their weapons and surrender. It doesn't work that way in the real world. Just turn round and start shooting. And don't miss. We won't have time to reload.'

'You've only got eight rounds in that magazine.'

'If I have to use more than five, we're in trouble.'

'I have to admit something to you, Allon. I'm just an intelligence officer. I've never shot anyone before.'

'Just remember to pull the trigger, Grigori. The gun works much better when you pull the trigger.'

THE THREE SECURITY GUARDS were still milling about the entrance of the warehouse when they returned. Someone must have found where Ivan kept the beer because all three were drinking from bottles of Baltika. As Gabriel walked towards the guards, he held his right wrist in his left hand to create the illusion that his hands were still cuffed. Bulganov walked a half-step behind, the Makarov pointed at the centre of Gabriel's back. The guards seemed only moderately interested in their reappearance.

It was precisely forty-two paces from the open loading door to the spot where Elena Kharkov sat chained to her metal chair. Gabriel knew this because he counted the steps in his head as he covered the distance now, with Colonel Grigori Bulganov at his side. Colonel Bulganov, who two months earlier had ordered Gabriel to be thrown down a flight of stairs in Lubyanka. Colonel Bulganov, who once said he would kill Gabriel if he ever returned to Russia, in whose hands Gabriel's life now resided.

Arkady Medvedev was standing before Elena in his shirtsleeves and screaming obscenities into her face. As Bulganov and Gabriel approached, he turned to face them, hands on his hips, his gun shoved down the front of his trousers.

Luka Osipov and the bald giant were standing directly behind Elena, each to one side. At least Elena was still handcuffed to the chair, Gabriel thought, and there was no chance of her getting into his line of fire. Bulganov spoke in Russian to Medvedev as they moved into point-blank range. Medvedev smiled and looked at Gabriel.

'So, you've come to your senses.'

'Yes, Arkady, I've come to my senses.'

'Tell me, then. Where are Ivan's children?'

'What children?'

Medvedev frowned and looked at Bulganov. Bulganov frowned in return and pointed his gun at Medvedev's heart. Gabriel took a step to his right while reaching beneath his coat for the Makarov. They fired their first shots simultaneously, Bulganov into Medvedev's chest, Gabriel into the flat forehead of the bald giant. Luka Osipov responded with a futile attempt to draw his weapon. Gabriel's shot caught him just beneath the chin.

At that instant, Gabriel heard the sound of shattering glass: the sound of three men dropping three bottles of Baltika beer. They came in through the doorway neatly spaced, like little floating ducklings in an arcade shooting gallery. Gabriel took them down in order: head shot, head shot, torso shot.

He spun round towards Elena. She was desperately trying to pull her wrists through her handcuffs, her mouth wide in a silent scream. Gabriel wanted to comfort her but could not; Arkady Medvedev was still alive and was struggling to get the Stechkin out of the front of his trousers. Gabriel kicked the gun out of Medvedev's hands and fired his last three shots into the Russian's head.

GABRIEL HELD ELENA tightly while Bulganov searched the bodies for a key to the handcuffs. He found one, a universal, on Luka Osipov. He freed Elena's hands first, then removed the cuffs from Gabriel's wrists.

While Bulganov led Elena out to the car, Gabriel searched the corpse of Arkady Medvedev. He found keys, passports and a wallet filled with cash. He ignored the money and removed a single item: a plastic card embossed with the image of a large apartment house on it.

Bulganov had the Volga's engine running by the time Gabriel stepped outside. He climbed into the back next to Elena, whose screams were no longer silent. Gabriel held her tightly as Bulganov drove away.

HER WAILING HAD CEASED by the time they saw the rusting sign that stood at the intersection of two dreadful roads. Bulganov explained that the road to Moscow was to the left, and that the border with Ukraine was to the right.

'We can be over the border before dawn,' he added.

'*We?*'

'I just helped an Israeli agent kill Arkady Medvedev and five of his security men. How long do you think I'll live if I stay in Moscow? A week, if I'm lucky. I'm coming with you.'

'Another defector? That's all we need.'

'I suspect you'll find I'm worth my weight in gold. You see, I've been privately investigating the ties between men like Ivan Kharkov and the FSB for years. I also know a great deal about Ivan's little arms-trafficking network. Are you sure you wouldn't like me to come with you, Allon?'

'We'd love the company, Colonel. Besides, I don't have a clue how to get out of here.' Bulganov let his foot off the brake and started to turn to the right. Gabriel told him to stop.

'What's the problem?' Bulganov asked. 'Ukraine is to the right.'

'We have a couple of errands to run before we leave.'

'Where?'

Gabriel pointed to the left.

ON THE OUTSKIRTS of Moscow was a supermarket that never closed. If it was not the world's largest supermarket, thought Gabriel, then it was surely a close second: two acres of frozen foods, a mile of biscuits and crackers, another mile of American soft drinks. And that was just the food. At the far end of the market was a section called Home and Garden, where one could buy everything from clothing to motorcycles to tractors.

Why the market remained open all night was a mystery because at 2 a.m. it was deserted. They walked the endless aisles quickly pulling items from the shelves: clean clothing, bandages and antiseptic, a pair of large sunglasses, enough snack food to fuel an early-morning road trip. When they wheeled their cart up to the check-out, the female clerk looked at Gabriel's eye and winced. Elena contemptuously explained that her 'husband' had crashed his car in a ditch—drunk out of his mind on vodka, of course. The check-out woman shook her head sadly as she rang up the items.

'Russian men,' she muttered. 'They never change.'

As Bulganov drove on towards central Moscow he told them the story of a young KGB officer who never truly believed the lies of Lenin and Stalin and who had quietly raised a glass of vodka when the empire of deception finally fell. This young officer had tried to resign after the collapse of communism but had been convinced by his mentor to stay on and help turn the KGB, now called the FSB, into a truly professional service. He had reluctantly agreed and had quickly risen through the ranks, only to see it deteriorate into something worse than the KGB had been. This young man, at great personal risk, had then joined forces with a group of officers who hoped to reform the FSB. 'Quietly,' said Bulganov. 'From the inside.' But they soon realised that their masters in the Kremlin were not interested in reform. So the group went underground. And started building a dossier.

'Our dossier does not paint a pretty picture. FSB involvement in murder for hire, prostitution and narcotics. My service is a criminal enterprise from top to bottom. And it is *running* Russia.'

'How did I end up on your plate that night in Lubyanka?'

'Ironically it was all by the book. We were watching you from the moment you hit the ground in St Petersburg. And I must admit, you were quite good. We had no suspicions. We thought you were Natan Golani of the Israeli Ministry of Culture.'

'So you didn't know that Arkady and Ivan were trying to have Olga and me killed that night?'

'No, not at all. At first, I thought you were just in the wrong place at the wrong time. But when you survived the attack and saved Olga, that caused Ivan a serious problem. He got on the phone to the chief. He knew you weren't Natan Golani of the Israeli Ministry of Culture. He knew your real name and your real job. He wanted you taken out into a field and shot. The top floor ordered me to do just that. I pretended to go along with it, and started stalling for time. Then, thankfully, your service made such a stink you became too hot, even for the likes of Ivan Kharkov. I persuaded the top floor to take you to the border and let you go. You came very close to dying that night, Allon—closer than you'll ever realise.'

'How did you end up in that warehouse tonight?'

'I've been plying my trade on both sides of the street.'

'You're on Ivan's payroll?'

Bulganov nodded. 'It made it much easier to gather information about the FSB's shady dealings. It also gave me protection. The real rotten elements thought I was one of them. I know a great deal about Ivan's operation. Maybe enough to track down those missiles *without* going back into the House on the Embankment. Even I get the creeps going into the place. It's haunted, you know. They say Stalin roams the halls at night.'

'I'm not leaving Russia without Ivan's disks.'

'You don't know if they're even still in the apartment,' Elena intervened. 'Ivan could have ordered someone to move them by now.'

'Even if they're still there, getting them out will cost valuable time,' Bulganov continued. 'It might also mean another dead body. There's going to be a new guard in the apartment. He might even have a helper or two. It could get ugly.'

Bolotnaya Square, Moscow

The Russian president frowned down in disapproval as Gabriel, Elena and Grigori Bulganov hurried across the street towards the House on the Embankment. Bulganov placed his FSB identification on the reception desk and threatened to cut off the porter's hand if he touched the telephone.

'We were never here. Do you understand me?' The terrified porter nodded.

Bulganov returned his ID to his coat pocket and walked over to the lift, where Gabriel and Elena were already inside. As the doors closed, Elena pressed herself into a rear corner while the two men drew their Makarovs and adopted firing positions. Their precaution proved unnecessary, however, because the vestibule, like the entrance hall of the apartment, was empty. It seemed the guard had fallen asleep on the couch in the living room while watching television.

Gabriel woke him by inserting the barrel of the Makarov into his ear. 'If you are a good dog, you will live to see the sunrise. If you are a bad dog, I'm going to make a terrible mess on Ivan's couch. Which is it going to be? Good dog or bad dog?'

'Good,' said the guard.

'Wise choice. Let's go.' Gabriel marched the guard into Ivan's fortified office, where Elena was already in the process of opening the interior vault. Her handbag was where Medvedev had left it. The disks were still inside. Bulganov ordered the guard into the vault and closed the steel door. Elena pressed the button behind *Anna Karenina* and the bookshelves slid shut. Inside, the guard began shouting, his muffled voice barely audible.

'Maybe we should give him some water,' Bulganov said.

'He'll be fine for a few hours.'

Gabriel and Bulganov led the way back to the lift, Makarovs levelled before them. The porter was still frozen in place behind the reception desk. Bulganov gave him one final reminder to keep his mouth shut, then walked out to the car.

'With a bit of luck, we can be across the border before dawn,' Bulganov said as he shoved his key into the ignition. 'Unless you have any more errands you'd like to run.'

'I do, actually. I need you to make one final arrest as an FSB officer.'

'Who?'

Gabriel told him.

'It's out of the question. There's no way I can get past all that security.'

'You're still a colonel in the FSB, Grigori. And FSB colonels take shit from no one.'

GABRIEL SAT behind the wheel of Colonel Grigori Bulganov's official car, with Elena beside him. The colonel was not present. He was on the eleventh floor, arresting Olga Sukhova.

'Do you think she'll come?' Elena asked.

'She'll come,' said Gabriel. 'She has no choice. She knows that if she ever sets foot outside that apartment, your husband will kill her.'

Elena reached out and touched the bandage on Gabriel's right eye. 'I did the best I could, but I think that beast managed to break something.'

'I'm sure he regretted his actions when he saw the gun in my hand.'

'I don't think he even saw your gun.' She touched his hand. 'Where did you learn to do that?'

'Unfortunately, I've had a lot of practice.'

'I'm glad you killed them. I know that must sound terrible, but I'm glad you killed them the way you did. Especially Arkady.'

'I should have waited until you were gone. I'm sorry for that, Elena.'

She looked at the mobile phone in her hand, and checked the strength of the signal.

'So is your name really Gabriel, or was that a deception, too?'

'It's my real name.' Elena smiled. 'Is there something humorous about my name?'

'No, it's a beautiful name. I was just thinking about the last words my mother said to me before I left her this afternoon, "May the angel of the Lord be looking over your shoulder." I suppose she was right after all.'

'We can pick her up on the way out of town if you like.'

'My mother? The last thing you want to do is drive to Ukraine with my mother in the back seat. Besides, there's no need to bring her out right away. Not even Ivan would harm an old woman.' She scrutinised him in silence for a moment. 'Is it true you don't know where my children are?'

He shook his head. 'I was lying to Arkady. I know where they are.'

'Tell me.'

'Not yet. I'll tell you when we're safely over the border.'

'Look!' She pointed up at the building. 'A light just came on. Does that mean she let him into the apartment?'

'Probably.'

She looked down at Bulganov's mobile phone. 'Ring, damn it. *Ring*.'

'Relax, Elena. It's three o'clock in the morning and an FSB colonel is telling her to pack a bag. Give her a moment to digest what's happening.'

Gabriel took the phone from her grasp and asked how she knew the Cassatt was a forgery.

'It was the hands. The brushstrokes were too impasto.'

'Sarah told me the same thing.'

'You should have listened to her.'

Just then the phone rang. Gabriel handed it to Elena.

'*Da?*' she said. Then, '*Da, da.*' She looked at Gabriel. 'She wants you to flash the headlights.'

Gabriel flicked the headlights twice. Elena spoke a few more words in Russian. The eleventh-floor window went dark.

Chapter 12

Villa dei Fiori, Umbria

The *vendemmia*, the annual harvest of the wine grapes, commenced at the Villa dei Fiori on the final Saturday in September. It coincided with the unwelcome news that the restorer was returning to Umbria. Count Gasparri briefly considered making the drive from Rome to inform the staff in person. In the end, he decided a telephone call to Margherita would suffice.

'Will he be alone or accompanied by Francesca?' she asked.

'That is unclear.'

'Should we assume he'll be working again?'

'That is the hope,' Gasparri said. 'But my friends at the Vatican tell me he's been in some sort of accident. Don't expect him to be in a good mood.'

'How will we tell the difference?'

'Be kind to him, Margherita. Apparently, the poor man's been through quite an ordeal.' And with that the line went dead.

The poor man's been through quite an ordeal . . .

Yes, she thought. *And now he's going to take it out on us.*

UNFORTUNATELY, Count Gasparri's predictions about the restorer's mood turned out to be accurate. Unlike in summer, when he had been predictably aloof, his moods now fluctuated between chilling silences and flashes of alarming temper. Francesca offered few clues about how he had sustained the injury, stating only that he had suffered 'a mishap' while working abroad. Naturally, the staff were left to speculate as to what had happened. But of one thing they were certain: the injury had left the restorer dangerously on edge.

At first, he did not venture beyond the walled garden. There, he would spend afternoons beneath the shade of the trellis, drinking his Orvieto wine and reading until his eye became too fatigued to continue.

Soon he felt strong enough to resume his walks. Some days, the woman accompanied him, but usually he walked alone, with only the dogs for company. Isabella greeted him each time he passed the stables, even though she usually received only a taciturn nod in return. With each passing day, he walked a little farther, and by the middle of October he was able to hike to the gate and back each morning. He even began venturing into the woods again.

ONE MORNING, the Villa dei Fiori, along with the rest of Europe, awoke to the stunning news that a disaster of unimaginable proportions had been narrowly averted. The story broke first in London, where the BBC reported that Scotland Yard was conducting 'major terrorism-related raids' in East London and in areas near Heathrow and Gatwick airports. Later that morning, the British prime minister went before the cameras to inform the nation that the security services had disrupted a major terrorist plot aimed at simultaneously destroying several airliners in British airspace. It was not the first time a plot such as this had been uncovered in Britain. What set this one apart, though, were the weapons involved: SA-18 shoulder-launch anti-aircraft missiles. British police had found twelve of the sophisticated weapons during their early-morning raids. Though the prime minister refused to say where the terrorists had obtained the missiles, he pointedly reminded reporters of the name of the country where the weapons were manufactured: Russia.

Ten minutes later, in Paris, the French president strode before the cameras at the Elysée Palace and announced that a similar round of police raids had been carried out that same morning in the suburbs of Paris and in the South of France. Twenty missiles had been found thus far. The French president said it was clear to him that the weapons had been supplied to the terrorists by a Russian source. He also suggested that the French security and intelligence services had played 'a major role in foiling the plot'.

Similar scenes played out in rapid succession in Madrid, Rome, Athens, Zurich, Copenhagen and, finally, in Washington, DC. Flanked by his senior national security staff, the president told the American people that eight SA-18 missiles had been discovered aboard a motor yacht bound for Miami from the Bahamas and six more had been found in the boot of a car attempting to enter the United States from Canada. Four suspected terrorists had been detained and were now undergoing interrogation. American and Israeli aircraft were said to be the primary targets of the terrorists.

By nightfall, all eyes were on Moscow. Shortly after 11 p.m., a spokesman for the Russian president finally issued a terse statement categorically denying any link between the terrorist plot and legitimate arms sales by Russia to its clients in the Middle East. If the missiles had indeed come from a Russian source, said the spokesman, then it was almost certainly a criminal act—one that would be investigated to the fullest extent possible by the Russian authorities. Within a few hours, however, the veracity of the Russian statement was called into question by a dramatic report in

London's *Daily Telegraph* written by Olga Sukhova, former editor-in-chief of *Moskovsky Gazeta*.

According to her front-page story, the missiles seized by European and American officials had originally been sold to the Democratic Republic of East Africa by Russian businessman and arms trafficker Ivan Kharkov. Kharkov had reportedly concluded the sale with the full knowledge that the weapons were to be transferred to an al-Qaeda affiliate in the Horn of Africa. The article also implicated Kharkov and his now-deceased chief of security, Arkady Medvedev, in the murders of *Gazeta* journalists Aleksandr Lubin and Boris Ostrovsky.

For the next few days, Olga Sukhova was a fixture on European and American television. So, too, was the man credited with facilitating her escape from Moscow earlier in the year: Colonel Grigori Bulganov of the FSB. He told tales of rampant corruption inside his old service and warned that the new masters of the Kremlin were nothing but KGB thugs who planned to confront the West at every turn.

By the end of the week, he and Olga Sukhova had both signed lucrative book deals. As for the man at the centre of the storm, Ivan Borisovich Kharkov, he had apparently vanished into thin air.

For a time, his grand palaces were surrounded day and night by reporters and cameramen. His assets had been seized; his bank accounts frozen. Finally, when it became clear Ivan was never coming back, the reporters moved on in search of other prey.

It was assumed by all that he had taken refuge somewhere inside Russia. How he had managed to get there from France, where he was last seen, was a matter of considerable contention.

Eventually, French aviation officials acknowledged that Ivan's private jet had departed Côte d'Azur International Airport on the morning of August 26, and that they *were* indeed aware of Ivan's involvement in the missile sale at the time of the flight in question. However, 'certain operational exigencies' required that Ivan be allowed to leave French soil. Those operational exigencies notwithstanding, French prosecutors now wanted Ivan back, as did their counterparts in Britain, where he faced a slew of criminal charges ranging from money laundering to involvement in a plot to commit an act of mass murder.

Forty-eight hours later, a photograph surfaced of Ivan and a young supermodel named Yekatarina Mazurov attending a Kremlin reception for the newly reelected Russian president. The Kremlin's only comment was that it was not possible under Russian law to extradite Mr Kharkov to face criminal charges. A week later, Ivan filed for divorce in a Russian court, accusing Elena Kharkov of sins ranging from infidelity to child abuse. Elena was not there to contest the charges. Elena, it seemed, had disappeared from the face of the earth.

None of this seemed to concern the staff of the Villa dei Fiori in Umbria, for they had more pressing matters with which to contend. There were crops to bring in and fences that needed mending. There was a horse with an injured leg and a leak in the roof that required fixing. And there was a melancholy man with a patch over one eye who feared he would never be able to work again. He could do nothing now but wait.

ARI SHAMRON telephoned a week later to invite himself to lunch. He arrived in a single embassy car, with Gilah at his side. The afternoon was windy and raw, so they ate indoors in the formal dining room with an olive-wood fire blazing in the open hearth. When lunch was over, Chiara and Gilah helped with the dishes. Gabriel and Shamron pulled on coats and walked along the gravel road between the umbrella pines. Shamron waited until they were a hundred yards from the villa before lighting his first Turkish cigarette. 'Don't tell Gilah,' he said. 'She's bothering me to quit again.'

'You should listen to her for once. Those things are going to kill you.'

'I'm as old as these hills, my son. Let me enjoy myself while I can.'

'Why didn't you tell me Gilah was coming with you?'

'I suppose it must have slipped my mind. We're going to Vienna to listen to Mozart next. Then we're going to London to see a play by Pinter.' Shamron made it sound as if he had been sentenced to a month in solitary.

'This is what people do when they retire, Ari. They travel. They relax.'

'I'm not *retired*. God, I hate that word.'

'Try to enjoy yourself, Ari—for Gilah's sake. She deserves a nice holiday in Europe.'

They walked in silence, Shamron trailing smoke like a steam engine. 'I hear we're sending a doctor up here tomorrow to remove your bandages.'

'Is that why you came? To see the great unveiling?'

'Gilah and I thought you would like to have some family around. Were we wrong to come?'

'Of course not, Ari. I just might not be very good company. That gorilla caused significant damage to my retina. Even under the best of circumstances, I'm going to have blurred vision for a while.'

'And the worst?'

'Significant loss of vision in one eye. Not exactly a helpful condition for someone who makes his living restoring paintings.'

'You make your *living* defending the State of Israel.' Greeted by Gabriel's silence, Shamron looked up at the treetops moving in the wind. 'Did I mention that Gilah and I had dinner at the Vatican last night with Monsignor Donati and His Holiness?'

'No, you didn't.'

'His Holiness was quite pleased that the Church was able to play a small role in Ivan's downfall. He's quite anxious it remain a secret, though.'

'You can see his point,' said Gabriel.

It was one of the many aspects of the affair that remained secret—the fact that Ivan's children, after leaving Saint-Tropez, had been taken to an isolated priory high in the Maritime Alps. They had stayed there for nearly a week—with the full knowledge and approval of the Supreme Pontiff—before boarding a CIA jet to the United States.

'Where are they?' Gabriel asked. 'Elena and the children?'

Shamron dropped his cigarette and crushed it out. 'I have no idea. She's Adrian's problem now. Ivan has started more than divorce proceedings. He's created a unit within his personal security service with one job: finding Elena and the children. He wants his children back. He wants Elena dead.'

'What about Olga and Grigori?'

'They're locked away in a safe house outside London, surrounded by armed guards. And so should you be.' Shamron didn't bother trying to conceal his irritation. 'If it were up to me, you'd be locked away someplace in Israel where Ivan would never think to look for you.'

'And you wonder why I'd rather be here.'

'Just don't think about setting foot outside this estate. Not until Ivan's had a chance to cool down.'

They had arrived at the stables. In an adjacent pen, a pair of pigs were rolling about in the mud. Shamron winced in disgust. 'I'm getting tired,' he said. 'Let's head back.'

They turned round and started towards the villa. Shamron produced an envelope from the breast pocket of his jacket and handed it to Gabriel. 'It's a letter from Elena,' he said. 'Adrian Carter had it couriered to Tel Aviv.'

'Did you read it?'

'Of course.'

Gabriel removed the letter and read it for himself.

'Are you up to it?' Shamron asked.

'I'll know after the great unveiling.'

'Maybe Gilah and I should stay here for a few days, just in case things don't go well.'

'What about Mozart and Pinter?'

'I'd rather be here'—he looked around theatrically—'with the pigs.'

'Then we'd love to have you.'

THE DOCTOR CAME the following morning. He wore a rabbinical beard and had the small, soft hands of a baby. He removed the dressing from Gabriel's eye, frowned heavily, and began snipping away the sutures.

'Let me know if anything I do hurts.'

'Trust me, you'll be the first to know.'

He shone a light directly into Gabriel's eye and frowned some more.

'How does it feel?'

'Like you're burning a hole in my cornea.'

The doctor switched off the light, then covered Gabriel's good eye. 'How many fingers am I holding up?'

'Four, I think, but I can't be sure.'

The doctor uncovered the good eye. He was holding up two fingers. He put some drops in the damaged eye that burned like battery acid and covered it with a black patch.

'Your retina looks remarkably good for what you've been through. You're a very lucky man. Wear the patch for a few days until your eye regains some of its strength. An hour on, an hour off. Avoid bright lights. And don't do anything that might give you unnecessary eyestrain.'

'How about painting?'

'Don't even think about it. Not for at least three days.'

THE DOCTOR'S OPTIMISM about the pace of his recovery turned out to be accurate. By the next morning, his vision had improved dramatically, and by the morning after it seemed almost normal. He felt ready to begin work on Elena's request but confined his efforts to preparing the canvas.

He slept poorly that night and woke at four. He tried to fall asleep again, but it was no use, so he slipped out of bed, headed downstairs, and started work. He applied the first layers of base paint, and by midday two small children were clearly visible on the canvas.

He took a break for lunch, then spent a second session before the canvas that lasted until dinner. He painted from memory, without even a photograph for reference, and with a swiftness and confidence he would not have thought possible a week earlier.

Chiara and the household staff knew better than to watch him while he worked, but Shamron was unaware of his rules and, with nothing else to occupy his time, was content now to sit silently at Gabriel's side as he worked, even if it meant forgoing his cigarettes.

'I should have left you at Bezalel in 1972,' he said late one night. 'I should have found someone else to execute those Black September murderers. You would have been one of the greatest artists of your generation.'

'I'm happy, Ari. I have Chiara.'

'Keep her close, Gabriel. Remember, *Ivan likes to break pretty things*.'

Gabriel laid down his brush, then stepped back and examined the painting for a long time, head tilted to one side. Chiara, who was watching from the top of the stairs, said, 'Is it finished?'

Gabriel was silent for a moment. 'Yes,' he said finally, 'it's finished. I just have to sign it.'

He dipped the brush in black paint and signed the name *Gabriel Allon* in the bottom left corner. 'Do you think she'll like it?'

'I'm sure she will. Is it finished now?'

'Not quite,' Gabriel said. 'I have to bake it for thirty minutes.'

'I should have left you at Bezalel,' Shamron said. 'You could have been great.'

DANIEL SILVA

Home: Washington, DC
Former profession: journalist
Website: danielsilvabooks.com

Moscow Rules is Daniel Silva's eleventh novel and the eighth featuring spy and art restorer Gabriel Allon. Below are extracts from a conversation with Daniel Silva, taken from his website.

Q: What are the Moscow Rules? Are they real?

A: They are real, and every intelligence officer and spy knows them. During the Cold War, Moscow was the toughest, most dangerous city in the world to work in, so the CIA created a set of operating principles. I tried to find an official list, but I discovered that the Agency never wrote them down. Some of the rules are chilling: 'Assume everyone you meet is under opposition control.' 'Assume every telephone is tapped and every room is bugged.' Some are hysterical: 'Murphy was right.' 'Technology will always let you down.' My personal favourite is: 'Don't look back. You are never completely alone.' That rule serves as the epigraph of the novel.

Q: Your thrillers take place all over the world, but this is the first time you've chosen to set a book in Russia. Why now?

A: Russia has been calling me for a long time. I grew up reading the classic novels of Cold War espionage and I studied Russian history and Soviet foreign policy. By the time I started writing novels, the Cold War was over and I'd always enjoyed the challenge of trying to catch history in the act. I knew enough about Russian history to bide my time. I told myself that, eventually, Russia would find a new tsar and challenge us again. The new tsar turned out to be Vladimir Putin, and his critics were soon dying under mysterious and violent circumstances. When Aleksandr Litvinenko was murdered in London in 2006 with a lethal dose of polonium-210, it was time for Gabriel Allon to go to Russia.

Q: You spent last summer in Moscow. What did you find?

A: I absolutely fell in love with Moscow. It's one of those places where you can't help but trip over history at every turn. It's a city of enormous contradictions. Within a few yards of Lenin's Tomb is some of the most expensive shopping in the world. Every night, we watched Russian millionaires making deals in the bar of our hotel. They dressed in the latest designer clothing, spoke fluent English, and were surrounded by bodyguards. Needless to say, I found it to be the perfect setting for a thriller.

Q: The action in *Moscow Rules* moves from Moscow to Italy, Israel, the Alps, the French Riviera and London. Did you spend time in those places, too?

A: Yes. That's the best part of my job. For example, at the start of the story, Gabriel is staying at an isolated cattle farm in Umbria. My family and I were lucky enough to stay on a farm just like it. I also spent a great deal of time chasing rich Russians around Western Europe, trying to get a glimpse of the way they're spending their money. And I can report that they're spending an enormous amount of it. In Courchevel, I visited a restaurant where the manager told me about a group of Russians who had just spent 300,000 euros for lunch. That's about a half million dollars. For lunch!

Q: You managed to get inside Lubyanka, the infamous former home of the KGB and current headquarters of its successor, the FSB. How did you get in, and what was it like?

A: The truth is, I am still not sure how we got in, but it was the experience of a life-time. We put in a request and waited. Finally, we were ordered to present ourselves at a side door of FSB headquarters, early on a Sunday morning. Waiting inside was a fit-looking colonel in his late fifties. He had a nice smile. He spoke only Russian, so our guide had to provide simultaneous translation. We followed him through darkened corridors and up darkened staircases. We didn't get to visit the notorious holding cells of Lubyanka, where poor Gabriel ends up in the story, but it was still fascinating.

Q: Your story deals with the dangers faced by Russian journalists. Were you able to talk to Russian reporters for your research?

A: I did, actually, and they were incredibly helpful. I was deeply moved by their courage and dedication. Russia is an extremely dangerous place to be a journalist. According to the Committee to Protect Journalists, forty-seven reporters, editors, cameramen and photographers have been killed in Russia since 1992. Fourteen of those deaths occurred during Putin's presidency. Very few have been solved or prose-cuted. I met a reporter who literally broke down in tears as he described the murder of his friend. It affected me deeply and had a profound impact on the book.

Q: Your last book was No 2 on the *New York Times* bestseller list, your highest ranking ever. Each one of your novels has been more successful than its predecessor. Why do you think Gabriel Allon has caught on the way he has?

A: No one is more surprised by the success of Gabriel and the series than I am. He really seems to have struck a chord with readers. There is no one else quite like him on the literary landscape: an Israeli assassin who also happens to be one of the world's finest art restorers and who lives in Italy under an assumed identity. He's not someone you'd actually like to spend a lot of time with for he's not the friendliest person. But he's incredibly gifted and very smart and he's by no means a gun-slinging, kill-all-the-bad-guys kind of superhero. He knows what it means to lose loved ones.

ELLY GRIFFITHS
THE CROSSING PLACES

When a child's remains are found buried
in a Norfolk saltmarsh, Detective Inspector
Harry Nelson asks Ruth Galloway, a local
forensic archaeologist, to date them.
But the results do not, as the police had
hoped, solve the ten-year-old mystery
of a missing local girl.
It's only when another disappearance
is reported that Ruth and Harry start
to find answers to tantalising mysteries
ancient and new . . .

Prologue

They wait for the tide and set out at first light.

It has rained all night and in the morning the ground is seething gently, the mist rising to join the overhanging clouds. Nelson calls for Ruth in an unmarked police car. He sits beside the driver and Ruth is in the back. They drive in silence to the car park near where the bones were found. As they drive along the Saltmarsh road, the only sounds are the sudden, staccato crackle of the police radio and the driver's heavy, cold-clogged breathing. Nelson says nothing. There is nothing to say.

They get out of the car and walk across the rain-sodden grass towards the marsh. The wind is whispering through the reeds and here and there they see glimpses of still, sullen water, reflecting the grey sky. At the edge of the marshland, Ruth stops, looking for the first sunken post, the twisting shingle path that leads through the treacherous water to the mud flats. When she finds it, half submerged by brackish water, she sets out.

Silently, they cross the marshes. As they get nearer the sea, the mist disperses and the sun starts to filter through the clouds. At the henge circle, the tide is out and the sand glitters in the early-morning light. Ruth kneels on the ground as she saw Erik doing all those years ago. Gently, she stirs the quivering mud with her trowel.

Suddenly everything is still; even the seabirds stop their mad skirling and calling up above. Or maybe they are still there and she just doesn't hear them. In the background she can hear Nelson breathing hard but Ruth herself feels strangely calm. Even when she sees it, the tiny arm still wearing the christening bracelet, even then she feels nothing.

She had known what she was going to find.

Chapter 1

Waking is like rising from the dead. The slow climb out of sleep, shapes appearing out of blackness, the alarm clock ringing like the last trump. Ruth flings out an arm and sends the alarm crashing to the floor, where it carries on ringing reproachfully. Groaning, she levers herself upright and pulls up the blind. Still dark. It's just not right, she tells herself, wincing as her feet touch the cold floorboards. Neolithic man would have gone to sleep when the sun set and woken when it rose. What makes us think this is the right way round? Falling asleep on the sofa during *Newsnight*, then dragging herself upstairs to lie sleepless over a Rebus book, listening to the World Service on the radio, counting Iron Age burial sites to make herself sleep and now this—waking in the darkness feeling like death.

In the shower, the water unglues her eyes and sends her hair streaming down her back. This is baptism, if you like. Ruth's parents are Born Again Christians and are fans of Full Immersion For Adults (capitals obligatory). Ruth can quite see the attraction, apart from the slight problem of not believing in God. Still, her parents are Praying For Her (capitals again).

Ruth rubs herself vigorously with a towel and stares unseeingly into the steamy mirror. She knows what she will see and the knowledge is no more comforting than her parents' prayers. Shoulder-length brown hair, blue eyes, pale skin and however she stands on the scales, which are at present banished to the broom cupboard, she weighs twelve and a half stone. She sighs (I am not defined by my weight, fat is a state of mind) and squeezes toothpaste onto her brush. She has a very beautiful smile, but she isn't smiling now and so this too is low on the list of comforts.

Clean, she pads back into the bedroom. She has lectures today so will have to dress slightly more formally than usual. Black trousers, black shapeless top. She likes colour and fabric; in fact, she has quite a weakness for sequins, bugle beads and diamanté. You wouldn't know this from her wardrobe though. A row of dark trousers and loose, dark jackets. The drawers in her pine dressing-table are full of black jumpers, long cardigans and opaque tights. She used to wear jeans until she hit size sixteen and now favours cords, black, of course. Jeans are too young for her anyhow. She will be forty next year.

Dressed, she negotiates the stairs. The cottage has steep stairs, more like a ladder than anything else. 'I'll never be able to manage those,' her mother had said on her only visit. Who's asking you to? Ruth had replied silently. Her parents had stayed at the local B&B as Ruth has only one bedroom; going upstairs was strictly unnecessary (there is a downstairs loo but it is by the kitchen, which her mother considers unsanitary). The stairs lead directly into the sitting room: sanded wooden floor, sofa, TV, books covering every available surface. Archaeology books mostly but also murder mysteries, cookery books, travel guides, doctor–nurse romances.

Ruth switches on the kettle and puts bread into the toaster. Then she collects her lecture notes and sits at the table by the front window. Beyond her front garden, with its wind-blown grass and broken blue fence, there is nothingness. Just miles of marshland, spotted with stunted gorse and criss-crossed by treacherous streams. Sometimes, at this time of year, you see flocks of geese, wheeling across the sky, feathers turning pink in the rays of the rising sun. But today, on this grey winter morning, there is not a living creature as far as the eye can see. Everything is pale and washed out, grey-green merging to grey-white as marsh meets sky. Far off is the sea, a line of darker grey. It is utterly desolate and Ruth has no idea why she loves it so.

She eats her toast and drinks her tea (she prefers coffee but is saving herself for a proper espresso at the university). As she does so, she leafs through her lecture notes. 'Gender and Prehistoric Technology', 'Excavating Artefacts', 'Life and Death in the Mesolithic', 'The Role of Animal Bone in Excavations'. Although it is only early November, the Christmas term will soon be over and this will be her last week of lectures. She teaches only post-graduates these days, and misses the casual, hung-over good humour of the undergraduates. Her students are so *keen*, waylaying her after lectures to talk about Lindow Man and Boxgrove Man and whether women would have played a significant role in prehistoric society.

Thought for the Day seeps into her unconscious, reminding her that it is time to leave. She puts her plate and cup in the sink and leaves food for her cats, Sparky and Flint. As she does so, she answers the ever-present sardonic interviewer in her head. 'OK, I'm a single, overweight woman on my own and I have cats. What's the big deal? And, OK, sometimes I do speak to them but I don't imagine that they answer back and I don't pretend that I'm any more to them than a convenient food dispenser.' Right on cue, Flint, a large ginger tomcat, squeezes through the cat flap and fixes her with an unblinking, golden stare.

Ruth strokes him and goes back into the sitting room to put her papers into her rucksack. She winds a red scarf (her only concession to colour: even fat people can buy scarves) round her neck and puts on her anorak. Then she turns out the lights and leaves the cottage. It's ten to nine.

Ruth's cottage is one in a line of three on the edge of the Saltmarsh. One is occupied by the warden of the bird sanctuary, the other by weekenders who come down in summer, have lots of barbecues and park their 4x4 in front of Ruth's view. The road is frequently flooded in spring and autumn and often impassable by midwinter. 'Why don't you live somewhere more convenient?' her colleagues ask. Ruth can't explain how a girl born and brought up in London can feel such a pull to these inhospitable marshlands, these desolate mud flats, this lonely, unrelenting view. It was research that brought her to the Saltmarsh but she doesn't know what makes her stay. 'I'm used to it,' is all she says. 'Anyway, the cats would hate to move.' And they laugh. *Good old Ruth, devoted to her cats, child substitutes of course, shame she never got married, she's really very pretty when she smiles.*

Today, though, the road is clear, with only the ever-present wind blowing a thin line of salt onto her windscreen.

Ruth teaches at the University of North Norfolk, just outside King's Lynn. She teaches archaeology, a new discipline there, specialising in forensic archaeology, which is newer still. Phil, her head of department, frequently jokes that there is nothing new about archaeology and Ruth always smiles dutifully. It is only a matter of time, she thinks, before Phil gets himself a bumper sticker. *'Archaeologists dig it.'* *'You're never too old for an archaeologist.'* Her special interest is bones. Last year her students bought her a life-size cut-out of Leonard 'Bones' McCoy from *Star Trek*. He stands at the top of her stairs, terrifying the cats.

The university consists of long, low buildings linked by glass walkways. On grey mornings like this, it looks inviting, the buttery light shining out across the car parks, a row of dwarf lamps lighting the way to the archaeology building. Closer up, it is less impressive. Though the building is only ten years old, cracks are appearing in the concrete façade, there is graffiti on the walls and a third of the dwarf lamps don't work. Ruth hardly notices this, however, as she parks in her usual space and hauls out her heavy rucksack—heavy because it is half full of bones.

Climbing the staircase to her office, she scrabbles for her key card in the corridor. Two people approach her. One is Phil, the head of department, the other she doesn't recognise. He is tall and dark, with greying hair cut very short and there is something hard about him, something contained and slightly dangerous that makes her think that he can't be a student and certainly not a lecturer. She stands aside to let them pass but, to her surprise, Phil stops in front of her and speaks in a serious voice.

'Ruth. There's someone who wants to meet you.'

A student after all, then. Ruth starts to paste a welcoming smile on her face but it is frozen by Phil's next words.

'This is Detective Chief Inspector Harry Nelson. He wants to talk to you about a murder.'

'Suspected murder,' Detective Chief Inspector Nelson says quickly.

'This is Dr Ruth Galloway,' says Phil. 'She's our forensics expert.'

'Pleased to meet you,' says Nelson without smiling. He gestures towards the locked door of Ruth's office. 'Can we?'

Ruth slides in her key card and pushes open the door. Her office is barely six feet across. One wall is taken up by bookshelves, another by the door and a third by a grubby window with a view of an even grubbier ornamental lake. Ruth's desk squats against the fourth wall, with a framed poster of Indiana Jones—ironic, she always explains hastily—hanging over it. When she has tutorials the students frequently spill out into the corridor and she props the door open with her cat doorstop. But now she shuts the door and Phil and the detective stand there looking too big for the space. Nelson, in particular, seems to block out the light as he stands, scowling, in the front of the window. He looks too broad, too tall, too *grown-up* for the room.

'Please . . .' Ruth gestures to the chairs stacked by the door. Phil makes a great performance of giving Nelson his chair first, practically wiping away the dust with his jumper sleeve.

Ruth squeezes behind her desk, which gives her an illusion of security. Nelson leans back, crosses his legs and addresses her in a brisk monotone. He has a slight northern accent, which serves only to make him sound more efficient, as if he hasn't time for the slow vowels of Norfolk.

'We've found some bones,' he says. 'They seem to be a child's but they look old. I need to know how old.'

Phil chips in eagerly. 'Where did you find them, Inspector?'

'Near the bird sanctuary. On the saltmarsh.'

Phil looks at Ruth. 'But that's right where you . . .'

'I know it,' Ruth cuts in. 'What makes you think the bones look old?'

'They're brown, discoloured, but they look in good condition. I thought that was your area?' he says, suddenly aggressive.

'It is,' says Ruth calmly. 'I assume that's why you're here.'

'Well, would you be able to tell if they are modern or not?' asks Nelson, again sounding rather belligerent.

'A recent discovery is usually obvious,' says Ruth, 'You can tell by appearance and surface. Older bones are more tricky. Sometimes it's almost impossible to tell fifty-year-old bones from two-thousand-year-old. You need radiocarbon dating for that.'

'Professor Galloway is an expert on bone preservation.' This is Phil again. 'She's worked in Bosnia, on the war graves . . .'

'Will you come and look?' Nelson interrupts.

Ruth pretends to consider but, of course, she is utterly fascinated. Bones! On the saltmarsh! Where she did that first unforgettable dig with Erik. It could be anything. It could be a find. It could be . . .

'You suspect it's a murder?' she asks.

Nelson looks uncomfortable for the first time. 'I'd rather not say,' he says heavily. 'Not at the present time. Will you come and look?'

Ruth stands up. 'I could come in my lunch break.'

'I'll send a car for you at twelve,' says Nelson.

Much to Ruth's secret disappointment, Nelson does not send a police car complete with flashing blue light. Instead he appears himself, driving a muddy Mercedes. She is waiting, as agreed, by the main gate and he does not even get out of the car, merely leans over and opens the passenger door. Ruth climbs in, feeling fat, as she always does in cars.

Nelson glances at Ruth's rucksack. 'Got everything you need?'

'Yes.' She has brought her instant excavation kit: pointing trowel, small hand shovel, plastic freezer bags for samples, tapes, notebook, pencils, paintbrushes, compass, digital camera. She has also changed into trainers and is wearing a reflective jacket. She is annoyed to find herself thinking that she must look a complete mess.

'So you live out the Saltmarsh way?' Nelson says, pulling out across the traffic with a squeal of tyres. He drives like a maniac.

'Yes,' says Ruth, feeling defensive. 'On New Road.'

'New Road!' Nelson lets out a bark of laughter. 'I thought only twitchers lived out there.'

'Well, the warden of the bird sanctuary is one of my neighbours,' says Ruth, keeping one foot clamped on an imaginary brake.

'I wouldn't fancy it,' says Nelson. 'Too isolated.'

'I like it,' says Ruth. 'I did a dig there and never left.'

'A dig? Archaeology?'

'Yes.' Ruth is remembering that summer, ten years ago. Sitting round the campfire in the evenings, eating burnt sausages and singing corny songs. The sound of birdsong in the mornings and the marsh blooming purple with sea lavender. The time when sheep trampled their tents at night. The time when Peter got stranded on the tidal marsh and Erik had to rescue him, crawling on hands and knees across the mud flats. The excitement when they found that first wooden post, proof that the henge existed. She remembers the exact sound of Erik's voice as he turned and shouted at them across the incoming tide, 'We've found it!'

She turns to Nelson. 'We were looking for a henge.'

'A henge? Like Stonehenge.'

'Yes. All it means is a circular bank with a ditch round it. Usually with posts inside the circle.'

'I read somewhere that Stonehenge is just a big sundial. A way of telling the time.'

'Well, we don't know exactly what it was for,' says Ruth, 'but it's safe to say that it involves ritual of some kind.'

Nelson shoots a strange look at her. 'Ritual?'

'Yes. Worship, offerings, sacrifices.'

'Sacrifices?' echoes Nelson. He seems genuinely interested now, the faintly condescending note disappearing from his voice.

'Well, sometimes we find evidence of sacrifices. Pots, spears, animal bones, sometimes human bones.'

There is a silence, then Nelson says, 'Funny place for one of those henge things, isn't it? Right out to sea.'

'This wasn't sea then. Landscapes change. Ten thousand years ago this country was still linked to the continent. You could walk to Scandinavia.'

'You're joking!'

'No. King's Lynn was once a huge tidal lake. That's what Lynn means. It's the Celtic word for lake.'

Nelson turns to look at her. 'So if this area wasn't sea, what was it?'

'Flat marshland. We think the henge was on the edge of a marsh.'

'Still seems a funny place to build something like that.'

'Marshland was very important in prehistory,' explains Ruth. 'It's a kind of symbolic landscape. We think that it was important because it was a kind of link between the land and the sea, or between life and death.'

Nelson snorts. 'Come again?'

'Well, marsh isn't dry land and it isn't sea. It's a sort of mixture of both. We know it was very special or sacred to prehistoric man.'

'How do we know?'

'We've found objects left on the edge of marshes. Offerings to the gods. And sometimes bodies. Have you heard of bog bodies? Lindow Man?'

'Might have,' says Nelson cautiously.

'Bodies buried in peat are almost perfectly preserved. But some people think the bodies were buried in the bogs to appease the gods.'

Nelson shoots her a look. They are approaching the saltmarsh now, driving towards the visitor car park. Notices listing the various birds to be found on the marshes stand around forlornly, battered by the wind. A boarded-up kiosk advertises ice creams, their lurid colours faded now. It seems impossible to imagine people picnicking here, enjoying ice creams in the sun. The place seems made for the wind and the rain.

The car park is empty apart from a solitary police car. The occupant gets out as they approach and stands there, looking cold and fed up.

'Dr Ruth Galloway,' Nelson introduces, 'Detective Sergeant Clough.'

DS Clough nods glumly. Ruth gets the impression that hanging about on a windy marshland is not his favourite way of passing the time. Nelson, though, looks positively eager, jogging slightly on the spot.

He leads the way along a gravel path marked 'Visitors' Trail'. They pass a wooden hide, built on stilts over the marsh. It is empty, apart from some crisp wrappers and an empty can of coke on the surrounding platform.

Nelson points at the litter and barks, 'Bag it.' It occurs to Ruth that police work must be similar to archaeology. She, too, would bag anything found at a site, labelling it carefully. She, too, would be prepared to search for days, weeks, in the hope of finding something significant. She, too, is concerned with death.

Ruth is out of breath before they find the spot marked out with the blue and white police tape. Nelson is now some ten yards ahead, hands in pockets, head forward as if sniffing the air. DS Clough plods behind him, holding a plastic bag containing the rubbish from the hide.

Beyond the tape is a shallow hole, half filled by muddy water. Ruth ducks under the tape and kneels down to look. Clearly visible in the rich mud are human bones.

'How did you find this?' she asks.

It is Clough who answers. 'Member of the public, walking her dog.'

Ruth takes a quick photo of the site and sketches a brief map in her note-book. This is the far west of the marsh; she has never dug here before. The beach, where the henge was found, is about two miles away to the east. Squatting down on the muddy soil, she begins laboriously baling out the water, using a plastic beaker from her excavation kit.

When the hole is almost free from water, Ruth can clearly see bones sticking out of the mud. Her heart starts to beat faster. Carefully she scoops out another beakerful of water and only then reaches into the mud and pulls free one of the bones. It emerges with a slight popping sound.

Sitting back on her haunches she examines the bone before placing it inside a freezer bag. It is a shin bone, but what is most exciting to Ruth is that it is clearly still attached to flesh. Shrivelled flesh, coloured dark brown from the peaty soil.

'Well?' Nelson is leaning eagerly over her shoulder.

'It's a child's,' says Ruth hesitantly, 'but . . .'

Where is the rest of the body? Slowly she reaches for her trowel. She mustn't rush things. She has seen entire excavations ruined because of one moment's carelessness. So, with Nelson grinding his teeth beside her, she gently lifts away the sodden soil. A hand, slightly clenched, wearing a bracelet of what looks like grass, lies exposed in the trench.

'Bloody hell!' murmurs Nelson over her shoulder.

Ruth lifts out the hand. She is working almost in a trance now. She plots the find on her map. Next she takes a photograph and places the hand care-fully in a freezer bag. Then she starts to dig again.

This time her trowel grates against metal. Ruth reaches down and pulls the object free from the mud. It gleams dully in the winter light: a lump of twisted metal, semicircular in shape.

'What's that?' Nelson's voice seems to come from another world.

'I think it's a torque,' says Ruth dreamily. 'A necklace. Probably from the Iron Age.'

'The Iron Age? When was that?'

'About two thousand years ago,' says Ruth.

Clough lets out a bark of laughter. Nelson turns away without a word.

NELSON GIVES RUTH a lift back to the university. He seems sunk in gloom, but Ruth is in a state of high excitement. The body must surely be from the Iron Age, that time of ritual slaughter and fabulous treasure hoards. It's a long way from the henge but could the two discoveries possibly be linked?

The henge is Bronze Age, some 2,000 years before the Iron Age. But surely another find on the same site can't be a coincidence? She can't wait to tell Phil. Perhaps they should inform the press; the publicity might be just what the department needs.

Nelson says suddenly, 'You're sure about the date?'

'I'm pretty sure the torque is Iron Age and it seems logical that the body was buried with it. But we can do carbon-14 dating to be sure.'

'What's that?'

'Carbon 14 is present in the atmosphere. Plants take it in, animals eat the plants, we eat the animals. We all absorb carbon 14 and, when we die, we stop absorbing it and the carbon 14 in our bones starts to break down. By measuring the amount of it left in a bone, we can tell its age.'

'How accurate is the test?'

'Well, it can be accurate within a range of a few hundred years. So we'll be able to tell if the bones are from the Iron Age.'

'Which was when exactly?'

'I can't be exact, but roughly eight hundred BC to AD forty-five.'

Nelson asks, 'Why would an Iron Age body be buried here?'

'As an offering to the gods. Possibly it would have been staked down. Did you see the grass round the wrist? That could have been a rope.'

'Jesus. Staked down and left to die?'

'Maybe, or maybe it was dead before they left it. The stakes could be just to keep it in place. Why did you think the bones might be modern?'

Nelson sighs. 'Some ten years ago there was a child that went missing. Near here. We never found the body. I thought it might be her.'

'Her?'

'Her name was Lucy Downey.' Nelson sighs again. 'It's funny, what you said earlier. About ritual and that. There was all sorts of rubbish in some letters sent to me about Lucy Downey. But one thing they said was that Lucy had been a sacrifice and that we'd find her where the earth meets the sky.'

'Where the earth meets the sky,' Ruth repeats. 'That could be anywhere.'

'Yes, but this place, it feels like the end of the world somehow. That's why, when I heard that bones had been found . . . It's hard for the parents when they don't know. Finding a body, it gives them a chance to grieve.'

'You're sure she's dead then?'

Nelson is silent for a moment, concentrating on overtaking a lorry. 'Yes,' he says at last. 'Five-year-old child, goes missing in November, no sign of her for ten years. She's dead all right.'

'November?'

'Yes. Almost ten years ago to the day.'

'The parents,' Ruth asks. 'Do they still live nearby?'

'Yes, they live out Fakenham way.' He swerves to avoid a lorry. Ruth closes her eyes. 'Cases like this,' he goes on, 'it's usually the parents.'

Ruth is shocked. 'The parents who killed the child?'

Nelson's voice is matter-of-fact, the northern vowels very flat. 'Nine cases out of ten. You get the parents all distraught, news conferences, floods of tears, then we find the child buried in the back garden.'

'How awful.'

'Yes. But this case, I'm sure it wasn't them. Nice couple, not young, been trying for a baby for years, then Lucy came along. They adored her.'

'How dreadful for them,' says Ruth inadequately.

'Dreadful, yes.' Nelson's voice is expressionless. 'But they never blamed me or the team. They still send me Christmas cards. That's why I'—he falters—'that's why I wanted a result for them.'

They are at the university now. Nelson screeches to a halt. Students turn and stare. Although it is only two thirty, it is already getting dark.

'Thanks for the lift,' says Ruth. 'I'll get the bones dated for you.'

'Thank you,' says Nelson. He looks at Ruth for what seems to be the first time. She is acutely aware of her wild hair and mud-stained clothes. 'This discovery, might it be important for you?'

'Yes,' says Ruth. 'It might be.'

'Glad someone's happy.' As soon as Ruth is out of the car he drives off without saying goodbye. She doesn't think she will ever see him again.

Chapter 2

Nelson cuts across two lanes of traffic as he heads into King's Lynn. His car is unmarked but he makes it a point of honour always to drive as if he is pursuing a suspect.

He is no fan of his adopted county. He is a northerner, born in Blackpool. He went to the Catholic grammar school and joined the police as a cadet, aged sixteen. From the start, he'd loved the job. The camaraderie, the long hours, the physical exertion, the sense of doing something worthwhile. And, though he would never admit it, he'd even liked the paperwork. Nelson is methodical; he likes lists and schedules, he is excellent at cutting through crap. He'd risen through the ranks and soon had a pretty good life: satisfying work, congenial mates, pub on Friday nights, the match on Saturdays, golf on Sundays.

But then the job in Norfolk had come up and his wife Michelle had been on at him to take it. Promotion, more money and 'the chance to live in the country'. Who in their right mind, thinks Nelson, would want to live in the bloody country? It's all cows and mud and locals who look like the result of several generations of keeping it in the family. But he'd given in and they had moved to King's Lynn. Michelle had started working for a posh hairdressing salon. They'd sent the girls to private schools and they'd come back laughing at his accent ('It's not bath, Daddy, it's ba-arth . . .'). He'd done well, become a detective inspector in double-quick time, people had talked of higher things . . . until Lucy Downey.

Nelson turns into the station car park. He is thinking of Lucy. He has always been sure that she is buried somewhere near the saltmarsh and, when the bones had been found, he had thought that he was near an ending at last. Not a happy ending, but at least an ending. And now this Dr Ruth Galloway tells him that the bones are from some bloody Stone Age body. All that stuff she'd spouted about henges and burials and being able to walk to Scandinavia—he'd thought she was taking the piss. But, when they got to the site, he could see she was a professional. He admired the way that she did everything carefully, making notes, taking photos, sifting the evidence. It's the way that police work should be done. Not that she'd ever make a policewoman. Too overweight, for one thing. What would Michelle say about a woman so out of condition that she is out of breath after a five-minute walk? She would be horrified. But, then, he can't think of any situation in which Michelle would meet Ruth Galloway. She's not likely to start popping into the salon, not from what he could see of her hair.

But she interests him. Like all forceful people, he prefers people who stand up to him. In his job, that doesn't happen often. People either despise him or kowtow to him. Ruth had done neither. She had looked him in the face, coolly, as an equal. He thinks he's never met anyone, any *woman*, quite as sure of themselves as Ruth Galloway. Even the way she dresses— baggy clothes, trainers—seems to be a way of saying she doesn't care what anyone thinks. She's not going to tart herself up just to please men. Not that there's anything wrong with pleasing men, muses Nelson, kicking open the door to his office, but there's something refreshing about a woman who doesn't care whether or not she's attractive.

And the things she said about ritual were interesting too. Nelson is frowning as he sits behind his desk. Talking about ritual and sacrifice has brought it all back: the days spent in fingertip searches, the anguished meetings with the parents, the station full to bursting, teams brought in from six different forces, all dedicated to finding one little girl. All in vain.

Nelson sighs. However much he tries not to, he knows that, before he goes home tonight, he will read through the Lucy Downey files.

IT IS PITCH BLACK by the time Ruth drives home, edging carefully along New Road. There are ditches on both sides of the road and the merest twitch on the wheel can send you plunging ignominiously downwards. Her headlights illuminate the raised tarmac of the road; the land drops away on either side so that she seems to be driving into nothingness. Nothing but the road ahead and the sky above. *Where the earth meets the sky.*

She parks outside her broken blue fence and pulls her rucksack out of the boot. The weekenders' house is in darkness but the warden has a light on upstairs. She assumes he goes to bed early to be up for the dawn chorus. Flint appears on her doorstep mewing for admittance even though he has his own cat flap and has, in fact, been snoozing inside all day. Ruth opens the door. Sparky, a small black cat with a white nose, is sleeping on the sofa. Ruth calls to her but she stays put. Sparky is a reserved character, unlike Flint who is now weaving around Ruth's legs.

'Stop it, you stupid cat.'

She drops her rucksack on the table and puts down food for the cats. Her answering-machine light is flashing. When she presses PLAY her mother's voice, aggrieved and slightly breathless, fills the room.

'. . . whether you're coming for Christmas. Really, Ruth, you could be a bit more considerate. I heard from Simon weeks ago. I assume you'll be coming because I can't imagine you'll want to spend Christmas on your own in that awful . . .'

Ruth clicks DELETE, breathing hard. Sloshing wine angrily into a glass, she composes a reply. She will never give it in person but it is comforting to stomp around the kitchen, cutting her mother down to size.

'The reason I haven't told you about Christmas is that I dread coming home and hearing you drone on about the Christ child and the true meaning of Christmas. Simon has been in touch because he's a creep. And if I don't come home I'll be with my friends or on some tropical island, not alone. And my house isn't awful, it's a hundred times better than your Eltham semi with its pine cladding and china ornaments. And Peter didn't finish with me, I finished with him.'

She has added the last one because she knows from experience that her mother will bring up the subject of Peter over Christmas. 'Peter sent us a card . . . such a shame . . . do you ever hear? . . . you know he's married now?' That her daughter could voluntarily end a relationship with a nice-looking, eligible man is something that Ruth's mother will never accept. Ruth noticed the same tendency in her friends and colleagues when she announced that she and Peter were no longer together. 'I'm so sorry . . . Has he found someone else? . . . Don't worry, he'll come back . . .' Ruth explained she had ended the relationship five years ago for the simple reason that she no longer loved him. 'That's right,' people would say, ignoring her. 'He'll soon get bored with the new woman. In the meantime, pamper yourself, have a massage, maybe even lose some . . .'

To cheer herself up, Ruth boils the water for some nice, fattening pasta and rings Erik. Her first tutor, Erik Anderssen, predictably nicknamed Erik the Viking, was the man responsible for getting her into forensic archaeology. He has been a huge influence on her life and is now a close friend. Smiling, she conjures him up: silver-blond hair pulled back in a ponytail, faded jeans, unravelling sweater. She knows he will be passionately interested in today's find.

Erik the Viking has, appropriately enough, moved back to Norway. Ruth visited him last summer, in his log cabin by the lake. She had freezing morning swims followed by steaming saunas, ate Magda's wonderful food and talked to Erik about Mayan civilisation as the stars came out at night. Magda, his wife, a voluptuous blonde goddess whose beauty manages to make you feel better, not worse, about yourself, is another good friend. *She* never once mentioned Peter, even though she had been there that summer when Ruth and Peter first fell in love; had, in fact, by her tact and gentle benevolence, actually brought them together.

But Erik is out. Ruth leaves a message and, feeling restless, gets the battered lump of metal out of her rucksack and examines it. Still in its freezer bag, carefully dated and labelled, it stares back at her. Phil had wanted her to leave it in the department safe but she had refused. She wanted to bring the torque home, to the Saltmarsh, at least for one night.

Stained dark green from its long immersion in the marsh, the metal nonetheless has a burnished sheen that looks like it might be gold. The piece in her hand is barely six inches long but she can imagine it as a full half-circle, imagine it round the neck of some savage beauty. Or round the neck of a child, a sacrificial victim?

She remembers Nelson's disappointment when he learned that the bones were not those of Lucy Downey. Ruth knows that for him the Iron Age bones are an irrelevancy, but for her they are as real as the five-year-old girl who went missing all those years ago. Why were the bones left on the edges of the marsh? Was she (from their size, Ruth thinks the bones are female but she cannot be sure) left for dead, sinking in the treacherous mud? Or was she killed somewhere else and buried at the start of the marshland, to mark the beginning of the sacred landscape?

When her pasta is cooked, Ruth eats it at the table by the window, Erik's book, *The Shivering Sand*, propped up in front of her. The title is from *The Moonstone* by Wilkie Collins and Ruth turns again to the first page where Erik quotes Collins's description of the sands.

> The last of the evening light was fading away; and over all the desolate place there hung a still and awful calm. The heave of the main ocean on the great sandbank out in the bay, was a heave that made no sound. The inner sea lay lost and dim, without a breath of wind to stir it. Patches of nasty ooze floated, yellow-white on the dead surface of the water. Scum and slime shone faintly in certain places, where the last of the light still caught them on the two great spits of rock jutting out, north and south, into the sea. It was now the time of the turn of the tide: and even as I stood there waiting, the broad brown face of the quicksand began to dimple and quiver —the only moving thing in all the horrid place.

Collins, surely, had understood about the haunted, uncanny places that lie between the sea and land. Ruth remembers that at least one character in *The Moonstone* meets their death on the sands. She remembers another phrase, 'What the Sand gets, the Sand keeps forever.' But the saltmarsh had given up some of its secrets: first the henge and now this body, just waiting there for Ruth to discover them. Surely there *must* be a link.

Reading again about the discovery of the henge (Erik wrote three books on the strength of the find), Ruth remembers how eerie it had looked in that first morning light: like a shipwreck that had risen to the surface, the wooden posts forming a sombre ring, black against the sky. She remembers Erik telling fireside stories about Norse water spirits: nixes, shape-shifters who lure unwary travellers into the water; Nokke, river sprites that sing at dawn and dusk. Water as a source of life and place of death . . .

Ruth reads on, her pasta forgotten. She has no lectures tomorrow; she will go back to the place where the bones were buried.

BUT IN THE MORNING it is raining; driving, slanting rain that batters against the windows and envelops the marsh in an impenetrable grey haze. Frustrated, Ruth busies herself with work, but she keeps coming back to the torque, which is lying in its freezer bag on the table by the window. Sensing her interest, Flint jumps up and sits heavily on the bag. Ruth pushes him off. She doesn't want Phil to notice the cat hairs. He is apt to be whimsical about the cats, calling them 'Ruth's familiars'. She grits her teeth. He is not going to be whimsical about this find. Phil has always been rather sceptical about Erik the Viking and his views on ritual landscape. The henge is probably late Neolithic. For the Iron Age people it was already ancient, probably as much of a mystery to them as it is to us. Did they bury this body in the mud to symbolise the beginning of this mystic landscape? Or was the victim ritually killed to appease the water spirits? If Ruth can prove a link between the body and the henge, then the whole area becomes significant. The Saltmarsh could become a major archaeological site.

By lunch time she thinks that the weather is improving slightly. She goes out as far as the gate and the rain is soft and friendly on her face. The trench will have filled with water and she can do no real work on her own, but she makes up her mind to walk to the site. It's not far, maybe a mile, and the exercise will do her good. She puts on a sou'wester and waders, puts a torch in her pocket and shrugs her rucksack onto her back. She's just going for a look, that's all. A nice brisk walk before it gets dark. Better than sitting at home wondering and eating biscuits.

At first it is pleasant. She is walking with her back to the wind and the sou'wester keeps her dry. In her pocket she has the very same Ordnance Survey map that they used on the henge dig. Looking at it earlier, she saw the henge marked in yellow, with green stickers where other pieces of prehistoric wood were found. They seemed to form a line radiating out from the henge and Erik thought at the time that they might have been part of a path, or causeway. Could the path be leading to Ruth's bones?

Rather than following the road to the car park, Ruth strikes out west, following a path intended for birdwatchers. As long as she sticks to the path she will be fine. The marsh lies on either side of her, huge clumps of reeds and mile upon mile of windswept grass. The ground looks solid enough but she knows from experience that it is full of hidden pools, treacherous and deep. When the tide comes in, the sea will come halfway up the marsh, covering the ground swiftly and silently. It was here that Peter was marooned all those years ago, stuck between the tidal and the freshwater marshes, lying on his face in the muddy water, clinging to a piece of driftwood, while Erik crept towards him across the mud flats shouting words of encouragement in Norwegian.

Ruth plods along the path. It is very narrow and the mist means she can see only a few yards in front of her. The rain falls steadily and the sky is heavy and grey. She disturbs a flock of snipe, who zigzag into the air, but otherwise she is quite alone. She hums as she walks, thinking of Erik and Peter and of the enchanted summer on the Saltmarsh. She thinks of the druids who came and camped out by the henge. Erik had been on their side, she remembers. After all, he had said, this is what it was built for, not for scientific study in a museum. But the university, who were sponsoring the dig, had wanted the timbers moved. They were being eroded by the tide, they had argued, they needed to be moved for own safety. 'But they were *meant* to be eroded,' Erik had argued. 'Life and death, ebb and flow, that's what it's all about.'

But Erik had lost and the timbers were removed to the university.

At last Ruth can see the hide where Nelson ordered Clough to bag up the litter. She can even see the car park, deserted now, of course. The ground is firmer here and she walks quickly despite being out of breath (she really *must* start going to the gym in January). The police tape is still fluttering in the breeze and Ruth ducks underneath it.

As she suspected, the trench is now almost filled with water. Ruth takes out her beaker and starts to scoop away water. She cannot hope to empty the trench but she just wants to see if there is anything else visible in the soil. Phil has promised to send a team from the university to excavate properly but she wants to see it first. This is her discovery.

After about half an hour, maybe more, she thinks she sees something. A dull, bronze-green gleam in the rich, dark soil. Gently she brushes away soil from its edges. It looks like another torque. Trembling, she takes out her original map of the site and marks in the new find. A second torque could mean the beginnings of a hoard, a ritual depositing of treasure.

It is definitely another torque, battered and scrunched up. But Ruth can see that this torque is intact. She can see both ends, rounded and smooth compared with the plaited quality of the rest of the metal. Ruth is sure it is from the same period—early to middle Iron Age. Is this a votive hoard? One find looks like chance, two starts to look like a ritual.

She sits back on her heels, her arms aching. It is only then that she realises how dark it has become. She looks at her watch. Four o'clock! The walk can only have taken half an hour so she has been squatting here in the mud for nearly two hours. She must be getting back. She straightens up, puts the bag containing the torque in her pocket and pulls up her hood. The rain, which had settled into a fine mist, now suddenly gathers in strength, hitting her in the face as she starts the climb back up towards the path. Ruth puts her head down and ploughs onwards; she has never been stuck on the marsh in the dark and she doesn't mean to start now.

For about twenty minutes she plods on, head down against the driving rain. Then she stops. She should have reached the gravel path by now. It is almost completely dark, with just a faint phosphorescent gleam coming from the marsh itself. Ruth gets out her torch but its shaky light shows her only flat marshland in all directions. Far off, she can hear the sea roaring as it thunders inland. She tries to get out her map but it is blown back in her face. It is too precious to lose so she packs it away again. She can hear the sea but from which direction? She gets out her compass. She is heading too far to the east. Slowly, trying not to panic, she revolves on the spot until she is facing south and she sets out again.

This time she stops because her foot steps into nothingness. One minute she is on dry land, the next she has sunk knee-high into bog. She almost falls on her face but manages to rock backwards until she is sitting on the firm ground. With an effort she pulls her leg from the liquid mud. It comes free with a horrible squelching sound but her wader, thank God, stays on. Panting, she stands up, then takes a step backwards. Firm ground. Steps forwards. Oozing mud. To the right, more mud. To the left, firmer ground. She starts to edge to the left, torch held out in front of her.

After a few yards, she falls into a ditch. Putting out her hands to save herself, she encounters icy water. She raises a hand to her lips. Salt. Oh God, she must have wandered right out to the tidal marsh. Scrambling to her feet she wipes mud off her face and checks her compass again. Due east. Has she missed the path altogether? Is she heading straight out to sea? The roaring in her ears is so loud now that she cannot tell if it is the sea or just the wind. Then a wave breaks right over her feet. There is no mistaking it, a freezing, briny-smelling swell of water. She is on the tidal mud flats, possibly at the very spot where Peter called for help all those years ago. But there is no Erik to save her. She will be drowned.

She is sobbing now, tears mingling with the rain and sea water on her face. Then she hears a voice. Calling her. She sees a light, a shaky hand-held light coming towards her. 'Help!' she shouts frantically, 'Help!'

The light comes nearer and a man's voice shouts, 'Come this way. Towards me.' Almost on all fours, she crawls towards the light and the voice. A figure looms out of the mist, a thick-set figure wearing a reflective jacket. A hand reaches out and grabs hers. 'This way,' says the voice.

Clinging to the yellow waterproof sleeve as if it were a life belt, she stumbles along beside the man. He seems familiar but all she can do is follow as he traces a circuitous path, first left then right, now into the wind, now away from the wind, through the mud flats. But, whatever route he is taking, it seems a remarkably effective one. Her feet are on firm ground almost all the time and, before too long, she can see the blue and white police tape and the car park where a battered Land Rover is waiting.

'Oh my God.' She lets go of the man and leans over to catch her breath.

The man steps back, shining his torch into her face. 'What the hell were you playing at?' he demands.

'I was trying to get home. I got lost. Thank you. I don't know what I would have done if you hadn't come along.'

'You'd have drowned, that's what you would have done.' Then his voice changes. 'You're the girl from the university, aren't you?'

Ruth looks at him, taking in close-cropped grey hair, blue eyes, official-looking jacket. It is her neighbour, the warden of the bird sanctuary. She smiles. Despite her feminist principles, she quite likes being called a girl.

'Yes. You're my neighbour aren't you?'

He holds out a hand. 'David.'

She shakes hands, smiling. 'I'm Ruth. Thanks again for saving me.'

He shrugs. 'That's OK. We'd better get you home. My car's over there.'

In the Land Rover, Ruth turns to David, who is coaxing the engine into life. 'How did you know the way back? It was amazing, the way you twisted and turned across the marsh.'

'I know this place like the back of my hand,' says David, putting the car into gear. 'There are wooden posts sunk into the ground. If you follow them, it leads you along a safe path through the marsh. I don't know who put them there, but, whoever did, they knew the land even better than I do.'

Ruth stares at him. 'Wooden posts?' she whispers.

'Yes. They're sunk deep into the ground, sometimes half submerged they'll lead you through the treacherous ground, right out to sea.'

Right out to sea. Right out to the henge. Ruth touches the freezer bag in her pocket but says nothing. Her mind is working furiously.

'What were you doing out on a night like this anyway?' asks David as they drive along the Saltmarsh road. The windscreen wipers are almost buckling under the weight of water.

'We found something. Over by the car park. I wanted to take a second look. I know it was stupid.'

'You found something old? You're an archaeologist, aren't you?'

'Yes. Some Iron Age bones. I think they might be linked to the henge. Do you remember, ten years ago, when we found the henge?' She dimly remembers David watching the excavations that summer. How terrible that they haven't spoken since.

'Yes,' he says slowly, 'I remember. That chap with a ponytail, he was in charge wasn't he? He was a good bloke. I had a lot of time for him.'

'Yes.' Funnily enough, there is something about David that reminds her of Erik. Perhaps it's the eyes, used to scanning far horizons.

'So, will there be all sorts of people here again? Druids and students and idiots with cameras?'

Ruth can tell that David thinks the saltmarsh should be left to him and the birds. How can she say she hopes there will be a major excavation, almost certainly involving students and idiots with cameras, if not druids.

'Not necessarily,' she says at last. 'It's very low-key at the moment.'

David grunts. 'The police were here the other day. What were they after?'

Ruth is not sure how much she should say. 'It was because of the bones, but, when they turned out to be prehistoric, they lost interest.'

They have reached Ruth's blue fence now. David turns to her and smiles for the first time. He has very white teeth. How old is he? she wonders. Forty? Fifty? Like Erik, he has an ageless quality.

'But you,' says David, 'you're more interested now, aren't you?'

Ruth grins. 'Yes I am.'

As she opens her front door, the phone is ringing. She knows, beyond any doubt, that it will be Erik.

'Ruthie!' Erik's singsong voice echoes across the frozen miles from Norway. 'What's all this about a find?'

'Oh, Erik,' says Ruth ecstatically, standing dripping onto the rug. 'I think I've found your causeway.'

IT IS DARK, but she is used to that. She stretches out a hand to see if she can touch the wall and encounters cold stone. No door. There is a trap door in the roof but she never knows when that will open. And sometimes it is worse when it does. No use screaming or crying; she has done this many times before and it never helps. Sometimes, though, she likes to shout just to hear her own voice. It sounds different somehow, like a stranger's voice. Sometimes it's almost company, this other voice. They have long talks, sometimes, whispering in the dark.

'Don't worry.'

'It'll all come right in the end.'

'Darkest before dawn.'

Words she can't even remember hearing, though now they seem lodged in her brain. Who was it told her it was darkest before dawn? She doesn't know. She only knows that the words give her a warm, ticklish feeling, like being wrapped in a blanket. She has an extra blanket when it's cold, but even then she shivers so much that in the morning her whole body aches. Sometimes it's warmer and a little light shines through the edges of the trap door. Once he opened the window in the roof. Usually it's only open at night when the sky is black, but this time it was bright and blue and it made her eyes hurt. The bars on the window turned into a little yellow ladder. Sometimes she dreams about climbing the ladder and escaping to . . . where? She doesn't know. She thinks of the sun on her face and being in a garden where there are voices and cooking smells and laughing and someone holding you tight, so tight they will never let you go.

And, at other times, she thinks there is nothing there at all, beyond these walls. Only more walls and iron bars and cold, concrete floors.

RUTH LEAVES HER PARENTS' house as soon as she decently can after Christmas. Phil is having a New Year's Eve party and, though she would rather chew her own arm off than attend, she tells her parents that it is her duty to go. 'It would be bad for my career. After all, he is head of department.'

So, on December 29, Ruth is driving along the M11 to Norfolk, singing along to her new Bruce Springsteen CD, a Christmas present to herself. According to her brother Simon, Ruth has the musical taste of a sixteen-year-old boy. 'A tasteless sixteen-year-old boy.' But Ruth doesn't mind. She loves Bruce and Rod and Bryan. All those ageing rockers with croaky voices and faded jeans and age-defying hair. She loves the way they sing about love and loss and the dark, soulless heart of America.

She takes the A11 towards Newmarket. It hadn't been such a bad Christmas really. Her parents hadn't nagged her too much about not going to church and not being married. Simon hadn't been too irritating and her nephews were at quite interesting ages, eight and six, old enough to go to the park and play at being Neolithic hunters. The children adored Ruth because she told them stories about cavemen and dinosaurs and never noticed when their faces needed washing. 'You've got quite a gift with kids,' said her sister-in-law Cathy, 'It seems a shame . . .'

'What's a shame?' Ruth had asked, although she knew only too well.

'That you haven't any of your own. Though, I suppose, by now . . .'

By now I have resigned myself to spinsterhood and godmotherhood and slowly going mad, knitting clothes for my cats out of my own hair, thinks Ruth. In the days when she'd been with Peter the only thing more annoying than people hinting at 'wedding bells' had been the suggestion that she might be 'getting broody'. When she'd bought the cats her mother had asked her straight out if they were 'baby substitutes'.

She reaches the Saltmarsh by mid-afternoon and the winter sun is low over the reed beds. The tide is coming in and the seagulls are calling. When Ruth gets out of her car she breathes in the wonderful sea smell and feels glad she is home. Then she sees the weekenders' monster car parked outside their cottage and feels a stab of irritation. Don't say they have come here for New Year. Why can't they stay in London like everyone else, flocking to Trafalgar Square?

Inside her cottage, Flint leaps on her, mewing furiously. Sparky, on the sofa, ignores her. Ruth's friend Shona has been coming in to feed the cats and Ruth finds welcome-home flowers on the table as well as milk and white wine in the fridge. God bless Shona, thinks Ruth, putting on the kettle.

Shona, who teaches English at the university, is Ruth's best friend in Norfolk. Like Peter, she had been a volunteer on the henge dig ten years ago. Fey and Irish, with wild Pre-Raphaelite hair, Shona declared herself in sympathy with the druids and even joined them for an all-night vigil, sitting on the sand chanting until the tide forced them inland and Shona was lured away by the promise of a Guinness in the pub. Shona is in a relationship with a married lecturer and sometimes she comes over to Ruth's cottage, weeping and flailing her hair around, declaring that she hates men and wants to become a nun or a lesbian or both. Then she will have a glass of wine and brighten up completely.

Her answering machine shows four messages. One is surprising.

'Hello . . . er . . . Ruth. This is Harry Nelson speaking, from the Norfolk police. Can you ring me? Thank you.'

Harry Nelson. She hasn't spoken to him since the day they found the Iron Age bones. She sent him the results of the carbon-14 dating, confirming that the bones were female, pre-pubescent, dating from about AD 650. She heard nothing back and didn't expect to. Once, before Christmas, when she was shopping in Norwich, she saw him striding along, looking discontented and weighed down with carrier bags. With him was a blonde woman, slim in a designer track suit, and two sulky-looking teenage daughters. Ruth hid and watched them. In this female environment of shopping bags and fairy lights, Nelson looked more inconveniently macho than ever.

The woman (his wife surely?) turned to him with a flick of hair and a smile of practised persuasiveness. Nelson said something, looking grumpy, and both girls laughed. They must gang up on him at home, Ruth decided, excluding him from their all-girl chats about boyfriends and mascara. But then Nelson caught up with his wife, whispered something that brought forth a genuine laugh, then ruffled one daughter's careful hairstyle and sidestepped neatly away. For a moment they looked united; a happy, teasing, slightly stressed family in the middle of their Christmas shopping.

Why was Harry Nelson ringing her now? And why is he so arrogant that he can't even leave a phone number? Irritated but curious, Ruth rifles through the phone book to find a number for the Norfolk police. Eventually she gets through to DCI Nelson.

'Nelson,' barks an impatient voice, sounding more northern and even less friendly than she remembers.

'It's Ruth Galloway from the university. You rang me.'

'Oh, yes. I rang you some days ago. Something's come up. Can you come into the station?'

Ruth is nonplussed. Of course, she wants to know what has come up but Nelson's request sounds more like an order.

'I've been away and I'm very busy—' she begins.

'I'll send a car,' says Nelson. 'Tomorrow morning all right?'

It is on the tip of Ruth's tongue to say no, tomorrow is not all right. I'm off to a very important jet-set conference in Hawaii so I'm far too busy to drop everything just because you order me to. Instead she says, 'I suppose I could spare you an hour or two.'

'Right,' says Nelson. Then he adds, 'Thank you.' It sounds as if he hasn't had much practice in saying it.

Chapter 3

The police car arrives at Ruth's door at nine. As she walks to the car, Ruth sees one of the weekenders looking furtively out of the window, so she waves and smiles cheerfully. They probably think she is being arrested. Guilty of living alone and weighing over ten stone.

She is driven into King's Lynn. The police station is in a detached Victorian house that still looks more like a family home. The reception desk is in what must have been the sitting room. Her escort, a uniformed policeman, ushers her through a door beside the desk. They climb a staircase, now marred with institutional carpeting, and enter a door marked CID.

Harry Nelson is sitting at a battered Formica desk surrounded by papers. This room was obviously once part of a bigger one; you can see where the plasterboard partition cuts into the elaborate coving round the ceiling. Now it is an awkward slice of a room, taller than it is wide, with a disproportionately large window, half covered by a broken white blind. Nelson, though, does not seem to be a man who bothers much about his surroundings.

He stands up when she enters. 'Ruth. Good of you to come.'

She can't remember telling him to call her by her first name.

'Coffee?' asks Nelson.

'Yes, please. Black.' She knows it will be horrible but it feels rude to refuse. Besides it will give her something to do with her hands.

'Two black coffees, Richards,' Nelson barks at the hovering policemen. Presumably he has the same problem with 'please' as with 'thank you'.

Ruth sits on a battered plastic chair opposite the desk. Nelson sits down too and, for a few minutes, seems just to stare at her, frowning. Ruth begins to feel uncomfortable. Surely he hasn't just asked her here for coffee? Is this silent treatment something he does to intimidate suspects?

The policeman marches back in with the coffees. Ruth thanks him profusely, noticing with a sinking heart the thin liquid and the strange wax film floating on the surface. Nelson waits until the door has shut again before saying, 'You must be wondering why I asked you to come in.'

'Yes,' says Ruth, sipping the coffee. It tastes even worse than it looks.

Nelson pushes a file towards her. 'There's been another child gone missing,' he says. 'You'll have read about it in the press.'

Ruth stays silent; she doesn't read the papers.

Nelson gives her a sharp look before continuing. He looks tired, she realises. There are dark circles around his eyes and he hasn't shaved.

'There's been a letter,' he says. 'Remember I told you about the letters that were sent during the Lucy Downey case? Well, this looks to be from the same person.'

'And you think this person may be the murderer?'

Nelson frowns into his coffee cup. 'It's dangerous to make assumptions. It's just . . . There is always the chance that they *could* be from the killer, in which case they could contain vital clues. And I remembered what you said, that day when we found the bones, about ritual and all that. There's a lot of that sort of thing in the letters. So I wondered if you'd take a look. Tell me what you think.'

Gingerly, Ruth takes the file and opens it. A typewritten letter faces her. She picks it up. It seems to have been written on standard printer paper using a standard computer.

Dear Detective Nelson,

To everything there is a season, and a time to every purpose under the heaven. A time to be born and a time to die; a time to plant and a time to pluck up what has been planted. A time to kill and a time to heal. A time to cast away stones and a time to gather stones.

She lies where the earth meets the sky. Where the roots of the great tree Yggdrasil reach down into the next life. All flesh is grass. Yet in death are we in life. She has become the perfect sacrifice. Blood on stone. Scarlet on white.

In peace.

'Well?' Nelson is watching her closely.

'Well, the first bit's from the Bible. Ecclesiastes.'

'What's all that about a tree?'

'In Norse legend, there's a tree called Yggdrasil. Its roots are supposed to stretch down to hell and up to heaven. There are all sorts of legends attached to it.' As she says this she remembers Erik, that great teller of Norse tales, sitting by the campfire, his face radiant in the half light, telling them about Odin and Thor, about Asgard, the home of the gods and Muspelheim, the land of fire.

'The letter says its roots reach *down* into the next life.'

'Yes.' This was the first thing to strike Ruth. She is surprised to find

Nelson so perceptive. 'Some people think prehistoric man believed that heaven was below the earth, not above. Have you heard of Seahenge?'

'No.'

'It was found on the coast, near the Saltmarsh at Holme-Next-the-Sea. A wooden henge, like the one at the Saltmarsh, except there was a tree buried in the centre of it. Buried upside down, its roots upwards, its branches going down into the earth.'

'Do you think this guy'—he picks up the letter—'may have heard of it?'

'Possibly. There was a lot of publicity at the time. Can you tell me something about the child? The one who's gone missing.'

He stares at her. 'It was in the papers. Local and national. Bloody hell, it was even on *Crimewatch*. Where have you been?'

Ruth is abashed. She seldom reads the papers or watches TV.

Nelson sighs and rubs his stubble. When he speaks, his voice is harsher than ever. 'Scarlet Henderson. Four years old. Vanished while playing in her parents' front garden in Spenwell.'

Spenwell is a tiny village about half a mile from Ruth's house.

'Scarlet?'

'Yes. *Scarlet on white. Blood on stone.* Quite poetic isn't it?'

Ruth is silent. She is thinking about Erik's theories of ritual sacrifice. Wood represents life, stone death. She asks, 'How long ago was this?'

'November.' Their eyes meet. 'About a week after we found those old bones. Almost ten years to the day since Lucy Downey vanished.'

'And you think the cases are connected?'

He shrugs. 'There are similarities. Then this letter arrives.'

'When?'

'Two weeks after Scarlet vanished. We'd done everything. Searched the area, drained the river, questioned everyone. Drawn a complete blank. Then this letter came. It got me thinking about the Lucy Downey case.'

'Hadn't you been thinking about it already?'

'I thought about it, yes,' Nelson says, slightly defensively. 'The similarities were there: similar age of child, same time of year. But there were differences too. Lucy Downey was taken from her own home. Actually snatched from her bed. This child was on her own, in the garden . . .'

There is a faint edge of censure in his voice that leads Ruth to ask, 'What about the parents? You said . . . it's sometimes the parents . . .'

'Hippies,' says Nelson contemptuously, 'New Agers. Got five children and don't look after 'em properly. Took two hours to notice Scarlet was missing. But we don't think they did it. No sign of abuse. Dad was away and Mum was in a trance or something, communing with the fairies.'

'May I see the other letters?' asks Ruth. 'The Lucy Downey letters.'

Nelson picks up another file on the desk and hands it to her. Ruth opens it. There are ten or more sheets inside.

'Twelve,' says Nelson, reading her mind. 'The last one was sent last year.'

'May I take these home and read them tonight?'

'I'll have them copied for you. The originals will have to stay here.'

AS NELSON ESCORTS RUTH OUT, he leads her through a room full of people, all working intently, crouched over phones or frowning at computer screens. On the wall is what looks like a roughly drawn mind map, full of arrows and scrawling writing. At the centre of it all is a photograph of a little girl with dark, curly hair and laughing eyes: Scarlet Henderson.

BACK HOME, RUTH POURS herself a glass of wine and spreads the letters out in front of her. Ten of the twelve seem to be on the same standard printer paper as the Scarlet Henderson letter. Two of them are handwritten on lined paper. The writing is legible but untidy. Ruth hardly ever sees handwriting these days; her students have laptops, her friends send emails or texts.

The hand-written letters come in the middle of the sequence. Ruth puts them back into order and starts to read.

November 1997

Nelson,

You are looking for Lucy but looking in the wrong places. Look to the sky, the stars, the crossing places. Look at what is silhouetted against the sky. You will find her where the earth meets the sky.

In peace.

December 1997

Nelson,

Lucy is the perfect sacrifice. Like Isaac, like Jesus, she carries the wood for her own crucifixion. Like Isaac and Jesus she is obedient to the father's will.

I would wish you the compliments of the season, make you a wreath of mistletoe, but, in truth, Christmas is merely a modern addition, grafted onto the great winter solstice. The pagan festival was here first, in the short days and long nights. Perhaps I should wish you greetings for St Lucy's Day. If only you have eyes to see.

In peace.

January 1998

Dear Detective Inspector Harry Nelson,

You see, I am calling you by your full name now. I feel we are old friends. Just because Nelson had only one eye, it doesn't follow that he couldn't see. 'A man may see how the world goes with no eyes.'

In peace.

January 1998

Dear Harry,

'A little touch of Harry in the night.' How wise Shakespeare was, a shaman for all time. Perhaps it is the wise men—and women—you should be consulting now.

For you still do not look in the right places, the holy places. You look only where trees flower and springs flow. Look again, Harry. Lucy lies deep below the ground but she will rise again.

In peace.

March 1998

Dear Harry,

Spring returns but not my friend. The trees are in bud and the swallows return. For everything there is a season.

Look where the land lies. Look at the cursuses and the causeways . . .

Ruth stops. She is so transfixed by the word 'cursuses' that it is a few minutes before she realises someone is knocking on the door.

It is the woman from next door; the weekender who watched her drive off in the police car that morning.

'Oh . . . hello,' says Ruth.

'Hi!' The woman flashes her a brilliant smile. She is older than Ruth, maybe early fifties, but fantastically well preserved: highlighted hair, tanned skin, honed figure in low-slung jeans. 'I'm Sammy. From next door. Isn't it ridiculous that we've hardly ever spoken to each other?'

Ruth doesn't think it is ridiculous at all. She spoke to the weekenders when they first bought the house about three years ago and since then has done her best to ignore them.

'Ed and I . . . we're having a little New Year's party. Just some friends from London. Very casual. We wondered if you'd like to come.'

Ruth says, 'Well, my head of department's having a party and I have—'

'Oh, I do understand. You work at the university, don't you?'

'Yes. I teach archaeology.'

'Archaeology! Ed would love that. He never misses *Time Team*. I thought you might have changed jobs.'

Ruth looks at her blankly, though she has a good idea what is coming. Sammy laughs gaily. 'The police car! This morning.'

'Oh, that,' says Ruth. 'I'm just helping the police with their enquiries.'

And with that, she thinks grimly, Sammy will just have to be content.

THAT NIGHT, Ruth finishes the Lucy Downey letters. She was halfway through the letter dated March 1998, with its surprising mention of cursuses. A cursus is a fairly obscure archaeological term meaning a shallow ditch. There is a cursus at Stonehenge, even older than the stones.

'. . . We crawl on the surface of the earth but we do not know its ways, or divine its intent.

In peace.

April 1998

Dear Harry,

Happy Easter. I do not think of you as a Christian somehow. You seem to belong to the older ways.

At Easter, Christians believe Christ died on the cross for their sins but did not Odin do this before him, sacrificing himself on the Tree of All Knowledge? Like Nelson, Odin had only one eye. How many eyes do you have, Detective Inspector? A hundred, like Argus?

Lucy is buried deep now. But she will flower again.

In peace.

Now come the two hand-written letters. They are undated but someone (Nelson?) has scribbled the date they were received:

Received 21st June, 1998

Dear Harry,

Greetings of the summer solstice. Hail to the Sun God. Beware water spirits and light bonfires on the beach. Beware the Wicker Man.

Now the sun turns southwards and evil spirits walk abroad. Follow the will-o'-the-wisps, the spirits of the dead children. Who knows where they will lead you?

In peace.

Received 24th June, 1998

Dear Harry,

Compliments of St John's Day. Sankt Hans Aften. *Herbs picked on St John's Eve have special healing powers. Did you know that?*

You are no nearer to Lucy and that makes me sad. But do not weep. I have rescued her and raised her up. I have saved her from a life of the mundane, a life spent worshipping false gods. I have made her the perfect sacrifice. Weep for yourself and your children and your children's children.

In peace.

Now the letters revert to typewriting and no longer is there the half-affectionate teasing, the assumption that Nelson and the writer are 'old friends' and share a special bond. Now the writer seems angry, resentful.

October 31, 1998

Dear Detective Inspector Nelson,

Now is the time when the dead walk. Graves have yawned and yielded up their dead. Beware the living and the dead. Beware the living dead. We who were living are now dying.

You have disappointed me, Detective Inspector. I have shared my wisdom with you and still you are no nearer to me or to Lucy . . .

Tomorrow is the Feast of All Saints. Will you find St Lucy there in all the holy pantheon? Or is she, too, bound to the earth?

In sadness.

November 25, 1998

Dear Detective Inspector Nelson,

It is now a year since Lucy Downey vanished. The world has turned full circle and what have you to show for it? Truly you have feet of clay.

A curse on the man who puts his trust in man, who relies on the things of flesh, whose heart turns from the Lord. He is like dry scrub in the wastelands, if good comes, he has no eyes for it.

In sadness.

December 1998

Dear Detective Inspector Nelson,

I nearly did not write to wish you compliments of the season but then I thought you would miss me. I am deeply disappointed in you.

A girl, a young girl, an innocent soul, vanishes, but you do not read the signs. A seer, a shaman, offers you the hand of friendship and you decline it. Look into your own heart, Detective Inspector. Truly it must be a dark place, full of bitterness and regret.

Yet Lucy is in light. That I promise you.

In sadness.

The last letter is dated January 2007:

Dear Detective Inspector Nelson,

With each New Year I think of you. Are you any nearer to the right path? Or have your feet strayed into the way of despair and lamentation?

I saw your picture in the paper last week. What sadness and loneliness is etched in those lines! Even though you have betrayed me, still I ache with pity for you.

You have daughters. Do you watch them? Do you keep them close?

I hope so for the night is full of voices and my ways are very dark. Perhaps I will call to you again one day?

In peace.

What did Nelson think, wonders Ruth, when he read that open threat to his daughters? She looks at the date on the final letter. Ten months later Scarlet Henderson vanished. Is the letter-writer responsible? Was he responsible for Lucy Downey? There is nothing concrete in these letters, only a web of allusion, quotation and superstition.

She recognises the Bible and Shakespeare, of course, but she wishes she could ask Shona for some of the other references. She is sure there is some T.S. Eliot in there somewhere . . . What interests her more are the Norse allusions: Odin, the Tree of all Knowledge, water spirits. And, even more than that, the signs of some archaeological knowledge. No layman, surely, would use the word 'cursuses'. She lies in bed, rereading, wondering.

'SO WHAT DO YOU THINK? Is he a nutter?'

Ruth is once again sitting in Nelson's shabby office, drinking coffee. Only this time she brought the coffee herself, from Starbucks.

'Starbucks, eh?' Nelson had said suspiciously.

'Yes. It's the closest. I don't normally go to Starbucks but . . .'

'Why not?'

'Oh, you know,' she shrugged, 'too global, too American.'

'I'm all for America myself,' said Nelson, looking doubtfully at his cappuccino. 'We went to Disneyland Florida a few years ago. It was champion.'

Ruth, for whom the idea of Disneyland is sheer hell, says nothing.

Now Nelson puts down his Styrofoam cup and asks, 'Is he a nutter?'

'I don't know,' says Ruth slowly. 'I'm not a psychologist.'

Nelson grunts. 'We had one of those. Talked complete bollocks.'

Ruth gets the letters out of her bag. 'I've categorised the references.'

'A list,' says Nelson approvingly. 'I like lists.'

'So do I.' She gets out a typed sheet of paper and passes it to Nelson.

Religious
Ecclesiastes
Isaac
Christmas
Christ dying on cross/Easter
St Lucy/St Lucy's Day (December 13)
St John's Day (June 24)
All Saints' Day (November 1)
Jeremiah

Literary
Shakespeare:
King Lear: 'A man may see how the world goes with no eyes.'
Henry V: 'A little touch of Harry . . .'
Julius Caesar: 'Graves have yawned and yielded up their dead.'
T.S. Eliot, *Ash Wednesday*: 'There, where trees flower, and springs
    flow, for there is nothing again.'
The Waste Land: 'We, who were living are now dying.'

Norse legend
Odin
The Tree of All Knowledge (the World Tree, Yggdrasil)

Pagan
Solstices
Wicker Man

Sun God
Shamanism
Will-o'-the-wisps
Mistletoe

Greek legend
Argus

Archaeological
Cursuses
Causeways

Nelson reads intently, his brows knitted together. 'It's good, seeing it all spread out like this,' he says at last. 'Otherwise you can't tell what is a quote and what is just mumbo jumbo. Lots of biblical stuff.'

'Maybe he had a religious upbringing,' says Ruth. 'My parents are Born Again Christians. They're always reading the Bible aloud.'

Nelson grunts. 'I was brought up a Catholic,' he says, 'but my parents weren't really into the Bible. It was more the saints. Praying to this one or that one, saying Hail Marys.'

'Are you still a Catholic?' asks Ruth.

'I had the girls baptised Catholic, but Michelle's not a Catholic. We never go to church. Don't know if I'd say I was a Catholic. A lapsed one maybe.'

'They never let you get away, do they? Even if you don't believe in God, you're still "lapsed". As if you might go back one day.'

'Maybe I will. On my deathbed.'

'I won't,' says Ruth, 'I'm an atheist. After you die, there's nothing.'

'Shame,' says Nelson with a grin, 'you never get to say "I told you so".'

Ruth laughs, rather surprised. Perhaps Nelson regrets this foray into levity because he turns back, frowning, to the list.

'This guy,' he says, 'what does *he* believe?'

'Well,' says Ruth, 'there's a strong theme of death and rebirth, the seasons, the cycle of nature. I would say his beliefs were pagan. There's the mention of mistletoe, for instance. The druids considered mistletoe sacred. That's where the tradition of kissing under the mistletoe comes from. Actually, our Iron Age girl had traces of mistletoe in her stomach.'

'In her stomach?'

'Yes, maybe she was forced to eat it before they killed her. As I said, ritual sacrifice was quite common in the Iron Age.'

Nelson winces. 'So does our guy know about all this Iron Age stuff?'

'It's possible. Take this stuff about sacrifice, the wicker man. Some people think that Iron Age man made human sacrifices every autumn to ensure that spring came again the next year. They put the victim in a wicker cage and burnt it.'

'I saw the film,' says Nelson, 'Christopher Lee. Great stuff.'

'Well, yes. It was sensationalised, of course, but there's a theme of sacrifice that runs through all religions. Odin was hung on the World Tree to gain all the knowledge of the world. Christ was hung on the cross. Abraham was prepared to sacrifice his son Isaac.'

'What did that mean, "Like Isaac, like Jesus, she carries the wood for her own crucifixion."'

'Well, Isaac carried the wood on which he was to be burned. There's a clear echo of Christ carrying his cross.'

There is a silence. Nelson is thinking of Lucy Downey, condemned, perhaps, to carry the instruments of her own death.

'Actually,' says Ruth, 'there's one very interesting Bible reference from Jeremiah, "*A curse on the man who puts his trust in man.*" I looked it up and this is how the next bit goes, "*. . . who relies on the things of flesh, whose heart turns from the Lord. He is like dry scrub in the wastelands, if good comes, he has no eyes for it, he settles in the parched places of the wilderness, a salt land, uninhabited.*"'

Nelson looks up. 'A salt land? The Saltmarsh . . .'

'Actually, there are a few things that point to the Saltmarsh,' says Ruth. She reads from one of the letters, '"Look to the sky, the stars, the crossing places. Look at what is silhouetted against the sky. You will find her where the earth meets the sky." Erik . . . an archaeologist I know, says that prehistoric man may have built structures on flat landscapes like the marshes because they would stand out, be silhouetted against the sky. He thinks that's one reason the henge was built on the marsh.'

'But other places are flat. Specially in this godforsaken county.'

'Yes, but . . .' How can she explain she thinks the letter writer shares Erik's views about a ritual landscape, about marshland being the link between life and death? 'Remember what I said about marshland?' she says at last. 'We quite often find votive offerings or occasionally bodies buried there. Maybe this man'—she gestures to the letters—'knows that too.'

'You think he's an archaeologist?'

Ruth hesitates. 'Not necessarily, but there's this word "cursuses".'

'Never heard of it.'

'Exactly! It's a technical term. It means a parallel ditch with banks on the inner sides. They're often found within early ritual landscape but we don't know what they were used for. At the Maxley Cursus, for example, they found shamans' batons.'

'Shamans' what?'

'Pieces of decorated deer antler. They would have been used by the shaman, the holy man.'

'What for?'

'We don't know, maybe as part of some ritual ceremony.'

'This guy'—Nelson points to the letters—'he talks about a shaman.'

'Yes, it's quite a popular idea among modern New Age thinkers. A holy man who works with natural magic.'

Nelson looks back at the list. 'What about causeways?'

'I think I've found one at the saltmarsh, leading to the henge. It's a sort of hidden path marked out by sunken posts. It's very exciting.'

RUTH ARRIVES HOME to find the phone ringing. She snatches it up and is rewarded by the voice of her favourite Viking.

'Ruthie! What news on the causeway?'

She tells him no one else knows of her discovery. However, when she visited David to give him a bottle of whisky as a thank-you present, he gave her a map of the saltmarsh with the posts marked in his own hand.

'Excellent,' purrs Erik. 'Don't let Techno Boy see anything until I get there.' Techno Boy is his nickname for Phil, who is addicted to all kinds of archaeological technology.

'When will that be?'

'That's why I'm ringing. I've managed to get a sabbatical next term.'

'That's wonderful!'

'Yes, I know. Magda's very jealous. It's the long nights, you know, a real killer in the winter. Anyway, I hope to be with you in a week or so.'

'Wonderful!' says Ruth again. 'Where will you stay?'

Erik laughs. 'Don't worry; I won't be after your sofa. I don't fancy sharing it with the cats. I'm sure they would put the evil eye on me. I remember a nice B&B quite near you. I'll book there.'

'Erik. There's just a chance you might get a call from someone called Detective Inspector Harry Nelson . . .'

Nelson had asked her if there was anyone she remembered hanging around the dig ten years ago, anyone who might have been fascinated by archaeology and mythology. Ruth could remember one name. A man who called himself Cathbad, who was the leader of the group of druids who wanted to save the henge. She had offered Nelson this name, which was met by a snort of contempt. Did Ruth have any idea what his real name was? No. Did she know anyone who might know? So Ruth had given him Erik's name. She remembers, many times, seeing Erik deep in conversation with Cathbad, the latter's purple cloak flying out behind him as they stood on the mud flats looking out to sea. Cathbad had been fairly young. He would only be in his late thirties or early forties now.

She explains the situation to Erik, telling him about the disappearance of Scarlet Henderson and the earlier case of Lucy Downey.

Erik whistles softly. 'So. You are helping the police with this case?'

'Well, there are some letters. They were sent when Lucy Downey vanished and Nelson thinks . . . Well, he'll explain if he speaks to you.'

'You sound as if you've got quite friendly with him.' There is an odd note in Erik's voice. Ruth remembers that he doesn't much like the police.

'I'm not friendly with him,' she hurries to defend herself. 'I don't know him very well. He's odd, complicated. He seems very northern and brash. Thinks archaeology is rubbish and mythology is nonsense and all New Agers should be shot but, I don't know, he's bright, brighter than you think at first. And he's interesting, I suppose.'

'I look forward to speaking to him,' says Erik politely. 'Am I to understand that I am a suspect?'

Ruth laughs. 'Of course not! It's just . . . he was asking whether I remembered anyone from the henge dig. And I thought of Cathbad.'

'Cathbad.' Erik takes a deep breath. 'Cathbad. I haven't thought of him for years. I wonder what he's doing now.'

'What was his real name?'

'Something Irish, I think. He was into the Celtic stuff too. Malone. Michael Malone.'

'Could he have been involved?'

'Cathbad? God, no. He was a real innocent. A simple soul. I think he really had magic powers, you know.'

After they have said goodbye and Ruth is bustling around, feeding herself and the cats, she reflects that Erik has a way of bringing you up short with something like that. Mentioning magic in the same quiet authoritative way that he talks about carbon dating or geophysics. Can Erik really believe that Cathbad, alias Michael Malone, has magical powers?

Chapter 4

Ruth did not intend to go to Sammy's New Year's Eve party. Having successfully pleaded a cold as an excuse to Phil, she planned to go to bed early with the new Rebus.

But, as she lies in bed with Rebus and listens to the thump of music coming from next door, she feels restless. She makes herself a hot drink but, downstairs, the lights from Sammy's house seem tempting. She dresses in black trousers and a red silk shirt, collects a bottle of red from her small store of wine and knocks on her neighbours' front door.

Sammy is thrilled. 'Ruth! How lovely. I didn't think you could come.'

'No. Well, I heard your music and—'

'I'm delighted to see you. *We're* delighted. Ed! Look who's here!'

Ed, a small, bright-eyed man who seems to be perpetually walking on tiptoe, bounds forward to shake Ruth's hand.

'Well, well, our mysterious neighbour. I'm very pleased you've come. I've been wanting to chat to you for ages. I'm a bit of an archaeology buff myself. Never miss *Time Team*. Come through.' Ed steers her into the house. Even in her flat shoes, he only comes up to Ruth's chin. The weekenders' house is larger than Ruth's because they have added a double-storey extension. Even so, it is on the cosy side for a party. The sitting room feels crowded, although there are actually only about five people in it.

'These are our friends Derek and Sue, up from London,' says Ed, bobbing up and down beside Ruth. He really makes her feel very large. 'And this is, well you must know each other, this is our mutual neighbour David.'

Ruth turns in surprise to see the warden of the bird sanctuary sitting uneasily on the sofa, a pint of beer held in front of him like a shield.

'Hello,' says David, smiling. 'I was hoping you'd come.'

'Oh ho,' says Ed jovially, 'what have we here? Romance blossoming on the mud flats?'

Ruth can feel herself blushing. Luckily the room is dark. 'David and I only really met a few weeks ago,' she says.

'Aren't we dreadful neighbours?' says Ed, striking himself theatrically on the forehead. 'All these years and we're only just getting to know each other. What'll you have to drink, Ruth? Red? White? Beer?'

'White would be lovely, thanks.'

Ed prances away and leaves Ruth sitting next to David on the sofa, still holding her bottle of red.

'Oh dear,' she says, 'I meant to give this to Ed. Now it looks as if I'm planning to drink it all myself.'

'I was worse,' says David. 'I brought some sloe gin. It was in a Lucozade bottle. I think they thought it was a bomb.'

Ruth laughs. 'I love sloe gin. Did you make it yourself?'

'Yes,' says David, 'the sloes are wonderful in autumn. And the blackberries. One year I made blackberry wine.'

'Was it good?'

'I think so,' he says, 'but I'm not much of a drinker. And I didn't really have anyone to offer it to.'

Ruth feels a sudden tug of understanding. She too has weekends when she doesn't speak to anyone but her cats.

Ed is back, carrying a huge glass of white wine. Ruth gives him the bottle of red.

'So, Ruth,' Ed says. 'Found any buried treasure recently?'

Ruth does not want to tell Ed about the body in the mud or the torques. 'I teach at the university,' she says. 'We don't really do many digs. The students do a dig every spring but they always find the same things.'

'Why's that?' asks Ed.

'Because we put them back every year,' explains Ruth. 'The Americans would ask for their money back if they didn't find something.'

'Americans,' says David. 'Dreadful people. We had some last year, trying to catch a sanderling. Apparently they thought it was wounded.'

'What's a sanderling?' asks Ed.

David looks astonished. 'It's a bird. Quite common. They run up and down the beach by the edge of the water, trying to catch sea creatures. These Americans, they thought it was hurt because it wasn't flying.'

'There must be some interesting birds round here,' says Ed.

David is transformed. 'Wonderful,' he says, his eyes shining. 'The mud flats are like heaven for them. So nutritious. You see whole flocks stopping by on their migration routes, just to feed here.'

'Like a motorway service station,' says Ruth.

David laughs. 'Exactly! In winter, the saltmarsh can be covered with birds, all trying to find something to eat on the mud flats. Sometimes there are as many as two thousand pink-footed geese coming from Iceland and

Greenland. There are lots of native waterfowl too: goldeneye, gadwall, goosander, shoveller, pintail. I've even seen a red-backed shrike.'

Ruth feels slightly dazed by all these names but she likes the sound of them and she likes being with another expert, someone else whose job is their enthusiasm. Ed, meanwhile, has drifted quietly away.

'I recognise snipe,' she offers. 'And I think I've heard a bittern. They've got such a sinister call.'

'Yes, we've a nesting pair on the marsh,' says David. 'Must have been the male you heard. They call in the morning, first thing. It's a kind of hollow boom; echoes for miles.'

Sammy bustles up and tells them that there is food in the kitchen. 'Then we've got to get you two mingling.'

They both get up obediently and follow her to the kitchen.

NELSON TOO IS AT A PARTY. His is rather more glamorous than Ruth's and certainly noisier. It is above a wine bar and sparkling wine is flowing like water. Discordant music blasts from the speakers and canapés are circulating. Nelson, who arrived straight from work, has eaten about twenty and now feels slightly sick. He is dying for a cigarette.

'All right?' His wife Michelle drifts by, elegant in a metallic gold dress.

'No. When can we go home?'

She laughs, pretending this is a joke. 'It's a New Year's Eve party, so the idea is to stay until midnight.'

'I've got a better idea. Let's go home and get a takeaway.'

'I'm enjoying myself.' She smiles widely and flicks her long blonde hair over her shoulder. She does look fantastic, he has to admit.

'And besides,' her face hardens, 'how would it look to Tony and Juan?' Tony and Juan are Michelle's bosses, joint owners of the hairdressing salon she manages. They are gay, which is fine by Nelson as long as he doesn't have to go to their parties.

'They won't notice. The place is packed.'

'They will notice, and anyway I don't want to leave. Come on, Harry.' She runs a manicured nail up his sleeve. 'Relax. Let your hair down.'

'I haven't got much hair. I'm the only person here without highlights.'

'I like your hair,' she says. 'It's very George Clooney.'

'Grey, you mean?'

'Distinguished. Come on, let's get you another drink.'

'Have they got any beer?' Nelson asks plaintively.

RUTH AND DAVID are at the conservatory window, watching Ed and Derek trying to light fireworks. The conservatory, another new addition to the house, faces towards King's Lynn and they can already see other small explosions in the sky as people greet the New Year.

'Interesting tradition,' says David, 'lighting fireworks at New Year.'

'Isn't it meant to symbolise lighting the way?' says Ruth.

Outside, a firework finally leaps into life. The sky is filled with green and yellow stars. Everyone cheers. In the background, on the television, excitable crowds of C-list celebrities count down alongside Big Ben.

'Ten, nine, eight . . .'

In the garden, Ed's capering figure looks suddenly demonic, outlined against the red glow of the fireworks.

'Seven, six, five . . .'

As he turns to Ruth, David is lit by technicolour flares. Red, gold, green.

'Four, three, two, one . . .'

'Happy New Year,' says David.

'Happy New Year,' echoes Ruth.

And, as Big Ben tolls mournfully in the background, the old year dies.

TONY AND JUAN are too cool for Big Ben and the C-list celebs so they organise their own countdown with the help of Juan's Rolex, live jazz and a rather elderly soprano who is going to warble 'Auld Lang Syne'.

Nelson has sloped out to smoke a cigarette and text his daughters. Laura, the eighteen-year-old, is out with her boyfriend. Rebecca, sixteen, is at a party. He thinks grimly of young lads like he had been, using the chimes of New Year as a chance for a snog. Or worse. A text message from their old dad might be just the thing to break the mood.

Happy New Year luv, he texts twice. Then, glancing down the menu, he sees the name after Rebecca's. Ruth Galloway.

He wonders what Ruth is doing tonight. He imagines her at a dinner party with other lecturers, all being very intellectual, word games over the brandy, that type of thing. Does she have a boyfriend? A partner, she'd probably call it. She has never mentioned anyone but he thinks Ruth is the sort to guard her privacy. Like him. Maybe she has a girlfriend? But she doesn't look like his idea of a lesbian. She might not dress for men but he doesn't think she dresses for women either. She looks, he searches for the word, *self-sufficient*, as if she doesn't much need other people. Maybe she's spending the evening on her own.

He wonders, for the hundredth time, if he's ever going to solve this case. Earlier in the evening he had heard two women talking about Scarlet Henderson. 'Still haven't found her . . . of course the police are doing nothing.' Nelson had had to control a murderous urge to storm over, seize the women by their necks and bellow, 'I'm working twenty-four hours a day on the case. I've cancelled all leave for my team. I've followed up every lead. I've looked at that little girl's face until it's imprinted on my eyelids. I dream about her at night. My wife says I'm obsessed. Every morning when I wake up, she's the first thing I think about. I haven't prayed since I was at school but I've prayed for her. Please God, let me find her; please God, let her be alive. So don't tell me I'm doing nothing, you emaciated bitches.'

He sighs. From inside he can hear the sounds of champagne corks popping. He looks down at his mobile phone with its glowing green numbers. On impulse he texts quickly, Happy New Year HN and presses SEND.

SHE WATCHES THE SQUARE of light in the roof turn green, then gold, then red. There are bangs too and sudden whizzing noises. At first she is frightened, then she thinks she has heard these sounds before. How many times? She doesn't know. Once before, he spoke to her and told her not to worry. It was only . . . What? She doesn't remember the word.

Usually she hears only the birds. The first ones come when it's still dark; long, wavy noises that she imagines like streamers wrapping themselves around everything. Then there are the low sounds, deep down, like a man clearing his throat. Like him, when he coughs in the dark and she doesn't know where he is. The sounds she likes best are the ones very high up, twisting and turning in the sky. She imagines herself flying up to meet them, high up where it's blue. But the window is shut during the day so she never sees the birds themselves.

She looks up at the trap door. She wonders if he will come down again. She thinks she hates him more than anyone in the world but, then again, there isn't anyone else in the world. And sometimes he is kind. He gave her the extra blanket when it was cold. He gives her food.

She thinks he gave her chocolate once. She was sick and her head hurt and he gave her water to drink. The glass had chattered against her teeth. She's got more teeth now. He took the old ones. The new teeth feel crowded and odd in her mouth. She tried to see her reflection once, in a metal tray, but this horrible creature stared back at her. A ghost face, white with wild black hair and terrible staring eyes. She doesn't want to look again.

'WE'VE FOUND HIM.'

There is nothing more annoying, thinks Ruth, than someone who thinks they don't have to introduce themselves on the phone, who assumes you must recognise their voice because it is so individual. But, then again, she *has* recognised his voice. Those flat northern vowels, the air of suppressed impatience, are unmistakable. Still, she says, 'Who is this?'

'It's Nelson. Harry Nelson. From the police.'

'Oh. Who have you found exactly?'

'Cathbad. His real name is Michael Malone.'

I knew that, Ruth wants to say. She asks, 'Where did you find him?'

'He's still in Norfolk. Lives in a caravan at Blakeney. I'm going to see him now. I wondered if you'd like to come.'

Ruth is silent for a moment. Of course, part of her wants very much to come. On the other hand, Nelson's assumption that she would be ready to drop everything at a moment's notice is rather insulting.

'Hello? Ruth?' Nelson is saying impatiently.

'OK,' says Ruth, 'I'll meet you in half an hour. At the car park in Blakeney. Be careful, though, it floods at high tide.'

AT BLAKENEY, the land juts out into the sea, forming a shingle spit that is a breeding ground for seals. Local fishermen offer trips out to watch them and in summer little boats shuttle to and fro all day, filled with excitable tourists. Ruth avoids Blakeney in the summer but today the car park contains only a few cars, one of them Nelson's dirty Mercedes. Ruth parks her Renault next to Nelson's car and gets her Wellingtons out of the boot.

'You're late,' Nelson greets her.

'Actually I'm early. It's only twenty-five minutes since you rang.'

As she pulls on her boots, Ruth wonders why Nelson has invited her. It is not as if he will need her archaeological knowledge and, unlike Erik, she barely knows Cathbad. Nelson is a mystery. Coming home late from Sammy's party, her mobile phone was flashing. The first message had been from Shona: Happy New Year. The second had been from Erik but the third had declared itself caller unknown. Pressing READ Ruth had at first wondered who 'HN' could be. It was not until she had read the fourth message that it had come to her. Harry Nelson. Texting to wish her a Happy New Year.

The fourth message had been from Peter.

'It's over there,' says Nelson, pointing.

Ruth sees an old caravan parked at the top of the beach. It is surrounded by upturned fishing boats and partly covered by a tarpaulin. It almost looks like just another boat apart from the fact that it is painted purple and has a lightning rod attached to the roof. Ruth looks quizzically at Nelson.

Nelson shrugs. 'Perhaps he's afraid of lightning.'

They plod across the stony beach, Ruth's boots holding up better than Nelson's brogues. As they reach the caravan, Nelson raises his hand to knock on the door but it is opened before he can connect. A figure wearing a long purple cloak and carrying a staff stands outlined in the doorway.

Cathbad. Ruth's first thought is that he hasn't changed much in ten years. Then, his hair had been long and dark, sometimes tied back in a ponytail, sometimes hanging loose about his shoulders. Now it is shorter and streaked with grey. He has grown a beard, which, strangely, remains jet black, so that it looks rather like a disguise, as if it is attached with elastic around the ears. His eyes are dark too and suspicious as he watches them. Ruth remembers him as nervous, edgy, likely to explode in either rage or laughter. Now he seems calmer, more in control. Ruth notices, though, that the hand gripping the staff is white around the knuckles.

'Michael Malone?' Nelson greets him formally.

'Cathbad.'

'Mr Malone, also known as Cathbad, I'm Detective Chief Inspector Nelson from the Norfolk police. May we come in?' As an afterthought, he adds, 'This is Dr Ruth Galloway from North Norfolk University.'

Cathbad turns his dark gaze on Ruth. 'I know you,' he says slowly.

'We met at a dig,' says Ruth, 'on the saltmarsh, ten years ago.'

'I remember.' Cathbad nods. 'You were with a red-headed man.'

To her annoyance, Ruth finds herself blushing. 'Yes, I was.'

'May we come in?' asks Nelson again.

Silently, Cathbad stands aside to let them into the caravan.

Inside, the first sensation is of being in a tent. Midnight-blue draperies hang from the ceiling and cover every piece of furniture. Ruth can just make out a bunk bed with cupboards under it; a cooker, covered with rust and food stains; a wooden bench seat and a table, this time covered with billowing red material. The blue drapes give a strangely dreamlike feeling, as do the twenty or so dream-catchers twinkling gently from the ceiling. The air is thick and musty. Ruth sees Nelson sniffing hopefully but she doesn't think it is cannabis. Joss sticks, more likely.

Cathbad gestures them towards the bench, before seating himself in a high-backed wizard's chair. First point to him, thinks Ruth.

'Mr Malone,' says Nelson, 'we're investigating a murder and we'd like to ask you a few questions.'

'You're very abrupt,' Cathbad says calmly. 'Are you a Scorpio?'

Nelson ignores him. From his pocket he pulls out a photograph and puts it on the table in front of Cathbad. 'Do you recognise this girl?'

Ruth looks curiously at the picture. She has never seen a picture of Lucy Downey and is struck by the resemblance to Scarlet Henderson. The same dark, curling hair, the same smiling mouth.

'No,' says Cathbad shortly. 'What's all this about?'

'This little girl vanished ten years ago,' says Nelson, 'when you were getting all worked up about that henge thing. I wondered if you'd seen her.'

Unexpectedly, Cathbad is angry. 'That henge thing,' he says in a voice shaking with rage, 'was a holy site, a place dedicated to worship and sacrifice. And Dr Galloway's *friends* proceeded to destroy it.'

'We didn't destroy it,' Ruth says. 'It's at the university. In the museum.'

'The museum!' mimics Cathbad savagely. 'A dead place.'

'Mr Malone,' cuts in Nelson. 'What were you doing ten years ago?'

'Looking up at the stars, listening to the music of the spheres.'

Nelson leans forward. He doesn't raise his voice but suddenly Ruth feels the temperature in the caravan drop. She is suddenly aware of an undercurrent of violence in the room. And it isn't coming from Cathbad.

'Look,' says Nelson softly, 'either you answer my questions civilly or we go down to the station and do it there. And, I promise you, when it gets out that you've been questioned in connection with this case, you won't be looking at the stars. You'll be looking at a gang of vigilantes trying to burn your bloody caravan down.'

Cathbad looks at Nelson for a long moment. Then he says, in a low monotone, 'Ten years ago I was living in a commune near Cromer.'

'And prior to that?'

'I was a student. Manchester.' Cathbad suddenly looks at Ruth and smiles, rather oddly. 'Studying archaeology.'

Ruth lets out at involuntary gasp. 'But that's where—'

'—Erik Anderssen taught. Yes. That's where I met him.'

Ruth's mind is racing. So Cathbad knew Erik long before the henge dig. Why hadn't Erik mentioned it? Erik had been her tutor when she did her doctorate at Southampton but she knew that previously he had been a lecturer at Manchester.

'So, what did you do, on this commune? Did any of you work?'

'We grew vegetables, we cooked them, we made music, we sang, we made love. And I was a postman,' Cathbad adds, as an afterthought.

'A *postman*?'

'Yes. It suited me fine. Early starts. I love the dawn, leaves you with the rest of the day free.'

'Free to disrupt the henge dig?'

'Disrupt!' The fire is back in Cathbad's eyes. 'We were trying to save it! Erik understood that. He wasn't like the rest of those . . . civil servants. He understood that the site was sacred. It wasn't about carbon dating and crap like that. It was about being at one with the natural world.'

Nelson cuts in again. 'And when the dig finished?'

'Life went on. I got another job. At the university. I still work there.'

Nelson looks at Ruth, who stares at him blankly. All these years, Cathbad has been working beside her at the university. Did Erik know?

'Doing what?'

'Lab assistant. My first degree was in chemistry.'

'Did you hear about the disappearance of Lucy Downey?'

'I think so. There was a lot in the papers, wasn't there?'

'And Scarlet Henderson?'

'Who? Oh, the little girl who went missing recently. I heard about it, yes. Look, Inspector . . .' Suddenly his voice changes and he draws himself up in the wizard's chair. 'What's all this about? You've got nothing that links me to these girls. This is police harassment.'

'No,' says Nelson mildly, 'just routine enquiries.'

'I won't say anything more without a solicitor present.'

Ruth expects Nelson to argue but he stands up. 'Thank you for your time, Mr Malone. May I have a sample of your handwriting?'

Cathbad looks about to refuse then goes to a filing cabinet, which is sitting incongruously in a corner of the caravan, unlocks a drawer and pulls out a sheet of paper.

Nelson looks down at the writing and his face darkens. Ruth sees his jaw muscles clench and wonders what's coming. But Nelson says in a bland, social voice, 'Thank you very much, Mr Malone. Good day.'

'Goodbye,' says Ruth weakly. Cathbad ignores her.

Ruth and Nelson scrunch away over the shingle.

'Well?' says Nelson at last, 'what do you think?'

'I can't believe he works at the university.'

'Why not? It's full of weirdoes, that place.'

'It's just . . . if Erik knew, he didn't tell me.'

Nelson looks at her. 'Are you close then, you and this Erik bloke?'

'Yes,' says Ruth, rather defiantly.

'He's coming to England soon, isn't he?'

'Next week.'

'I'll look forward to meeting him.'

Ruth smiles. 'He said the same about you.'

Nelson grunts sceptically. They have almost reached their cars.

'What about his writing?' asks Ruth. In reply, Nelson hands her the piece of paper. It seems to be a poem entitled 'In praise of James Agar'.

'Who's James Agar?' she asks.

'Bastard who killed a policeman.'

'Oh.' She begins to see why Cathbad chose this particular piece of paper. She glances down the lines. The handwriting is extravagant, full of swirls and loops. It is nothing like the writing in the Lucy Downey letters.

'It's not the same,' she says.

'Doesn't mean he's off the hook.'

'Do you suspect him then?'

Nelson pauses, one hand on his car door. 'I'm not ruling him out,' he says at last. 'He's a slippery character. He was in the area at the time and he knows all about that mystic stuff. He's clever too and he's got something to hide. Why was that cabinet locked?'

Not knowing why, Ruth volunteers, 'Erik says he has magic powers.'

Nelson laughs. 'Magic powers! Nothing magic about him that a kick up the arse won't cure.' He gets into his car but pauses before putting the key in the ignition. 'Mind you, he did get one thing right. I am a Scorpio.'

AS RUTH TURNS INTO New Road she sees a familiar red sports car parked in front of her house. She hasn't seen Shona since before Christmas and wonders what new dramas her friend will have to report. She quite enjoys Shona's love life—secondhand; she wouldn't want to live it herself, just as she wouldn't drive a scarlet Mazda. Fat chance of either, she thinks, as she parks behind Shona's car—number plate: FAB 1.

Shona, huddled up in a sheepskin coat, is standing looking out over the saltmarsh. Dark clouds are gathering over the sea; shadows race over the mud flats and the seagulls are flying inland, a sure sign of a storm to come.

'I don't know how you can live here, Ruth,' Shona says, turning round. 'This place gives me the creeps.'

'I like it,' says Ruth mildly. 'I like being able to look right out to the horizon, with nothing in the way. Do you want some lunch?'

In the cottage, Ruth goes into the kitchen and arranges cheese, pâté and salami on a plate. Shona sits at the table by the window, talking.

'I'm definitely going to end it with Liam. He says he loves me but he's obviously never going to leave Anne. It was awful on New Year's Eve. Liam kept shoving me into cupboards and saying he loved me and trying to feel me up, then the next minute he was back with his arm round Anne talking about their extension. And Phil kept asking me if I'd got a bloke yet. Creep. Just because I wouldn't go to bed with him.'

She pauses to eat a piece of bread, shaking out her red-gold hair so that it shimmers in the dim afternoon light. Ruth wonders what it must be like to be so beautiful. Exhausting, to judge from what Shona says. Yet it must be exciting too—imagine if every man you met wanted to go to bed with you. Briefly, she flicks through a mental card index of the men in her life: Phil, Erik, her students, Ed next door, David, Harry Nelson. She can't really imagine any of them panting with desire for her. The thought is absurd and oddly disturbing—

'Ruth!'

'What?'

'What about this highly mysterious police work you've been doing?'

'Who told you about that?'

'Phil.'

'It's not very mysterious really. This policeman asked me to look at some bones he'd found but they weren't modern, they were Iron Age.'

'Why did he think they might be modern?'

'He was looking for the body of a girl who disappeared ten years ago.'

'There's been another little girl gone missing recently, hasn't there?'

Ruth nods. 'Scarlet Henderson.'

'Are you involved in that too?'

Ruth hesitates. Nelson has told her that the contents of the letters are confidential but, then again, Shona is the literature expert.

'A little. There are some letters . . . Written after the first disappearance and now after Scarlet Henderson. This policeman, he thinks they might be linked.' Has she said too much?

Shona looks out of the window 'This policeman, what's his name?'

'Nelson. Harry Nelson.'

Shona swings round to look hard at Ruth. 'Are you sure?'

'Yes. Why?'

'Oh nothing.' Shona goes back to the window. 'It's just that I think I heard something about him once. Something about police brutality. God, look at that sky! I'd better get home before it tips down.'

TEN MINUTES AFTER SHONA has left, the storm breaks. Rain and hail hurl themselves at the windows and Ruth feels as if she is under siege. The wind is roaring in from the sea with a noise like thunder and Ruth feels as if her whole cottage is shaking. The windows rattle under the onslaught and Ruth draws the curtains and turns on the lights. She'll do some work; that'll take her mind off the weather.

But instead of clicking onto LECTURES 07, Ruth finds her finger hovering over the Google logo. She types in the words Harry Nelson. ENTER. A stream of Nelsons floods the screen. Ruth scrolls down. There he is. DI Harry Nelson, decorated for bravery in 1992. And again, Harry Nelson (back row, second left) in a police rugby team. Ruth has another idea and clicks onto Friends Reunited, a guilty late-night fix of hers. Yes, here he is. Henry (Harry) Nelson at a Catholic grammar school in Blackpool. What does he say about himself? His contribution is brief in the extreme, 'Married to Michelle, two daughters. Living in Norfolk (God help me).'

Ruth ponders this. It must be significant that his marriage to Michelle is the first thing he mentions, as if it were the achievement of his life. Ruth thinks back to that sighting before Christmas. Michelle certainly looked attractive enough, a definite prize for a man who is letting himself go a bit, a man who doesn't look as if he has a gym membership or spends more than five pounds on a haircut. And Michelle looked like a woman who knows her own worth, as if she knows the value of her good looks and also how to use them for her own purposes. She remembers seeing her laughing up at Nelson, her hand on his arm, soothing, cajoling. She looked, in short, like the sort of woman Ruth dislikes intensely.

What else? Well, he doesn't like Norfolk much. Ruth has already gathered as much from his references to 'this godforsaken county'. And God gets a mention here too. God help me. It is meant light-heartedly, Ruth knows, but the fact remains that Nelson has one thing in common with the mysterious letter writer. He too likes to mention God.

Ruth scrolls back and clicks on the first mention, the decoration for bravery. She sees a much younger Nelson, less battered and wary-looking. He is holding a certificate and looking embarrassed. She reads:

PC Harry Nelson was awarded the Police Medal for Bravery in connection with the poll-tax riots in Manchester. The riots, which quickly became violent, culminated in the death of a policeman, PC Stephen Naylor. PC Nelson, at great risk to his own life, broke through the lines of protestors to carry away PC Naylor's body. PC Naylor later died of his injuries. A twenty-four-year-old man, James Agar, was charged with the murder.

James Agar. Ruth looks at the name, clicking through her internal search engine. Then it comes to her. Cathbad's poem, 'In praise of James Agar'. No wonder Nelson's face had turned black when he read it. No wonder Cathbad had been so careful to choose this particular example of his handwriting. Manchester. That must have been when Cathbad was a student. Maybe he was involved in the riots. Lots of students were. She remembers similar riots when she was a student in London, watching from a window at University College, sympathising with the cause but too prudent to join in. Cathbad, typically, would have shown no such reserve. And James Agar was convicted. She wonders on whose evidence.

Ruth clicks on 'James Agar' and finds page after page of tributes to James Agar—'framed by the police for the killing of PC Stephen Naylor'. There had been one key witness at Agar's trial: PC Harry Nelson.

Ruth clicks back onto her lecture notes. The wind continues to howl across the marshes. Flint, his fur soaked flat, dashes in through the cat flap and sits on the sofa looking martyred. Sparky is nowhere to be seen.

Ruth adds a few notes about soil erosion and is just about to make herself a sandwich when the phone rings. She snatches it up.

'Ruth! How are you?' It is Peter.

After they split up, Peter made a concerted attempt to stay in touch. He was living and working in London but he used to phone a lot and once or twice came up to see her. On these occasions they ended up in bed together and this felt so right that Ruth came to the conclusion that it must be wrong.

'If we're apart, we must stay apart,' she had said. 'It's no good carrying on like this. It'll stop either of us finding someone new.'

Peter had been terribly hurt. 'But I want to be with you,' he had said. 'Don't you see, if we can't stay away from each other, it must mean that we were meant to be together?'

But Ruth had been adamant and eventually Peter had stormed back to London. Six months later he had married someone else.

That had been five years ago. Ruth had heard very little from Peter in that time. She knew that he and his wife, Victoria, had had a baby, a boy called

Daniel. He must be about four now. After Daniel's birth (she sent a teddy), Ruth had heard nothing until the text message on New Year's Eve. Happy New Year love Peter. Just for a second, Ruth had felt her heart contract.

'Peter. Hello.'

'Bit of blast from the past, eh?'

'You could say that, yes.'

A brief silence. Ruth tries to imagine Peter at the other end of the phone. Is he calling from work? From home? She imagines Victoria, whom she has never met, sitting by his side with Daniel on her lap. 'What's Daddy doing?' 'Shh, darling, he's ringing his ex-girlfriend.'

'So.' Very hearty. 'How've you been, Ruth?'

'I've been fine. How about you?'

'Fine. Working hard.'

Peter teaches history at University College, London, where Ruth did her first degree.

'Still at UCL?'

'Yes. What about you?'

'Still at North Norfolk. Still digging up bones and fighting with Phil.'

Peter laughs, but the laugh ends rather abruptly. 'Look, Ruth. The thing is, I've got a sabbatical next term—'

'You too?' The words are out before she can stop them.

'What do you mean?'

'Oh, it's just—Erik's got a sabbatical too. He's coming over next week.'

'Erik! The old Viking himself? So you're still in touch?'

'Yes.' Slightly defensively.

'Well, the thing is . . . I'm writing a book on Nelson.'

'*Who?*'

A confused pause. 'Horatio Nelson. Admiral Nelson.'

'Oh . . . yes.' The other Nelson in her life has temporarily caused her to forget the most famous Nelson of all. Of course, he was from Norfolk, too.

'Well, I'm planning to visit Burnham Thorpe. Where he was born. I'm renting a cottage nearby and I thought I could pop over to see you.'

Several things cross Ruth's mind. Will your wife be there? Is this only about research? Aloud she says, 'That would be great.'

'Good.' Peter sounds relieved. 'And I'd like to see the Saltmarsh again. God, I remember that summer. Finding the henge in the mud, those hippies who kept putting spells on us, old Erik telling ghost stories around the campfire. Do you remember when I nearly drowned?'

'Yes.' Peter is suffering from an attack of nostalgia, she knows the symptoms. She mustn't join in otherwise she'll be swept away too, drowning in the quicksand of the past.

Peter sighs. 'Well, I'll be in touch. It'll probably be next week or the week after. Will you be around?'

'Yes, I'll be around.'

'Great. Bye then.'

'Bye.' Ruth replaces the receiver. The past seems to be converging on her. First Erik, then Cathbad, now Peter. Before she knows it, she will have gone back in time ten years and will be walking along the beach, hand-in-hand with Peter, her hair six inches longer and her waist four inches thinner. She shakes her head. The past is dead. She, an archaeologist, knows that better than most. But she knows too that it can be seductive.

Rain is still drumming against the windows. Getting up, she strokes Flint, now stretched out on the sofa. She'd better check that Sparky isn't outside meowing to be let in—although she has a cat flap, Sparky prefers having the door opened for her. Ruth opens the door.

The rain flies in her face and she wipes her eyes on her sleeve. And then she sees it. Sparky is on the doorstep. But she isn't meowing or making any other sound. She is lying on her back and her throat has been cut.

Chapter 5

Nelson is, for once, driving slowly. It is still raining hard, turning the narrow lanes into treacherous gullies, but Nelson isn't usually the sort of driver who worries about weather conditions. No, Nelson is dawdling because he has just been to see Scarlet's parents and feels he needs time to recover before getting back to the station. He has had to tell Delilah and Alan that not only has the investigation made no progress, but the police want to bring sniffer dogs to search the family garden.

He's ruling out nothing, but he doesn't really suspect Scarlet's parents. Alan was away and Delilah—Delilah is a fading flower child in bare feet and fringed skirts. She irritates the hell out of him but he can't imagine her as a killer. 'Never make assumptions about people or circumstances,' Derek Fielding, his first boss, used to say laboriously. Delilah Henderson could have killed her daughter. She was in the right location and probably had the means to hand. It had taken her three hours to report Scarlet missing. 'I thought they were just playing hide and seek,' she had sobbed. Nelson disapproves (what sort of mother would not notice, for three hours, that her four-year-old was missing?) but he puts it down to hippyish, lackadaisical parenting. She had been distraught when she realised Scarlet had gone. She was still distraught, had hardly taken in the news about the garden, just clutched at Nelson, begging him to find her baby. Christ. Nelson slows down almost to walking pace as the windscreen wipers battle against the onslaught of water. Sometimes he hates his job.

When his phone rings he almost doesn't answer; not for safety reasons, but because he just can't be bothered with anything else today. When he does press RECEIVE an almost inhuman sound greets him, a sort of sobbing wail. Nelson squints at the caller identification. Ruth Galloway. Jesus.

'Ruth? What is it?'

'She's dead,' wails Ruth.

Now Nelson does stop the car, almost skidding into a water-logged ditch. 'Who's dead?'

'Sparky.' Long, gulping pause. 'My cat.'

'Are you ringing me up to tell me about a dead cat?'

'Someone cut her throat.'

'*What?*'

'Someone cut her throat and left her on my doorstep.'

'I'll be right over.'

Nelson turns his car and heads back towards the Saltmarsh. It is pitch black by the time he reaches the row of houses and, though the rain has stopped, it is still blowing a gale. The car door is almost ripped out of his hand and, as he walks up the path, he can feel the full force of the wind pushing him forward. Jesus, what a place to live. Nelson's home is a modern, four-bedroom house outside King's Lynn; civilised, with speed bumps and security lights and double garages. Ruth's cottage seems little better than a hovel and it's so isolated, stuck out here on the edge of nowhere with only the twitchers for company. Why on earth does she live here?

Ruth opens the door immediately as if she were waiting for him.

'Thanks for coming,' she sniffs.

The door opens straight into a sitting room, which, to Nelson's eyes, looks a mess. Books and papers everywhere, a half-drunk cup of coffee sits on the table, along with the remains of a meal. But then he stops noticing anything because, on the sofa, lies the corpse of a black and white cat. Ruth has covered the body with a pink, fluffy blanket.

'Have you touched it? The body?'

'Only to put her on the sofa I . . . stroked her a bit.' Ruth turns away. When she turns back, her face is quite composed. 'Do you think it was him?' she asks. 'The murderer?'

'We haven't got a murder yet,' says Nelson, pulling back the blanket and bending over Sparky's body. After a moment, he straightens up. 'Does anyone know you're involved in this investigation?'

'Phil, my boss, knows,' says Ruth, 'and maybe some other people at the university. My neighbour saw me leaving in a police car that time.'

Nelson turns away from Sparky then, almost as an afterthought, he stoops to cover the little body again with the pink blanket. Then he touches Ruth's arm and says in a surprisingly gentle voice, 'Let's sit down.'

Ruth sits in a sagging armchair. She looks towards the curtained window. The wind is still roaring outside, making the panes rattle.

Nelson perches on the edge of the sofa. 'Ruth,' he says. 'We know there's a dangerous man out there. He may have murdered two girls and he may be the person who did this to your cat. In any event, you've got to be careful. Someone is trying to frighten you and I think it's safe to assume that it has something to do with this case.'

Still looking past him, Ruth asks, 'Do you need to take Sparky away?'

'Yes,' says Nelson, 'we need to test for fingerprints and DNA.'

'So really,' says Ruth in a high, hard voice, 'this is a breakthrough.'

'Ruth,' says Nelson, 'look at me.'

She does so. Her face is swollen with crying.

'I'm sorry about your cat. About Sparky. I had a German Shepherd once called Max. I thought the world of that dog. My wife used to say she felt quite jealous sometimes. When he was run over, I was beside myself, wanted to charge the driver with dangerous driving though it wasn't his fault. But this is a possible murder investigation and your cat is a valuable clue. You want to find out what has happened to Scarlet, don't you?'

'Yes,' says Ruth, 'of course I do.'

'I promise you, Ruth, that, when the lab has finished, I'll bring Sparky back and help you bury her. I'll even light a candle in church. Deal?'

Ruth manages a watery smile. 'Deal.'

Nelson picks up Sparky's body, ensures it is covered with the blanket. 'And Ruth? Lock all your doors tonight.'

WHEN HE HAS GONE, Ruth heads for the kitchen, hell-bent on finding some wine. Splashing Pinot Grigio into a glass, Ruth looks across to the table by the window where her laptop is still open. She clicks back through her history until she is once again on the page of Nelsons.

Then she hears it. A sound outside her window. A muffled cough, then footsteps, coming closer. Her heart thumps with such huge, irregular beats that she wonders if she is going to have a coronary. The knock on the door makes her cry out with fear. She is shaking so much she drops her wine-glass. The knock again. Should she ring Nelson? Her phone is across the room, by the sofa, and the idea of moving seems impossible.

'Ruth!' shouts a voice. 'Are you in there?'

Oh thanks be to the God she doesn't believe in. It is Erik.

Half laughing, half crying, Ruth dives to open the door. Erik Anderssen, dressed in a black raincoat and carrying a bottle of whisky, stands smiling in the doorway.

'Hello, Ruthie,' he says, 'fancy a nightcap?'

'DROWNED LANDSCAPES,' says Erik, his singsong voice echoing across the wind-flattened grass, 'have a magic of their own. Think of the drowned forest on this very beach, the trees buried beneath our feet. There is something deep within us that fears what is buried, what we cannot see.'

Ruth and Erik are walking along the beach. Yesterday's rain has given way to a beautiful winter's day, cold and bright. He has been a true friend, thinks Ruth. Despite everything, it is wonderful to see him again, to be striding over the saltmarsh with him once more.

Last night she had flung herself into Erik's arms, almost incoherent with crying. He had been very kind, had sat her down and made her coffee with whisky in it. She had told him about Sparky and he had said that, when they got the body back, they should give her a Viking funeral, a burning pyre drifting out to sea. Ruth, who wanted to bury Sparky in her garden, under the apple tree, had said nothing but had been aware that Erik was paying Sparky a huge compliment, considering her a soul worthy of such an honour. Ruth hadn't wanted to be alone and so Erik had spent the night on the sofa, folding up his long limbs under Ruth's sleeping-bag.

After breakfast, he had suggested going to look at the henge site and Ruth had agreed readily. She feels the need to be out of doors, away from the house. It is good to be walking along the wide expanse of beach, under the high, blue sky. Mind you, she has forgotten how far it is when the tide is out. The sand stretches for miles, glittering with secret inlets. It looks vast and completely featureless but Erik seems to know exactly where he is going. He strides on, looking at the horizon.

Last night's wind has blown the sand into odd shapes and ridges. Little streams run across it to join the sea and, occasionally, there are larger expanses of water. Ruth splashes through one of these pools, remembering the summer of the henge dig.

'Do you still think we should have left the henge here?' she asks.

Erik raises his face to the sun, shutting his eyes. 'Yes,' he says. 'It belonged here. It marked a boundary. We should have respected that.'

'Boundaries were important to Neolithic people, weren't they?'

'Yes indeed.' Erik steps over a stream. 'Which is why they marked them with burial mounds, religious shrines, offerings to the ancestors.'

'Do you think that my Iron Age body marks a boundary?' Over breakfast, Ruth had told him more about the girl with branches twisted round her arms and legs, and about the torques and the coins and the tantalising location of the body.

'Yes, I do,' Erik says at last. 'Boundaries in the ancient landscape were often marked by isolated burials. He stops suddenly. He is looking at the sand, which has suddenly become dark and silty. He traces a line with his shoe. Underneath, the sand is quite startlingly blue. 'Burnt matter,' he says, 'the roots of ancient trees. We're getting near.'

Looking back, Ruth sees a clump of trees to the left and the spire of a church away in the distance. She remembers the view perfectly; they are very near the henge circle. But the sand, grey in the winter sun, gives nothing away. *What the Sand gets, the Sand keeps forever.*

Ruth remembers how the henge had looked that summer evening ten years ago, the ring of gnarled wooden posts sinister and otherworldly as if it had risen out of the sea. She remembers Erik kneeling before them.

'It's here,' says Erik.

There is nothing to see, just a slightly raised circle, darker than the surrounding sand, but Erik acts as if he has entered a church. He stands completely still, his eyes closed, and then touches the ground, as if for luck.

'Sacred ground,' he says.

'That's what Cathbad would say.'

'Cathbad! Have you seen him?'

'Yes . . . Erik? Why didn't you tell me that you knew Cathbad quite well, that he'd been a student of yours?'

Erik is silent, looking at her. She can't read his cool, blue stare.

'Does it matter?'

'Of course it matters!' Ruth explodes. 'He's a suspect in a murder inquiry.'

'Is he?'

Ruth hesitates. She knows that Nelson suspects and distrusts Cathbad but is that enough to make him a suspect? Probably. Aloud she says, 'I don't know. The police think he's hiding something.'

'The police! What do they know? Do you remember when they removed the protesters from the site? The unnecessary violence they used?'

'Yes.' The police had been heavy-handed when they removed the protestors. 'Did you put Cathbad up to it?' asks Ruth. 'The protest?'

Erik smiles. 'No, the local pagans were up in arms already. Let's just say that I encouraged him a bit.'

'Did you get him the job at the university too?'

'I gave him a reference.'

'Why didn't you tell me he was working there?'

'You didn't ask.'

Ruth turns away, stomping her way over the wet sand.

Erik catches her up, puts his arm round her. 'Don't be angry, Ruthie. Didn't I always tell you, it's the questions that matter, not the answers?'

Ruth looks at Erik's familiar, weather-beaten face. His hair is whiter and there are more lines around his eyes, but he is still the same. He is smiling, his blue eyes sparkling. Reluctantly, Ruth smiles back.

'Come on,' says Erik, 'let's see if we can find that causeway of yours.'

They set off, walking inland across the dunes.

Ruth has David's map, showing the buried posts. She unfurls it and hands it to Erik. He makes a hissing noise of satisfaction. 'So . . . Now we have it.' He examines the map. Ruth watches him with admiration. No one is better at reading a map or a landscape than Erik. For him, hills and streams and villages are signposts pointing directly to the past. She remembers him saying to her when she first started his postgraduate course, 'If you wanted to make a map of your sitting room for archaeologists of the future, what would be the most important thing?'

'Er . . . making sure I have a full inventory of objects.'

He had laughed. 'No, no. Inventories are all very well but they do not tell us how people *lived*, what was important to them. No, the most important thing would be the *direction*. The way your chairs were facing. That would show archaeologists of the future that the most important object in the twenty-first-century home was the large grey rectangle in the corner.'

Now Erik looks up from the map, sniffs the air and smiles. 'This way, I think.' They set off at a brisk pace. The wind is behind them now, blowing the coarse grass flat against the ground. They pass the tidal reed beds, the shallow water dark and mysterious. Above them a bird calls.

'Here.' Erik stops and bends down. Ruth squats beside him. There, half-buried in the peaty ground between the reeds and the mud flats, is a post. It extends about four inches above the soil.

'Bog oak,' says Erik. Ruth looks more closely. The wood is dark, almost black, its surface dotted with little holes, like woodworm.

'Molluscs,' says Erik laconically, 'they eat away at the wood.'

'How old is it?' asks Ruth.

'Don't know for sure. But it looks old.'

'As old as the henge?'

'Possibly.'

Ruth reaches out to touch the post. It feels soft, like black toffee.

'Come on,' says Erik. 'Let's find the next one.'

The next post is about eight feet away. This one is harder to see, almost submerged by water. Erik paces between the posts.

'Incredible. The land between the two is completely dry, although it's marshland on either side. It must be a shingle spit.'

Ruth can sense his excitement. 'So it could be a pathway through the marsh?'

'Yes, a crossing place. It was as important as marking a boundary, marking a crossing place over sacred ground. One step wrong and you're dead, straight to hell. Keep on the path and it will lead you to heaven.'

He is smiling, but Ruth shivers, remembering the letters. *Look to the sky, the stars, the crossing places. . . You will find her where the earth meets the sky.* Did the letter writer know about the pathway? He spoke about causeways and cursuses. Had he brought Lucy here?

They find a total of twelve posts, leading them back almost to the car park and the place where Ruth found the Iron Age body.

'Do you think we have found a link between my Iron Age body and the henge?' Ruth asks.

Erik looks at her quizzically. '*Your* Iron Age body?'

'I found it,' says Ruth defiantly.

'We own nothing in this life,' says Erik.

'You sound like Cathbad.'

Erik looks at her, then says, 'Come and meet him properly.'

Ruth hesitates. Part of her, the amateur detective part, wants to see Cathbad again, to assess him without Nelson's sceptical presence clouding her judgment. But as she thinks, watched quizzically by Erik, her phone rings. 'Excuse me.' Ruth turns away.

'Ruth. It's Nelson. Are you busy? Can you come to Spenwell? I'm at Scarlet Henderson's house. We've found some human bones in the garden.'

SPENWELL IS A TINY VILLAGE. One street of houses, a phone box and a shop that is open for only two hours in the afternoon. Scarlet's family live in a bungalow of ugly brown brick slightly redeemed by ivy. Ruth parks her car behind Nelson's Mercedes and two police vans. A group of children watches, wide-eyed, from the other side of the road and, up and down the street, faces appear in windows.

As Ruth approaches, Nelson appears round the side of the house. The front garden has been reduced to mud by police boots. Someone has put down planks, presumably for a wheelbarrow.

'Ruth,' Nelson greets her, 'how are you this morning?'

Ruth feels slightly embarrassed. Today she is the professional, the expert once more. She doesn't want to be reminded that last night she was sobbing over a dead cat. 'Better,' she says. 'Erik . . . you know, my ex-tutor, he came round after you left.'

Nelson looks at her slightly quizzically. But all he is says is, 'Good.'

'Where are the bones?' asks Ruth.

'Round the back. The dogs found the place.'

The back garden is long and untidy, littered with old sofas, broken bicycles and a half-constructed climbing frame built out of reclaimed timber. Scene-of-crime officers in white overalls cluster round a large hole. Sniffer dogs are straining at their leads, tails wagging madly. With a shock, Ruth realises that the Hendersons are here too. Scarlet's father and mother, standing by the back door. The mother is youngish, pale and pretty with long dark hair and a waifish look. She is wearing a purple velvet skirt and is barefoot, despite the cold. The father is older and has a rat-like face, thin with watery eyes. In the garden three of their children are playing on the half-finished climbing frame.

'This is Dr Ruth Galloway,' says Nelson to one of the white-clad men, 'She's an expert on buried bones.' Like a dog, thinks Ruth.

Ruth looks at the hole, which seems to run along the dividing line between the Hendersons' garden and the garden next door. Nearer the house, there is a timber fence but, here, at the end of the garden, there is only flint and rubble. A boundary, thinks Ruth. She hears Erik's voice in her head. *It marked a boundary. We should have respected that.*

'Was there once a wall here?' she asks. She addresses the nearest officer but Scarlet's father must have heard because he steps forward.

'There used to be an old flint wall here. I took the flints about five years ago, to make a kiln.'

The white suits step back and Ruth, carrying her excavation kit in her backpack, moves forward. She kneels on the edge of the hole, takes out her small trowel and gently scrapes away at the sides. The digging is clean; she can see the marks of the shovels and the soil is arranged in neat layers, like a terrine. A thin layer of topsoil, then the characteristic peaty soil of the area, then a line of flint. At the bottom, about three feet down, Ruth sees the yellow-white of the bones.

Wearing gloves, Ruth lifts a bone and holds it up to the light.

Nelson leans forward and speaks into Ruth's ear. She smells cigarettes and aftershave.

'Are they human?'

'I think so, yes. But . . . They weren't buried.'

Nelson squats down beside her. 'What do you mean?'

'A burial disturbs the layers. Look at this.' She gestures to the sides of the hole. 'The layers are all perfect. These bones were laid on the ground and, over the centuries, the earth has covered them.'

'Over the centuries?'

'I think they're Iron Age. Like the other ones.'

Nelson looks at her for a moment before straightening and calling to the scene-of-crime men. 'Right, that's it, boys. Excitement over.'

'What is it, boss?' asks one. *Boss!* Ruth can hardly believe her ears.

'The good news is it's a dead body. The bad news is it's been dead about two thousand years. Come on. Let's get out of here.'

AN HOUR LATER, Ruth has bagged up the bones and sent them to the university lab for carbon-14 dating. She is sure they are Iron Age but what does that mean? There were no traces of any votive hoard here. It appears to be simply a skeleton, the bones of someone who died, or was killed, over two thousand years ago. Could these bones be linked to that other body, found on the edge of the saltmarsh? And is there a link between bones, body, causeway and henge? Her mind is buzzing but she tries to concentrate on drinking herbal tea and talking to Scarlet's parents.

She is not quite sure how she ended up here, in the Hendersons' chaotic kitchen, sitting on a stool, balancing a mug in her hand. All she knows is that Nelson seemed keen to accept the invitation on her behalf.

'We'd love to,' he had said. 'Thanks very much, Mrs Henderson.'

'Delilah,' corrected Mrs Henderson wearily.

So now they are in the kitchen listening to Ocean, the Hendersons' youngest child, grizzling in her highchair.

'She misses Scarlet,' says Delilah with resignation.

'I'm sure she does,' mumbles Ruth. 'How old is . . . er . . . Ocean?'

'She's two, Scarlet's four, Euan and Tobias are seven, Maddie's sixteen.'

'You don't look old enough to have a sixteen-year-old daughter.'

'I was only sixteen when I had her. She's not Alan's, of course.'

Ruth glances briefly at Alan, who is lecturing Nelson on ley lines. Nelson looks up and catches Ruth's eye.

Two dark-haired boys race into the room. To Ruth's surprise they head straight for Nelson. 'Harry! Did you bring your handcuffs?'

'Can I try them on?'

'It's my turn.'

Solemnly, Nelson pulls a pair of handcuffs from his pocket and fits them round one of the boy's hands.

'My turn! Let me!'

'I've only had a second. *Less* than a second.'

Ruth turns back to Delilah and sees that she is now breastfeeding Ocean. Averting her eyes, her gaze falls on a cork board over the kitchen table. It is covered in multicoloured bits of paper: party invitations, children's drawings, photographs. She sees a picture of the twins holding a football trophy. Then she sees another photo. It is a faded snapshot of Delilah and Alan next to a standing stone, probably Stonehenge or possibly Avebury. But it is not the stone that catches Ruth's attention; it is the other person in the picture. Wearing jeans and a T-shirt and with normal-length hair it is nonetheless definitely Cathbad.

'ARE YOU SURE it was him?'

'Certain. He had short hair and ordinary clothes but it was him without a doubt.'

'Bastard! I knew he was hiding something.'

'It could be quite innocent.'

'Then why didn't he mention it when I interviewed him? He acted as if he'd hardly heard the name Henderson.'

Ruth and Nelson are in a pub near the harbour. Ruth had been surprised when Nelson suggested lunch, not least because it was three o'clock when they left the Hendersons'. But it seems no landlord will refuse to serve a policemen complete with warrant card, and now they are sitting in an empty bar looking out onto the quayside.

Ruth tucks into a ploughman's lunch. Nelson eats sausages and mash like someone refuelling, not noticing what he puts into his mouth. He has insisted on paying. Ruth drinks diet coke. Nelson chooses the full-fat variety.

'My wife keeps nagging me to drink diet drinks,' he says. 'She says I'm overweight.'

'Really,' says Ruth drily.

Nelson chews meditatively for a few minutes, then asks, 'How long ago do you think the picture was taken?'

'Hard to tell. Cathbad's hair was dark and it's quite grey now.'

'More than ten years ago? Before you first met him?'

'Maybe. Delilah looked young.'

'She dresses like a teenager now.'

'She's very beautiful.'

Nelson grunts, then says, 'What did you think of Alan? Bit of an unlikely partner for her, wouldn't you say? With her being so beautiful and all.'

Ruth thinks of Alan Henderson, with his sharp, rodent's face and darting eyes. He does seem an unlikely husband for Delilah who, even in her distress, seemed somehow exotic. But then they have four children together so presumably the marriage works. 'The eldest child, Maddie, isn't his,' she says. 'Maybe she married him on the rebound.'

'How the hell do you know that?'

'She told me.'

Nelson smiles. 'I thought she'd talk to you.'

'Is that why you made us have tea with them?'

'I didn't. They offered.'

'And you accepted. For both of us.'

Nelson grins. 'I'm sorry. I just thought we might need to build bridges with them. After all, we'd been there all morning digging their garden up. I thought they might appreciate a nice friendly chat. And I thought Delilah might open up to you.'

'Open up? About what?'

'Oh, I don't know. You'd be surprised what turns out to be useful.'

'It was just horrible,' Ruth says, 'to see them suffering so much and not to be able to do anything about it.'

Nelson nods. 'It is horrible. That's when I hate my job the most.'

'It was so sad, the way Delilah kept referring to Scarlet in the present tense but we don't know if she's alive or dead.'

Nelson nods soberly. 'It's every parent's worst nightmare. When you have children, you realise you'd do anything to keep them safe. But sometimes there just isn't anything you can do. And that's the hardest thing.'

He stops and takes a swig of coke, embarrassed at saying so much. Ruth watches him with wonder. She thought she could understand what Delilah Henderson felt, losing a beautiful child like Scarlet, but the thought that Nelson should feel like that about the two stroppy adolescents she had seen him with at the shopping centre seems almost unbelievable. Yet looking at his face as he stares into his glass, she does believe it.

NOW THERE IS a new noise at night. Three cries, very low and echoey, the third cry always the longest and most frightening. She's used to the other sounds at night, the snufflings and rustlings, the wind. Sometimes it feels as if the wind is going to roar through the trap door and snatch her up. She imagines herself thrown high into the air, sailing through the clouds, looking down on all the houses and people. Funny, she knows exactly what she will see: a little white house with a swing in the garden. Sometimes there's a girl on the swing, laughing as she flies into the air. If she closes her eyes, she can still see the house and it's hard to believe she hasn't actually floated there on the clouds, looking down on the girl and the swing and the neat rows of bright flowers.

Once she saw a face at the window. A monster's face. Grey-white with black stripes on either side. She kept very still, waiting for the monster to see her and gobble her up. But it hadn't. It had sort of sniffed at the bars with its wet black nose like those shoes that she had once had for best. Then it had gone away, clattering horribly over the glass.

The new sound is very close sometimes. It happens when the night is very dark and very cold. It wakes her up and she shivers, wrapping her blanket round her. She doesn't know why but she thinks it might be calling to her. Once she calls back, 'I'm here! Let me out!' and the sound of her own voice is the scariest thing of all.

Chapter 6

In the morning, Nelson brings Sparky's body back. He stands on the doorstep, holding the ominous-looking cardboard box.

Ruth, still bleary-eyed before her first coffee, squints at him.

'I did promise.' Nelson indicates the box.

'Yes, thank you. Come in. I'll make us some coffee.'

'Coffee would be grand.'

Nelson puts the box on the floor by the sofa. Ruth busies herself with the coffee and Nelson stands in the sitting room, looking around with a slight frown. Ruth is reminded of the first time she saw him, at the university, and the impression she had of him being too big for the room. That is certainly the case here. Nelson, looming in his heavy black jacket, makes the tiny cottage seem even smaller. Erik is tall but he had seemed able to fold himself up into the space. Nelson looks as if he might, at any second, knock something over or bash his head against the ceiling.

'Lots of books,' he says, when Ruth comes in with coffee and biscuits.

'Yes, I love reading.'

Nelson grunts. 'The wife belongs to a book club. All they do is moan about their husbands. They never talk about the bloody book at all.'

'How do you know?'

'I've listened when they meet at our place.'

'Maybe they talk about the books when you're not listening.'

Nelson acknowledges this with a slight smile.

'Did you find anything?' asks Ruth, 'from . . . from Sparky?'

Nelson takes a gulp of coffee and shakes his head. 'We won't know until tomorrow at the earliest. I've had the letters tested again as well. We're checking the prints and DNA results against known offenders.'

Ruth wonders what has prompted this course of action. Nelson sounds very much as if he has a 'known offender' in mind. Before she can ask, Nelson puts down his coffee cup and looks at his watch.

'Have you got a spade?' he asks briskly.

Reluctant to bury Sparky, Ruth wants to stay inside drinking coffee and pretending that nothing bad has happened. But she knows it can't be put off and so she gets her coat and shows Nelson to the tool shed.

Ruth's garden is a tiny square of wind-blown grass. When she first moved in, she had tried to plant things, but they were always the wrong things and nothing ever seemed to grow except thistles and wild lavender. Next door, the weekenders have a smart deck, which, in summer, they adorn with terracotta pots. Today, though, it looks as forlorn and empty as Ruth's garden. David's garden is even more overgrown though it does contain an elaborate bird table complete with a device to repel cats.

There is a dwarf apple tree at the end of the garden and it is here that Ruth asks Nelson to dig the grave. He does the job quickly, then hands Ruth the box. She wants to look inside but she knows this would not be a good idea. Instead, she drops a kiss on the lid and places the box in the grave.

Ruth gets another spade and helps Nelson fill in the hole. For a few minutes, the only sound in the garden is their breathing as they shovel in the earth. Nelson has taken off his jacket and hung it on the apple tree.

When the hole is filled in, Nelson and Ruth look at each other. Ruth understands why burials are therapeutic. Earth to earth. She has buried Sparky but her cat will always be there, part of the garden, part of her life.

'What about the candle?' she asks Nelson.

'I'll do it on Sunday. A decade of the rosary too.'

They look at each other over the newly dug grave and smile. Geese call, high overhead, and a light rain starts to fall.

'I'd better be going,' says Nelson, but he doesn't move.

Ruth looks at him, the rain falling softly on her hair. Nelson smiles, an oddly gentle smile. Ruth opens her mouth to speak but the silence is broken by a voice that seems to come from another world, another existence.

'Ruth! What are you doing out here?'

It is Peter.

WHEN NELSON DRIVES AWAY, gruff and professional once more, Ruth makes more coffee and sits at the table with Peter.

He looks good, thinks Ruth. His gingery blond hair is shorter, he is about a stone lighter and he even has a tan, something so unusual (Peter has typical redhead's skin) that it makes him look almost shockingly different.

'Who was that man again?' asks Peter.

'It's a long story,' says Ruth.

Peter is a good audience. He is shocked at the death of Sparky—he loved the cats, she remembers—and fascinated by the Iron Age bodies and the causeway. She tells him a little about the police investigations, but not the letters, and he says he has read about the Scarlet Henderson case.

'Poor little girl. Terrible for the parents. Do the police really think that the murderer might have killed Sparky as a sort of warning to you?'

'It's a possibility, they think.'

'God, Ruth. You do live, don't you?'

Ruth detects a tinge of envy in Peter's voice for her supposedly exciting life. She wants to tell him, that far from being excited, she actually feels lonely and scared. She looks at him, wondering how honest to be.

It is odd to see Peter in the cottage again. He and Ruth had lived here together for a year. Ruth bought the cottage a few years after the henge dig, drawn to the Saltmarsh and its desolate beauty. By that time she and Peter had been living together for two years and there was talk of their buying the place together. Ruth had resisted, at the time not even sure why, and Peter had given in. The cottage was hers alone and she remembers that, when Peter moved out, the place didn't even seem to notice. There were a few gaps on the walls and in her bookshelves but, on the whole, the house seemed to close in on her, satisfied. At last they were alone.

'I've missed this place,' says Peter, looking out of the window. 'Living in London you never get to see the sky. There's so much sky here.'

Ruth looks out at the expanse of stormy, gunmetal sky over the marshes. 'Lots of sky,' she agrees, 'But not much else.'

'I like it,' says Peter, 'I like the loneliness.'

'So do I,' says Ruth.

Peter is looking sadly into his coffee cup. 'Poor little Sparky,' he says. 'I remember when we first brought her home. She was no bigger than that squeaky mouse toy we bought her.'

Ruth can't take much more of this. 'Come on,' she says, 'Let's go for a walk. I'll show you the causeway.'

THE WIND HAS GROWN stronger and, as they walk, they have to lower their heads to stop the sand blowing into their eyes. Ruth would be happy to stomp along in silence but Peter seems keen to chat. He tells her about his work, his recent skiing trip and his views on the government. He doesn't, once, mention Victoria or Daniel. Ruth tells him about her work, her family and the Iron Age bodies.

'What does Erik think?' asks Peter.

'He thinks they're all connected.'

'Oh, indeed.' Peter adopts a thick Norwegian accent. 'The sacred site, the power of the landscape, the gateway between life and death.'

Ruth laughs. 'Exactly. Phil, on the other hand, thinks it's all coincidence pending geophysics reports and radiocarbon dating.'

'What do *you* think?'

'I think they're connected,' Ruth says. 'The first Iron Age body marks the beginning of the marsh; the causeway leads almost straight to the henge, which marks the point where the marsh became tidal. I don't know about the Spenwell bones but they must mark a boundary of some sort.'

They have reached the first buried post. Ruth points out the soft bog oak, scored by the tiny teeth of molluscs.

'Erik's getting it dated, but we think it's from the same era as the henge.'

Peter pats the oak stump. 'Will you have to uproot the posts?'

'Erik doesn't want to.'

'I remember all that fuss when we dug up the henge. The druids tying themselves to the posts. The police dragging them away.'

'Yes.' Ruth remembers it too. Vividly. 'The thing is . . . we did find out a lot about the henge by excavating. The type of axe used to chop the wood down, for example. We even found some of the rope used to tow it.'

'Mistletoe rope wasn't it?'

'You've got a good memory.'

'I remember everything about that summer.' Seeing Peter looking at her, Ruth avoids his gaze. She stares out to sea, where the waves are breaking. A stone skims past her, jumping once, twice, three times.

Ruth turns to look at Peter who grins, flexing his arm.

'You were always good at that,' says Ruth.

'It's a man thing.'

They are silent for a moment, watching the waves, then, 'Peter,' says Ruth at last, 'why are you here?'

'I told you, to research my book.'

The wind is whipping the sand up into their faces, like a fine gritty rain. Ruth rubs her eyes. Peter, too, brushes sand out of his eyes. When he looks back at Ruth, his eyes are red.

'Victoria and I, we've split up. I suppose I just wanted to come back.'

Ruth takes a deep breath that is almost a sigh. Somehow, she thinks, she had known this all along. 'I'm sorry. Why didn't you tell me before?'

'I don't know,' Peter speaks into the wind so it is hard for her to catch his words. 'I suppose I wanted everything to be like it was before.'

After a few minutes, they turn round and walk back towards the house.

HALFWAY BACK, it starts to rain; sharp, horizontal rain that stings their faces. Ruth has her head down and doesn't realise they have drifted northwards, until she sees the hide in front of her. She remembers it from the map. It is on a shingle spit, almost at the tide mark. You would need to be a determined birdwatcher, she thinks, to venture this far across the marsh.

'Ruth!'

Ruth looks up to see David standing by the hide holding a plastic bag.

'Hello,' she says. 'Clearing up?'

'Yes,' David's face is dark. 'They never learn. There are notices everywhere and still they leave their crap all over the place.'

Ruth tuts and introduces Peter, who comes forward to shake hands.

'David is the warden of the bird sanctuary,' she explains.

'Must be an interesting job,' says Peter.

'It is,' says David with animation. 'This is a wonderful place for birds.'

'I came here years ago, for a dig,' says Peter, 'but I've never really got it out of my system. It's so lonely and so peaceful.'

David says, 'I saw a police car outside your house, Ruth.'

'Yes,' Ruth sighs. 'You know I'm helping the police with an investigation, with the forensic side.'

'Ruth's cat was killed,' Peter cuts in, to Ruth's annoyance. 'The police think it might be significant.'

Now David looks shocked. 'Your cat was killed? How?'

Frowning at Peter, Ruth says shortly, 'Her throat was cut. They think it could be linked to the investigation.'

'My God. How awful!' David makes a gesture as if to touch Ruth's arm.

'Yes, well, I was upset. I was . . . fond of her.'

'Of course you were. She was company.' He says it like he knows the importance of company.

They stand there awkwardly for a few minutes, in the rain, then Ruth says, 'We'd better be getting back.'

'Yes,' says David, squinting towards the horizon. 'The tide's coming in.'

'I nearly drowned once on these mud flats,' says Peter chattily. 'Got cut off by the tide.'

'The tide comes in faster than a galloping horse, they say,' says David.

'Let's gallop off then,' says Ruth. She is fed up with both of them.

As they trudge away, Ruth's phone rings. For some reason she knows it will be Nelson.

It is a text: Have arrested Malone. His prints on letters. HN.

'WE'VE GOT TO DO SOMETHING,' says Erik. 'The police haven't got a suspect so they're trying to frame Cathbad. We can't let them get away with it.'

'Apparently his fingerprints were on the letters,' says Ruth cautiously.

'Fingerprints, huh! You think they aren't capable of faking evidence?'

Erik paces angrily round the tiny office. They are at the university. Ruth has a student consultation in ten minutes. However, Erik, who has been ranting against the police for the past half-hour, shows no sign of leaving.

'Anyway, writing a letter doesn't make him a murderer. There's nothing that links him to that little girl. Nothing.'

Ruth thinks back to the photo in the Hendersons' kitchen. She knows there *is* something that links Cathbad to the Hendersons. Does this make him a murderer? His fingerprints were on the letters. Does this make him the author? Ruth thinks about the letters. Cathbad knows about mythology, he knows about archaeology, he is fanatically interested in the saltmarsh. He is a likely candidate. But why? Is he really capable of killing a little girl and taunting the police? And Lucy Downey? Could he have killed her too?

'I don't know,' she says. 'I don't know any more than you.'

This isn't quite true. After receiving his text, Ruth rang Nelson. His phone was switched off but he rang her that evening. Peter had gone home.

Nelson sounded excited, almost jubilant. 'Turned out we had his prints on file. He'd been arrested before, demonstrations, that sort of thing. That's why I tested again. And we've got a link to Scarlet.'

'Does he admit anything?'

'No.' A harsh laugh. 'Says it's all a set-up, wicked police state and all that. But he can't deny he knows the Hendersons. Turns out he's the father of the eldest girl.'

'*What?*'

'Yes. He knew Delilah Henderson when she was still at school. He was a student at Manchester, she lived nearby. They had an affair and the result was Madeleine. Apparently they lived together for a bit but then she left him for another bloke.'

'Alan Henderson?'

'No, someone else. He came later. Anyway, she left Malone and he claims he hasn't seen her to this day. Had no idea she was living nearby.'

'He must have seen her on the TV. When Scarlet first went missing.'

'Hasn't got a TV. Harmful rays, apparently, polluting the atmosphere.'

'Will you tell the press?'

'Not if I can help it.'

But someone had told them because that night, on the radio, Ruth heard that 'a local man has been arrested in connection with the disappearance of four-year-old Scarlet Henderson'. She had switched on the TV news and, immediately, Nelson's face, dark and forbidding, had filled the screen. 'Detective Chief Inspector Harry Nelson,' intoned the newsreader, 'who, up to now, had had to admit no progress in the case of little Scarlet Henderson, was tonight unavailable for comment.' As if to prove this, Nelson swept past the hovering reporters and bounded up the steps to the police station. 'The man is believed to be forty-two-year-old Michael Malone, a lab technician at North Norfolk University.'

Jesus, thought Ruth, they know his name. Now all hell will break loose.

And it had. That morning, Ruth had been stopped at the university gates and asked to show her ID. Nodding her through, the policeman had told her to avoid the chemistry wing. Naturally this had aroused her curiosity and she had driven straight round to find the entrance to the chemistry department completely blocked by cars, trailers, even a portaloo. TV camera crews jostled to and fro, waving giant fluffy microphones. Anyone entering the building was greeted by a hysterical babble of questions, 'Do you know Michael Malone? Who is he? What sort of . . .' Hastily Ruth backed away to the relative calm of the archaeology block.

Erik had arrived an hour later, eyes blazing, white hair flying.

'Have you heard? Have you heard?'

'Yes.'

'What are you going to do about it?'

'Me? What can I do?'

'You're friendly with this policeman, this Neanderthal, aren't you?'

'Not exactly friendly . . .'

Erik had looked at her narrowly. 'That's not what Cathbad said. He said you and this Nelson turned up together to interview him. Very cosy. He said there was a definite chemistry between you.'

'Bollocks.' Unthinkingly, Ruth employs a favourite word of Nelson's.

Erik didn't seem to have heard her. 'Nelson is using Cathbad as a scapegoat and you, Ruth, delivered Cathbad to him. On a plate.'

'I didn't! I asked *you* if you remembered his name. *You* told me.'

'And you told Nelson.'

'He would have found him anyway.'

'Would he? He seems a complete incompetent to me. No, he used you to deliver Cathbad. He used you, Ruth.'

'What if Cathbad did do it?' Ruth countered angrily. 'Don't you want the murderer to be found?'

Erik smiled pityingly. 'Ruth, Ruth. He has really got to you, hasn't he? You're even thinking like a policeman.'

Ruth is angry that Erik thinks her a patsy, a fool who has been used by the cynical Nelson in his attempt to pin the crime on Cathbad. But, secretly, she does feel slightly guilty. She suggested Cathbad to Nelson. If Cathbad didn't do it, his life could be ruined by this notoriety. He could even go to prison for a crime he didn't commit. But what if he did do it?

'I don't know what's going on,' she says again.

Erik looks at her, his blue eyes cold. 'Then find out, Ruthie.' And he sweeps out.

RUTH HAS TO BATTLE past the reporters again on her way home. The news reports gave no further developments in the case. 'Police have been granted another twenty-four hours to question the suspect, believed to be forty-two-year-old Michael Malone from Blakeney.'

Ruth switches off the radio. She still feels uneasy about Cathbad's arrest. Although she doesn't, like Erik, think that Cathbad is simply a scapegoat; equally it is hard to think of him as a murderer. Yet he *could* conceivably be the author of those letters. Erik hasn't read them. He can't hear the erudite, sinister, taunting voice. *She lies where the earth meets the sky. Where the roots of the great tree Yggdrasil reach down into the next life. . . . She has become the perfect sacrifice.* Thinking of Cathbad in his wizard's chair, the dream-catchers glittering around him, Ruth can imagine him writing these lines. But abducting and killing a little girl? He is the father of Scarlet's half-sister. How could he possibly have done this to Scarlet? To Delilah, whom, presumably, he had once loved?

And what about Lucy Downey, all those years ago? Ruth thinks of Cathbad in his prime, purple cloak fluttering, exhorting his followers to stand firm against the police and the archaeologists. She has a vision of him standing within the timber circle, arms aloft, as the sea water swirls around his feet and the other druids clamber to safety. She had thought at the time that, if conviction could stop the tide, the sea would surely turn in its tracks. But, of course, ten minutes later, Cathbad too was scrambling for the higher ground, holding his sodden robe above his knees. Could this man—ridiculous, impressive, passionate—really be a killer?

When she reaches the Saltmarsh, the tide is out and the birds are coming in to feed. Watching them, Ruth thinks of David, his face transformed as he talked about the migrating birds, and of Peter, saying sadly that he just wanted to come back.

Going back. When Ruth met Peter she was not yet thirty. She had been newly appointed to the job at North Norfolk University and was full of energy and enthusiasm. Peter, a history research fellow at the University of East Anglia, had heard on the academic grapevine about the dig. He had simply turned up one morning with his backpack and bedroll and asked if they wanted help. They had teased him for being a city boy. They laughed at his lack of archaeological knowledge. Yet he was obsessed with the henge and listened enthralled to Erik's tales of ritual and sacrifice. It was he who had found the first oak stump, exposed when a summer storm had blown the sand away from its base. Peter had been frantically digging around the stump when he had been caught by the tide and eventually rescued by Erik.

It was that evening that she realised she loved him, Ruth remembers. They had always got on well together, teaming up on the dig, laughing at the same things. Erik's wife, Magda, had noticed and often seemed to contrive to leave the two of them together.

Once Ruth had cut herself and Peter had helped her put on the plaster; the touch of his hand had made her tremble. And, as they sat by the campfire on the evening of his near-drowning, Ruth had looked at Peter and thought, Now, it has to be now. He could have drowned today, we mustn't waste any more time. Peter had looked up and met her eyes. He had got up and suggested a walk to collect samphire. They had walked to the water's edge, the sound of the sea rustling in the dark and, smiling, had walked into each other's arms.

And now, as Ruth lets herself into her cottage, she wonders if she really wants Peter back in her life. After the walk on Sunday, he has called twice but she hasn't seen him again. He is staying nearby. She could call him tonight, suggest going out for a drink, but she knows she won't.

Inside the cottage, a clock ticks and the seabirds are calling from the marshes. Otherwise, all is silent.

Ruth makes some tea and sits at her computer, meaning to work. But the Lucy letters insist on running through her mind. *You are looking for Lucy but looking in the wrong places . . . Look where the land lies. Look at the cursuses and the causeways.*

Ruth is missing something, she knows it. It is as if she has all the evidence from a dig, all the pottery shards and flakes of flint, all the soil samples, and she can't put it together to make a proper picture. What did Erik say? *The most important thing is the direction.*

Ruth gets out her map of north Norfolk. She traces a line from Spenwell, where the bones were found in the Hendersons' garden, to the bones at the edge of the saltmarsh. She continues the line along the route marked by the causeway. It leads where she thought it would: straight as an arrow, to the centre of the henge circle. To the sacred ground.

She looks down at her page of notes. Under the heading CURSUSES she has written: *Can be seen as lines pointing to sacred places. Longest cursus in Britain: 4 miles. Sight lines—tell you where to look.*

With a shaking hand Ruth reaches for her phone.

'Nelson? I think I know where Scarlet is buried.'

THEY WAIT FOR THE TIDE and set off at first light. When they return from the henge circle, with Scarlet's body zipped into a police body bag, Ruth is driven back to her house. She has left Nelson in the car park where they first found the bones. He is waiting for a policewoman to arrive so they can break the news to Scarlet's parents.

On the way home Ruth asks the driver to stop so she can be sick. She is sick again, back in the cottage, listening to the radio news. 'Police searching for four-year-old Scarlet Henderson have found a body believed to be that of the missing child . . .' *The missing child.* How can those few words convey the horrific pathos of the little arm encircled by the silver bracelet? The little girl taken from the people who loved her: murdered, buried in the sand, covered by the sea.

She calls Phil and tells him that she won't be coming in. He is agog but remembers to feel sorry for Scarlet's parents. 'Poor people, it doesn't bear thinking about.' But Ruth has to think about it, all day long. Ten minutes later, Peter phones. Does Ruth want him to come over? She says no, she is fine. She doesn't want to see Peter; she doesn't want to see anyone.

By midday, the Saltmarsh is seething with people. It has started to rain again but still she can see little figures crawling over the sands. A new gaggle of journalists swarms past. At least the press haven't caught up with her yet. Ruth sees David standing outside his house, binoculars in hand, looking thunderous. He must hate the saltmarsh being invaded like this. The birds have been frightened away and the skies are low and dark. Thank God Sammy and Ed have gone back to London so Ruth doesn't have to bear their curiosity and concern. She pulls the curtains.

Erik rings. He is conciliatory, concerned. Ruth wishes she didn't think that he is as much concerned with the archaeological site as with Scarlet's fate. The police are digging madly in the very centre of the henge circle. For Erik, as for David, the site will be contaminated for ever. He can hardly say this, though, and after a few platitudes he rings off.

The rain continues to fall, somewhat thwarting the journalists, whom Ruth hears tramping back along New Road. Ruth, who hasn't eaten all day, pours herself a glass of wine. The phone rings. She picks it up wearily. Peter? Erik? Her mother?

'Dr Ruth Galloway?' An unfamiliar voice, slightly breathless.

'Yes?'

'I'm from the *Chronicle*.' The local paper. 'I hear you were involved with the discovery of Scarlet Henderson's body?'

'I've got nothing to say.' Ruth slams down the phone, hands shaking. Immediately it rings again and she takes it off the hook.

Flint crashes in through the cat flap, making Ruth jump sky high. She feeds him and tried to get him to sit on her lap, but he too is twitchy, prowling round the room with his whiskers quivering.

It is nine o'clock. Ruth, who has been up since four, is exhausted but feels too strung out to go to bed. Neither, for some reason, can she read or watch TV. She just sits there, in the dark, watching Flint circling the room.

Ten o'clock and a heavy knock on the door sends the cat running upstairs. Though she doesn't know why, Ruth is trembling from head to foot. She switches on a light and edges towards the door. Though the rational archaeologist in her tells her that it is probably only Peter or Erik or Shona, the irrational side tells her that something dreadful lurks outside the door. Something terrible arisen from the mud and the sand.

'Who is it?' she calls out, trying to keep her voice steady.

'Me. Nelson,' comes the reply.

Ruth opens the door. Nelson looks terrible. He is unshaven, red-eyed, his clothes soaking. He steps into the sitting room and sits down on the sofa. It seems, at that moment, completely right that he should be there.

'Do you want anything to drink?' she asks. 'Tea? Coffee? Wine?'

'Coffee, please.'

When she comes back with the coffee, Nelson is sitting, leaning forward, his head in his hands. Ruth notices the amount of grey in his thick, dark hair. Surely he can't have aged in just a couple of months?

Ruth puts a mug on the table beside him. 'Was it terrible?' she asks.

Nelson groans, rubbing his hands over his face. 'Terrible,' he says at last. 'Delilah just . . . just crumpled up like someone had squeezed all the life out of her. She just collapsed and lay there, curled up in a ball, crying, calling out for Scarlet. Judy, the WPC, was very good, but what could anyone say?' He picked up a mug. 'Jesus. I've broken bad news before in my time but never anything like this. If I go to hell tomorrow, it can't be worse than this.'

He is silent again for a few moments, frowning into his coffee mug. Ruth puts her hand on his arm but says nothing.

Eventually Nelson says, 'I hadn't really understood how much she believed that Scarlet was still alive. I think we all thought . . . after two months . . . she must be dead. Like with Lucy, you gradually stop hoping. But Delilah really believed her little girl was going to walk back through the front door one day. She kept saying, "She can't be dead." I had to tell her, "I've seen her", and then, Christ, I had to ask them to identify the body.'

'Did they both go?'

'I wanted Alan to go on his own but Delilah insisted on coming too. I think, right up to the moment that she saw the body, Delilah was hoping it wasn't Scarlet. When she saw the body, that's when she collapsed.'

'Do they know how long . . . how long Scarlet had been dead?'

'No. We'll have to wait for the forensic report.' He sighs. Then, speaking for the first time in his business-like, policeman's voice, 'She didn't look like she'd been dead long, did she?'

'That was the peat,' says Ruth. 'It's a natural preservative.'

They are silent again for a moment, deep in their own thoughts.

'I've had another letter,' Nelson says, breaking the silence. He brings a crumpled piece of paper out of his pocket. 'It's a copy,' he explains. 'Original's with forensics.'

Ruth leans forward to read.

Nelson,
You seek but you do not find. You find bones where you hope to find flesh. All flesh is grass. I have told you this before. I grow tired of your foolishness, your inability to see. Do I have to draw a map for you? Point a line to Lucy and to Scarlet?
The nearer the bone, the sweeter the flesh. Do not forget the bones.
In sorrow.

Ruth looks at Nelson. 'When did you get this?'

'Today. In the post. It was sent yesterday.'

'So, when Cathbad was in custody?'

'Yes.' Nelson looks up. 'Doesn't mean he couldn't have arranged to have it sent though.'

'Do you think that's what he did?'

'Maybe. Or this letter could be from a different person.'

'It reads like the others,' says Ruth, examining the typewritten paper. 'Biblical quotation, the tone, the reference to sight. It even says, "I have told you this before."'

'Yes. That struck me too. Almost as if he was trying too hard to tie it to the other letters.'

Ruth looks at the words. *Point a line to Lucy and to Scarlet.* She remembers last night tracing the path on the map from the Spenwell bones to the marsh bones to the henge circle. She shivers. It is as though the writer was at her shoulder, watching her as she drew the line that led to Scarlet.

'So, do you still think Cathbad did it?'

Nelson sighs, running his hands through his hair so that it stands up like a crest. 'I don't know, but I haven't got enough to charge him. No DNA, no motive, no confession. We've been over his caravan with a toothcomb, found nothing. I'll keep him until I get the forensics report. If I find a trace of his DNA on Scarlet then he's finished.'

Ruth looks at Nelson. He looks younger somehow, almost vulnerable. Maybe it's the rumpled hair and dishevelled clothes.

'But you don't think he did it, do you?'

Nelson looks at her. 'No, I don't,' he says.

'Then who did?'

'I don't know.' Nelson lets out another sigh, almost a groan. 'That's the terrible thing. All those hours of investigation, all that police time, all that searching and questioning and I've still no bloody idea who killed those two girls. No wonder the media are shouting for my head.'

'I got a call from the *Chronicle* this evening.'

'How did they know about you? I've kept your name out of it.'

Who could have told them? Erik? Shona? Peter?

'They'll make life hard for you,' warns Nelson. 'Is there anywhere you could go for a few days?'

'I could stay with my friend Shona.'

'Good. I've sent my wife and kids to my mum. Until the worst is over.'

'When *will* the worst be over?'

'I don't know.' Nelson looks at her again, his dark eyes troubled. She can hear the rain and the wind outside but somehow it seems a long way away, as if this room, this tiny circle of light, is all that is left in the world.

Nelson is still looking at her. 'I don't want to go home,' he says at last.

Ruth reaches out to lay her hand on his. 'You don't have to,' she says.

THE SILENCE WAKES RUTH. The wind and rain have stopped and the night is still. She thinks she hears an owl hooting and, far off, the sigh of the waves.

The moon shines serenely through the open curtains and illuminates the crumpled bed, the strewn clothes and the sleeping figure of DCI Harry Nelson, breathing heavily, one arm flung out across Ruth's breasts. Gently, Ruth lifts the arm and gets up to put on some pyjamas. She can't believe she went to bed naked. Somehow that is even harder to accept than the fact that she went to bed with Nelson. That she laid her hand on his, that, seconds later, she reached over to touch his lips with hers. She remembers his slight hesitation, a whisper of indrawn breath, before his hand reached up behind her head and he pulled her to him. They had clung to each other, kissing desperately, hungrily, as the rain battered against the windows. She remembers the roughness of his skin, the surprising softness of his lips, the feel of his body against hers.

How could this have happened? She hardly knows Harry Nelson. All she does know is that last night they seemed to share something that set them apart from all the world. They had seen Scarlet's body as it rose, lifeless, from the sand. They had, in some small way, shared her family's pain. They had read the letters. They knew of the evil presence out there in the dark. They knew of Lucy Downey too, feared that the next discovery would be her body. And it had seemed only natural that this knowledge should draw them into each other's arms, that they should blot out the pain with the comforts of the body. They might never do it again but last night . . . last night had been right.

Even so, thinks Ruth, pulling on her pyjamas, he'd better leave soon. The press knows about her. The last thing either of them wants is for the media to discover the leading policeman in the Scarlet Henderson case in bed with the bones expert. She looks down at Nelson. In sleep his dark eyelashes fan out against his cheeks, his harsh mouth is gentle.

'Nelson?' Ruth shakes him. 'You'd better go.'

He groans. 'What time is it?'

'Almost four.'

He wakes immediately, then looks at her as if wondering who she is and then smiles. The surprisingly sweet smile that she has seen only once or twice before. 'Good morning, Dr Galloway.'

'Good morning, DI Nelson,' says Ruth. 'You'd better get dressed.'

As Nelson reaches for his clothes, Ruth sees a tattoo high on his shoulder, blue writing around some kind of shield.

'What does your tattoo say?' she asks.

'Seasiders. It's a nickname for my team, Blackpool. Michelle hates it.'

There, he has said her name. Michelle, the perfect wife, who hovered between them all last night, is suddenly there in the room. Nelson, pulling on his trousers, seems unconscious of what he has said.

Dressed, he looks a different person. A policeman, a stranger. He comes over to her, sits on the bed and takes her hand. 'Thanks,' he says.

'What for?'

'Being there.'

'Just doing my duty as a citizen.'

He grins. 'You should get a medal.'

Ruth watches as he retrieves his mobile from under the bed. She feels oddly detached, as if she is watching something on television.

'Will you go to your friend's house?' Nelson shrugs on his jacket.

'I think so, yes.'

'Well, keep in touch. Any trouble from the press, give me a shout.'

'I will.'

At the doorway he turns and smiles. 'Goodbye, Dr Galloway,' he says.

Chapter 7

Unable to get back to sleep, Ruth gets up and showers. Afterwards, she dries herself briskly and goes into her bedroom. She strips the bed and dresses quickly in trousers and fleece. Then she gets out a bag and starts to pack some clothes. She will take Nelson's advice and go to Shona's for a few days. She'll call her from the university.

Packing her pyjamas, she thinks of Nelson. Did he sleep with her only to blot out the horror of finding Scarlet's body? He can't possibly fancy her, not with Miss Blonde Housewife 2008 waiting for him at home. Does she fancy him? If she is honest, yes. She has been attracted to him ever since she saw him in the corridor that first time, looking too big and grown-up for his surroundings. He is an antidote to the weedy academic types around her: men like Phil and Peter, even Erik. Nelson would never sit and pore over dusty reference books; his preference is for doing things: striding over the marshes, questioning suspects, driving too fast. Sleeping with women who aren't his wife? Well, maybe. She senses it isn't the first time he has been unfaithful to Michelle. There was something practised about his demeanour this morning, gathering up his clothes, not making any promises about when they might meet next. But there had been emotion too last night, something surprisingly tender. She remembers his sharp intake of breath when she first kissed him, the way he had murmured her name, the way he had kissed her, softly at first and then much harder.

Stop thinking about it, she tells herself as she lugs the bag downstairs. It was a one-off. It will never happen again. How can it? He is married, they have almost nothing in common. It was only the circumstances of last night that conjured up that particular spell.

Flint purrs at her ankles and Ruth wonders what to do about him. She can't take him to Shona's. She'll have to ask David to feed him.

It is still only six o'clock. She makes herself coffee and toast. The sky is still dark but there is a faint line of gold against the horizon.

At seven, she goes to call on David. She is sure he gets up early, for the dawn chorus or something. It is light now and the day is cold and clear, the sky washed clean by yesterday's rain. There will be nothing to stop the journalists today. Nelson is right: she must get away.

David takes a long time to open the door but when he does he is wearing waterproofs and looks like he has already been outside.

'I'm sorry to call so early,' says Ruth, 'but I've got to go away for a few days. Could you possibly feed Flint, my cat? I'd be really grateful.'

'Flint?' he repeats.

'My cat. Could you come in and feed him for a few days?'

David seems to be registering her for the first time. 'Ruth,' he says. 'Were you involved in all that drama yesterday?'

Drama? The word seems wrong for what has happened.

'Yes,' says Ruth shortly. 'I found the body.'

'My God!' David looks really shocked. 'How awful.'

'The press were after me yesterday. I want to lie low for a bit.'

'The press.' David's face darkens. 'Vermin. Trampling over the reed beds, dropping litter everywhere. Will they be back today, do you think?'

'I'm afraid so.'

'I'd better be on patrol.' David looks grim. Ruth thinks it might be time to remind him about Flint. She proffers her key.

'So, is it all right about the cat? His food's in the kitchen. He has one small tin every day and some biscuits. Otherwise, he'll just come and go. He's got a cat flap. I'll leave my contact details on the table.'

David takes the key. 'Food. Cat flap. Contact details. Fine. Yes. OK.'

Ruth hopes that he will remember.

The roads are clear and she gets to the university in record time. The car parks are empty. It seems that journalists, like academics, are not early risers. She punches in the code to open the doors and escapes to her office with a sigh of relief. Three cups of coffee and several pages of lecture notes later, there is a knock at the door.

'Come in,' says Ruth. She assumes it will be Phil, but it's Shona. Ruth is surprised. Shona hardly ever ventures over from the arts faculty.

'Ruth'—Shona gives her a hug—'I've just heard about yesterday.'

'Who told you?' asks Ruth.

'Erik. I saw him in the car park.'

'Yes. She was buried right in the centre of the henge circle.'

'My God.' Shona had been on the dig ten years ago. 'Does Erik know where she was found?' she asks, sitting down.

'Yes. I think he's more upset about that than anything. The police digging up the site.' Ruth surprises herself with the bitterness in her voice.

'Why are they still digging?'

'Well, they think the other girl may be buried there. Lucy Downey.'

'The one who disappeared all that time ago?'

'Ten years ago. Just after the henge dig.'

'Do the police think they were killed by the same person?'

Shona's face is soft, concerned, but Ruth also catches a trace of the slightly shamefaced curiosity that she recognises all too well. In herself.

'I don't know,' she says. 'I don't know what the police think.'

'Are they going to charge that druid chap?'

'Cathbad? I'm sorry, Shona, I just don't know.'

'Erik says he's innocent.'

'Yes,' agrees Ruth. She wonders how much Erik has told Shona.

'What do *you* think?' persists Shona.

'I don't know,' says Ruth for what feels like the hundredth time. 'He always seemed harmless. Into peace and nature and all that. But the police must have some evidence otherwise they wouldn't be able to hold him.'

'That Detective Nelson sounds a real hard bastard.'

Briefly Ruth thinks of Nelson. Sees, as if projected in technicolour onto the wall opposite, his face above hers. Feels his stubble against her cheek.

'I really don't know him that well,' she says. 'Look, Shona, I've got a favour to ask you. Can I stay with you for a few days? You see, the press have got wind that I was involved. I think they might come round to my house and I'd just like to get away for a bit.'

'Of course,' says Shona at once. 'You're more than welcome. Tell you what, we'll have a takeaway and a few bottles tonight. Have a real girls' night in. Forget about everything and just unwind. What do you think?'

RUTH DOESN'T ENJOY her girls' night in. She is exhausted and after a few glasses of Pinot Grigio she feels her eyelids begin to droop. Then, for perhaps the first time in her adult life, she isn't hungry. Usually she loves takeaways. But, tonight, after a few mouthfuls of crispy aromatic duck, the smell of soya sauce starts to make her feel sick.

'What's up?' asks Shona, her mouth full. 'Dig in. There's loads.'

'I'm sorry,' says Ruth, 'I'm not very hungry.'

'You have to eat,' intones Shona, as if Ruth were an anorexic schoolgirl rather than an overweight woman in her thirties. 'At least have another drink.' She sloshes more wine into Ruth's glass. 'Come on, chill out.'

Shona lives in a terraced house on the outskirts of King's Lynn. It is near the centre of town, the perfect urban antidote to the Saltmarsh. When she arrived, Ruth installed herself in Shona's spare room (polished floor, pine bed). Now I can relax, she told herself. No one knows where I am. I can have a nice meal and a few glasses of wine. I'll be a new person tomorrow.

But it hasn't worked out like that. She feels ill at ease. She worries that David will forget to feed Flint. She misses her cottage. She feels tired but she knows she won't be able to sleep tonight. As soon as she shuts her eyes the whole thing will play again, like some X-rated movie on a continuous loop: the trek over the mud flats, the discovery of Scarlet's body, Nelson at her door, red-eyed and unshaven, his body moving against hers . . .

Everything is a reminder. Shona's ambient music playing softly in the background reminds her of the rain and the voices of the birds, suddenly stilled. When she looks at Shona's bookshelves and sees T.S. Eliot nestling next to Shakespeare she thinks of the Lucy Downey letters. *We who were living are now dying.*

'So do you think he will?' asks Shona, pouring wine into Ruth's glass.

'What?' Ruth has completely lost track of the conversation.

'Leave Anne. Do you think Liam will leave Anne?'

Not in a million years, thinks Ruth. Just as Nelson will never leave Michelle.

'Maybe. Are you sure you want him to?'

'I don't know. I think I would be terrified, to be honest. There's something safe about going out with a married man. You always think, if it wasn't for his wife, he'd be with me. You don't have to face up to anything else that might be wrong with the relationship. And it stays exciting. You don't have a chance to get bored.'

'Have you done this before then?' As far as Ruth knows, Liam is Shona's first married lover but she is talking like a veteran of extramarital affairs. Like Nelson, she thinks cynically.

Shona's face takes on a closed, watchful expression. She fills up her own glass, splashing wine onto the trendy rush-matting rug. 'Oh, once or twice,' she says, with what sounds like deliberate casualness. 'Before I met you. Now, for heaven's sake drink up, Ruth. You're way behind.'

RUTH WAS RIGHT about not being able to sleep. She tries to immerse herself in Ian Rankin's Inspector Rebus but Rebus and Siobhan become, embarrassingly and explicitly, herself and Nelson. She even opens her laptop and starts to work but, although way behind Shona, she has drunk too much to be interested in Mesolithic burial sites.

She drinks some water, turns over her pillow and determinedly shuts her eyes. A hundred, ninety-nine, ninety-eight, ninety-seven . . . Scarlet's arm hanging down below the tarpaulin . . . ninety-six, ninety-five . . . *We who were living are now dying* . . . ninety-four, ninety-three . . . he'll never leave his wife . . . why are the Iron Age bodies in a line, why did the line point to Scarlet . . . ninety-two, ninety-one . . .

The bleeping of her phone is a welcome relief. She snatches it up gratefully. A text message. The screen gleams green in the dark. Caller unknown.

I know where you are.

THE SKY IS FULL OF NOISES. Thumping noises, crackling noises like very large birds hooting and calling. She knows it is daytime because the window is closed. She can't see anything, hears only the noises. She is scared and huddles in the corner of the room, under the blanket.

For a long time he doesn't come and she is hungry and more scared than ever. She finishes her water and looks in the dark for the piece of bread she thinks she dropped a few days ago.

He doesn't come for a long time and her mouth is dry and the bucket in the corner starts to smell.

She can see lights through the sides of the trap door and she wants to call out but is afraid to. The stone walls are damp and mossy, smooth when she runs her hands over them. She can reach higher now, almost to the dry bits at the top where the stones are crumbly like breadcrumbs. Why can she reach higher? Is she getting bigger? He says so. Too big, he says.

She reaches as high as she can and pulls at one of the stones. It comes away in her hands. She sits on the floor and feels the edge of the stone with her thumb. It is sharp, it cuts her. She licks the blood until it has gone.

She takes the stone to the corner of the room where there is soil, not floor. She digs a hole and, very carefully she places the stone in the hole and covers it with earth. Then she stamps on the soil until it is all smooth again and no one but her would know that something is buried there.

It is the first time she has had a secret. It tastes good.

EXHAUSTION FINALLY SENDS RUTH to sleep at 2 a.m. For several hours she had just listened to her heart pounding and looking at the text message. Who could have sent it? Is it the letter writer, the murderer? Who knows where she is? Who has her mobile phone number? Must it—her stomach contracts—must it be someone she knows?

She has to ring Nelson but, somehow, she doesn't want to call him in the middle of the night. She doesn't want him to think she is hassling him.

She falls asleep and wakes a few hours later. Her phone has fallen to the floor and, hand trembling, she picks it up. No new messages. Ruth sighs and burrows down inside the bed.

When she wakes again there is daylight outside the window and Shona is standing by her bed holding a cup of tea.

'You have slept well,' she says brightly, as Ruth sits up. 'It's past nine.'

Ruth sips the tea gratefully. Sitting in Shona's sunny spare room, she feels ready to fight. She gets up, showers and dresses in her toughest, most uncompromising clothes (black suit, white shirt, scary earrings). Then she goes downstairs ready to kick ass.

She is in her car, ready to drive to work, when her phone goes off. Despite her scary earrings, she is terrified, breathing hard, palms clammy.

'Hi Ruth. It's Nelson.'

'Oh. Nelson. Hello.' For some reason, her heart is still thumping.

'Just wanted you to know, we're releasing Malone tomorrow. Forensic reports have come back and there's none of his DNA on Scarlet. So we're charging him with writing the letters and that's all. He'll come up in court tomorrow and I expect he'll get bail.'

'Is he still a suspect?'

Nelson laughs humourlessly. 'Well he's the only one we've got.'

'What did the . . . the post-mortem say?'

'Death was by asphyxiation. Something was shoved in her mouth and she choked on it. Her hands were tied with some sort of plant plaited together. Looks like honeysuckle and—you'll like this—mistletoe.'

Ruth thinks of the letters and their mention of mistletoe. Does this mean that the writer was the murderer? Does this mean that it was Cathbad after all? Then she thinks of the ropes that had hauled the henge timbers into place. Mistletoe rope. As Peter had remembered.

'Body had been in the ground about six weeks,' Nelson is saying. 'Hard to tell because of the peat. No sign of sexual abuse.'

'That's something,' says Ruth hesitantly.

'Yes,' says Nelson, his voice bitter. 'And we'll be able to let the family have the body for burial. That'll mean a lot to them.' He sighs. Ruth imagines him scowling as he sits at his desk, looking through files, making lists, deliberately not looking at the photo of Scarlet Henderson.

'Any road,' Nelson's voice changes gear, rather jerkily, 'how are you? No more calls from the press, I hope.'

'No, but I had an odd message last night.' Ruth tells him about the text message. She imagines Nelson's eyes shooting heavenwards. *How much more trouble is this woman going to cause me?*

'I'll get someone on to it,' he says. 'Give me the number.'

She does so. 'Can you trace a mobile phone number?'

'Yes. Mobile phones have a unique number they send out every time they make a call. If we have the number, it won't be hard to trace the call. Of course, if he's clever, he'll have ditched the phone. We need to get you some protection. How long are you staying with your mate?'

'I don't know.'

'I'll send some men to watch her house and to keep your place under surveillance. Try not to worry too much. I don't think the murderer'll come out into the open. He's too clever.'

'Is he?'

'Well, he's been too clever for me, hasn't he?'

'You'll catch him,' says Ruth with more conviction that she feels.

'Wish the press agreed with you. Take care, love.'

As she clicks off her phone, Ruth thinks, *love?*

AT THE UNIVERSITY, the first person she sees is Peter. He's waiting outside her room and the memory comes back, unbidden, of seeing Nelson in the same place, so harsh and unyielding next to the conciliatory Phil. Unlike Nelson on that occasion, Peter looks nervous, flattening himself apologetically against the wall every time a student goes past.

'Ruth!' He steps forward to greet her.

'Peter. What are you doing here?'

'I wanted to see you.'

Ruth sighs inwardly. 'You'd better come in,' she says ungraciously.

In her office, Peter swoops on her cat doorstop. 'I remember buying you this. I can't believe you've still got it.'

'It's useful,' says Ruth shortly. She's not about to tell him she has kept it for sentimental reasons.

Peter sinks down in her visitor's chair. 'Great office,' he says. Ten years ago, she hadn't been important enough for an office of her own.

'Bit small,' she says.

'You should see my office at UCL. I share it with an archivist with a personal freshness problem. I only get the desk Mondays and Thursdays.'

Ruth laughs. Peter could always make her laugh, she thinks grudgingly.

Peter smiles too, looking fleetingly like his old self, but then his face looks grave again. 'What a terrible business on the saltmarsh,' he says, 'you finding that little girl's body. How did you know she was there?'

Ruth looks up sharply. This seems an odd question. Who was to say that it wasn't the police who discovered the location?

'It was a hunch,' she says. 'I was looking at the map and saw a line leading from the Spenwell body to my Iron Age body to the henge. The posts I showed you, the causeway, they seemed to mark the route. I thought of cursuses, underground paths that seem to point to significant things in the landscape. I suddenly realised that the causeway was a cursus.'

'But are you saying it was deliberate? That someone buried her there knowing all about causeways and cursuswhatsits?'

'The police think that maybe the murderer knows about archaeology.'

'*Do* they?' Peter is silent for a few seconds. Then he says, 'That reminds me, Erik's set up a dig next week to look at the causeway.'

'Has he got police permission?'

'Apparently so. He spoke to your mate Nelson. He says it's OK as long as they don't go into the henge circle. And, obviously, they've got to show the police anything they find.'

Erik has spoken to Nelson, whom apparently he dislikes and distrusts. Nelson has given permission for the dig. Ruth's head swims in a miasma of contradictions, loyalties, memories.

'When did you see Erik?' she asks at last.

'Yesterday. We had lunch together.'

'Did he say anything about Cathbad? Michael Malone?'

'Only that the police had got the wrong man. He seemed quite heated. Kept going on about a police state. You know what an old hippie he is.'

Yet Erik was quite prepared to go to Nelson for permission to dig, thinks Ruth. Nothing, *nothing*, comes in the way of the archaeology.

'They're releasing Cathbad,' says Ruth. 'It'll probably be on the news today.' Well, Nelson didn't tell her to keep it a secret.

'Really?' says Peter with interest. 'Releasing him without charge?'

'There may be some charges, I don't know.'

'Come off it, Ruth, you seem to know everything.'

'I don't,' snaps Ruth, unreasonably irritated.

'Sorry.' Peter slumps in his chair. It's going to take a rocket to shift him.

'Peter,' says Ruth, lighting the touch paper, 'look, did you want something? I ought to be getting on.'

He looks hurt. 'Just to see how you were. I wondered if you'd like to go out for a drink tonight?'

Ruth thinks of going back to another girls' night in: Pinot Grigio, Liam, takeaway, mysterious text messages. 'Ok,' she says. 'That'd be nice.'

THEY GO TO A RESTAURANT in King's Lynn, near the pub where Ruth had lunch with Nelson. This place, though, has pretensions: blond wooden floors, square plates, banks of flickering candles. Chasing a lone scallop over acres of white china, Ruth says, 'Where did you find this place? It's great,' she adds hastily.

'Phil recommended it.' That figured.

It's early and there are only two other couples dining; two thirtysome-things who are clearly counting the minutes until they can be in bed together and an elderly couple who eat but do not exchange one word.

'Blimey, why don't they get a room?' mutters Ruth as the thirtysomething woman starts licking wine off the man's fingers.

'Probably married to other people.'

'Why do you say that?'

'If they were married to each other, they wouldn't even be talking,' says Peter in a low voice. 'Take a look at the old dears over there. Fifty years of wedded bliss and not a word to say to each other.'

Ruth wants to ask if this was what his marriage was like. Say nothing, she tells herself, and he'll come out with it.

Sure enough, Peter sighs and takes a gulp of overpriced red wine. 'Like me and Victoria. We just . . . drifted apart. We ran out of things to say to each other. Woke up one morning and discovered that, apart from Daniel, we had nothing in common. Oh, we still like each other, it's all very friendly, but that vital something has gone.'

But that's what happened to us, Ruth wants to say. She remembers that feeling of looking at Peter—intelligent, kind, good-looking Peter—and thinking, Is this it? Is this what I have to settle for? A nice man who, when he touches me, I sometimes don't even notice?

But Peter has his rose-tinted spectacles on again. 'With us, we had so much in common,' he says dreamily. 'Archaeology, history, books. Victoria's only serious reading matter is *Hello* magazine.'

'That's very patronising,' says Ruth.

'Don't get me wrong,' says Peter hastily, 'Victoria's a wonderful woman. I'm very fond of her and we're both devoted to Daniel but it's not a marriage any more. We're more like flatmates, sharing childcare and housework, only talking about who's picking up Daniel the next day or when the Tesco delivery is coming.'

'Well, what did you expect to be talking about? Renaissance architecture? The early poems of Robert Browning?'

Peter grins. 'Something like that. Well, *we* talked didn't we? Do you remember the nights round the campfire talking about whether Neolithic man was a hunter-gatherer or a farmer?'

Ruth leans forward. 'Look, Peter, the henge dig was ten years ago. That was then. This is now. We're different people. We had a relationship and that was great but it's in the past. You can't go back.'

'Can't you?' asks Peter, looking at her very intently.

'No,' says Ruth gently.

Peter stares at her in silence for a minute or two, then he smiles. 'Well, let's just get pissed then,' he says, leaning forward to fill up her glass.

She doesn't get pissed but she's probably slightly over the limit when she gets into her car.

'Drive carefully,' says Peter as he heads towards a new Alfa Romeo.

'I will.' Ruth drives slowly, following more decisive cars. Despite her tough words, she sympathises with Peter and his yearning for the past. There is something very tempting about the idea of going back to him, accepting that the mysterious perfect man is not going to turn up, that Peter is the best she is going to get. What's stopping her? Is it Nelson? She knows that nothing will come of the night with Nelson—it is just that imaging herself in bed with Peter seems comforting and familiar; it does not, for one minute, seem exciting.

She finds a parking space and walks towards Shona's house. Out of reflex, she checks her text messages. Just one:

I know where you are.

SCARLET HENDERSON'S FUNERAL takes place on a rainy Friday afternoon.

'It's bad luck to have a funeral on a Friday,' says Shona, looking out of her sitting-room window at the water cascading down the street.

'For Christ's sake,' explodes Ruth. 'When is it good luck to have a funeral?'

She shouldn't have snapped at Shona. She's only trying to be supportive. She has even offered to come to the funeral with her but Ruth says she should go alone. She feels that she owes it to Scarlet, the little girl she knows only in death. Owes it too to Delilah and Alan. And to Nelson? Maybe. She hasn't spoken to him in days. Cathbad's release was on every newscast with Nelson, stony-faced, claiming to be following up new leads. Ruth suspects this is a lie, a suspicion shared, apparently, by most of the press.

The church, on the outskirts of Spenwell, is packed. Ruth finds a space at the back. She can just see Nelson at the front. He is wearing a dark grey suit and looking straight ahead. He is flanked by other burly figures who she thinks must be policemen. There is a policewoman too. Ruth wonders if it is the one who helped to break the news to Scarlet's parents.

The arrival of the tiny coffin, accompanied by a shell-shocked Delilah and Alan, the chrysanthemums spelling out the name 'Scarlet', the siblings, cowed and wide-eyed in their dark clothes, the reedy singing of 'All things bright and beautiful' – all seem designed to break your heart. Ruth feels the tears prickling at the back of her eyes.

The vicar makes a few remarks about angels and innocence and God's right hand. Then, to Ruth's surprise, Nelson steps forward to do a reading. He reads very badly, stumbling over the words, eyes downcast.

'"I am the resurrection and the life," says the Lord. "Those that believe in me even though they die, will live and everyone who lives and believes in me will never die."'

Ruth is reminded uncomfortably of the letters. The writer of the Lucy Downey letters would love this, all his old favourites are here: life, death, the certainty of the afterlife and a comforting pall of mysticism thrown over the whole. Did Cathbad write those letters? And, if so, why? To frustrate the police? She knows that Cathbad dislikes the police—and archaeologists too, for that matter—but is that enough of a reason?

At last it's over and the little white coffin passes so close that Ruth could almost touch it. The final hymn is playing, people are getting to their feet.

Outside the rain has stopped and the air is cold and clammy. The coffin, followed by Scarlet's family, is driven away for a private cremation.

Ruth finds herself next to the policewoman. She introduces herself and the officer's face lights up with recognition.

'Oh, I know about you. The boss's talked about you. I'm Detective Constable Judy Johnson.'

'You're the one who . . .' Ruth stops, not knowing if she should go on.

'Who broke the news. Yes. I've had the training, you see, and they like a woman to go, especially if there's a child involved.'

'Nelson . . . DCI Nelson, said you were very good.'

'That's kind of him but I'm not sure how much anyone could do.'

They are silent for a moment looking at the undertaker's cars lining the road outside. Nelson is getting into one of them. He doesn't look round.

'See those people over there?' DC Johnson indicates a grey-haired couple walking away from the church. 'They're Lucy Downey's parents.'

'How do they know the Hendersons?'

'When Scarlet went missing, Mrs Downey contacted Delilah Henderson to offer support.'

Ruth watches them. Lucy Downey's mother looks old, grey-haired and round-shouldered. Her husband is more robust, he has his arm round her as if he is used to protecting her. How must they feel, attending this funeral when they have never been able to say goodbye to their own daughter? Do they, in some corner of their hearts, still think she is alive?

'Can I give you a lift home?' asks DC Johnson.

Ruth looks at her, thinking of the drive back to Shona's house; Shona's solicitude, tinged with curiosity, the night in the tasteful spare room.

'No, thank you,' she says. 'I've got my car. I'm going straight home.'

And she does. She drives straight back to New Road. She knows she will have to return to Shona's house to pick up her clothes but, at this moment, all she wants to do is go home.

The marshes are grey and dreary under the lowering skies but Ruth is still unaccountably glad to be back. She parks in her usual spot beside the broken fence and lets herself in, shouting joyfully for Flint. He must have been waiting for her because he comes running in from the kitchen, looking ruffled and hard done by. Ruth picks him up, breathing in the lovely, outdoor smell of his fur.

The house is as she left it. David has collected her post and put it in a neat pile. Flint seems fine so he must have remembered to feed him.

The post is mostly boring: bills, overdue library books, a flier from a local theatre, charity appeals, a postcard from a friend in New York. Ruth goes into the kitchen to make a cup of tea. Flint jumps onto the work surface and meows loudly. He must have been getting into bad habits.

Ruth puts him back on the floor whereupon he immediately jumps up again. 'Stupid cat. What are you playing at?'

'Cats aren't stupid,' says a voice behind her. 'They have highly developed mystical powers.'

Ruth swings round. A man wearing a muddy cloak over jeans and an army jacket stands smiling, quite at ease, at her kitchen door. Cathbad.

Ruth backs away. 'How did you get in?' she asks.

'I came in when that man came in to feed the cat. He didn't see me. I can make myself invisible, didn't you know? I've been watching the house for a while. I knew you'd be back. This place has quite a hold over you, hasn't it?'

'What are you doing here?' Ruth says, trying to steady her voice.

'I wanted to talk to you. Have you got any herbal teas?' He gestures towards her mug. 'Caffeine's a poison.'

'I'm not making you a cup of tea. I want you out of my house.'

'It's natural for you to be upset,' says Cathbad kindly. 'Have you been to the funeral? Poor little girl. Poor, undeveloped soul. I've been sitting here sending positive thoughts to Delilah.'

'I'm sure she was very grateful.'

'Don't be angry, Ruth,' says Cathbad with a surprisingly sweet smile. 'We've got no quarrel after all. Erik says you've got a good heart.'

'Very kind of him.'

'He says you understand about the saltmarsh, about the henge. It wasn't your fault the barbarians destroyed it. I remember you that summer, hand in hand with your boyfriend. It was a magical time, wasn't it?'

Ruth lowers her eyes. 'Yes,' she admits. 'What do you want?'

'To talk to you,' says Cathbad again. He picks up Flint, who disgusts Ruth by purring loudly. 'This is a wise cat,' he announces. 'An old soul.'

'He's not that bright,' says Ruth. 'My other cat was cleverer.'

'Yes. I'm sorry about what happened to her.'

'How did you know?' asks Ruth, her voice trembling slightly.

'Erik told me. Why? Did you think I did it?'

Ruth doesn't know what to think. Is she trapped in the kitchen with a cat killer, or worse, a child murderer? She looks at Cathbad at he stands there, holding Flint in his arms. His face is open, slightly hurt-looking. He doesn't look like a killer but then what does a killer look like?

'I don't know what to think,' she says. 'The police have charged you with writing those letters.'

Immediately, Cathbad's face darkens. 'The police! That bastard Nelson has it in for me. I'm going to sue him for wrongful arrest.'

'*Did* you write them?'

Cathbad smiles and puts Flint gently back on the floor. 'I think you know I didn't,' he says. 'You've read them, after all.'

'How did you . . . ?'

'Nelson's not as clever as he thinks. Yakking on about archaeology terms. There's only one person who could have told him all that. You're very friendly, you two, aren't you? There's a definite energy between you.'

Ruth says nothing. Cathbad may not, as Erik claims, be magic, but there is no denying that some of his shots hit the mark.

'I know you, Ruth,' says Cathbad. 'I watched you fall in love with that red-haired fellow all those years ago. I know what you're like when you're in love. You were in love with Erik too, weren't you?'

'Of course not!'

'Oh yes you were. I felt sorry for you because you didn't get a look-in, what with his wife and girlfriend both on the dig.'

'Girlfriend? What do you mean?'

'That beautiful girl with all the hair. Looks like a Renaissance picture. She was sympathetic to us, I remember. Joined in the protests.'

'Shona?' Ruth whispers. 'That's not true.'

'No?' Cathbad looks at her, while Ruth shuffles quickly through her memories. Shona and Erik always liked each other. Erik called Shona 'The Lady of Shalott'. An image comes to Ruth, clear as a film flashback, of Shona plaiting Erik's grey ponytail. 'Like a horse,' she is saying, 'a Viking cart-horse.' And then her hand rests just lightly on his cheek.

Cathbad smiles, satisfied. 'I need you to clear my name, Ruth,' he says.

'I thought the police didn't press charges?'

'Oh, no, they didn't charge me with the murders, but if they never find the killer, it'll always be me, don't you see? Everyone will always think I did it, that I killed those two little girls.'

'And did you?' asks Ruth, greatly daring.

Cathbad's eyes never leave her face. 'No,' he says. 'And I want you to find out who did.'

HE HAS COME BACK. When she sees him climbing in through the trap door she doesn't know if she is pleased or sorry. She is hungry though. She tears at the food he has brought—crisps, sandwiches, an apple—stuffing another mouthful in her mouth before she has finished the first.

'Steady,' he says. 'You'll make yourself sick.'

She doesn't answer. She hardly speaks to him. She saves talking for when she is alone, which, after all, is most of the time, when she can chat to the friendly voices in her head, the ones that tell her it is darkest before dawn.

He gives her a drink in a funny orange bottle. It tastes odd but she gulps it down. Briefly she wonders if it is poison, like the apple the wicked witch gave Snow White, but she is so thirsty she doesn't care.

'I'm sorry I couldn't come before,' he says. She ignores him.

'I'm sorry,' he says again. He often says this but she doesn't really know what it means. 'Sorry' is a word from long ago, like 'love' and 'good night'. What does it mean now? She isn't sure. One thing she knows, if he says it, it can't be a good word. He isn't good, she is sure of it now. At first she was confused, he brought her food and drink and a blanket and sometimes he talked to her. Those were good things, she thought. But now she thinks that he keeps her locked up, which isn't good. After all, if he can climb through the trap door, up into the sky, why can't she? Now she is taller she has tried to jump up to the door and the barred window but she never manages it. Maybe one day, if she keeps getting taller, as tall as . . . what was it called? As tall as a tree, that's it. She'll push her branches through the hole and carry on, up to where she hears the birds singing.

Chapter 8

Ruth is woken from confused dreams by a furious knocking at the door. She staggers downstairs, groggy with sleep, to find Erik, dressed in army surplus and a bright yellow sou'wester, standing on the doorstep.

'Good morning, good morning,' he says brightly, like some crazed holiday rep. 'Any chance of a cup of coffee?'

'Erik,' Ruth says weakly, 'what are you doing here?'

Erik looks at her incredulously. 'The dig,' he says. 'It starts today.'

Of course. Erik's dig. The one approved by Nelson. The dig that aims to answer the riddle of the Iron Age body and the buried causeway.

'I didn't know it was today,' says Ruth, backing into the house. Erik follows, rubbing his hands together. He has probably been up for hours. Ruth remembers that one of his traditions on a dig was to see the sun rise on the first day and set on the last.

'Yes,' Erik is saying casually. 'Nelson said it had to be after the funeral and that was yesterday, I believe.'

'It was. I was there.'

'Were you?' Erik looks at her in surprise. 'Why ever did you go?'

'I don't know,' says Ruth, putting on the kettle. 'I felt involved somehow.'

'Well, you aren't involved,' says Erik, removing his sou'wester. 'High time you stopped all this detective nonsense and concentrated on archaeology. That's what you're good at. One of my best students, in fact.'

'Archaeologists *are* detectives,' Ruth says. 'That's what you always said.'

'The poor girl is dead,' says Erik gently, his accent like a lullaby. 'She is buried, she is at peace. Leave it at that.'

Ruth looks at him. Erik is sitting by the window, smiling at her. The sun gleams on his snowy hair. He looks utterly benign.

'I'm going to get dressed,' says Ruth. 'Help yourself to coffee.'

THE DIG IS ALREADY well underway by the time Ruth arrives. Three trenches have been marked out with string and pegs, one by the original Iron Age body, the other two along the path of the causeway.

Ruth remembers from the henge excavation that digging on this marshy land is a tricky business. The farthest trench, which is beyond the tide mark, will fill with water every night. And the tide can take you by surprise. Ruth remembers that Erik always used to have one person on 'tide watch'; sometimes the tide comes in slowly, creeping silently over the flat landscape. At other times the earth becomes water before you have time to catch your breath. These fast tides, called rip tides, could cut you off from land in the blink of an eye.

Ruth finds Erik leaning over the farthest trench. Because of the shifting ground, the trench is narrow and reinforced with sandbags.

Ruth kneels beside Erik, who is examining one of the posts.

'Are you going to take it out?' she asks.

Erik shakes his head. 'No, I want to keep it in place but I'm worried the waves will loosen it if we dig too far down.'

Ruth looks at the post. The outer, softer wood has been worn away by the tide. What's left is the hard centre of the wood, ragged. 'It looks like the wood that was used for the henge posts,' she says.

Erik looks at her. 'Yes, it does. We'll have to see what the dendrochronology says.'

Ruth goes to help with the trench where the Iron Age body was discovered. She still has a fellow feeling with this girl, fed mistletoe and tied down to die. She sees her as somehow linked to Lucy and Scarlet. She can't help thinking that, if she solves the riddle of the Iron Age girl, she might just throw some light on the deaths of the other two girls. She settles down to trowelling, getting into a rhythm. After yesterday's rain the ground is sticky and sodden.

Cathbad eventually left last night after Ruth promised to help clear his name. She would have promised almost anything to get him out of the house. But, despite herself, as she trowels, she can't stop his words running on a continuous loop in her head, *I felt sorry for you because you didn't get a look-in, what with his wife and girlfriend both on the dig . . .*

Did Erik and Shona have an affair on the henge dig? Shona is gorgeous and Ruth knows that no man is impervious to beauty. But Erik has a beautiful wife of his own, and one, moreover, who seemed to share his interests and enthusiasms. Ruth thinks of Magda, whom she has always liked and admired. Magda, with her sea-blue eyes and ash-blonde hair, her voluptuous figure in fisherman's jumpers and faded jeans, her gleam of Nordic jewellery at the neck and wrists. How could Erik have risked all this for an affair with Shona?

Is she jealous, Ruth asks herself as she trowels and sifts? Not sexually jealous. She has always known that Erik could never be interested in her, but she had thought that she was special to him. Hadn't he written on the title page of his book, *The Shivering Sand*: *To Ruth, my favourite pupil*? But it turns out that she hadn't been his favourite after all.

'Ruth!'

Eager to be distracted from her buzzing, unpleasant thoughts, Ruth looks up. Standing in the trench, she sees the newcomer from the bottom up: walking boots, waterproof trousers, mud-coloured jacket. David.

He kneels down on the edge of the trench. 'What's going on?'

Ruth pushes a lock of hair out of her eyes. 'It's an archaeological dig,' she says. 'We're excavating the Iron Age grave and the causeway.'

'Causeway?'

'Those buried posts you showed me. We think it's a Neolithic causeway. A kind of pathway leading to the henge.' Ruth looks down, hoping David won't realise that it was she who told the archaeologists about the posts.

But David has other things on his mind. 'Well, mind you don't go near the hide. The farthest one. There's a rare long-eared owl nesting there.'

Ruth can see that David is genuinely worried. 'I'm sure we won't go near the hide,' she says soothingly. 'The trenches are all over towards the south.'

David stands up, still looking anxious. 'By the way,' Ruth calls after him, 'thanks for looking after Flint. My cat.'

His face is transformed by a smile. 'That's OK,' he says. 'Any time.'

David is now looking over towards the car park. Following his gaze, Ruth sees a familiar dirty Mercedes coming to a halt by the bird-sanctuary notice board. Nelson, wearing jeans and a battered Barbour, gets out and strides towards the trench. Unconsciously, Ruth rubs her muddy hands on her trousers and tries to smooth her hair.

'Hello, Ruth.'

Ruth is fed up with looking up at people. She heaves herself out of the trench. 'Hello.'

'Bit of a circus, isn't it?' says Nelson, looking round disapprovingly at the archaeologists swarming over the site.

'It's organised,' says Ruth. 'Anyway, you gave permission for the dig.'

'Yes, well, I need all the help I can get.'

'Did you find anything at the henge circle?'

'Not a thing.' Nelson is silent, looking past the trenches to the sea. He is thinking, she's sure, of the morning they found Scarlet's body.

'I saw you yesterday,' says Nelson, 'at the funeral.'

'Yes,' says Ruth.

'Good of you to go.'

'I wanted to.'

Nelson looks as if he is going to say something else but a familiar lilting voice cuts in. 'Ah, Chief Inspector . . .' It is Erik.

As far as Ruth knows, this is a promotion for Nelson, but he doesn't offer a correction. He greets Erik cordially and the two men walk away, talking intently. Ruth feels unaccountably irritated.

By lunchtime she is tired. She is considering sneaking back to her cottage for a cup of tea when two slim hands wrap themselves over her eyes.

'Guess who?'

Ruth breaks free. She has recognised the perfume anyhow. Shona.

Shona flops down on the grass next to Ruth. 'Well?' she asks, smiling, 'found anything interesting?' Her long hair is caught up in a messy bun and she is wearing jeans that make her legs look like pipe-cleaners. A puffy silver jacket only emphasises her slimness. She looks stunning.

'Just some more coins,' Ruth says. 'Nothing much.'

'Where's Erik?' asks Shona, slightly too casually.

'Talking to Nelson.'

Shona raises her eyebrows. 'I thought they couldn't stand each other.'

'So did I but they seem matey enough now.'

'Men,' says Shona lightly, pulling her jacket more tightly round her. 'It's bloody freezing. How long are you going to stay?'

'I was just thinking of going back home for a cup of tea.'

'What are we waiting for then?'

On the way back to the cottage, Ruth wrestles with her conscience. Shona has been very kind to her, letting her stay at a moment's notice. Ruth hasn't even thanked her. She just disappeared yesterday leaving a brief message on the answering machine. Shona has been a good friend to her over the years. When Ruth split up with Peter, she provided a shoulder to cry on plus several vats of white wine. They have spent countless evenings together, laughing, talking, crying. They even went on holiday together, to Italy and Greece. Is Ruth really going to let Cathbad's spiteful rumours get in the way of this friendship?

'I'm sorry about taking off like that yesterday,' she says at last. 'For some reason after the funeral I just wanted to be at home.'

They have reached that home now. Ruth opens the door for Shona.

'That's OK,' says Shona. 'I understand. Was it awful, the funeral?'

'Yes,' says Ruth, putting on the kettle. 'It was terrible.'

'I can imagine,' says Shona, sitting down and taking off the silver jacket.

Ruth makes tea and sandwiches and they sit companionably in silence. Outside it has started to rain.

Eventually Ruth says, 'I saw Cathbad yesterday.'

'Who?'

'Michael Malone. The one they questioned about Scarlet's murder.'

'Jesus! Where did you see him?'

'Here. He came to talk to me.'

'Bloody hell, Ruth.' Shona shivers. 'I'd have been terrified.'

'Why?' asks Ruth, though she had been so scared she had slept last night with a kitchen knife by her bed. 'He wasn't charged with the murder.'

'I know, but even so. What did he want?'

'Said he wanted me to clear his name.'

'What a cheek.'

'Yes, I suppose so,' said Ruth, who had been obscurely flattered.

'What's he like, this Cathbad?'

Ruth looks at her. 'Don't you remember him? He remembers you.'

'What?' Shona has taken out her combs and shaken out her hair. She stares at Ruth, apparently bewildered.

'Don't you remember him from the henge dig? He was the leader of the druids. Always wore a big, purple cloak. He remembers you were sympathetic to them, joined in the protests.'

Shona smiles. 'Cathbad. I remember him. He was quite a gentle soul as I recall.'

'Erik says he has magic powers.'

Now Shona laughs aloud. 'Dear old Erik.'

'Cathbad says you had an affair with Erik.'

'What?'

'Cathbad. He says you and Erik had an affair on the henge dig.'

'Cathbad! What does he know?'

'Did you?'

Instead of answering, Shona twists her hair into a tight knot and puts the combs back in, their little teeth digging viciously into her skull. She doesn't look at Ruth, but Ruth knows the answer now.

'How could you do it, Shona?' she asks. 'What about Magda?'

She is shocked at the virulence with which Shona turns on her.

'What do you care about Magda all of a sudden? You don't know any-thing about it, sitting there, judging me. What about you and Peter? He's married now, didn't you know?'

'Peter and I aren't . . .' stammers Ruth. 'We're just friends,' she finishes. Inside, though, she knows that Shona is right. She is a hypocrite. What did she care about Michelle when she invited Nelson into her bed?

'Oh yeah?' sneers Shona. 'You think you're so perfect, Ruth, so above all those feelings like love and hate and loneliness. Well, it's not as simple as that. I was in love with Erik,' she adds, in a slightly different tone.

'Were you?'

Shona flares up again. 'Yes, I bloody well was! *You* remember what he was like. I'd never met anyone like him. I thought he was so wise, so charis-matic, I would have done anything for him. When he told me that he was in love with me, it was the most wonderful moment of my life.'

'He told you that he was in love with you?'

'Yes! Does that surprise you? Did you think he had the perfect marriage with Magda? Jesus, Ruth, they both have affairs all the time. Did you know about Magda's toy boy, back home in Sweden?'

'I don't believe you.'

'Ruth, you're such an innocent! Magda has a twenty-year-old lover called Lars. He fixes her sauna, then hops into bed with her. And he's one of many. In return, Erik does what he likes.'

To rid her mind of the image of Magda with her twenty-year-old handy-man lover, Ruth turns to the window. The saltmarsh has almost disappeared beneath the slanting, grey rain.

'Did you think I was the first?' asks Shona bitterly. 'No, there are gradu-ate students all over England who can say they went to bed with the great Erik Anderssen. It's almost an essential part of your education.'

But not of my education, thinks Ruth. Erik treated me as a friend, a col-league, a promising student. He never, once, said a single word that could be construed as a sexual invitation.

'If you knew he was like that,' she asks, 'why did you sleep with him?'

Shona sighs. 'I thought I was different, of course. Like all the other silly little cows. I thought I was the one he really loved. He said he'd never felt like that before, he said he'd leave Magda, that we'd get married, have chil-dren . . .' She stops, biting her lip.

And then Ruth remembers Shona's abortion, just a few months after the henge dig. 'The baby . . .' she begins.

'Was Erik's,' says Shona wearily, 'Yes. It was then I realised he didn't mean any of it. When I told him I was pregnant, he went mad, pressured me to have an abortion.' She looks at Ruth with a strange, dispassionate smile. 'Poor Ruth. All this is very hard for you. You always admired him so much.'

'Yes,' says Ruth hoarsely. 'Yes, I did.'

'He's still a great archaeologist,' says Shona. 'I'm still friends with him. And with Magda,' she adds with a slight laugh. 'It's just the way he is.'

'I guess so,' says Ruth tightly.

Shona rises, picking up her silver jacket. At the door she turns. 'Don't blame either of us too much, Ruth,' she says.

When Shona has gone, Ruth is amazed to find that she is shaking. What is so surprising about finding out that two grown-up people have had an affair? Why does she feel let down, angry, *betrayed*?

She supposes that she must really have been in love with Erik all these years. She remembers when she first met him, as a graduate student in Southampton, the way that he seemed to take her mind apart, shuffle it and put it back together a different shape. He changed her view of everything: archaeology, landscape, nature, art, relationships.

She had thought nobody could be good enough for Erik but Magda was. She had loved their relationship, that affectionate companionship. They lived the perfect life, climbing mountains, sailing, spending the winters writing and researching and the summers digging. She remembers the log cabin by the lake in Norway, the meals eaten on the deck, the hot tub, the evenings eating, drinking and talking. Erik and Magda had argued sometimes, but always they had listened to each other's views.

Ruth is not stupid. She knows that she created idealised parents in Magda and Erik and that is why she feels so let down. And, if she was in love with Erik, too . . . well, that makes a perfect Freudian hole-in-one.

She knows it is childish, but Ruth feels that she needs to be reminded of Erik's good opinion. So she takes down her copy of Erik's book, *The Shivering Sand*. She opens it at the title page. *To Ruth, my favourite pupil.*

Ruth looks at the words for a long moment. Then, almost staggering, she gets up and goes to the desk where she keeps her copies of the Lucy Downey letters. Hands shaking, she leafs through them until she gets to the two that are hand-written.

She lays them on the table next to Erik's dedication. The handwriting is the same.

For what seems like hours, Ruth just stands there, unable to move.

Almost unable to breathe. Think, Ruth, think. Breathe. Can Erik really have written these letters? Is it possible that Erik, as well as being a hypocrite and a serial seducer, is also a murderer?

The worst thing is that she can almost believe it. Erik knows about archaeology. He knows about Norse legends and Neolithic ritual and the power of the landscape. She can hear his voice, that beloved singsong voice, telling campfire stories of water spirits and shape-changers and the creatures of the dark.

Can it be true? Erik was still living in England when Lucy Downey vanished. It was just after the henge dig. He could have sent the early letters. He didn't go back to Norway until eight years later. But could he have sent the recent letters about Scarlet? He has only been back in England since January. Nelson showed her a letter dated last November. Could Erik have sent that letter or arranged to have someone send it?

It's crazy, Ruth tells herself. Erik would not be capable of writing those evil, taunting, *warped* letters. He is a humanitarian, the first to support striking miners or victims of natural disasters. He is kind and thoughtful, comforting Ruth in the shock of Peter's marriage, grieving with Shona when her father died. But he is also, thinks Ruth, the man who speaks approvingly of human sacrifice ('isn't the same thing happening in Christian Holy Communion?'), who advised Ruth to forget Peter with another lover ('it's the easiest way') and who, presumably, was sleeping with Shona and encouraging her to abort their child while weeping with her about her father. Erik is amoral, he is somehow outside normal human rules; that is one of the most attractive things about him. But is it also something that makes him capable of unimaginable evil?

If he wrote the letters, did he kill the two little girls? She remembers a conversation she had with him about her Iron Age body. 'How could anyone do that?' she had asked. 'Kill a child for some religious ritual?'

'Look at it this way,' Erik had said calmly. 'Maybe it's a good way to go. Saves the child the disillusionment of growing up.' He had smiled as he said it, but Ruth remembers feeling chilled.

She can't bear it any more. Grabbing her coat and bag, she rushes out into the rain. She is going to speak to Shona.

SHONA IS STILL OUT when she arrives. Ruth slumps down on the doorstep, too exhausted to remember that she still has a key. She just sits there.

When Shona eventually appears, swinging down the road carrying a

Thresher's bag and a rented DVD, she looks so innocent that Ruth thinks that she must be mistaken. No way can her friend be mixed up in any of this. But, then, Shona sees Ruth, and a curious trapped look comes over her face, like a fox cornered in a suburban garden. Almost instantly though, charm breaks out again and she smiles, proffering the bag and the DVD.

'Girls' night in,' she says. 'Want to join me?'

'Shona, I've got to talk to you.'

'OK,' Shona says, opening the door. 'You'd better come in.'

Ruth doesn't even give her time to take off her coat.

'Did Erik write those letters?'

'What letters?' asks Shona. She looks positively terrified.

Ruth looks around the room, at the sanded floor and the trendy rugs, at the photos in decorated frames—almost all of Shona herself, she notices now—at the patchwork throw over the sofa, at the new novels stacked on the table, at the bookshelves with their battered copies of the classics, from T.S. Eliot to Shakespeare. Then she looks back at Shona.

'Jesus,' she says. 'You helped him, didn't you?'

Shona seems to look around for a means of escape, but then collapses onto the sofa and covers her face.

Ruth comes nearer. 'You helped him, didn't you?' she says. 'Of course, he'd never have thought of all that T.S Eliot stuff by himself, would he? You're the literature expert. Your Catholic background probably helped too. He supplied the archaeology and the mythology, you did the rest. Quite the perfect little team.'

'It wasn't like that,' says Shona dully. 'It was him. Nelson.'

'*What?*'

'Erik hated him,' says Shona. 'That's why he wrote the letters, to get at Nelson. To distract him. To stop him solving the case. To punish him.'

'What for?' whispers Ruth.

'James Agar,' says Shona. 'He was Erik's student. At Manchester. It was during the poll-tax riots. Apparently a group of students attacked a policeman and he was killed. James Agar was only on the outskirts of the group. He didn't do anything but Nelson framed him.'

'Who told you this? Erik?'

'It was common knowledge. Everyone knew it. Even the police. Nelson wanted a scapegoat so he picked on James.'

'He wouldn't do that,' says Ruth. Wouldn't he? she thinks.

'Oh, I know you like him. Erik says you've been totally taken in by him.'

'Does he? And you weren't taken in by Erik, I suppose?'

'Yes, I was,' says Shona wearily. 'I was obsessed with him. I would have done anything for him.'

'Even help him to write those letters?'

Shona looks up, her face defiant. 'Yes,' she says. 'Even that.'

'But why, Shona? This was a murder investigation. You were probably helping the murderer get away.'

'Nelson's a murderer,' snaps Shona. 'James Agar died in prison, a year after Nelson framed him. He killed himself.'

Ruth thinks of Cathbad's poem, 'In praise of James Agar'. She thinks of the locked cabinet in Cathbad's caravan.

'Cathbad,' she says at last. 'Where does he come into this?'

Shona laughs, slightly hysterically. 'He was the postman,' she says.

NELSON HAS HAD a tough day. But then again he almost can't remember a time when his life didn't consist of defending himself against people who wanted him sacked, trying to motivate an increasingly depressed team, ignoring Michelle's demands to come home while trying to catch a murderer. He had thought that Scarlet's funeral yesterday must be the lowest point. Seeing that little white coffin. Seeing Lucy Downey's parents again, remembering how he had let them down. He had caught sight of Ruth in the congregation and wondered if she was thinking what he was thinking: the letter writer would love this.

And then there is Ruth. He knows he shouldn't have gone to bed with her. It was unprofessional as well as wrong. He has betrayed Michelle, whom he loves. But, that night, he has to admit, was something else. Ruth seemed to understand him totally, in a way that Michelle has never done. But why had she slept with him? She can't possibly fancy him; he's not intellectual enough for her.

He can only suppose that, like him, she was caught up in the horror of finding Scarlet's body, telling the parents. The only escape was in simple, straightforward sex. Some of the best, he has to admit, that he has ever had.

He doesn't know where he stands with her now. She's not the sort who will go soppy, declaring undying love and begging him to leave Michelle. He has spoken to her on the phone a few times and she has seemed fine, professional and calm, despite having some scary stuff to cope with. He admires that. Ruth is tough, like him. He'd watched her as he approached her at the dig yesterday. She was totally absorbed in her work and he didn't know why, but suddenly he had wanted her to look up, to wave, smile, but of course, she hadn't. She had simply carried on with her job, just as he was carrying on with his. It was the sensible, adult way to behave.

He had a good chat with that Anderssen bloke at the dig. Of course he's an old hippie, way too old to have his hair in a ponytail. But he had told Nelson that there's a prehistoric forest buried underneath the saltmarsh. That's why you sometimes find odd-looking stumps of trees and bits of timber. Anderssen had also talked about ritual. 'Think of a burial,' he'd said. 'From the body to the wood of the coffin to the stone of the graveyard.'

Nelson had returned from the dig to be met by his boss. Superintendent Whitcliffe is a career policeman, a graduate who favours linen suits and slip-on shoes. Just standing near him makes Nelson feel more than usually untidy. Still, Nelson is not about to let the superintendent push him around. He's a good cop; he knows it and Whitcliffe knows it. He's not going to be the scapegoat on this case.

'Ah, Harry,' Whitcliffe had said. 'Been out and about?'

'Following up leads.' He was damned if he was going to add 'sir'.

'We need to talk, Harry,' Whitcliffe had said, sitting down behind Nelson's desk and establishing superiority. 'We need another statement.'

'We've got nothing to say.'

'That's just it, Harry,' sighed Whitcliffe, 'we need to have something to say. The press are after our blood. You arrest Malone and then release him—'

'On bail.'

'Yes, on bail,' said Whitcliffe tetchily. 'That doesn't change the fact that you've got no evidence to charge him with the murders. And without him you've got no suspects. With all the coverage of the little girl's funeral, we need to be seen to be doing something.'

'I am *doing something*,' said Nelson, 'I've been working flat out for months. We've searched every inch of the saltmarsh . . .'

'I hear you've let the archaeologists loose there today.'

'Have you seen how they work?' demanded Nelson. 'They examine every inch of ground. It's all planned, nothing overlooked. Our forensic teams could never match it. If there's anything to find, they'll find it.'

The superintendent nods brusquely, then gets to his feet and crosses to the door.

Left alone, Nelson sinks into his chair. He knows he can't stall Whitcliffe for ever. He will have to give a statement to the press and what the hell will he say? Malone was the only suspect, and, for a while he had seemed quite promising. He had links with the Henderson family, he was a drifter and he was full of all that New Age crap, just like the writer of the letters. But then they had found Scarlet's body and there was DNA all over it. The only problem was that none of it matched Malone's. He'd had to let the man go.

Scarlet had been tied up, gagged and strangled. Then someone had carried her body out to the peat beds and buried her where that henge thing used to be. Does this mean the murderer had to know about the henge? Ruth had said that there was a path, a causeway or something, leading right to the place where Scarlet was buried. Were the police meant to find her?

Nelson knows he'll be blamed if they don't find Scarlet's killer. He knows too that it won't be long before the press makes the link with Lucy Downey. They don't know about the letters, of course, and he'll be crucified if that gets out, but in some ways none of that bothers him. He's got no time for the press. No, he wants to find the killer for the sake of Lucy's and Scarlet's families. He wants to put the bastard away for ever. It won't bring Lucy and Scarlet back, but it will, at least, mean that justice has been done.

A sound downstairs makes him sit up. He hears the desk sergeant's voice. It sounds as if he is remonstrating with someone. Nelson gets up and starts towards the door. And finds himself colliding with his expert witness, Dr Ruth Galloway.

'Jesus,' says Nelson, putting out both hands to steady her.

'I'm OK.' Ruth leaps away as if he is infectious. For a second they stare awkwardly at each other. Ruth looks a mess, her hair wild.

'Sorry,' she is saying, taking off her dripping jacket, 'but I had to come.'

'What's the matter?' asks Nelson neutrally, retreating behind his desk.

Ruth slams a book and a piece of paper down on his desk. He recognises the paper as a copy of one of the letters. The book means nothing to him though Ruth has opened it and is pointing at some writing on the first page.

'Look!' she is saying urgently.

To humour her, he looks. Then he looks again. 'Who wrote this?'

'Erik. Erik Anderssen.'

'Are you sure?'

'Of course I'm sure. His girlfriend confirms it. He wrote the letters.'

'His girlfriend?'

'Shona. My . . . my colleague at the university. His ex-girlfriend, if you like. Anyway, she admits Erik wrote the letters and she helped him.'

'Why?'

'Because he hates you. Because of James Agar.'

Whatever he expected it wasn't this. James Agar. The poll-tax riots, police bussed in from five forces, the streets full of tear gas and placards, trying to hold the line, students spitting in his face, the alley where Stephen Naylor's body had been found. Naylor, a recruit, only twenty-two, stabbed to death with a kitchen knife. Agar, coming towards him, eyes unfocused, carrying the bloody knife as if it didn't belong to him.

'James Agar was guilty,' says Nelson flatly.

'He committed suicide in prison,' says Ruth. 'Erik blames you. James Agar was his student. He says you framed him.'

'Bollocks. There were a dozen witnesses. You mean to tell me that Anderssen wrote all this . . . *crap* . . . because of some student?'

'Shona says Erik hated you and wanted to stop you solving the Lucy Downey case. He thought the letters would distract you.'

'He wanted the murderer to go free?'

'He sees you as a murderer.'

'I'm sure you agree with him,' Nelson says bitterly.

'I don't know anything about it,' says Ruth wearily.

She looks tired, Nelson realises; her hands are shaking. He relents slightly. 'What about Malone?' he asks. 'He wrote a poem about James Agar. Remember? He even offered it as an example of his handwriting.'

'Cathbad was Agar's friend,' says Ruth. 'They were students together at Manchester. He posted the letters. Remember he told us he was a postman.'

'What about the recent letters? I thought Anderssen had been out of the country.'

'Erik emailed them to Cathbad. He printed them out and posted them.'

Nelson leans forward and puts his hand on Ruth. 'Ruth, do you think Anderssen killed Lucy and Scarlet?'

And Ruth answers, so quietly he can hardly hear her. 'Yes.'

THERE ARE THE SOUNDS AGAIN. *She crouches, holding her stone. When he comes down with her food, she watches the back of his head as he puts the plates on the floor. Where would be the right place? On top, where the hair is going all straggly? At the back of his neck, horribly red and raw-looking? He turns to look at her and she wonders if this isn't the best way, right in the face, between the eyes, in his gaping mouth, across his horrid, gulpy neck.*

He examines her, which she hates. Looks into her mouth, feels her arm muscles, makes her turn round and lift up her feet, one after the other.

'You're growing,' he says, 'You need some new clothes.'

Clothes. The word reminds her of something. A smell, that's it. A soft, comforting smell. Something held against her face, silky, smooth, rubbing between her thumb and forefinger. But he is talking about what's on her body: a long scratchy top and trousers that seem too short. She can see her legs sticking out at the bottom. They look white, like the inside of a twig. They look like they can't possibly work, but they do. She has been practising running, round this little room, on the spot, up and down. She knows that soon she will have to run for real.

He cuts her nails with a funny red knife he keeps in his pocket.

'Don't worry about the noises outside,' he says, 'It's just . . . animals.'

Animals. Pony, dog, cat, rabbit, incy wincey spider climbing the water spout. She says nothing, feeling the stone in her pocket.

He looks at her. 'Are you all right?' he asks.

She doesn't answer. Instead she hangs her head so she can't see him. Her hair is long; it smells of dust. Sometimes he cuts her hair with the little knife. She remembers a story where someone escapes by climbing on hair. It doesn't sound possible; it's one of those things that only happens in stories. Escape. Does that only happen in stories too?

Chapter 9

Ruth sits in Nelson's office, a cup of undrinkable coffee in front of her. It is cold in the high-ceilinged room. She is still wearing her digging trousers, baggy army surplus, but had taken off her thick jumper back at her house. It seems days ago. Her coat is still dripping and far too thin. She wishes she had worn an anorak. She wraps her hands round the plastic cup. At least it is hot.

Nelson has disappeared to round up some officers to arrest Erik.

He crashes back into the room accompanied by Judy Johnson, the police-woman Ruth had met at the funeral. 'Right,' he says. 'I'll go in the first car with Cloughie. Ruth, you follow behind with DC Johnson. On no account are you to get out of the car. Do you understand?'

'Yes,' says Ruth, rather sulkily. She wants to remind Nelson that she is not one of his officers.

The cars set off through the night. It is still raining, a steady drizzle. The cars head out of King's Lynn and along the coast road.

Nelson's Mercedes comes to a halt in front of the blameless-looking seaside guesthouse. The look is traditional seaside kitsch: net curtains, gnomes in the garden, stained glass over the front door. Nelson and Sergeant Clough climb the crazy-paving steps and Clough leans heavily on the doorbell. *The Sandringham Guesthouse*, reads the sign. *Bed and Breakfast, En suite rooms, colour TV, home cooking. Vacancies.*

It is nearly ten o'clock and there is only one light on inside the guesthouse. It's upstairs, directly above the door. Ruth remembers Erik telling her that he was the only guest. Is that his light then? Is he inside, calmly working on some scholarly article about Bronze Age Field Systems?

After what seems like hours, Ruth sees the front door open. Nelson leans forward, speaking to the unseen opener. The door shuts and Nelson and Clough make their way slowly back to the car.

Nelson leans in through the window. His forearm rests on the window frame a few inches from Ruth. She has to fight a desire to touch it.

'He's gone,' says Nelson. 'His room's empty. He left a cheque.'

'What now?' asks DC Johnson.

Nelson looks at Ruth. 'Any ideas, Dr Galloway?'

Ruth doesn't meet his eye. 'He could be with Shona, I suppose.'

When they reach Shona's house, it is in darkness. At first Ruth thinks that she must be out but, after a few minutes, she appears at the door wearing a dressing gown. She looks rumpled and slightly drunk.

DC Johnson has gone to the door this time.

Shona steps back to allow the police constable to enter. Alone in the car, Ruth starts to shiver. She jumps when the passenger door opens.

Nelson leans in. 'Are you OK?'

'Fine,' she says, setting her jaw to stop her teeth chattering.

'You're freezing. Hang on.'

He pulls off his heavy police jacket and hands it to her. 'Put this on.'

'But it's yours.'

He shrugs. 'I'm not cold. Keep it.'

Ruth pulls on the jacket gratefully. It smells of garages and, faintly, of Nelson's aftershave. The DI, in his shirtsleeves, does not seem cold. He jogs slightly on the balls of his feet, impatient for Judy Johnson to come back.

At last she appears in the doorway and Nelson goes to meet her. They confer quickly, then DC Johnson gets back in the car.

'He's not there,' she tells Ruth. 'She hasn't seen him. I'm putting out a call to all units. The boss says I've to take you to a safe house.'

Ruth watches Nelson getting into the other car. Suddenly, she feels incredibly tired.

'Is there anyone you could stay with?' asks Johnson. 'A friend? Family?'

'There is someone,' says Ruth.

THE HOUSE IS ONE of a row of squat, whitewashed fishermen's cottages on the seafront near Burnham Ovary. Ruth stands irresolute on the doorstep. What if he isn't there? Will she have to sleep under her desk at the university? At the moment, even that seems quite an attractive proposition.

Ruth looks back at the police car, which is waiting discreetly in the street. She wonders if the neighbours are watching behind their curtains.

'Ruth!' She swings round to see Peter silhouetted in a rectangle of light. Ruth opens her mouth to tell him about Erik and Shona and to ask him for a place to sleep but, to her intense embarrassment, she starts to cry. Huge, gulping, unromantic sobs.

Peter reaches out and draws her inside. 'It's OK,' he says. 'It's OK.'

And he shuts the door behind them.

'I'm sorry,' says Ruth, walking into the sitting room and sinking down on Peter's sofa. As in all rented houses, the furniture looks the wrong shape for the room. The sofa is mysteriously uncomfortable.

'What's going on?' asks Peter, standing in the doorway.

'You'd better come and sit down,' says Ruth.

IN THE KITCHEN, Peter makes omelettes and opens a bottle of red wine, then brings it all through to the sitting room. Ruth eats hungrily. They both drink a good deal, keen to blot out the evening's revelations. Ruth has told him about the letters, about Shona and Erik, and, finally, about the match with Erik's handwriting.

'You know,' Peter keeps saying, 'I just can't believe it of Erik. He always seemed a real New Ager to me. Into peace and love and free dope for all. I just can't imagine that he would kill a little girl.'

'But what if he really believed all that stuff—about sacrifices and offerings to the gods? Maybe he felt he needed to make an offering to appease them for taking the henge away?'

'You're saying that he's mad?'

'Who are we to say what is mad and what is sane?'

'You're quoting Erik!'

'Yes.' Ruth tucks her feet under her on the sofa. Despite everything, she is beginning to feel very sleepy.

'You loved him, didn't you?' says Peter. 'All the time I thought it was me but it was Erik. He was the one you really loved.'

'No,' protests Ruth. 'I did love him, but as a friend. As a teacher, I suppose. I loved Magda, too. It was different with you.'

Peter leans over and kisses her and, for a second, she feels herself dissolving into his arms. Would this be so wrong, she asks herself? She is single; he is separated from his wife. Who would they be hurting?

'God, Ruth,' Peter murmurs, 'I've missed you so much. I love you.'

That does it. Ruth pushes Peter away. 'No.'

'What?' Peter still has his arms round her. 'I made a mistake, marrying Victoria. You and I were always meant to be together.'

'No, we weren't.'

'Why not?'

'I don't love you,' Ruth says. 'Is it OK if I sleep on the sofa?'

SHE WAKES TO FIND HERSELF covered with Nelson's jacket and a duvet. Grey light streams in through the thin curtains. Ruth sits up. The time on her mobile is 07:15. Her head hurts and her eyes feel gritty. She can't even remember going to sleep. But she does remember Peter slamming out of the room after she told him she didn't love him. He must have come back, though, to put the duvet over her. She feels sick.

She gets up, intending to find a loo and a shower but, when she opens the door, she comes face to face with Peter, who is carrying a cup of tea.

'Thank you,' she says, taking the cup. 'I feel terrible.'

Peter smiles. 'So do I. We're not young any more. Bathroom's upstairs, by the way. First on the left. Towels in the airing cupboard next door.'

'Thanks,' says Ruth. Perhaps it's not going to be so bad after all.

It's horrible putting her old clothes on after her shower, but at least she is clean. She goes downstairs. Peter is in the tiny kitchen.

'What are you going to do now?' he asks, putting toast in front of her.

'Go into work, tidy up. Then go away for a bit. See my parents.'

'Blimey. Things must be desperate.'

Ruth smiles but, when she looks at Peter, his face is suddenly dark. He looks, for a second, like a stranger.

'Remember, Ruth,' he says. 'I know where you are.'

'Is ERIK REALLY A SUSPECT?' asks Phil, shutting his office door behind her.

'I'm not sure,' lies Ruth. 'I just know the police want to talk to him.'

All the way to the university, she has been thinking about Peter's words. *I know where you are.* Could Peter have sent her those messages? But why would Peter want to scare her like that? It doesn't make sense.

'What's going on?' asks Phil.

'I don't know,' says Ruth wearily. 'Look, Phil, I've got a favour to ask you. The police think I should get away for a few days and I was thinking of going to my parents in London. Is it OK if I have a few days off?'

Phil stares at her.

'Do they think you're in danger? From Erik?'

'Sorry, Phil,' answers Ruth, 'I can't say more. Is it OK if I have the time off?'

'Of course,' says Phil. Then, 'Can I ask you something, Ruth?'

'Yes,' says Ruth warily.

'Why are you wearing a policeman's jacket?'

SHE HAD MEANT to leave early but it's getting dark by the time she reaches the Saltmarsh. All at once there seemed to be so many things to do.

Then, in the middle of it all, Nelson had rung. 'Ruth. You OK?'

'Fine.'

'DC Johnson said she took you to a friend's house last night. I don't want you to do that again. I want you in a safe house.'

'I'm going to my parents. In London.'

'Good. That's good.'

'Have you found Erik yet?' she asked.

'No. But we've got people watching the guesthouse, his girlfriend's house, the university. There's an alert at all the airports.'

'What about Cathbad's place?'

'I paid a visit to our friend Malone this morning. Says he hasn't seen Anderssen for days but we're watching him too.'

Ruth had taken a taxi to the police station to pick up her car but she hadn't seen Nelson. The desk sergeant had told her that he was out 'following up on information received'. She had almost left Nelson's jacket at the police station but something made her keep it. It reminded her of him and, in some strange way, made her feel braver. Besides, it was very warm.

As she turns into New Road, ominous grey clouds are gathering over the sea. A storm is on its way. The wind has dropped and the air is heavy.

There is a livid yellow line on the horizon and even the birds are still.

She lets herself into her house and Flint greets her hysterically. God, she had forgotten him last night. She fills up his bowl. She'll have to take him with her to her parents. She can't face asking David again and she doesn't know how long she'll be away. She goes up to the attic to get Flint's travelling basket and hears the first distant rumble of thunder.

She packs quickly and hurries downstairs with her suitcase. She checks her mobile. Five o'clock. Damn, at this rate it will be midnight before she gets to London. She looks out of the window. It is pitch black now and the wind has started up again. Her gate is swinging wildly to and fro. She grabs Flint and shoves him, protesting, into the cat basket. She must hurry up.

And yet, despite everything, she finds herself going to her desk for one last look at the Iron Age torque that started the whole thing. She doesn't know why she does this. She should have given the torque to Phil to put with the other finds but, for some reason, she can't bear to let it go.

It gleams dully in her hand, the twisted metal somehow both sinister and beautiful. Why was it put into the grave? To show the status of the dead girl? Or as an offering to the gods of the underworld and of the crossing places? The gods who guard the entry to the marshlands. For a full minute, Ruth stands there, weighing the heavy gold object in her hand.

Then a voice says informatively, 'Around seventy BC, I think. The time of the Iceni.'

It is Erik.

Ruth swings round, heart hammering. At the same moment a violent blast of wind throws itself against the house. The storm has arrived.

'A rough night,' says Erik in a conversational voice. He is wearing a black raincoat. He steps forward, smiling. 'Hello, Ruth. Did you think I would leave without saying goodbye?' He takes a step closer. He's still smiling but his blue eyes are cold. As cold as the North Sea.

'The police are looking for you,' says Ruth.

'I know.' He smiles. 'But they won't look here.'

Ruth starts to back towards the door.

'What's wrong, Ruthie? Don't you trust me?'

'No.'

'I didn't kill them, you know. I'm not a nix. I'm not an evil sea spirit. I'm just Erik.' His voice is as hypnotic as ever.

Ruth shakes her head to clear it. She mustn't be taken in.

'You wrote the letters. The letters told me where to find Scarlet.'

'Rubbish,' says Erik. 'You twisted the facts to suit your theory just as all academics do.'

'Aren't you an academic?'

'Me?' Erik smiles. 'No. I am a teller of tales. A weaver of mysteries.'

He is, she understands suddenly, quite mad.

Slowly, she moves towards the door. Her hand is touching the handle. Then Flint, realising that he is about to be left behind in the basket, sets up an unearthly yowl. Erik starts and jumps towards Ruth. What he means to do she doesn't know, but one look at his eyes decides her. She throws herself through the door and out into the night.

The wind is so strong that she can hardly stay upright. It is coming directly from the sea, racing across the marshes, flattening everything in its path. Rain beats against her face but she stumbles on. At last she reaches her car. Her trusty, rusty Renault. She scrabbles at the door.

'Looking for these?' She looks round and there is Erik holding up her car keys. He is still smiling, his white hair now flattened by the rain.

Ruth runs. She darts across New Road, jumps over the ditch that leads to the marshes and sets out into the dark.

'Ruth!' She can hear Erik behind her, stumbling over the coarse grass and low bushes. Ruth stumbles too, falling heavily on the muddy ground, grazing her hands on loose stones. But she gets up and keeps going, panting, gasping, weaving through the stunted trees, with no idea where she's headed. Erik will kill her, she knows, just as he killed those two little girls. For no reason. For the reason that he is mad.

Despite his age, he's much fitter than she is. But desperation drives her on. She falls into a stream and knows she must be getting near the tidal saltmarshes. The wind is even louder now and the rain stings her face. She stops. Where is Erik? She can't hear anything except the wind.

Exhausted, she sinks down on the ground. It is soft and reed stalks brush her face. Where is the sea? She mustn't wander onto the mud flats or that will be the end of her. *The tide comes in like a galloping horse*, David, her neighbour had said. It is easy to imagine wildly galloping hoofs in the noise of the wind, the white horses of the waves storming in across the marshes. She tries to gather her wits. She must ring Nelson, get help, but, as she scrambles for her mobile, she realises that she has packed it in her case. The wind screams around her and, in the background, she hears a roaring, rushing sound.

She is lost on the saltmarsh and the tide is coming in.

NELSON'S MOOD IS DARK as he drives back to the station. The so-called 'information received' has turned out to be a load of bollocks. A man answering Erik Anderssen's description had been spotted at a King's Lynn pub. But, when Nelson arrived at the pub, it turned out to be folk music night, which meant that every man in the place answered to Erik Anderssen's description: grey ponytail, smug expression and all.

He prays Ruth is safely on her way to London now. Not that he thinks Erik will try to contact her. Privately, he's sure that the man has already left the country, probably leaped on a late flight last night. He'll be sitting in a café in Oslo now, drinking whatever Norwegians drink and laughing his bearded head off.

The desk sergeant tells him Ruth collected her car an hour ago. Nelson frowns. That's too late for his liking. What was she doing, hanging about? He'd spoken to her at lunchtime, she should have left straight away.

At his office door he is stopped by a WPC. He doesn't know her name, but he composes his face into something like a smile. She is young and looks nervous.

'Er . . . there's someone to see you, Detective Chief Inspector. He's in your office. He wouldn't leave a name.'

Why the hell hadn't he been stopped downstairs? thinks Nelson irritably. He pushes open the door and the first thing he sees is a swirl of purple cloak. He shuts the door behind him, very quickly indeed.

Cathbad is sitting, quite at his ease, on Nelson's side of the desk. He has his feet, encased in muddy trainers, actually on the desk.

'Get your feet off my desk!' he bellows.

'You really must watch that anger, Detective Chief Inspector,' says Cathbad. But he takes his feet off the desk.

'Now get out of my chair,' says Nelson, breathing heavily.

'We own nothing in this world,' counters Cathbad, getting up fairly quickly all the same.

'Did you just come here to spout rubbish at me?' snarls Nelson.

'No,' says Cathbad calmly. 'I've come to give you some information about Erik Anderssen. I thought I would bring the news in person so I slipped out when your two . . . er . . . guards were otherwise occupied.'

Nelson's hands clench into fists as he thinks of the officers sent to watch Cathbad. What the hell were they doing?

'Erik telephoned me an hour ago. He told me that he was on his way to see Ruth Galloway.'

Nelson's heart starts to beat faster. He forces himself to speak calmly. 'Why are you so keen to help the police all of a sudden?'

'I dislike the police,' says Cathbad loftily, 'but I abhor all forms of violence. Erik sounded distinctly violent to me. I think your friend Dr Galloway could be in danger.'

RUTH LIES in the reed bed, listening to the roar of the tide and the howling of the wind. Soon the tide will come in and she has no idea if she is already on the tidal mud flats. But Ruth has no intention of cowering in the mud. She may as well run as lie here waiting for Erik catch her. She gets to her feet and moves on, zigzagging through the reeds, head down against the wind.

A mighty crack of thunder almost throws her off her feet. Immediately, a lightning blast turns the sky white. The storm must be right overhead. Is she going to be struck by lightning? Another explosion of thunder sends her, instinctively, down among the reeds again with her arms over her head. This time she is lying in a shallow stream. This is dangerous. Water conducts electricity, doesn't it? She edges forward, on her stomach. This is how she imagines the First World War: face down in the mud while mortar shells exploded in the sky. Hand over hand, she crawls forward.

JAW CLENCHED, Nelson drives like a maniac towards the saltmarsh. Next to him, humming softly, sits Cathbad. While there is no one whose company Nelson desires less, there are two important reasons why Cathbad is currently occupying the passenger seat of Nelson's Mercedes. One, he claims to know the saltmarsh 'like the back of his hand', and two, Nelson does not trust him to be out of his sight for a second.

Sergeant Clough and Constable Johnson follow in a police car. Both cars have their sirens blaring but there is little traffic as they scorch through the country lanes. The storm, raging unnoticed above them, has driven everyone inside.

At New Road, Nelson recognises Ruth's car and his breathing eases a little. Then he sees the open door of the cottage swinging in the wind and he feels his heart contract. When he enters the sitting room, however, his heart almost jumps out of his chest. The room is filled with a terrible, unearthly wailing. He stops dead and Cathbad cannons into the back of him.

To Nelson's eternal shame it is then Cathbad who notices the cat basket and goes to rescue Flint. 'Go free, little cat,' he murmurs.

Flint disappears through the open front door.

By the time Clough and WPC Johnson arrive, Nelson has already searched the tiny cottage. There is no sign of Erik or Ruth, though a packed suitcase sits by the door.

Cathbad is examining a piece of metal that was lying on the table.

'What's that?' asks Nelson.

'Looks like an Iron Age torque,' replies Cathbad. 'Full of magic.'

Nelson loses interest immediately. 'They can't have gone far,' he says. 'Johnson, Clough, go and ask the neighbours if they heard anything, then radio for an armed response team.'

BENT DOUBLE, Ruth is running across the saltmarsh. Falling headlong into muddy streams, clawing herself out, tasting blood in her mouth, getting up again and falling again, this time into a pond about a foot deep. Spluttering, she staggers to her feet. The marsh is full of water like this, some stretches several feet wide. She finds some firmer ground.

She has lost a shoe and her trousers are ripped to pieces. Thank God, though, for the police jacket, which has kept her top half dry. She must keep going; she owes it to Nelson if no one else. It would finish his career if another body was found on the marshes. She pulls the coat more tightly round her and feels a faint glow of courage, as if it is transferred to her via the coat. Nelson wouldn't be scared by a bit of wind and rain, would he?

But where is Erik? She stops, tries to listen but she can hear only the wind and the rain and the thunder. *What the thunder said*. Isn't that T.S. Eliot? For a second she thinks of the letters. Does she really believe that Erik killed Scarlet Henderson? Does she really believe that he would kill her? Trust no one, she tells herself, staggering on over the uneven ground. Trust no one but yourself.

Then she hears a sound that makes her heart stop. A voice like no human voice she has ever heard. It is as if the dead themselves are calling her. Three calls, low and even, the last shuddering away into silence.

The call comes again. For no reason that she knows, she starts to move towards it and suddenly finds herself facing a solid wall.

She can't believe it at first. But it is, unmistakably, a wall. Gingerly, she puts out a hand to touch it. No, it isn't a mirage. It is a solid wall of wood, made of rough boards nailed together.

Of course! It's the hide! She has reached the hide. She almost laughs in her relief. This must be the farthest hide, the one where she and Peter met David that day. This hide, she remembers, is above the tide mark. She is safe. She can shelter inside until the storm passes. Thank God for birdwatchers.

Half drunk with relief, she staggers into the hut. It's open on one side so it doesn't offer brilliant shelter but it's wonderful to be out of the wind and the rain. Her face aches as if she has been repeatedly slapped, and her ears are ringing. She rests her head against the rough wood and closes her eyes. It's crazy but she could almost go to sleep.

Outside the storm is still raging but she has almost become used to it. Now the wind sounds like children's voices calling. How sad they sound, like the cries of sailors lost at sea, like will-o'-the-wisps searching the world for comfort and warmth. Ruth shivers. She mustn't get spooked now and start thinking about Erik's fireside tales. About the long green fingers reaching out of the water, about the undead creatures roaming the night, about the drowned cities, the church bells ringing deep below the sea . . .

She jumps. She has heard a cry coming from beneath her feet. She listens again. For a moment, the storm is still and she hears it again. Unmistakably a human voice. 'Help me! Help me!'

Ruth looks at the wooden floor of the hide. It is covered by a carpet of rush matting. She tears at the carpet. It is pinned down but comes away after the third or fourth tug. Below are floorboards and a trap door. Why on earth would there be a trap door in a birdwatching hide? And there is the voice again. Calling from beneath the floor.

Ruth bends and puts her face to the trap door. 'Who's there?' she calls.

There is a silence and then a voice answers, 'It's me.'

The response strikes Ruth to the heart. It presupposes that Ruth knows the owner of the voice. And, almost at once, she feels she does.

'Don't worry,' she shouts. 'I'm coming.'

There is a bolt on the trap door. It slides back easily as if it is used regularly. Ruth opens the door and peers down in the darkness. At the same time a flash of lightning illuminates the surroundings.

A face looks back up at her. A girl, a teenager perhaps, painfully thin with long, matted hair. She's wearing a man's jumper and tattered trousers and has a blanket round her shoulders.

'What are you doing here?' asks Ruth stupidly.

The girl shakes her head. Her eyes are huge, her skin grey.

'What's your name?' asks Ruth.

But, all of a sudden she knows. It is as if she has known all along.

'Lucy,' she says gently. 'You're Lucy, aren't you?'

Chapter 11

Johnson and Clough report that there is no response from either of Ruth's neighbours. 'Houses look shut up, boss.' Nelson tells them to stay and wait for the dog handlers. He will search on the saltmarsh.

'In this?' DS Clough gestures towards the dark expanse of the marsh, where the trees are almost blown flat by the wind. 'You'll never find them.'

'There's quicksand,' says WPC Judy Johnson, as a savage blast almost knocks her off her feet. 'And the tide comes in really fast. It's not safe.'

'I know a way,' says Cathbad. 'It's a hidden way. I discovered it ten years ago. It's as sort of shingle spit. It leads from the lowest hide right up to the henge circle. Solid ground all the way.'

That must have been the path Ruth took to find Scarlet's body, thinks Nelson. 'Can you find it in the dark?' he asks.

'Trust me,' says Cathbad.

THE SOUND of her name seems to have a devastating effect on the girl and she starts to cry loudly. 'Let me out!' she sobs. 'Oh, let me out!'

'I will,' says Ruth grimly.

She reaches down and grabs the girl's arm. It feels brittle, as if it might snap. Then she hauls but she is not strong enough to take the girl's weight.

'I'm coming down,' she says, 'then I'll give you a leg up.'

The girl backs away but Ruth jumps in through the trap door and falls heavily onto the concrete floor below. The girl is standing against the opposite wall, her teeth bared like an animal. In her hand she holds a stone. A flint, decides Ruth, giving it a professional look. A sharp one.

Ruth tries a smile. 'Hello,' she says, 'Hello, Lucy. I'm Ruth.'

She looks around. She is in a small, square underground dungeon. Looking up, she sees the trap door in the ceiling plus a barred window, which also has a wooden cover. The room is empty apart from a low bed, a bucket and a plastic box that seems to contain baby's toys. The walls and the floor are all concrete, rough in places, and there is moisture running down the walls. The whole place smells of damp and urine and fear.

My God, thinks Ruth. Has Erik really kept her a prisoner all this time? What about when he was in Norway? Cathbad, that must be the answer.

This is the link between Erik and Cathbad. Cathbad must be his jailer.

And now they must escape.

Ruth turns to the girl, who is still cowering against the wall. 'Come on.' She holds out her hand. 'I'm going to help you get out of here.'

But the girl just whimpers and shakes her head.

'Come on, Lucy,' says Ruth, trying to make her voice sound as calm and gentle as possible. Trying to make it sound as if they have all the time in the world and there isn't a madman on their trail and a raging tempest outside. 'Come on. I'll take you home. You'd like to go home, wouldn't you, Lucy? To see your mum and dad?'

She'd expected the girl to react to the words 'mum and dad', but Lucy is still looking terrified. Ruth edges slowly towards her, dredging her mind for every soothing platitude she can think of.

'There, there. It's OK. Don't worry. It'll be all right.'

What were some of the things her mother used to say to her? Annoying little catchphrases but nevertheless as soothing as a cup of cocoa when you can't sleep. Ruth has never had children so it is her own childhood she must conjure up. Remember the days when her mother was not just someone who annoyed her on the phone, but the most important person in the word. The litany of motherhood.

'There, there. Don't worry. It'll be all right. No use crying over split milk. Tears before bedtime. Tomorrow's another day. All's well that ends well. Don't cry. It's darkest before dawn.'

And, as if the last words are the magic spell that releases the princess from the tower, Lucy throws herself into Ruth's arms.

NELSON DRIVES CATHBAD to the car park in silence. The only sounds are the overloaded windscreen wipers swishing to and fro and Nelson's fingers drumming impatiently on the steering wheel.

The trees round the car park are blown into a frenzy and the boarded-up kiosk looms eerily out of the dark. Grimly, Nelson gets a rope and a heavy-duty torch out of the boot. Cathbad hums serenely.

They walk up the gravel track to the first hide. Nelson leads, shining the torch in front of him. He's not an imaginative man but the noise of the wind howling across the marshes is starting to give him the creeps. Thunder rumbles overhead. They pass the first hide and Cathbad pushes in front.

'The path,' he says calmly. 'It's near here.'

Nelson hands him the torch.

After a few yards, Cathbad veers off the gravel track and starts to head out over the marsh. Despite the torch, it's pitch black. Here and there, Nelson can see glimpses of water, dark and dangerous. It's like walking into the unknown. It takes all of his self-control now not to elbow Cathbad out of the way and insist on turning back to the track.

Suddenly Cathbad stops. 'Here it is,' he murmurs. Nelson sees him shine the torch onto the ground. A bolt of lightning turns the sky white. Cathbad grins at him. 'Follow me,' he says.

ABOUT A MILE AWAY, across the black marshland, Ruth holds Lucy in her arms. It feels strange, cuddling this thin, vulnerable body. Ruth doesn't know many teenagers and those she does know are hardly likely to fling their arms around her and sob.

'Come on. Before *he* gets back,' Ruth is forced to say at last.

That does the trick. Lucy breaks away, her eyes round with fear.

'Is he coming?' she whispers.

'I don't know,' says Ruth. Hopefully Erik is lost out there on the dark marshes, but knowing him he probably has a sea sprite's sixth sense that will allow him to walk unharmed through the storm and arrive just as they are trying to escape. Taking advantage of the girl's loosened grip, she propels her gently below the trap door.

'I'm going to give you a leg up. You know,' she adds desperately, 'like on a pony.'

'A pony,' Lucy repeats carefully.

'Yes. I'm going to push you up through that hole and then climb up myself. OK?' she finishes brightly.

Almost imperceptibly, Lucy nods.

'Put your arms up,' says Ruth. Lucy does so. Clearly she is used to obeying orders. In the event, Ruth does not give her a leg up, instead she clasps Lucy round the waist and lifts her. To her amazement, the girl grasps the edge of the trap door and swings herself up. Then she peers down at Ruth, her lips curved in something like a smile.

'Well done, Lucy! Well done!' Ruth is so elated that she has almost forgotten that she has to get herself up. She looks around for something to climb on. She spots the plastic box of toys and pulls it over. She stands on top. Not high enough. So she gets the bucket, tipping its pungent smelling contents into the corner, and puts it upside-down on top of the box. She balances on the bucket and is able to grab the rim of the trap door. Her fingers scrabble madly on the hide's wooden floor and then, amazingly, she feels something else pulling at her hand. It is Lucy trying to help her.

Suddenly Ruth's torso is up through the trap door. One final heave and her legs are up too. She struggles to her feet and takes Lucy's hand. She can hear the rain drumming on the roof but the thunder seems to have stopped. She looks at Lucy's thin, shivering body, then takes off the policeman's jacket and wraps it round the girl. It comes to below her knees.

'There,' she says in her bright 'mother' voice. 'Now you'll be fine.'

But Lucy is looking beyond her. Staring at the entrance to the hide. She has heard something and now Ruth hears it too. A man's footsteps.

PURPLE CLOAK FLYING behind him, Cathbad leads the way across the marshes. Occasionally he stops and shines the torch at the ground, then turns slightly to the right or left. Nelson feels his jaw locked with frustration, but he has to admit that, so far, Cathbad hasn't put a foot wrong. On either side of them he can see still water and dark, treacherous marshland, but their feet remain on the twisting stony path. Thunder is rolling above them, the rain beats down. Nelson is soaked.

It is so dark that sometimes he almost loses sight of Cathbad, though he is only a few paces in front. Then he sees a glimmer of purple again.

Where the hell is Ruth? And Erik? Nelson sighs. When he thinks of Ruth, a reluctant tenderness constricts his throat. He thinks of her lists, her love for her cats, the calm way she can dig through layers of mud and come up with treasure. He thinks of the way she fed him coffee and listened, the night Scarlet was found. He thinks of her body, actually rather magnificent unclothed, white in the moonlight. He thinks of her at Scarlet's funeral, her eyes red, and of her face when she told him that Erik was the author of the letters. He sighs again. He's not in love with Ruth but somehow she gets to him. If anything happens to her, he will never forgive himself.

Cathbad stops again and Nelson almost bumps into him.

'What's the matter?' He has to shout to be heard above the wind.

'I've lost the path.' Cathbad sweeps the beam of the torch over the ground. 'Some of the posts are submerged . . . I think this is it.'

He takes a step forward and disappears. He doesn't even have time to scream. He just vanishes, swallowed by the night. Nelson jumps forward and is just in time to catch a handful of cloak. The cloak tears but now he has hold of Cathbad's arm. Cathbad is up to his neck in the mud and it takes all Nelson's strength to haul him out. Finally, with a ghastly sucking noise, the marsh relinquishes its prey. Cathbad kneels on the path, panting.

Nelson yanks him to his feet. 'Come on, Cathbad, you're not dead yet.' It is the first time he has called Malone by his adopted name, but neither of them notices this.

Cathbad grasps Nelson's arm, his eyes look white and wild in his blackened face. 'I am in your debt,' he says, fighting for breath. 'The spirits of the ancestors are strong, they are all about us.'

'Well, we're not about to join them yet,' Nelson tells him briskly. 'Where's that torch?'

RUTH AND LUCY stare at each other, terrified. The footsteps are coming nearer. They are trapped. Ruth moves in front of Lucy. She looks wildly around the hide but it is completely empty. If only she had a stone or a piece of wood. Where is the stone that Lucy was carrying?

The footsteps come nearer and, at the same moment, the moon slides out from behind the clouds. A man's figure approaches, wearing yellow waterproofs. The man reaches the steps to the hide and, in the moonlight, Ruth sees his face.

It isn't Erik. It is David.

'David!' shouts Ruth. 'Thank God!' David has come to save her again. She feels giddy with relief.

But, behind her, Lucy starts to scream.

NELSON HEARS the scream. He grabs Cathbad's arm.

'Where did that come from?'

Cathbad points over to the right. 'From over there,' he says vaguely.

'Come on.' Nelson sets out, running, staggering over the waterlogged ground.

'No!' shouts Cathbad. 'You're off the path!'

But Nelson keeps running.

Lucy screams and, in that second, Ruth understands everything.

'You!' she stares at David. 'It was you.'

David looks calmly back at her. He looks no different from the kind, diffident, slightly eccentric David she thought she knew.

'Yes,' he says. 'Me.'

'You killed Scarlet? You kept Lucy a prisoner here for all these years?'

'I didn't mean to kill Scarlet. I brought her as company for Lucy. Lucy was growing up. I wanted a younger one. But she struggled. I tried to make her be quiet and . . . she died. I didn't mean to do it. I buried her in the sacred place. Erik told me it was the right thing to do.'

'Erik? So he knew about this?'

'He didn't know but he talked to me, all those years ago, about burial places and sacrifices. He told me that in prehistoric times they buried children on the marshland, as an offering to the gods. So I buried Scarlet where the wooden circle used to be. But you dug her up again.'

'You killed my cat,' bursts out Ruth.

'Yes. I hate cats. They kill birds.' David takes a step closer.

Ruth grabs hold of Lucy, who is shaking violently. 'Keep away from her.'

'Oh, I can't let you go now,' says David, in a sweet, reasonable voice. 'She'd never survive in the wild. She's been in captivity too long. I'll have to kill you both.'

And then Ruth sees that he is holding a knife. The moonlight gleams on its jagged blade.

'Run!' she yells and, dragging Lucy after her, she sprints past David and into the night. She doesn't know where she is going and she doesn't give a thought to the tide or the marshes. All she knows is that they are running for their lives.

Beside her, Lucy runs surprisingly well, hardly making a sound. Ruth hangs on grimly to her hand. She mustn't let Lucy go. Alone, in the dark, on the tidal marsh, she would have no chance at all.

Ruth can hear David behind them. He is wading through the stream they have just crossed. She must change direction, head for home. But where is home? She makes a random left turn and finds herself facing a pool of water. She runs on and finds the ground getting softer and softer. Oh God, she must be on the mud flats.

And then she hears something. She stops, listening. It sounds almost like 'Police'. She must be hallucinating.

But it was a mistake to stop. With horrifying suddenness, David's face suddenly looms out of the dark. Ruth screams and Lucy breaks free. David lunges forward, grabbing Ruth's foot. She kicks out. He falls back. Ruth takes to her heels again; she must find Lucy before David does.

But David is right behind her. She can hear his ragged breathing; hear the splashing as he wades through the pool. Frantically, Ruth turns and finds herself scrambling up a sandy slope. A sand dune. She must be right by the sea but she barely has time to think this when she is falling down the other side of the dune and landing in water. Salt water. Looking ahead, she can see nothingness. Only the ink-black sea, flecked with white foam, coming relentlessly towards her. She turns and wades inland, along a narrow channel of water. Where's Lucy? She must find Lucy.

Ahead of her, she can see a square dark shape in the water. She heads for it and sees a Second World War pillbox, a small, low concrete structure. They are dotted all over the marshes. She climbs on top of the box. If she jumps, she can reach the higher ground, where she should be safe from the tide. She jumps and lands heavily on the opposite bank. A brief thrill of elation runs through her. She has done it! But then the elation vanishes. Standing over her, knife in hand, is David.

NELSON RUNS across the saltmarsh. He falls many times, staggering in and out of the water. Behind him he can hear Cathbad shouting about the tide but he ignores him. Someone is screaming. Ruth is in danger.

'Police!' he yells. 'Freeze!'

He hasn't even got a gun—what's he going to do when he gets there? He doesn't pause to think about that, he just runs doggedly on. And then he sees the hide, looming up out of the featureless dark, and runs towards it.

The hide is deserted. Nelson climbs the steps and looks down into the dark hole left by the trap door. Thank God he took the torch from Cathbad. Its bright beam illuminates the underground room.

'Jesus,' breathes Nelson.

'SORRY RUTH,' says David, again sounding like the shy helpful neighbour who had looked after her cat and to whom she had given her mobile phone number. 'I have to kill you now you know about Lucy.'

'Why did you do it?' asks Ruth. She genuinely wants to know the truth, even though she knows it might be the last thing she hears.

'Why?' asks David, surprised. 'For company, of course.'

He moves towards her, holding out the knife. Ruth backs away. They are standing on a raised bank; behind David is the pool she passed earlier. She has no idea how deep it is. Even if she manages to get past him, she can hardly swim across the water in the dark. Behind her are the sand dunes and the sea, crashing relentlessly forwards. She is exhausted and overweight; she knows David would catch her easily. Then, a noise fills the night. Three echoing calls, harsh and even. It is the sound she heard earlier, beside the hide. David looks at Ruth, his face transfixed.

'Did you hear that?' he whispers.

Without waiting for an answer, he turns and starts walking away from her, towards the sound. It comes again. Calling, calling across the black marshes. Is it the voice of a dead child? At this moment, Ruth will believe anything. She too starts to move towards the sound.

As if hypnotised, David walks straight into the pool. He is waist deep but does not seem to notice. Ruth sees his yellow jacket moving steadily through the inky water. Then the clouds move and Ruth sees a figure on the opposite bank. A figure wearing a dark jacket that comes almost to its knees. Lucy. There is something in her stance, something poised and purposeful, that is almost terrifying. Suddenly Ruth has no doubt that it is Lucy who is making the strange, unearthly call.

David, though, is beyond thought. He walks through the water, pulled as if on invisible strings. And then a huge, white-edged wave comes crashing over the sandbank and into the pool. David loses his balance and disappears under the surface. Another wave follows, turning the pool into a cauldron of foamy water. Ruth feels spray on her face and shuts her eyes. When she opens them again, the pool is still and David has vanished.

Now Ruth screams but she knows no one can hear her. She knows too that there is nothing anyone can do for David.

Another figure appears on the opposite bank. A tall, thick-set figure. Nelson. He is shouting something but Ruth can't make out the words. She starts to make her way towards him, on hands and knees, crawling along the shingle bank that surrounds the pool. It is farther than it looks but, finally, she reaches the far side, where Nelson is looking, with wonder, into the face of the girl beside him.

'Nelson,' says Ruth, 'meet Lucy Downey.'

Epilogue

Ruth is walking along the sand. It is early March and although the wind is cold there is a faint promise of spring in the air. She is barefoot and the clamshells cut into her feet.

She is near the henge circle. The sand, rippling like a frozen sea, stretches far in front of her. She walks jauntily. She is due to meet Nelson, who is going to give her the latest news of Lucy. This is one legacy of that terrible night, three weeks ago. Ruth feels bound to Lucy and knows that this connection will last for ever, whether Lucy wants it or not. Ruth may soon fade in Lucy's mind—indeed, she hopes many things will fade from Lucy's mind; one day she will become just the strange, large lady who comes with presents at Christmas and birthdays, bringing with her a faint memory of a dark night, a wild sea and the end of a nightmare. But for Ruth, that moment when she held Lucy in her arms was a turning point. She knew then that she would do anything to protect Lucy. She knew then what it is to be a mother.

Nelson told her about Lucy's reunion with her actual parents. 'We called them, didn't tell them what was up, just asked them to come to the station. It was four in the morning. God knows what they thought. The mother thought we'd found Lucy's body, I could see it in her eyes. We had a child psychologist standing by; nobody knew what would happen. Would Lucy even recognise her parents? She was very calm, just sat there, huddled in my jacket, as if she was waiting for something. We made her a cup of tea and she screamed. Hadn't expected it to be hot. Probably hadn't had a hot drink for ten years. She screamed and dropped the drink on the floor, then she cringed away from me, as if she expected me to hit her. So I left her with WPC Johnson. Then, when I came in with the parents . . . she made this noise, this little cry, like a baby. The mother said, 'Lucy?' And Lucy just howled, 'Mummy!' and flung herself into her arms. The parents hugged her as if they'd never let her go. Then the mother looked at me, over Lucy's head, and said, "Thank you. *Thank you!*"'

'Will Lucy be all right, do you think?'

'Well, she's seeing an army of psychiatrists but they say she's remarkably resilient. She has to learn to be a teenager, not a little girl. In some ways, she's stuck at five years old but, in others, she's amazingly mature.'

And Ruth, remembering the way that Lucy had used the bird call (the call, she is sure, of the long-eared owl) to lure David to his death, believes him.

They have not found David's body. It must have been washed out to sea.

They did find Erik though. The great shaman, who knew the marshes like the back of his hand, had drowned in a marshy pool just a few hundred yards from Ruth's cottage.

Ruth went to Norway for Erik's funeral. Despite everything, she found that she still had some love left for him—and for Magda. Erik had always said that he wanted a Viking funeral. So they had taken his ashes and put them in a wooden boat built specially by Lars, Magda's lover. They had set fire to the boat and sent it sailing out onto the lake where it burned all through the night.

'You know—'Magda had turned to Ruth, her face lit by the glow from the boat—'we were happy.'

'I know,' said Ruth.

And she did know. Magda and Erik were happy, despite Shona and Lars and all the others. And she, Ruth, still loved Erik, despite the letters and the adultery and the cold light behind the blue eyes. She seemed to have learned a lot about love over the last few weeks. After Norway, she went home to Eltham where she went shopping with her mother, played Scrabble with her father and even attended church with them. She doesn't think she will ever be a believer herself but these days it does not seem so important to remind her parents of this. Somehow, when she held Lucy in her arms in that terrible cellar, she found a way back to her own mother. Perhaps it is just that she learned the value of the maternal cliché, the love that is always the same, no matter how many years pass, and burns no less strongly by being expressed in time-worn phrases.

Erik was never charged with any crime. Cathbad was quietly cleared of the charge of wasting police time. The letters were never made public. Ruth thinks about them sometimes. Thinks about why Erik wrote them. Was it grief for James Agar? Or was it arrogance? The chance to pit his wits against the police, that embodiment of a philistine state?

Cathbad celebrated the dropping of the charges by performing a spiritual cleansing session on the beach, not unlike a Viking funeral, involving much dancing around a ceremonial fire. He invited Nelson but the detective inspector declined to attend.

Ruth sees Nelson approaching over the sand dunes. He looks wary, as if he expects the sand to leap up and attack him. Nelson will never love the Saltmarsh. He has always found it a spooky place and now it will always be associated in his mind with Lucy's long imprisonment and with death.

He has reached Ruth, who is standing at the start of the henge circle.

'What a place to meet,' grumbles Nelson, 'miles from anywhere.'

'The exercise will do you good,' says Ruth.

'You sound like Michelle.'

Ruth has met Michelle now and, to her surprise, quite likes her. She admires the way that Harry's wife always does exactly what she wants, while retaining the image of the perfect spouse. This, she realises, is a skill she could usefully learn . . . not that she is planning to be anyone's wife.

Peter has gone back to Victoria. Ruth is relieved that it was David, not Peter, who sent the text messages. Her memories of him can stay intact.

The discovery of Lucy Downey was, of course, a media sensation. There seemed to have been little else in the papers for weeks—one reason why Ruth escaped to Norway and Eltham. Nelson came in for his share of criticism; after all, Lucy was found in an area that had been searched many times by the police. But, then again, Nelson did get the credit for rescuing Lucy. Ruth was happy for her part to be downplayed and Cathbad, too, had reasons for remaining in the shadows. Also, Lucy's parents refused to criticise Nelson, saying instead that it was his tireless searching that had eventually resulted in their daughter's discovery.

'How's Lucy?' asks Ruth as they walk along the sea's edge. The tide is going out, leaving a line of shells and glistening stones.

'Good,' says Nelson. 'I went round yesterday and she was playing on a swing. Apparently she remembered the house and the garden perfectly. But she'd forgotten lots of things. When she first saw a cat, she screamed.'

Ruth thinks of Flint, who stayed with Shona while she was away. Shona, desperate to make amends, fed Flint almost entirely on smoked salmon.

'Has Lucy said anything about what it was like?' she asks.

'The psychiatrist's been getting her to draw pictures. The most disturbing things you ever saw. Little black boxes, clutching hands, iron bars.'

'Was she abused by him? David.'

'Abused? Of course she was abused. But, sexually, there's no sign. I think he was quite squeamish about sex, actually.'

'How did he make that underground room?'

'It was an old Second World War bunker. He built the hide on top of it.'

'Does anyone know why he did it?' she asks at last.

'The shrinks have got a million theories but it's all guesswork.'

'For company, that's what he said to me.' Ruth thinks of what David said when she told him of her grief for Sparky. *She was company.*

'Company.' Nelson grunts. 'Couldn't he have joined a club?'

Why not indeed, thinks Ruth, looking out at the sea. Why does anyone do anything? Why does she remain here, on the Saltmarsh, where so many awful things have happened? Why does Nelson still love his wife, though they have nothing in common? Why is she fat and Shona thin? There's no answer to any of it. But, she thinks, smiling as the cold water foams over her bare feet, somehow none of that matters today. She's happy with her life, here on the desolate coast. She wouldn't change any of it. She likes her job, her friends, her home. And besides, she thinks, smiling even more widely to herself, I'm not fat, I'm pregnant. She has no intention of telling Nelson, though. Not yet.

Nelson too is gazing out to sea. 'What's happened about the Iron Age girl?' he asks suddenly. 'The one who started all this?'

Ruth smiles. 'They're calling her Ruth, you know, after me. I call her the lost girl of the marshes. I'm writing a paper about her.'

'Do you know any more about why she died?'

'Not really. She seems to be from a wealthy family, her nails are manicured and we've done tests on her hair that prove she had good nutrition. But no one knows why she was tied down on the marsh and left to die. Maybe it was to ensure safe passage over the marsh. Maybe she was an offering to the gods. But, really, we don't know.'

'Seems to me it's all a lot of guesswork,' says Nelson.

Ruth smiles. 'The questions are more important than the answers.'

'If you say so.'

And they turn and walk back towards the dunes.

ELLY GRIFFITHS

Born: London, August 17, 1963
Home: Saltdean, near Brighton
Website: www.ellygriffiths.co.uk

RD: What made you choose the name Elly Griffiths as a pseudonym?
EG: Apparently it's a real cliché, but I decided to adopt my grandmother's name, Eleanor Griffiths, because I know she always wanted to write a book but never did. I'm half-Italian and I've had four books published under my real name, Domenica de Rosa, all of which are set in Italy, so I thought, Let's give the old Welsh side an airing.

RD: Why did you choose to set *The Crossing Places* in Norfolk?
EG: We often spend family holidays in Norfolk. My aunt owns a boat there and I have happy memories of sailing on the Broads with her when I was a child. I am fascinated by the Norfolk scenery—the huge sky, and those big, open spaces. There's also a very spooky side to it, a sense of things buried or covered by the sea.

RD: When did you discover that burial sites exist beneath the marshes?
EG: My husband's an archaeologist, and one day, when we were trudging over Titchwell Marsh, he told me that Iron Age people considered marshland sacred because it was neither land nor sea, and so did not belong to either this life or the next. That's why they buried offerings there, and that's what gave me the idea of a sacred landscape.

RD: You mention a henge at Holme-next-the-Sea. Were you influenced by the timber circle known as 'Seahenge' that was discovered there?
EG: Very much so. And by Francis Pryor's wonderful book *Seahenge*, in which he expounds a lot of theories about ritual landscape and Seahenge.

RD: What made you choose a forensic archaeologist as your heroine?
EG: I think people are interested in forensic archaeology and in the kind of skills that Ruth Galloway has. My husband has a friend who works in this field and the police often call her in to help them, so I don't think it's too far-fetched.

RD: It's easy to relate to Ruth Galloway. Did she step effortlessly into your novel?
EG: She did and, really, I don't know where she came from. But I do feel that I love her more than anyone else I've ever written about. I think she's probably an amalgam of a lot of strong women in my life, especially my mother, my aunt and my two older sisters. I wanted to avoid making her a dolly-bird type.

RD: Is her relationship with Detective Inspector Harry Nelson going to develop?
EG: Yes, Nelson loves his wife but he does have strong feelings for Ruth. In the second book, *The Two-Faced God*, which I've almost finished writing, their relationship becomes more complicated. The book starts with Ruth finding bones beneath Roman walls.

RD: Your writing is very atmospheric. Are you influenced by particular writers?
EG: Wilkie Collins, especially the descriptions of the shivering sands in *The Moonstone*. I love Victorian writers. I also like books written by Reginald Hill and Kate Atkinson.

RD: Are you superstitious?
EG: I'm not, but superstition is a big part of my life because my father was Italian and Italians are very superstitious. At my wedding reception my cousins were throwing bread and my dad was going mad because it's bad luck if bread touches the floor!

RD: If you could sail away for a year and a day, where would you go?
EG: Six months along the Amalfi coast and six months off the coast of northern Scotland. I'd take my husband and children, and my aunt as skipper. I'd have complete confidence that she'd get me to where I wanted to go. I'd spend the extra day sleeping!

A HISTORIC RING OF OAK

Seahenge is the Bronze Age timber circle that Elly Griffiths describes in *The Crossing Places*, and it was once at Holme-next-the-Sea in Norfolk. Discovered in 1999, it is pictured here before the 55 oak timber posts and the upturned oak tree in the centre were lifted controversially from the saltmarsh. After their removal, the endangered timbers were taken for dating and analysis by English Heritage scientists. A variety of tests have shown that the tree died some time between April and June 2050 BC, and experts state that the henge was almost certainly used as a ceremonial site. The timbers are now on display in the Bronze Age Gallery at the Lynn Museum in King's Lynn, Norfolk.

COPYRIGHT AND ACKNOWLEDGMENTS

THE BRASS VERDICT: Copyright © 2008 by Hieronymus, Inc.
Published at £18.99 by Orion Books, an imprint of the Orion Publishing
Group Ltd, an Hachette Livre UK Company.
Condensed version © The Reader's Digest Association Limited, 2009.

FATHERS & SONS: Copyright © 2008 by Richard Madeley.
Published at £18.99 by Simon & Schuster UK Ltd, a CBS Company.
Condensed version © The Reader's Digest Association Limited, 2009.

MOSCOW RULES: Copyright © Daniel Silva, 2008.
Published at £12.99 by Michael Joseph, an imprint of the Penguin Group.
Condensed version © The Reader's Digest Association Limited, 2009.

THE CROSSING PLACES: Copyright © 2009 by Elly Griffiths.
Published at £12.99 by Quercus.
Condensed version © The Reader's Digest Association Limited, 2009.

The right to be identified as authors has been asserted by the following in accordance with
sections 77 and 78 of the Copyright, Designs and Patents Act, 1988: Michael Connelly,
Richard Madeley, Daniel Silva, Elly Griffiths.

Dustjacket spine: Digital Vision; illustrator: Rhett Podersoo@Advocate-Art. 6–8 Panoramic
Images; illustrator: Narrinder Singh@velvet tamarind; 4 and 152 Photo by Wendy Werris; 153
Getty Images/David McNew. 154–6 Courtesy of Simon & Schuster; 4 and 268–9 © Courtesy
of Simon & Schuster; 270–2 © Stone; illustrator: Kate Baxter@velvet tamarind; 476, 526 and
527: the line 'We who were living are now dying' from T.S. Eliot 'The Wasteland', Collected
Poems (Faber and Faber 1974) is quoted by permission. 5 and 442 © John Earle. 444–6
Digital Vision; illustrator: Rhett Podersoo@Advocate-Art. 5 and 574 © Jerry Bauer; 575 ©
English Heritage Photo Library.

Printed and bound by GGP Media GmbH, Pössneck, Germany

020-258 DJ0000-1